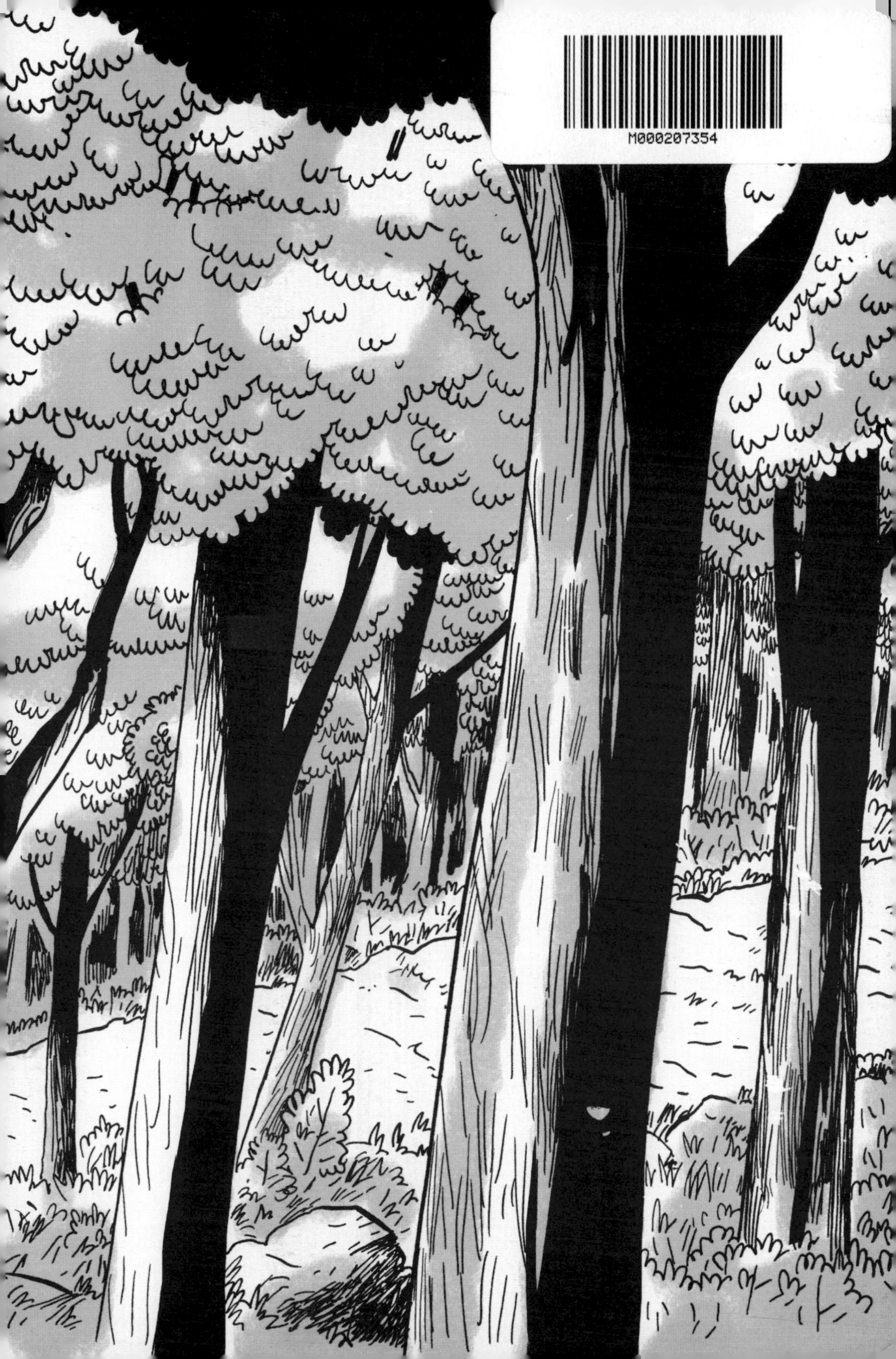

MAP OF PINEWOOD FOREST BOY SCOUT CAMP

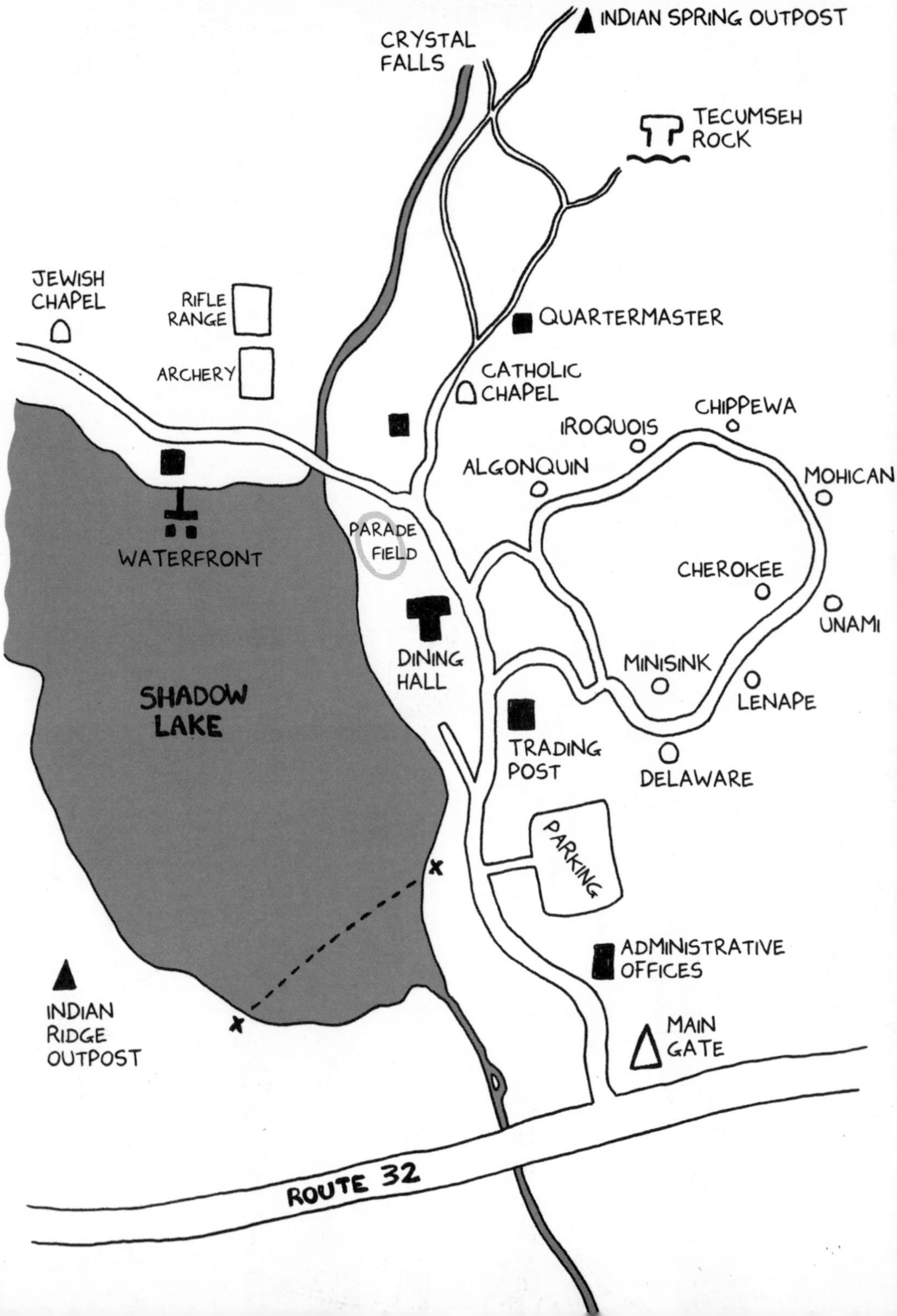
INDIAN SPRING OUTPOST
CRYSTAL FALLS
TECUMSEH ROCK
JEWISH CHAPEL
RIFLE RANGE
ARCHERY
QUARTERMASTER
CATHOLIC CHAPEL
CHIPPEWA
IROQUOIS
ALGONQUIN
MOHICAN
PARADE FIELD
WATERFRONT
CHEROKEE
UNAMI
DINING HALL
MINISINK
LENAPE
SHADOW LAKE
TRADING POST
DELAWARE
PARKING
ADMINISTRATIVE OFFICES
INDIAN RIDGE OUTPOST
MAIN GATE
ROUTE 32

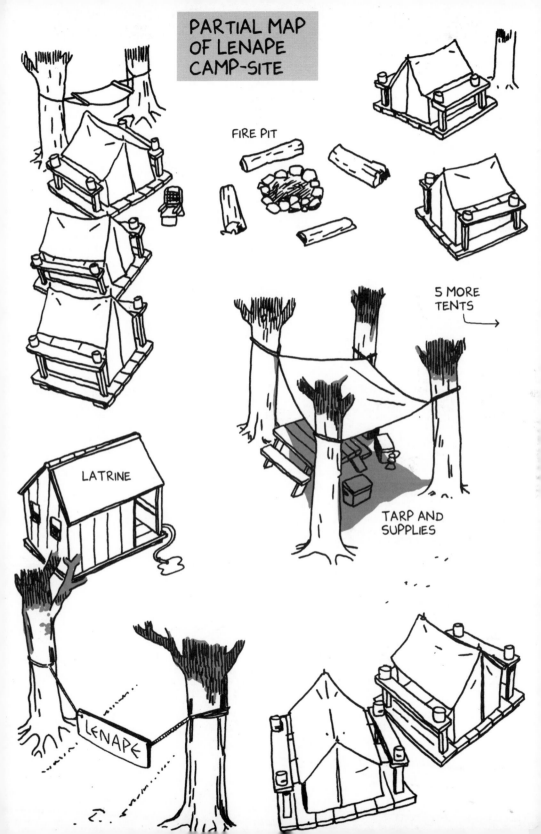

PARTIAL MAP OF LENAPE CAMP-SITE

FIRE PIT

5 MORE TENTS →

LATRINE

TARP AND SUPPLIES

LENAPE

TROOP 142 © 2011 MIKE DAWSON
PUBLISHED BY SECRET ACRES
DESIGNED BY MIKE DAWSON

SECRET ACRES
75-22 37TH AVENUE, #452
JACKSON HEIGHTS, NY, 11372

PRINTED IN SINGAPORE

LIBRARY OF CONGRESS PCN: 2011924536

ISBN 10: 0-9799609-9-1
ISBN 13: 978-0-9799609-9-4

MIKE
DAWSON
TROOP 142

BE PREPARED.

- BOY SCOUT MOTTO

SUNDAY

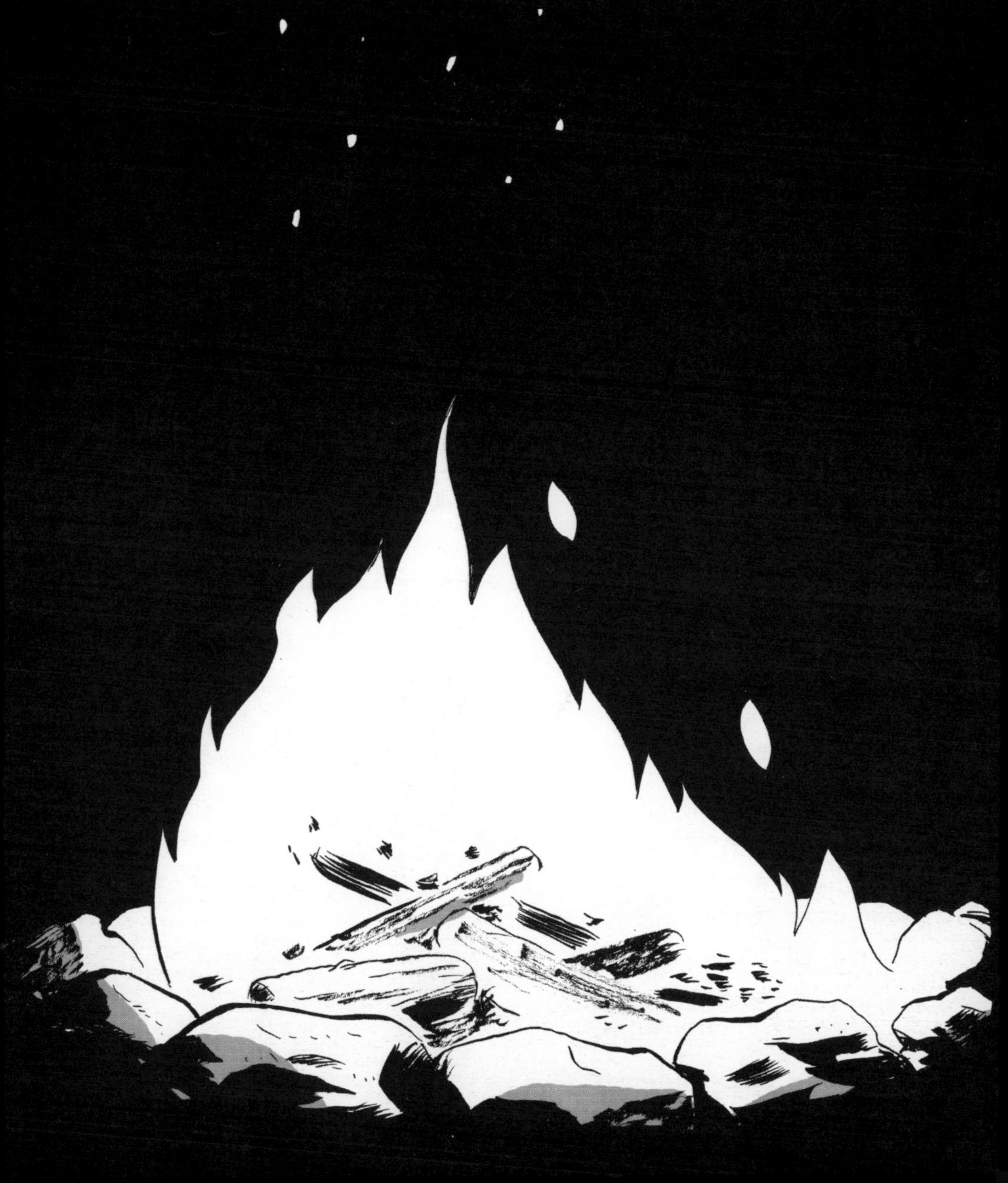

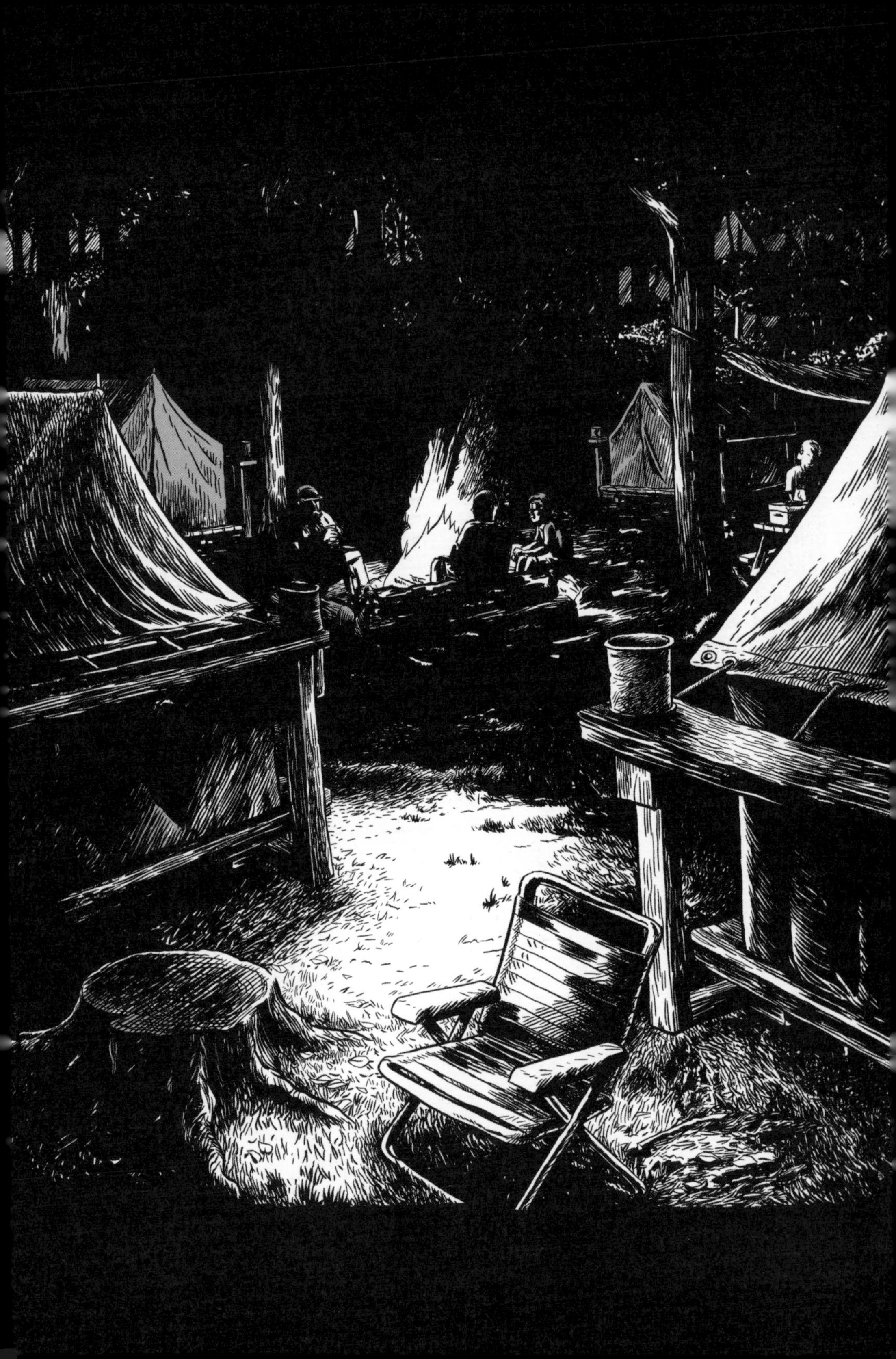

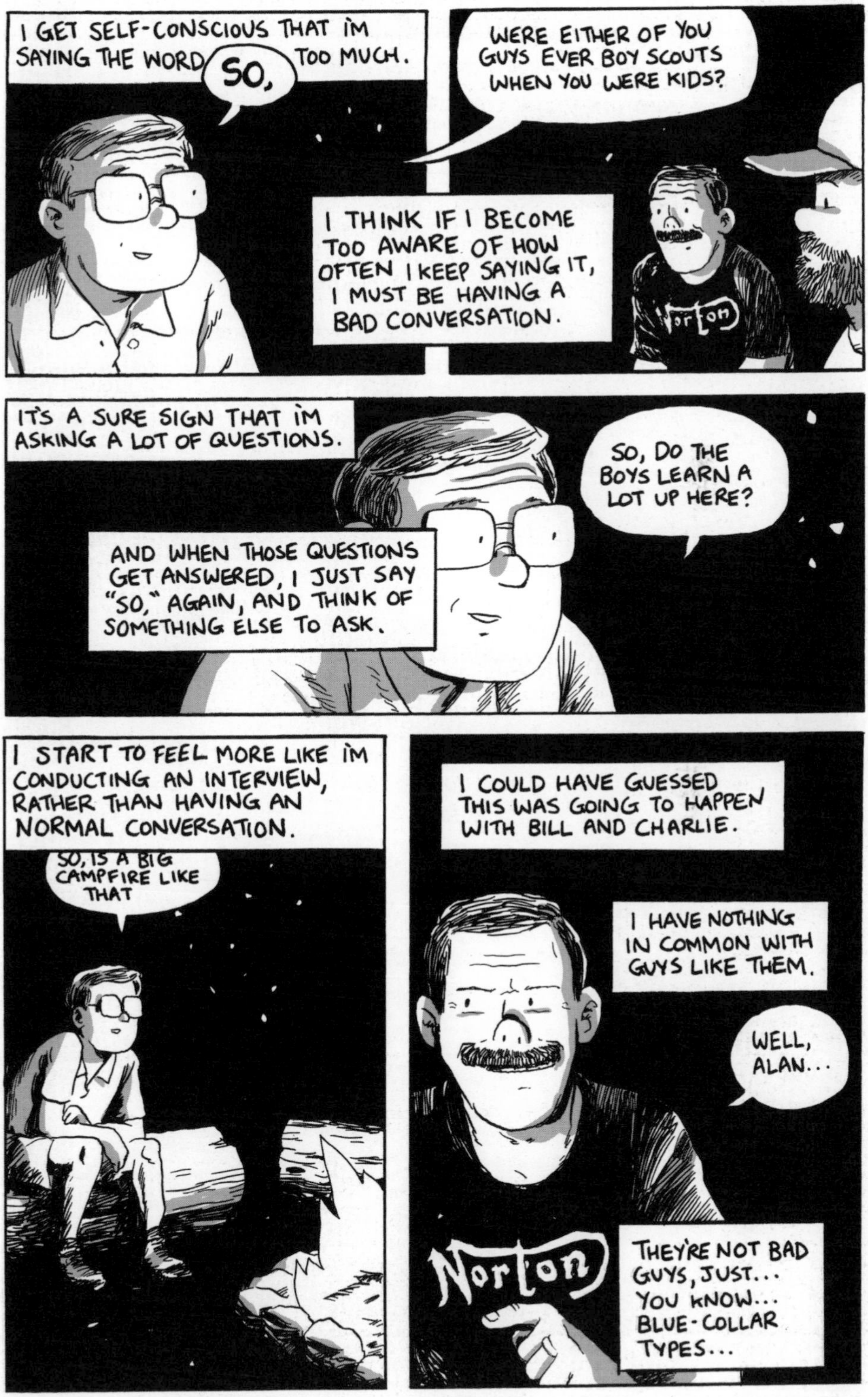
I GET SELF-CONSCIOUS THAT I'M SAYING THE WORD
SO,
TOO MUCH.
WERE EITHER OF YOU GUYS EVER BOY SCOUTS WHEN YOU WERE KIDS?
I THINK IF I BECOME TOO AWARE OF HOW OFTEN I KEEP SAYING IT, I MUST BE HAVING A BAD CONVERSATION.
Norton
IT'S A SURE SIGN THAT I'M ASKING A LOT OF QUESTIONS.
SO, DO THE BOYS LEARN A LOT UP HERE?
AND WHEN THOSE QUESTIONS GET ANSWERED, I JUST SAY "SO," AGAIN, AND THINK OF SOMETHING ELSE TO ASK.
I START TO FEEL MORE LIKE I'M CONDUCTING AN INTERVIEW, RATHER THAN HAVING AN NORMAL CONVERSATION.
SO, IS A BIG CAMPFIRE LIKE THAT
I COULD HAVE GUESSED THIS WAS GOING TO HAPPEN WITH BILL AND CHARLIE.
I HAVE NOTHING IN COMMON WITH GUYS LIKE THEM.
WELL, ALAN...
Norton
THEY'RE NOT BAD GUYS, JUST... YOU KNOW... BLUE-COLLAR TYPES...

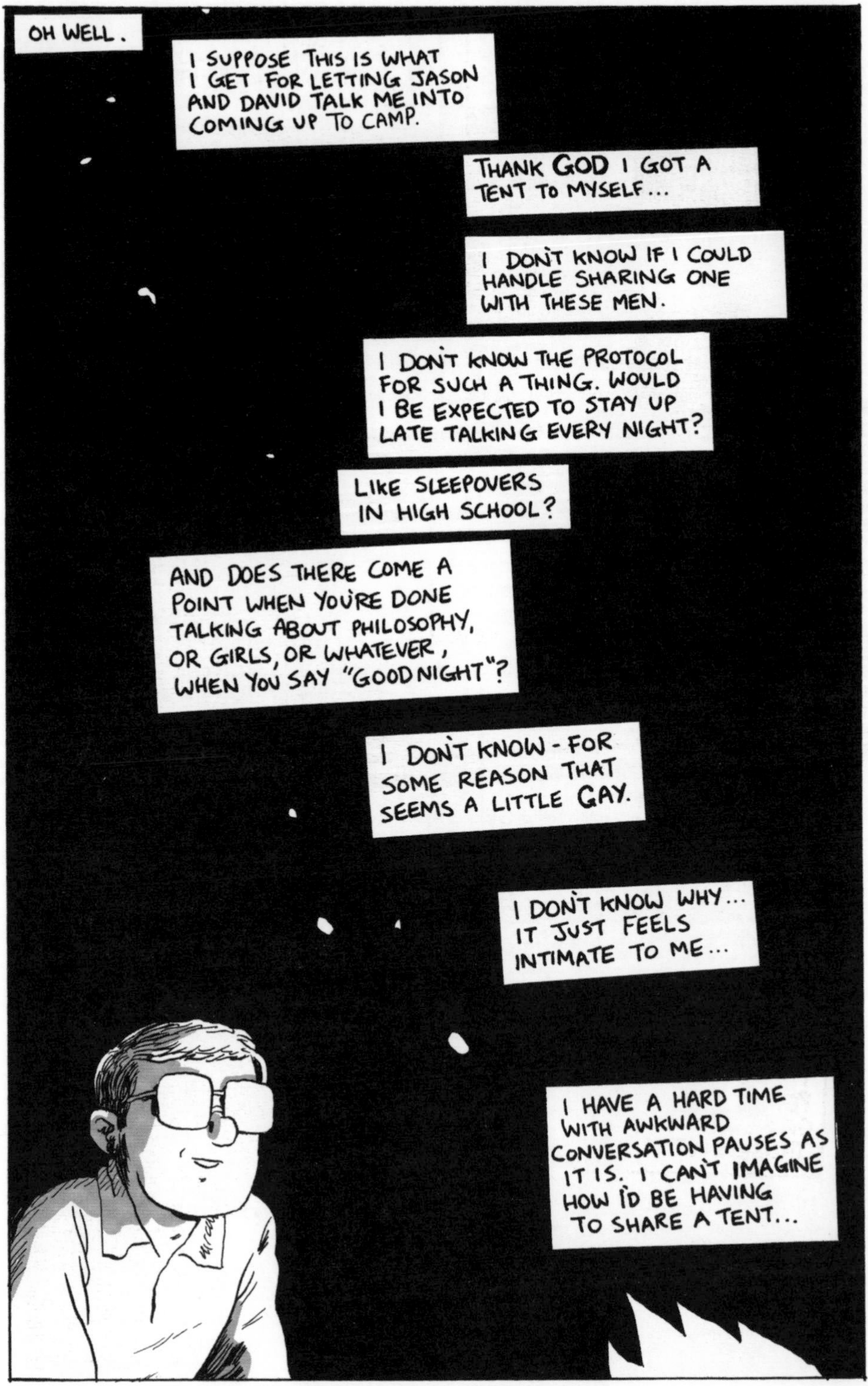
OH WELL.
I SUPPOSE THIS IS WHAT I GET FOR LETTING JASON AND DAVID TALK ME INTO COMING UP TO CAMP.
THANK GOD I GOT A TENT TO MYSELF...
I DON'T KNOW IF I COULD HANDLE SHARING ONE WITH THESE MEN.
I DON'T KNOW THE PROTOCOL FOR SUCH A THING. WOULD I BE EXPECTED TO STAY UP LATE TALKING EVERY NIGHT?
LIKE SLEEPOVERS IN HIGH SCHOOL?
AND DOES THERE COME A POINT WHEN YOU'RE DONE TALKING ABOUT PHILOSOPHY, OR GIRLS, OR WHATEVER, WHEN YOU SAY "GOOD NIGHT"?
I DON'T KNOW - FOR SOME REASON THAT SEEMS A LITTLE GAY.
I DON'T KNOW WHY... IT JUST FEELS INTIMATE TO ME...
I HAVE A HARD TIME WITH AWKWARD CONVERSATION PAUSES AS IT IS. I CAN'T IMAGINE HOW I'D BE HAVING TO SHARE A TENT...

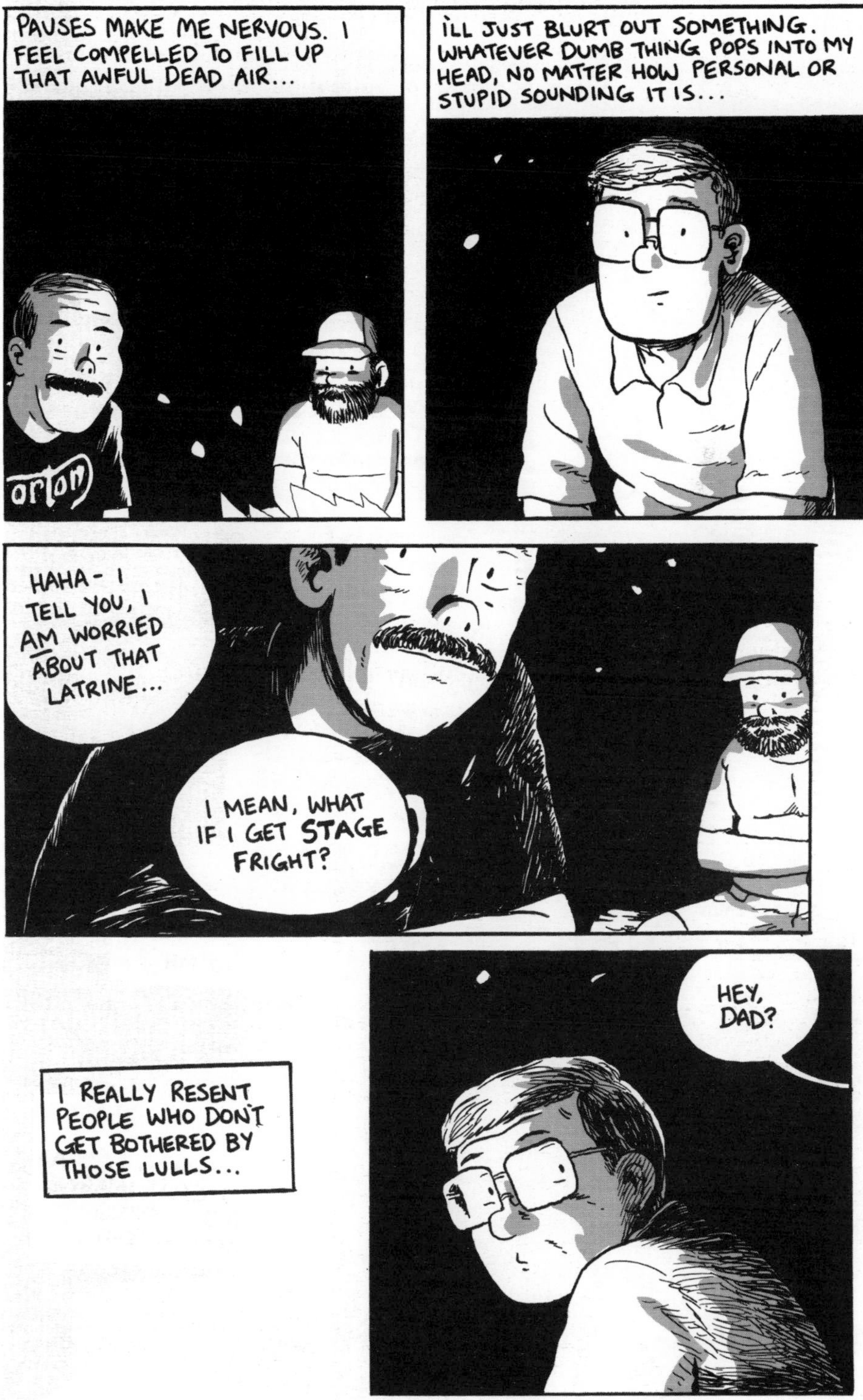
PAUSES MAKE ME NERVOUS. I FEEL COMPELLED TO FILL UP THAT AWFUL DEAD AIR...
orton
I'LL JUST BLURT OUT SOMETHING. WHATEVER DUMB THING POPS INTO MY HEAD, NO MATTER HOW PERSONAL OR STUPID SOUNDING IT IS...
HAHA- I TELL YOU, I AM WORRIED ABOUT THAT LATRINE...
I MEAN, WHAT IF I GET STAGE FRIGHT?
I REALLY RESENT PEOPLE WHO DON'T GET BOTHERED BY THOSE LULLS...
HEY, DAD?

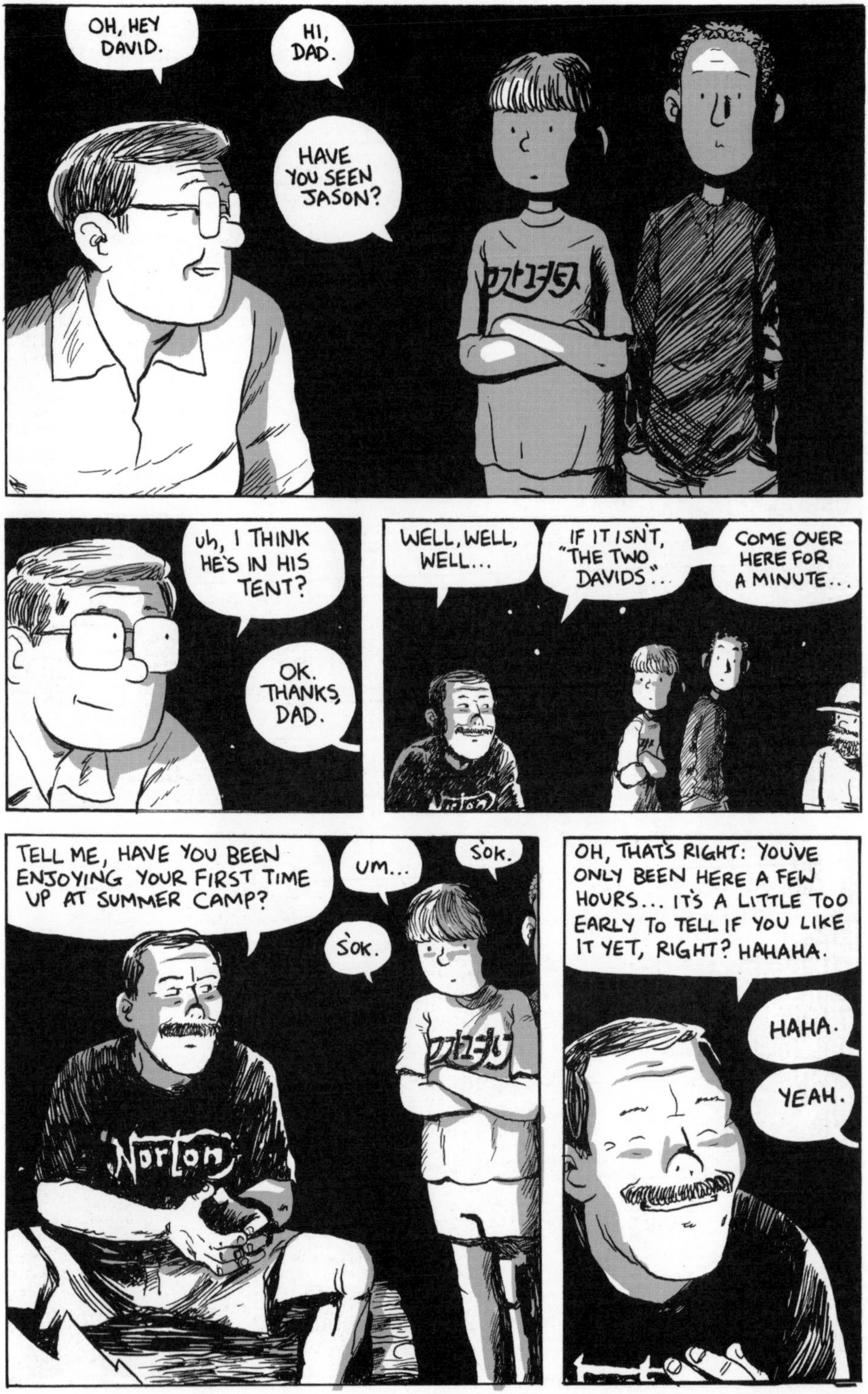
OH, HEY DAVID.
HI, DAD.
HAVE YOU SEEN JASON?
uh, I THINK HE'S IN HIS TENT?
OK. THANKS, DAD.
WELL, WELL, WELL...
IF IT ISN'T, "THE TWO DAVIDS"...
COME OVER HERE FOR A MINUTE...
TELL ME, HAVE YOU BEEN ENJOYING YOUR FIRST TIME UP AT SUMMER CAMP?
UM...
S'OK.
S'OK.
OH, THAT'S RIGHT: YOU'VE ONLY BEEN HERE A FEW HOURS... IT'S A LITTLE TOO EARLY TO TELL IF YOU LIKE IT YET, RIGHT? HAHAHA.
HAHA.
YEAH.

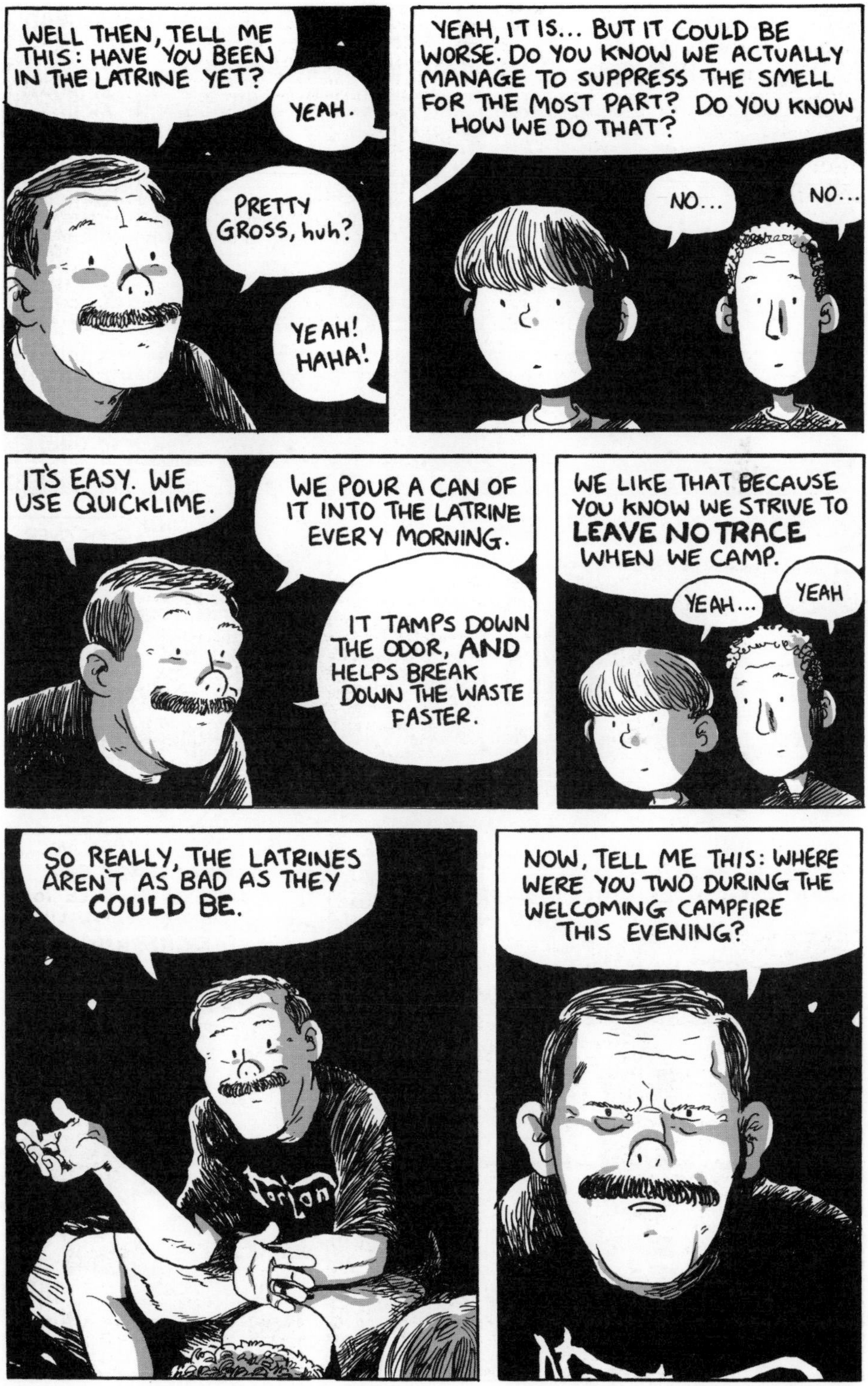
WELL THEN, TELL ME THIS: HAVE YOU BEEN IN THE LATRINE YET?
YEAH.
PRETTY GROSS, huh?
YEAH! HAHA!
YEAH, IT IS... BUT IT COULD BE WORSE. DO YOU KNOW WE ACTUALLY MANAGE TO SUPPRESS THE SMELL FOR THE MOST PART? DO YOU KNOW HOW WE DO THAT?
NO...
NO...
IT'S EASY. WE USE QUICKLIME.
WE POUR A CAN OF IT INTO THE LATRINE EVERY MORNING.
IT TAMPS DOWN THE ODOR, AND HELPS BREAK DOWN THE WASTE FASTER.
WE LIKE THAT BECAUSE YOU KNOW WE STRIVE TO LEAVE NO TRACE WHEN WE CAMP.
YEAH...
YEAH
SO REALLY, THE LATRINES AREN'T AS BAD AS THEY COULD BE.
NOW, TELL ME THIS: WHERE WERE YOU TWO DURING THE WELCOMING CAMPFIRE THIS EVENING?

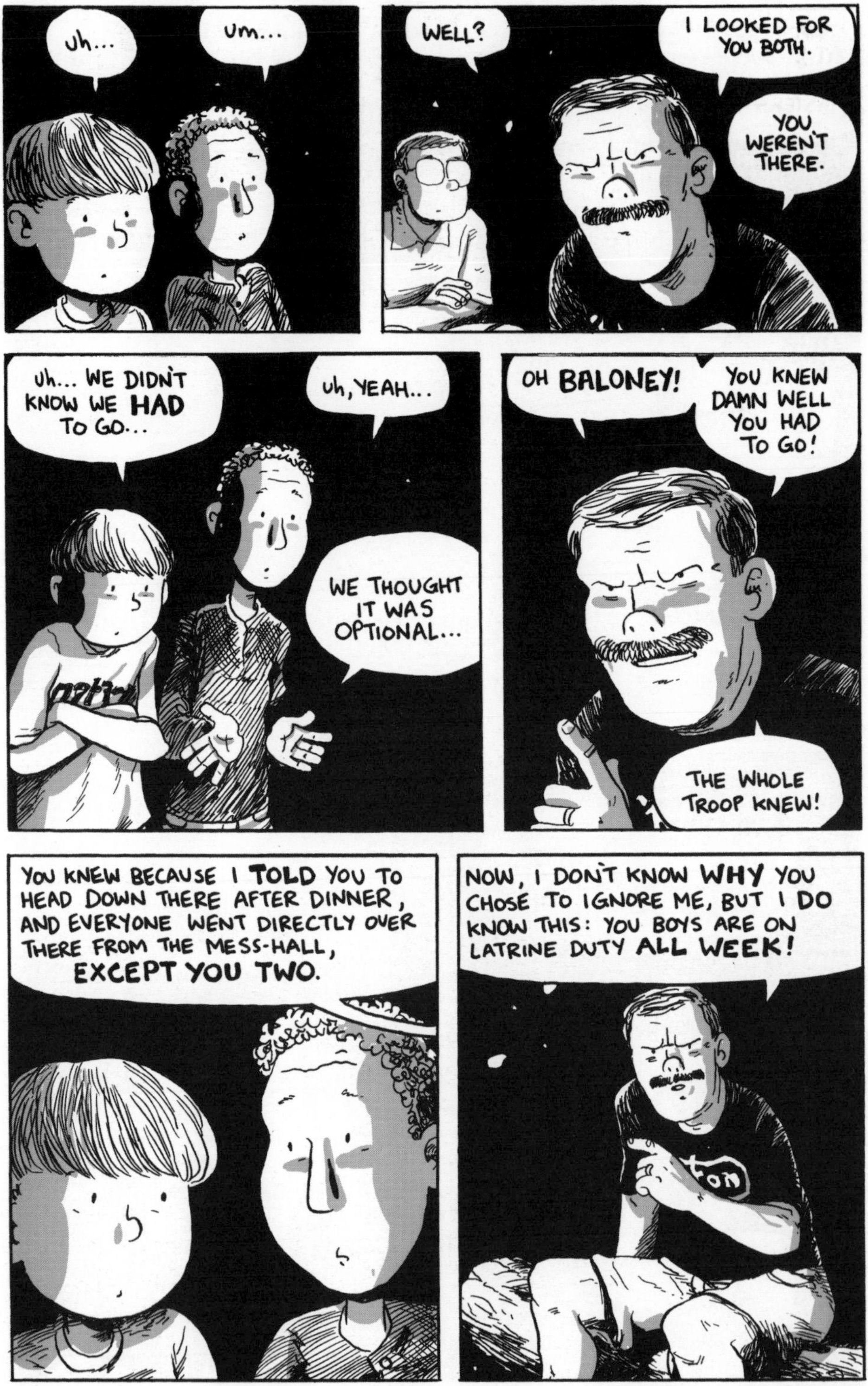
uh...
um...
WELL?
I LOOKED FOR YOU BOTH.
YOU WEREN'T THERE.
uh... WE DIDN'T KNOW WE HAD TO GO...
uh, YEAH...
WE THOUGHT IT WAS OPTIONAL...
OH BALONEY!
YOU KNEW DAMN WELL YOU HAD TO GO!
THE WHOLE TROOP KNEW!
YOU KNEW BECAUSE I TOLD YOU TO HEAD DOWN THERE AFTER DINNER, AND EVERYONE WENT DIRECTLY OVER THERE FROM THE MESS-HALL, EXCEPT YOU TWO.
NOW, I DON'T KNOW WHY YOU CHOSE TO IGNORE ME, BUT I DO KNOW THIS: YOU BOYS ARE ON LATRINE DUTY ALL WEEK!

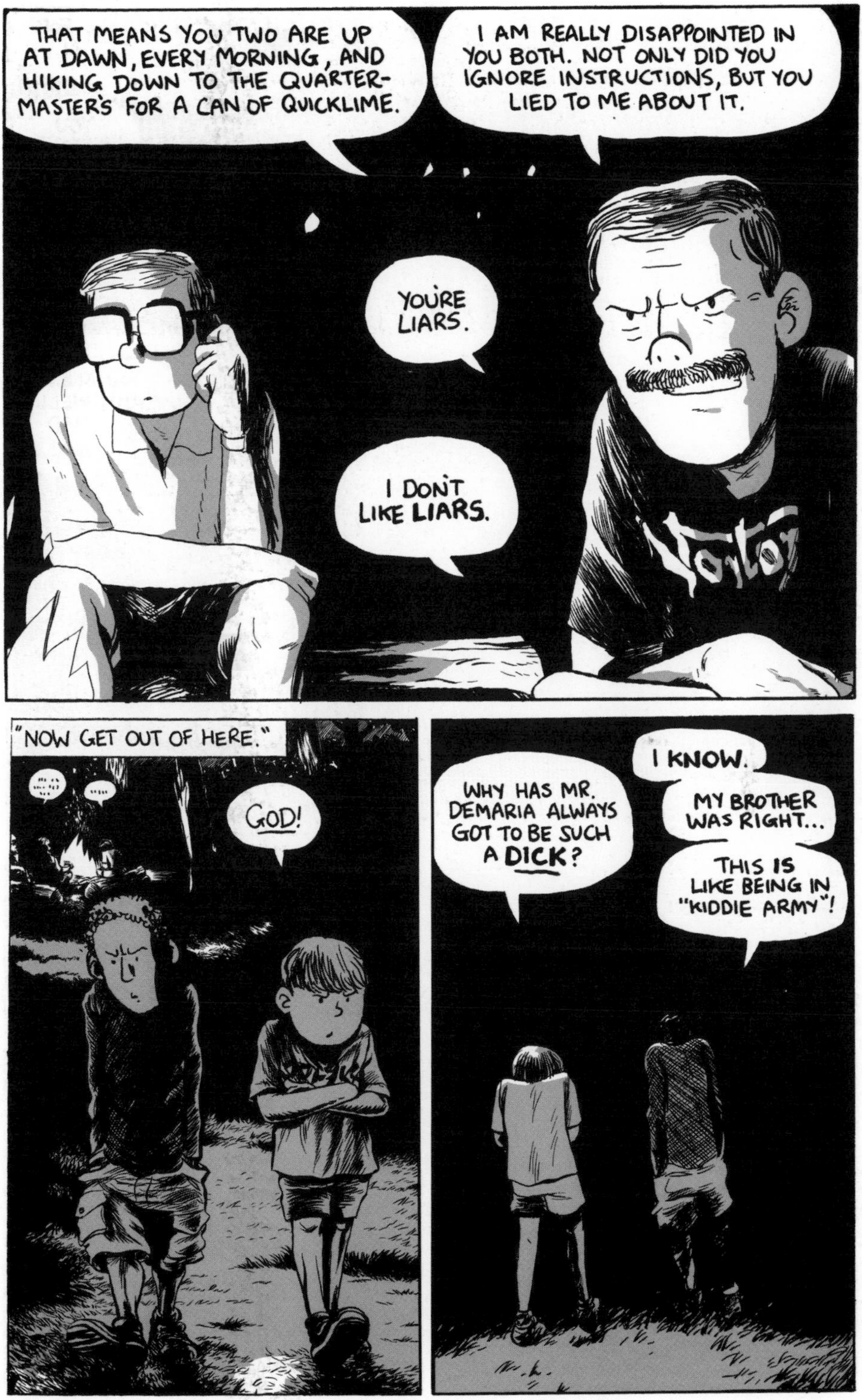
THAT MEANS YOU TWO ARE UP AT DAWN, EVERY MORNING, AND HIKING DOWN TO THE QUARTER-MASTER'S FOR A CAN OF QUICKLIME.
I AM REALLY DISAPPOINTED IN YOU BOTH. NOT ONLY DID YOU IGNORE INSTRUCTIONS, BUT YOU LIED TO ME ABOUT IT.
YOU'RE LIARS.
I DON'T LIKE LIARS.
"NOW GET OUT OF HERE."
GOD!
WHY HAS MR. DEMARIA ALWAYS GOT TO BE SUCH A DICK?
I KNOW.
MY BROTHER WAS RIGHT...
THIS IS LIKE BEING IN "KIDDIE ARMY"!

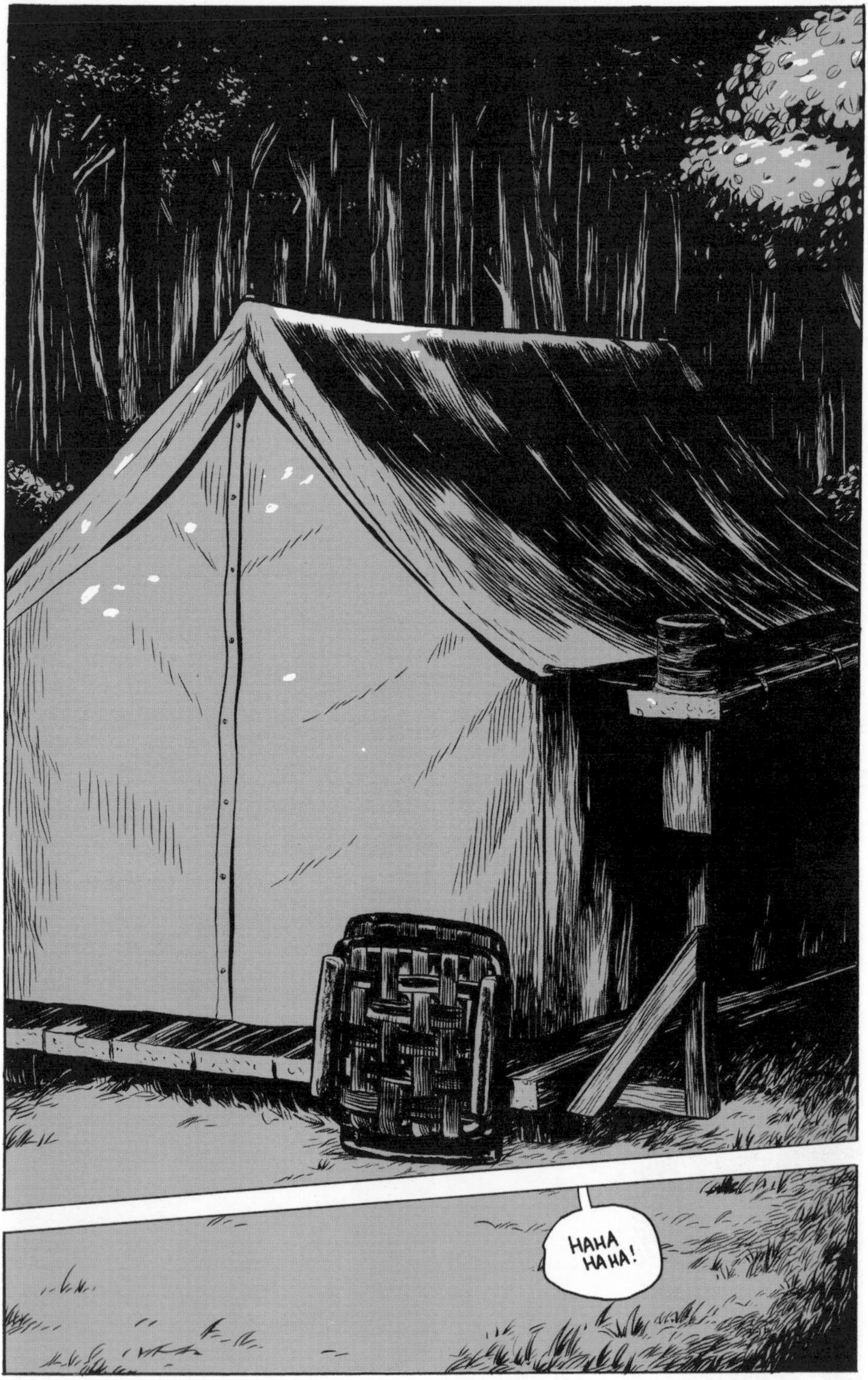
HAHA HAHA!

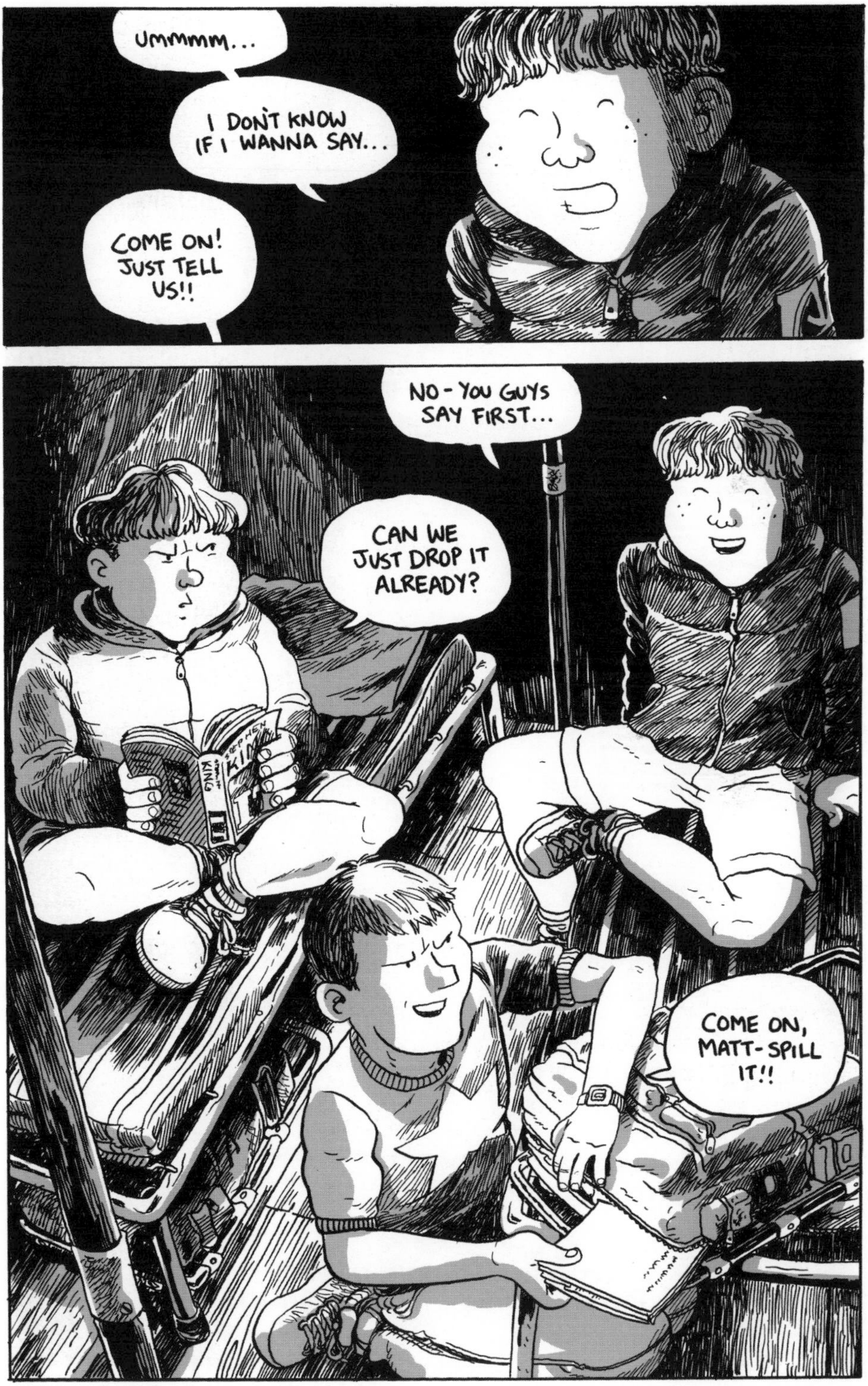
UMMMM...
I DON'T KNOW IF I WANNA SAY...
COME ON! JUST TELL US!!
NO - YOU GUYS SAY FIRST...
CAN WE JUST DROP IT ALREADY?
COME ON, MATT- SPILL IT!!

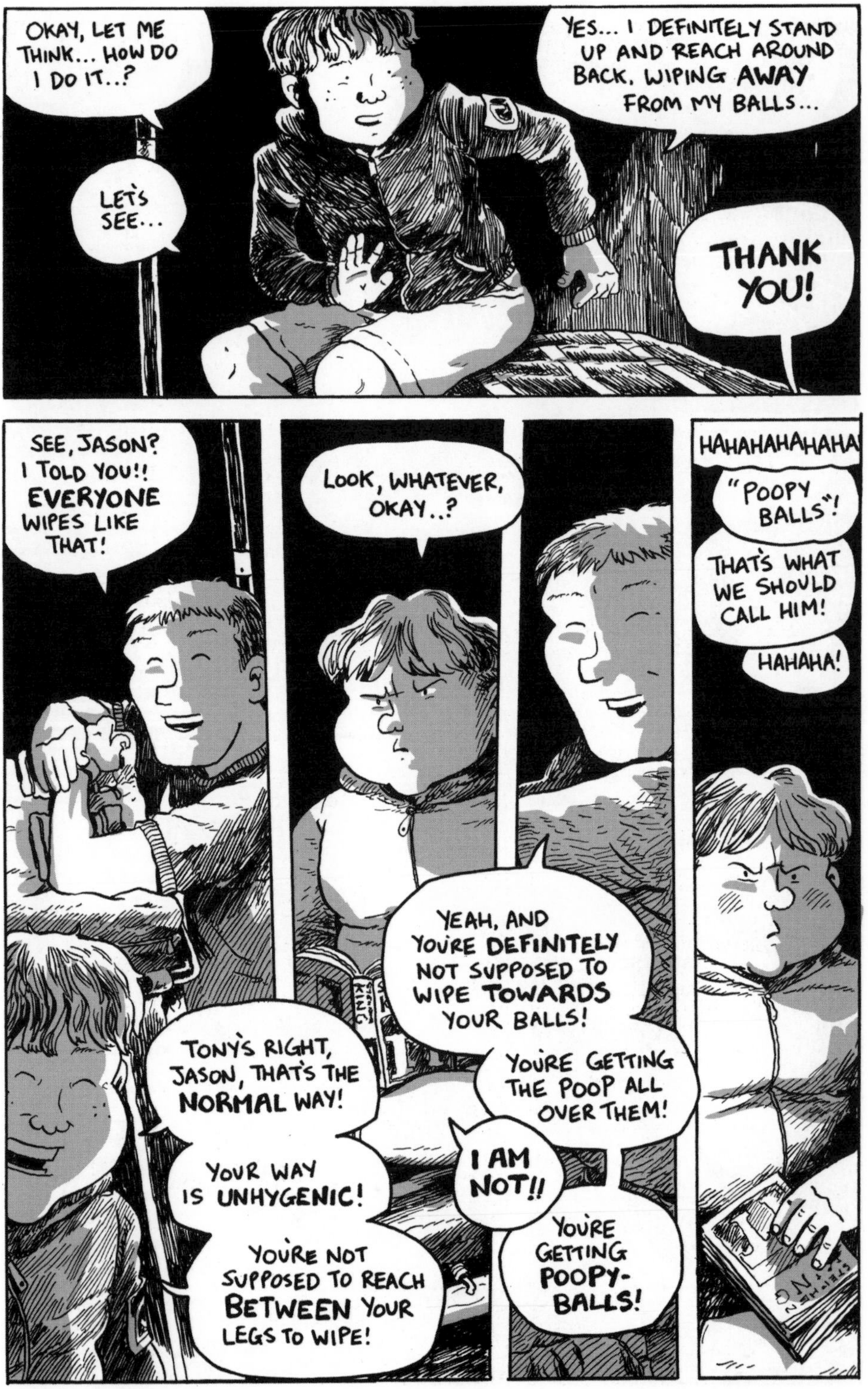
OKAY, LET ME THINK... HOW DO I DO IT..?
LET'S SEE...
YES... I DEFINITELY STAND UP AND REACH AROUND BACK, WIPING AWAY FROM MY BALLS...
THANK YOU!
SEE, JASON? I TOLD YOU!! EVERYONE WIPES LIKE THAT!
TONY'S RIGHT, JASON, THAT'S THE NORMAL WAY!
YOUR WAY IS UNHYGENIC!
YOU'RE NOT SUPPOSED TO REACH BETWEEN YOUR LEGS TO WIPE!
LOOK, WHATEVER, OKAY..?
YEAH, AND YOU'RE DEFINITELY NOT SUPPOSED TO WIPE TOWARDS YOUR BALLS!
YOU'RE GETTING THE POOP ALL OVER THEM!
I AM NOT!!
YOU'RE GETTING POOPY-BALLS!
HAHAHAHAHAHAHA
"POOPY BALLS"!
THAT'S WHAT WE SHOULD CALL HIM!
HAHAHA!

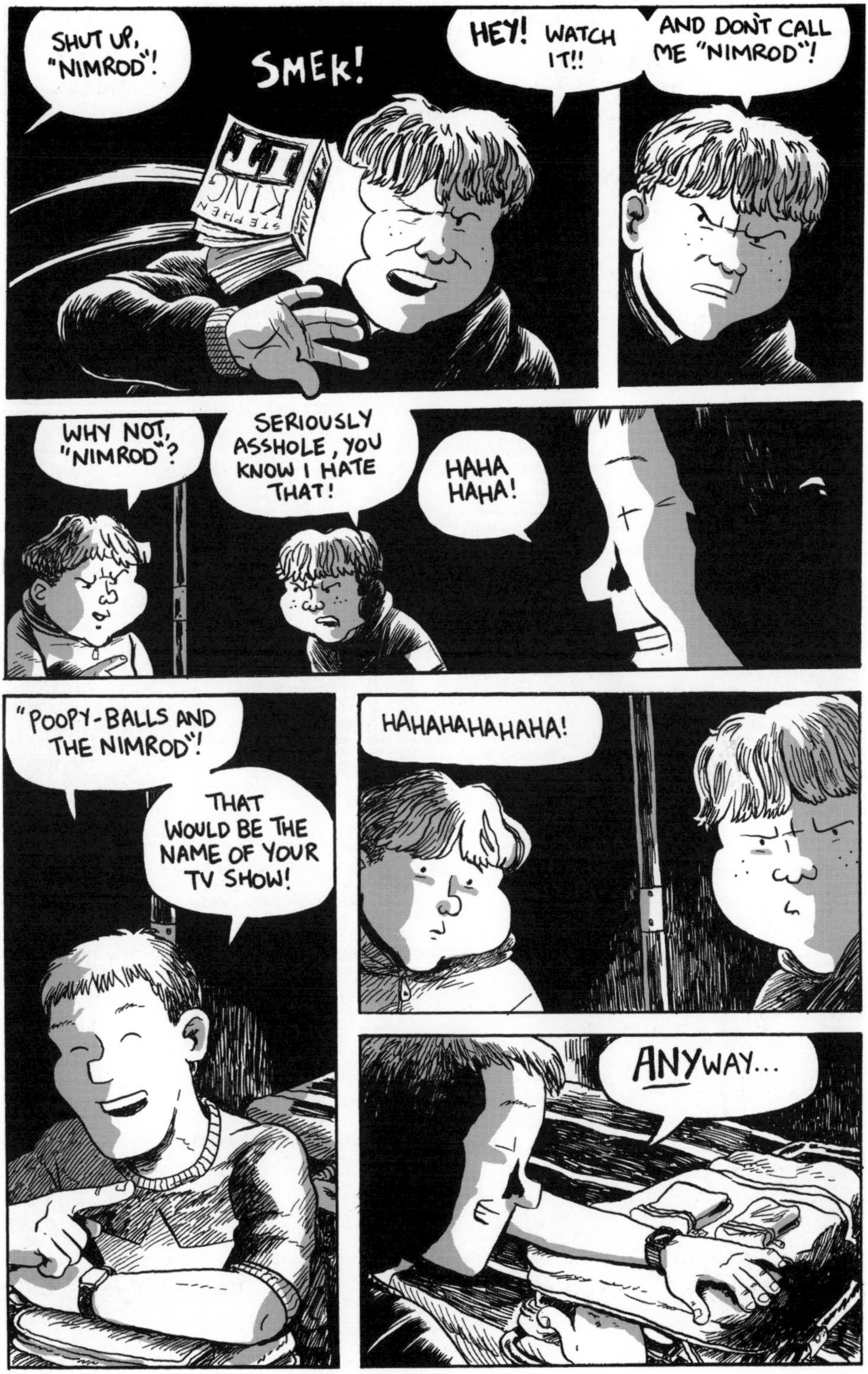
SHUT UP, "NIMROD"!
SMEK!
STEPHEN KING IT
HEY! WATCH IT!!
AND DON'T CALL ME "NIMROD"!
WHY NOT, "NIMROD"?
SERIOUSLY ASSHOLE, YOU KNOW I HATE THAT!
HAHA HAHA!
"POOPY-BALLS AND THE NIMROD"!
THAT WOULD BE THE NAME OF YOUR TV SHOW!
HAHAHAHAHAHA!
ANYWAY...

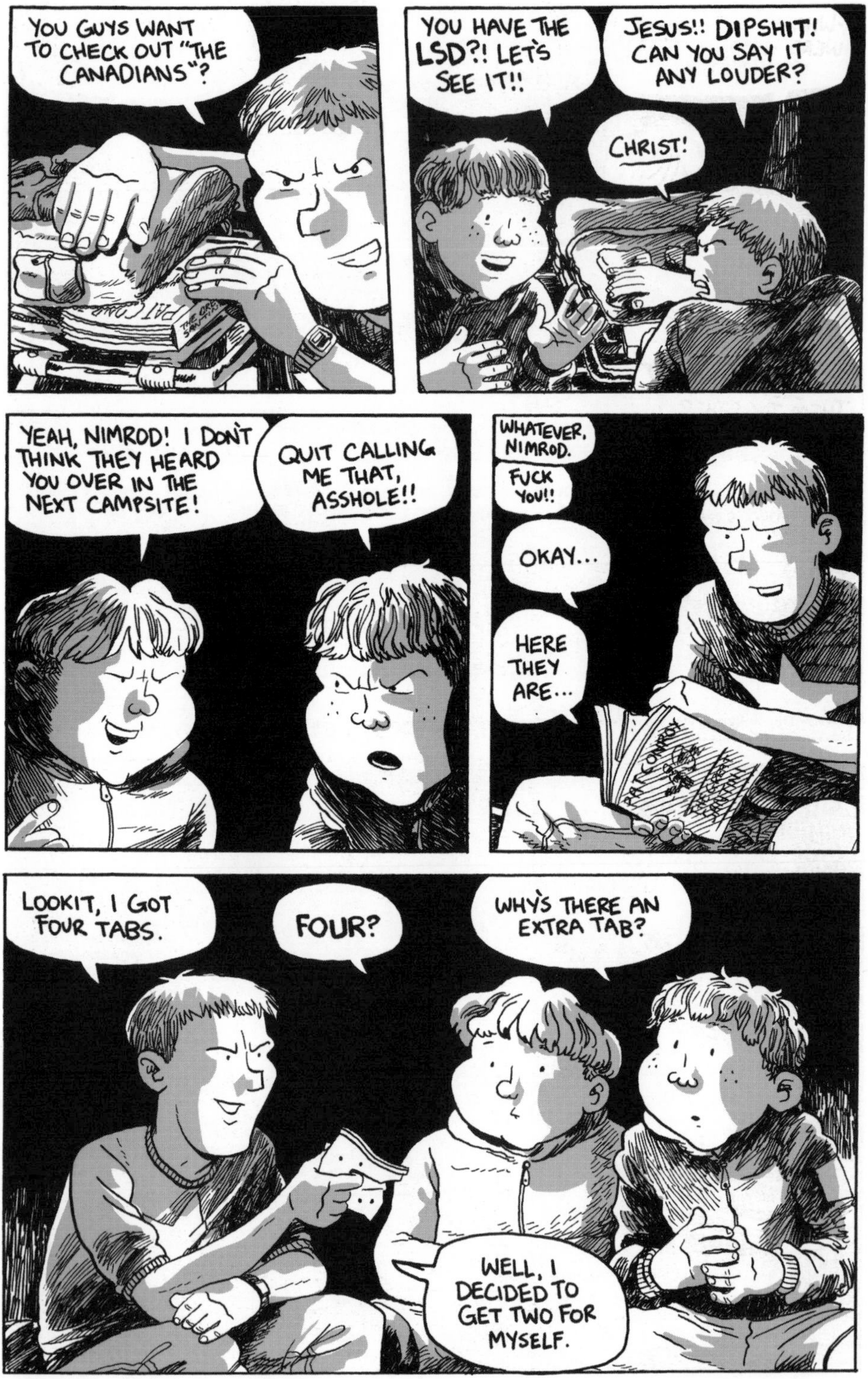
YOU GUYS WANT TO CHECK OUT "THE CANADIANS"?
YOU HAVE THE LSD?! LET'S SEE IT!!
JESUS!! DIPSHIT! CAN YOU SAY IT ANY LOUDER?
CHRIST!
YEAH, NIMROD! I DON'T THINK THEY HEARD YOU OVER IN THE NEXT CAMPSITE!
QUIT CALLING ME THAT, ASSHOLE!!
WHATEVER, NIMROD.
FUCK YOU!!
OKAY...
HERE THEY ARE...
LOOKIT, I GOT FOUR TABS.
FOUR?
WHY'S THERE AN EXTRA TAB?
WELL, I DECIDED TO GET TWO FOR MYSELF.

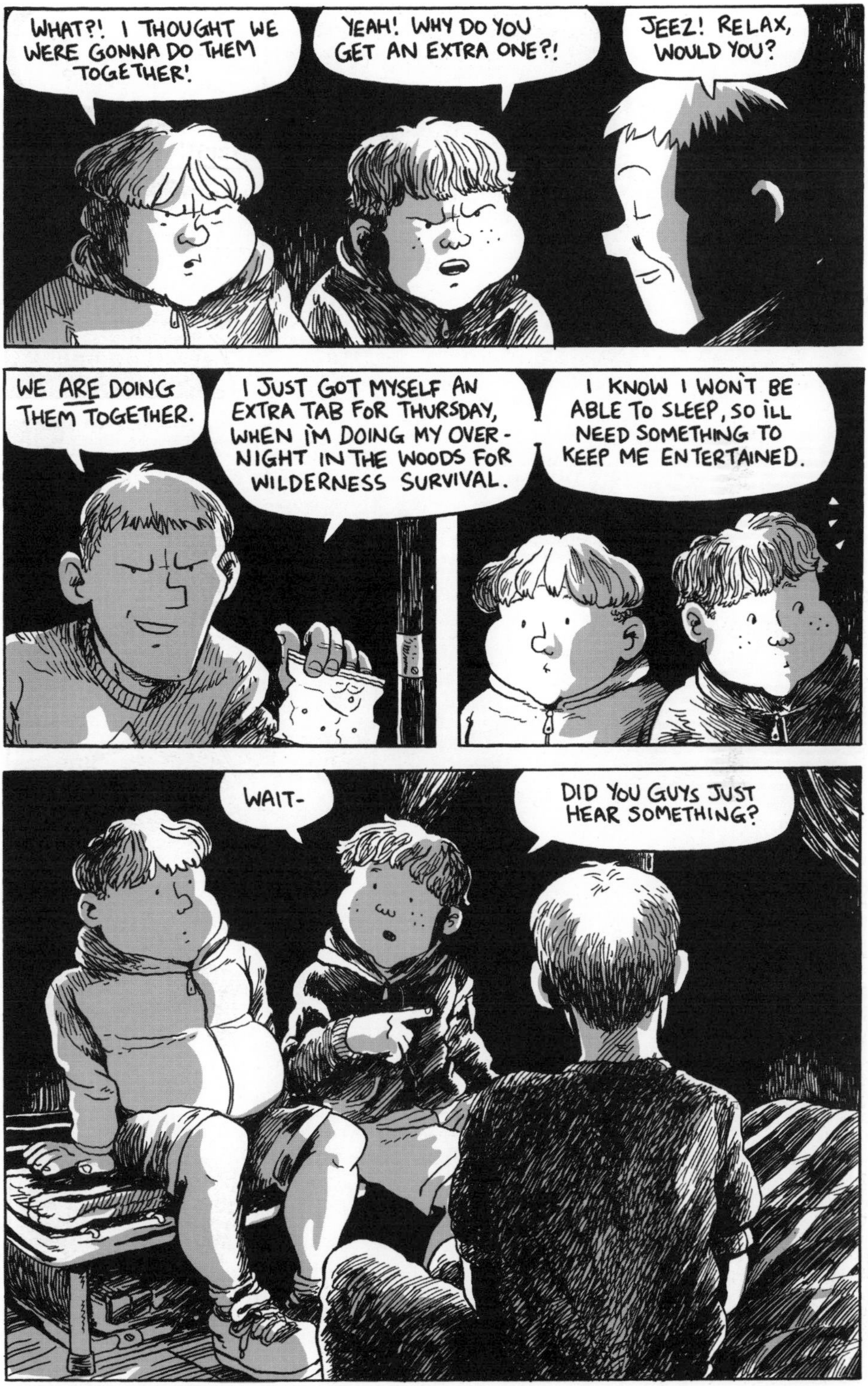
WHAT?! I THOUGHT WE WERE GONNA DO THEM TOGETHER!
YEAH! WHY DO YOU GET AN EXTRA ONE?!
JEEZ! RELAX, WOULD YOU?
WE ARE DOING THEM TOGETHER.
I JUST GOT MYSELF AN EXTRA TAB FOR THURSDAY, WHEN I'M DOING MY OVER-NIGHT IN THE WOODS FOR WILDERNESS SURVIVAL.
I KNOW I WON'T BE ABLE TO SLEEP, SO I'LL NEED SOMETHING TO KEEP ME ENTERTAINED.
WAIT-
DID YOU GUYS JUST HEAR SOMETHING?

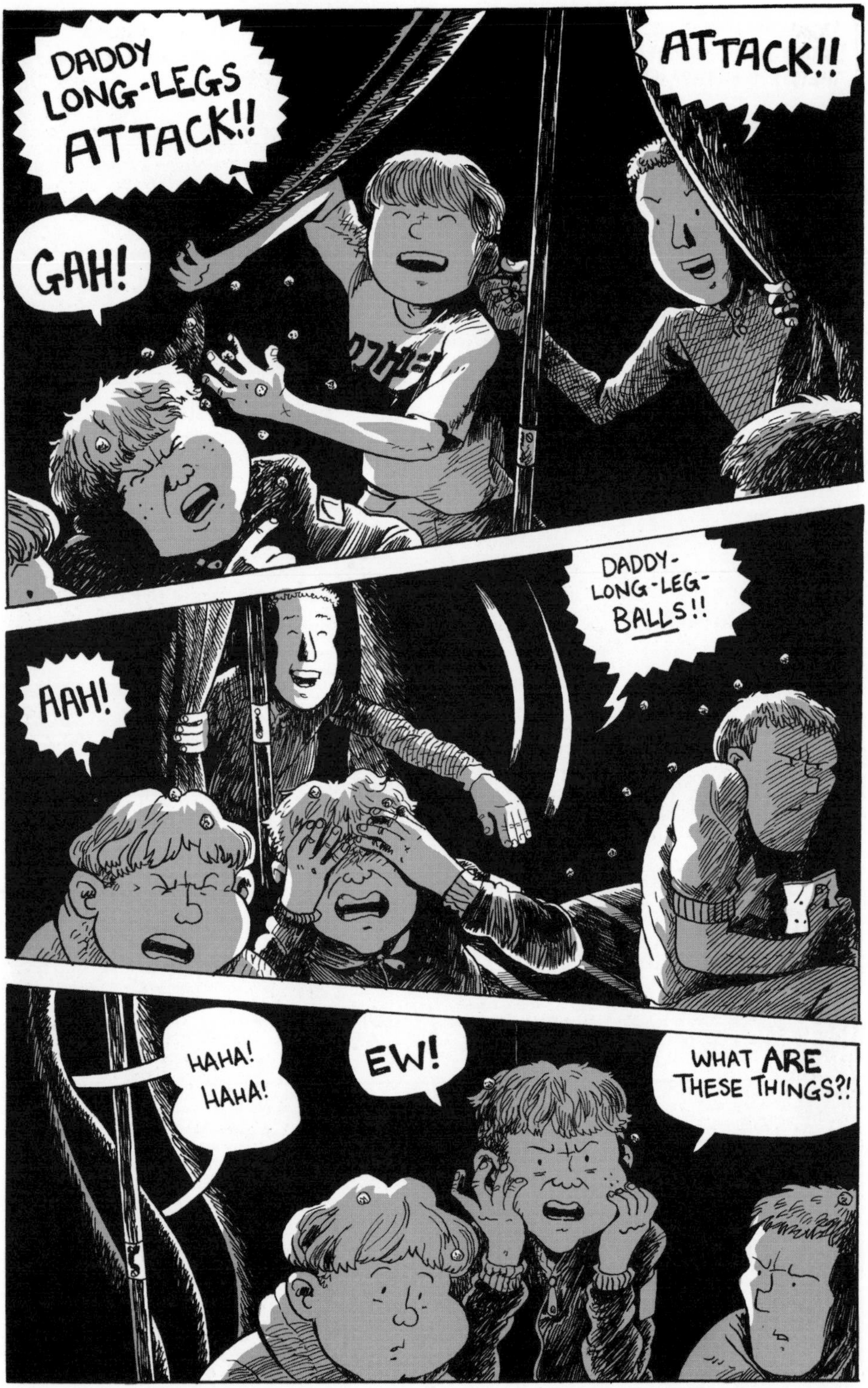
DADDY LONG-LEGS ATTACK!!
ATTACK!!
GAH!
DADDY-LONG-LEG-BALLS!!
AAH!
HAHA! HAHA!
EW!
WHAT ARE THESE THINGS?!

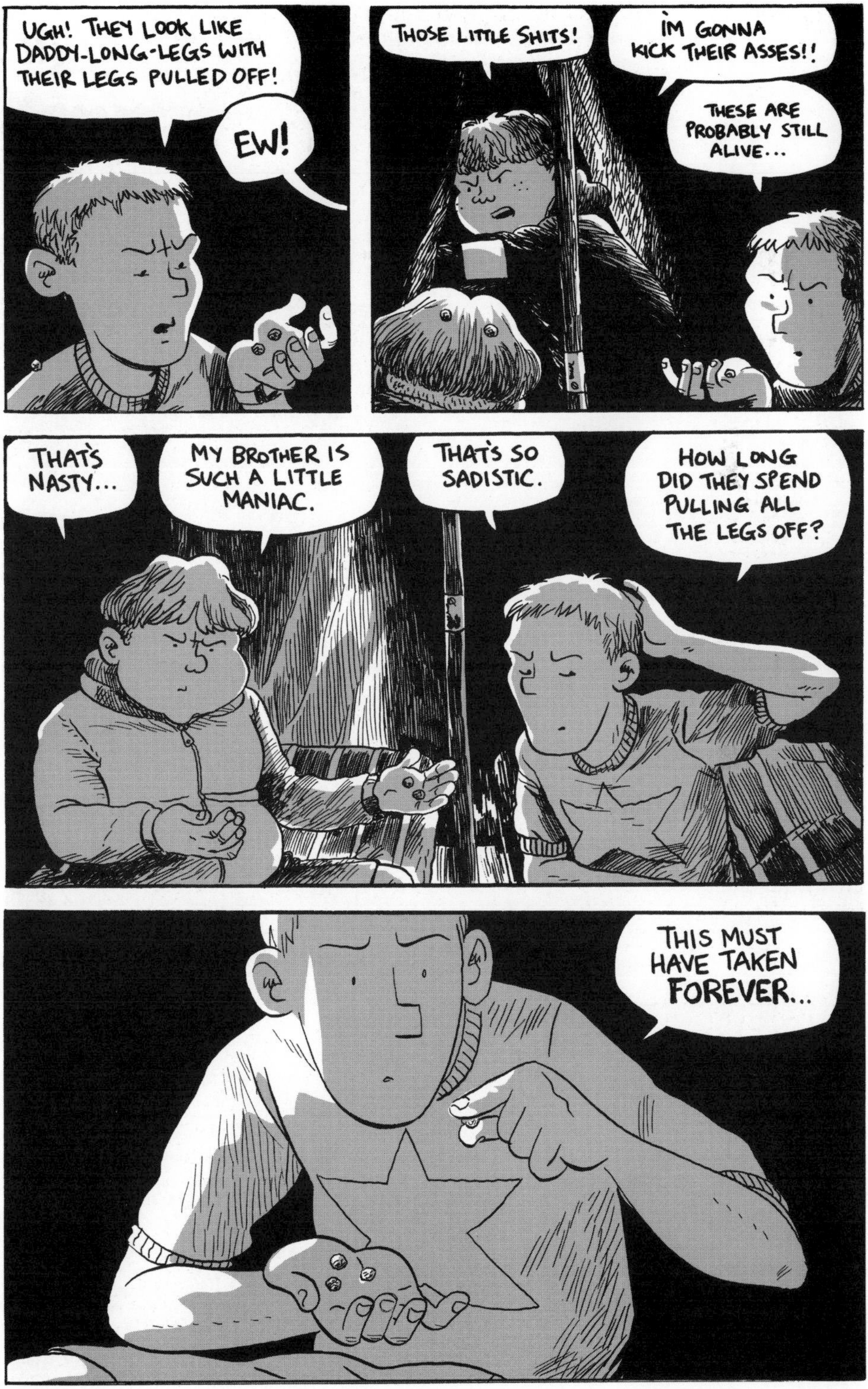
UGH! THEY LOOK LIKE DADDY-LONG-LEGS WITH THEIR LEGS PULLED OFF!
EW!
THOSE LITTLE SHITS!
IM GONNA KICK THEIR ASSES!!
THESE ARE PROBABLY STILL ALIVE...
THAT'S NASTY...
MY BROTHER IS SUCH A LITTLE MANIAC.
THAT'S SO SADISTIC.
HOW LONG DID THEY SPEND PULLING ALL THE LEGS OFF?
THIS MUST HAVE TAKEN FOREVER...

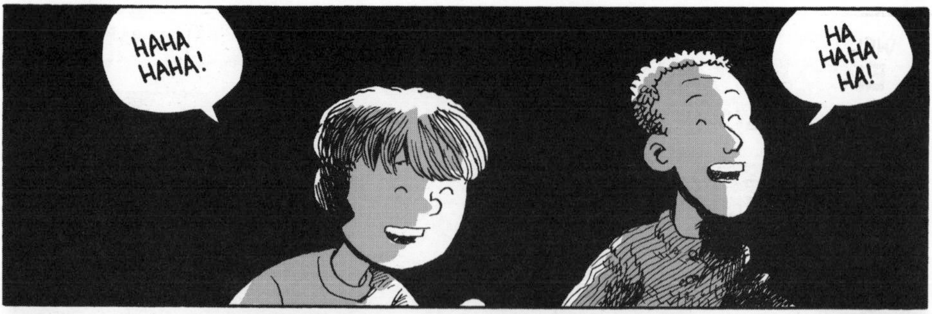
HAHA HAHA!
HA HAHA HA!
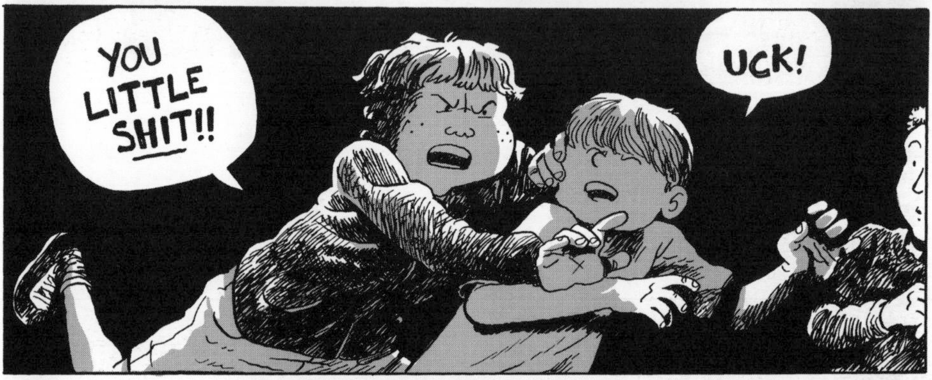
YOU LITTLE SHIT!!
UCK!
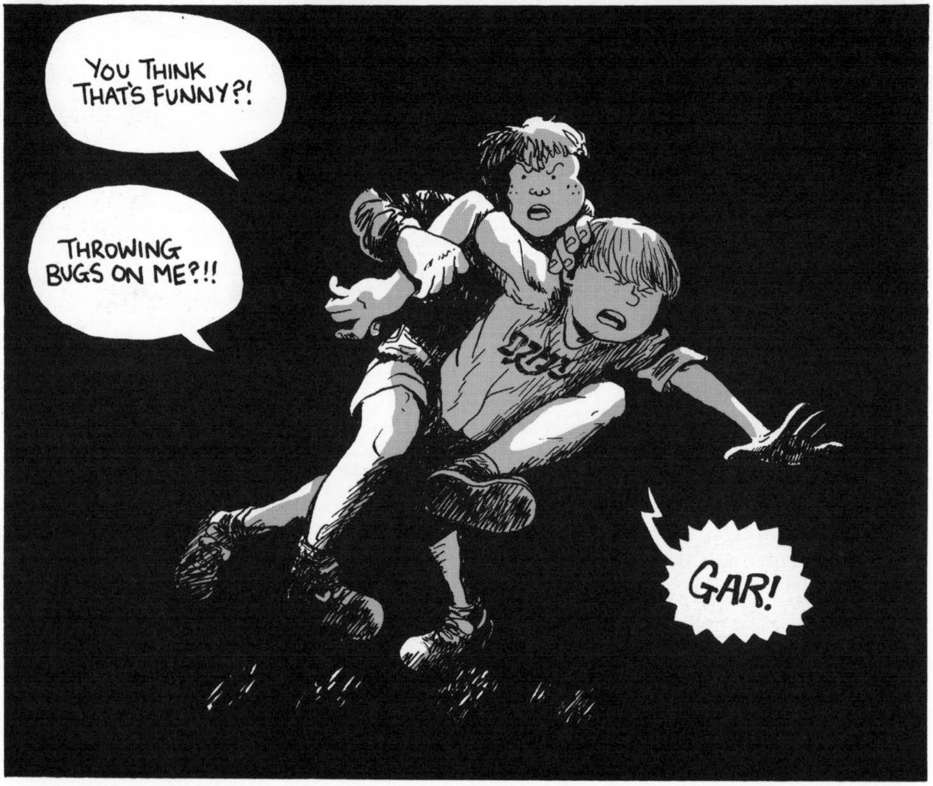
YOU THINK THAT'S FUNNY?!
THROWING BUGS ON ME?!!
GAR!

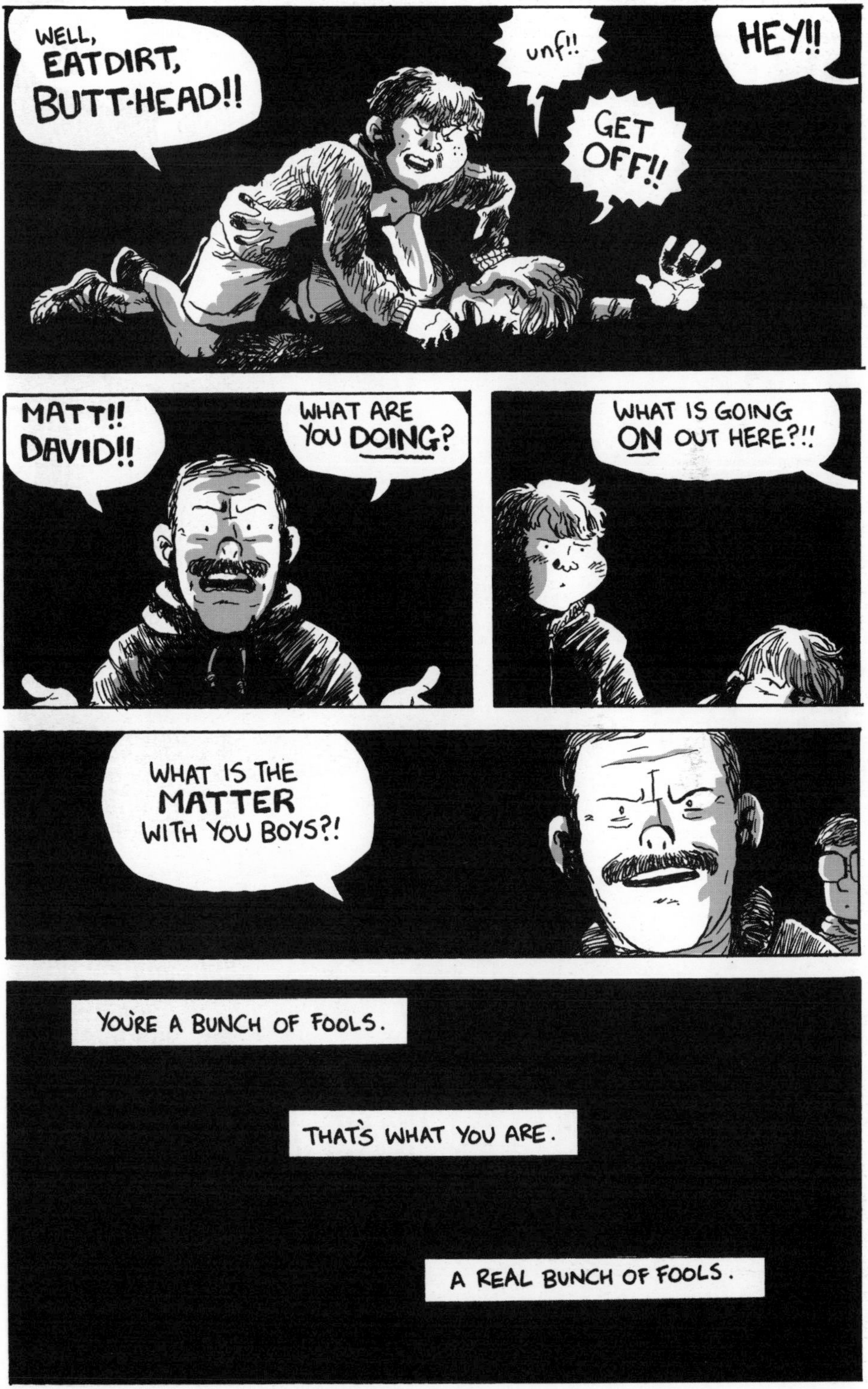
WELL, EATDIRT, BUTT-HEAD!!
unf!!
HEY!!
GET OFF!!
MATT!! DAVID!!
WHAT ARE YOU DOING?
WHAT IS GOING ON OUT HERE?!!
WHAT IS THE MATTER WITH YOU BOYS?!
YOU'RE A BUNCH OF FOOLS.
THAT'S WHAT YOU ARE.
A REAL BUNCH OF FOOLS.

TROOP 142
Eatontown, NJ

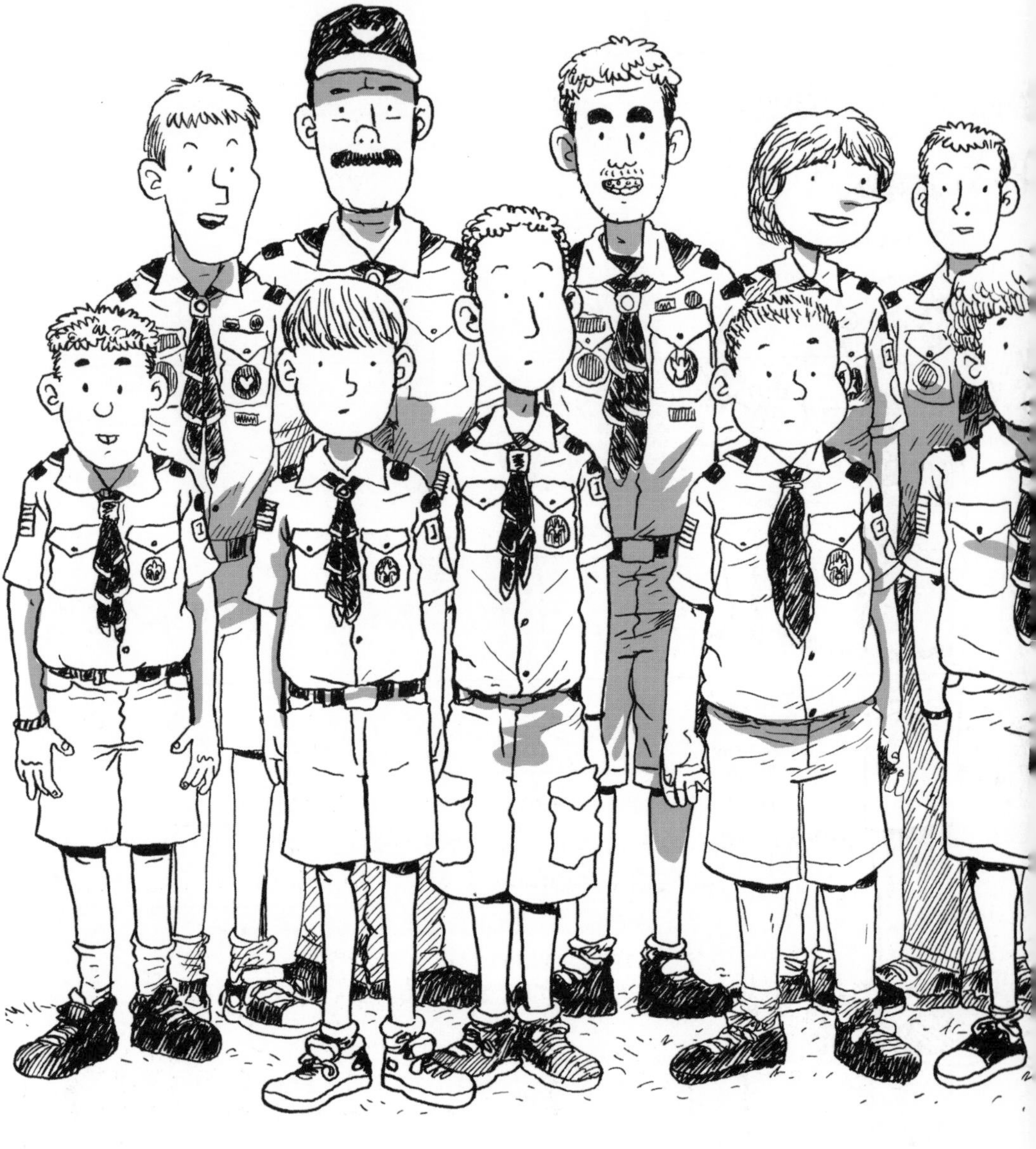

PINEWOOD
FOREST, 1995

b-deep

b-deep

b-deep

b-deep

b-deep

b-deep

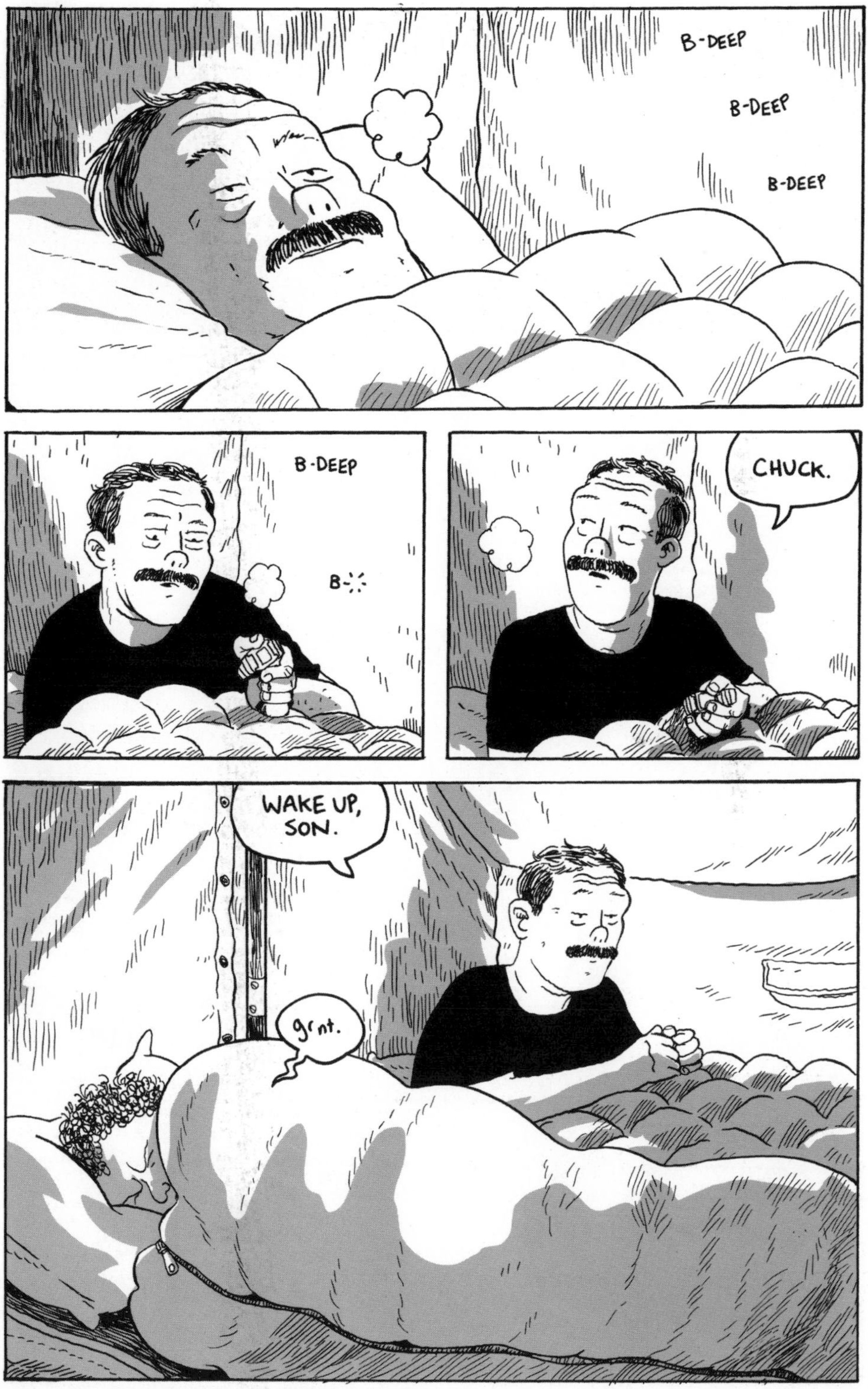

B-DEEP
B-DEEP
B-DEEP
B-DEEP
B-
CHUCK.
WAKE UP, SON.
grnt.

MONDAY

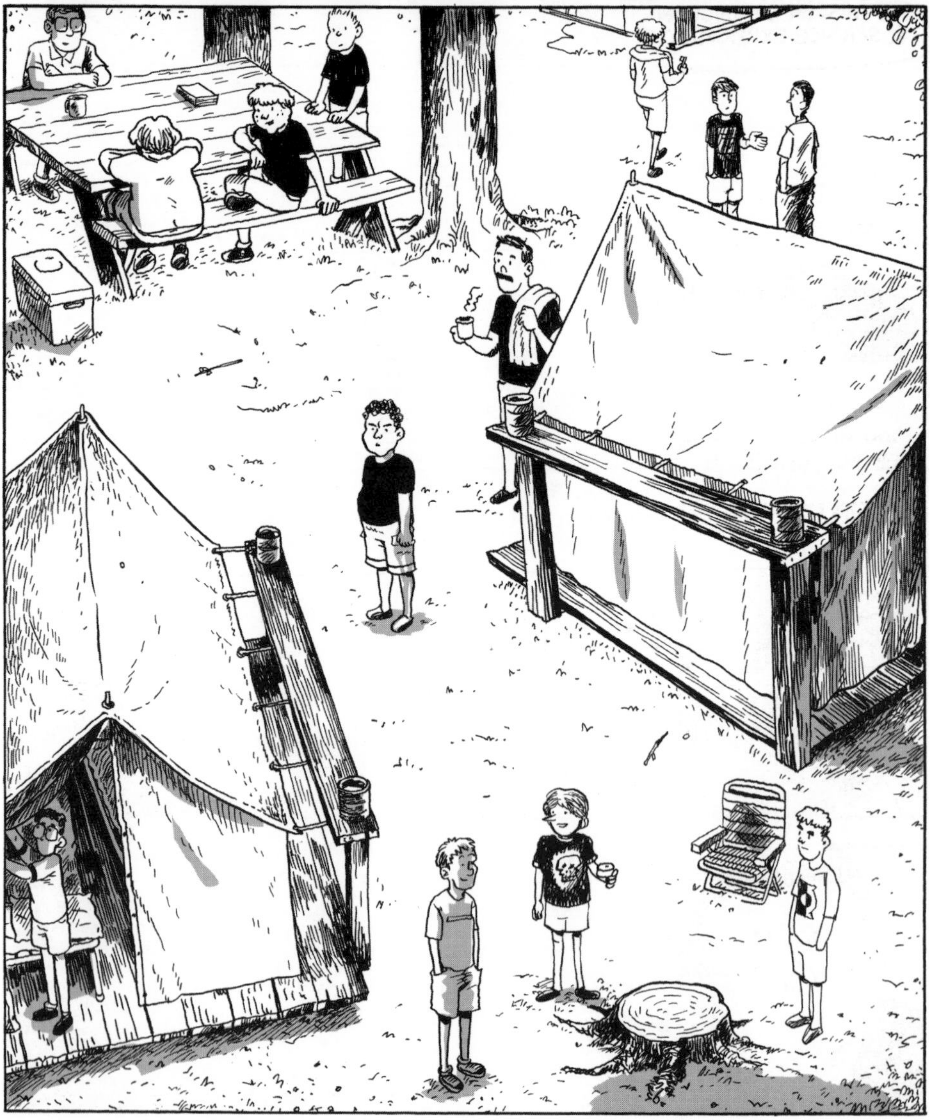

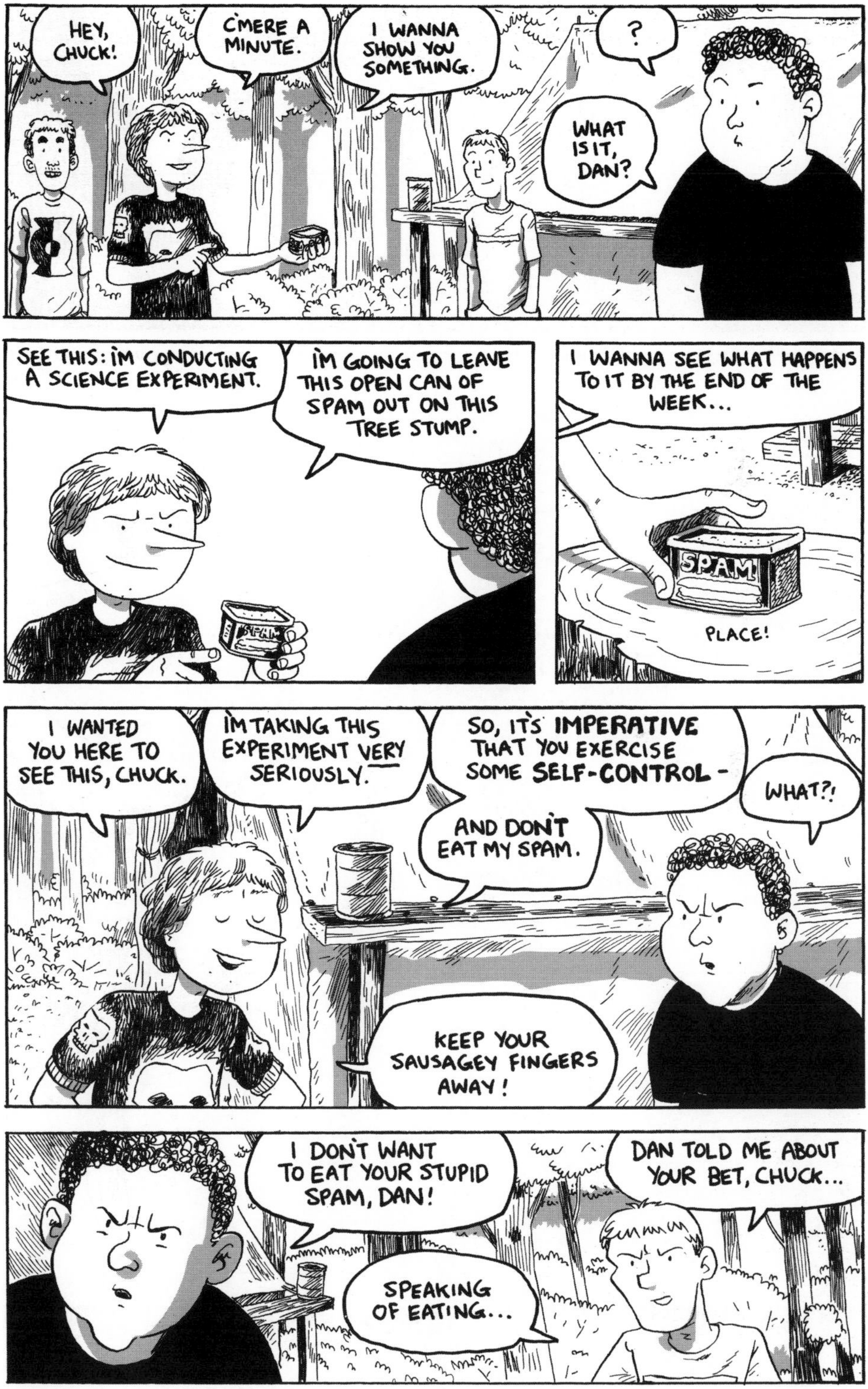
HEY, CHUCK!
C'MERE A MINUTE.
I WANNA SHOW YOU SOMETHING.
?
WHAT IS IT, DAN?
SEE THIS: I'M CONDUCTING A SCIENCE EXPERIMENT.
I'M GOING TO LEAVE THIS OPEN CAN OF SPAM OUT ON THIS TREE STUMP.
I WANNA SEE WHAT HAPPENS TO IT BY THE END OF THE WEEK...
SPAM
PLACE!
I WANTED YOU HERE TO SEE THIS, CHUCK.
I'M TAKING THIS EXPERIMENT VERY SERIOUSLY.
SO, IT'S IMPERATIVE THAT YOU EXERCISE SOME SELF-CONTROL -
AND DON'T EAT MY SPAM.
WHAT?!
KEEP YOUR SAUSAGEY FINGERS AWAY!
I DON'T WANT TO EAT YOUR STUPID SPAM, DAN!
SPEAKING OF EATING...
DAN TOLD ME ABOUT YOUR BET, CHUCK...

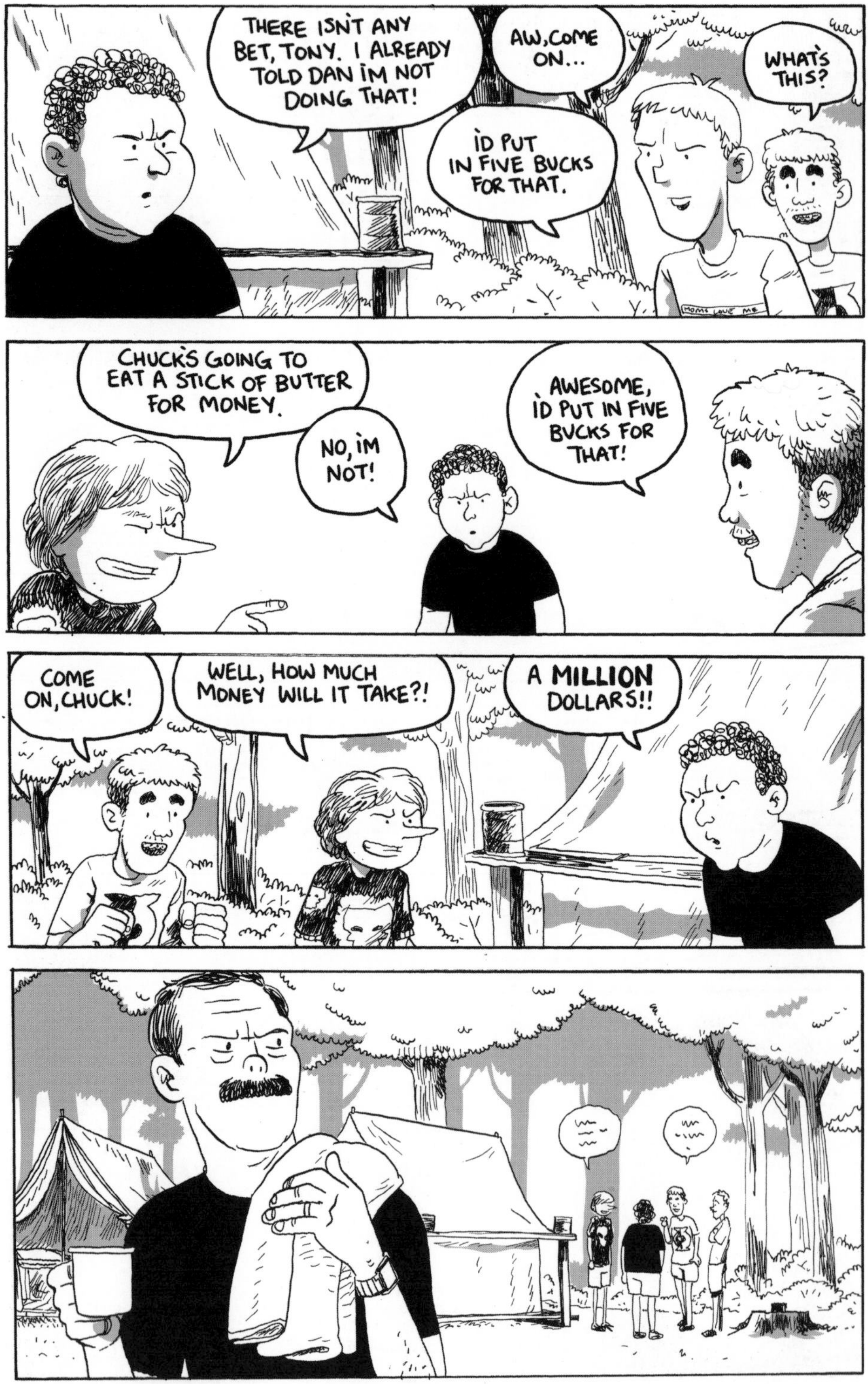
THERE ISN'T ANY BET, TONY. I ALREADY TOLD DAN I'M NOT DOING THAT!
AW, COME ON...
I'D PUT IN FIVE BUCKS FOR THAT.
WHAT'S THIS?
MOMS LOVE ME
CHUCK'S GOING TO EAT A STICK OF BUTTER FOR MONEY.
NO, I'M NOT!
AWESOME, I'D PUT IN FIVE BUCKS FOR THAT!
COME ON, CHUCK!
WELL, HOW MUCH MONEY WILL IT TAKE?!
A **MILLION** DOLLARS!!

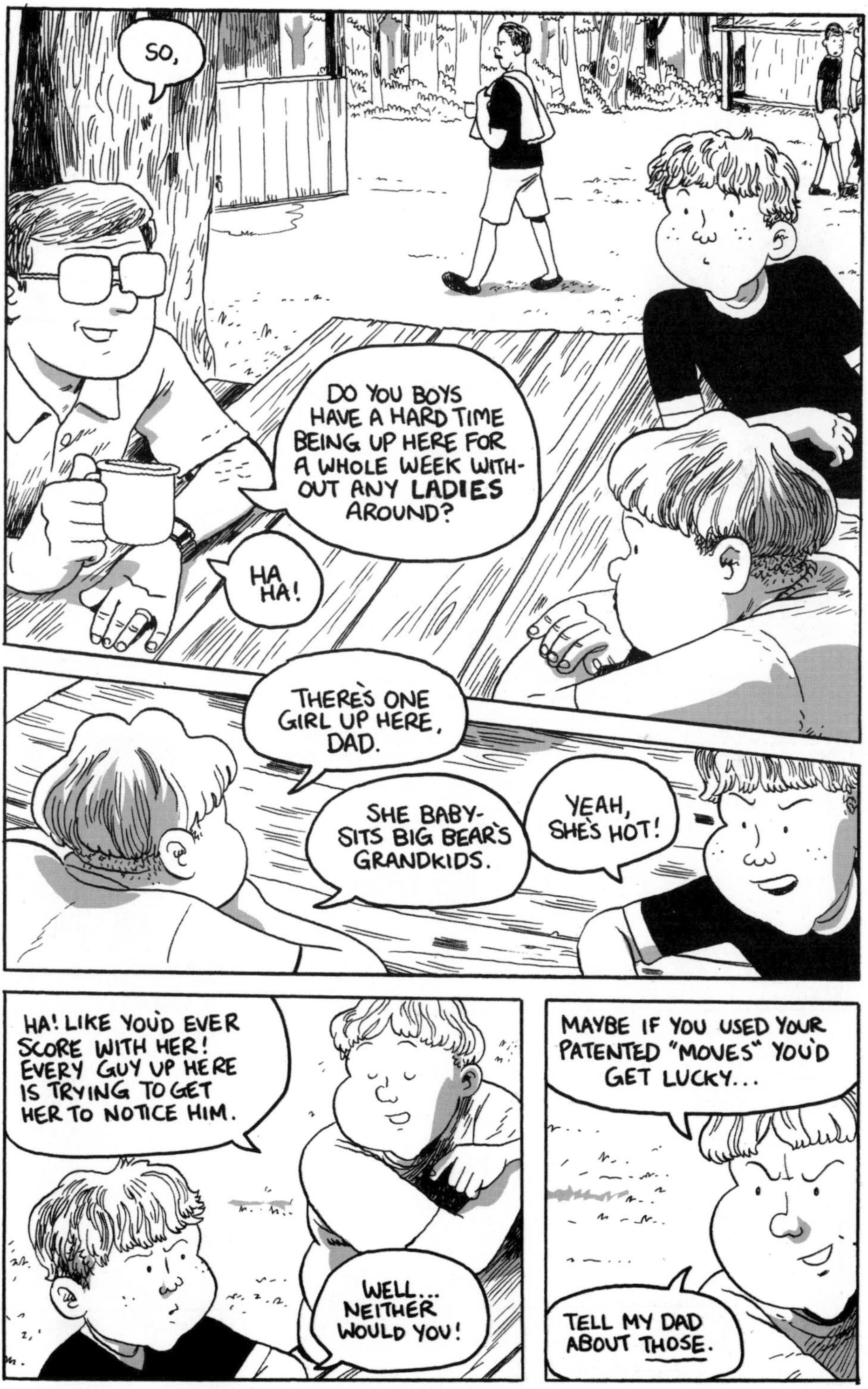
SO,
DO YOU BOYS HAVE A HARD TIME BEING UP HERE FOR A WHOLE WEEK WITHOUT ANY LADIES AROUND?
HA HA!
THERE'S ONE GIRL UP HERE, DAD.
SHE BABY-SITS BIG BEAR'S GRANDKIDS.
YEAH, SHE'S HOT!
HA! LIKE YOU'D EVER SCORE WITH HER! EVERY GUY UP HERE IS TRYING TO GET HER TO NOTICE HIM.
WELL... NEITHER WOULD YOU!
MAYBE IF YOU USED YOUR PATENTED "MOVES" YOU'D GET LUCKY...
TELL MY DAD ABOUT THOSE.

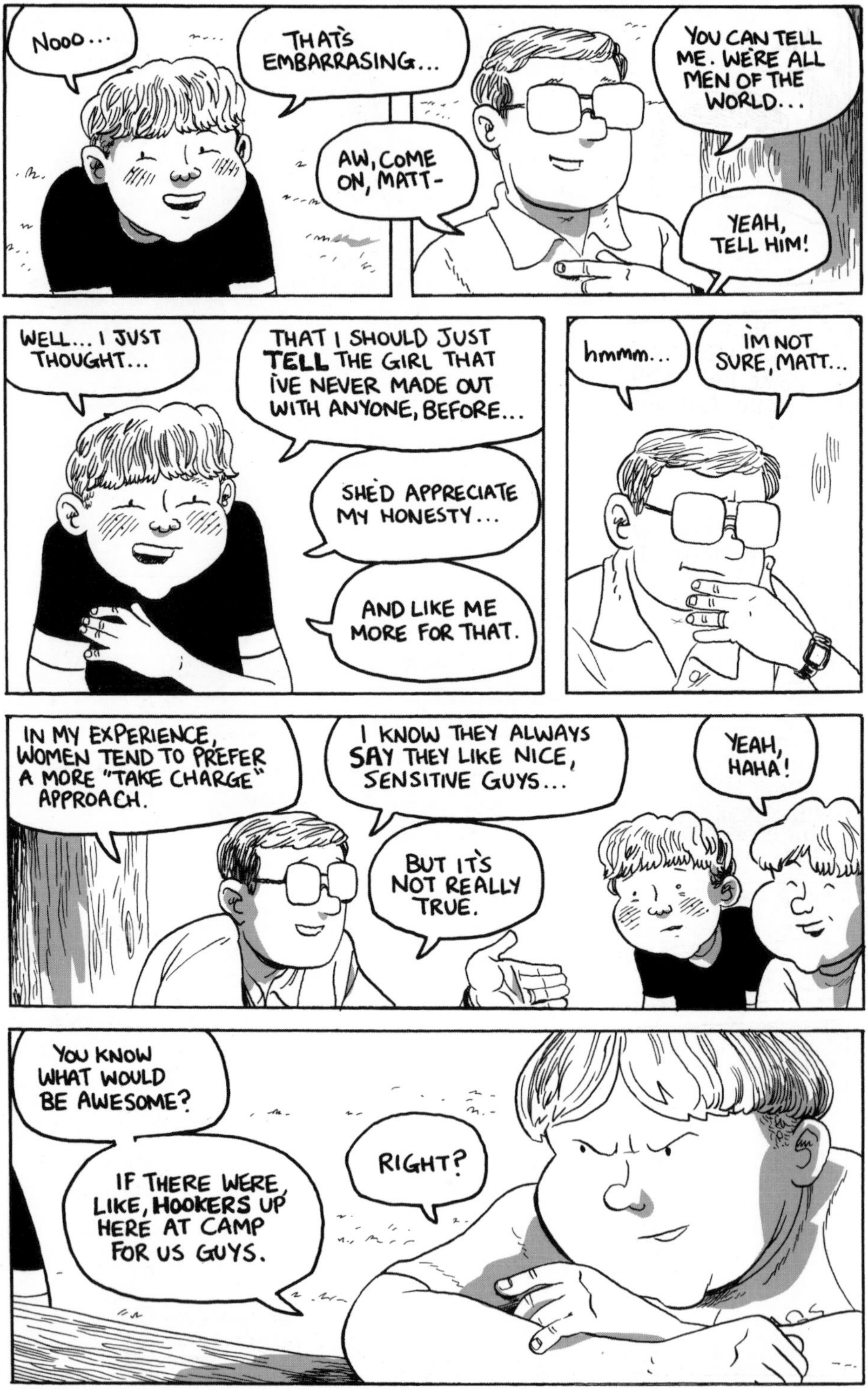
Nooo...
THAT'S EMBARRASING...
AW, COME ON, MATT-
YOU CAN TELL ME. WE'RE ALL MEN OF THE WORLD...
YEAH, TELL HIM!
WELL... I JUST THOUGHT...
THAT I SHOULD JUST **TELL** THE GIRL THAT I'VE NEVER MADE OUT WITH ANYONE, BEFORE...
SHE'D APPRECIATE MY HONESTY...
AND LIKE ME MORE FOR THAT.
hmmm...
I'M NOT SURE, MATT...
IN MY EXPERIENCE, WOMEN TEND TO PREFER A MORE "TAKE CHARGE" APPROACH.
I KNOW THEY ALWAYS **SAY** THEY LIKE NICE, SENSITIVE GUYS...
BUT IT'S NOT REALLY TRUE.
YEAH, HAHA!
YOU KNOW WHAT WOULD BE AWESOME?
IF THERE WERE, LIKE, **HOOKERS** UP HERE AT CAMP FOR US GUYS.
RIGHT?

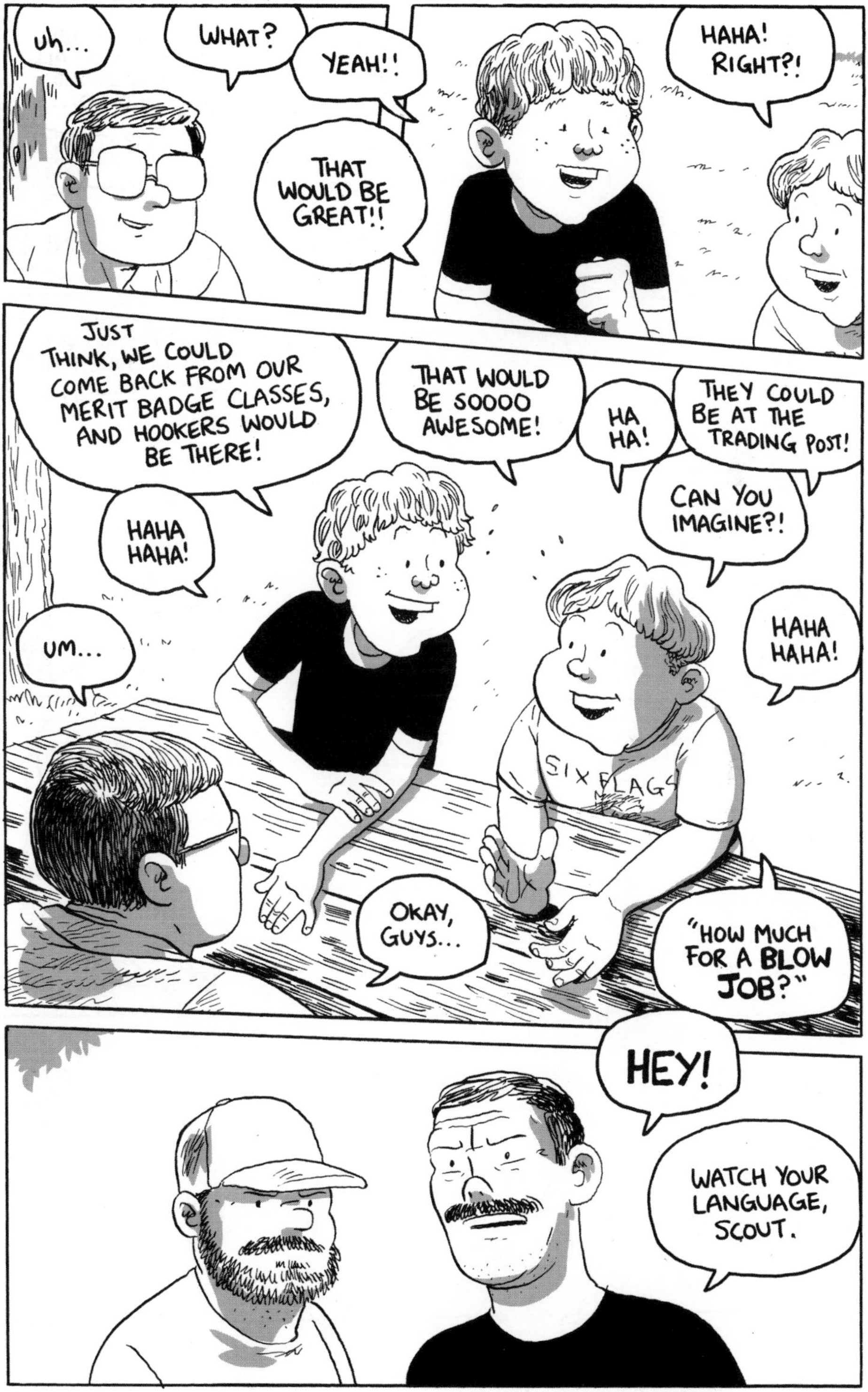
uh...
WHAT?
YEAH!!
THAT WOULD BE GREAT!!
HAHA! RIGHT?!
JUST THINK, WE COULD COME BACK FROM OUR MERIT BADGE CLASSES, AND HOOKERS WOULD BE THERE!
THAT WOULD BE SOOOO AWESOME!
HA HA!
THEY COULD BE AT THE TRADING POST!
HAHA HAHA!
CAN YOU IMAGINE?!
UM...
HAHA HAHA!
SIX FLAGS
OKAY, GUYS...
"HOW MUCH FOR A **BLOW JOB**?"
HEY!
WATCH YOUR LANGUAGE, SCOUT.

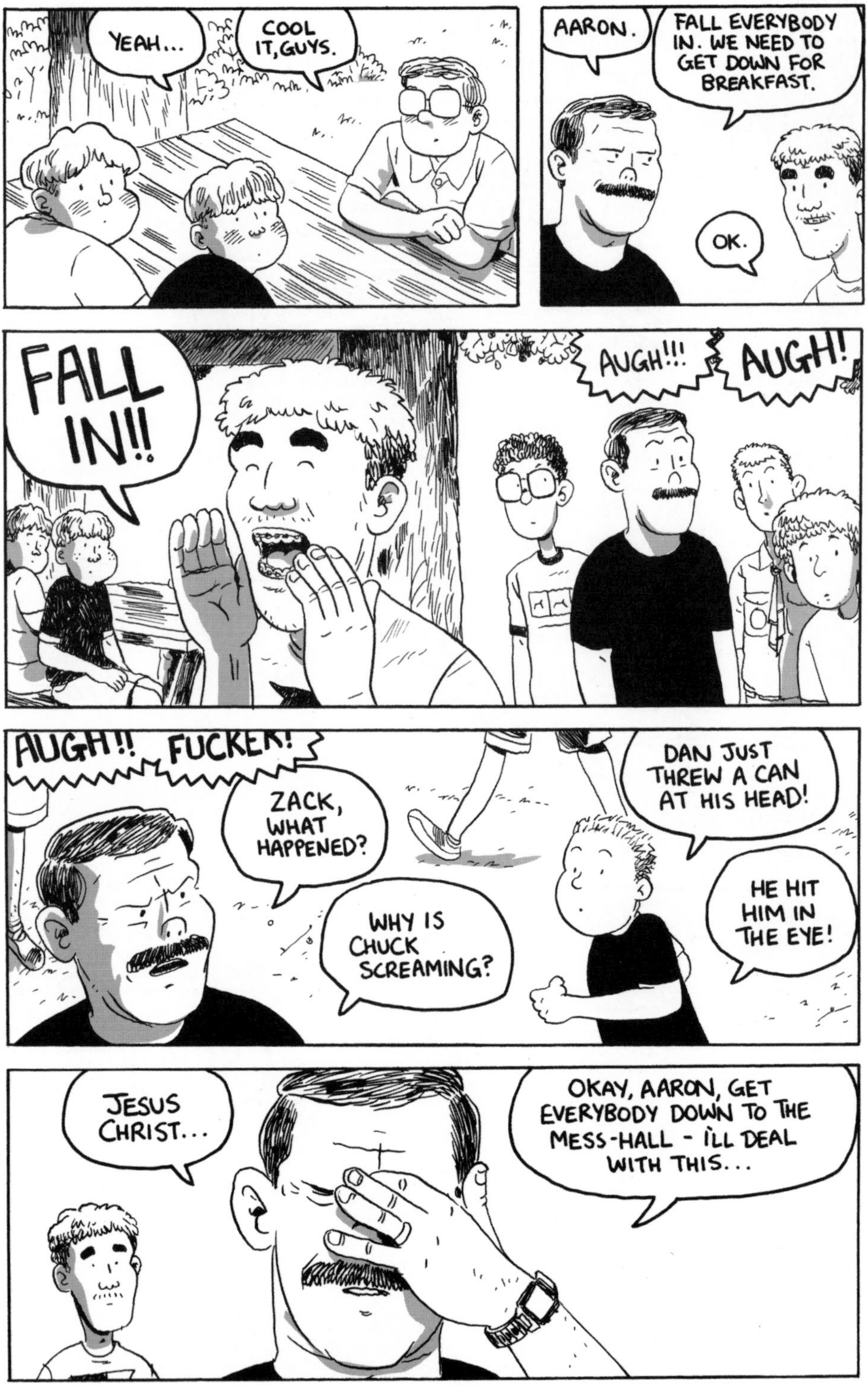
YEAH...
COOL IT, GUYS.
AARON.
FALL EVERYBODY IN. WE NEED TO GET DOWN FOR BREAKFAST.
OK.
FALL IN!!
AUGH!!!
AUGH!
AUGH!!
FUCKER!
ZACK, WHAT HAPPENED?
WHY IS CHUCK SCREAMING?
DAN JUST THREW A CAN AT HIS HEAD!
HE HIT HIM IN THE EYE!
JESUS CHRIST...
OKAY, AARON, GET EVERYBODY DOWN TO THE MESS-HALL - I'LL DEAL WITH THIS...

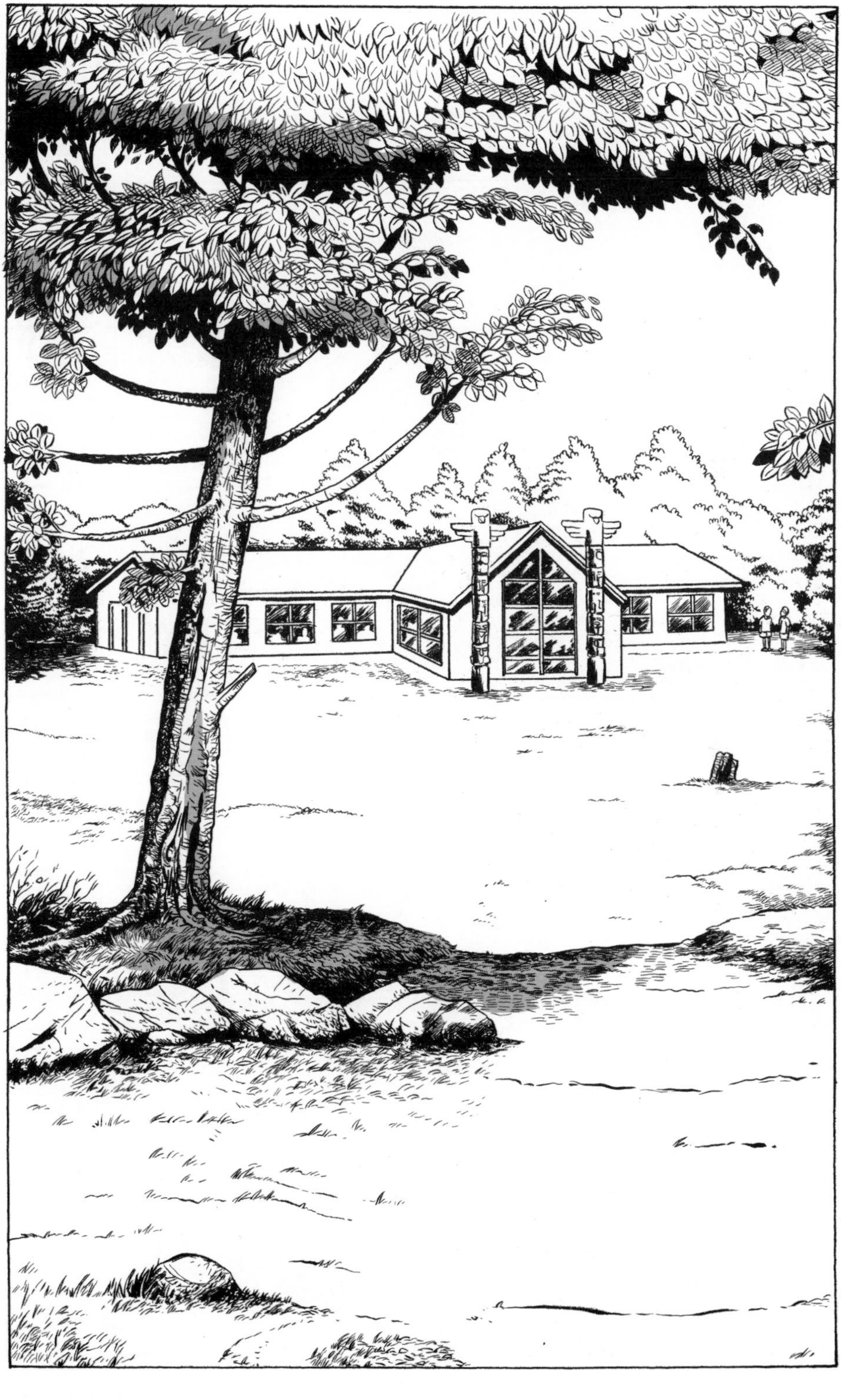

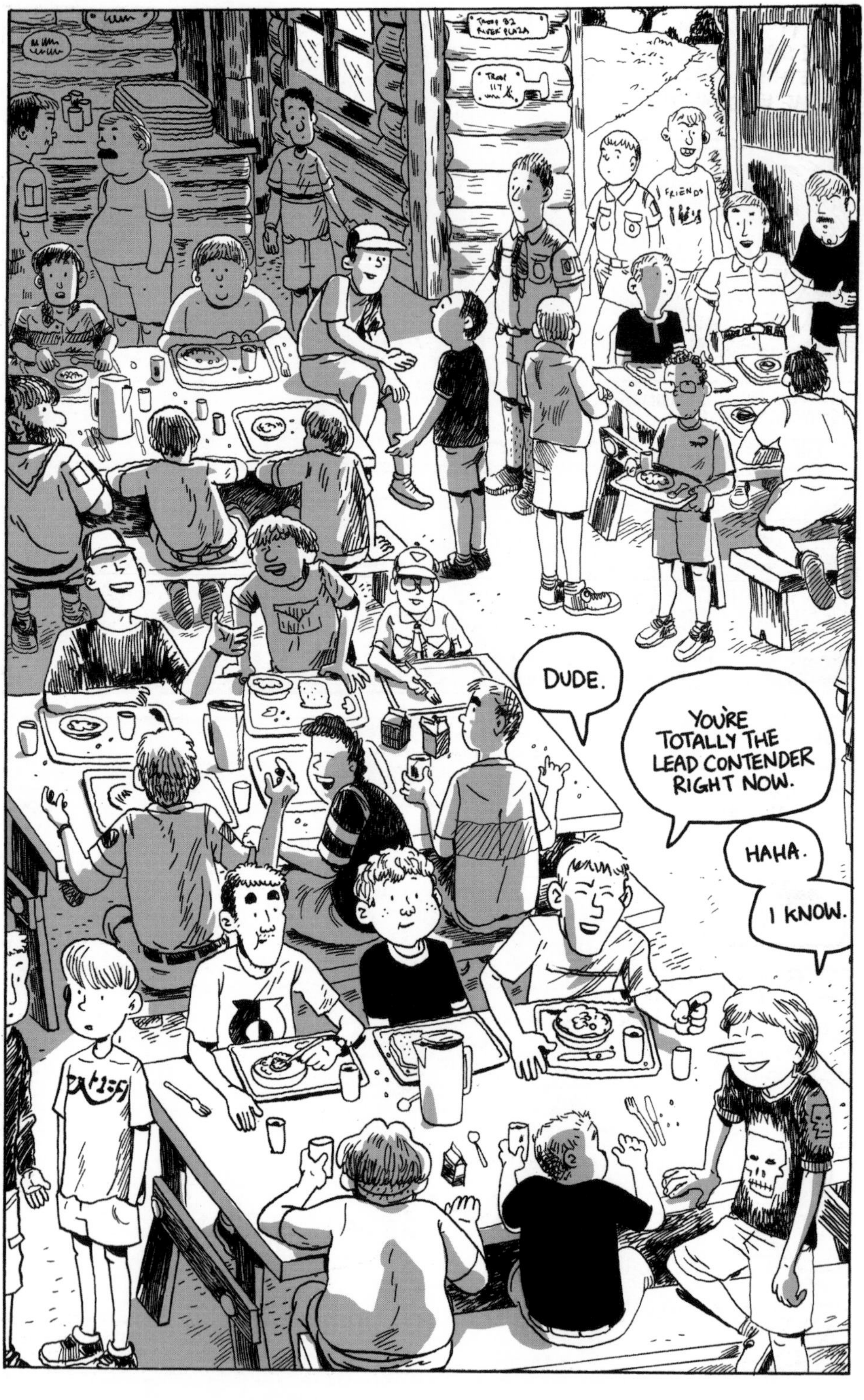
DUDE.
YOU'RE TOTALLY THE LEAD CONTENDER RIGHT NOW.
HAHA.
I KNOW.

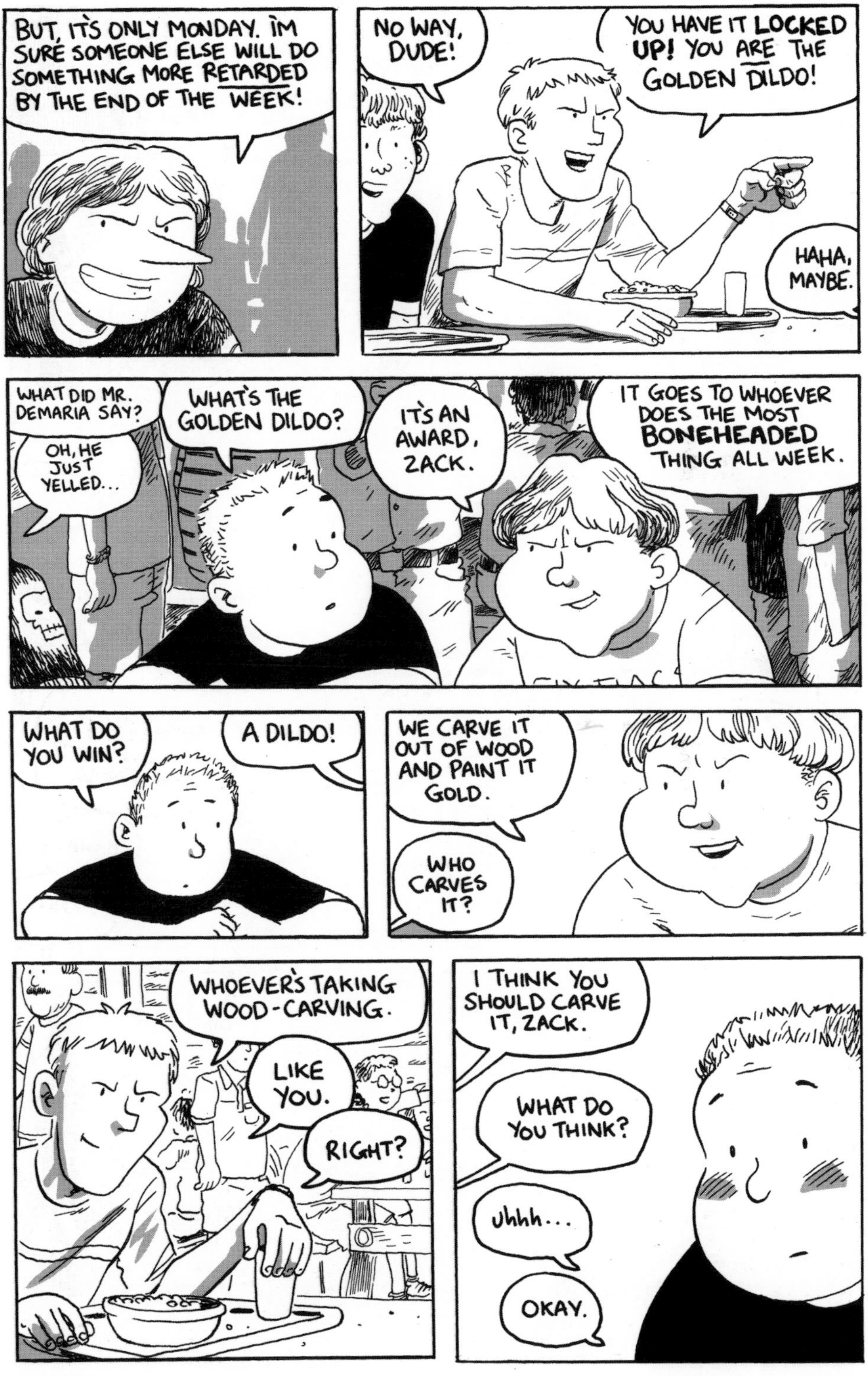

BUT, IT'S ONLY MONDAY. I'M SURE SOMEONE ELSE WILL DO SOMETHING MORE RETARDED BY THE END OF THE WEEK!
NO WAY, DUDE!
YOU HAVE IT LOCKED UP! YOU ARE THE GOLDEN DILDO!
HAHA, MAYBE.
WHAT DID MR. DEMARIA SAY?
OH, HE JUST YELLED...
WHAT'S THE GOLDEN DILDO?
IT'S AN AWARD, ZACK.
IT GOES TO WHOEVER DOES THE MOST BONEHEADED THING ALL WEEK.
WHAT DO YOU WIN?
A DILDO!
WE CARVE IT OUT OF WOOD AND PAINT IT GOLD.
WHO CARVES IT?
WHOEVER'S TAKING WOOD-CARVING.
LIKE YOU.
RIGHT?
I THINK YOU SHOULD CARVE IT, ZACK.
WHAT DO YOU THINK?
uhhh...
OKAY.

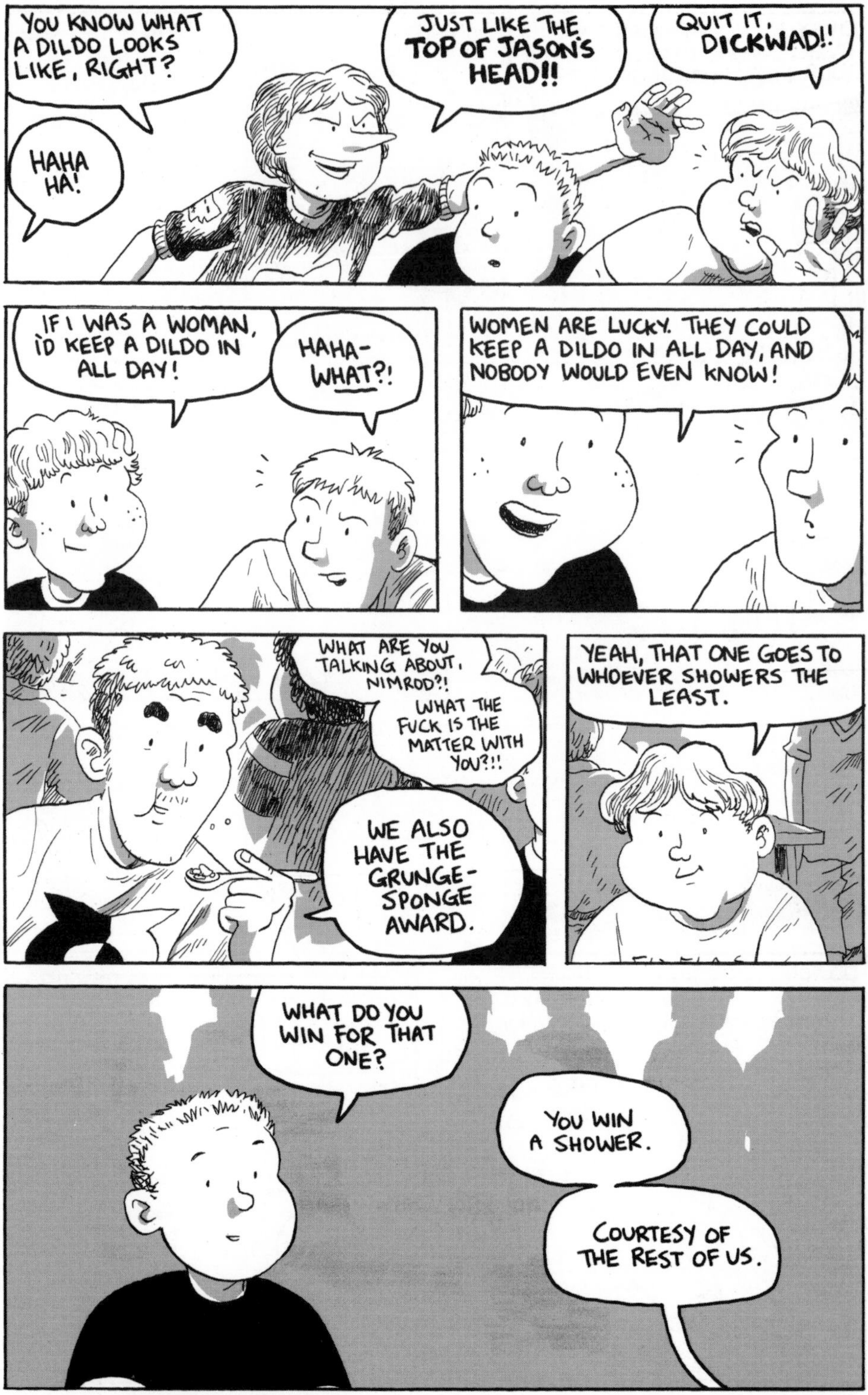

YOU KNOW WHAT A DILDO LOOKS LIKE, RIGHT?
HAHA HA!
JUST LIKE THE TOP OF JASON'S HEAD!!
QUIT IT, DICKWAD!!
IF I WAS A WOMAN, I'D KEEP A DILDO IN ALL DAY!
HAHA- WHAT?!
WOMEN ARE LUCKY. THEY COULD KEEP A DILDO IN ALL DAY, AND NOBODY WOULD EVEN KNOW!
WHAT ARE YOU TALKING ABOUT, NIMROD?!
WHAT THE FUCK IS THE MATTER WITH YOU?!!
WE ALSO HAVE THE GRUNGE-SPONGE AWARD.
YEAH, THAT ONE GOES TO WHOEVER SHOWERS THE LEAST.
WHAT DO YOU WIN FOR THAT ONE?
YOU WIN A SHOWER.
COURTESY OF THE REST OF US.

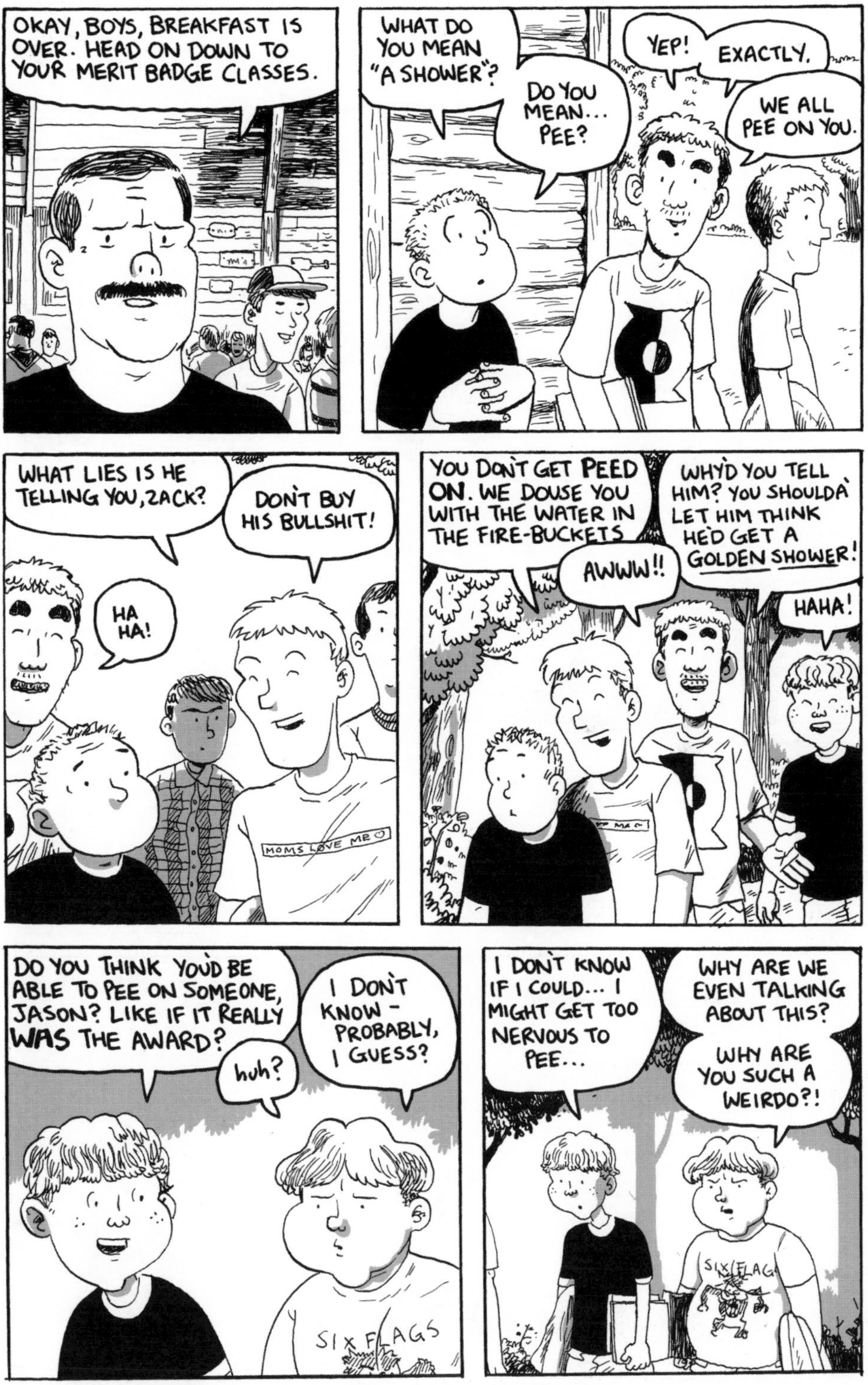
OKAY, BOYS, BREAKFAST IS OVER. HEAD ON DOWN TO YOUR MERIT BADGE CLASSES.
WHAT DO YOU MEAN "A SHOWER"?
DO YOU MEAN... PEE?
YEP!
EXACTLY.
WE ALL PEE ON YOU.
WHAT LIES IS HE TELLING YOU, ZACK?
DON'T BUY HIS BULLSHIT!
HA HA!
MOMS LOVE ME
YOU DON'T GET PEED ON. WE DOUSE YOU WITH THE WATER IN THE FIRE-BUCKETS
AWWW!!
WHY'D YOU TELL HIM? YOU SHOULDA' LET HIM THINK HE'D GET A GOLDEN SHOWER!
HAHA!
DO YOU THINK YOU'D BE ABLE TO PEE ON SOMEONE, JASON? LIKE IF IT REALLY WAS THE AWARD?
huh?
I DON'T KNOW - PROBABLY, I GUESS?
SIX FLAGS
I DON'T KNOW IF I COULD... I MIGHT GET TOO NERVOUS TO PEE...
WHY ARE WE EVEN TALKING ABOUT THIS?
WHY ARE YOU SUCH A WEIRDO?!
SIX FLAGS

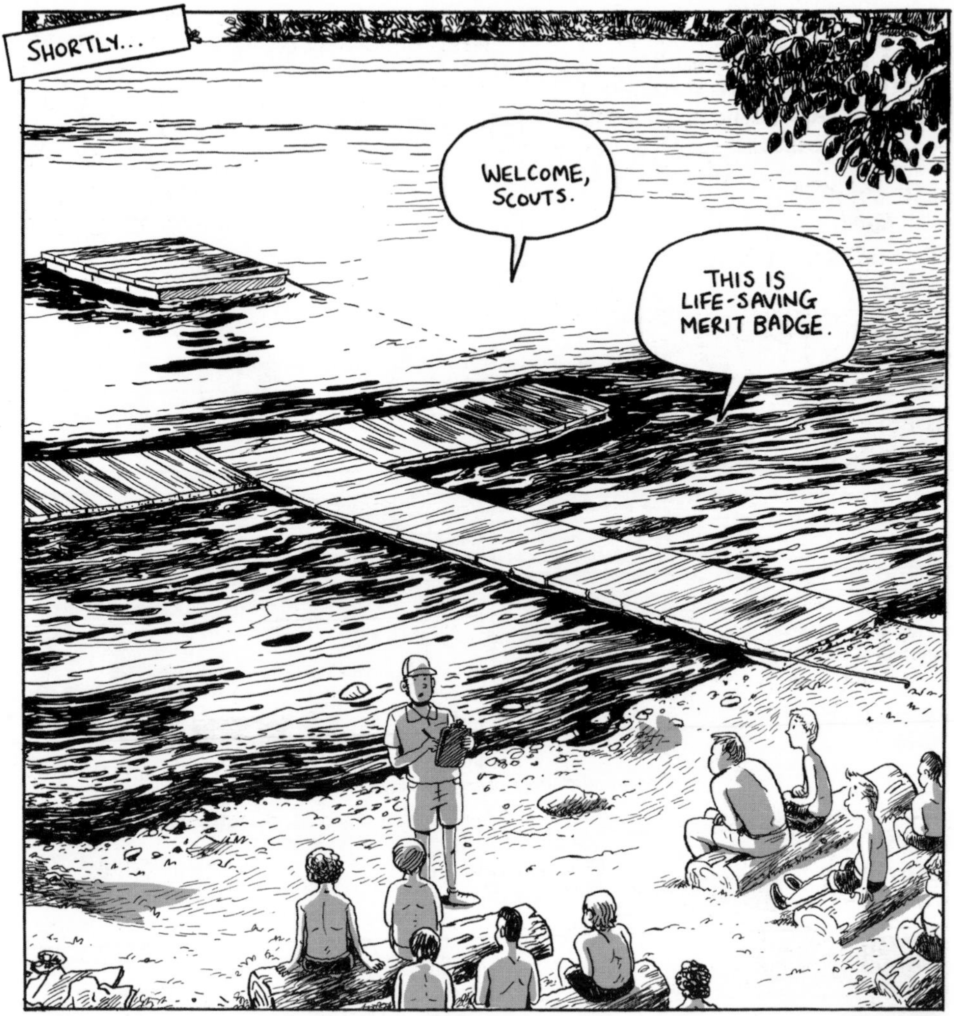
SHORTLY...
WELCOME, SCOUTS.
THIS IS LIFE-SAVING MERIT BADGE.

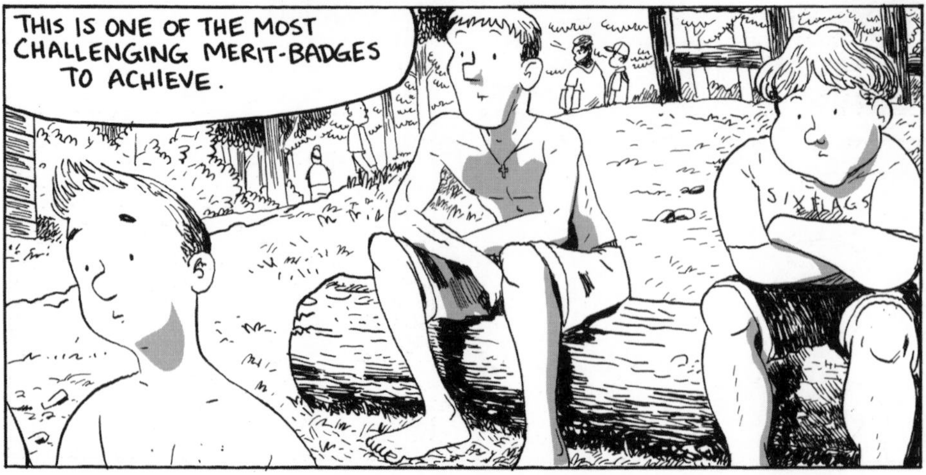
THIS IS ONE OF THE MOST CHALLENGING MERIT-BADGES TO ACHIEVE.
SIX FLAGS

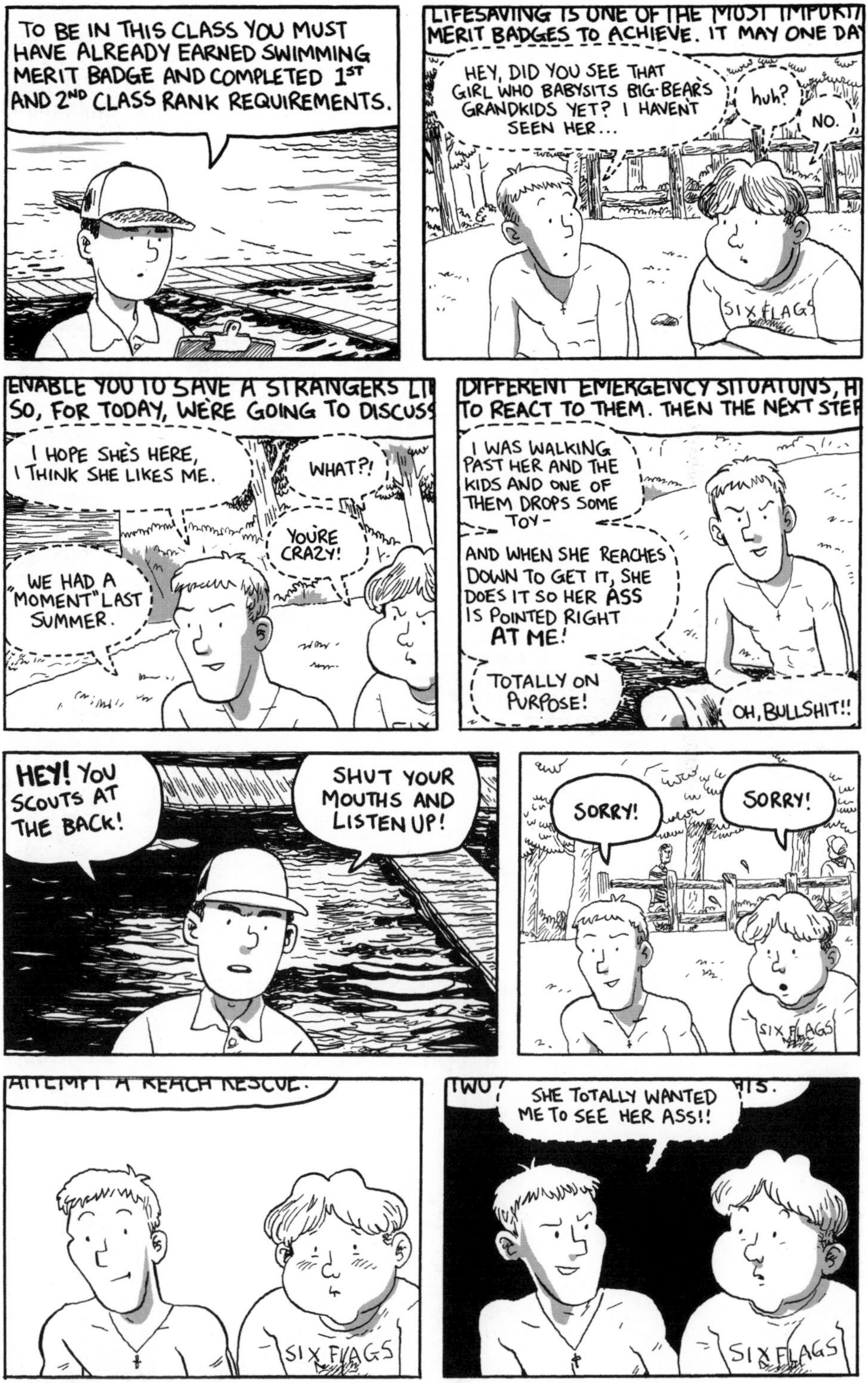

TO BE IN THIS CLASS YOU MUST HAVE ALREADY EARNED SWIMMING MERIT BADGE AND COMPLETED 1ST AND 2ND CLASS RANK REQUIREMENTS.
LIFESAVING IS ONE OF THE MOST IMPORT MERIT BADGES TO ACHIEVE. IT MAY ONE DAY
HEY, DID YOU SEE THAT GIRL WHO BABYSITS BIG-BEAR'S GRANDKIDS YET? I HAVENT SEEN HER...
huh?
NO.
SIX FLAGS
ENABLE YOU TO SAVE A STRANGERS LI SO, FOR TODAY, WE'RE GOING TO DISCUSS
I HOPE SHE'S HERE, I THINK SHE LIKES ME.
WHAT?!
YOU'RE CRAZY!
WE HAD A "MOMENT" LAST SUMMER.
DIFFERENT EMERGENCY SITUATIONS, H TO REACT TO THEM. THEN THE NEXT STEP
I WAS WALKING PAST HER AND THE KIDS AND ONE OF THEM DROPS SOME TOY-
AND WHEN SHE REACHES DOWN TO GET IT, SHE DOES IT SO HER ASS IS POINTED RIGHT AT ME!
TOTALLY ON PURPOSE!
OH, BULLSHIT!!
HEY! YOU SCOUTS AT THE BACK!
SHUT YOUR MOUTHS AND LISTEN UP!
SORRY!
SORRY!
SIX FLAGS
ATTEMPT A REACH RESCUE.
SIX FLAGS
SHE TOTALLY WANTED ME TO SEE HER ASS!!
SIX FLAGS

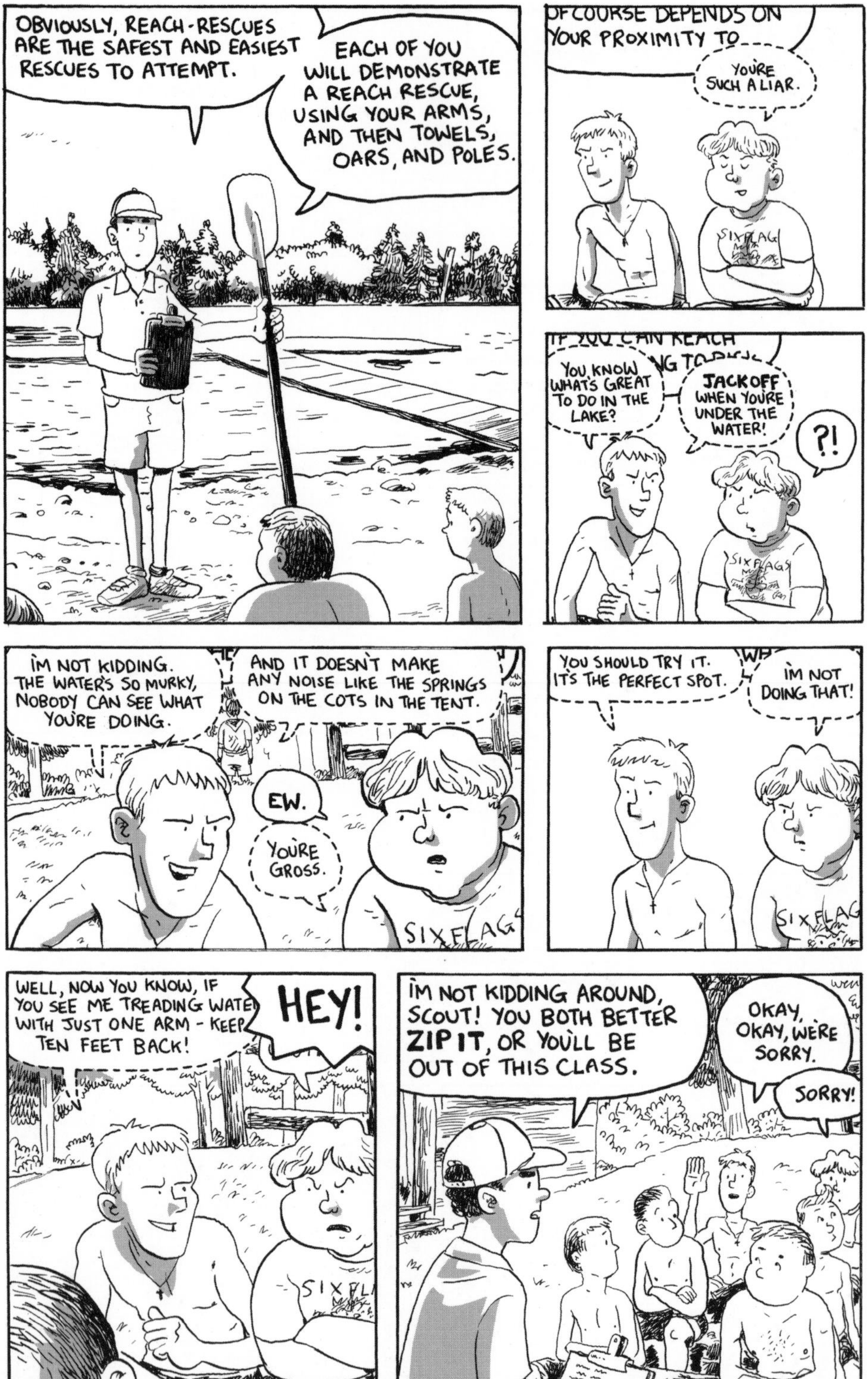
OBVIOUSLY, REACH-RESCUES ARE THE SAFEST AND EASIEST RESCUES TO ATTEMPT.
EACH OF YOU WILL DEMONSTRATE A REACH RESCUE, USING YOUR ARMS, AND THEN TOWELS, OARS, AND POLES.
OF COURSE DEPENDS ON YOUR PROXIMITY TO
YOU'RE SUCH A LIAR.
IF YOU CAN REACH
YOU KNOW WHAT'S GREAT TO DO IN THE LAKE?
JACKOFF WHEN YOU'RE UNDER THE WATER!
?!
I'M NOT KIDDING. THE WATER'S SO MURKY, NOBODY CAN SEE WHAT YOU'RE DOING.
AND IT DOESN'T MAKE ANY NOISE LIKE THE SPRINGS ON THE COTS IN THE TENT.
EW.
YOU'RE GROSS.
YOU SHOULD TRY IT. IT'S THE PERFECT SPOT.
I'M NOT DOING THAT!
WELL, NOW YOU KNOW, IF YOU SEE ME TREADING WATE WITH JUST ONE ARM - KEEP TEN FEET BACK!
HEY!
I'M NOT KIDDING AROUND, SCOUT! YOU BOTH BETTER ZIP IT, OR YOU'LL BE OUT OF THIS CLASS.
OKAY, OKAY, WE'RE SORRY.
SORRY!

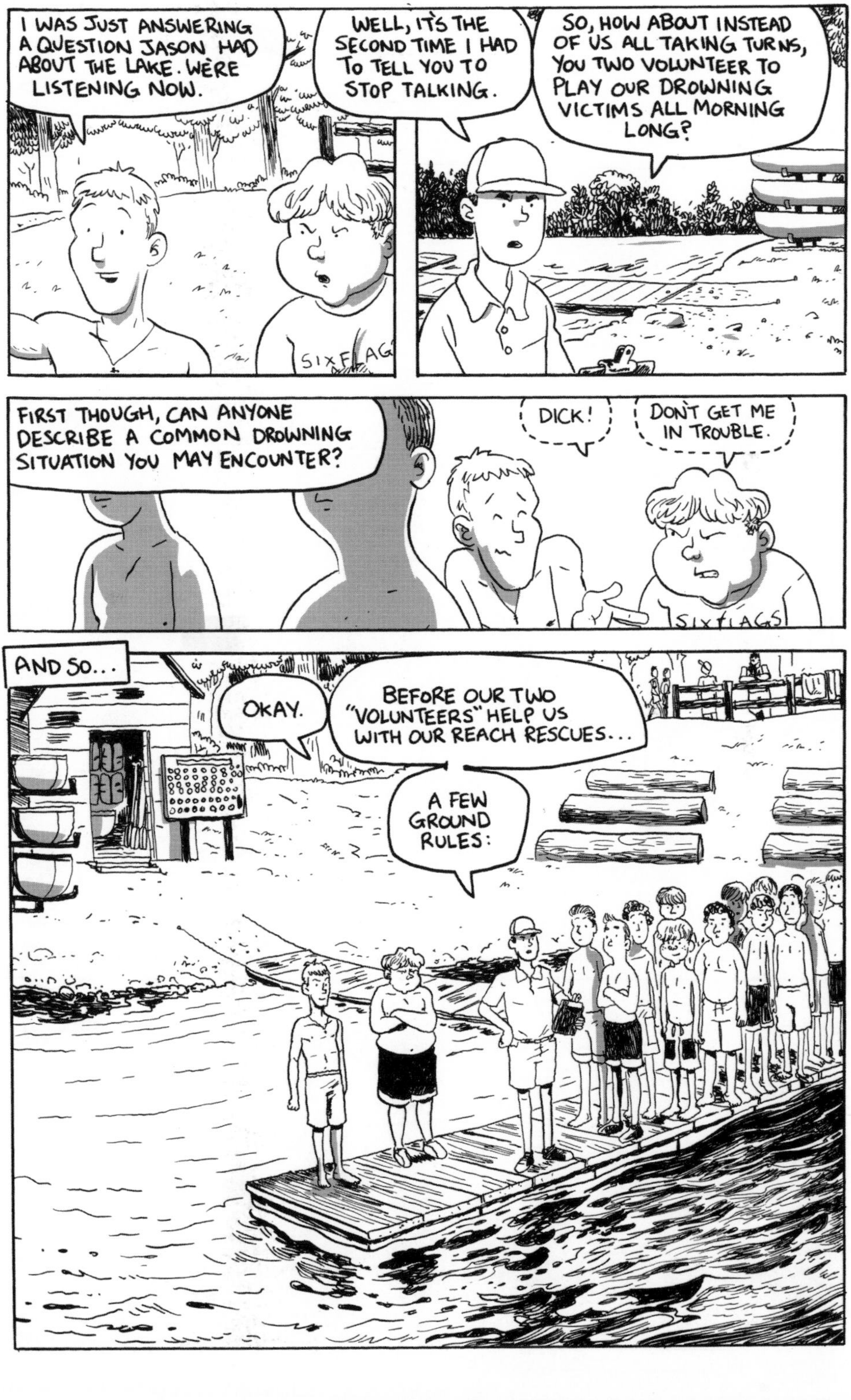
I WAS JUST ANSWERING A QUESTION JASON HAD ABOUT THE LAKE. WE'RE LISTENING NOW.
WELL, IT'S THE SECOND TIME I HAD TO TELL YOU TO STOP TALKING.
SO, HOW ABOUT INSTEAD OF US ALL TAKING TURNS, YOU TWO VOLUNTEER TO PLAY OUR DROWNING VICTIMS ALL MORNING LONG?
FIRST THOUGH, CAN ANYONE DESCRIBE A COMMON DROWNING SITUATION YOU MAY ENCOUNTER?
DICK!
DON'T GET ME IN TROUBLE.
AND SO...
OKAY.
BEFORE OUR TWO "VOLUNTEERS" HELP US WITH OUR REACH RESCUES...
A FEW GROUND RULES:

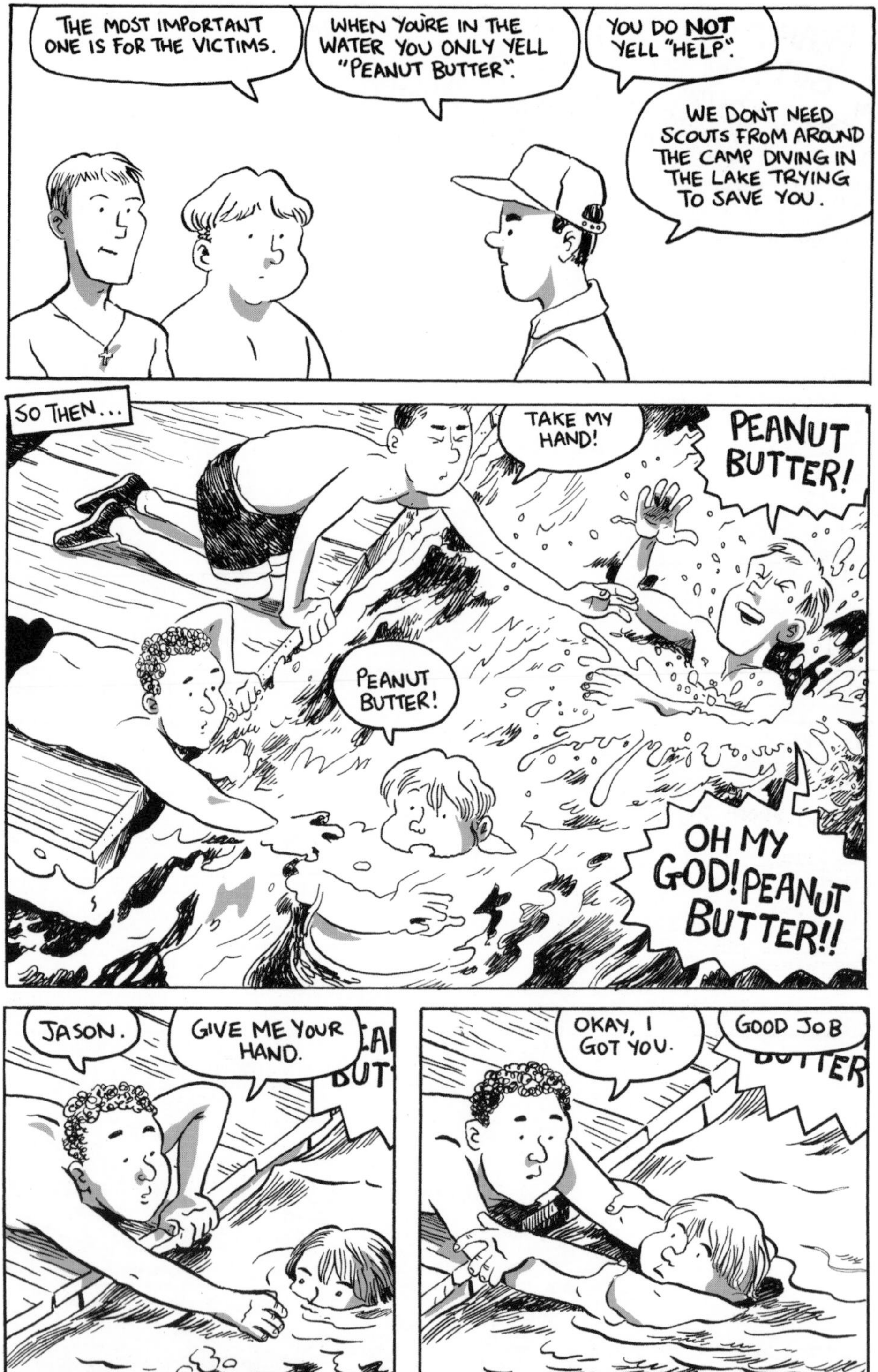
THE MOST IMPORTANT ONE IS FOR THE VICTIMS.
WHEN YOU'RE IN THE WATER YOU ONLY YELL "PEANUT BUTTER".
YOU DO NOT YELL "HELP".
WE DON'T NEED SCOUTS FROM AROUND THE CAMP DIVING IN THE LAKE TRYING TO SAVE YOU.
SO THEN...
TAKE MY HAND!
PEANUT BUTTER!
PEANUT BUTTER!
OH MY GOD! PEANUT BUTTER!!
JASON.
GIVE ME YOUR HAND.
OKAY, I GOT YOU.
GOOD JOB

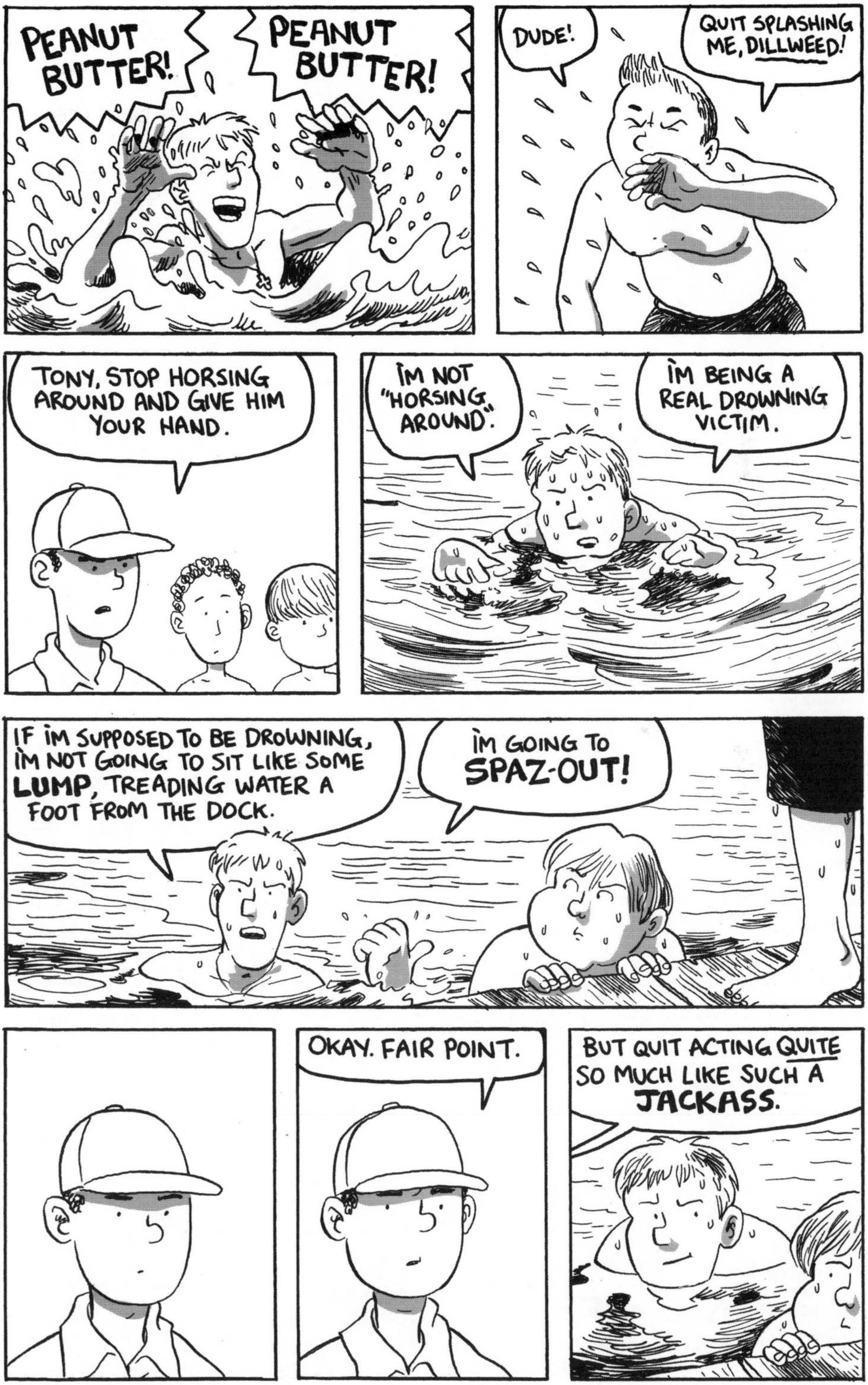
PEANUT BUTTER!
PEANUT BUTTER!
DUDE!
QUIT SPLASHING ME, DILLWEED!
TONY, STOP HORSING AROUND AND GIVE HIM YOUR HAND.
I'M NOT "HORSING AROUND".
I'M BEING A REAL DROWNING VICTIM.
IF I'M SUPPOSED TO BE DROWNING, I'M NOT GOING TO SIT LIKE SOME LUMP, TREADING WATER A FOOT FROM THE DOCK.
I'M GOING TO SPAZ-OUT!
OKAY. FAIR POINT.
BUT QUIT ACTING QUITE SO MUCH LIKE SUCH A JACKASS.

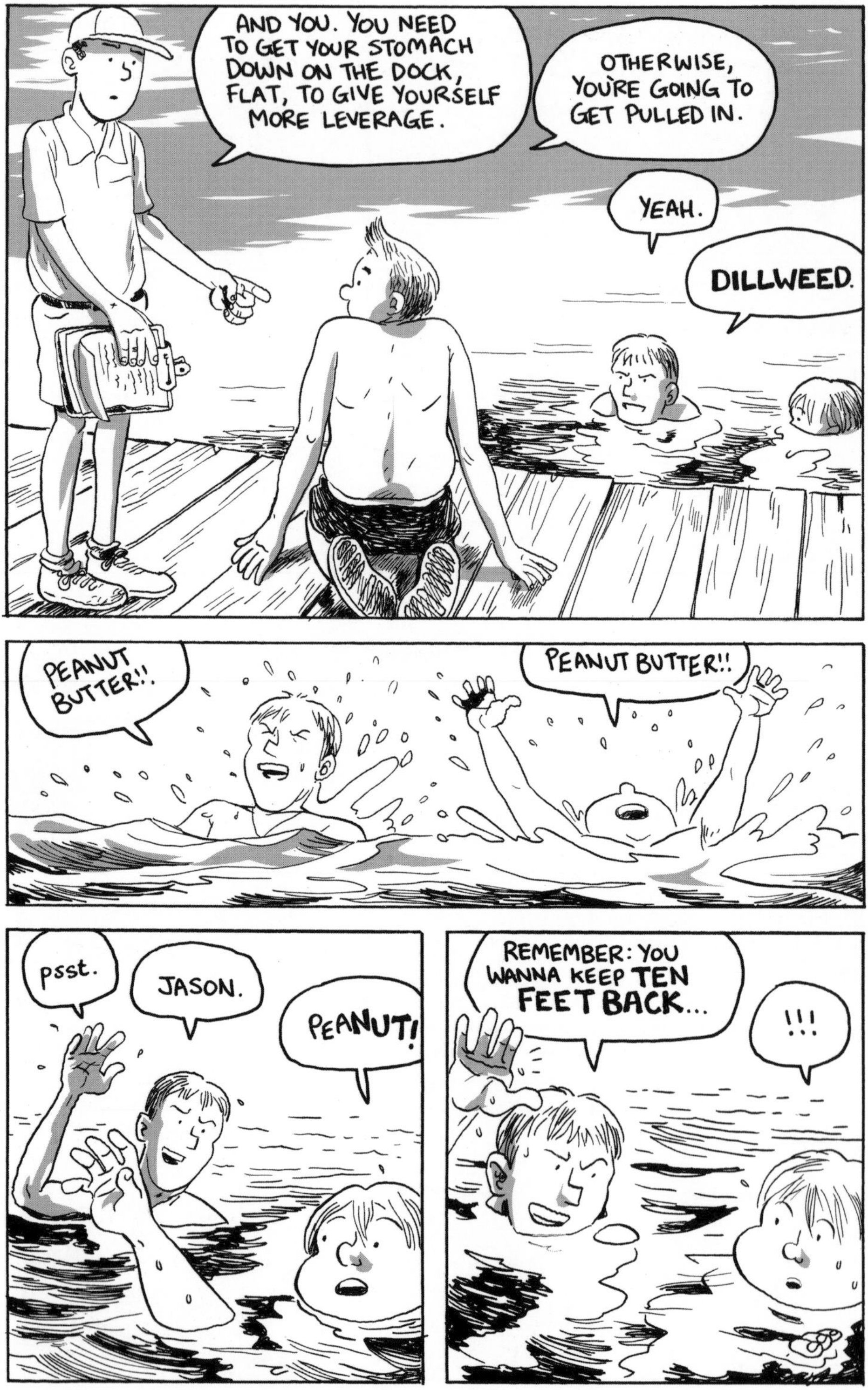
AND YOU. YOU NEED TO GET YOUR STOMACH DOWN ON THE DOCK, FLAT, TO GIVE YOURSELF MORE LEVERAGE.
OTHERWISE, YOU'RE GOING TO GET PULLED IN.
YEAH.
DILLWEED.
PEANUT BUTTER!!
PEANUT BUTTER!!
psst.
JASON.
PEANUT!
REMEMBER: YOU WANNA KEEP TEN FEET BACK...
!!!

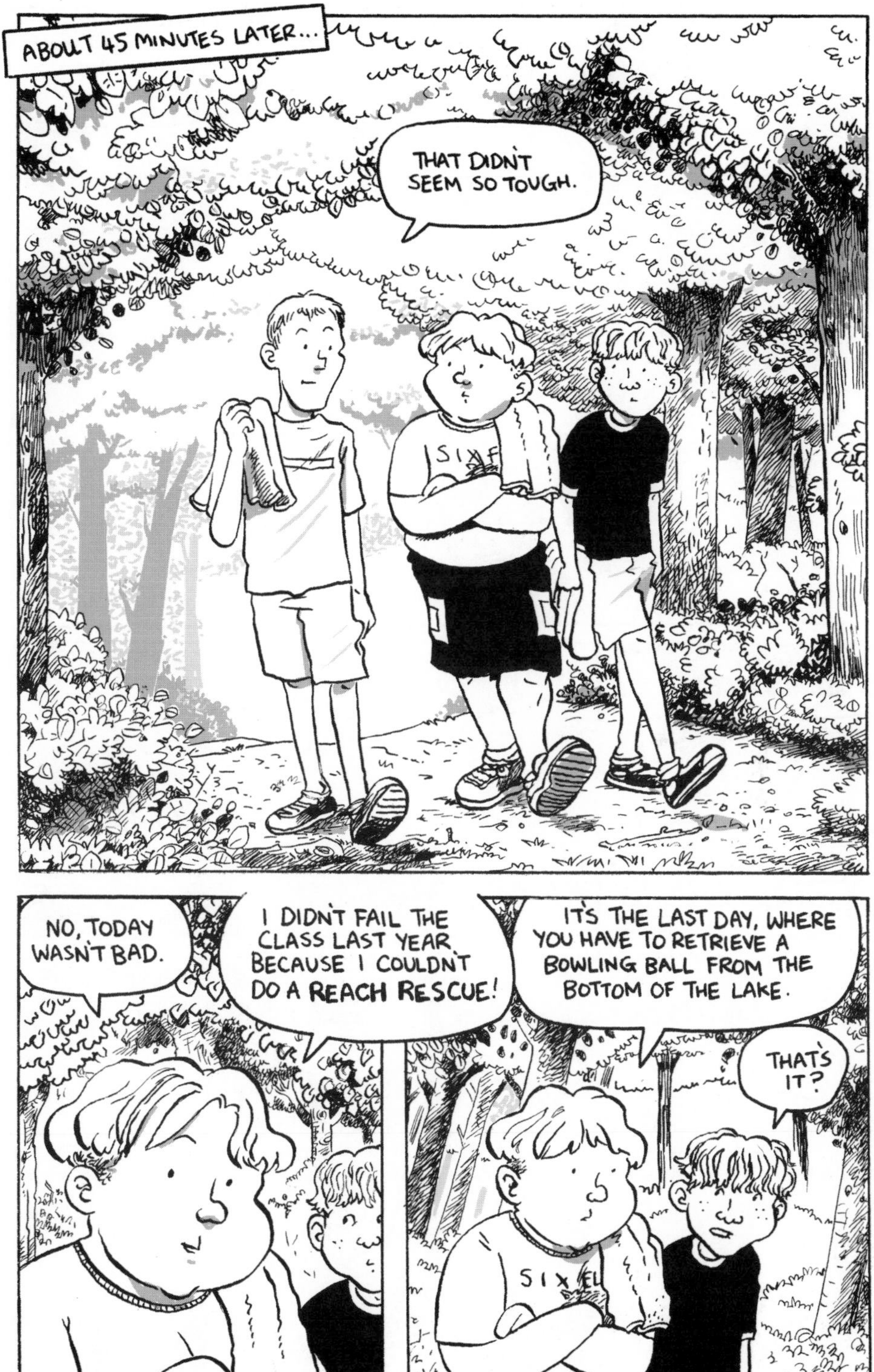
ABOUT 45 MINUTES LATER...
THAT DIDN'T SEEM SO TOUGH.
NO, TODAY WASN'T BAD.
I DIDN'T FAIL THE CLASS LAST YEAR BECAUSE I COULDN'T DO A REACH RESCUE!
IT'S THE LAST DAY, WHERE YOU HAVE TO RETRIEVE A BOWLING BALL FROM THE BOTTOM OF THE LAKE.
THAT'S IT?

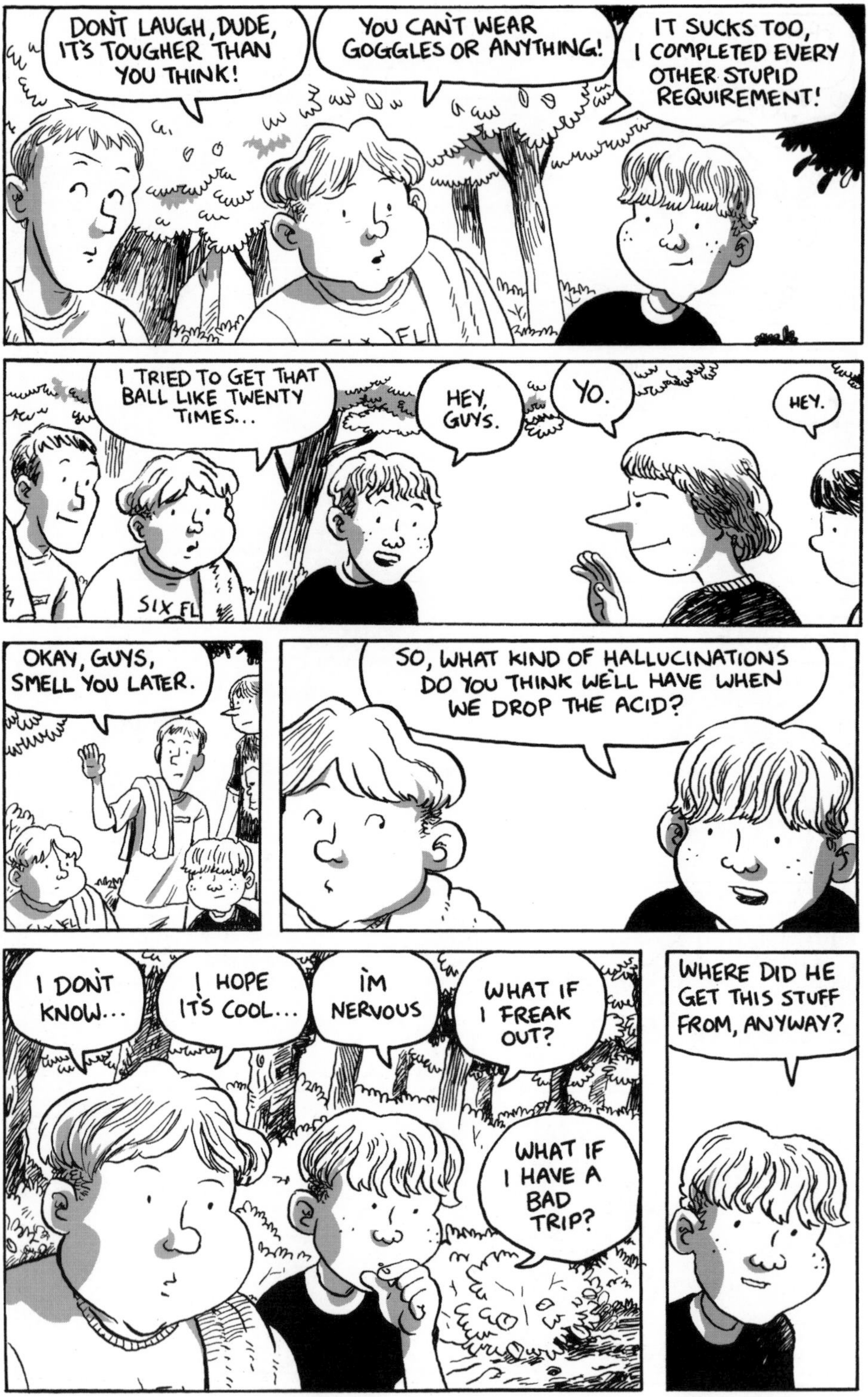
DON'T LAUGH, DUDE, IT'S TOUGHER THAN YOU THINK!
YOU CAN'T WEAR GOGGLES OR ANYTHING!
IT SUCKS TOO, I COMPLETED EVERY OTHER STUPID REQUIREMENT!
I TRIED TO GET THAT BALL LIKE TWENTY TIMES...
SIX FL
HEY, GUYS.
YO.
HEY.
OKAY, GUYS, SMELL YOU LATER.
SO, WHAT KIND OF HALLUCINATIONS DO YOU THINK WE'LL HAVE WHEN WE DROP THE ACID?
I DON'T KNOW...
I HOPE IT'S COOL...
I'M NERVOUS
WHAT IF I FREAK OUT?
WHAT IF I HAVE A BAD TRIP?
WHERE DID HE GET THIS STUFF FROM, ANYWAY?

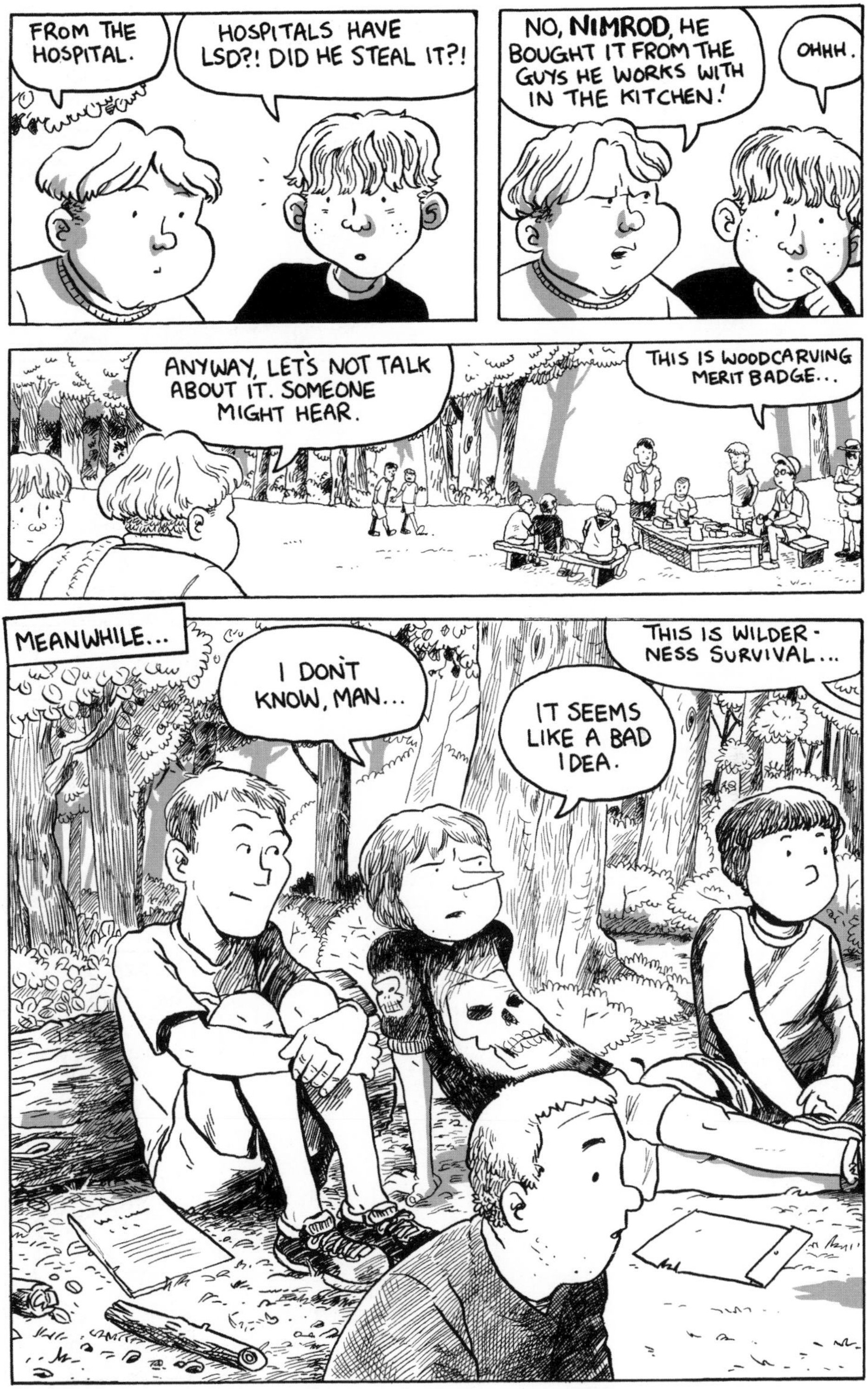
FROM THE HOSPITAL.
HOSPITALS HAVE LSD?! DID HE STEAL IT?!
NO, NIMROD, HE BOUGHT IT FROM THE GUYS HE WORKS WITH IN THE KITCHEN!
OHHH.
ANYWAY, LET'S NOT TALK ABOUT IT. SOMEONE MIGHT HEAR.
THIS IS WOODCARVING MERIT BADGE...
MEANWHILE...
I DON'T KNOW, MAN...
IT SEEMS LIKE A BAD IDEA.
THIS IS WILDERNESS SURVIVAL...

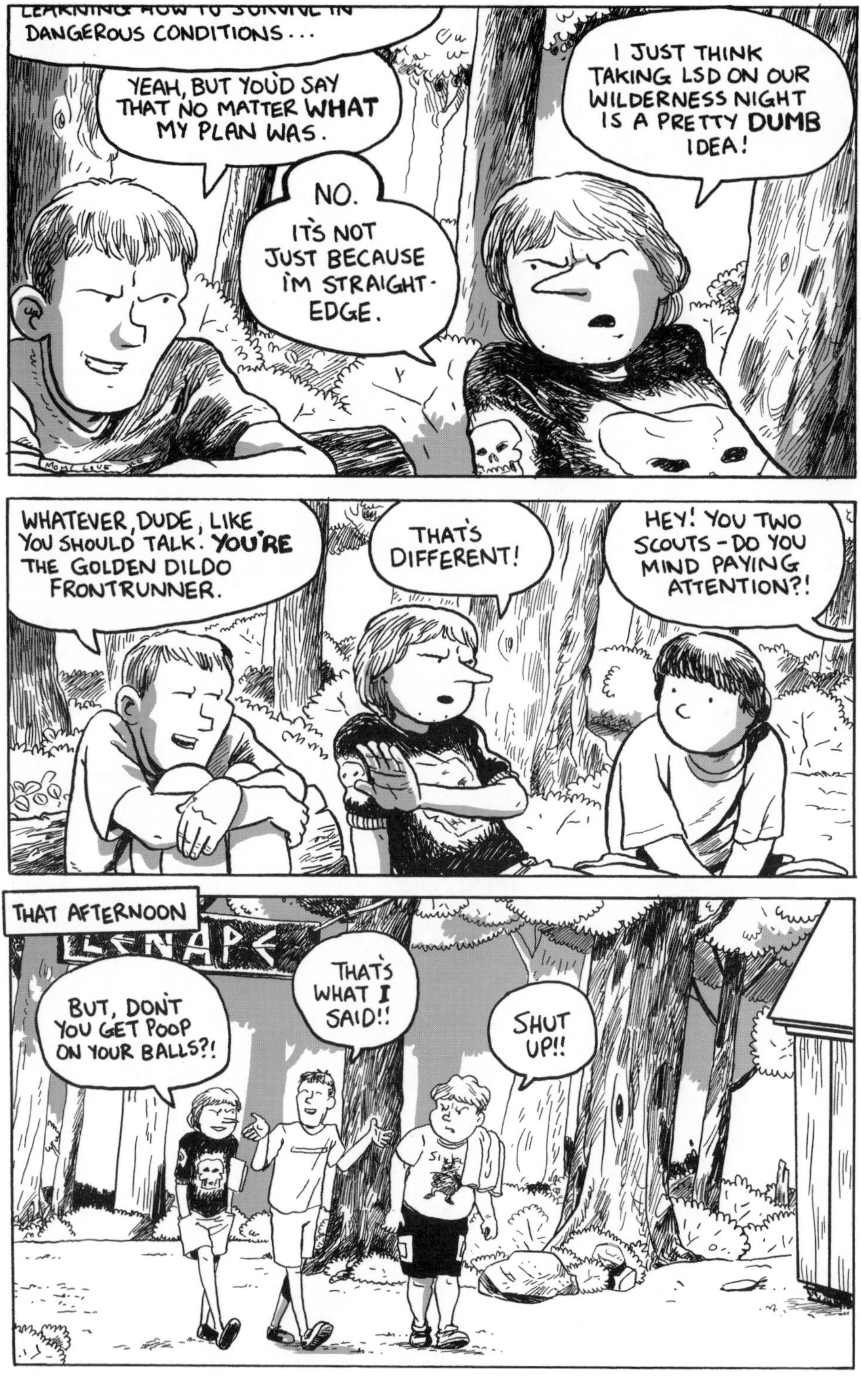
DANGEROUS CONDITIONS . . .
YEAH, BUT YOU'D SAY THAT NO MATTER **WHAT** MY PLAN WAS.
I JUST THINK TAKING LSD ON OUR WILDERNESS NIGHT IS A PRETTY **DUMB** IDEA!
NO.
IT'S NOT JUST BECAUSE I'M STRAIGHT-EDGE.
WHATEVER, DUDE, LIKE YOU SHOULD TALK. **YOU'RE** THE GOLDEN DILDO FRONTRUNNER.
THAT'S DIFFERENT!
HEY! YOU TWO SCOUTS - DO YOU MIND PAYING ATTENTION?!
THAT AFTERNOON
BUT, DON'T YOU GET POOP ON YOUR BALLS?!
THAT'S WHAT **I** SAID!!
SHUT UP!!

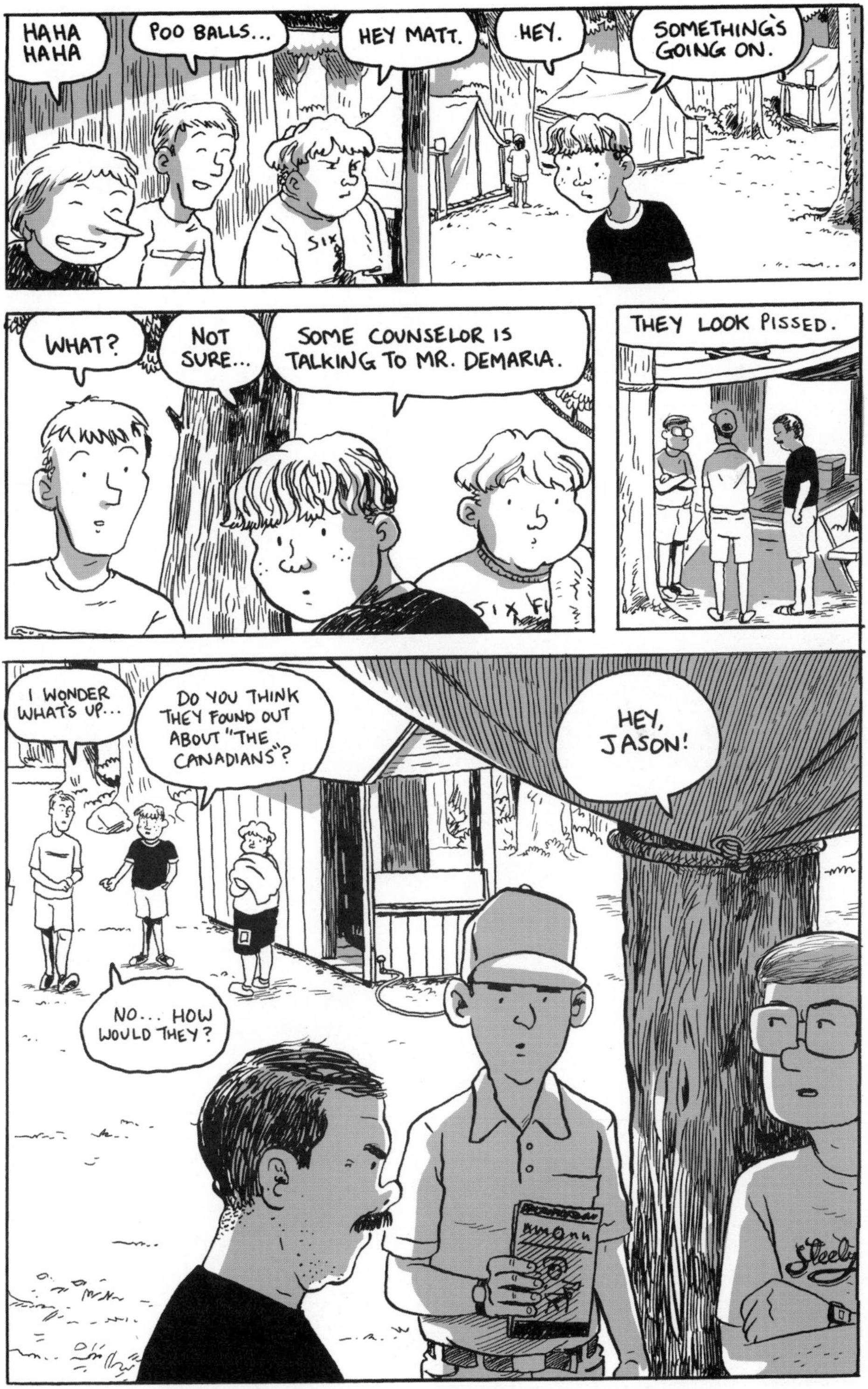
HAHA HAHA
POO BALLS...
HEY MATT.
HEY.
SOMETHING'S GOING ON.
WHAT?
NOT SURE...
SOME COUNSELOR IS TALKING TO MR. DEMARIA.
THEY LOOK PISSED.
I WONDER WHAT'S UP...
DO YOU THINK THEY FOUND OUT ABOUT "THE CANADIANS"?
NO... HOW WOULD THEY?
HEY, JASON!

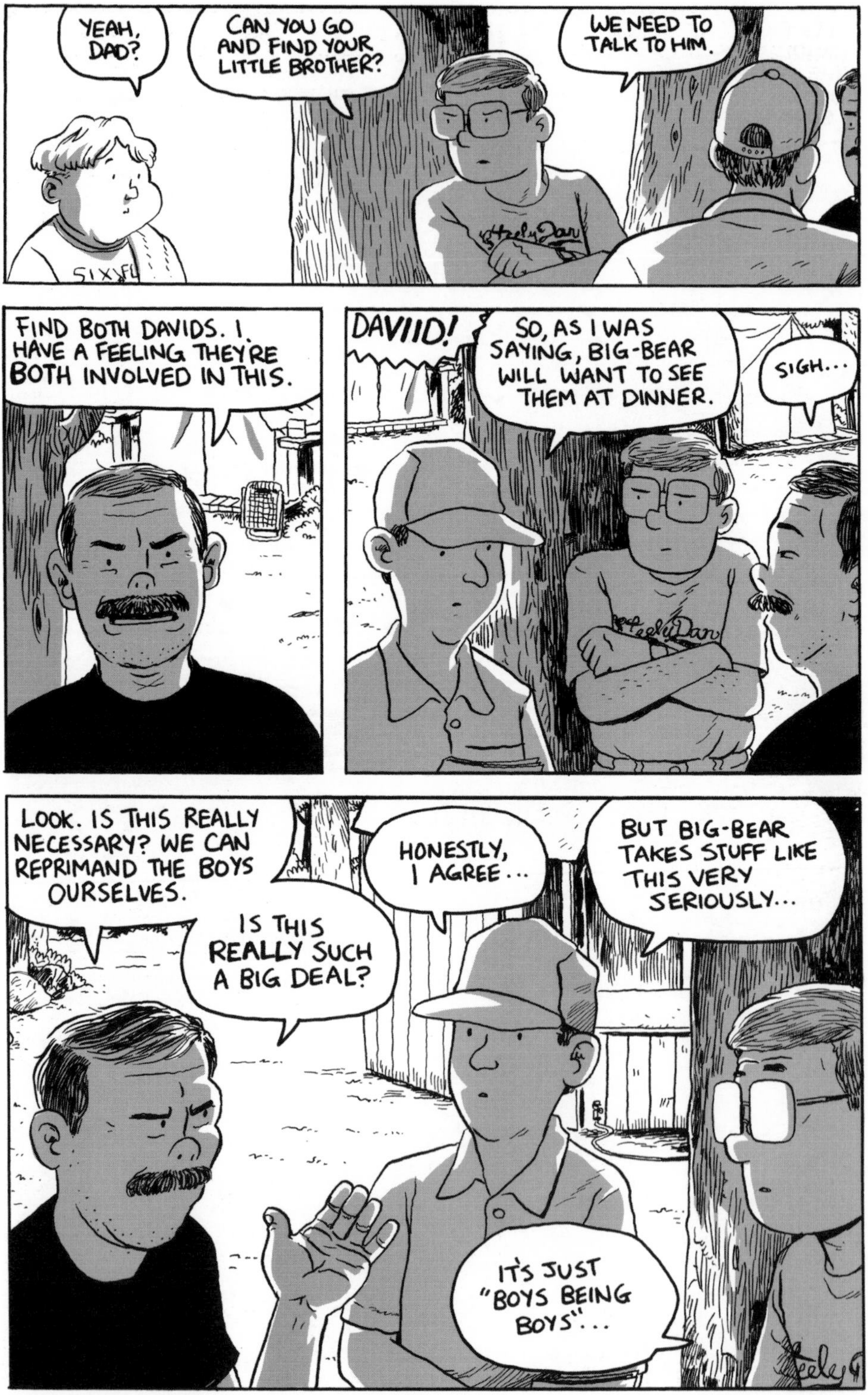
YEAH, DAD?
CAN YOU GO AND FIND YOUR LITTLE BROTHER?
WE NEED TO TALK TO HIM.
FIND BOTH DAVIDS. I HAVE A FEELING THEY'RE BOTH INVOLVED IN THIS.
DAVIID!
SO, AS I WAS SAYING, BIG-BEAR WILL WANT TO SEE THEM AT DINNER.
SIGH...
LOOK. IS THIS REALLY NECESSARY? WE CAN REPRIMAND THE BOYS OURSELVES.
IS THIS REALLY SUCH A BIG DEAL?
HONESTLY, I AGREE...
BUT BIG-BEAR TAKES STUFF LIKE THIS VERY SERIOUSLY...
IT'S JUST "BOYS BEING BOYS"...

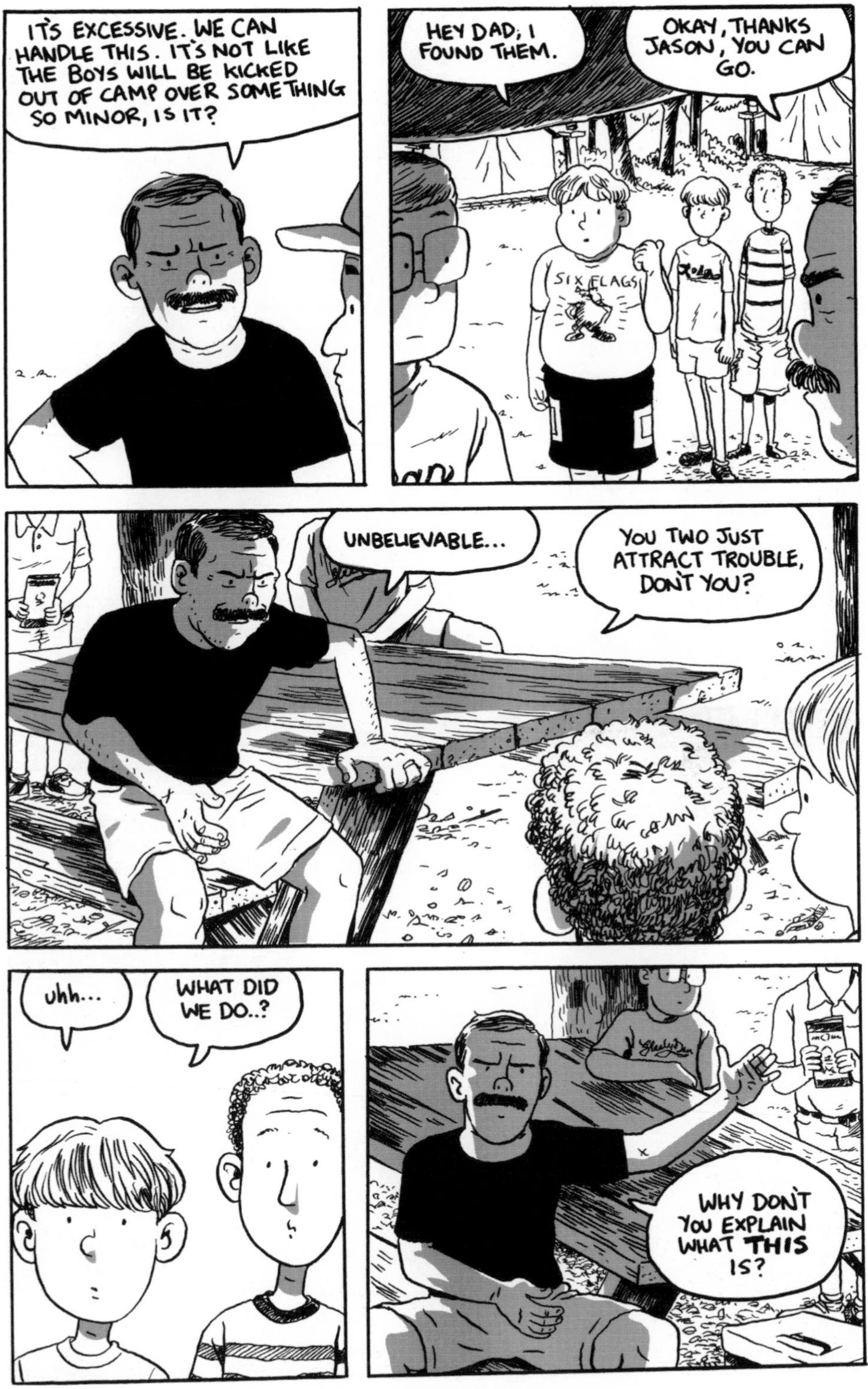
IT'S EXCESSIVE. WE CAN HANDLE THIS. IT'S NOT LIKE THE BOYS WILL BE KICKED OUT OF CAMP OVER SOMETHING SO MINOR, IS IT?
HEY DAD; I FOUND THEM.
OKAY, THANKS JASON, YOU CAN GO.
SIX FLAGS
UNBELIEVABLE...
YOU TWO JUST ATTRACT TROUBLE, DON'T YOU?
uhh...
WHAT DID WE DO..?
WHY DON'T YOU EXPLAIN WHAT **THIS** IS?

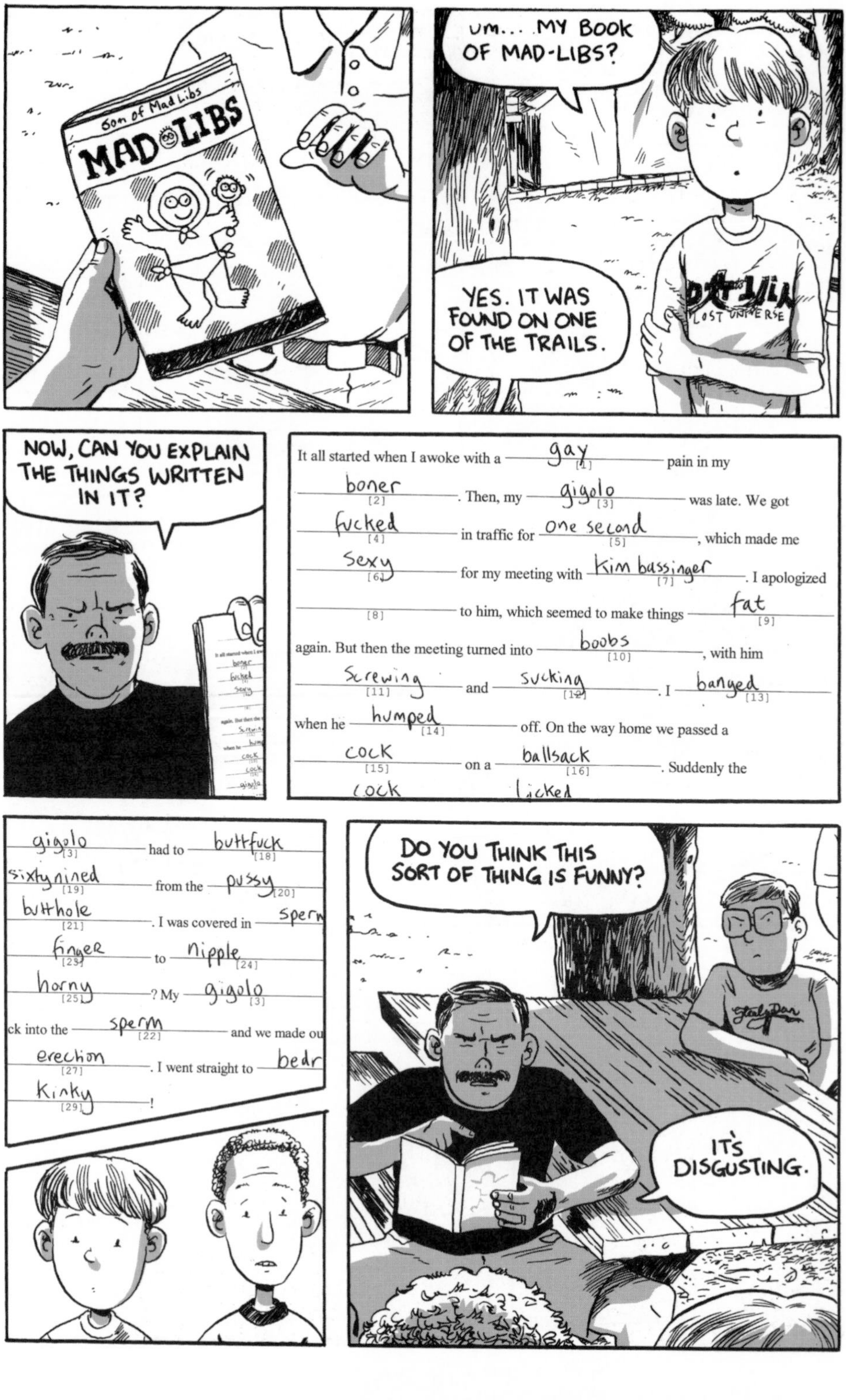
Son of Mad Libs
MAD LIBS
UM... MY BOOK OF MAD-LIBS?
LOST UNIVERSE
YES. IT WAS FOUND ON ONE OF THE TRAILS.
NOW, CAN YOU EXPLAIN THE THINGS WRITTEN IN IT?
It all started when I awoke with a gay [1] pain in my
boner [2]. Then, my gigolo [3] was late. We got
fucked [4] in traffic for one second [5], which made me
sexy [6] for my meeting with kim bassinger [7]. I apologized
[8] to him, which seemed to make things fat [9]
again. But then the meeting turned into boobs [10], with him
Screwing [11] and sucking [12]. I banged [13]
when he humped [14] off. On the way home we passed a
cock [15] on a ballsack [16]. Suddenly the
cock licked
gigolo [3] had to buttfuck [18]
sixtynined [19] from the pussy [20]
butthole [21]. I was covered in sperm
finger [23] to nipple [24]
horny [25]? My gigolo [3]
ck into the sperm [22] and we made ou
erection [27]. I went straight to bedr
kinky [29]!
DO YOU THINK THIS SORT OF THING IS FUNNY?
IT'S DISGUSTING.

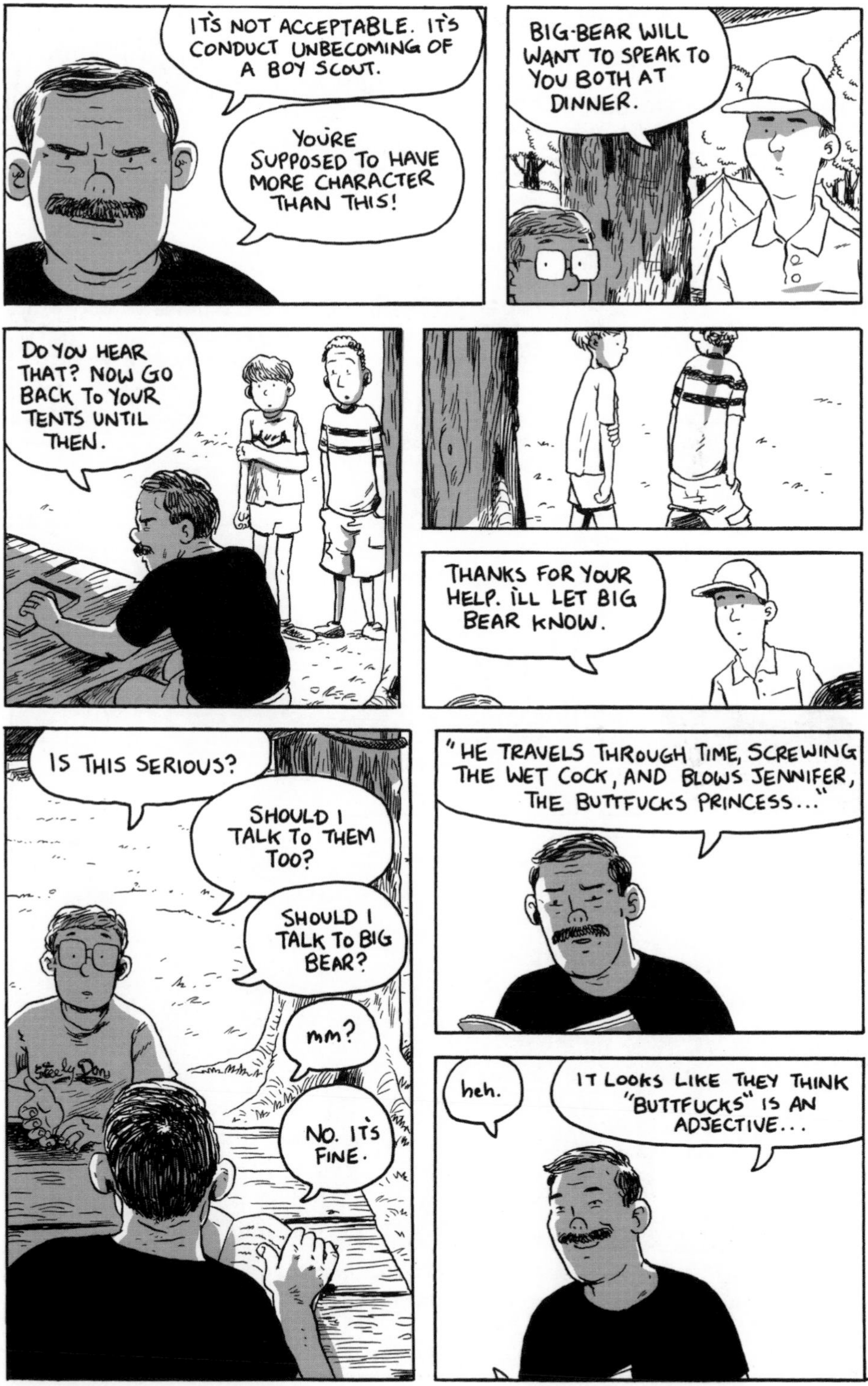
IT'S NOT ACCEPTABLE. IT'S CONDUCT UNBECOMING OF A BOY SCOUT.
YOU'RE SUPPOSED TO HAVE MORE CHARACTER THAN THIS!
BIG-BEAR WILL WANT TO SPEAK TO YOU BOTH AT DINNER.
DO YOU HEAR THAT? NOW GO BACK TO YOUR TENTS UNTIL THEN.
THANKS FOR YOUR HELP. I'LL LET BIG BEAR KNOW.
IS THIS SERIOUS?
SHOULD I TALK TO THEM TOO?
SHOULD I TALK TO BIG BEAR?
mm?
NO. IT'S FINE.
Steely Dan
"HE TRAVELS THROUGH TIME, SCREWING THE WET COCK, AND BLOWS JENNIFER, THE BUTTFUCKS PRINCESS..."
heh.
IT LOOKS LIKE THEY THINK "BUTTFUCKS" IS AN ADJECTIVE...

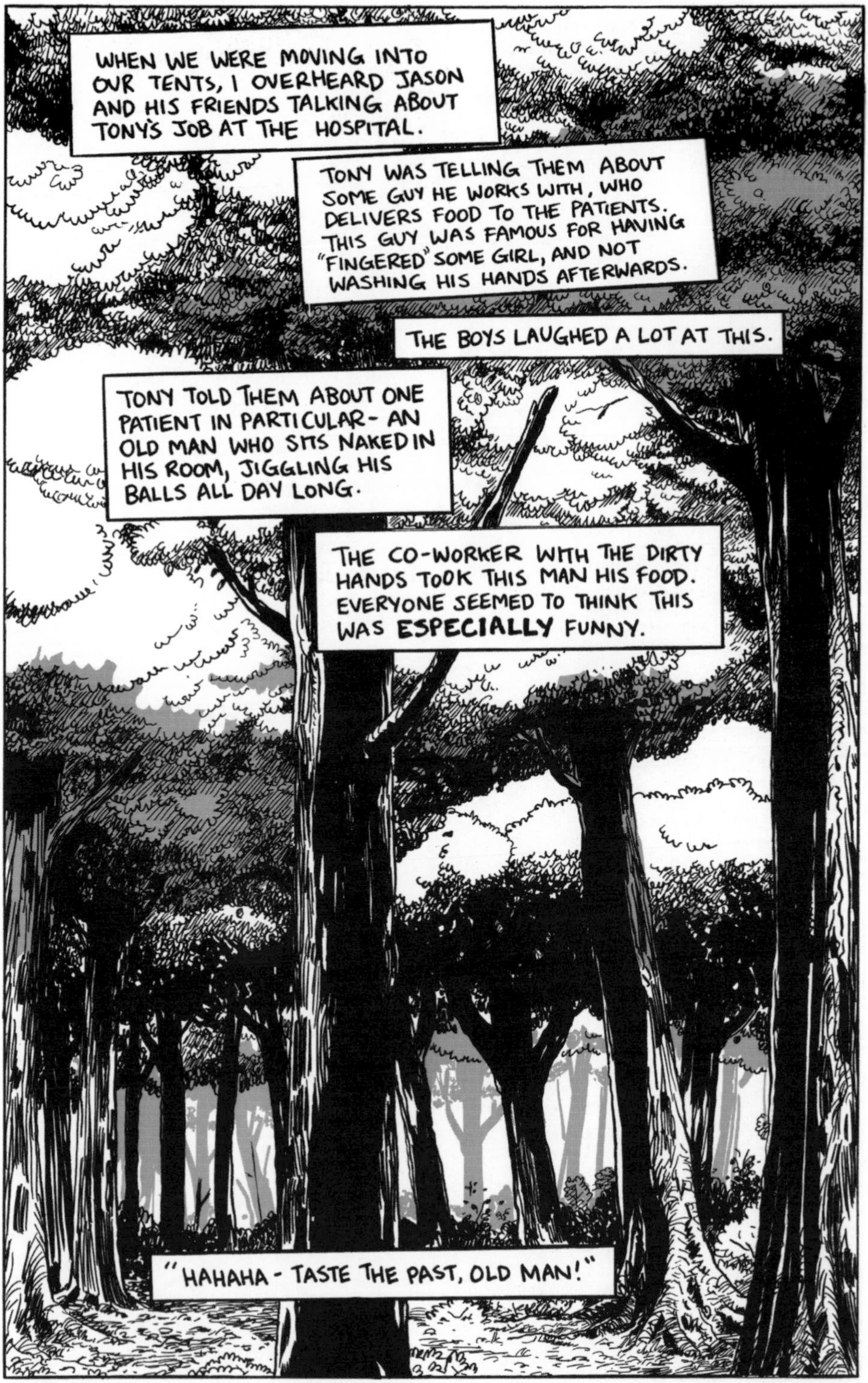
WHEN WE WERE MOVING INTO OUR TENTS, I OVERHEARD JASON AND HIS FRIENDS TALKING ABOUT TONY'S JOB AT THE HOSPITAL.
TONY WAS TELLING THEM ABOUT SOME GUY HE WORKS WITH, WHO DELIVERS FOOD TO THE PATIENTS. THIS GUY WAS FAMOUS FOR HAVING "FINGERED" SOME GIRL, AND NOT WASHING HIS HANDS AFTERWARDS.
THE BOYS LAUGHED A LOT AT THIS.
TONY TOLD THEM ABOUT ONE PATIENT IN PARTICULAR- AN OLD MAN WHO SITS NAKED IN HIS ROOM, JIGGLING HIS BALLS ALL DAY LONG.
THE CO-WORKER WITH THE DIRTY HANDS TOOK THIS MAN HIS FOOD. EVERYONE SEEMED TO THINK THIS WAS **ESPECIALLY** FUNNY.
"HAHAHA - TASTE THE PAST, OLD MAN!"

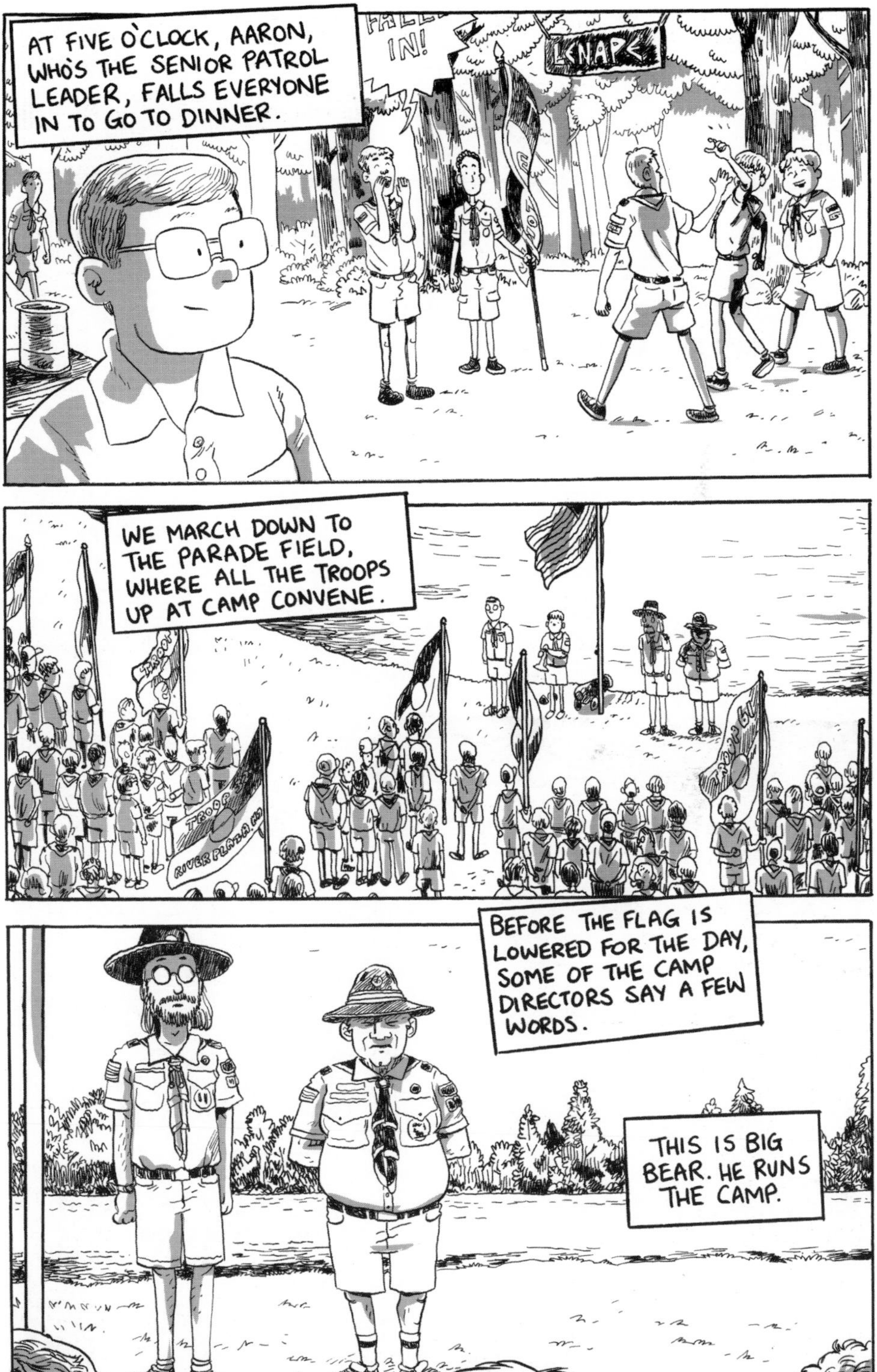
AT FIVE O'CLOCK, AARON, WHO'S THE SENIOR PATROL LEADER, FALLS EVERYONE IN TO GO TO DINNER.
IN!
LENAPE
WE MARCH DOWN TO THE PARADE FIELD, WHERE ALL THE TROOPS UP AT CAMP CONVENE.
RIVER PLAZA, NJ
BEFORE THE FLAG IS LOWERED FOR THE DAY, SOME OF THE CAMP DIRECTORS SAY A FEW WORDS.
THIS IS BIG BEAR. HE RUNS THE CAMP.

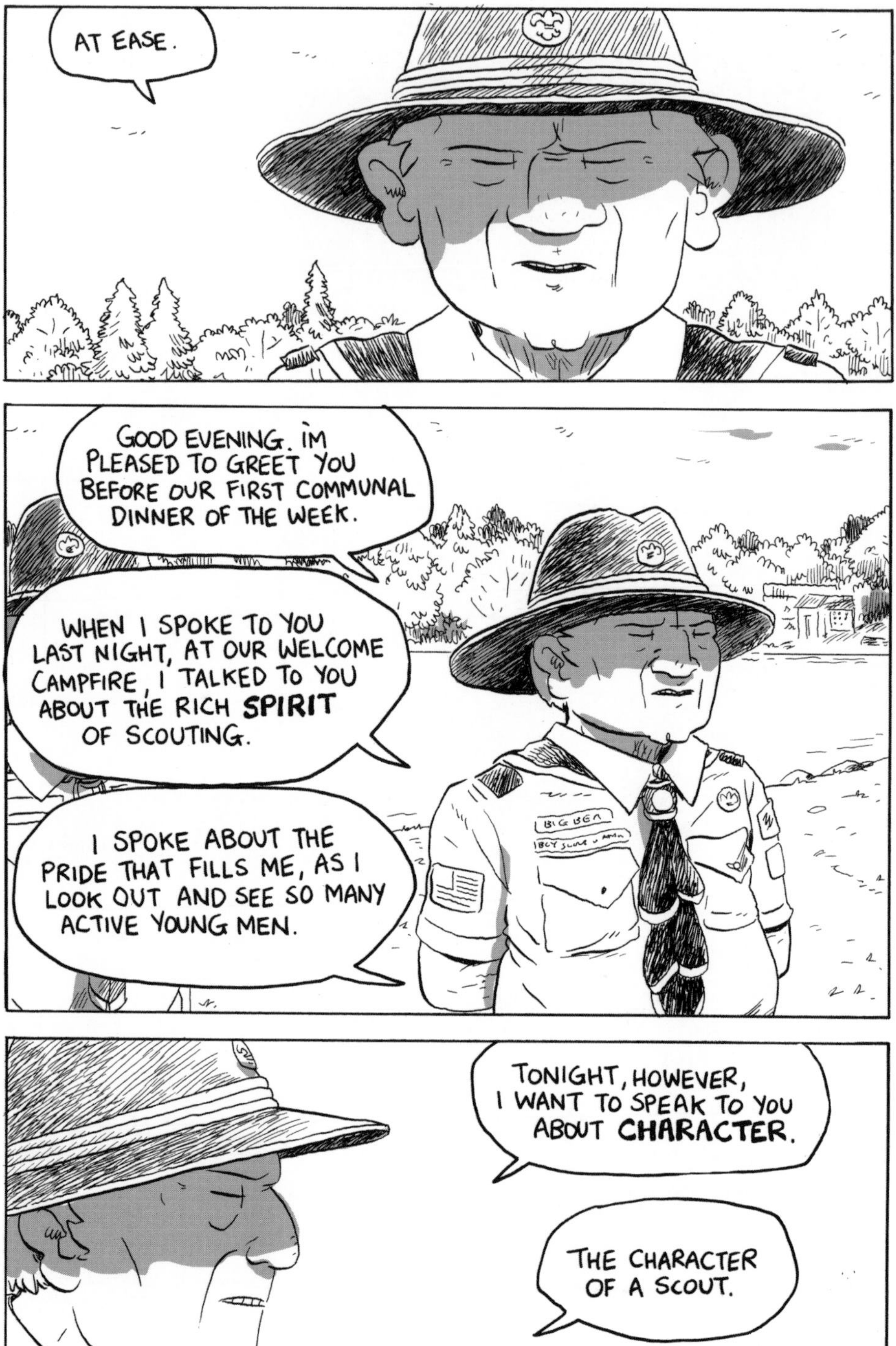
AT EASE.
GOOD EVENING. I'M PLEASED TO GREET YOU BEFORE OUR FIRST COMMUNAL DINNER OF THE WEEK.
WHEN I SPOKE TO YOU LAST NIGHT, AT OUR WELCOME CAMPFIRE, I TALKED TO YOU ABOUT THE RICH **SPIRIT** OF SCOUTING.
I SPOKE ABOUT THE PRIDE THAT FILLS ME, AS I LOOK OUT AND SEE SO MANY ACTIVE YOUNG MEN.
BIG BEN
TONIGHT, HOWEVER, I WANT TO SPEAK TO YOU ABOUT **CHARACTER**.
THE CHARACTER OF A SCOUT.

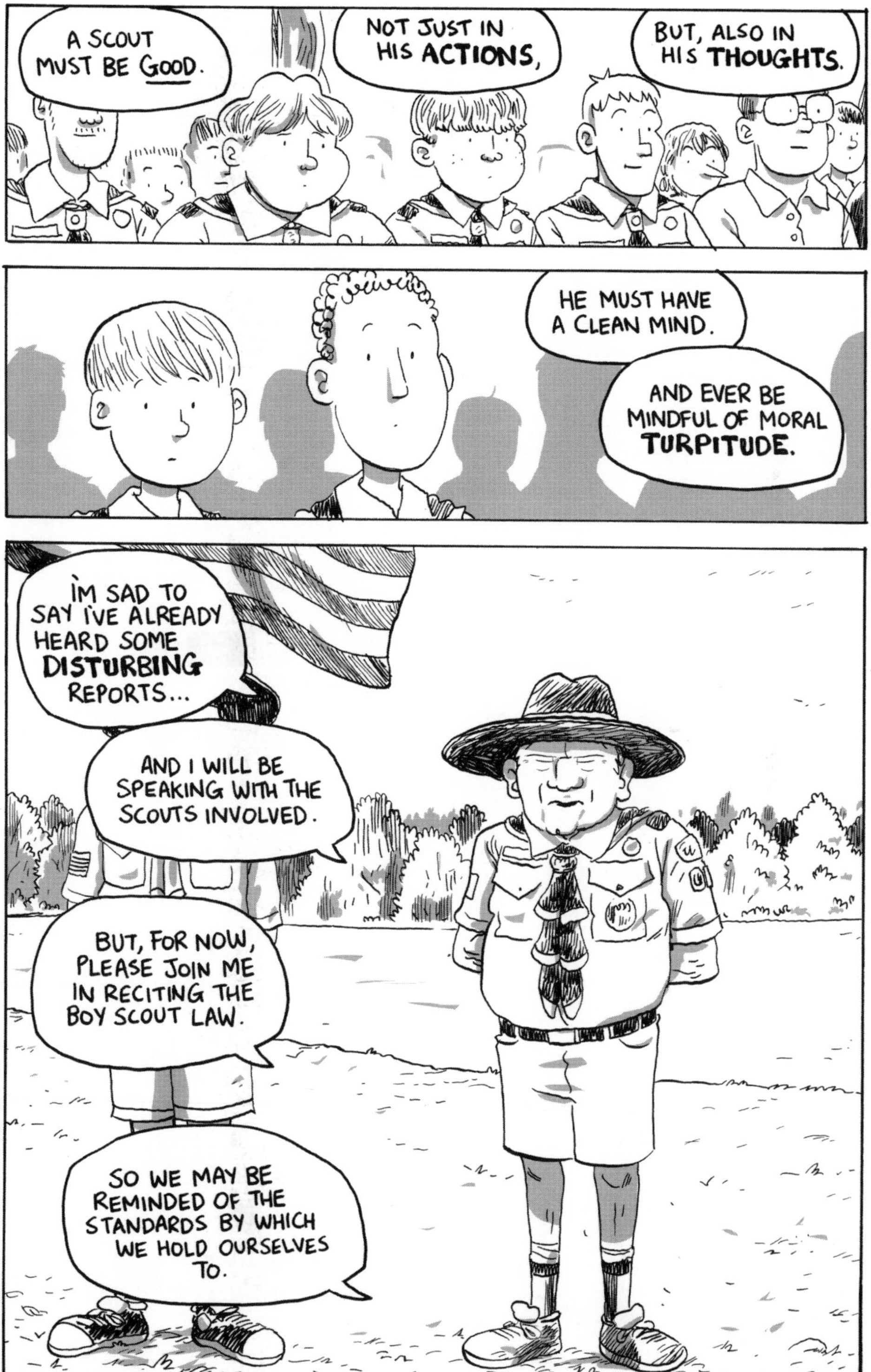
A SCOUT MUST BE GOOD.
NOT JUST IN HIS ACTIONS,
BUT, ALSO IN HIS THOUGHTS.
HE MUST HAVE A CLEAN MIND.
AND EVER BE MINDFUL OF MORAL TURPITUDE.
I'M SAD TO SAY I'VE ALREADY HEARD SOME DISTURBING REPORTS...
AND I WILL BE SPEAKING WITH THE SCOUTS INVOLVED.
BUT, FOR NOW, PLEASE JOIN ME IN RECITING THE BOY SCOUT LAW.
SO WE MAY BE REMINDED OF THE STANDARDS BY WHICH WE HOLD OURSELVES TO.

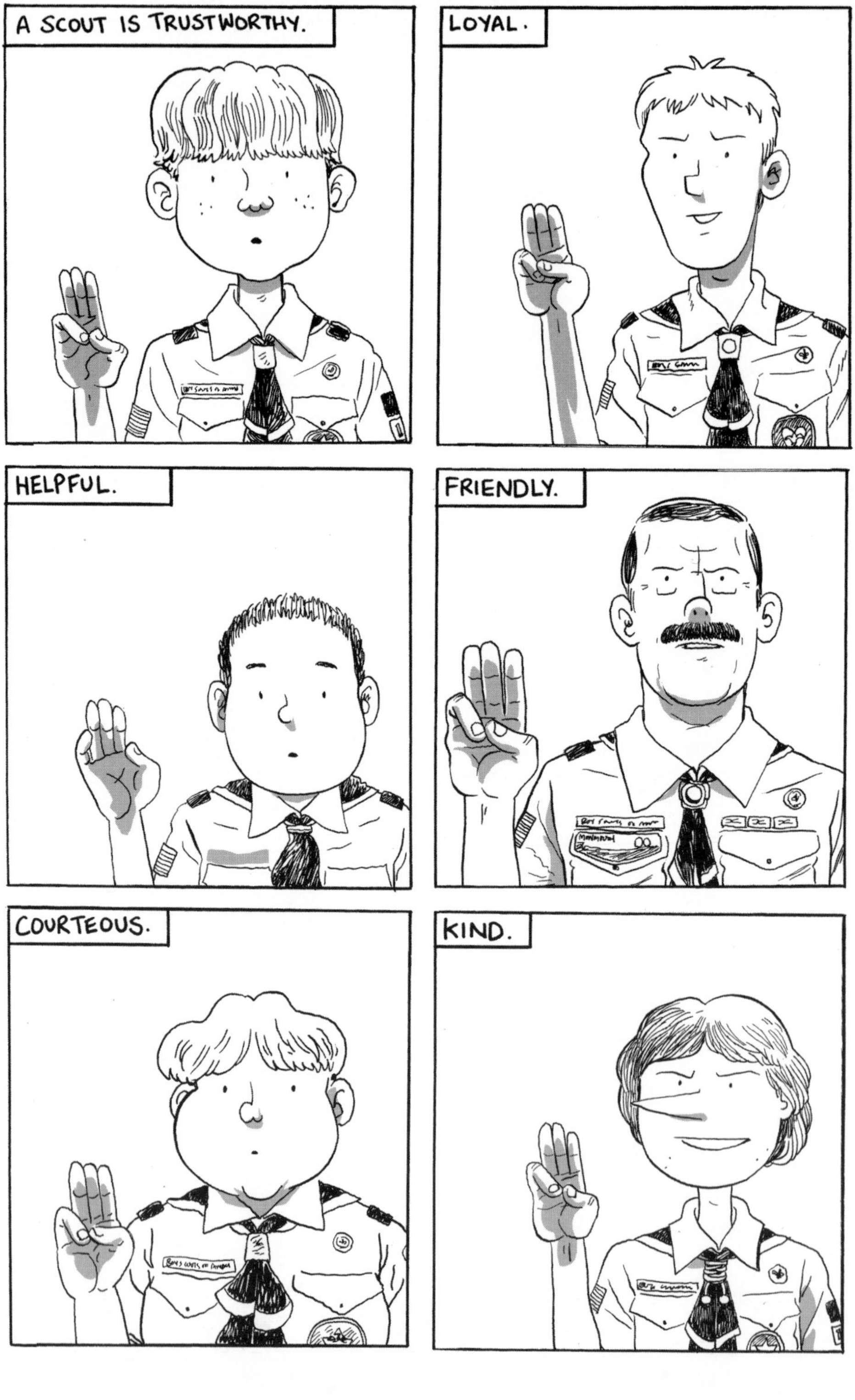
A SCOUT IS TRUSTWORTHY.
LOYAL.
HELPFUL.
FRIENDLY.
COURTEOUS.
KIND.

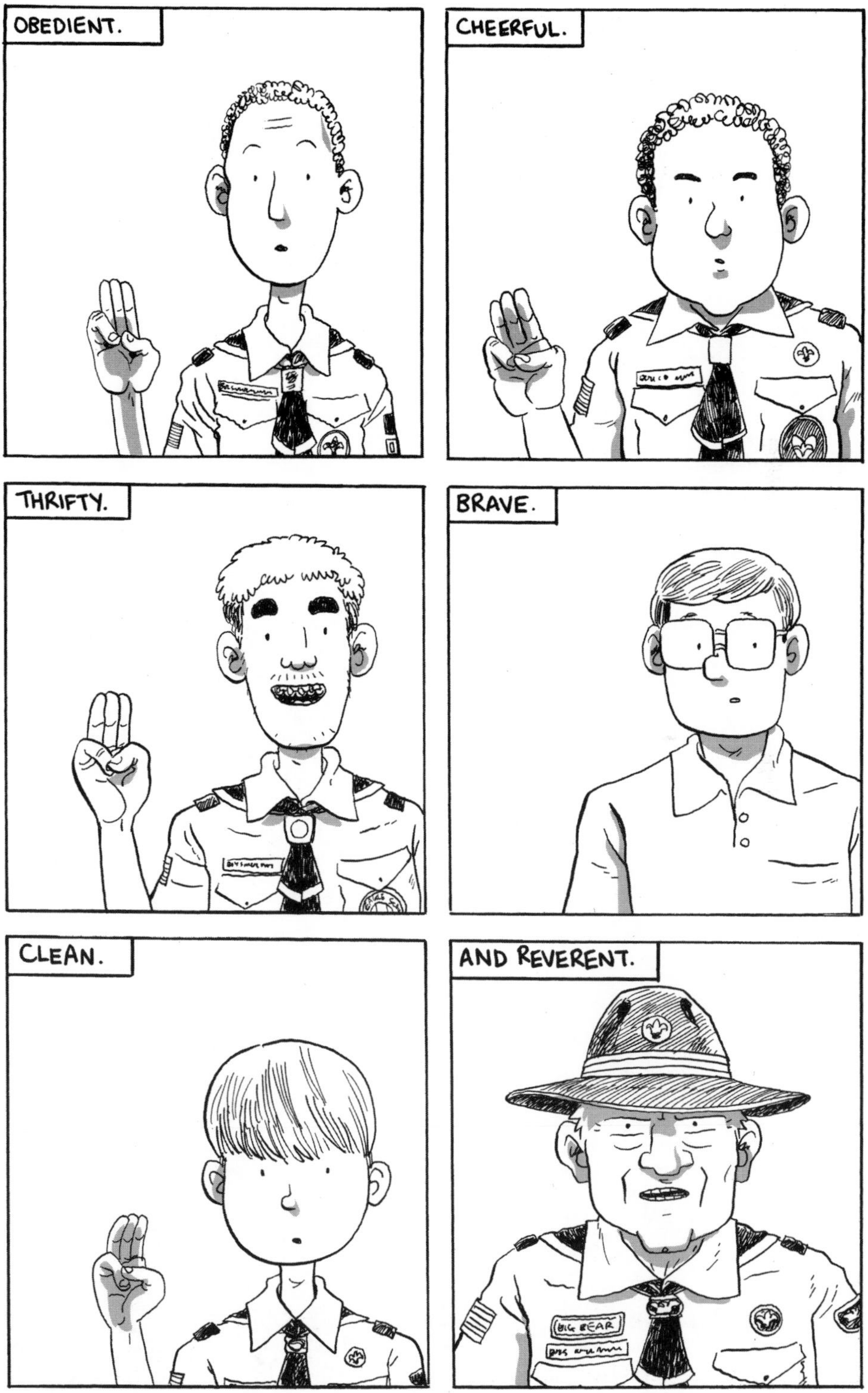
OBEDIENT.
CHEERFUL.
THRIFTY.
BRAVE.
CLEAN.
AND REVERENT.
BIG BEAR

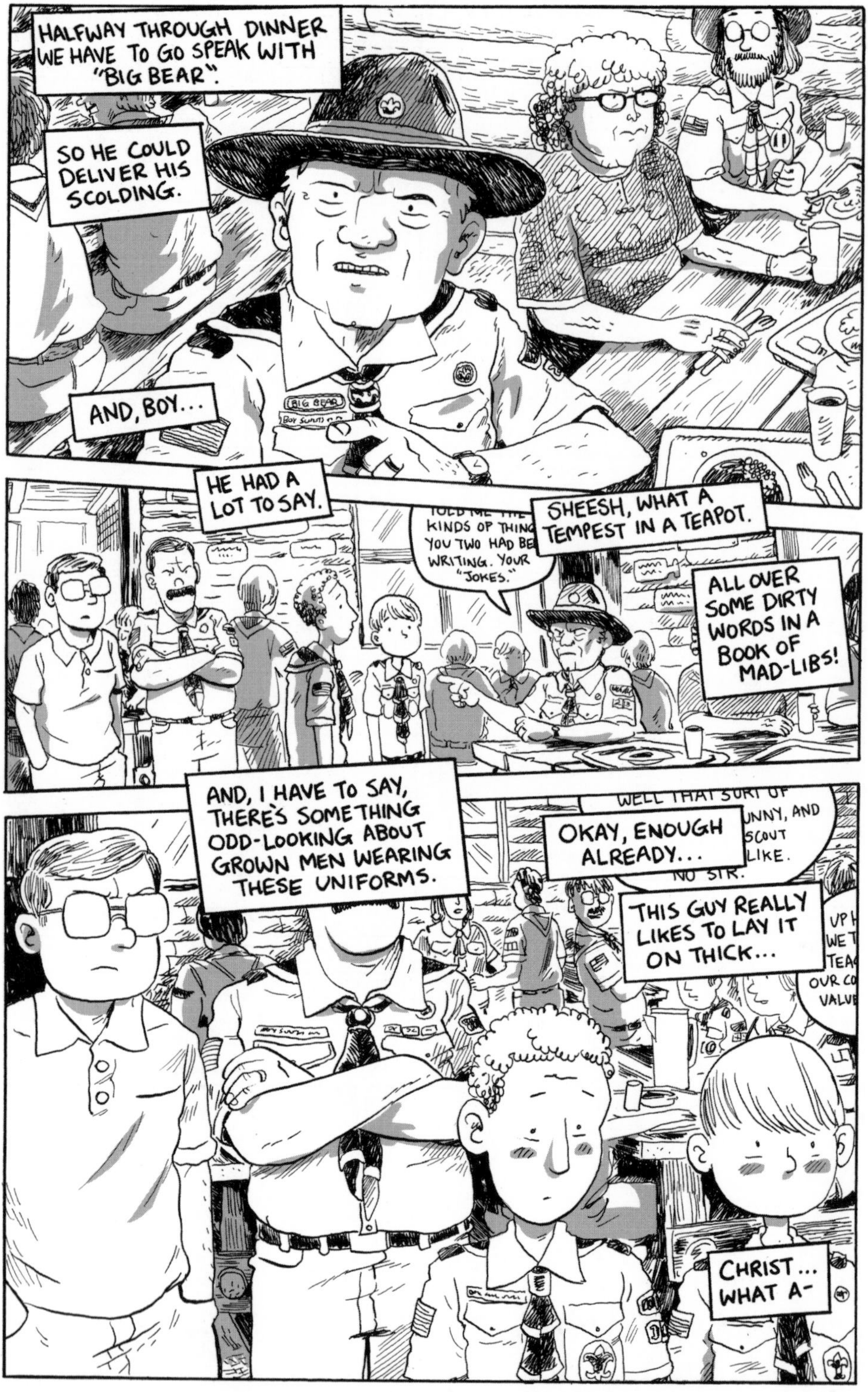
HALFWAY THROUGH DINNER WE HAVE TO GO SPEAK WITH "BIG BEAR".
SO HE COULD DELIVER HIS SCOLDING.
BIG BEAR
AND, BOY...
HE HAD A LOT TO SAY.
KINDS OF THING YOU TWO HAD BE WRITING. YOUR "JOKES."
SHEESH, WHAT A TEMPEST IN A TEAPOT.
ALL OVER SOME DIRTY WORDS IN A BOOK OF MAD-LIBS!
AND, I HAVE TO SAY, THERE'S SOMETHING ODD-LOOKING ABOUT GROWN MEN WEARING THESE UNIFORMS.
OKAY, ENOUGH ALREADY...
NO SIR.
THIS GUY REALLY LIKES TO LAY IT ON THICK...
CHRIST... WHAT A-

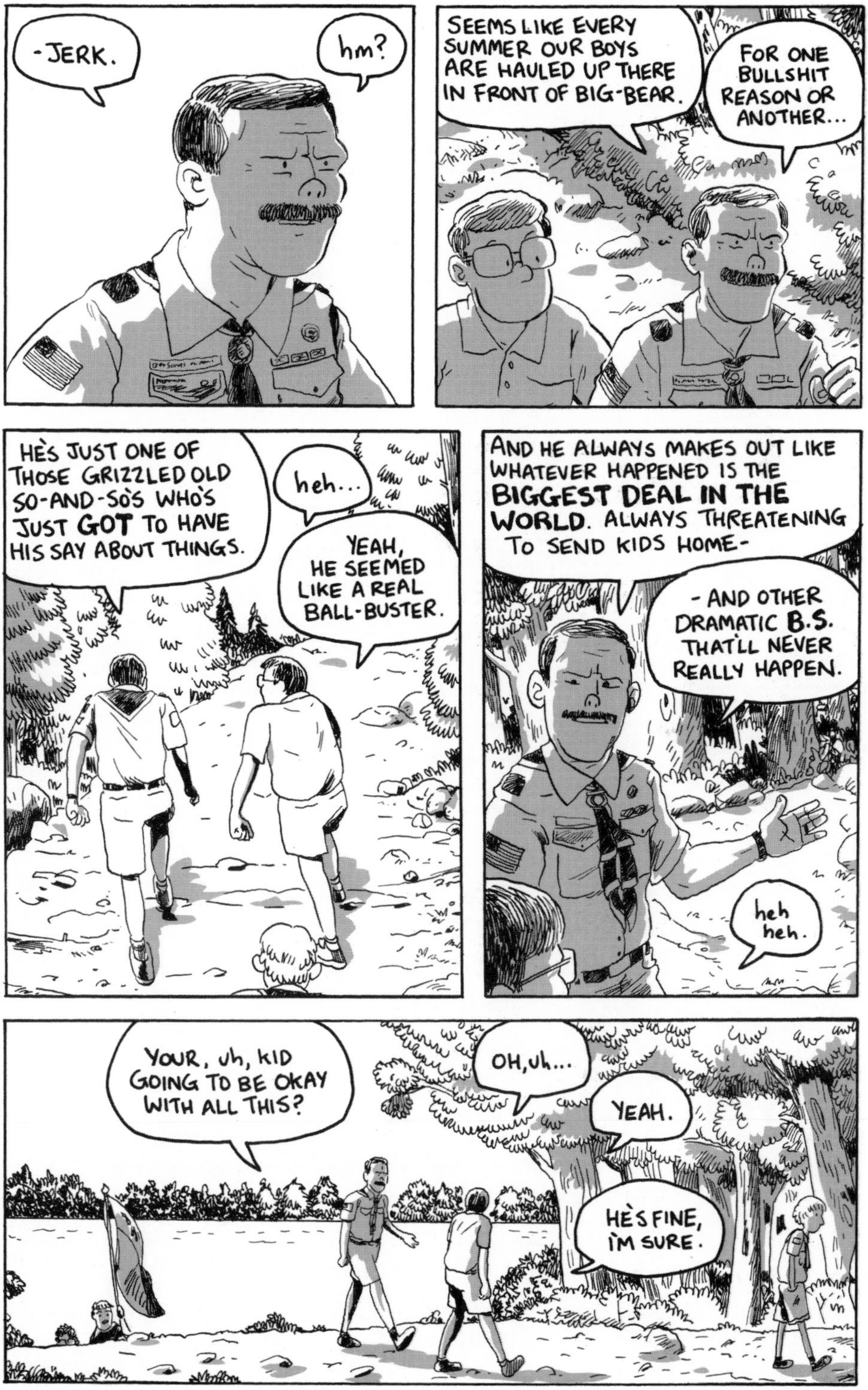
-JERK.
hm?
SEEMS LIKE EVERY SUMMER OUR BOYS ARE HAULED UP THERE IN FRONT OF BIG-BEAR.
FOR ONE BULLSHIT REASON OR ANOTHER...
HE'S JUST ONE OF THOSE GRIZZLED OLD SO-AND-SO'S WHO'S JUST GOT TO HAVE HIS SAY ABOUT THINGS.
heh...
YEAH, HE SEEMED LIKE A REAL BALL-BUSTER.
AND HE ALWAYS MAKES OUT LIKE WHATEVER HAPPENED IS THE BIGGEST DEAL IN THE WORLD. ALWAYS THREATENING TO SEND KIDS HOME-
- AND OTHER DRAMATIC B.S. THAT'LL NEVER REALLY HAPPEN.
heh heh.
YOUR, uh, KID GOING TO BE OKAY WITH ALL THIS?
OH, uh...
YEAH.
HE'S FINE, I'M SURE.

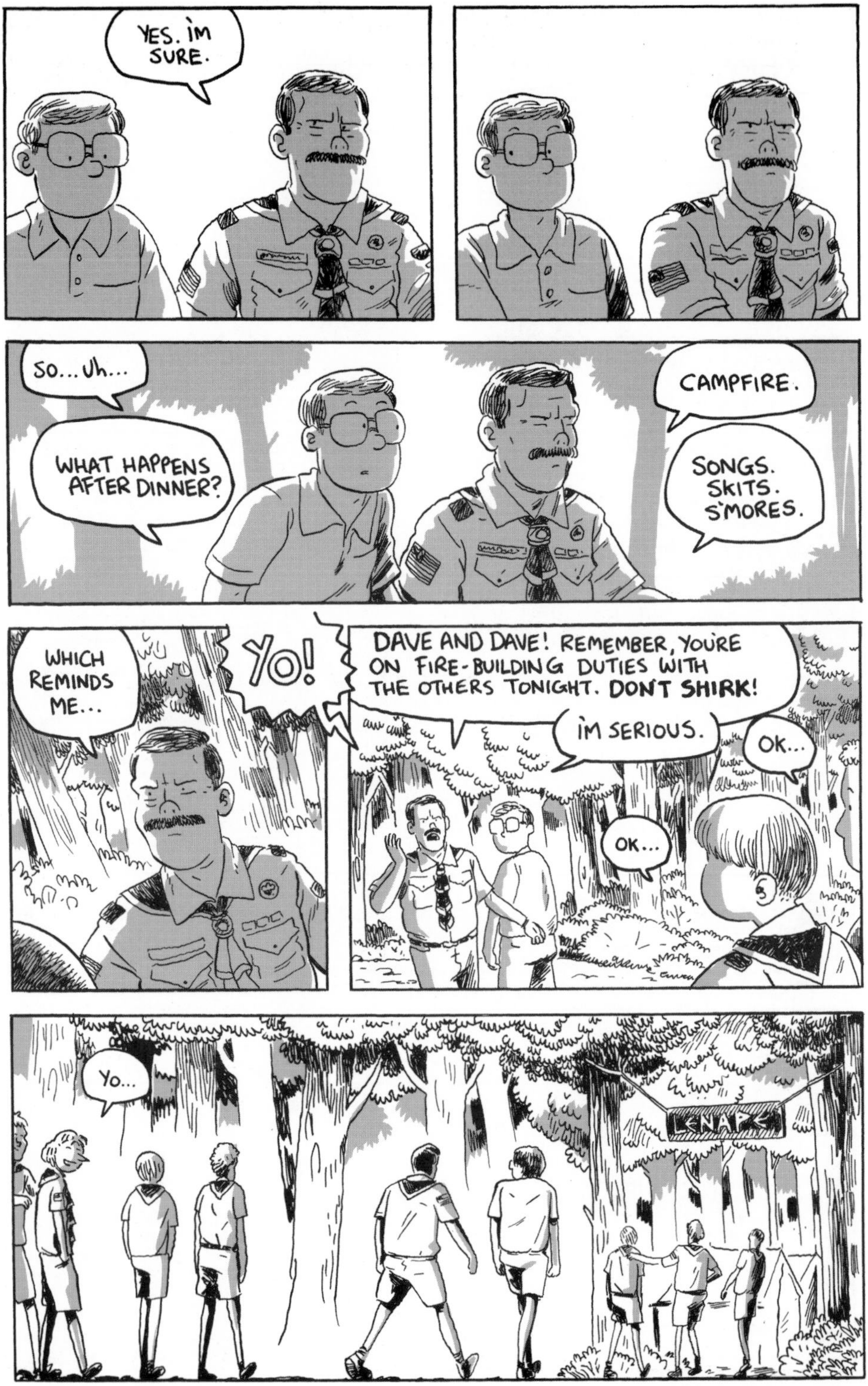
YES. IM SURE.
SO... UH...
WHAT HAPPENS AFTER DINNER?
CAMPFIRE.
SONGS. SKITS. S'MORES.
WHICH REMINDS ME...
YO!
DAVE AND DAVE! REMEMBER, YOU'RE ON FIRE-BUILDING DUTIES WITH THE OTHERS TONIGHT. DON'T SHIRK!
IM SERIOUS.
OK...
OK...
YO...
LENAPE

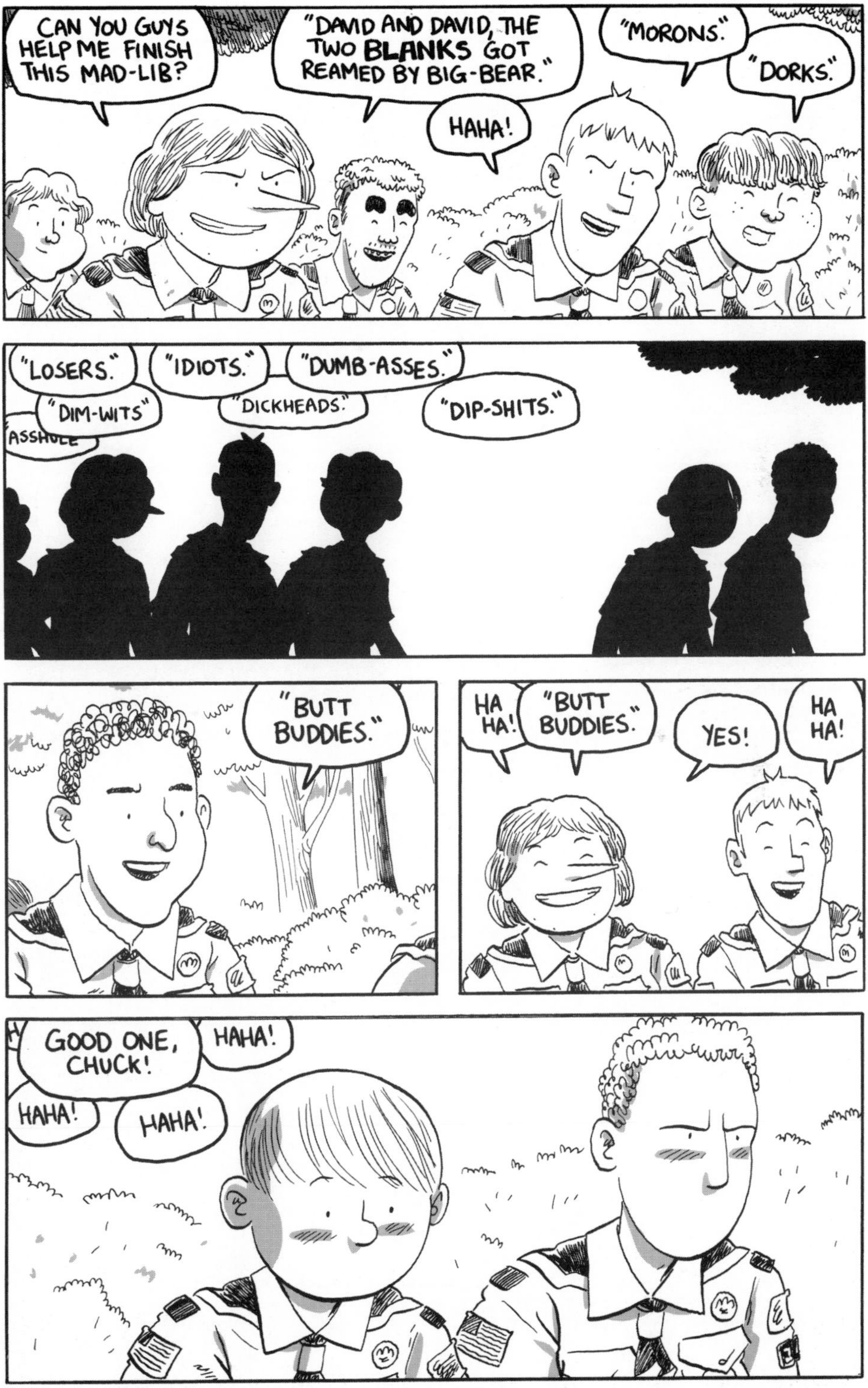
CAN YOU GUYS HELP ME FINISH THIS MAD-LIB?
"DAVID AND DAVID, THE TWO BLANKS GOT REAMED BY BIG-BEAR."
HAHA!
"MORONS."
"DORKS."
"LOSERS."
"IDIOTS."
"DUMB-ASSES."
"DIM-WITS"
"DICKHEADS."
"DIP-SHITS."
ASSHOLE
"BUTT BUDDIES."
HA HA!
"BUTT BUDDIES."
YES!
HA HA!
GOOD ONE, CHUCK!
HAHA!
HAHA!
HAHA!

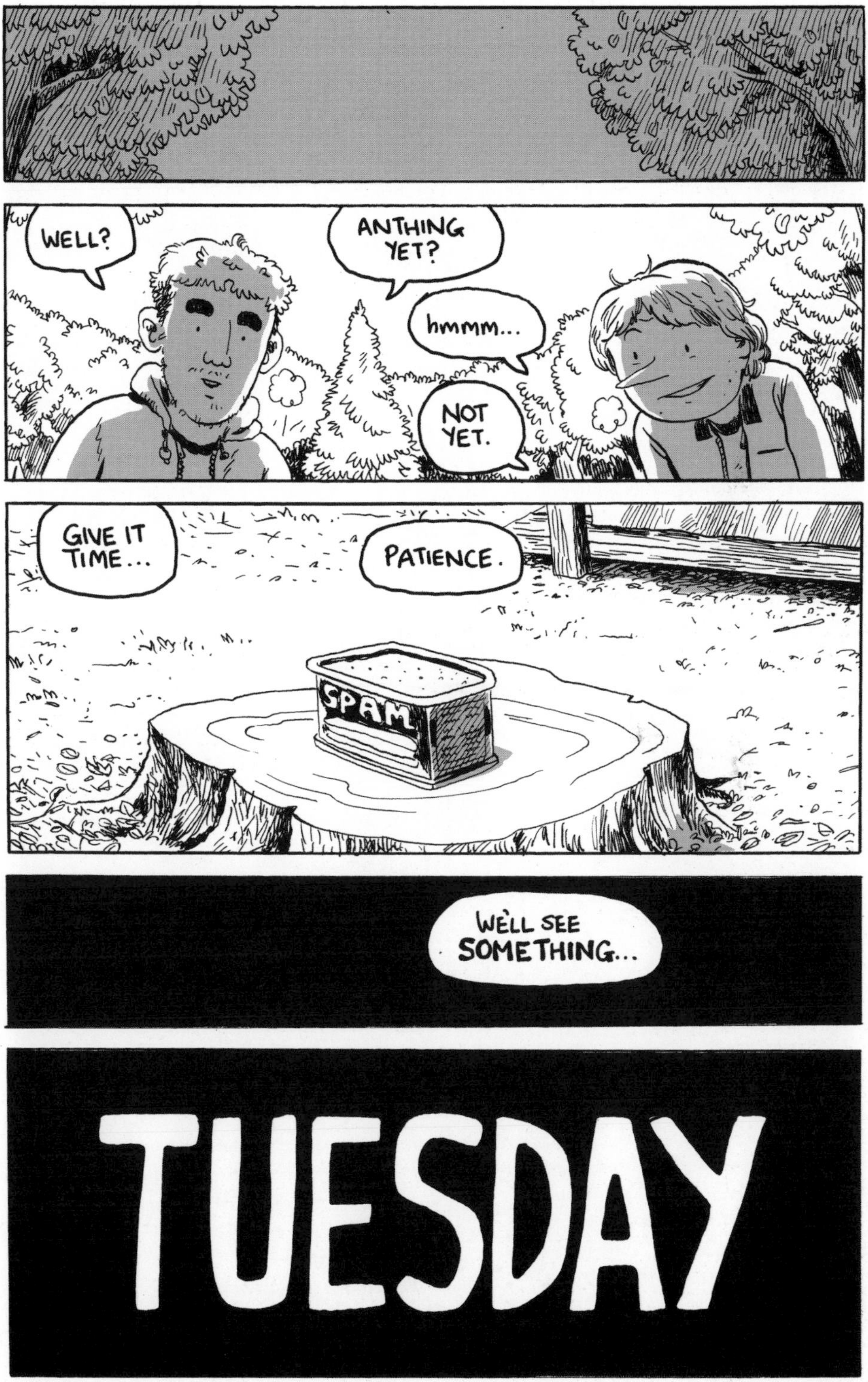
WELL?
ANTHING YET?
hmmm...
NOT YET.
GIVE IT TIME...
PATIENCE.
SPAM
WE'LL SEE SOMETHING...
TUESDAY

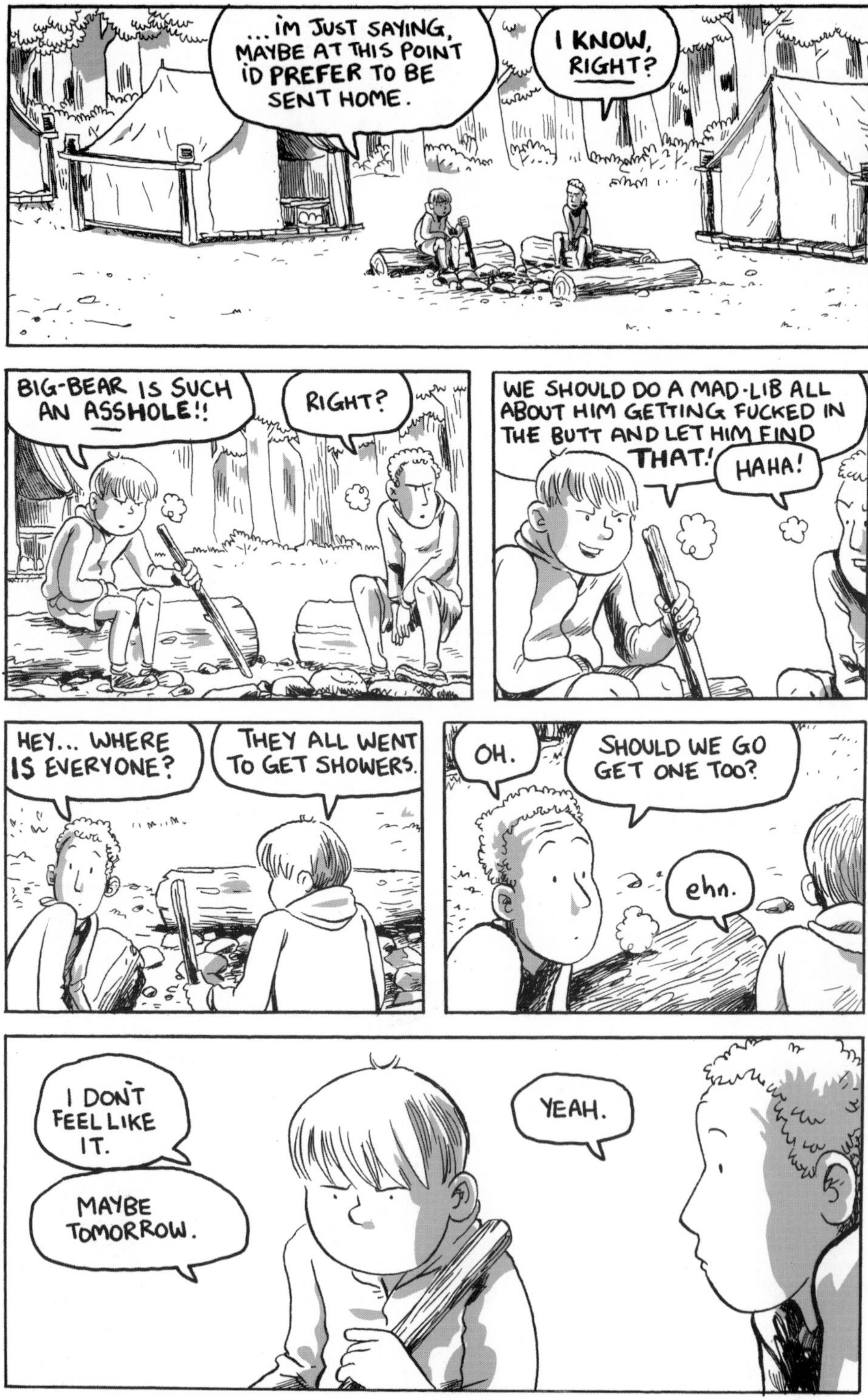
...IM JUST SAYING, MAYBE AT THIS POINT ID PREFER TO BE SENT HOME.
I KNOW, RIGHT?
BIG-BEAR IS SUCH AN ASSHOLE!!
RIGHT?
WE SHOULD DO A MAD-LIB ALL ABOUT HIM GETTING FUCKED IN THE BUTT AND LET HIM FIND THAT!
HAHA!
HEY... WHERE IS EVERYONE?
THEY ALL WENT TO GET SHOWERS.
OH.
SHOULD WE GO GET ONE TOO?
ehn.
I DON'T FEEL LIKE IT.
MAYBE TOMORROW.
YEAH.

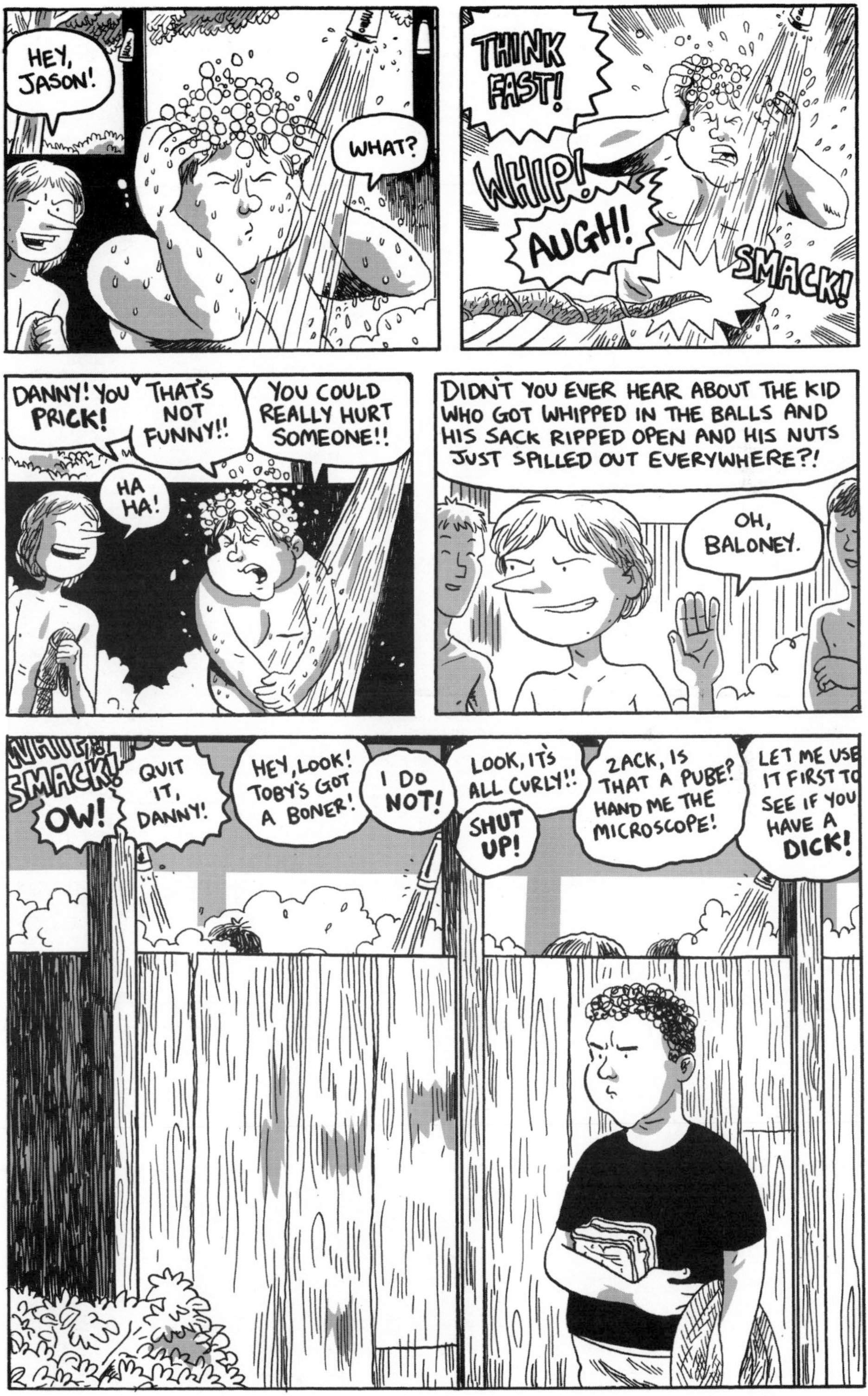
HEY, JASON!
WHAT?
THINK FAST!
WHIP!
AUGH!
SMACK!
DANNY! YOU PRICK!
THAT'S NOT FUNNY!!
YOU COULD REALLY HURT SOMEONE!!
HA HA!
DIDN'T YOU EVER HEAR ABOUT THE KID WHO GOT WHIPPED IN THE BALLS AND HIS SACK RIPPED OPEN AND HIS NUTS JUST SPILLED OUT EVERYWHERE?!
OH, BALONEY.
SMACK!
OW!
QUIT IT, DANNY!
HEY, LOOK! TOBY'S GOT A BONER!
I DO NOT!
LOOK, IT'S ALL CURLY!!
SHUT UP!
ZACK, IS THAT A PUBE? HAND ME THE MICROSCOPE!
LET ME USE IT FIRST TO SEE IF YOU HAVE A DICK!

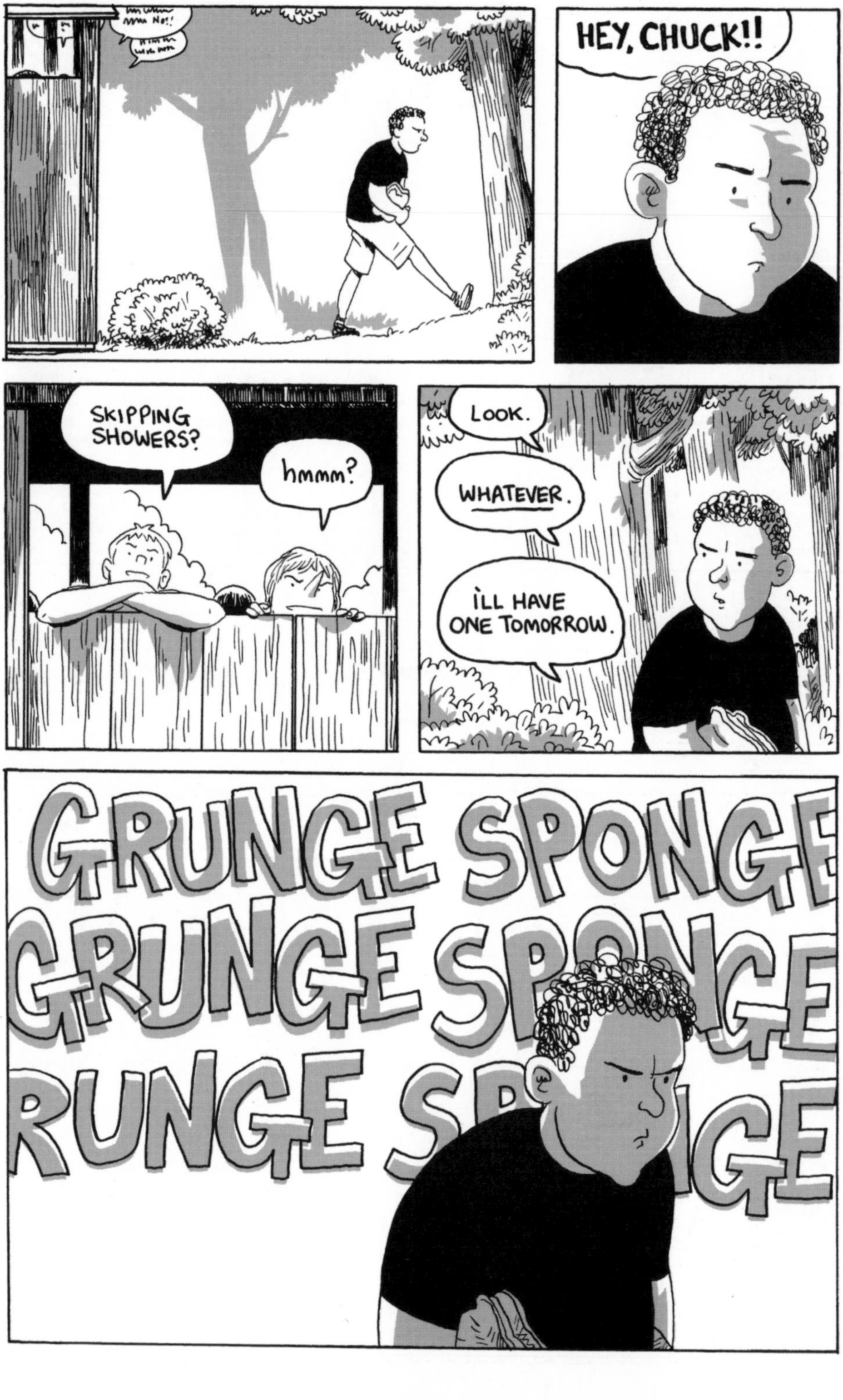
HEY, CHUCK!!
SKIPPING SHOWERS?
hmmm?
LOOK.
WHATEVER.
ILL HAVE ONE TOMORROW.
GRUNGE SPONGE
GRUNGE SPONGE
RUNGE

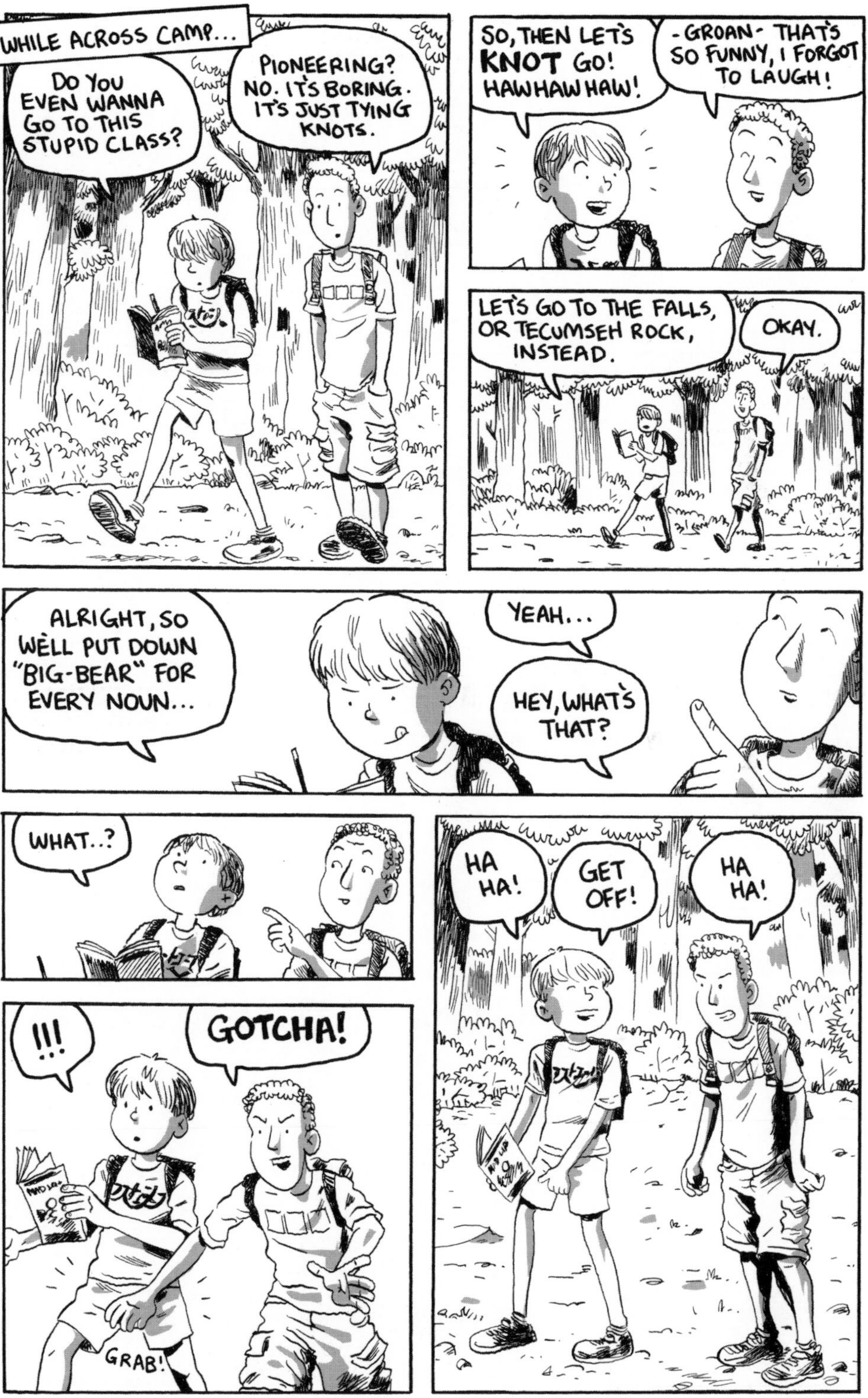
WHILE ACROSS CAMP...
DO YOU EVEN WANNA GO TO THIS STUPID CLASS?
PIONEERING? NO. IT'S BORING. IT'S JUST TYING KNOTS.
SO, THEN LET'S KNOT GO! HAWHAWHAW!
-GROAN- THAT'S SO FUNNY, I FORGOT TO LAUGH!
LET'S GO TO THE FALLS, OR TECUMSEH ROCK, INSTEAD.
OKAY.
ALRIGHT, SO WE'LL PUT DOWN "BIG-BEAR" FOR EVERY NOUN...
YEAH...
HEY, WHAT'S THAT?
WHAT..?
!!!
GOTCHA!
GRAB!
HA HA!
GET OFF!
HA HA!

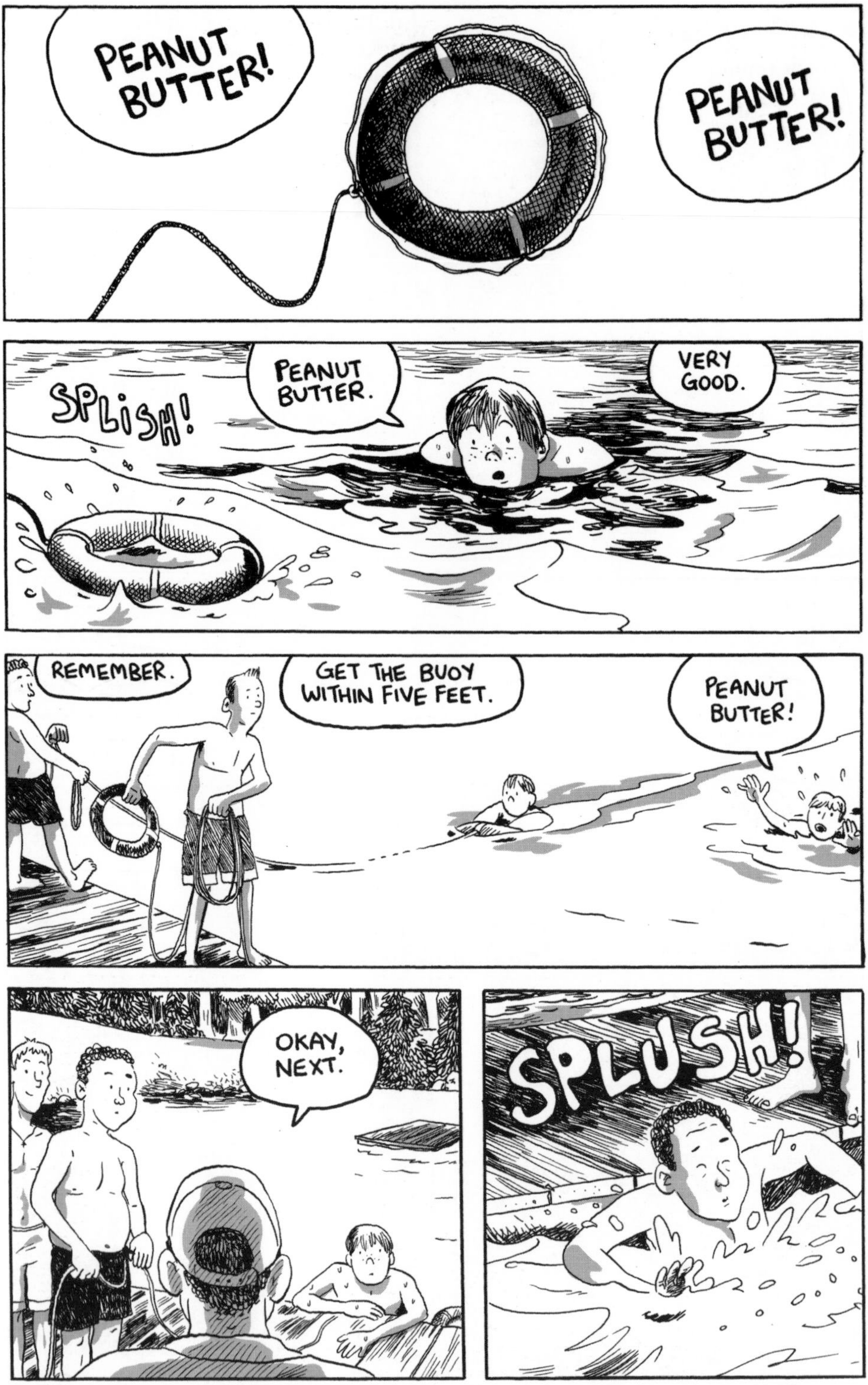
PEANUT BUTTER!
PEANUT BUTTER!
SPLISH!
PEANUT BUTTER.
VERY GOOD.
REMEMBER.
GET THE BUOY WITHIN FIVE FEET.
PEANUT BUTTER!
OKAY, NEXT.
SPLUSH!

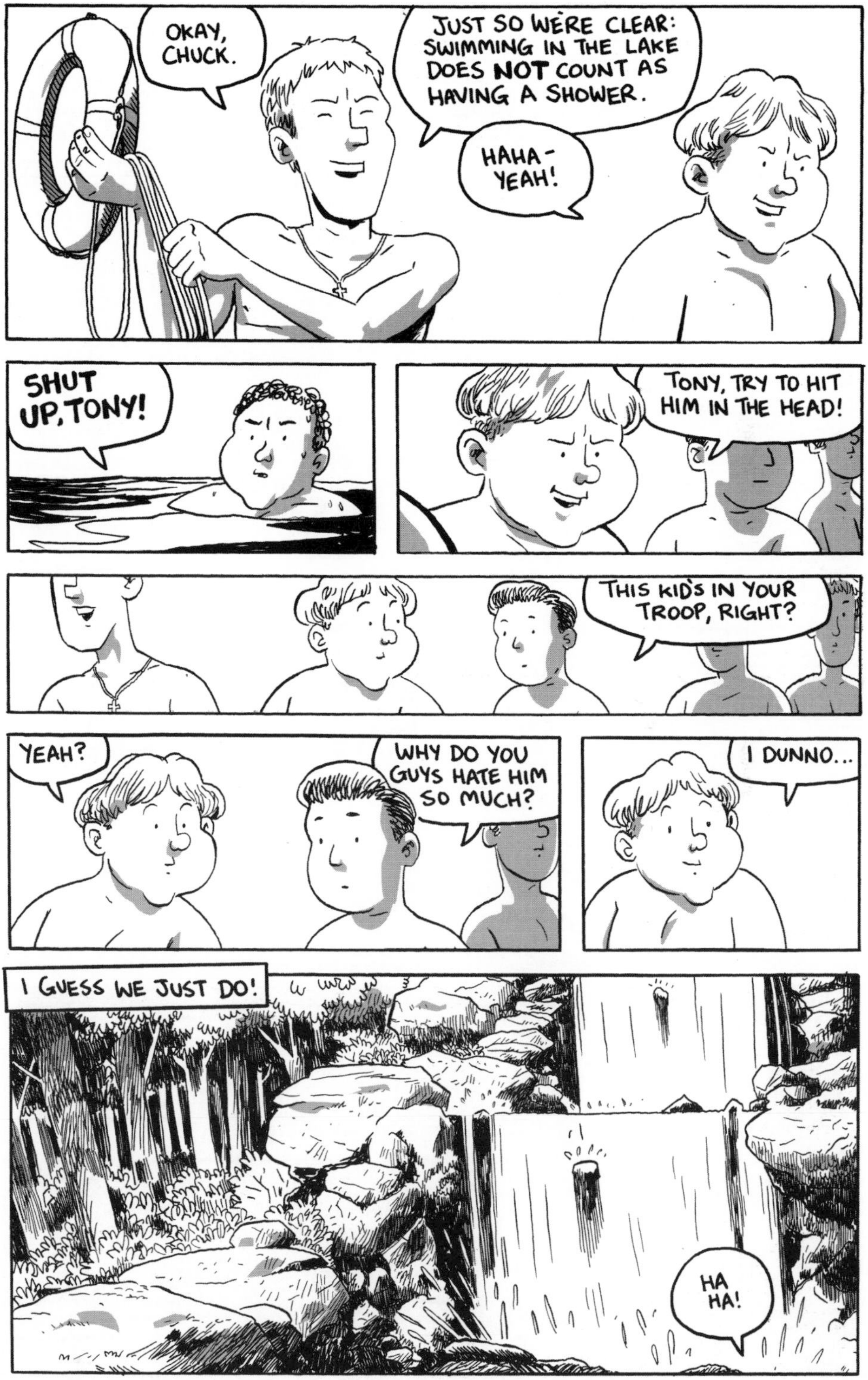
OKAY, CHUCK.
JUST SO WE'RE CLEAR: SWIMMING IN THE LAKE DOES NOT COUNT AS HAVING A SHOWER.
HAHA- YEAH!
SHUT UP, TONY!
TONY, TRY TO HIT HIM IN THE HEAD!
THIS KID'S IN YOUR TROOP, RIGHT?
YEAH?
WHY DO YOU GUYS HATE HIM SO MUCH?
I DUNNO...
I GUESS WE JUST DO!
HA HA!

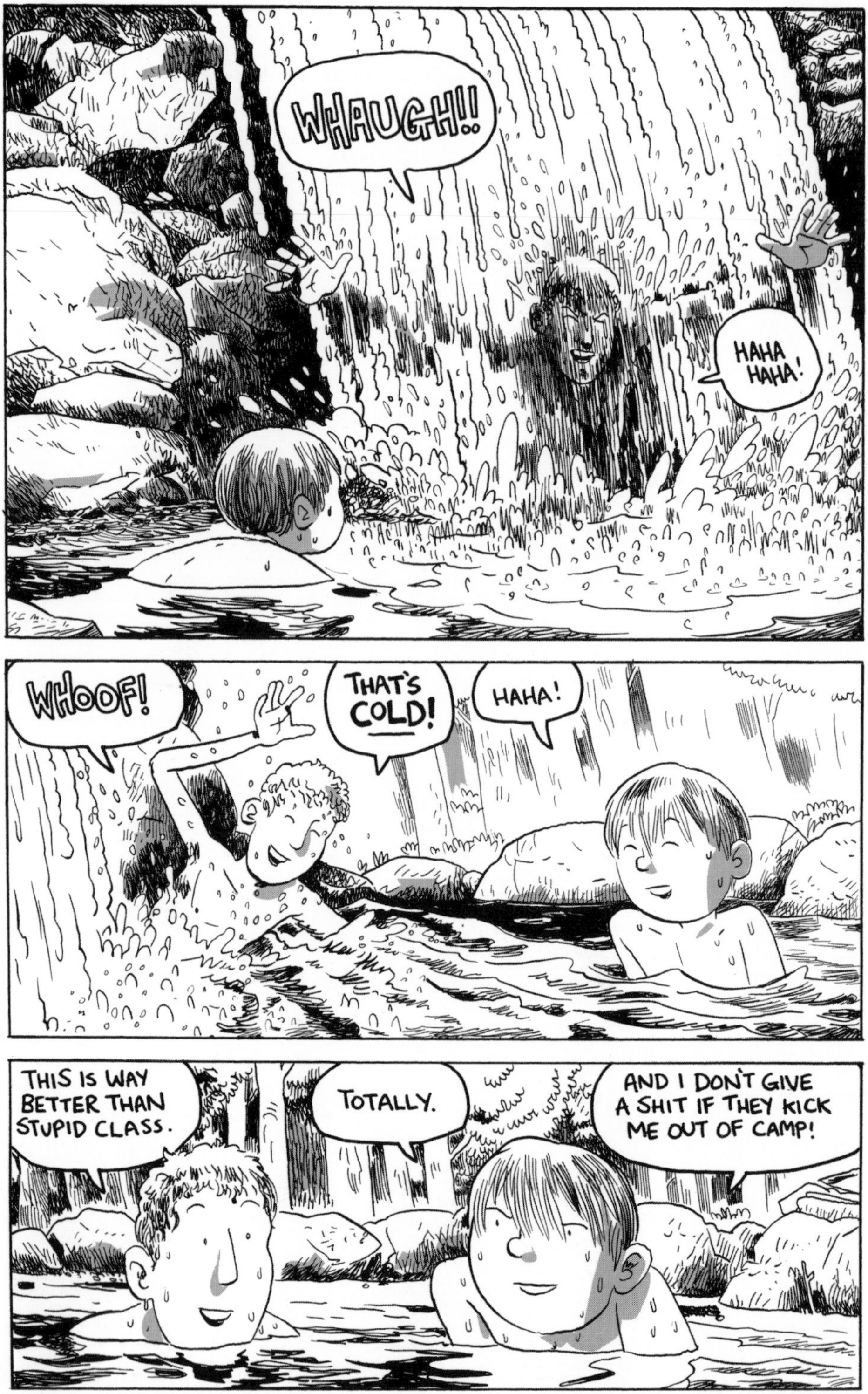
WHAUGH!!
HAHA HAHA!
WHOOF!
THAT'S COLD!
HAHA!
THIS IS WAY BETTER THAN STUPID CLASS.
TOTALLY.
AND I DON'T GIVE A SHIT IF THEY KICK ME OUT OF CAMP!

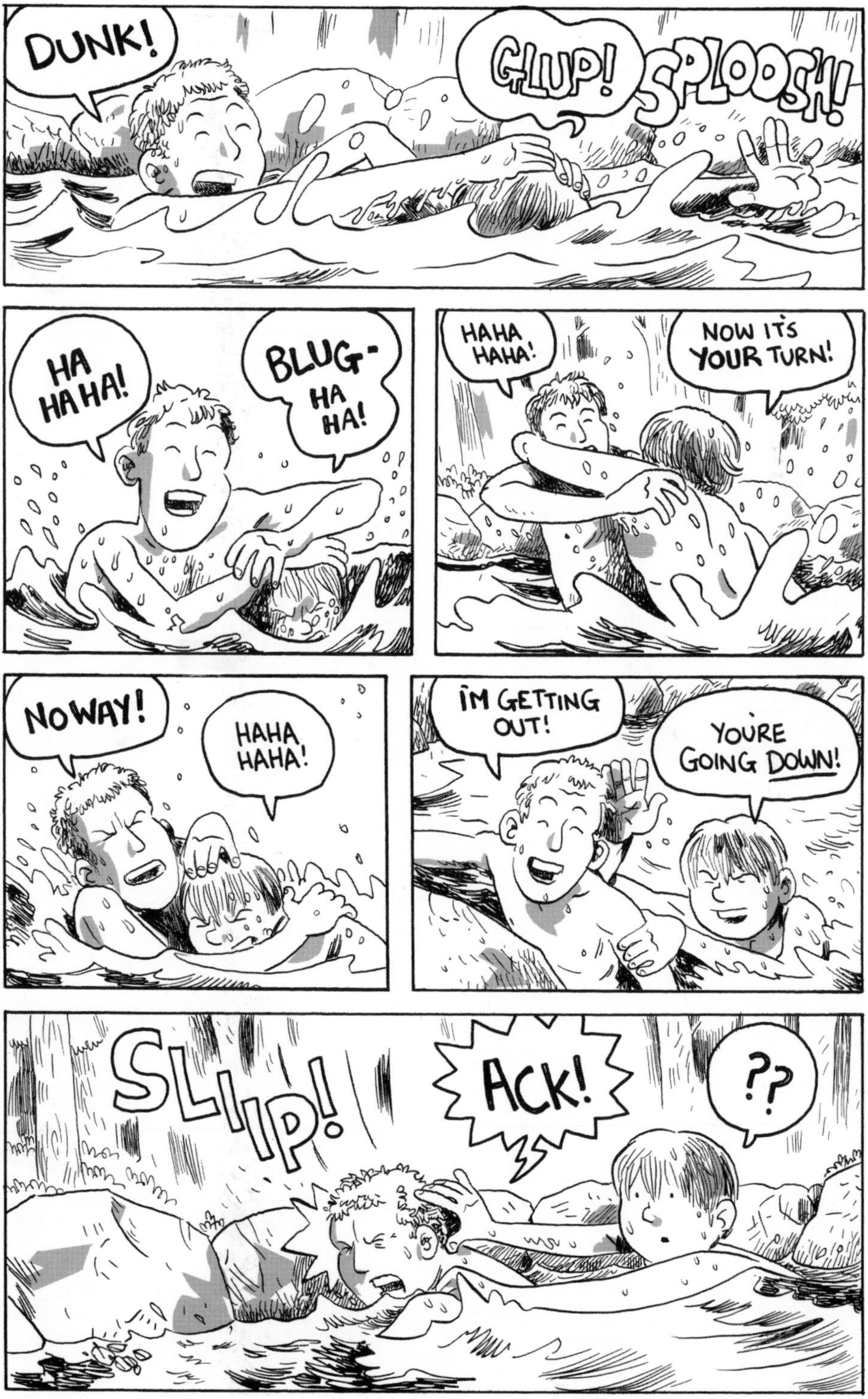
DUNK!
GLUP!
SPLOOSH!
HA HAHA!
BLUG- HA HA!
HAHA HAHA!
NOW IT'S YOUR TURN!
NO WAY!
HAHA HAHA!
I'M GETTING OUT!
YOU'RE GOING DOWN!
SLIIP!
ACK!
??

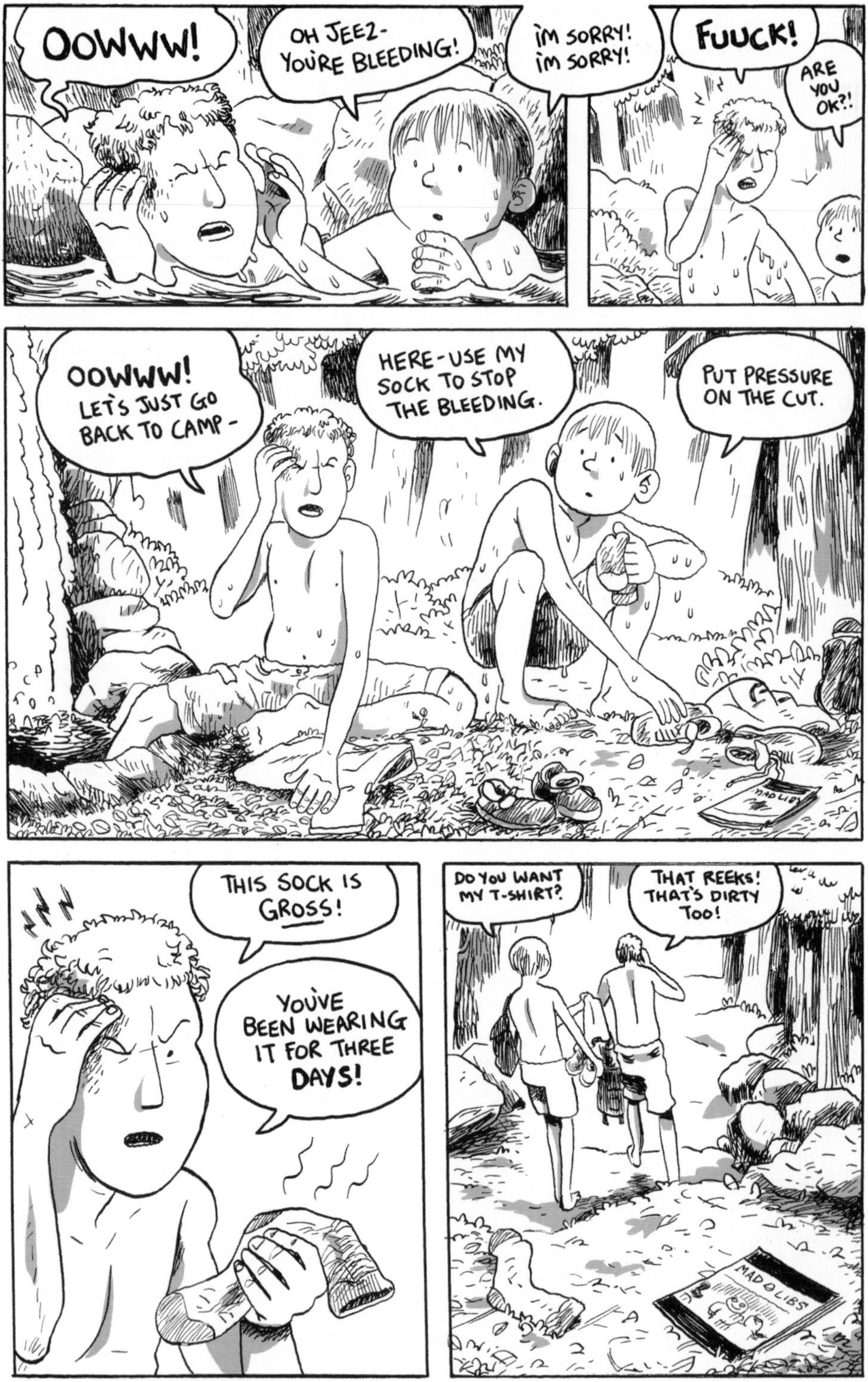
OOWWW!
OH JEEZ- YOU'RE BLEEDING!
I'M SORRY! I'M SORRY!
FUUCK!
ARE YOU OK?!
OOWWW! LET'S JUST GO BACK TO CAMP-
HERE-USE MY SOCK TO STOP THE BLEEDING.
PUT PRESSURE ON THE CUT.
MAD LIBS
THIS SOCK IS GROSS!
YOU'VE BEEN WEARING IT FOR THREE DAYS!
DO YOU WANT MY T-SHIRT?
THAT REEKS! THAT'S DIRTY TOO!
MAD LIBS

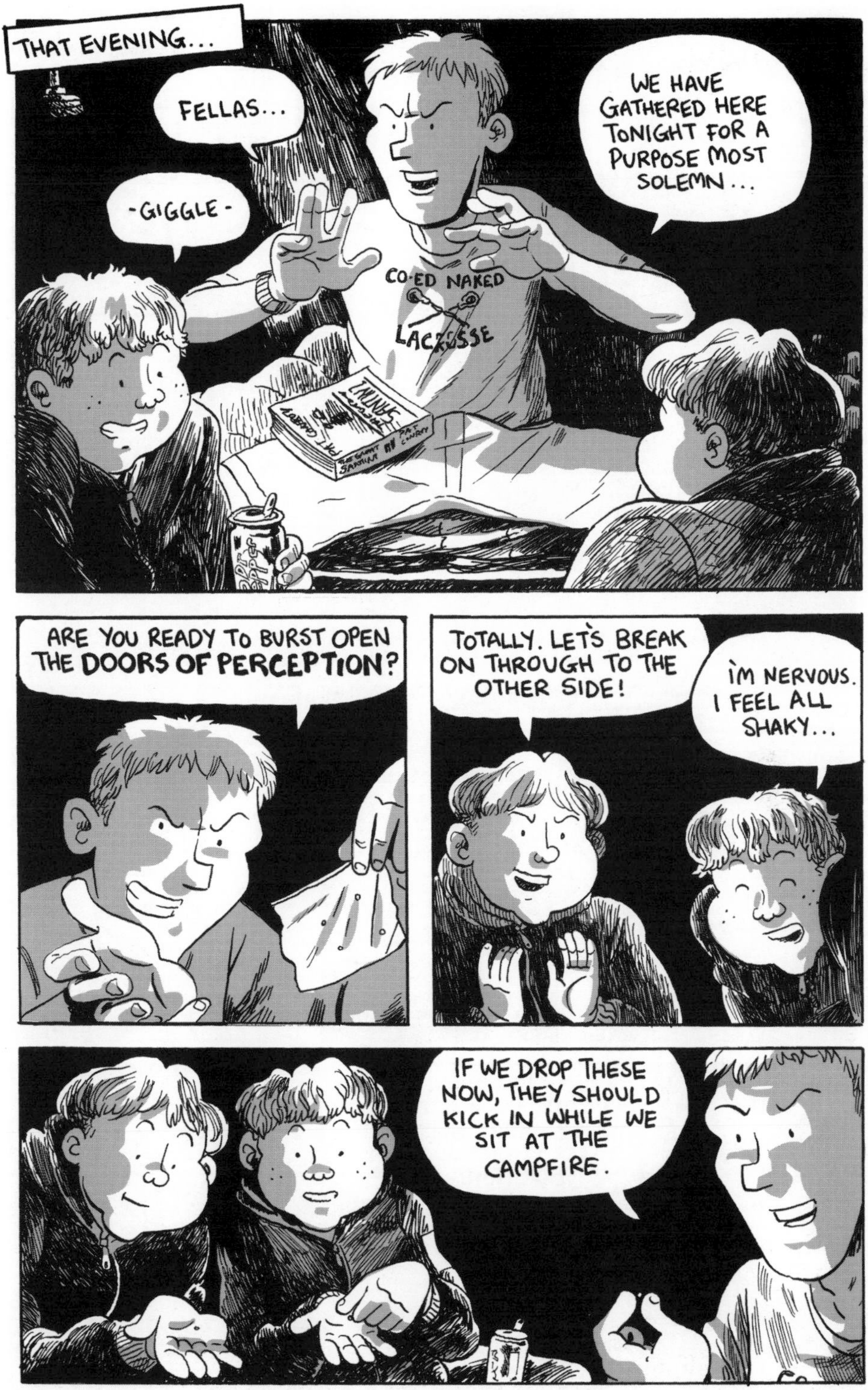
THAT EVENING...
FELLAS...
-GIGGLE-
WE HAVE GATHERED HERE TONIGHT FOR A PURPOSE MOST SOLEMN...
CO-ED NAKED LACROSSE
ARE YOU READY TO BURST OPEN THE DOORS OF PERCEPTION?
TOTALLY. LET'S BREAK ON THROUGH TO THE OTHER SIDE!
I'M NERVOUS. I FEEL ALL SHAKY...
IF WE DROP THESE NOW, THEY SHOULD KICK IN WHILE WE SIT AT THE CAMPFIRE.

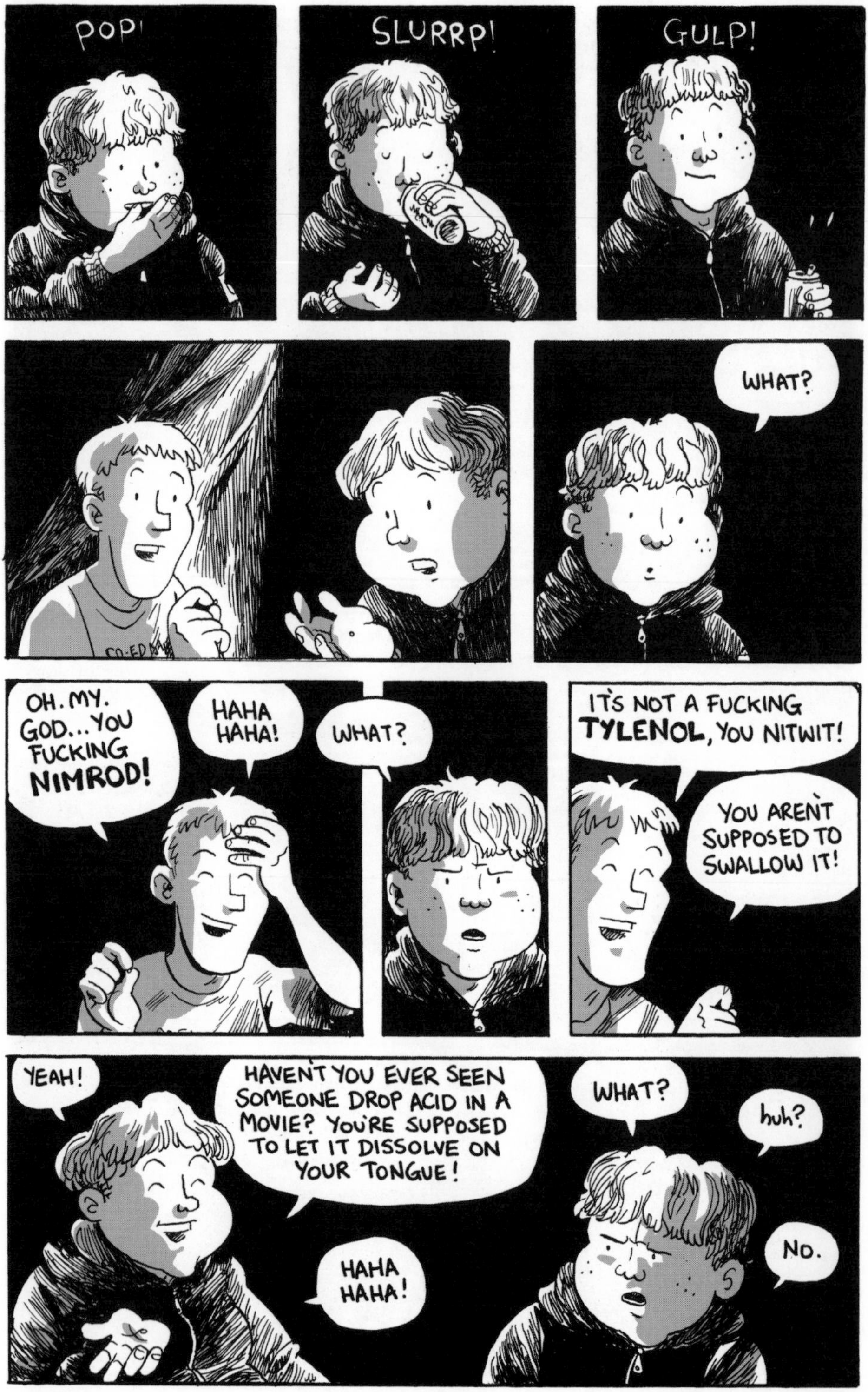
POP!
SLURRP!
GULP!
WHAT?
OH. MY. GOD... YOU FUCKING NIMROD!
HAHA HAHA!
WHAT?
IT'S NOT A FUCKING TYLENOL, YOU NITWIT!
YOU AREN'T SUPPOSED TO SWALLOW IT!
YEAH!
HAVEN'T YOU EVER SEEN SOMEONE DROP ACID IN A MOVIE? YOU'RE SUPPOSED TO LET IT DISSOLVE ON YOUR TONGUE!
HAHA HAHA!
WHAT?
huh?
NO.

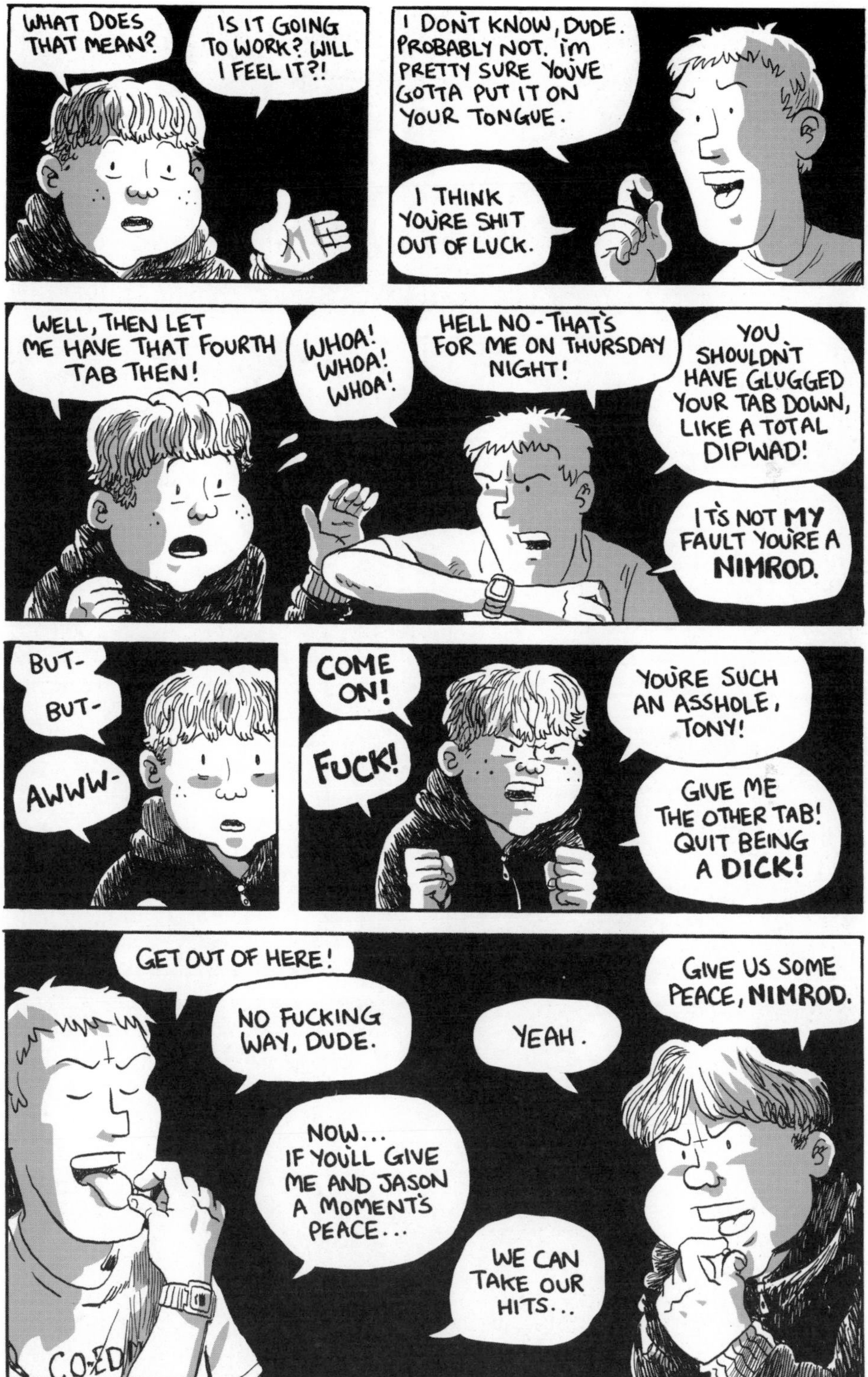
WHAT DOES THAT MEAN?
IS IT GOING TO WORK? WILL I FEEL IT?!
I DON'T KNOW, DUDE. PROBABLY NOT. I'M PRETTY SURE YOU'VE GOTTA PUT IT ON YOUR TONGUE.
I THINK YOU'RE SHIT OUT OF LUCK.
WELL, THEN LET ME HAVE THAT FOURTH TAB THEN!
WHOA! WHOA! WHOA!
HELL NO - THAT'S FOR ME ON THURSDAY NIGHT!
YOU SHOULDN'T HAVE GLUGGED YOUR TAB DOWN, LIKE A TOTAL DIPWAD!
IT'S NOT MY FAULT YOU'RE A NIMROD.
BUT-
BUT-
AWWW-
COME ON!
FUCK!
YOU'RE SUCH AN ASSHOLE, TONY!
GIVE ME THE OTHER TAB! QUIT BEING A DICK!
GET OUT OF HERE!
NO FUCKING WAY, DUDE.
YEAH.
GIVE US SOME PEACE, NIMROD.
NOW... IF YOU'LL GIVE ME AND JASON A MOMENT'S PEACE...
WE CAN TAKE OUR HITS...
CO-ED

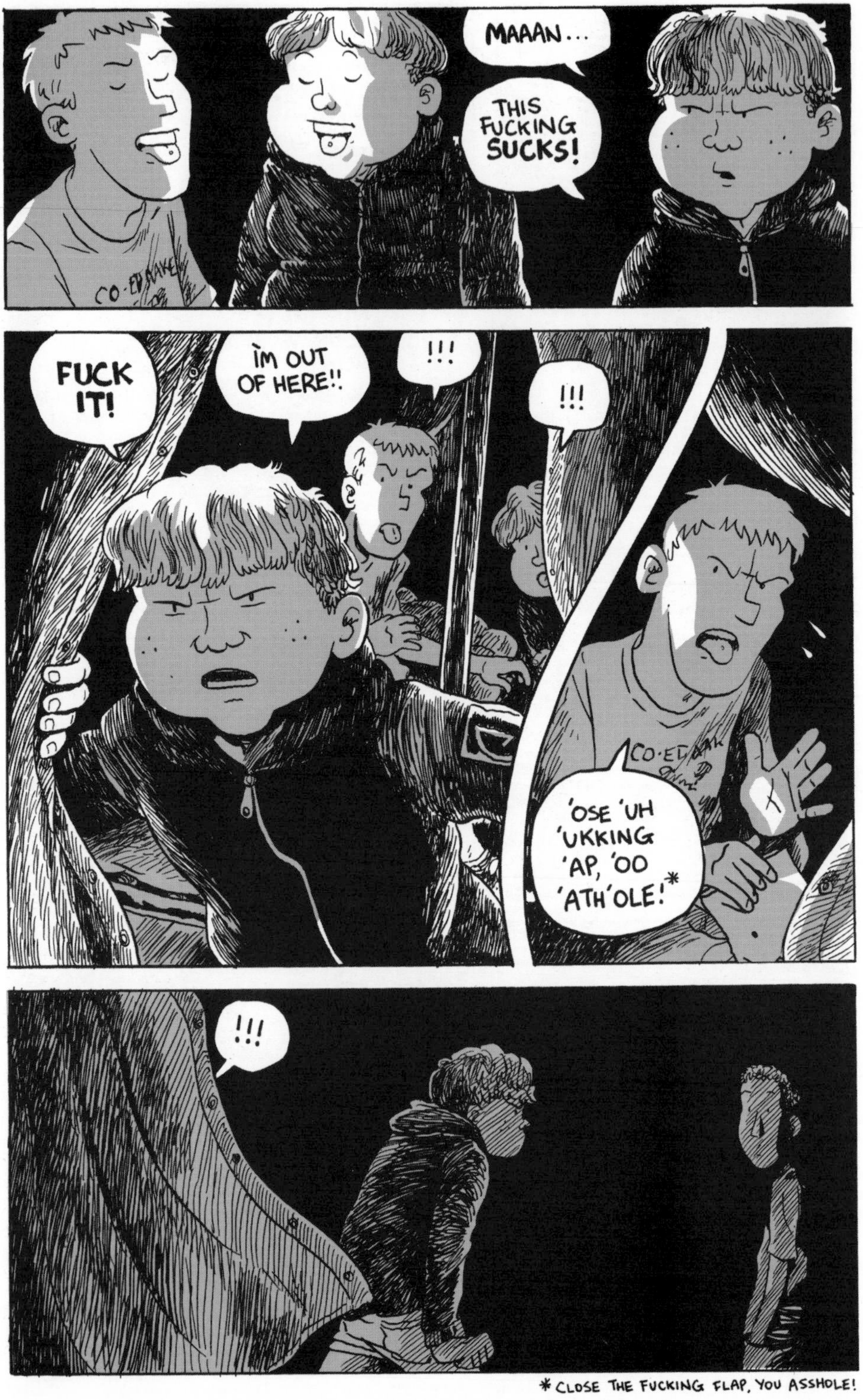
MAAAN...
THIS FUCKING SUCKS!
FUCK IT!
I'M OUT OF HERE!!
!!!
!!!
'OSE 'UH 'UKKING 'AP, 'OO 'ATH'OLE!*
!!!

* CLOSE THE FUCKING FLAP, YOU ASSHOLE!

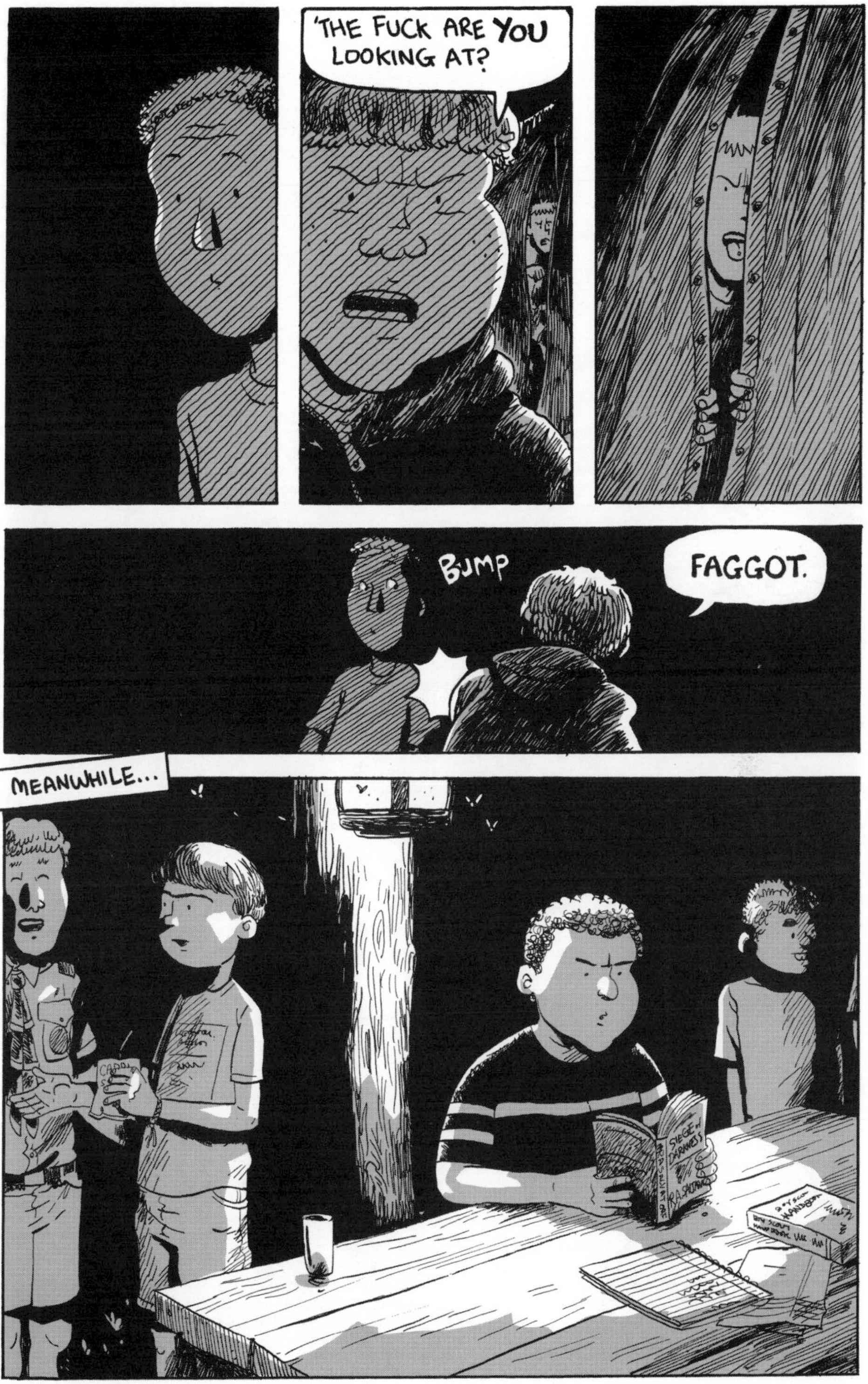
'THE FUCK ARE YOU LOOKING AT?
BUMP
FAGGOT.
MEANWHILE...
SIEGE OF DARKNESS

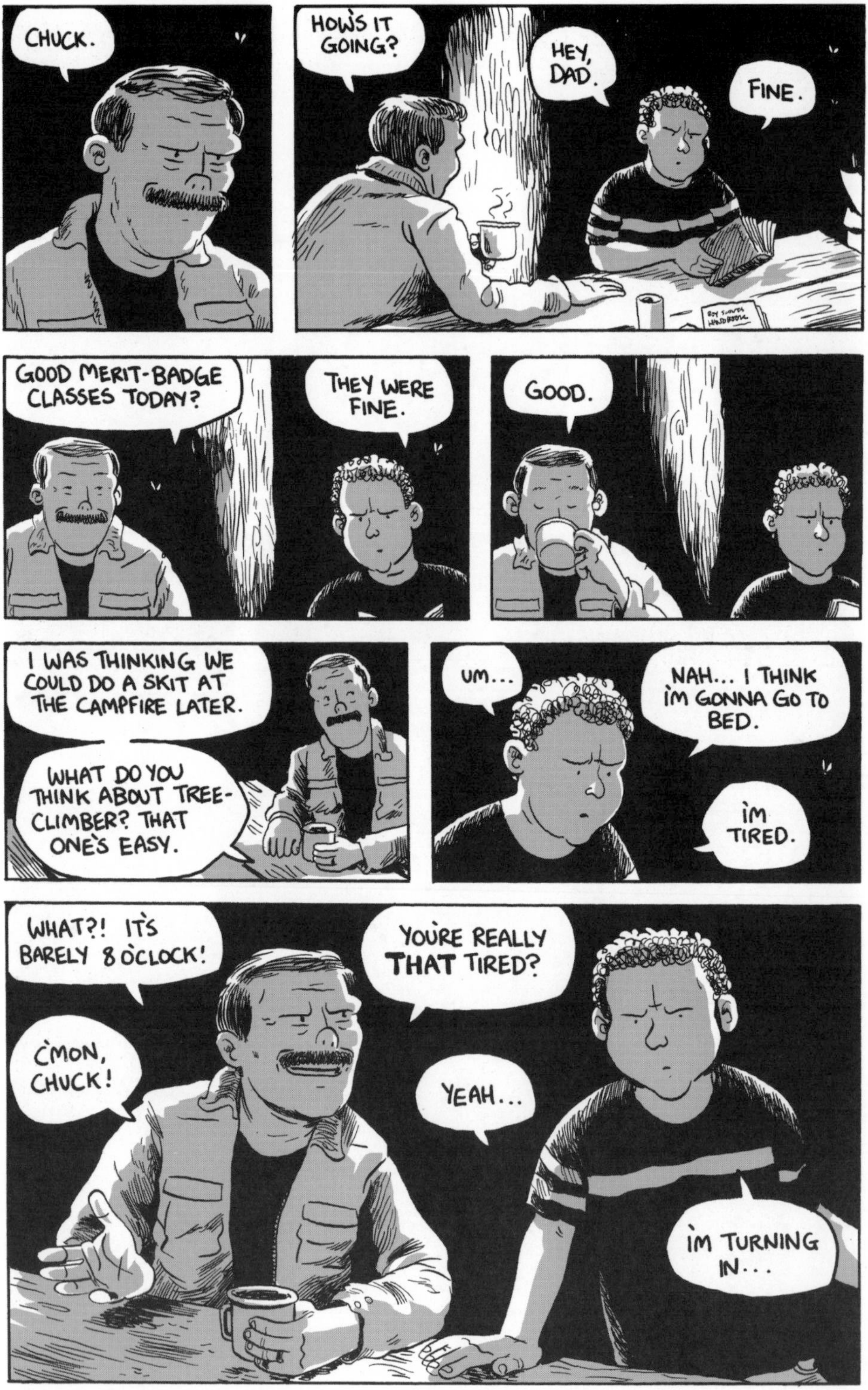
CHUCK.
HOW'S IT GOING?
HEY, DAD.
FINE.
GOOD MERIT-BADGE CLASSES TODAY?
THEY WERE FINE.
GOOD.
I WAS THINKING WE COULD DO A SKIT AT THE CAMPFIRE LATER.
WHAT DO YOU THINK ABOUT TREE-CLIMBER? THAT ONE'S EASY.
UM...
NAH... I THINK I'M GONNA GO TO BED.
I'M TIRED.
WHAT?! IT'S BARELY 8 O'CLOCK!
YOU'RE REALLY THAT TIRED?
C'MON, CHUCK!
YEAH...
I'M TURNING IN...

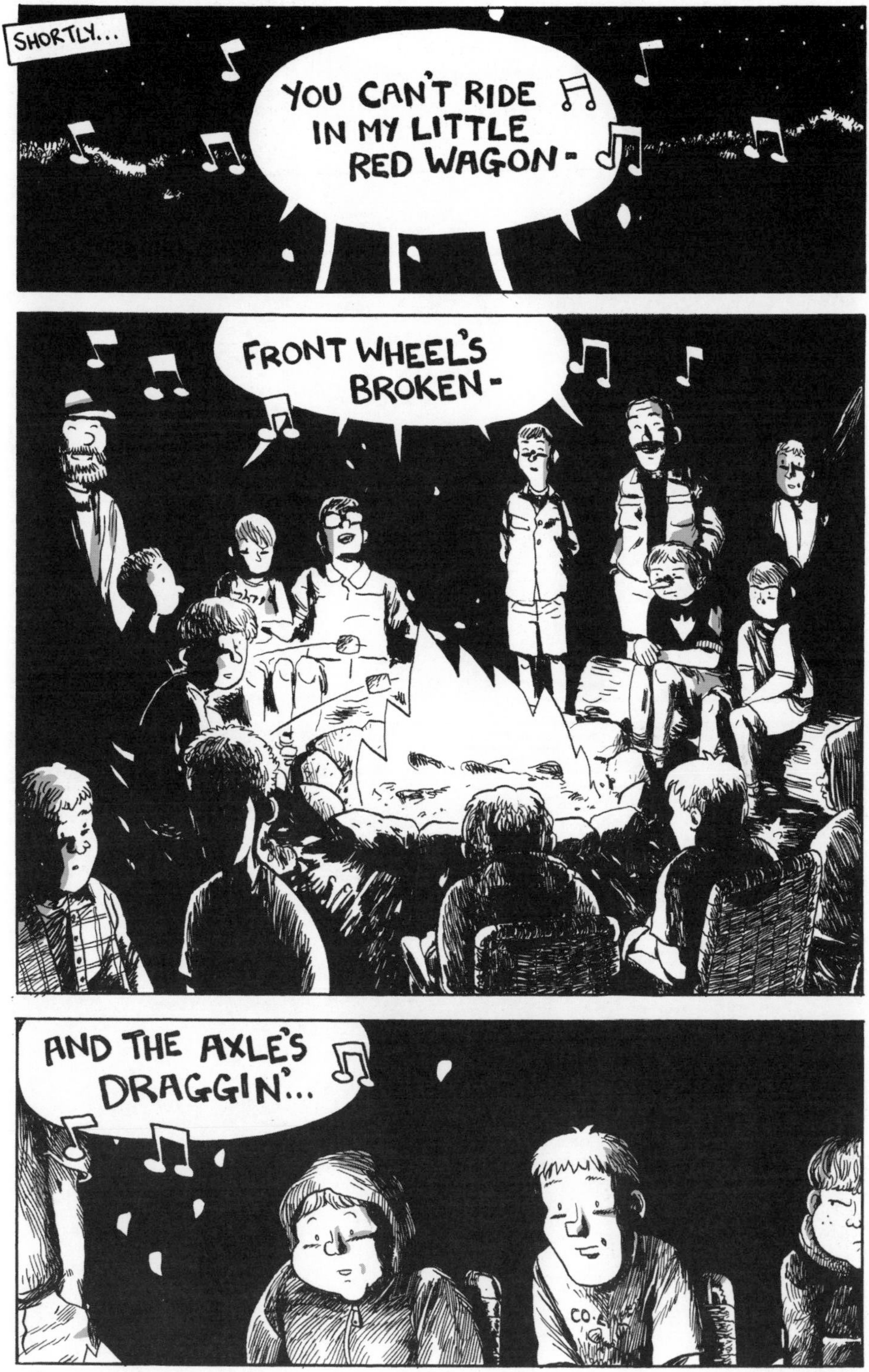
SHORTLY...
YOU CAN'T RIDE IN MY LITTLE RED WAGON-
FRONT WHEEL'S BROKEN-
AND THE AXLE'S DRAGGIN'...

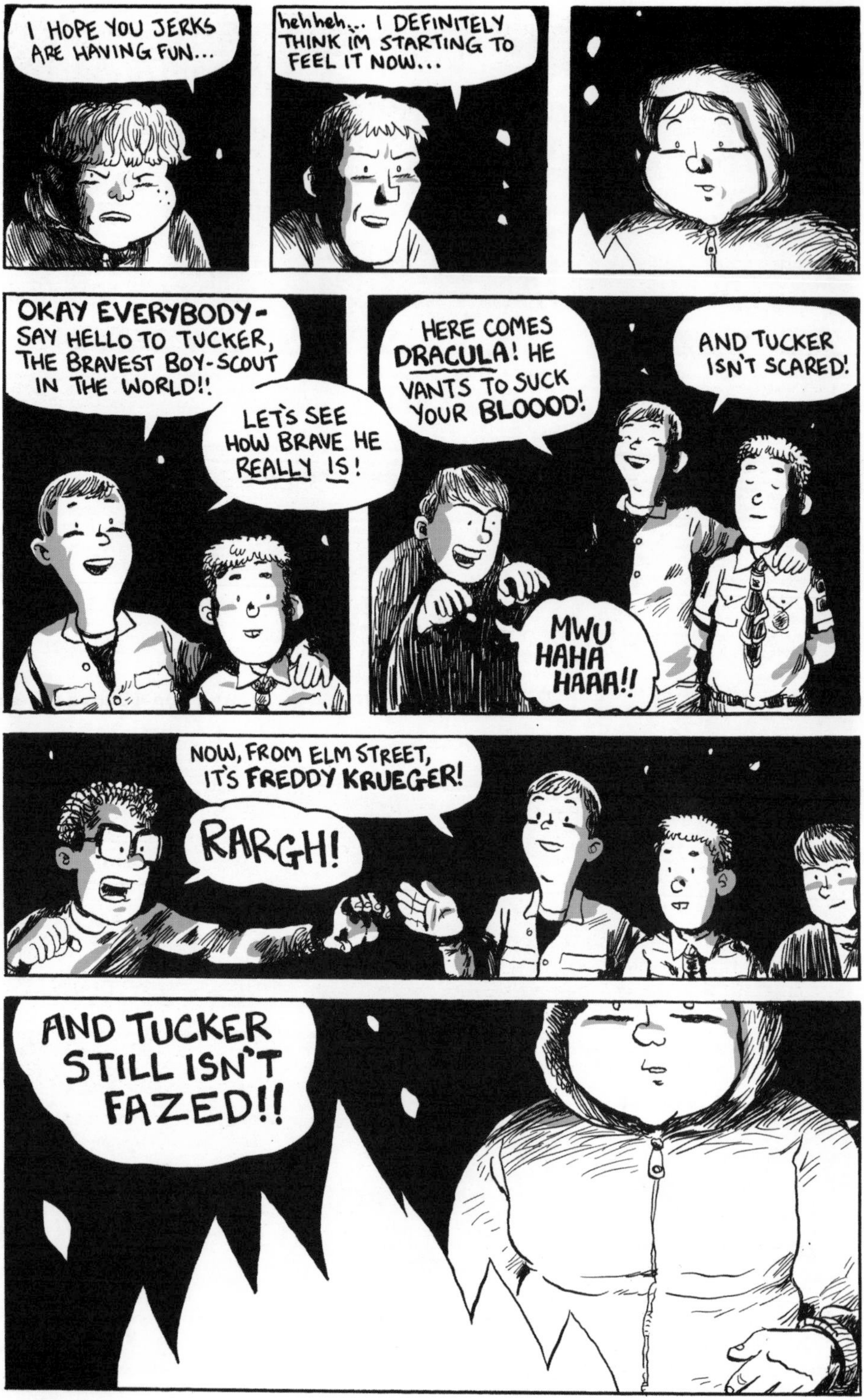

I HOPE YOU JERKS ARE HAVING FUN...
hehheh... I DEFINITELY THINK I'M STARTING TO FEEL IT NOW...
OKAY EVERYBODY- SAY HELLO TO TUCKER, THE BRAVEST BOY-SCOUT IN THE WORLD!!
LET'S SEE HOW BRAVE HE REALLY IS!
HERE COMES DRACULA! HE VANTS TO SUCK YOUR BLOOOD!
AND TUCKER ISN'T SCARED!
MWU HAHA HAAA!!
NOW, FROM ELM STREET, IT'S FREDDY KRUEGER!
RARGH!
AND TUCKER STILL ISN'T FAZED!!

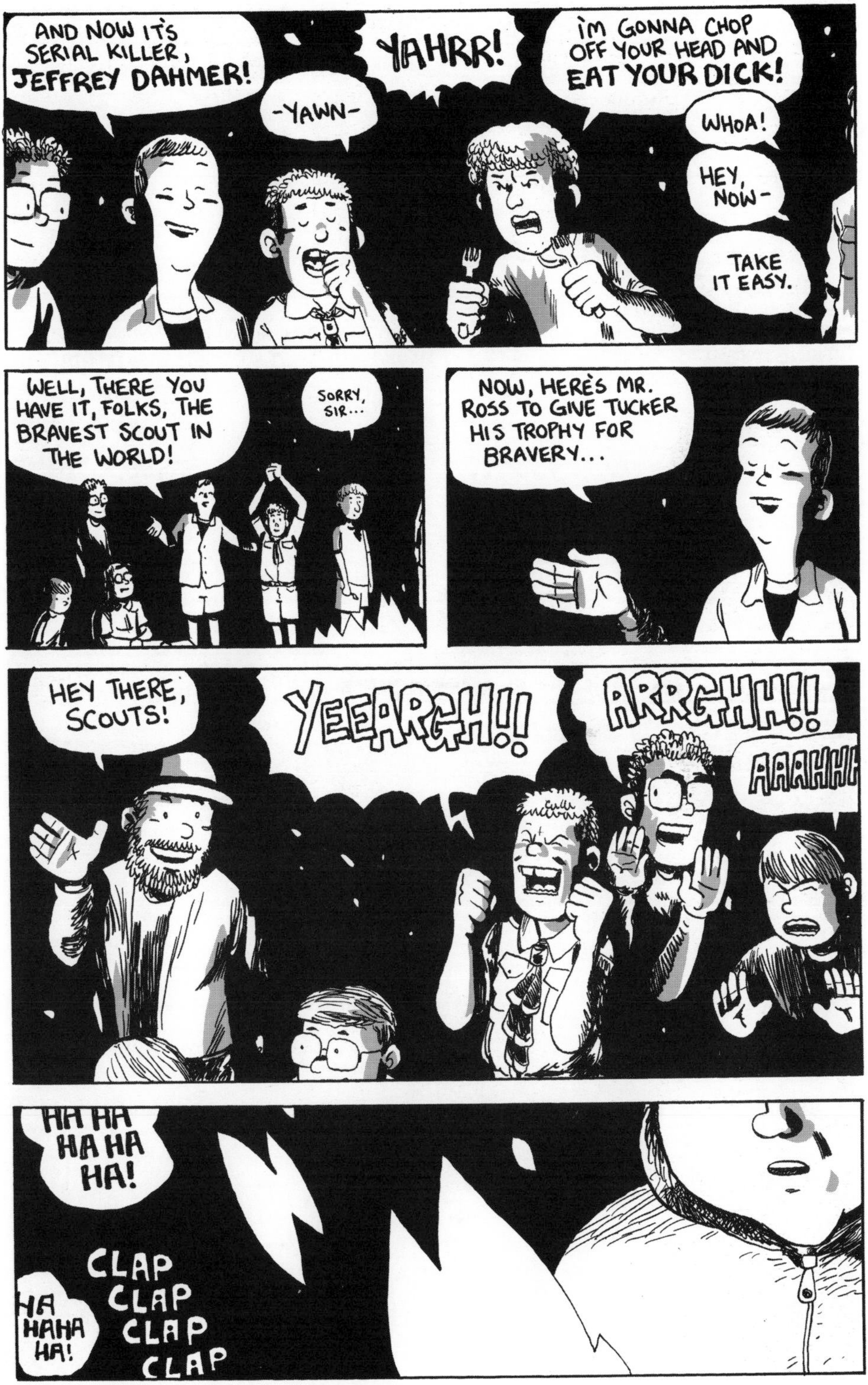
AND NOW IT'S SERIAL KILLER, JEFFREY DAHMER!
-YAWN-
YAHRR!
I'M GONNA CHOP OFF YOUR HEAD AND EAT YOUR DICK!
WHOA!
HEY, NOW-
TAKE IT EASY.
WELL, THERE YOU HAVE IT, FOLKS, THE BRAVEST SCOUT IN THE WORLD!
SORRY, SIR...
NOW, HERE'S MR. ROSS TO GIVE TUCKER HIS TROPHY FOR BRAVERY...
HEY THERE, SCOUTS!
YEEARGH!!
ARRGHH!!
HA HA HA HA HA!
CLAP CLAP CLAP CLAP
HA HAHA HA!

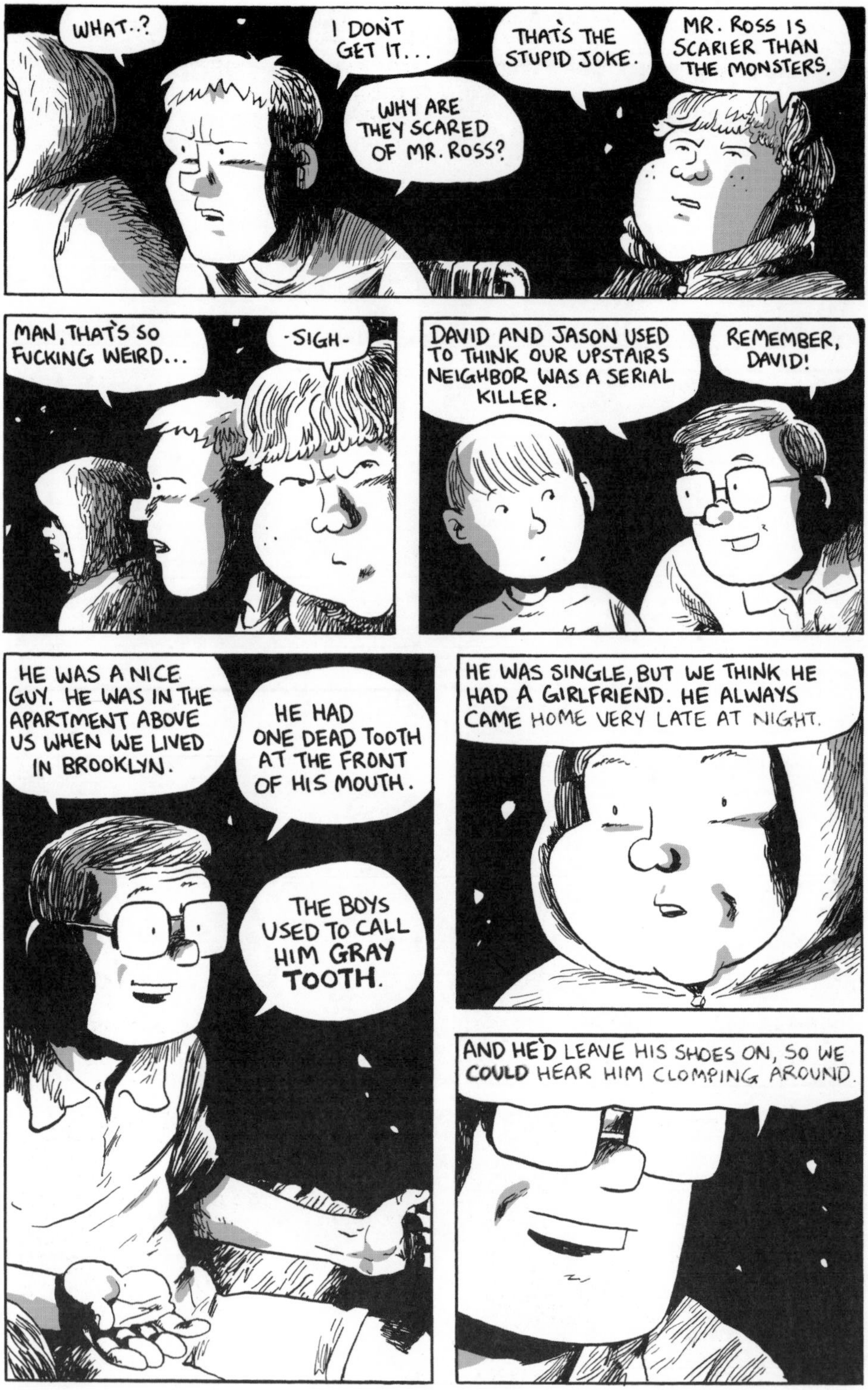
WHAT..?
I DON'T GET IT...
WHY ARE THEY SCARED OF MR. ROSS?
THAT'S THE STUPID JOKE.
MR. ROSS IS SCARIER THAN THE MONSTERS.
MAN, THAT'S SO FUCKING WEIRD...
-SIGH-
DAVID AND JASON USED TO THINK OUR UPSTAIRS NEIGHBOR WAS A SERIAL KILLER.
REMEMBER, DAVID!
HE WAS A NICE GUY. HE WAS IN THE APARTMENT ABOVE US WHEN WE LIVED IN BROOKLYN.
HE HAD ONE DEAD TOOTH AT THE FRONT OF HIS MOUTH.
THE BOYS USED TO CALL HIM GRAY TOOTH.
HE WAS SINGLE, BUT WE THINK HE HAD A GIRLFRIEND. HE ALWAYS CAME HOME VERY LATE AT NIGHT.
AND HE'D LEAVE HIS SHOES ON, SO WE COULD HEAR HIM CLOMPING AROUND.

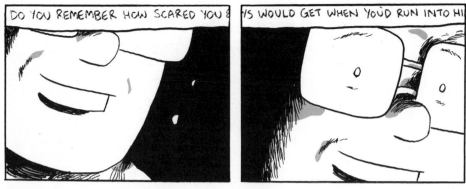

DO YOU REMEMBER HOW SCARED YOU & /S WOULD GET WHEN YOU'D RUN INTO HI

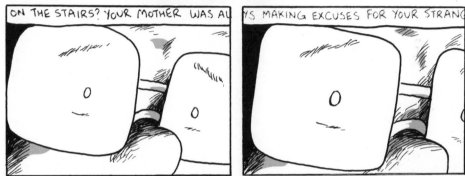

ON THE STAIRS? YOUR MOTHER WAS AL /S MAKING EXCUSES FOR YOUR STRANG

BEHAVIOR. POOR GUY, I WONDER WH HE THOUGHT WHAT WAS HIS NAME?

JASON? DO YOU REMEMBER HIS NAM

JASON?

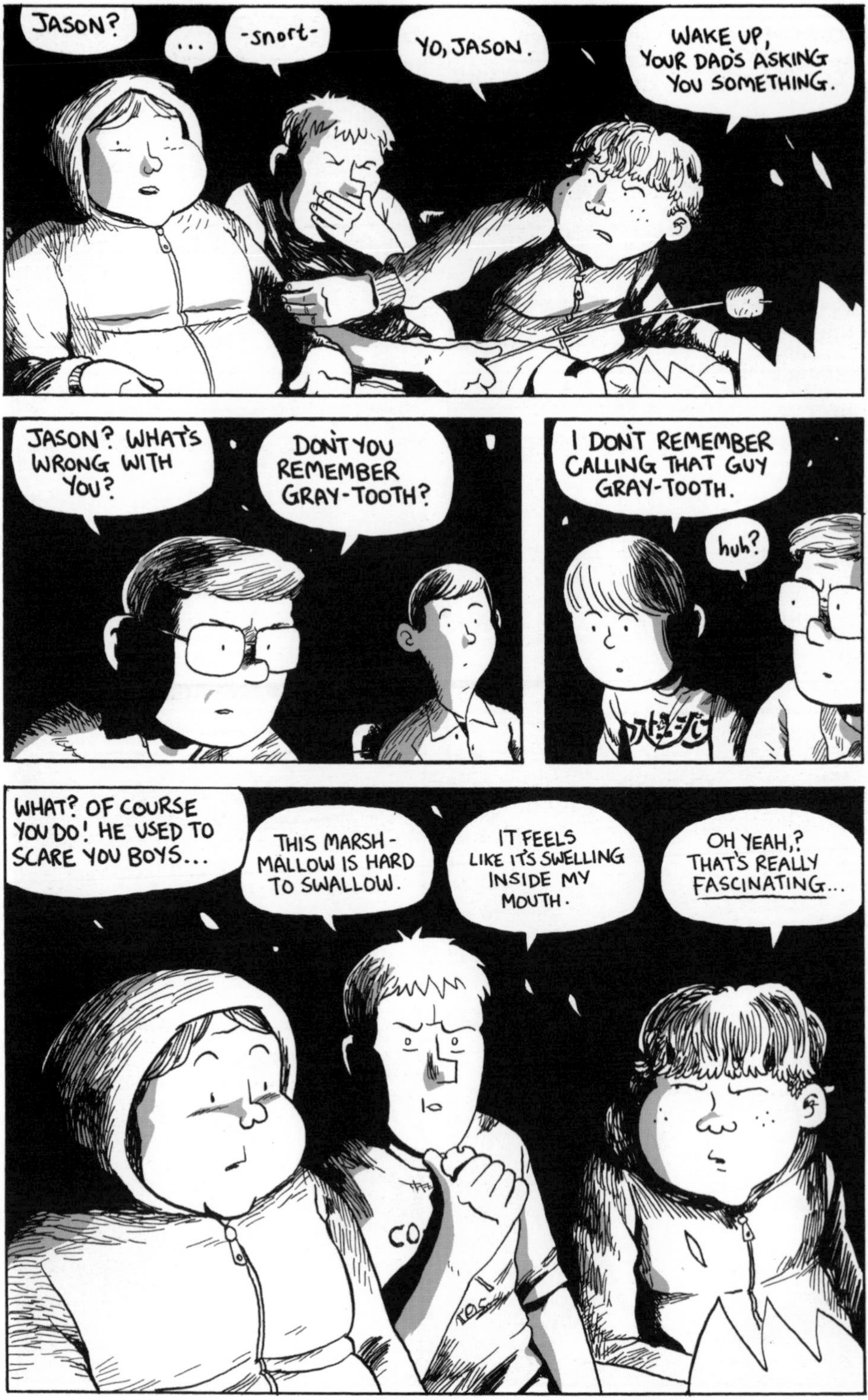
JASON?
...
-snort-
YO, JASON.
WAKE UP, YOUR DAD'S ASKING YOU SOMETHING.
JASON? WHAT'S WRONG WITH YOU?
DON'T YOU REMEMBER GRAY-TOOTH?
I DON'T REMEMBER CALLING THAT GUY GRAY-TOOTH.
huh?
WHAT? OF COURSE YOU DO! HE USED TO SCARE YOU BOYS...
THIS MARSH-MALLOW IS HARD TO SWALLOW.
IT FEELS LIKE IT'S SWELLING INSIDE MY MOUTH.
OH YEAH,? THAT'S REALLY FASCINATING...

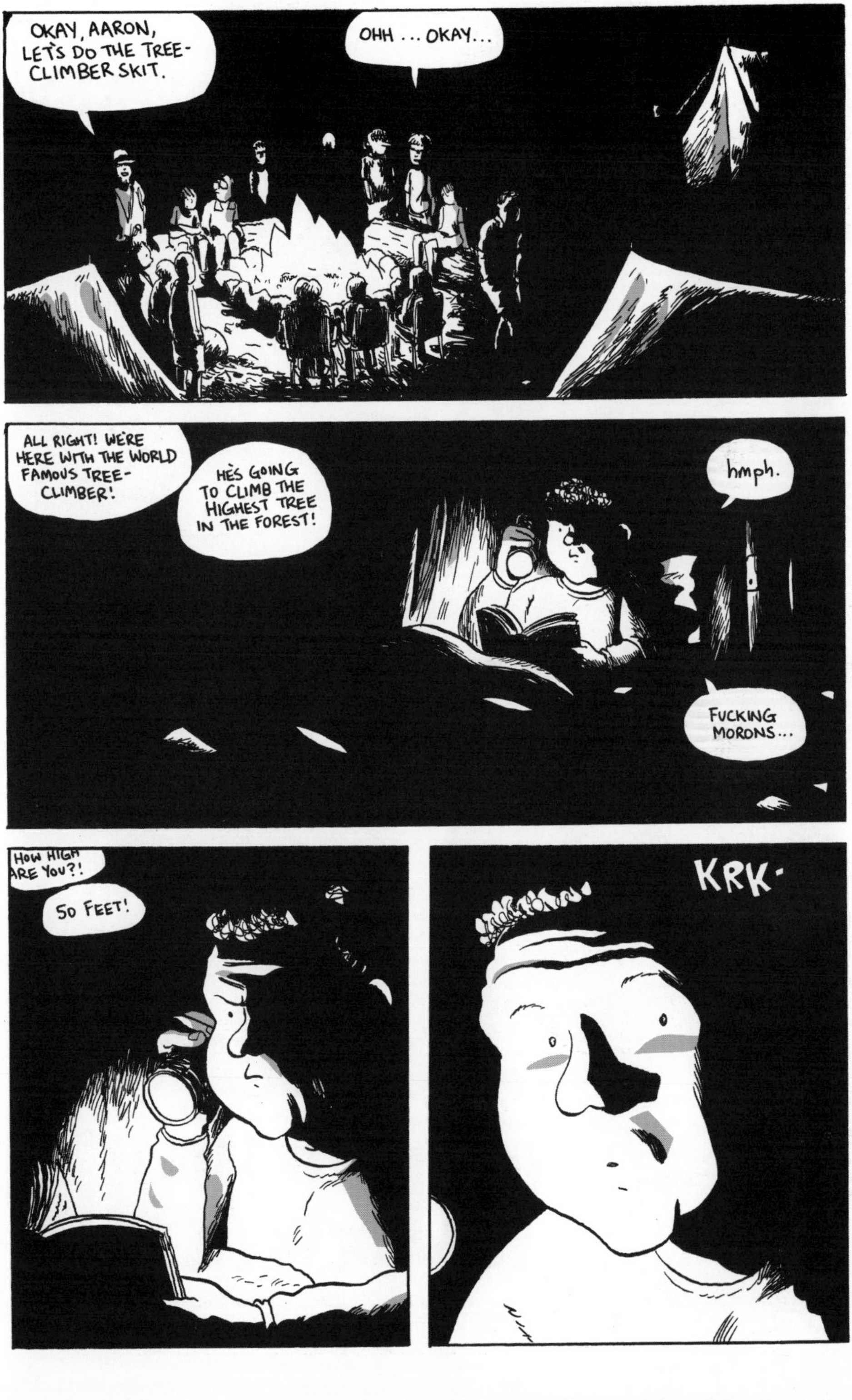
OKAY, AARON, LET'S DO THE TREE-CLIMBER SKIT.
OHH ... OKAY...
ALL RIGHT! WE'RE HERE WITH THE WORLD FAMOUS TREE-CLIMBER!
HE'S GOING TO CLIMB THE HIGHEST TREE IN THE FOREST!
hmph.
FUCKING MORONS...
HOW HIGH ARE YOU?!
50 FEET!
KRK-

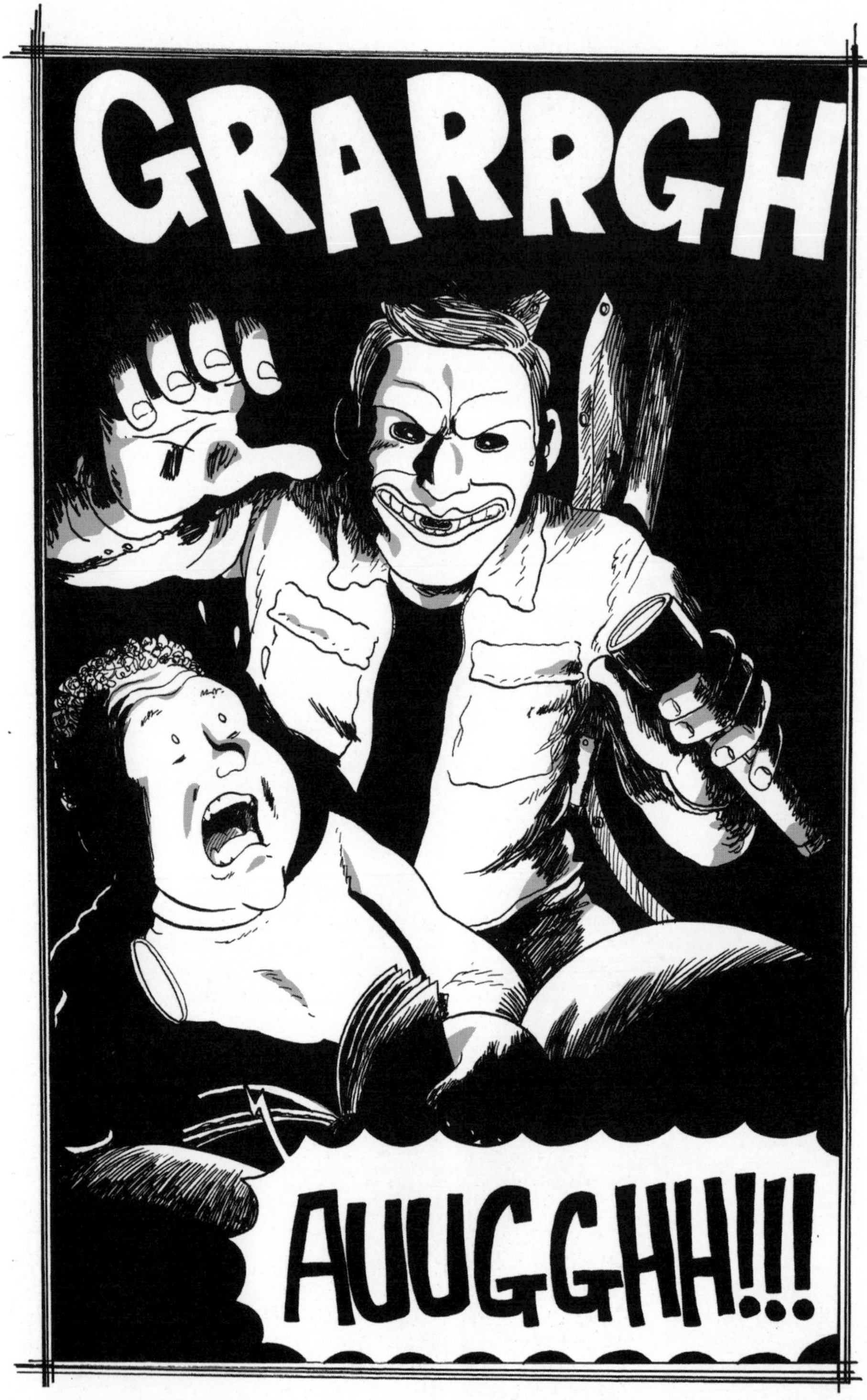
GRARRGH
AUUGGHH!!!

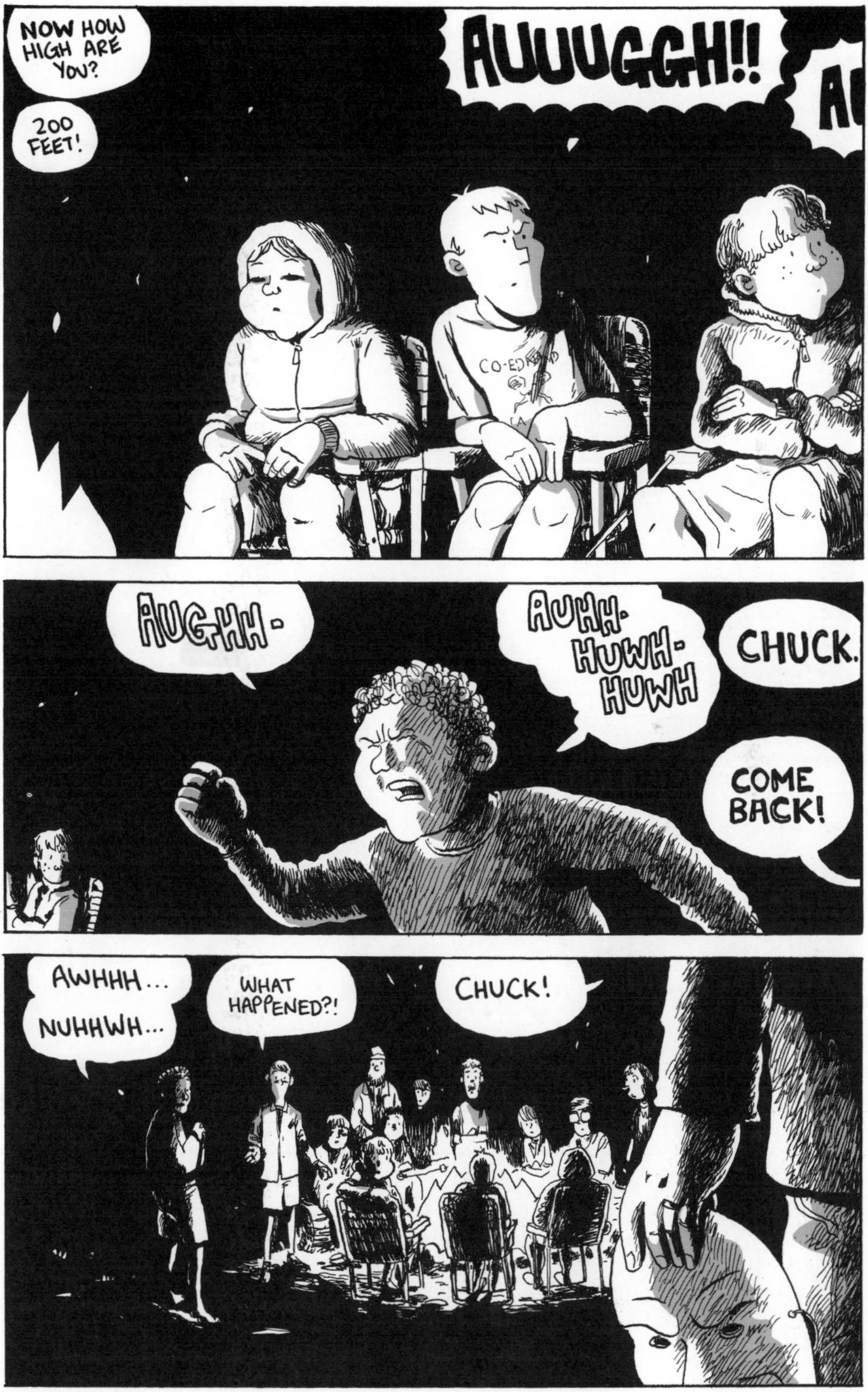
NOW HOW HIGH ARE YOU?
200 FEET!
AUUUGGH!!
CO-ED
AUGHH-
AUHH-HUWH-HUWH
CHUCK.
COME BACK!
AWHHH... NUHHWH...
WHAT HAPPENED?!
CHUCK!

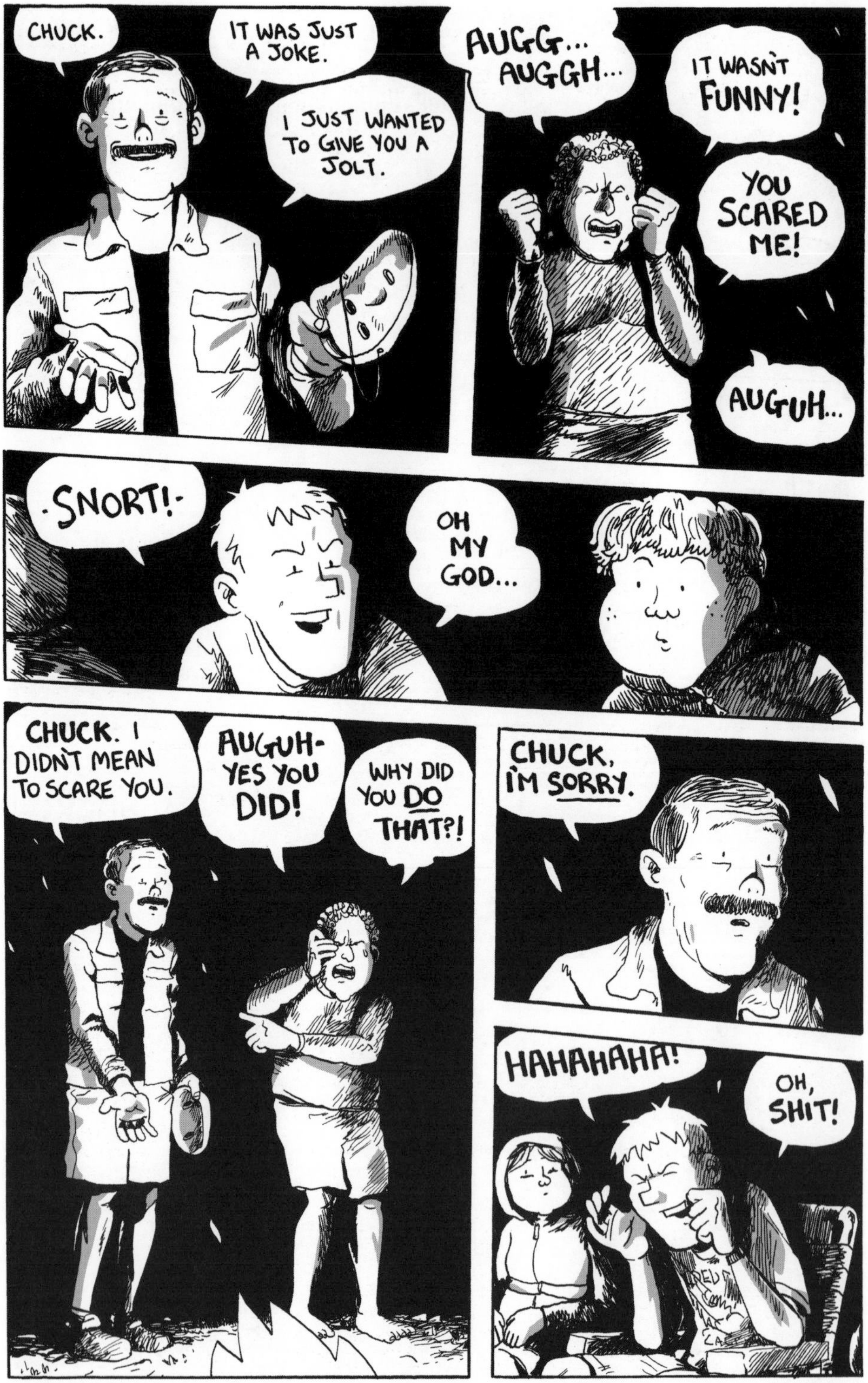
CHUCK.
IT WAS JUST A JOKE.
I JUST WANTED TO GIVE YOU A JOLT.
AUGG... AUGGH...
IT WASN'T FUNNY!
YOU SCARED ME!
AUGUH...
·SNORT!·
OH MY GOD...
CHUCK. I DIDN'T MEAN TO SCARE YOU.
AUGUH- YES YOU DID!
WHY DID YOU DO THAT?!
CHUCK, I'M SORRY.
HAHAHAHA!
OH, SHIT!

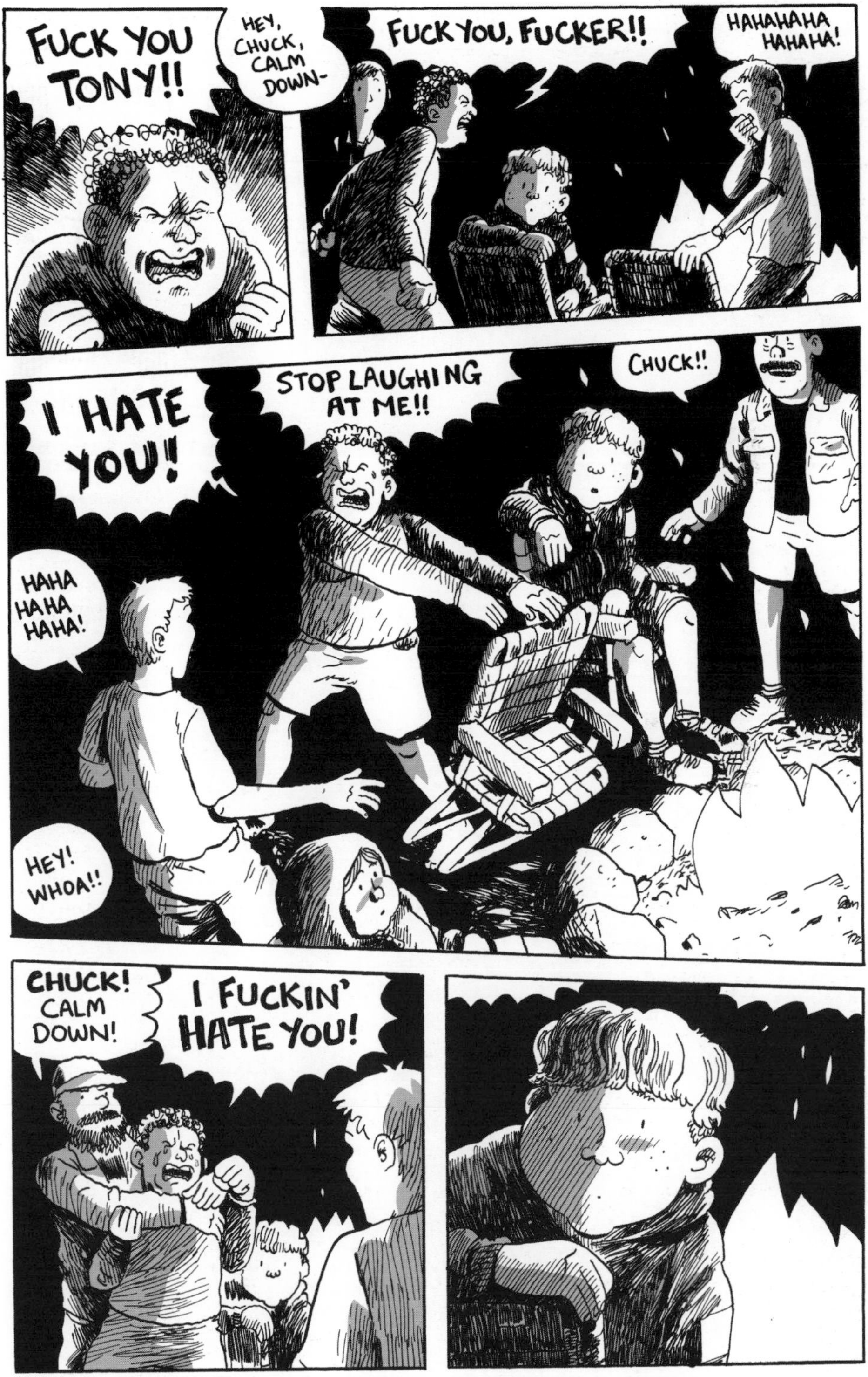
FUCK YOU TONY!!
HEY, CHUCK, CALM DOWN-
FUCK YOU, FUCKER!!
HAHAHAHA HAHAHA!
I HATE YOU!
STOP LAUGHING AT ME!!
CHUCK!!
HAHA HAHA HAHA!
HEY! WHOA!!
CHUCK! CALM DOWN!
I FUCKIN' HATE YOU!

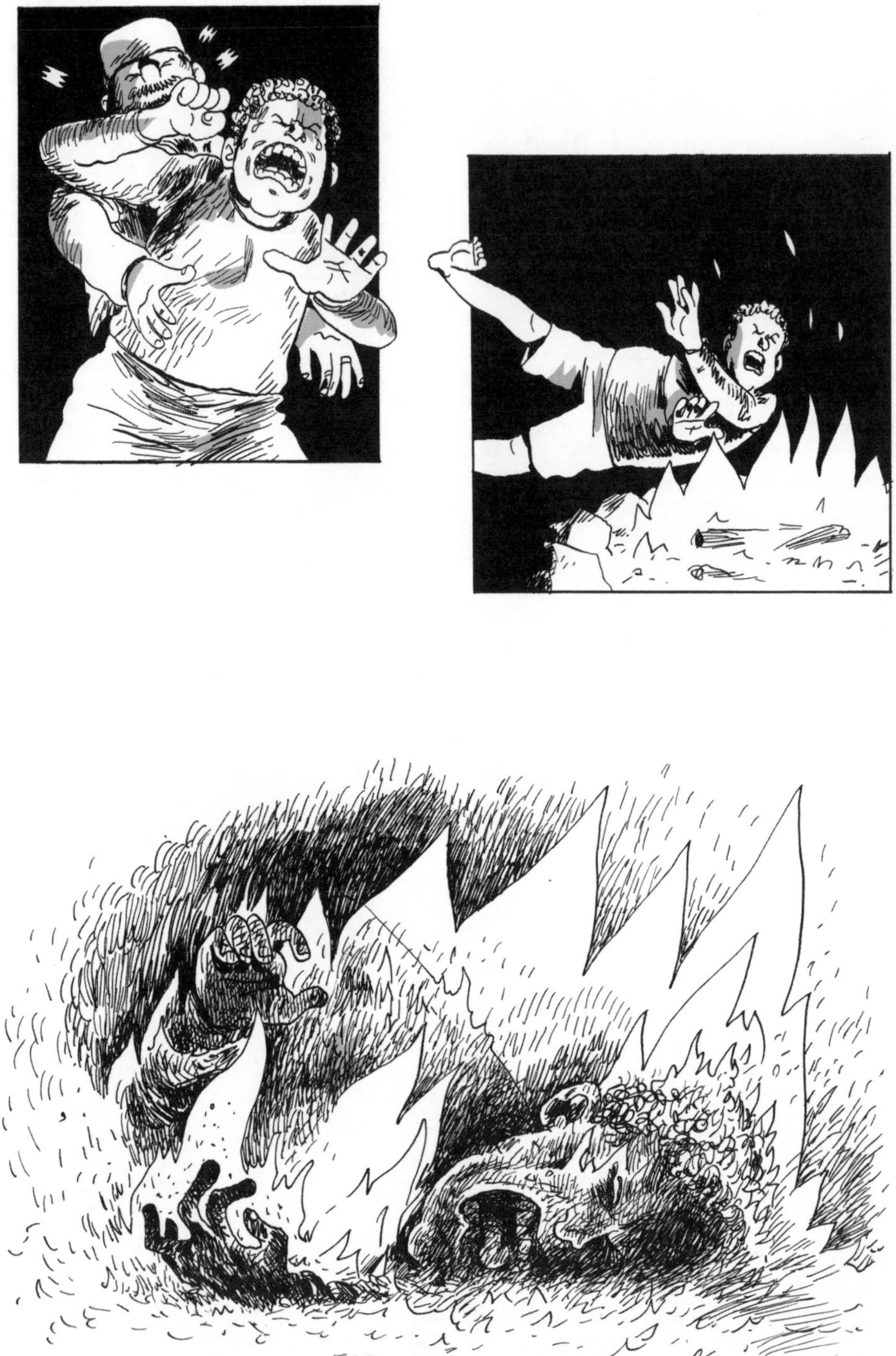

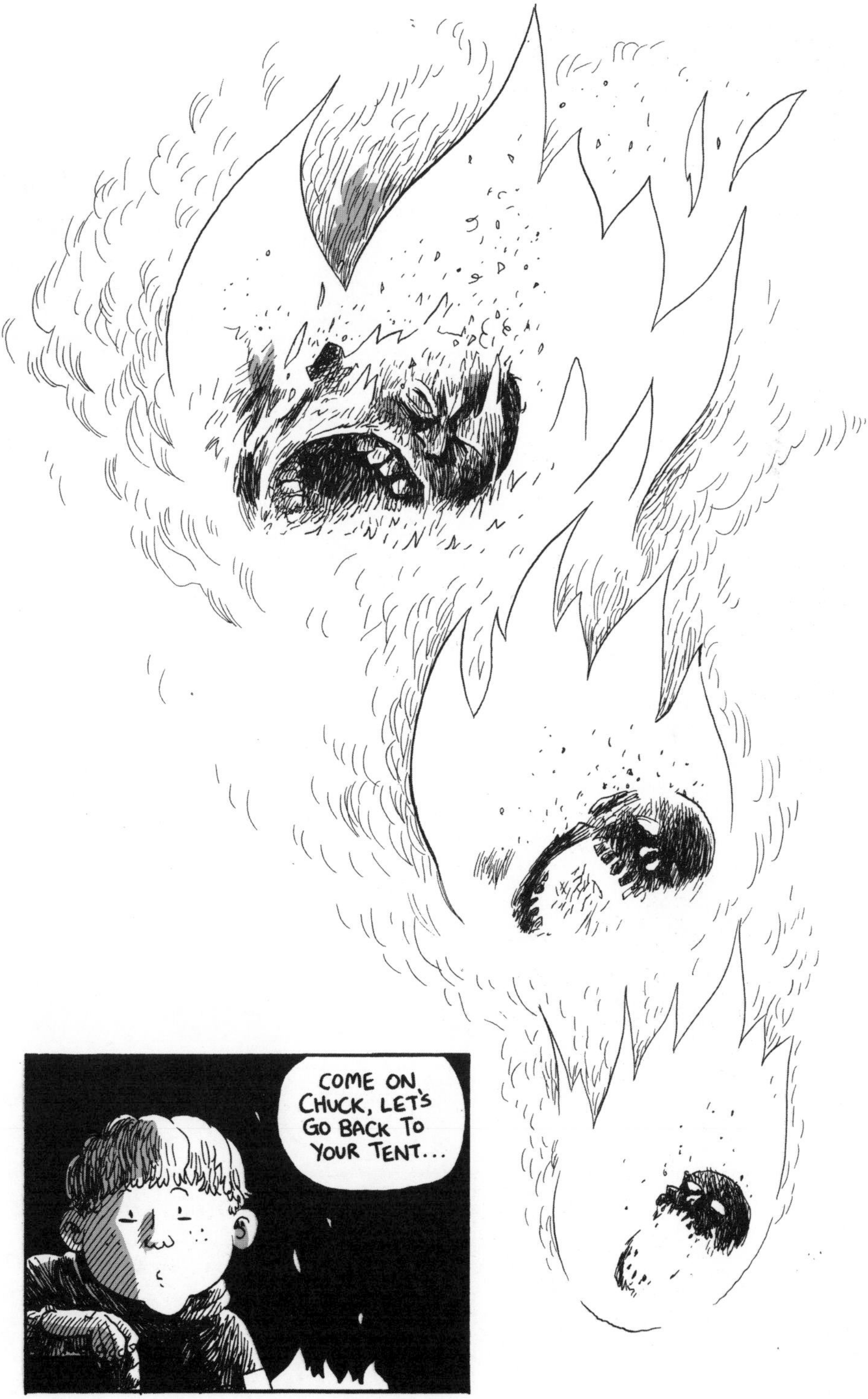
COME ON CHUCK, LET'S GO BACK TO YOUR TENT...

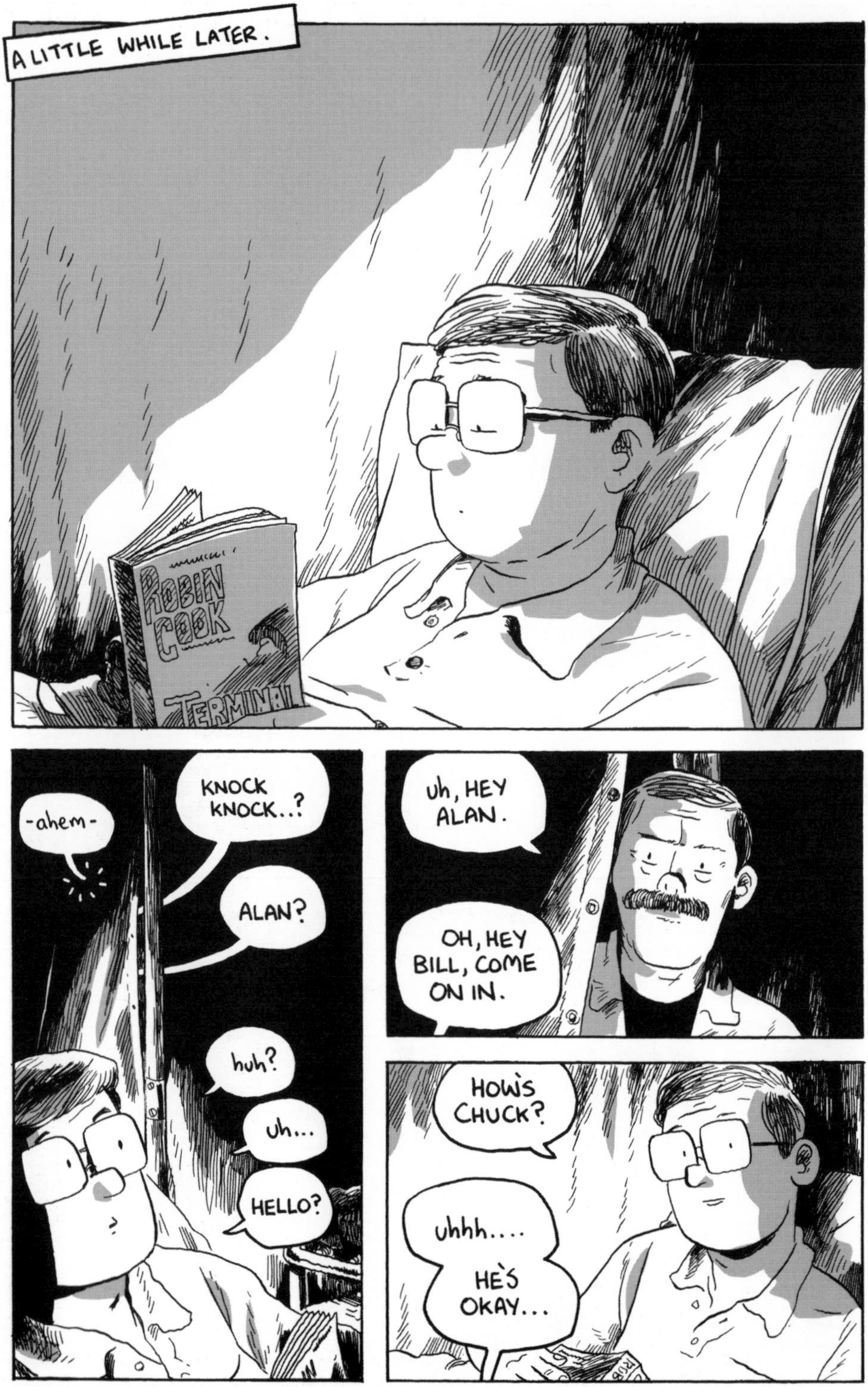
A LITTLE WHILE LATER.
ROBIN COOK
TERMINAL
-ahem-
KNOCK KNOCK..?
ALAN?
huh?
uh...
HELLO?
uh, HEY ALAN.
OH, HEY BILL, COME ON IN.
HOW'S CHUCK?
uhhh....
HE'S OKAY...

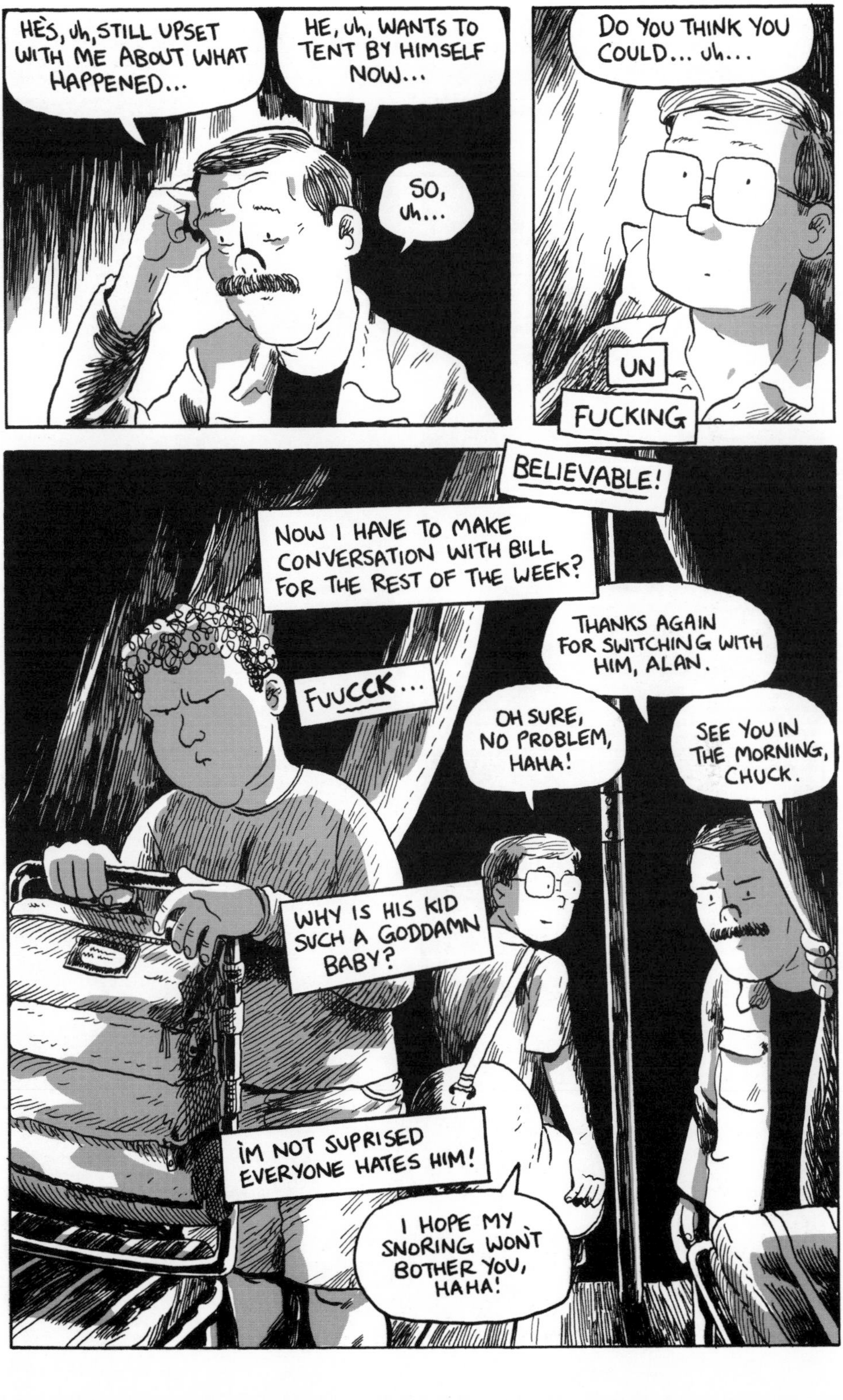
HE'S, uh, STILL UPSET WITH ME ABOUT WHAT HAPPENED...
HE, uh, WANTS TO TENT BY HIMSELF NOW...
SO, uh...
DO YOU THINK YOU COULD... uh...
UN
FUCKING
BELIEVABLE!
NOW I HAVE TO MAKE CONVERSATION WITH BILL FOR THE REST OF THE WEEK?
FUUCCK...
THANKS AGAIN FOR SWITCHING WITH HIM, ALAN.
OH SURE, NO PROBLEM, HAHA!
SEE YOU IN THE MORNING, CHUCK.
WHY IS HIS KID SUCH A GODDAMN BABY?
I'M NOT SUPRISED EVERYONE HATES HIM!
I HOPE MY SNORING WON'T BOTHER YOU, HAHA!

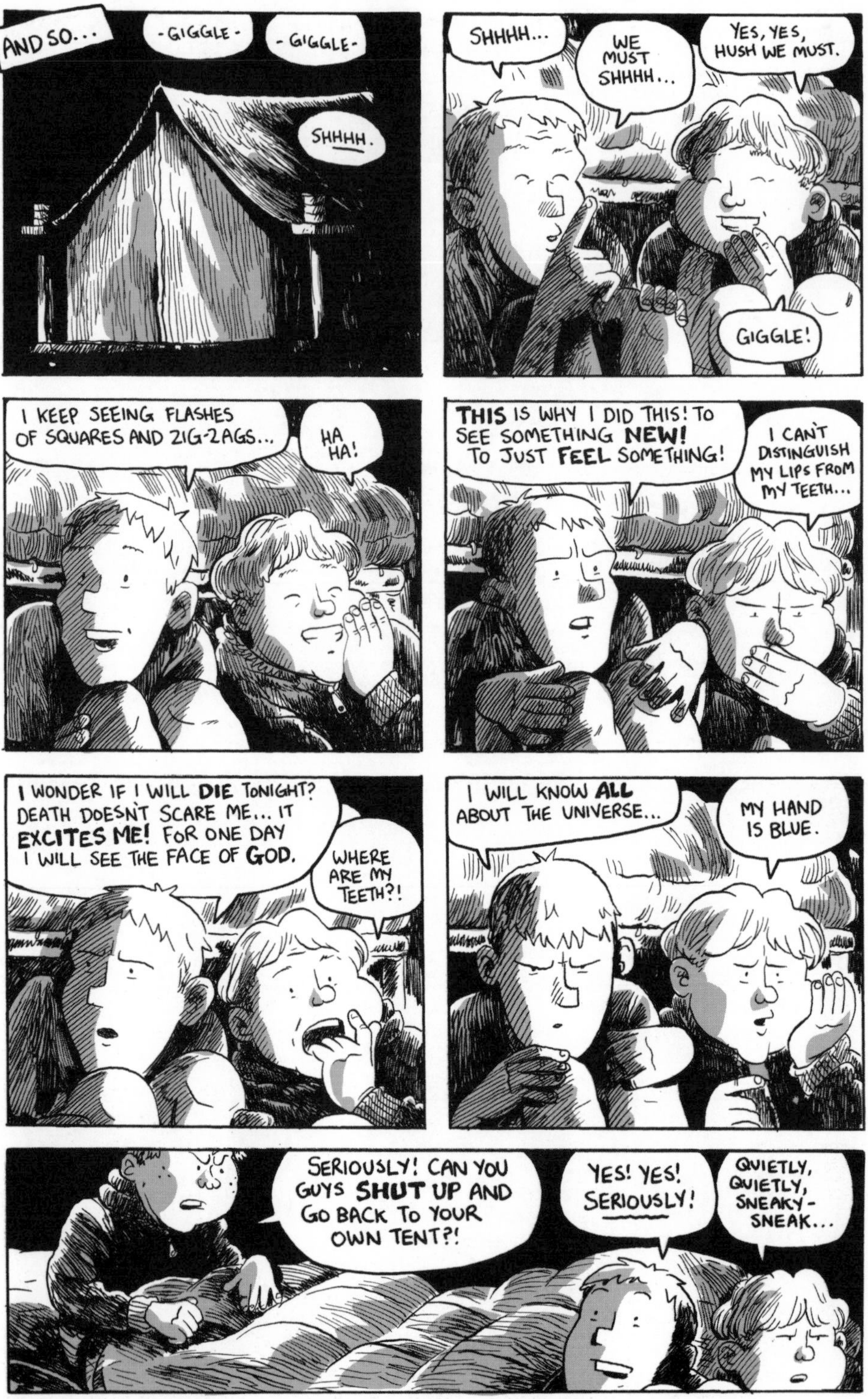
AND SO...
-GIGGLE-
-GIGGLE-
SHHHH.
SHHHH...
WE MUST SHHHH...
YES, YES, HUSH WE MUST.
GIGGLE!
I KEEP SEEING FLASHES OF SQUARES AND ZIG-ZAGS...
HA HA!
THIS IS WHY I DID THIS! TO SEE SOMETHING NEW! TO JUST FEEL SOMETHING!
I CAN'T DISTINGUISH MY LIPS FROM MY TEETH...
I WONDER IF I WILL DIE TONIGHT? DEATH DOESN'T SCARE ME... IT EXCITES ME! FOR ONE DAY I WILL SEE THE FACE OF GOD.
WHERE ARE MY TEETH?!
I WILL KNOW ALL ABOUT THE UNIVERSE...
MY HAND IS BLUE.
SERIOUSLY! CAN YOU GUYS SHUT UP AND GO BACK TO YOUR OWN TENT?!
YES! YES! SERIOUSLY!
QUIETLY, QUIETLY, SNEAKY-SNEAK...

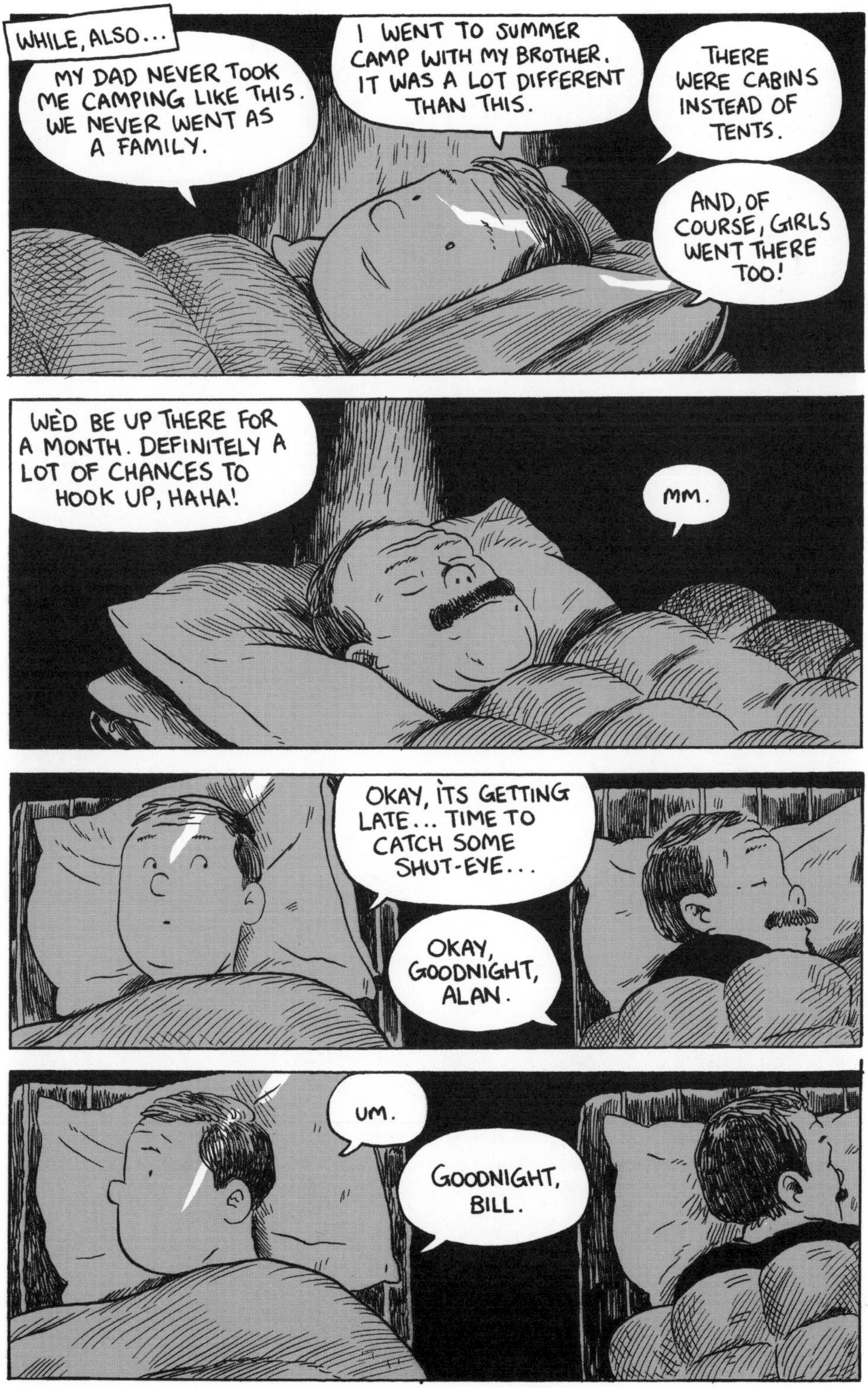
WHILE, ALSO...
MY DAD NEVER TOOK ME CAMPING LIKE THIS. WE NEVER WENT AS A FAMILY.
I WENT TO SUMMER CAMP WITH MY BROTHER. IT WAS A LOT DIFFERENT THAN THIS.
THERE WERE CABINS INSTEAD OF TENTS.
AND, OF COURSE, GIRLS WENT THERE TOO!
WE'D BE UP THERE FOR A MONTH. DEFINITELY A LOT OF CHANCES TO HOOK UP, HAHA!
MM.
OKAY, ITS GETTING LATE... TIME TO CATCH SOME SHUT-EYE...
OKAY, GOODNIGHT, ALAN.
UM.
GOODNIGHT, BILL.

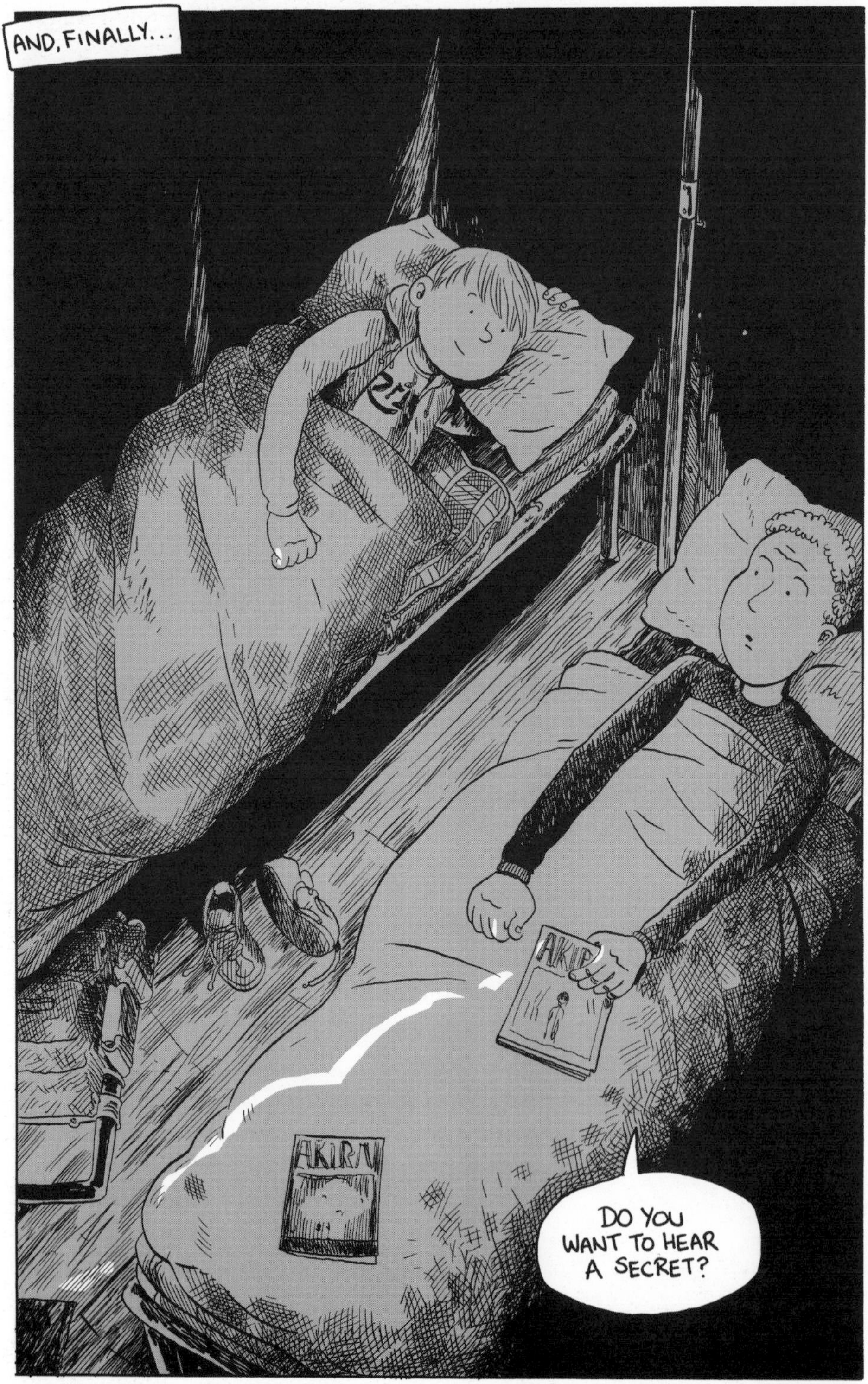
AND, FINALLY...
AKIRA
AKIRA
DO YOU WANT TO HEAR A SECRET?

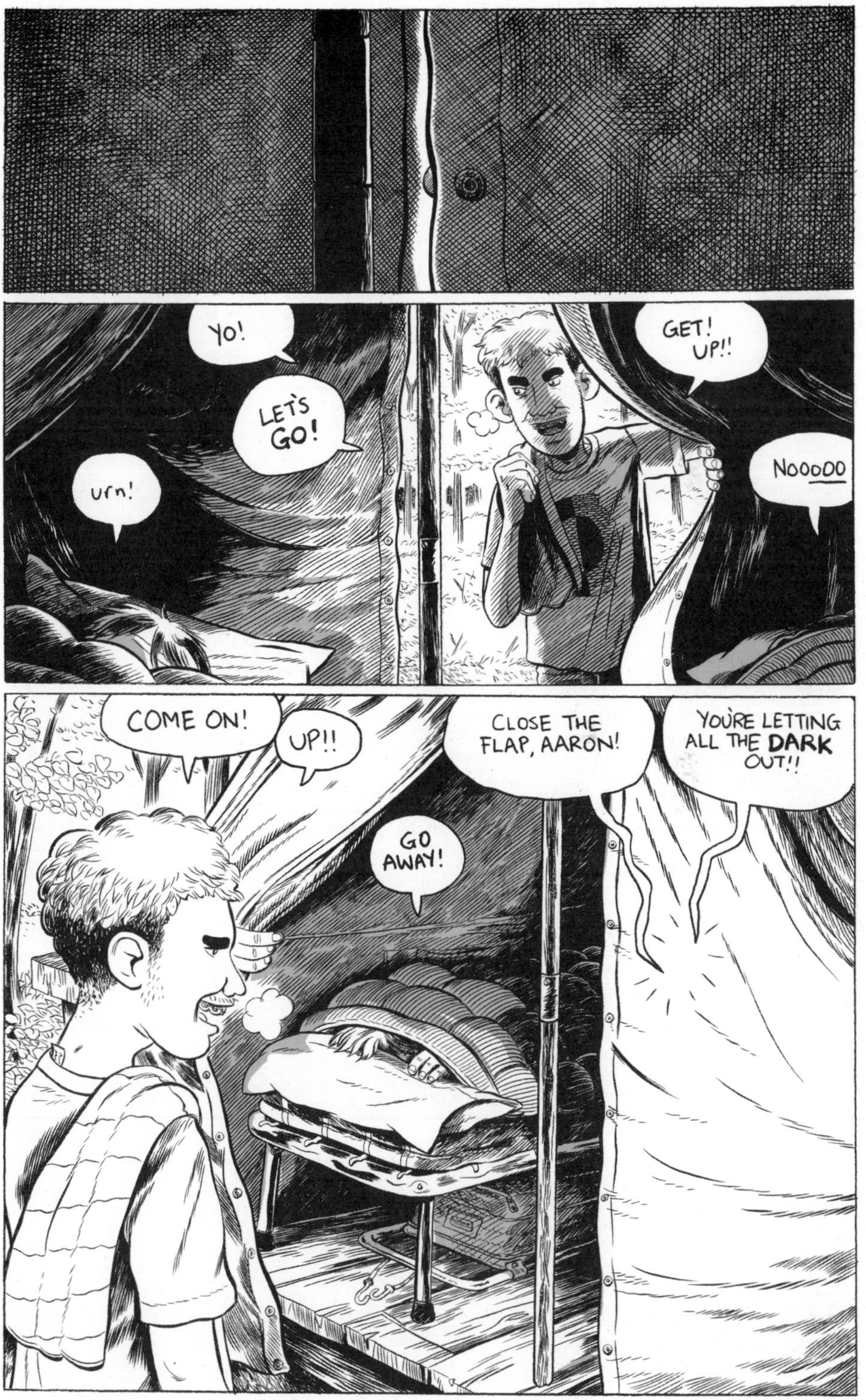

YO!
LET'S GO!
urn!
GET! UP!!
NOOOOO
COME ON!
UP!!
CLOSE THE FLAP, AARON!
YOU'RE LETTING ALL THE **DARK** OUT!!
GO AWAY!

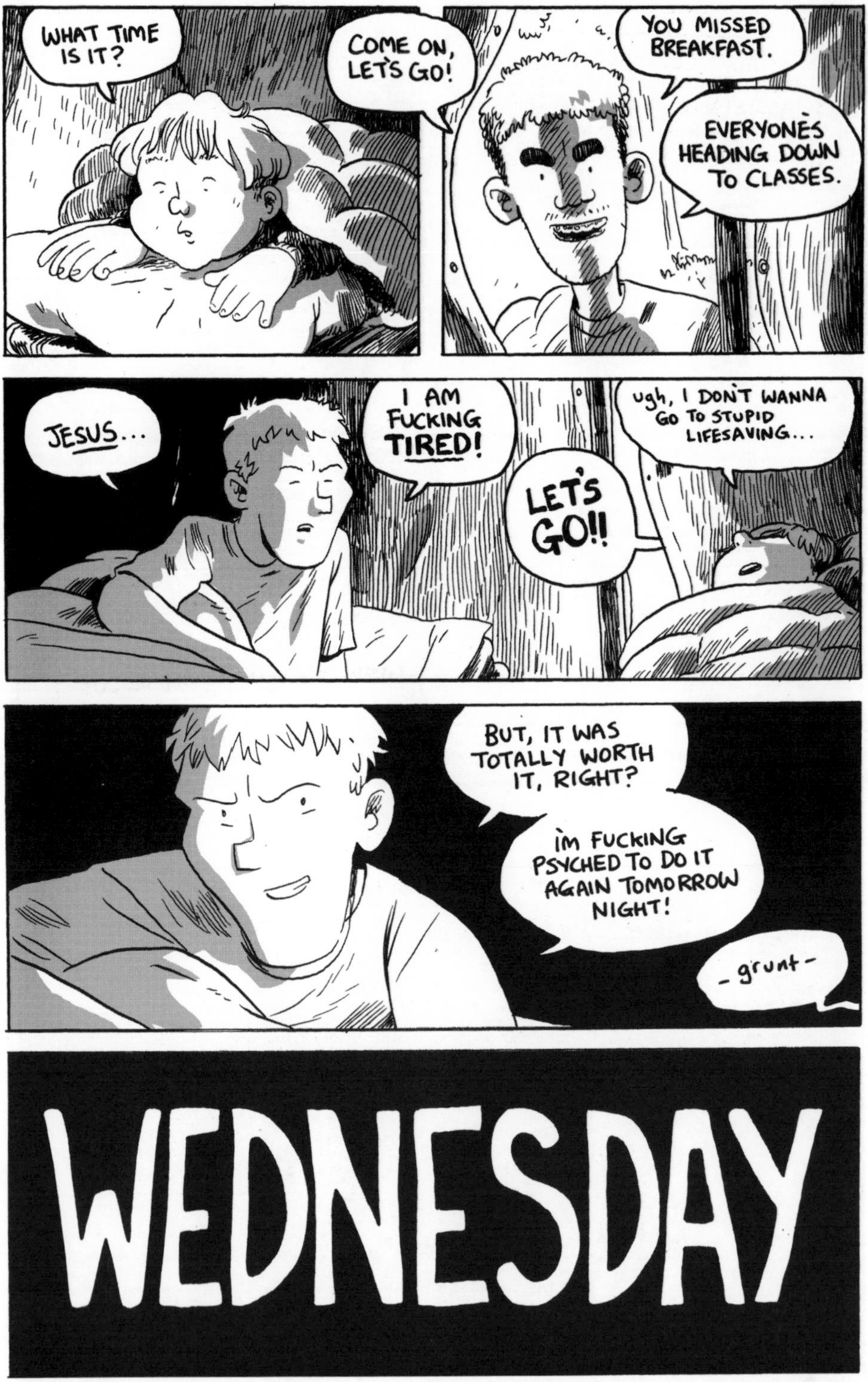
WHAT TIME IS IT?
COME ON, LET'S GO!
YOU MISSED BREAKFAST.
EVERYONE'S HEADING DOWN TO CLASSES.
JESUS...
I AM FUCKING TIRED!
LET'S GO!!
ugh, I DON'T WANNA GO TO STUPID LIFESAVING...
BUT, IT WAS TOTALLY WORTH IT, RIGHT?
I'M FUCKING PSYCHED TO DO IT AGAIN TOMORROW NIGHT!
-grunt-
WEDNESDAY

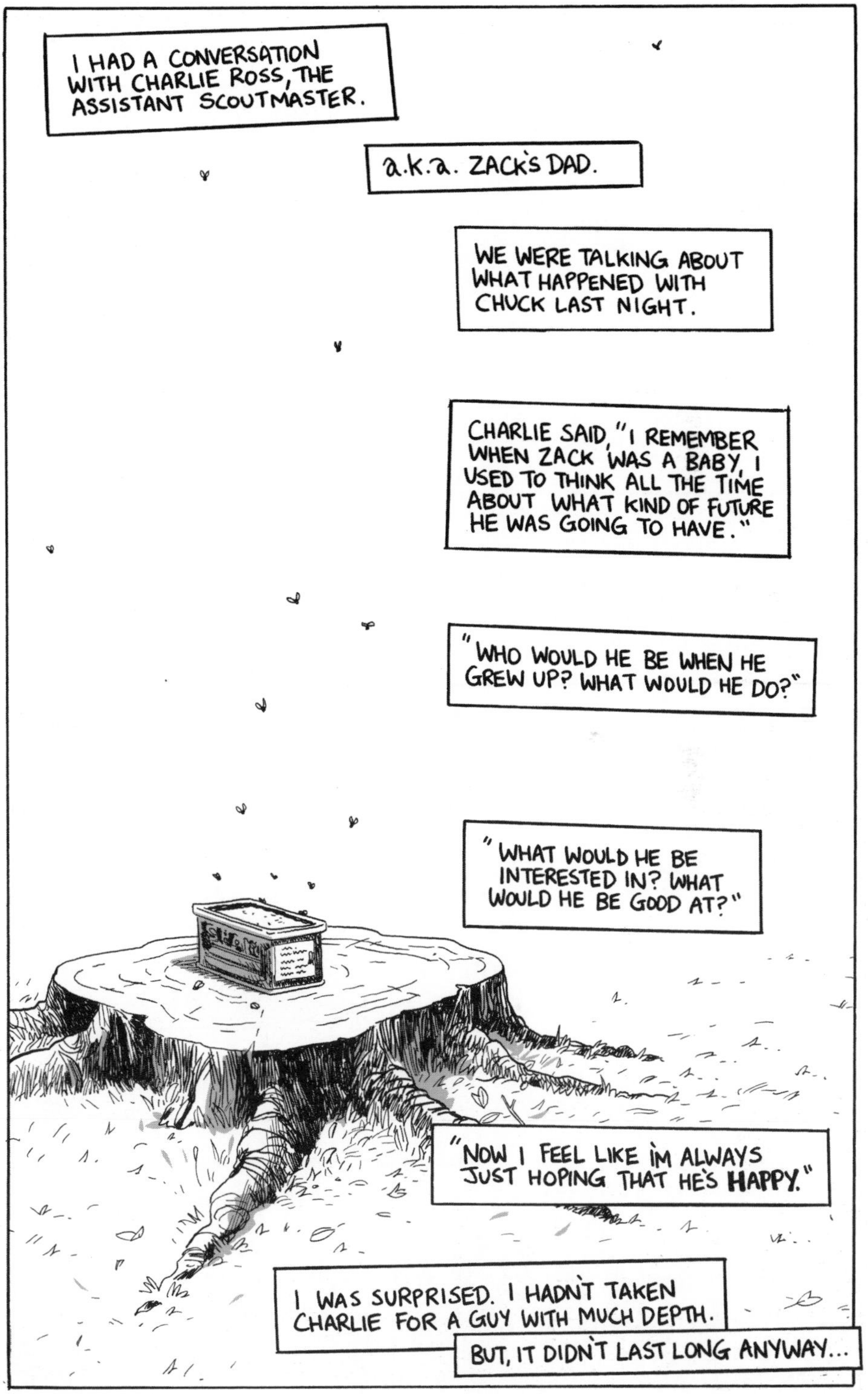

I HAD A CONVERSATION WITH CHARLIE ROSS, THE ASSISTANT SCOUTMASTER.
a.k.a. ZACK'S DAD.
WE WERE TALKING ABOUT WHAT HAPPENED WITH CHUCK LAST NIGHT.
CHARLIE SAID, "I REMEMBER WHEN ZACK WAS A BABY, I USED TO THINK ALL THE TIME ABOUT WHAT KIND OF FUTURE HE WAS GOING TO HAVE."
"WHO WOULD HE BE WHEN HE GREW UP? WHAT WOULD HE DO?"
"WHAT WOULD HE BE INTERESTED IN? WHAT WOULD HE BE GOOD AT?"
"NOW I FEEL LIKE I'M ALWAYS JUST HOPING THAT HE'S **HAPPY**."
I WAS SURPRISED. I HADN'T TAKEN CHARLIE FOR A GUY WITH MUCH DEPTH.
BUT, IT DIDN'T LAST LONG ANYWAY...

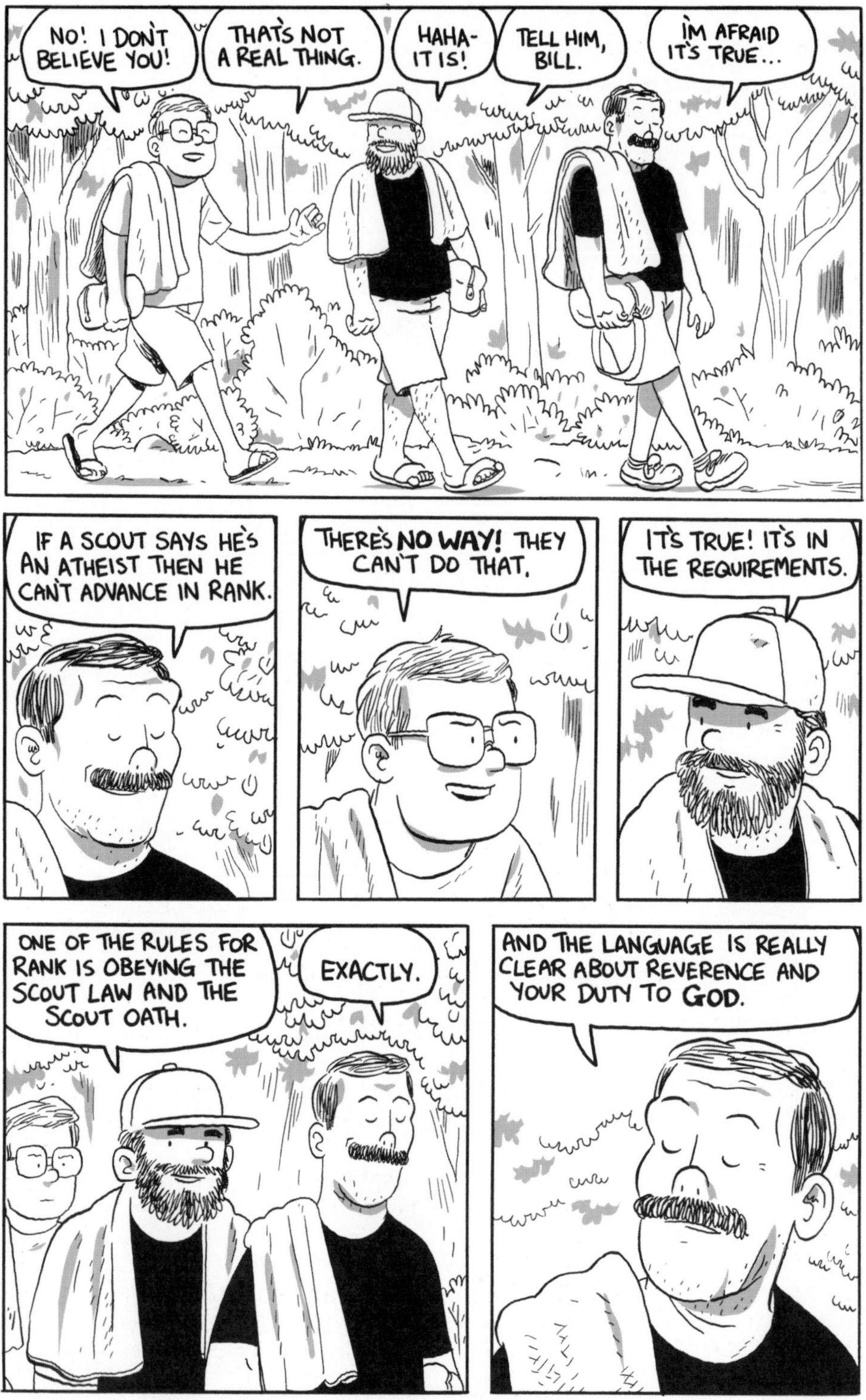
NO! I DON'T BELIEVE YOU!
THAT'S NOT A REAL THING.
HAHA- IT IS!
TELL HIM, BILL.
I'M AFRAID IT'S TRUE...
IF A SCOUT SAYS HE'S AN ATHEIST THEN HE CAN'T ADVANCE IN RANK.
THERE'S NO WAY! THEY CAN'T DO THAT.
IT'S TRUE! IT'S IN THE REQUIREMENTS.
ONE OF THE RULES FOR RANK IS OBEYING THE SCOUT LAW AND THE SCOUT OATH.
EXACTLY.
AND THE LANGUAGE IS REALLY CLEAR ABOUT REVERENCE AND YOUR DUTY TO GOD.

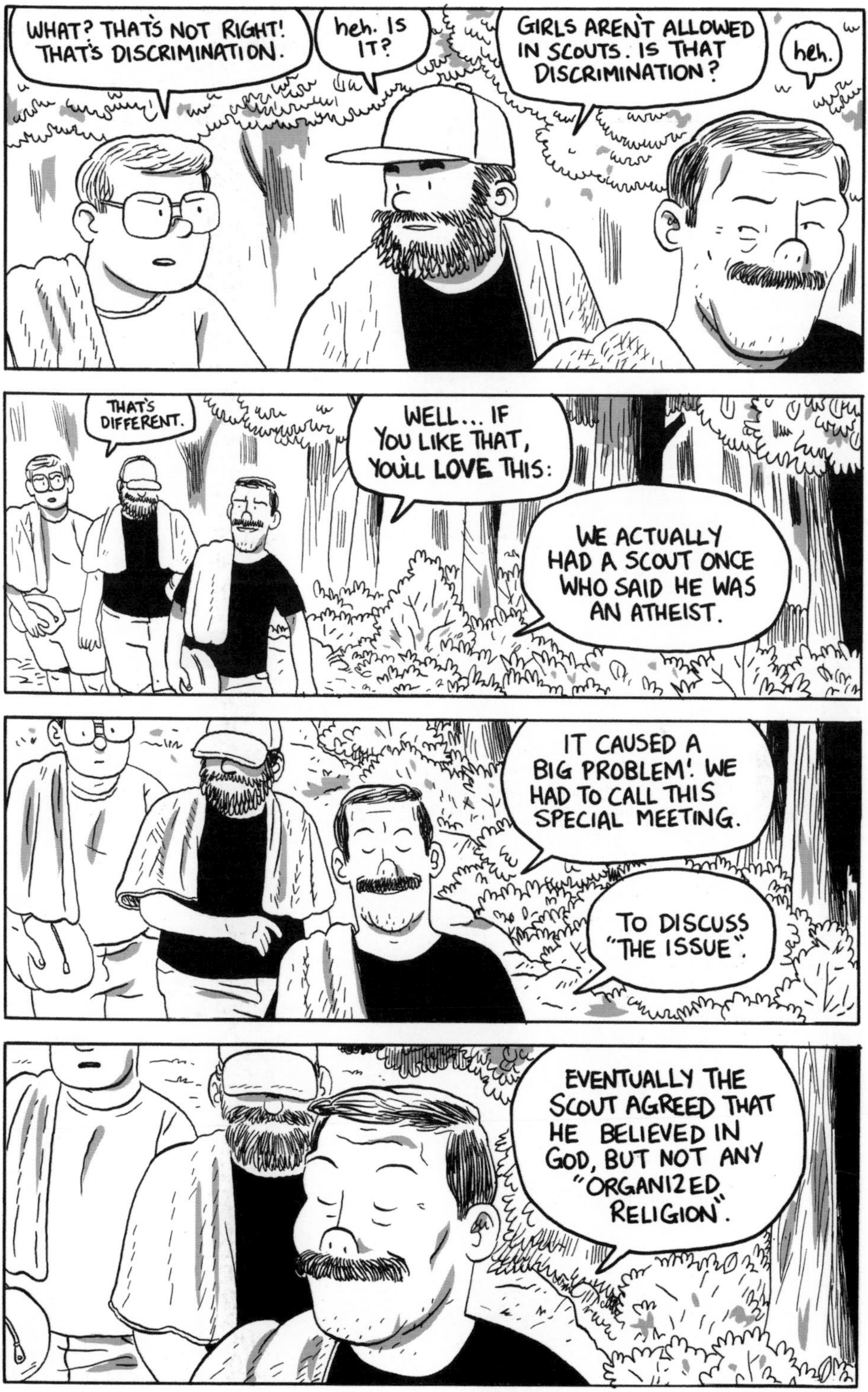
WHAT? THAT'S NOT RIGHT! THAT'S DISCRIMINATION.
heh. IS IT?
GIRLS AREN'T ALLOWED IN SCOUTS. IS THAT DISCRIMINATION?
heh.
THAT'S DIFFERENT.
WELL... IF YOU LIKE THAT, YOU'LL LOVE THIS:
WE ACTUALLY HAD A SCOUT ONCE WHO SAID HE WAS AN ATHEIST.
IT CAUSED A BIG PROBLEM! WE HAD TO CALL THIS SPECIAL MEETING.
TO DISCUSS "THE ISSUE".
EVENTUALLY THE SCOUT AGREED THAT HE BELIEVED IN GOD, BUT NOT ANY "ORGANIZED RELIGION".

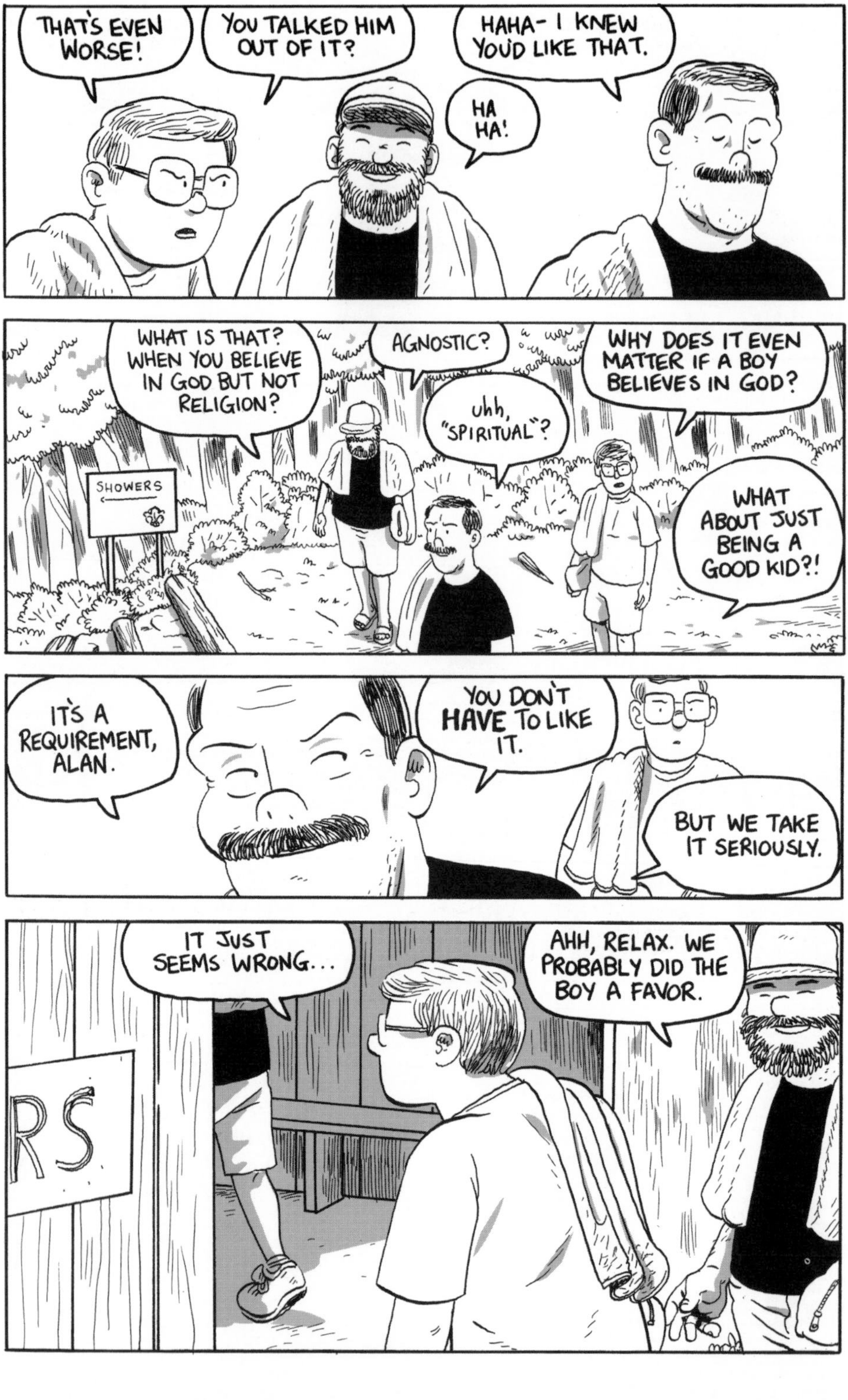
THAT'S EVEN WORSE!
YOU TALKED HIM OUT OF IT?
HA HA!
HAHA- I KNEW YOU'D LIKE THAT.
SHOWERS
WHAT IS THAT? WHEN YOU BELIEVE IN GOD BUT NOT RELIGION?
AGNOSTIC?
uhh, "SPIRITUAL"?
WHY DOES IT EVEN MATTER IF A BOY BELIEVES IN GOD?
WHAT ABOUT JUST BEING A GOOD KID?!
IT'S A REQUIREMENT, ALAN.
YOU DON'T **HAVE** TO LIKE IT.
BUT WE TAKE IT SERIOUSLY.
IT JUST SEEMS WRONG...
AHH, RELAX. WE PROBABLY DID THE BOY A FAVOR.
RS

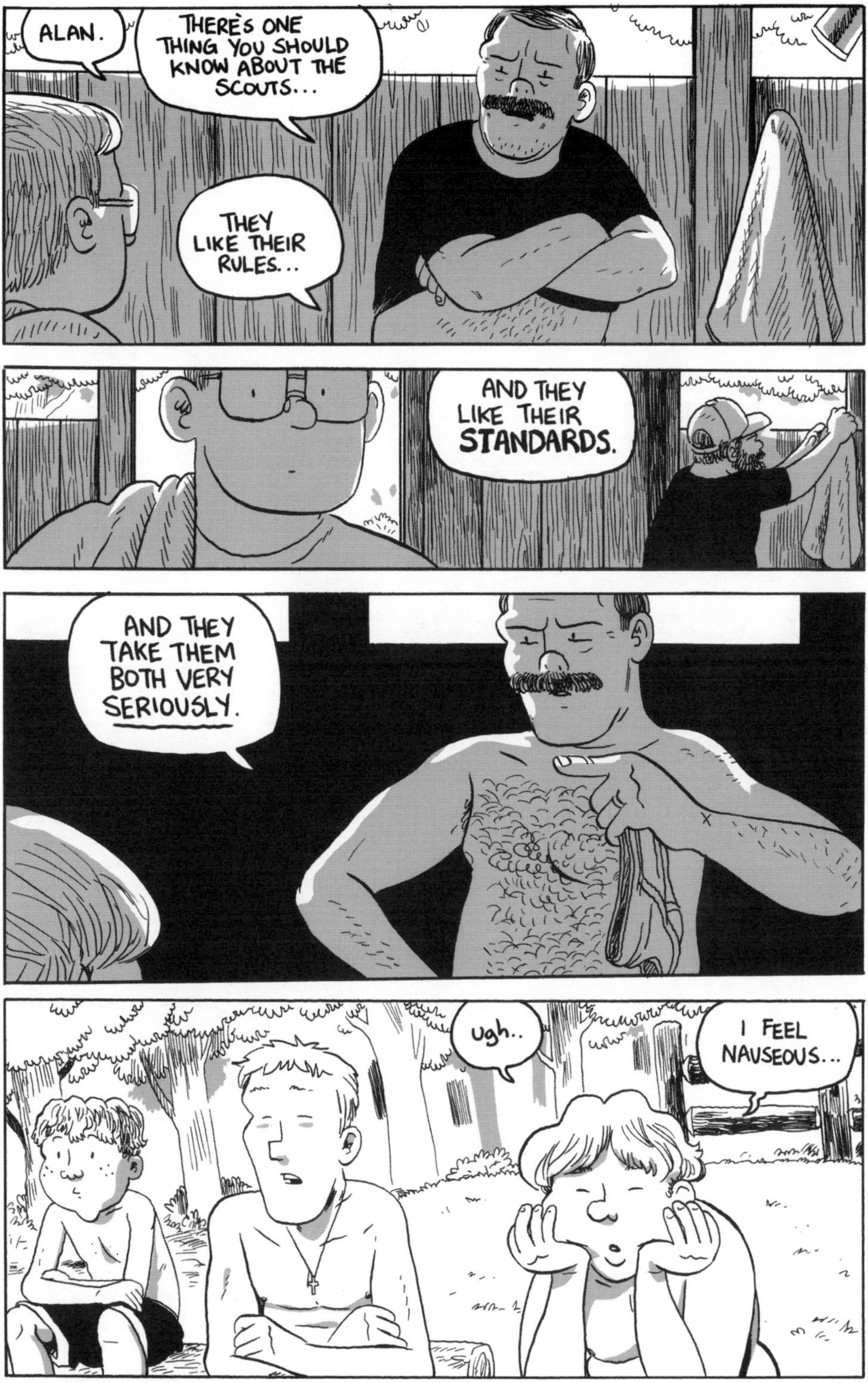
ALAN.
THERE'S ONE THING YOU SHOULD KNOW ABOUT THE SCOUTS...
THEY LIKE THEIR RULES...
AND THEY LIKE THEIR STANDARDS.
AND THEY TAKE THEM BOTH VERY SERIOUSLY.
Ugh..
I FEEL NAUSEOUS...

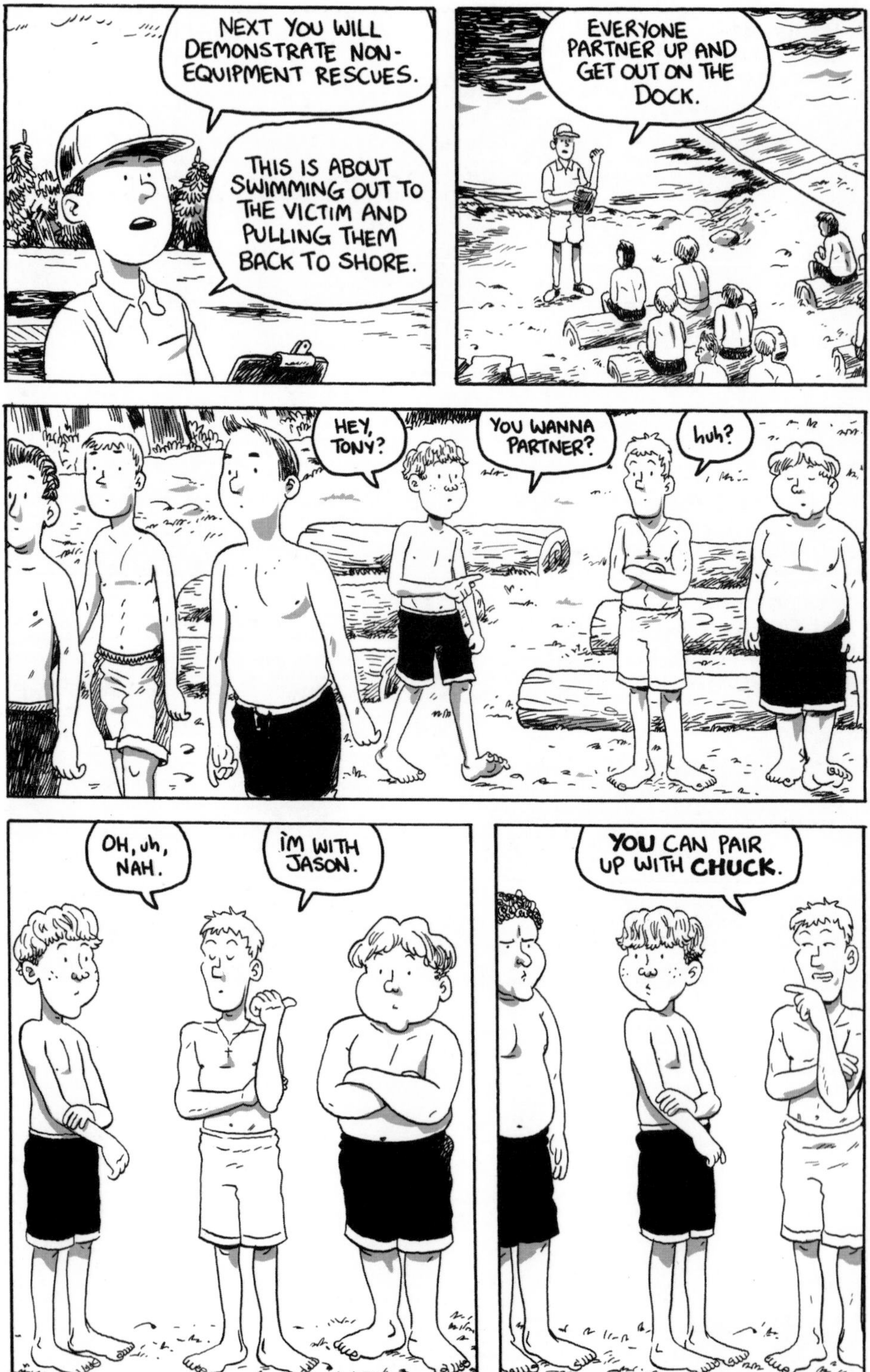
NEXT YOU WILL DEMONSTRATE NON-EQUIPMENT RESCUES.
THIS IS ABOUT SWIMMING OUT TO THE VICTIM AND PULLING THEM BACK TO SHORE.
EVERYONE PARTNER UP AND GET OUT ON THE DOCK.
HEY, TONY?
YOU WANNA PARTNER?
huh?
OH, uh, NAH.
I'M WITH JASON.
YOU CAN PAIR UP WITH CHUCK.

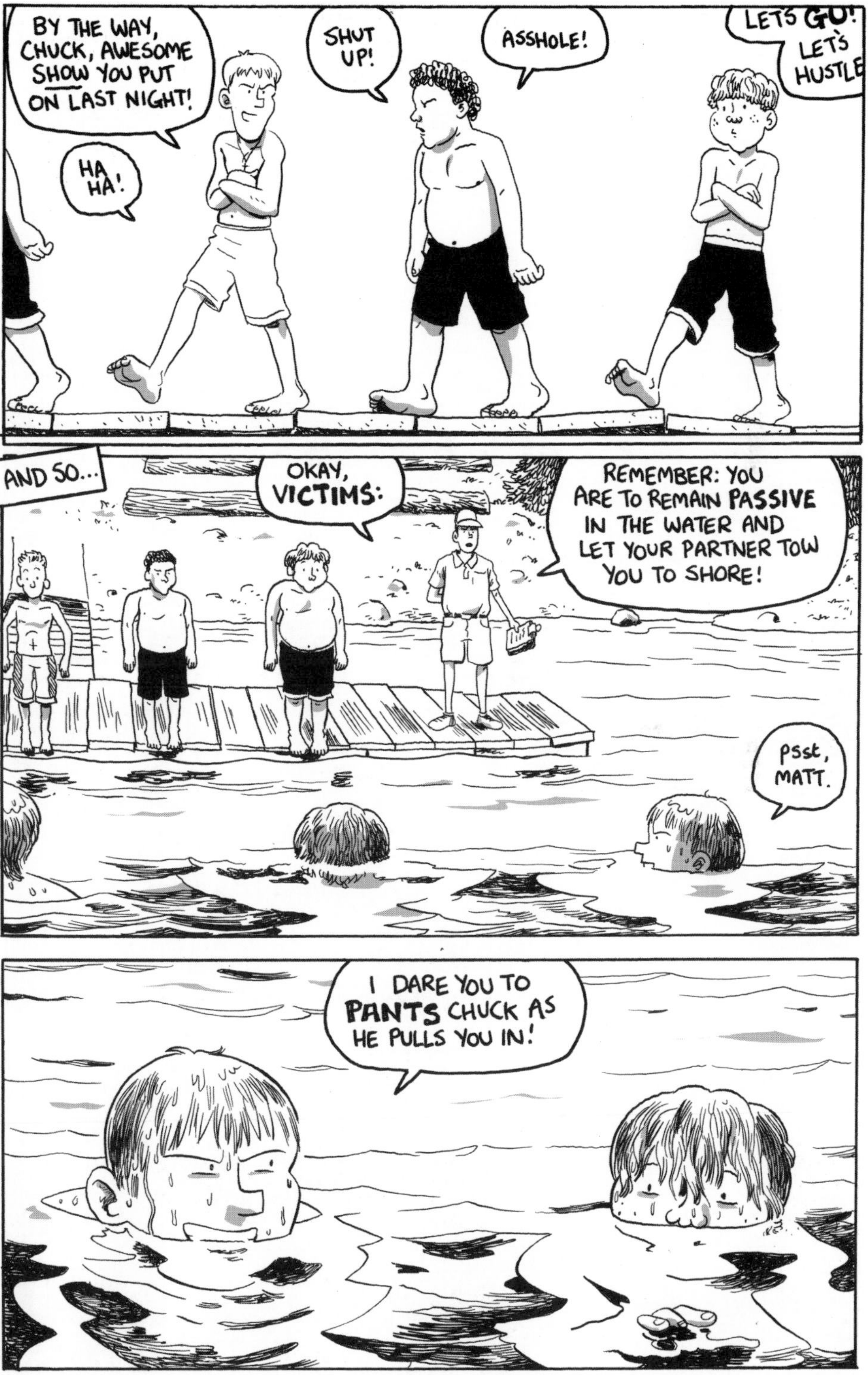
BY THE WAY, CHUCK, AWESOME SHOW YOU PUT ON LAST NIGHT!
HA HA!
SHUT UP!
ASSHOLE!
LETS GO! LET'S HUSTLE
AND SO...
OKAY, VICTIMS:
REMEMBER: YOU ARE TO REMAIN PASSIVE IN THE WATER AND LET YOUR PARTNER TOW YOU TO SHORE!
psst, MATT.
I DARE YOU TO PANTS CHUCK AS HE PULLS YOU IN!

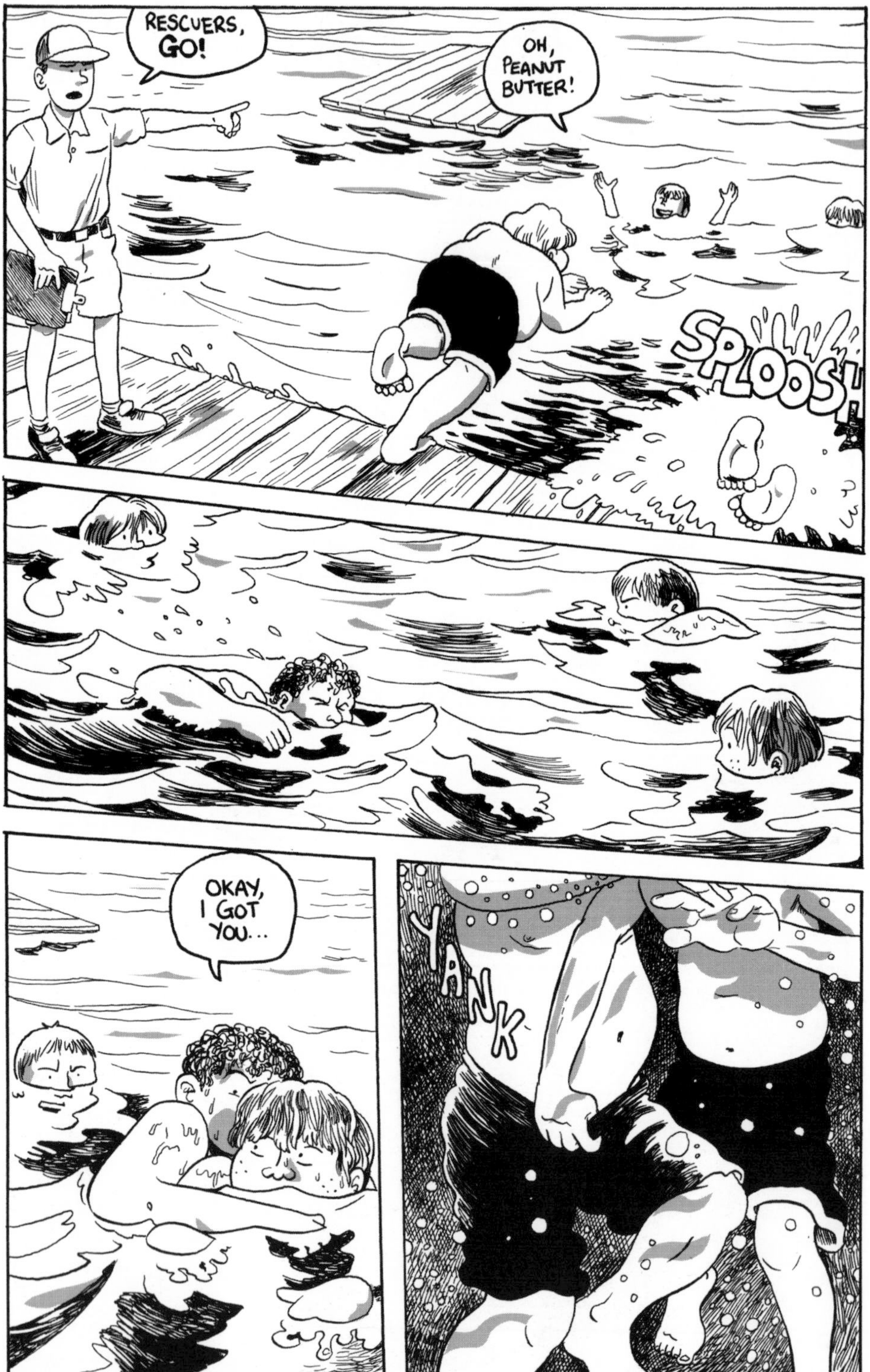
RESCUERS, GO!
OH, PEANUT BUTTER!
SPLOOSH
OKAY, I GOT YOU...
YANK

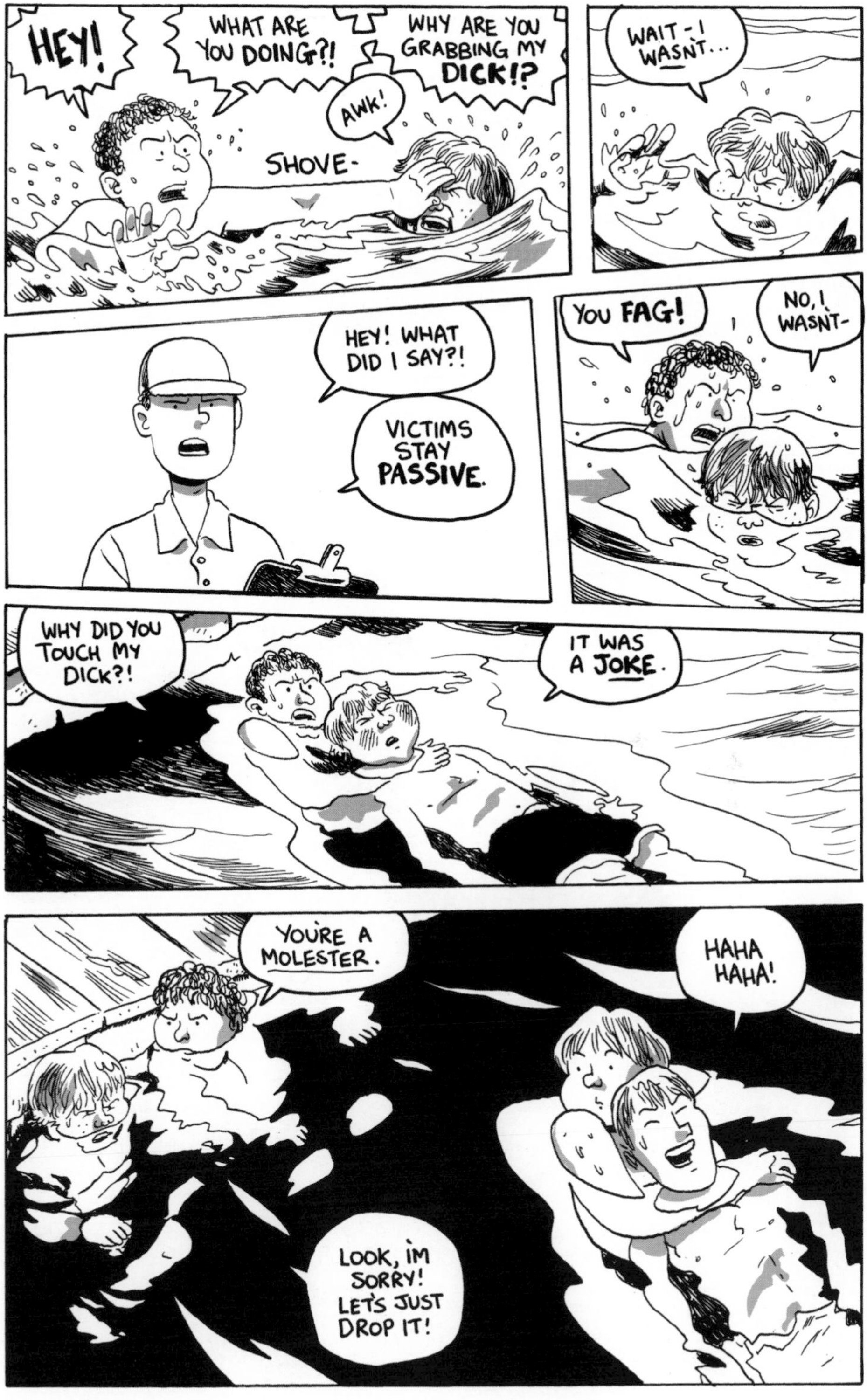
HEY!
WHAT ARE YOU DOING?!
WHY ARE YOU GRABBING MY DICK!?
AWK!
SHOVE-
WAIT-I WASN'T...
HEY! WHAT DID I SAY?!
VICTIMS STAY PASSIVE.
YOU FAG!
NO, I WASN'T-
WHY DID YOU TOUCH MY DICK?!
IT WAS A JOKE.
YOU'RE A MOLESTER.
HAHA HAHA!
LOOK, I'M SORRY! LET'S JUST DROP IT!

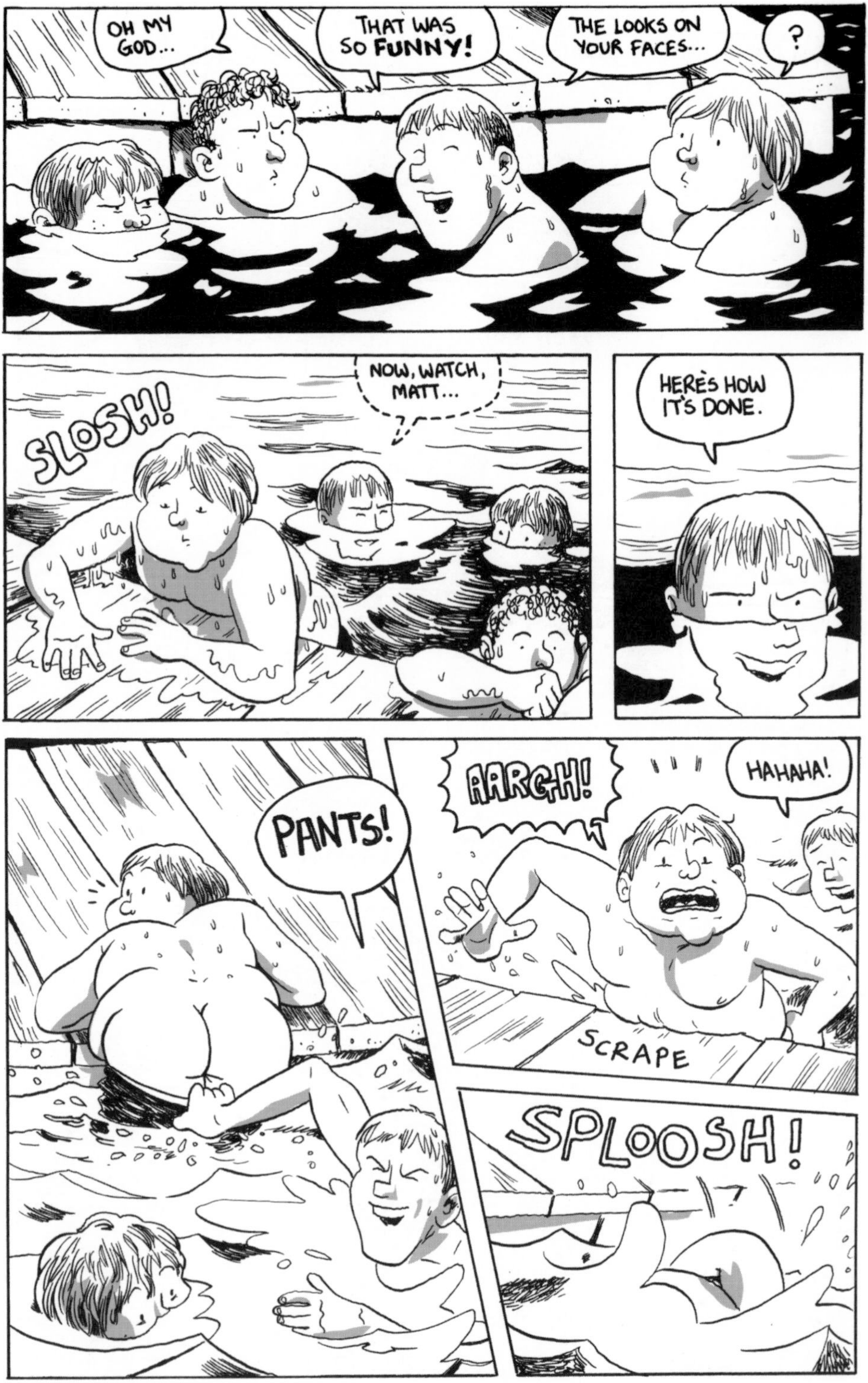
OH MY GOD...
THAT WAS SO FUNNY!
THE LOOKS ON YOUR FACES...
?
SLOSH!
NOW, WATCH, MATT...
HERE'S HOW IT'S DONE.
PANTS!
AARGH!
HAHAHA!
SCRAPE
SPLOOSH!

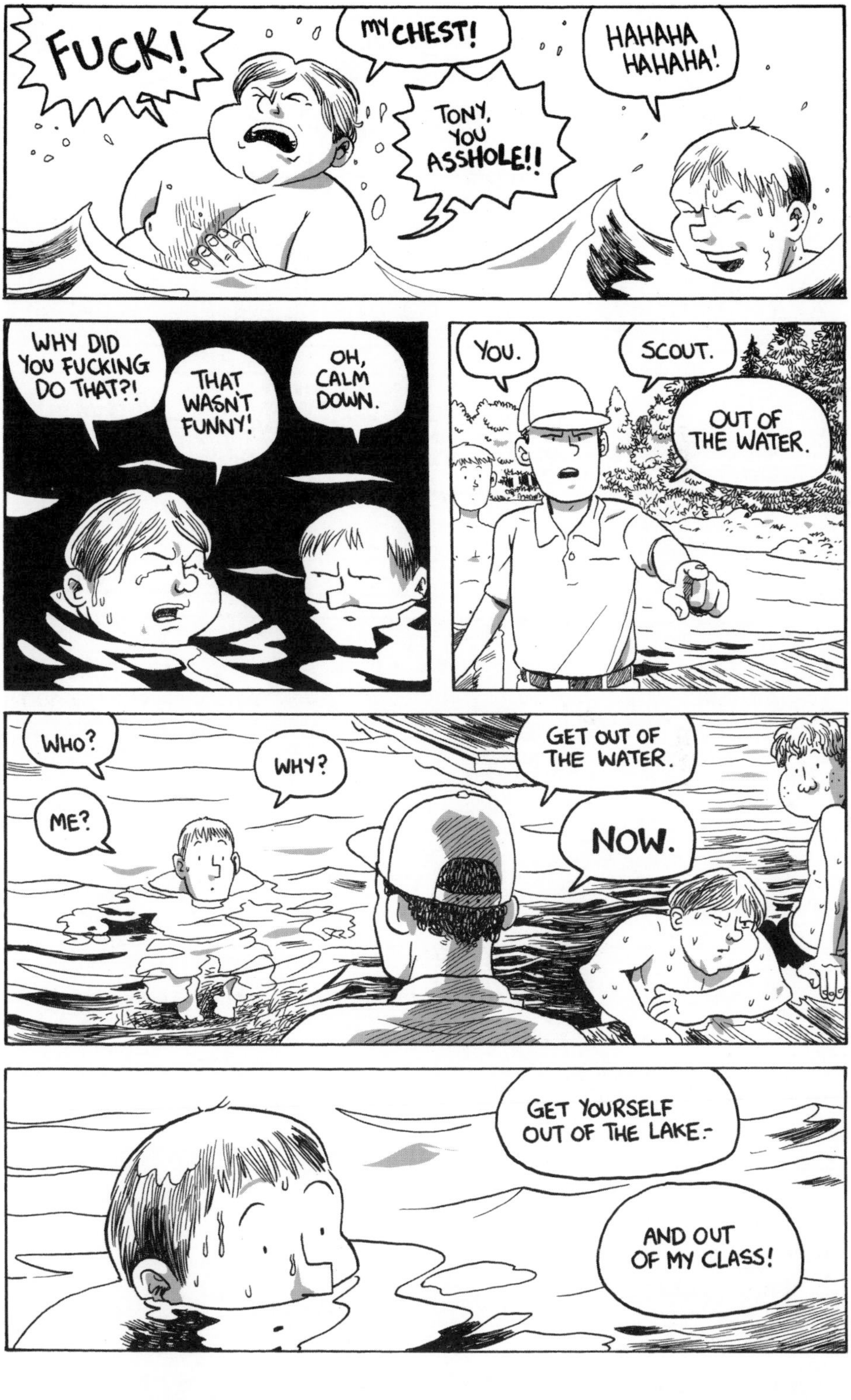
FUCK!
MY CHEST!
TONY, YOU ASSHOLE!!
HAHAHA HAHAHA!
WHY DID YOU FUCKING DO THAT?!
THAT WASN'T FUNNY!
OH, CALM DOWN.
YOU.
SCOUT.
OUT OF THE WATER.
WHO?
ME?
WHY?
GET OUT OF THE WATER.
NOW.
GET YOURSELF OUT OF THE LAKE-
AND OUT OF MY CLASS!

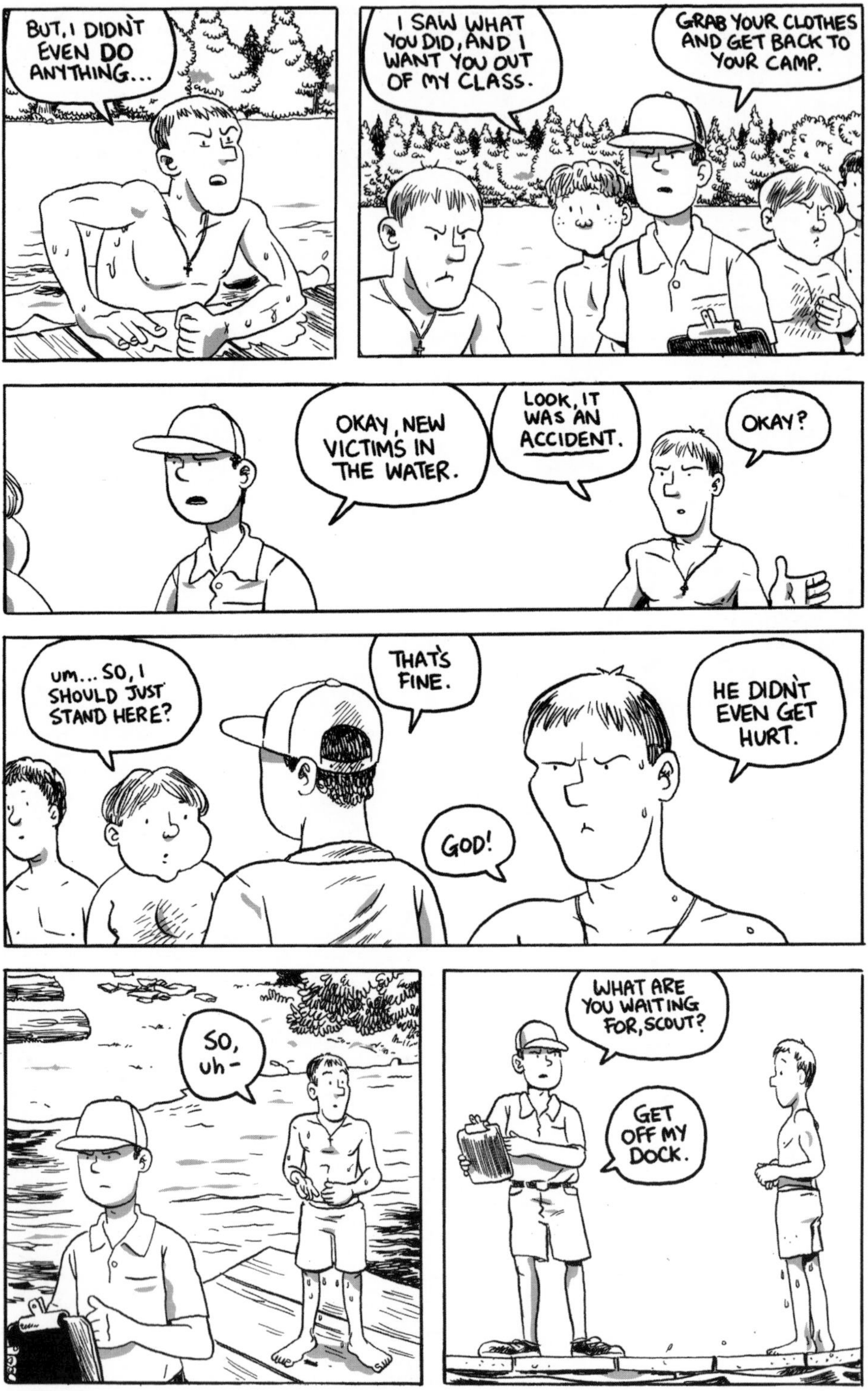
BUT, I DIDN'T EVEN DO ANYTHING...
I SAW WHAT YOU DID, AND I WANT YOU OUT OF MY CLASS.
GRAB YOUR CLOTHES AND GET BACK TO YOUR CAMP.
OKAY, NEW VICTIMS IN THE WATER.
LOOK, IT WAS AN ACCIDENT.
OKAY?
um... SO, I SHOULD JUST STAND HERE?
THAT'S FINE.
HE DIDN'T EVEN GET HURT.
GOD!
SO, uh-
WHAT ARE YOU WAITING FOR, SCOUT?
GET OFF MY DOCK.

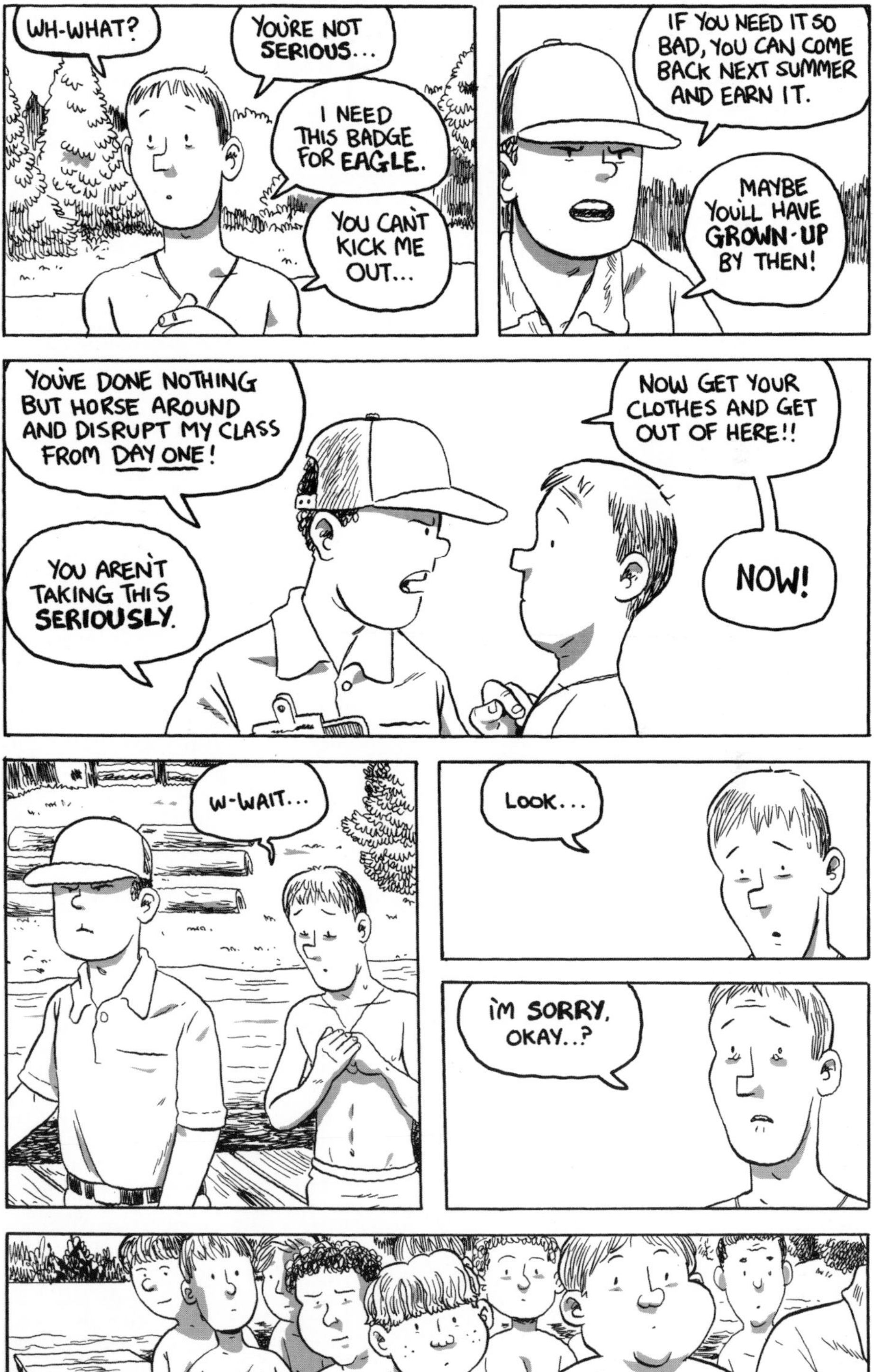
WH-WHAT?
YOU'RE NOT SERIOUS...
I NEED THIS BADGE FOR EAGLE.
YOU CAN'T KICK ME OUT...
IF YOU NEED IT SO BAD, YOU CAN COME BACK NEXT SUMMER AND EARN IT.
MAYBE YOU'LL HAVE GROWN-UP BY THEN!
YOU'VE DONE NOTHING BUT HORSE AROUND AND DISRUPT MY CLASS FROM DAY ONE!
YOU AREN'T TAKING THIS SERIOUSLY.
NOW GET YOUR CLOTHES AND GET OUT OF HERE!!
NOW!
W-WAIT...
LOOK...
I'M SORRY, OKAY..?

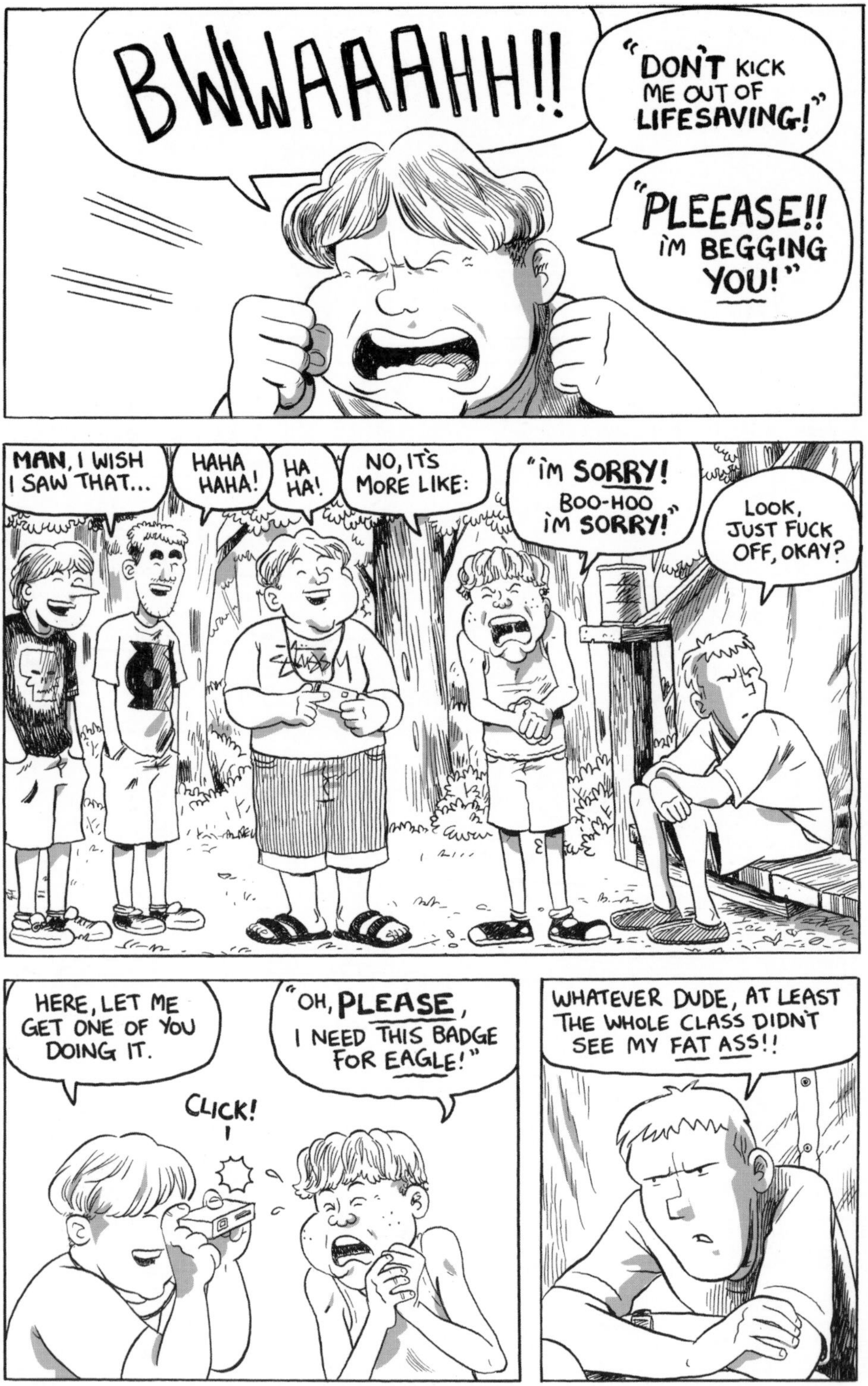
BWWAAAHH!!
"DON'T KICK ME OUT OF LIFESAVING!"
"PLEEASE!! I'M BEGGING YOU!"
MAN, I WISH I SAW THAT...
HAHA HAHA!
HA HA!
NO, IT'S MORE LIKE:
"I'M SORRY! BOO-HOO I'M SORRY!"
LOOK, JUST FUCK OFF, OKAY?
HERE, LET ME GET ONE OF YOU DOING IT.
"OH, PLEASE, I NEED THIS BADGE FOR EAGLE!"
CLICK!
WHATEVER DUDE, AT LEAST THE WHOLE CLASS DIDN'T SEE MY FAT ASS!!

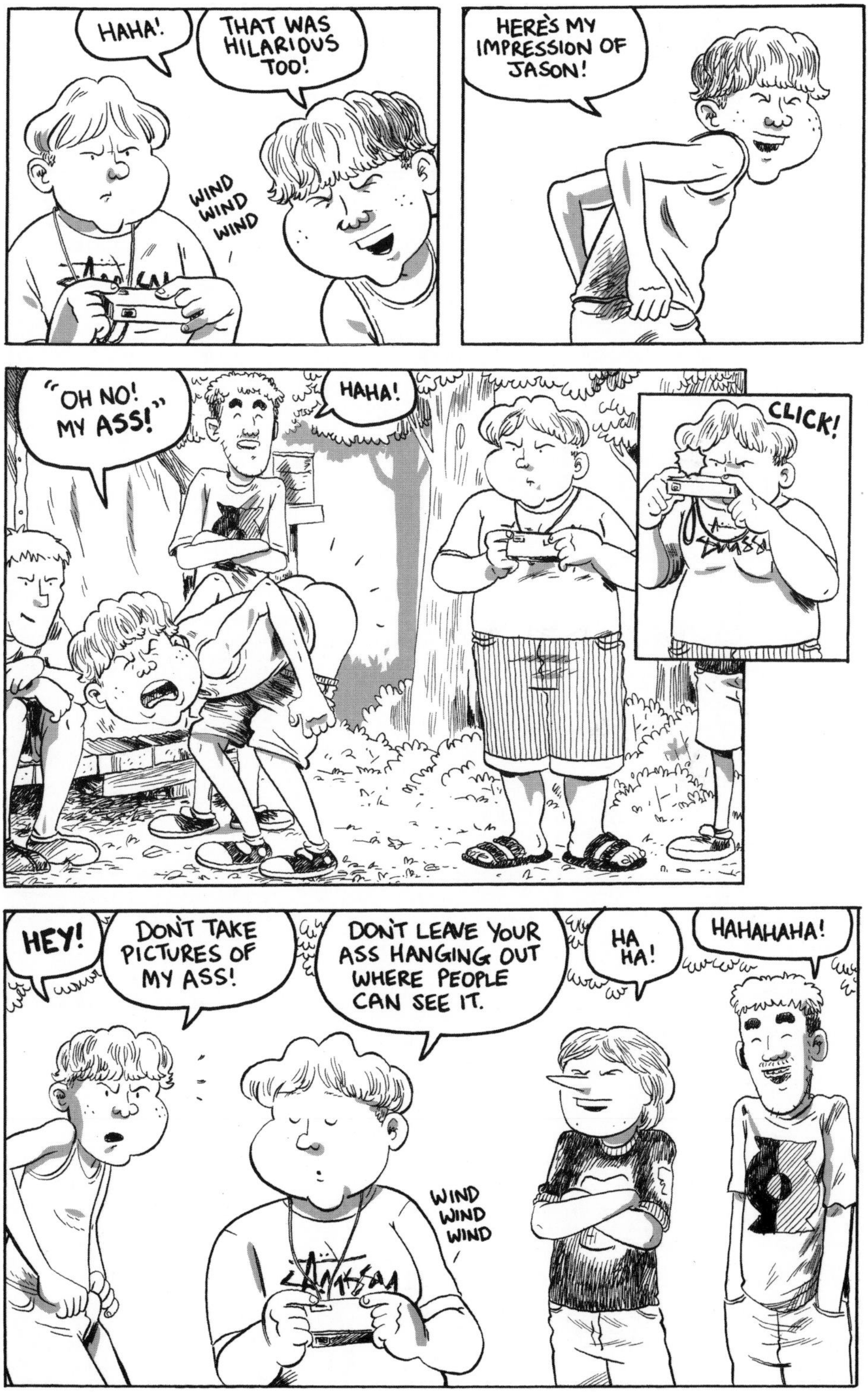
HAHA!
THAT WAS HILARIOUS TOO!
WIND WIND WIND
HERE'S MY IMPRESSION OF JASON!
"OH NO! MY ASS!"
HAHA!
CLICK!
HEY!
DON'T TAKE PICTURES OF MY ASS!
DON'T LEAVE YOUR ASS HANGING OUT WHERE PEOPLE CAN SEE IT.
HA HA!
HAHAHAHA!
WIND WIND WIND

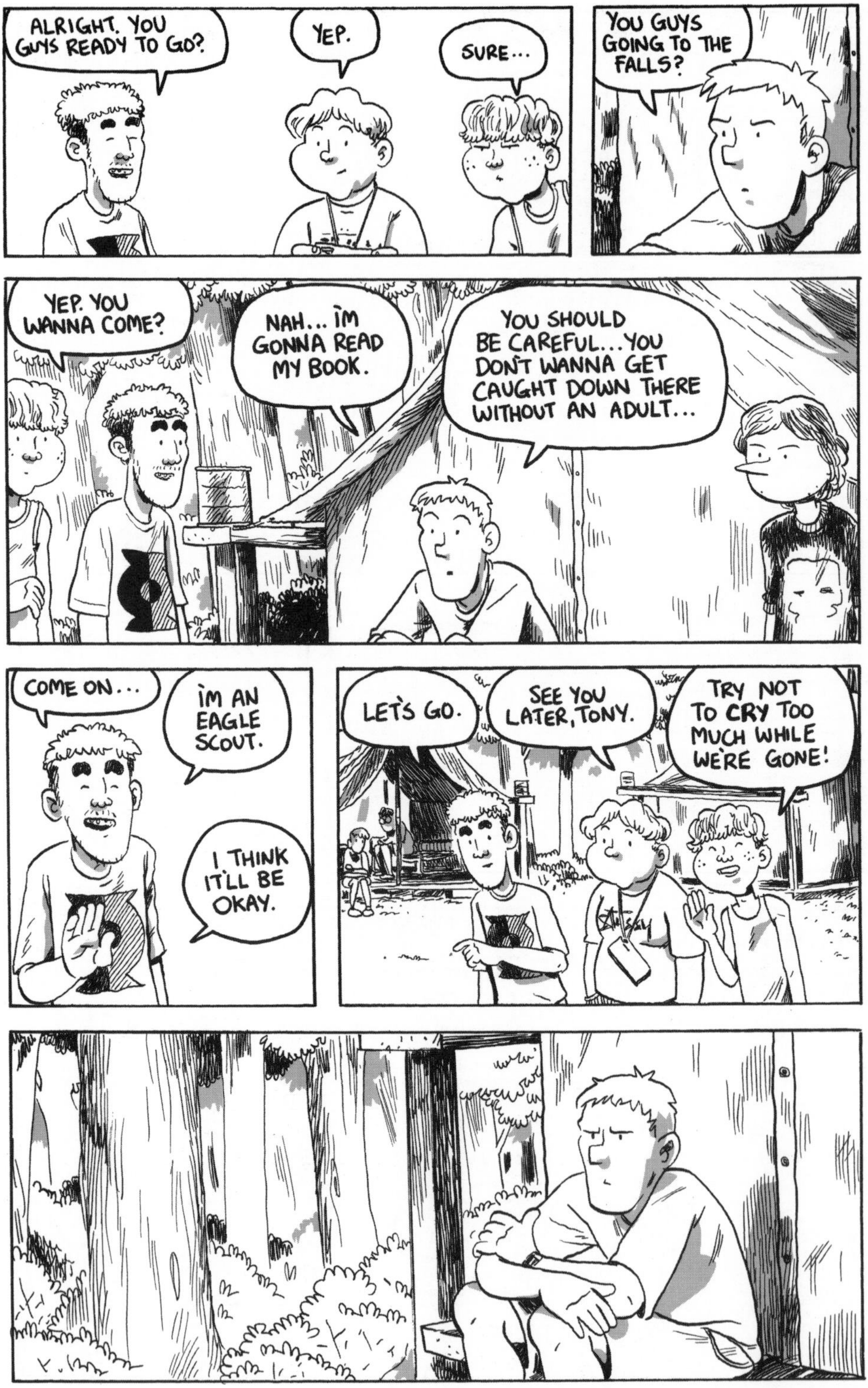
ALRIGHT. YOU GUYS READY TO GO?
YEP.
SURE...
YOU GUYS GOING TO THE FALLS?
YEP. YOU WANNA COME?
NAH... I'M GONNA READ MY BOOK.
YOU SHOULD BE CAREFUL... YOU DON'T WANNA GET CAUGHT DOWN THERE WITHOUT AN ADULT...
COME ON...
I'M AN EAGLE SCOUT.
I THINK IT'LL BE OKAY.
LET'S GO.
SEE YOU LATER, TONY.
TRY NOT TO CRY TOO MUCH WHILE WE'RE GONE!

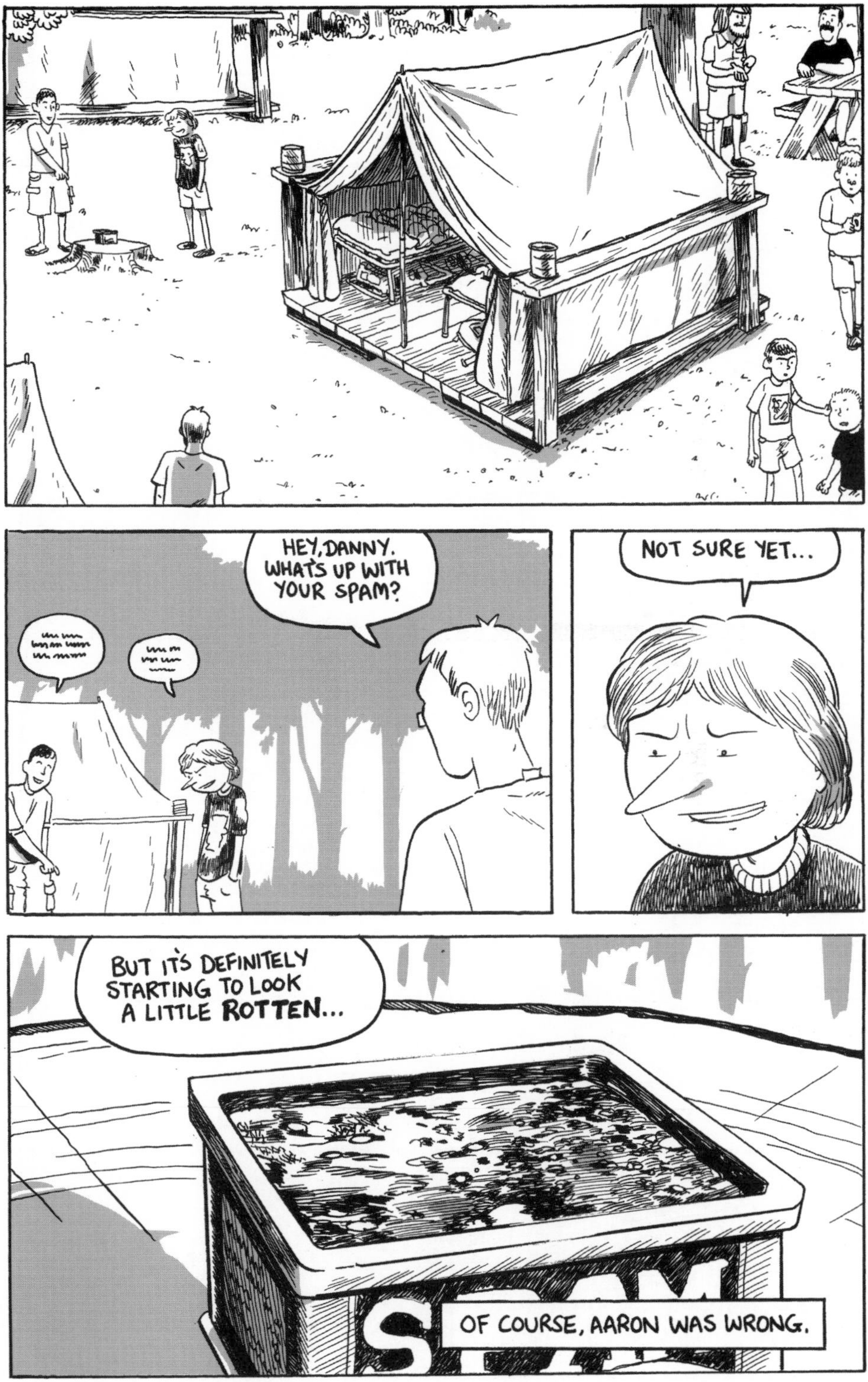
HEY, DANNY. WHAT'S UP WITH YOUR SPAM?
NOT SURE YET...
BUT IT'S DEFINITELY STARTING TO LOOK A LITTLE **ROTTEN**...
OF COURSE, AARON WAS WRONG.

THE CAMP RULES ARE QUITE CLEAR.

MONKEY BRIDGE SIGNUP SHEET

#142

SCOUTS CANNOT GO DOWN TO THE FALLS WITHOUT ADULT SUPERVISION.

MOMS LOVE ME ♡

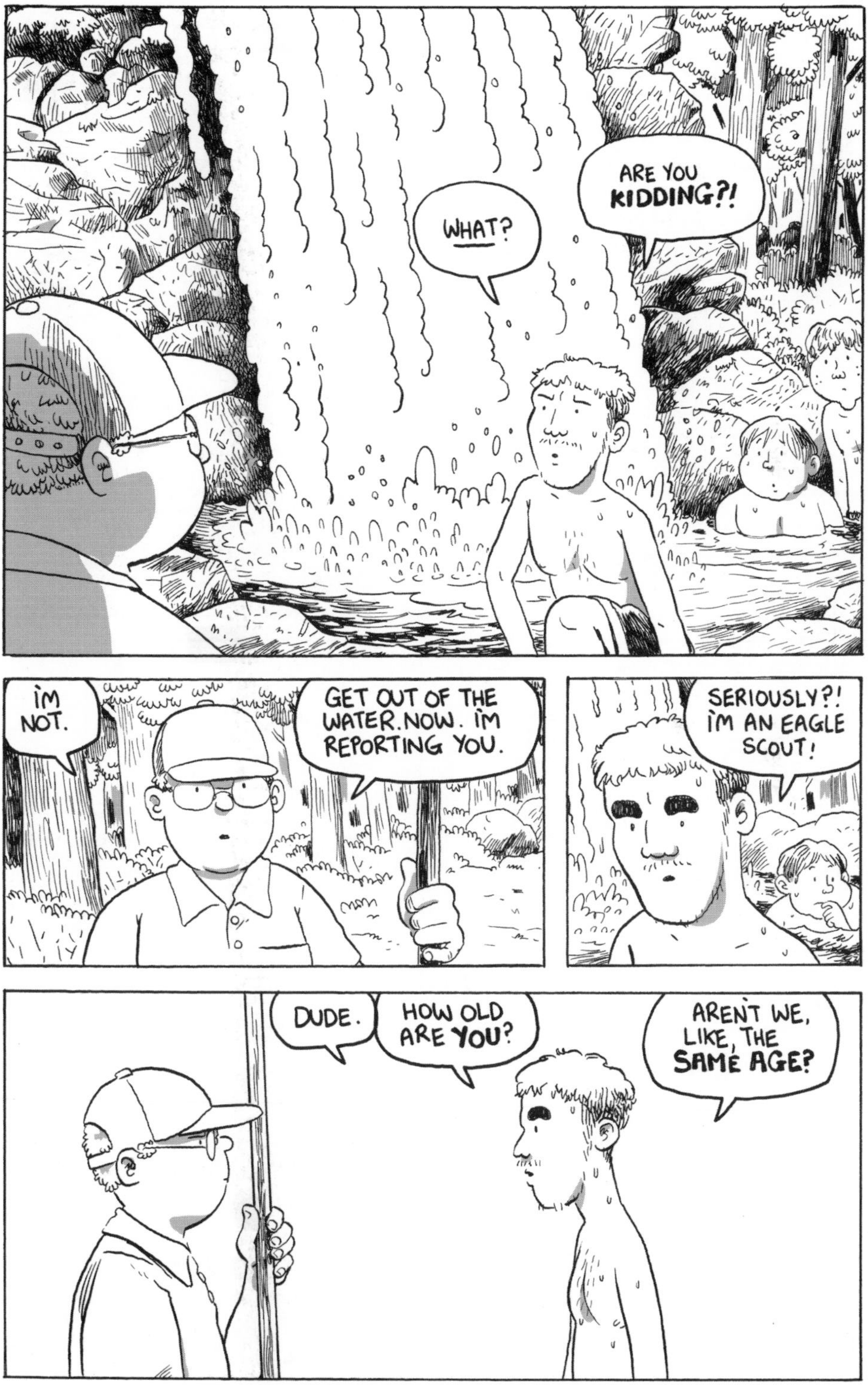

WHAT?
ARE YOU KIDDING?!
I'M NOT.
GET OUT OF THE WATER. NOW. I'M REPORTING YOU.
SERIOUSLY?! I'M AN EAGLE SCOUT!
DUDE.
HOW OLD ARE YOU?
AREN'T WE, LIKE, THE SAME AGE?

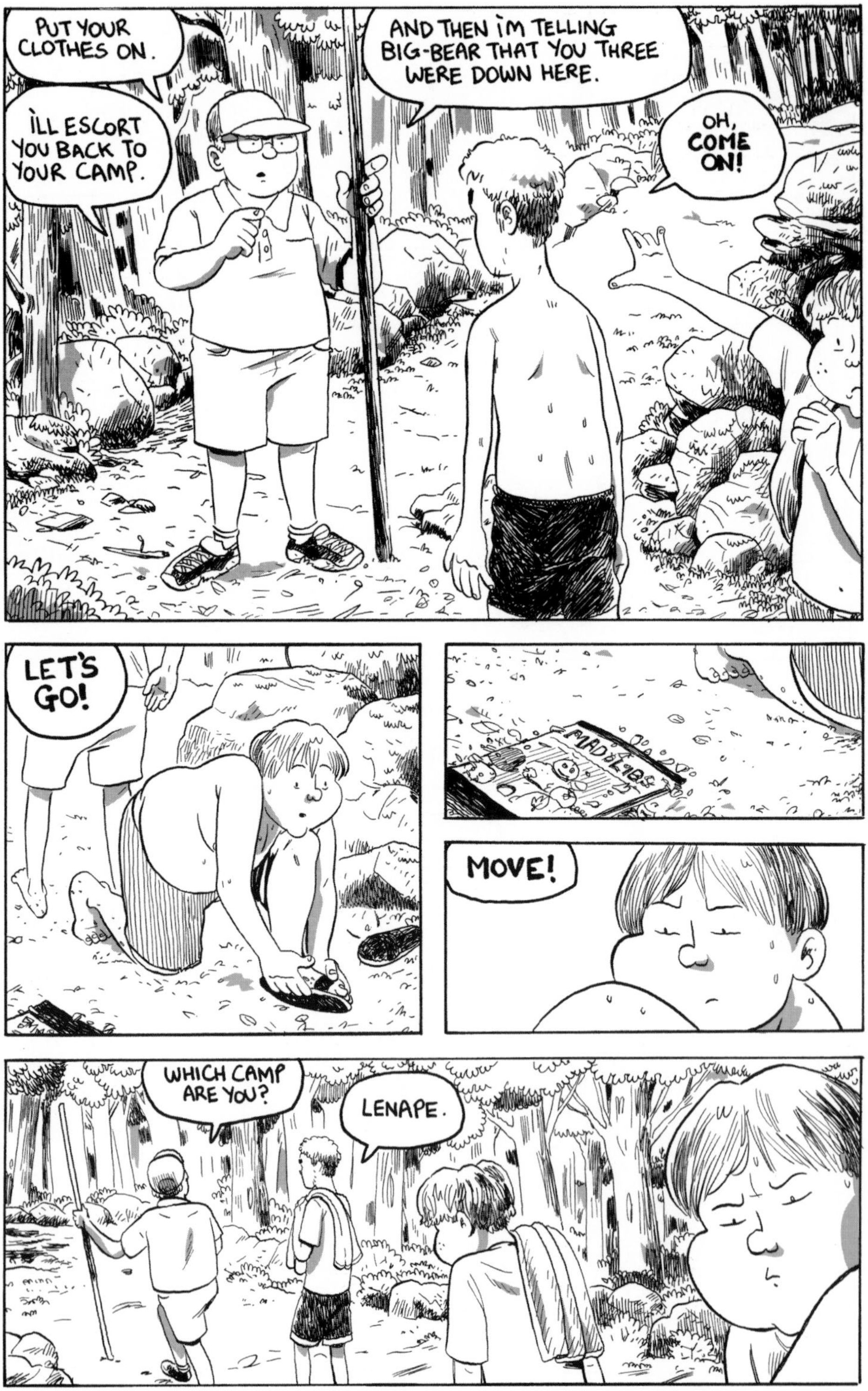
PUT YOUR CLOTHES ON.
I'LL ESCORT YOU BACK TO YOUR CAMP.
AND THEN I'M TELLING BIG-BEAR THAT YOU THREE WERE DOWN HERE.
OH, COME ON!
LET'S GO!
MOVE!
WHICH CAMP ARE YOU?
LENAPE.

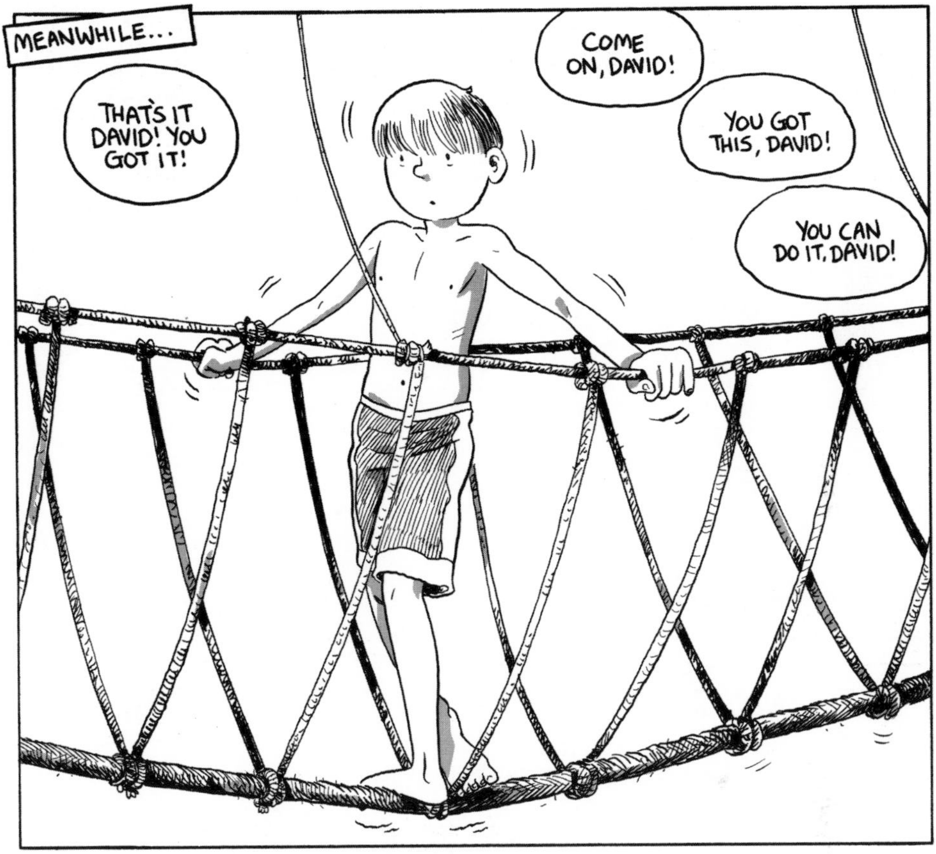
MEANWHILE...
THAT'S IT DAVID! YOU GOT IT!
COME ON, DAVID!
YOU GOT THIS, DAVID!
YOU CAN DO IT, DAVID!

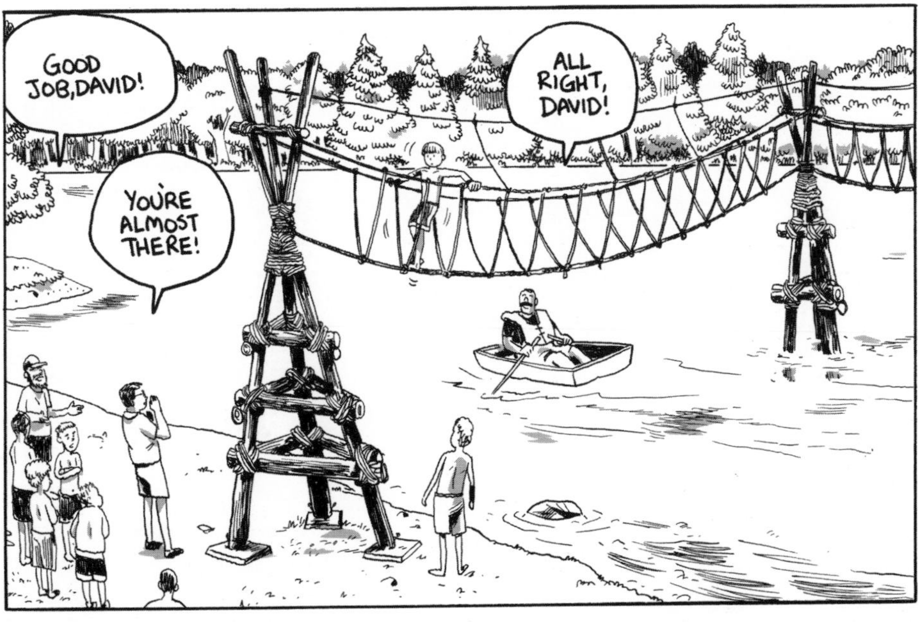
GOOD JOB, DAVID!
YOU'RE ALMOST THERE!
ALL RIGHT, DAVID!

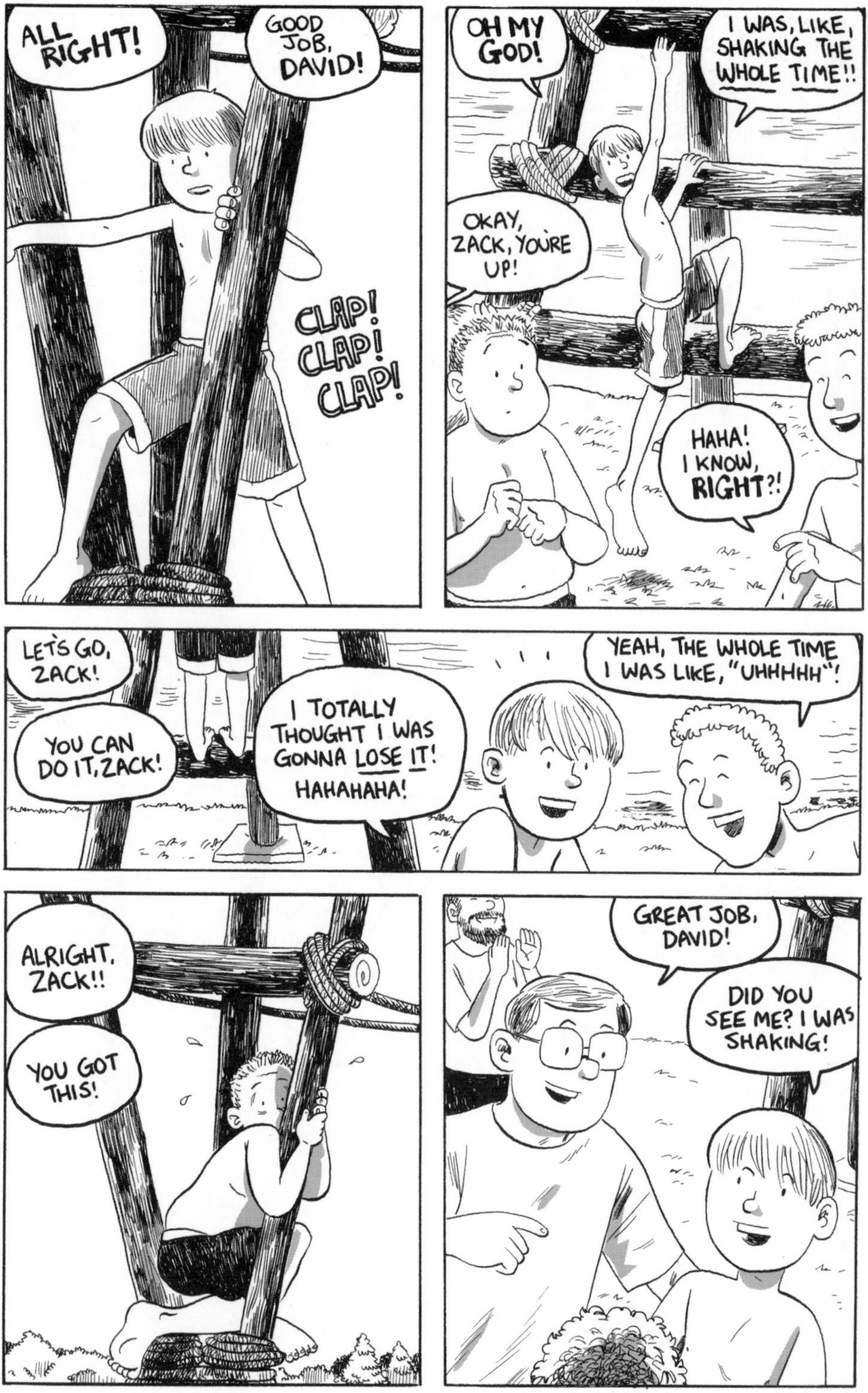
ALL RIGHT!
GOOD JOB, DAVID!
CLAP! CLAP! CLAP!
OH MY GOD!
I WAS, LIKE, SHAKING THE WHOLE TIME!!
OKAY, ZACK, YOU'RE UP!
HAHA! I KNOW, RIGHT?!
LET'S GO, ZACK!
YOU CAN DO IT, ZACK!
I TOTALLY THOUGHT I WAS GONNA LOSE IT! HAHAHAHA!
YEAH, THE WHOLE TIME I WAS LIKE, "UHHHHH"!
ALRIGHT, ZACK!!
YOU GOT THIS!
GREAT JOB, DAVID!
DID YOU SEE ME? I WAS SHAKING!

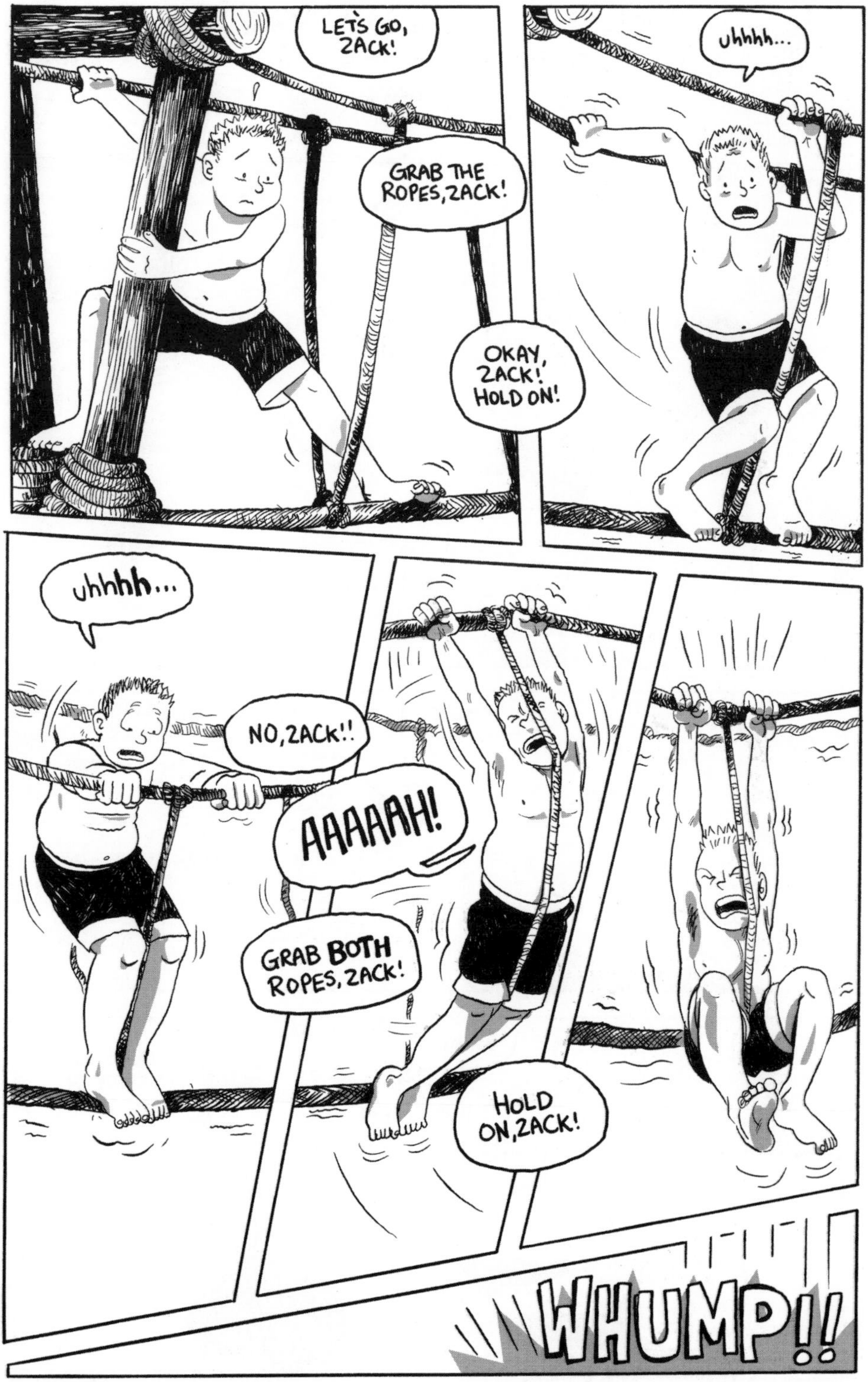
LET'S GO, ZACK!
GRAB THE ROPES, ZACK!
OKAY, ZACK! HOLD ON!
uhhhh...
uhhhh...
NO, ZACK!!
AAAAAH!
GRAB BOTH ROPES, ZACK!
HOLD ON, ZACK!
WHUMP!!

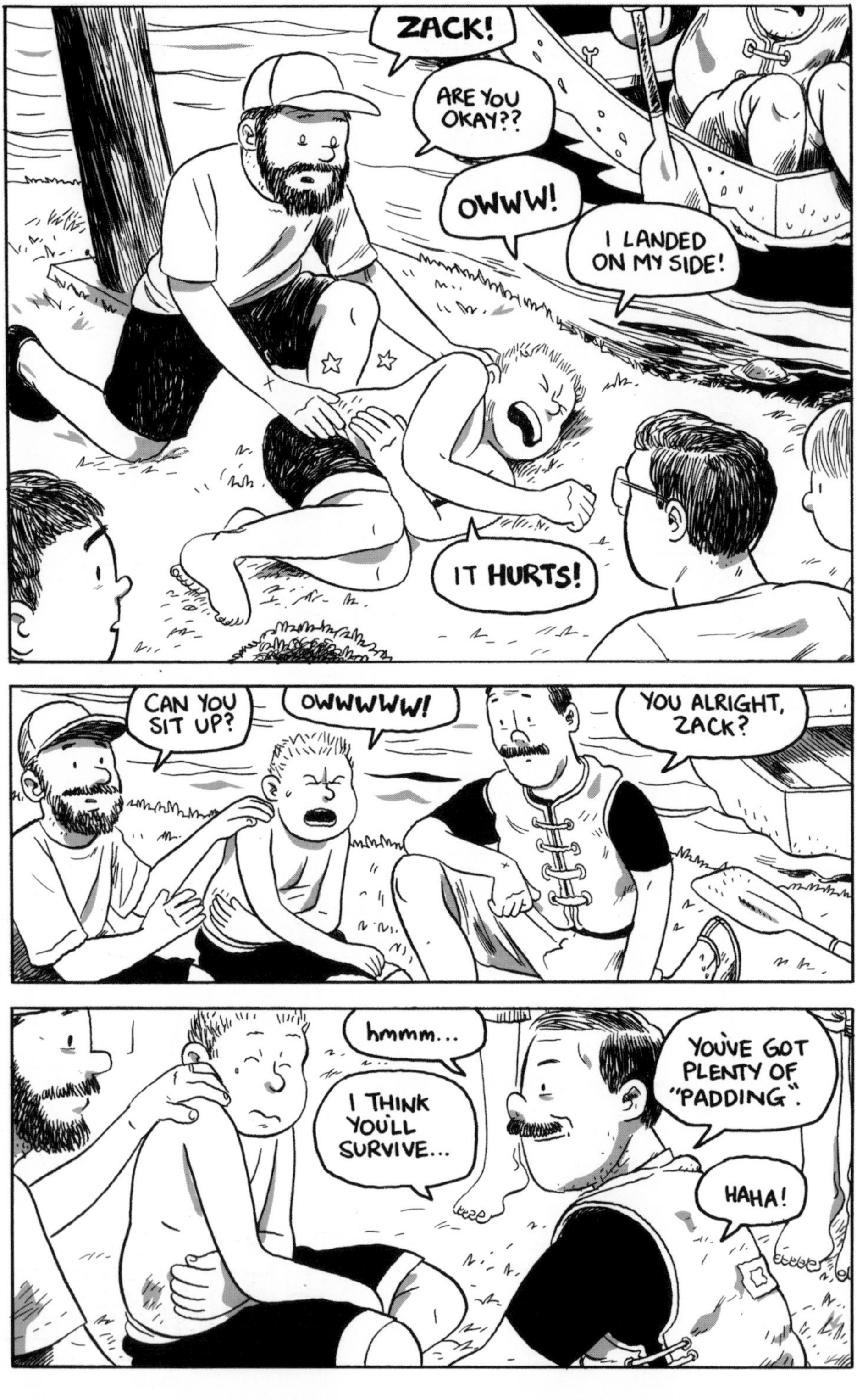
ZACK!
ARE YOU OKAY??
OWWW!
I LANDED ON MY SIDE!
IT HURTS!
CAN YOU SIT UP?
OWWWWW!
YOU ALRIGHT, ZACK?
hmmm...
I THINK YOU'LL SURVIVE...
YOU'VE GOT PLENTY OF "PADDING".
HAHA!

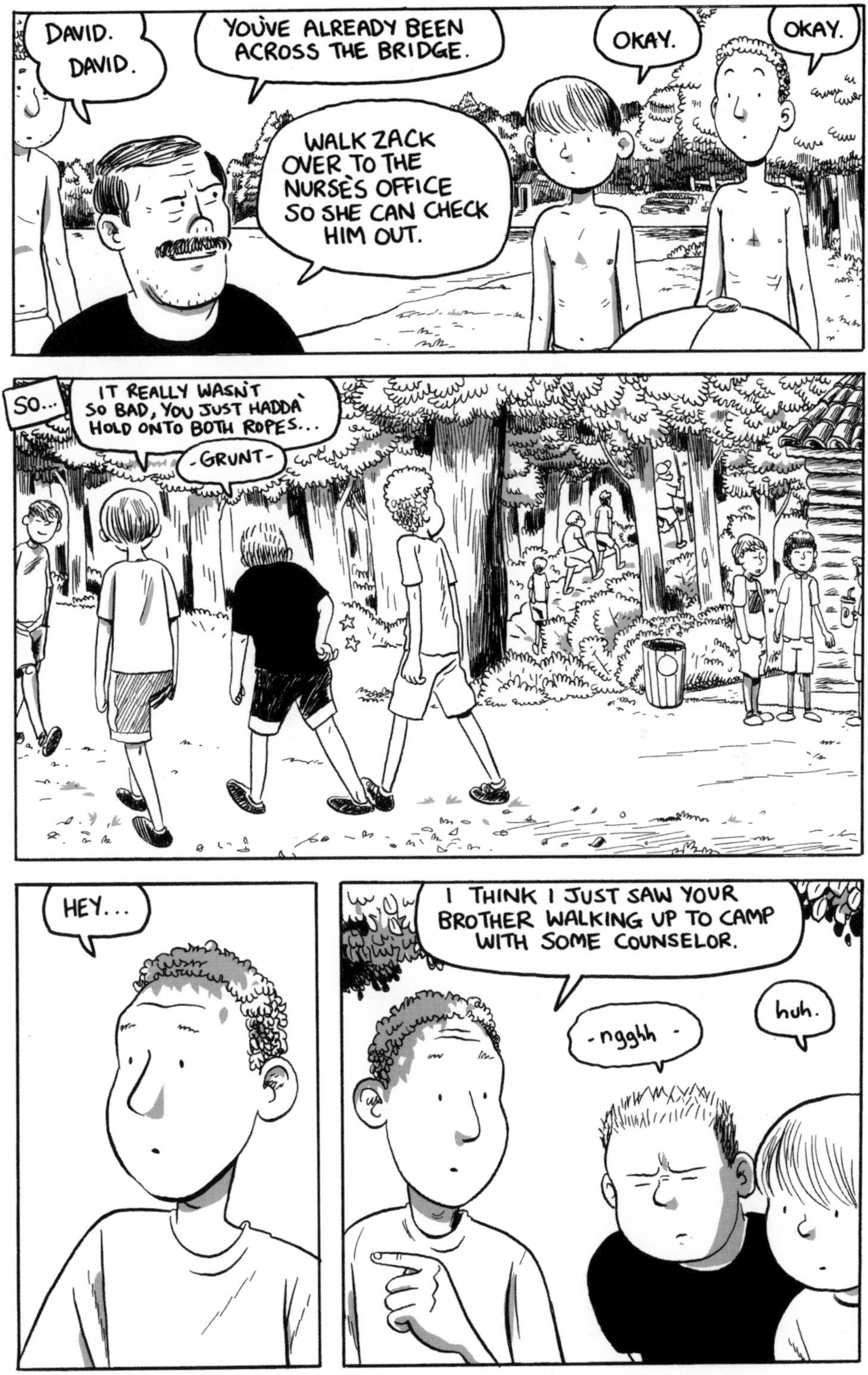
DAVID. DAVID.
YOU'VE ALREADY BEEN ACROSS THE BRIDGE.
WALK ZACK OVER TO THE NURSE'S OFFICE SO SHE CAN CHECK HIM OUT.
OKAY.
OKAY.
SO...
IT REALLY WASN'T SO BAD, YOU JUST HADDA HOLD ONTO BOTH ROPES...
-GRUNT-
HEY...
I THINK I JUST SAW YOUR BROTHER WALKING UP TO CAMP WITH SOME COUNSELOR.
-ngghh-
huh.

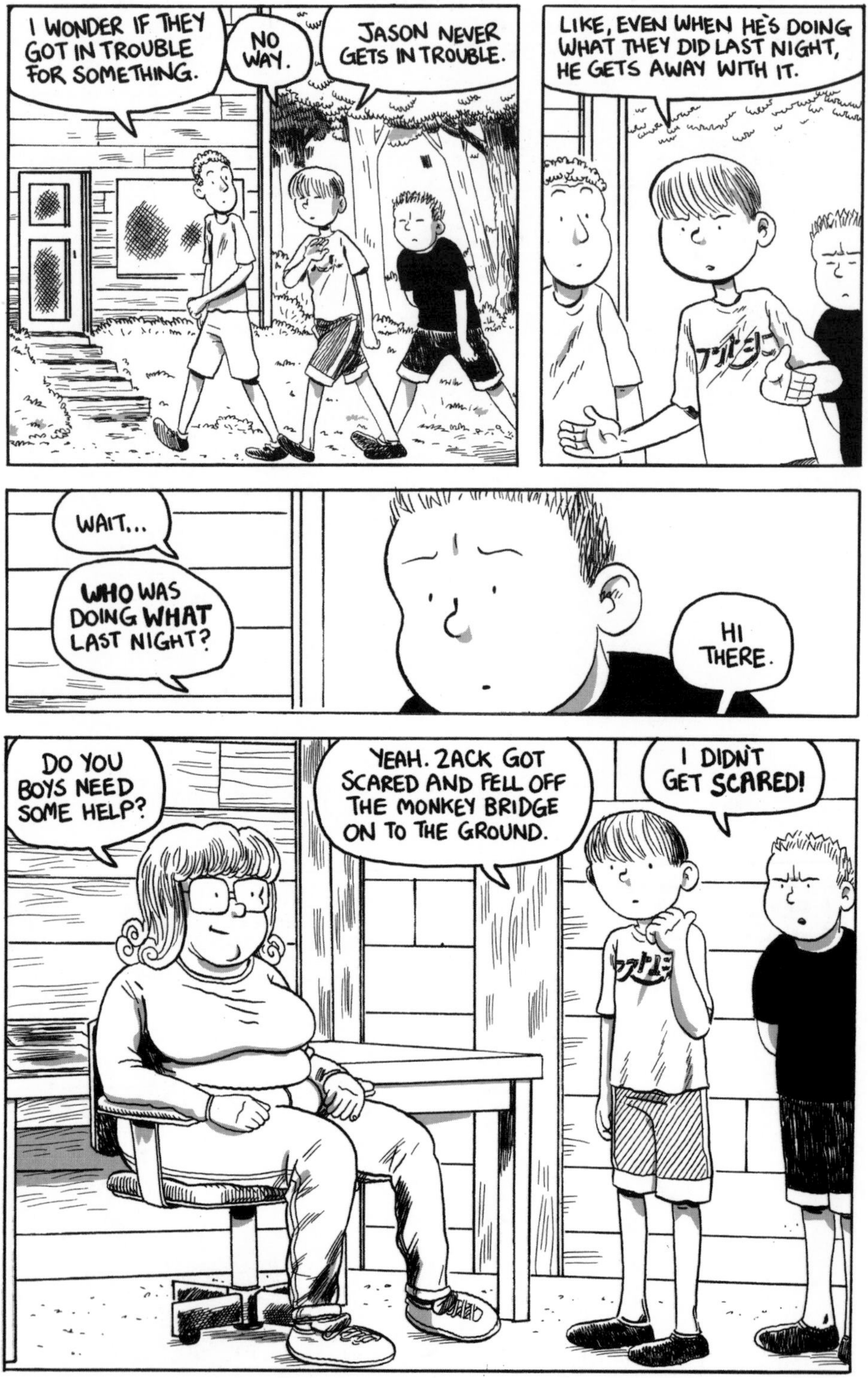
I WONDER IF THEY GOT IN TROUBLE FOR SOMETHING.
NO WAY.
JASON NEVER GETS IN TROUBLE.
LIKE, EVEN WHEN HE'S DOING WHAT THEY DID LAST NIGHT, HE GETS AWAY WITH IT.
WAIT...
WHO WAS DOING WHAT LAST NIGHT?
HI THERE.
DO YOU BOYS NEED SOME HELP?
YEAH. ZACK GOT SCARED AND FELL OFF THE MONKEY BRIDGE ON TO THE GROUND.
I DIDN'T GET SCARED!

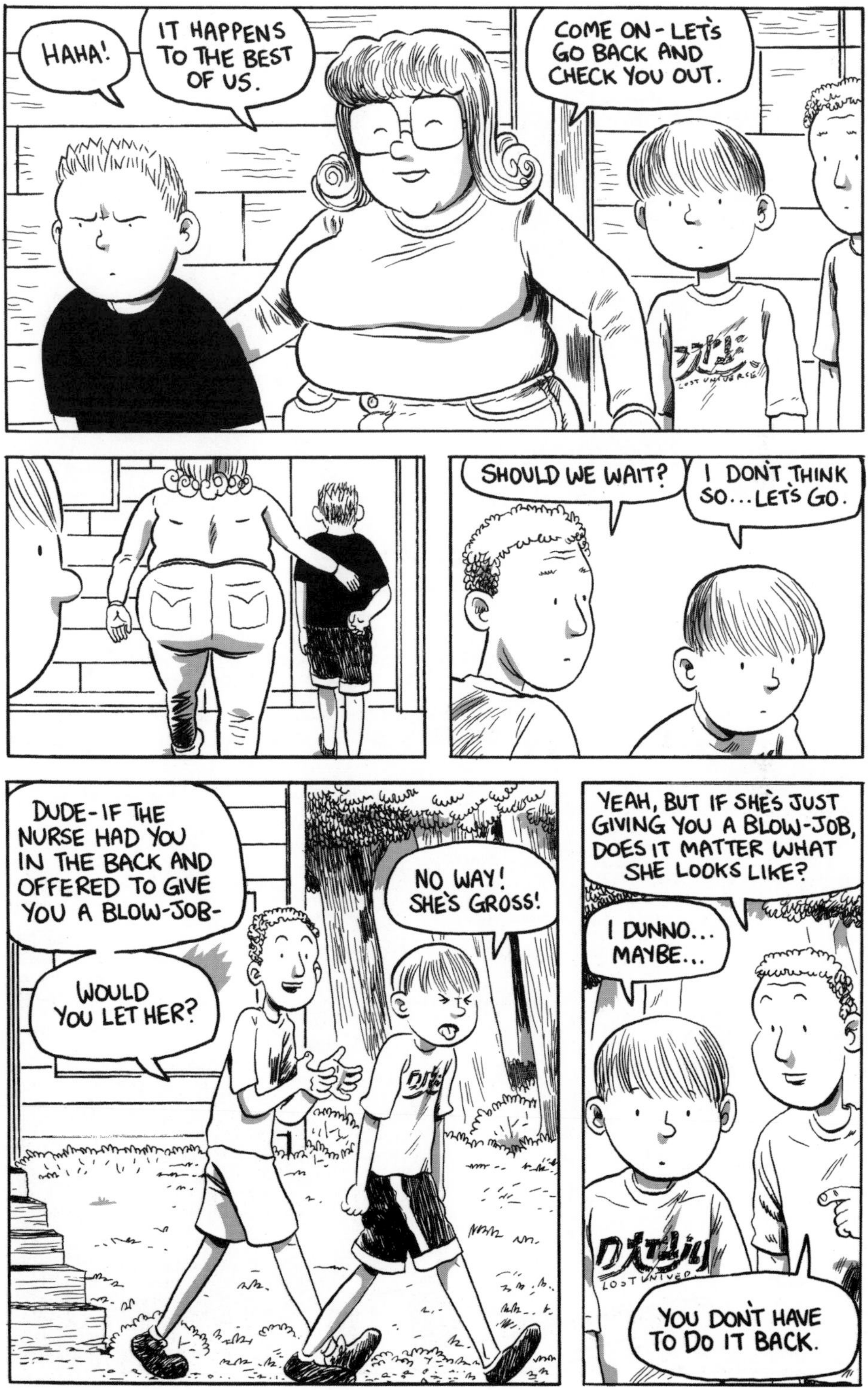
HAHA!
IT HAPPENS TO THE BEST OF US.
COME ON - LET'S GO BACK AND CHECK YOU OUT.
SHOULD WE WAIT?
I DON'T THINK SO... LET'S GO.
DUDE - IF THE NURSE HAD YOU IN THE BACK AND OFFERED TO GIVE YOU A BLOW-JOB-
WOULD YOU LET HER?
NO WAY! SHE'S GROSS!
YEAH, BUT IF SHE'S JUST GIVING YOU A BLOW-JOB, DOES IT MATTER WHAT SHE LOOKS LIKE?
I DUNNO... MAYBE...
YOU DON'T HAVE TO DO IT BACK.

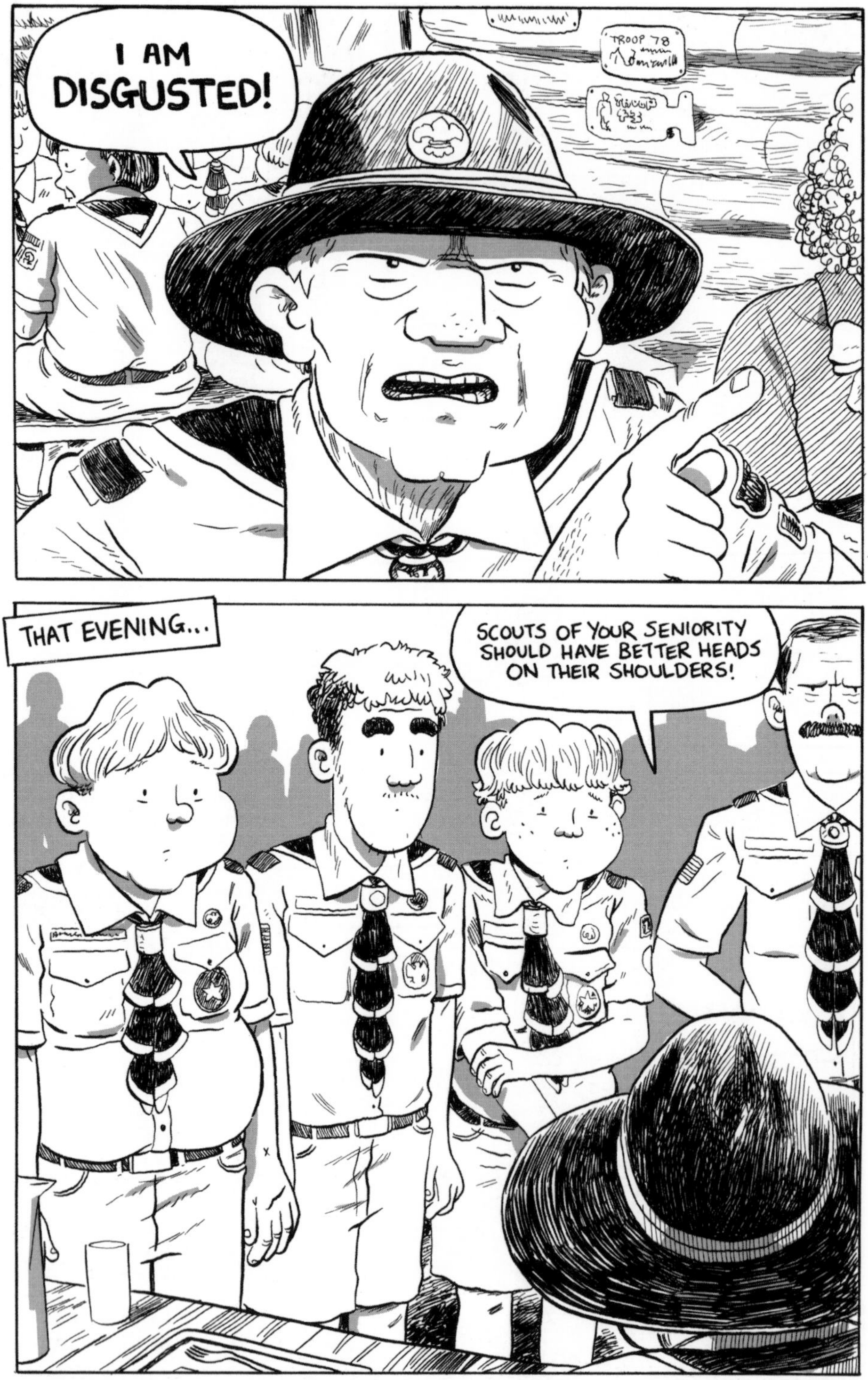

I AM DISGUSTED!
TROOP 78
THAT EVENING...
SCOUTS OF YOUR SENIORITY SHOULD HAVE BETTER HEADS ON THEIR SHOULDERS!

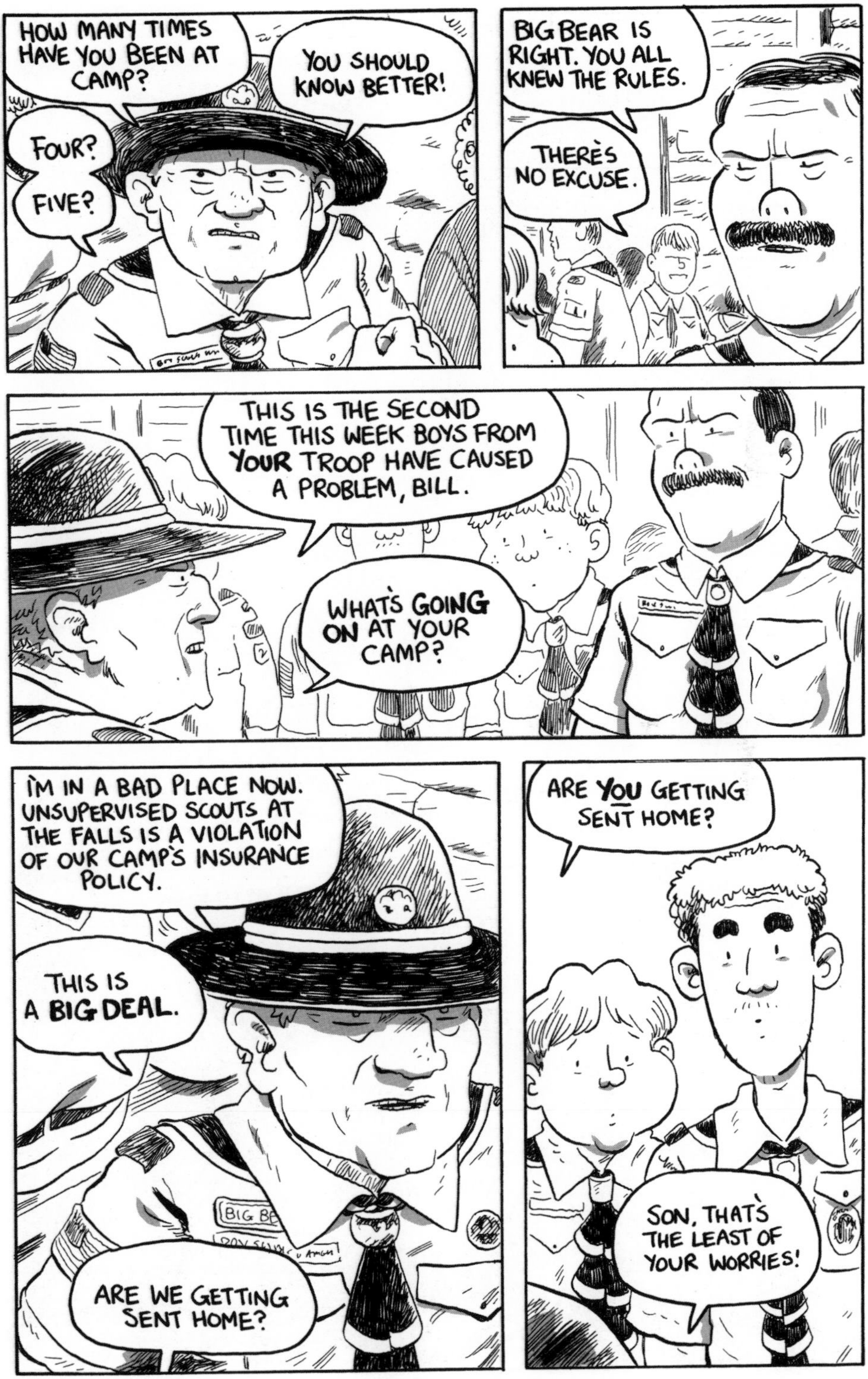
HOW MANY TIMES HAVE YOU BEEN AT CAMP?
YOU SHOULD KNOW BETTER!
FOUR?
FIVE?
BIG BEAR IS RIGHT. YOU ALL KNEW THE RULES.
THERÈS NO EXCUSE.
THIS IS THE SECOND TIME THIS WEEK BOYS FROM YOUR TROOP HAVE CAUSED A PROBLEM, BILL.
WHAT'S GOING ON AT YOUR CAMP?
I'M IN A BAD PLACE NOW. UNSUPERVISED SCOUTS AT THE FALLS IS A VIOLATION OF OUR CAMP'S INSURANCE POLICY.
THIS IS A BIG DEAL.
ARE WE GETTING SENT HOME?
ARE YOU GETTING SENT HOME?
SON, THAT'S THE LEAST OF YOUR WORRIES!

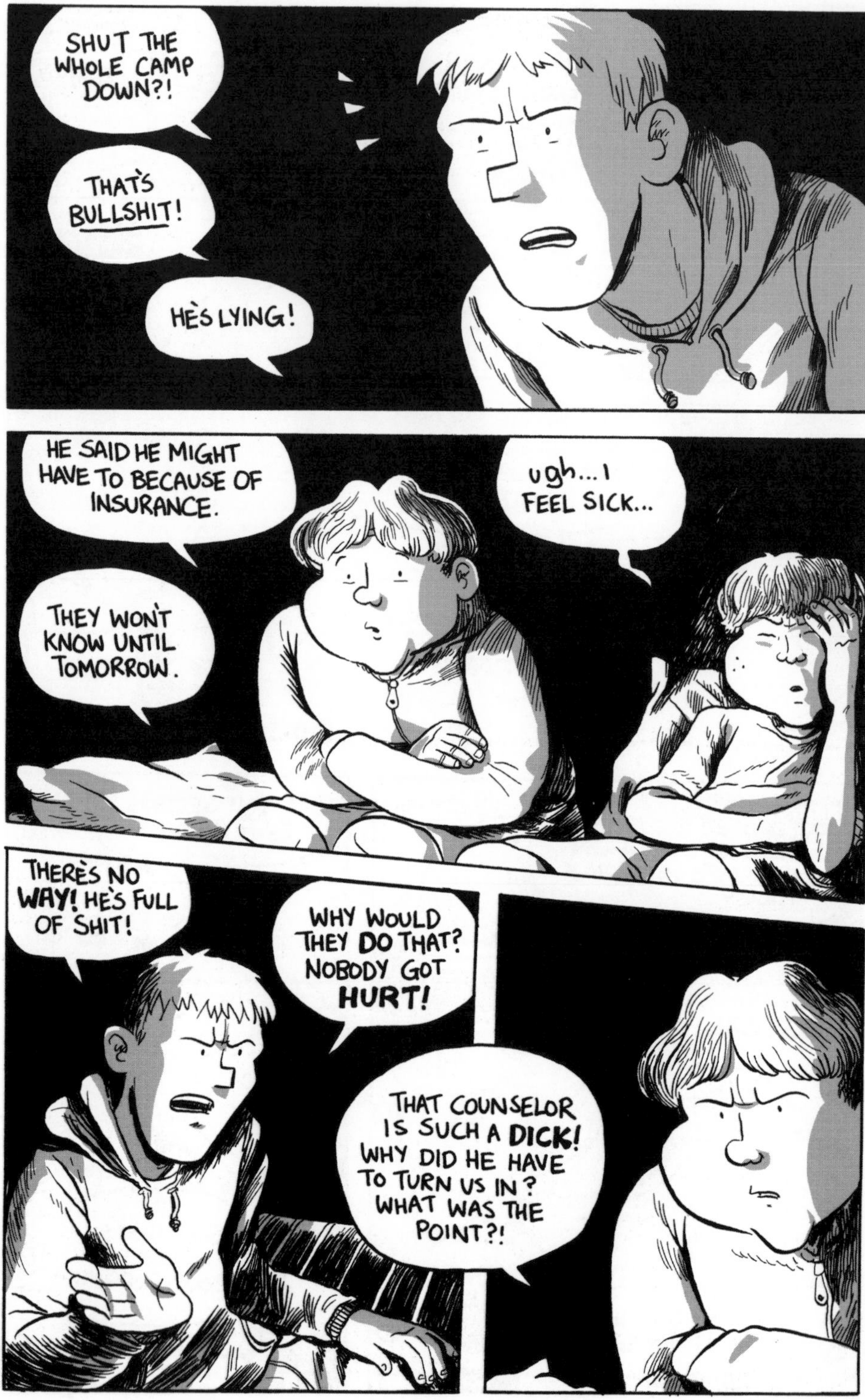
SHUT THE WHOLE CAMP DOWN?!
THAT'S BULLSHIT!
HE'S LYING!
HE SAID HE MIGHT HAVE TO BECAUSE OF INSURANCE.
THEY WON'T KNOW UNTIL TOMORROW.
ugh... I FEEL SICK...
THERE'S NO **WAY!** HE'S FULL OF SHIT!
WHY WOULD THEY **DO** THAT? NOBODY GOT **HURT!**
THAT COUNSELOR IS SUCH A **DICK!** WHY DID HE HAVE TO TURN US IN? WHAT WAS THE POINT?!

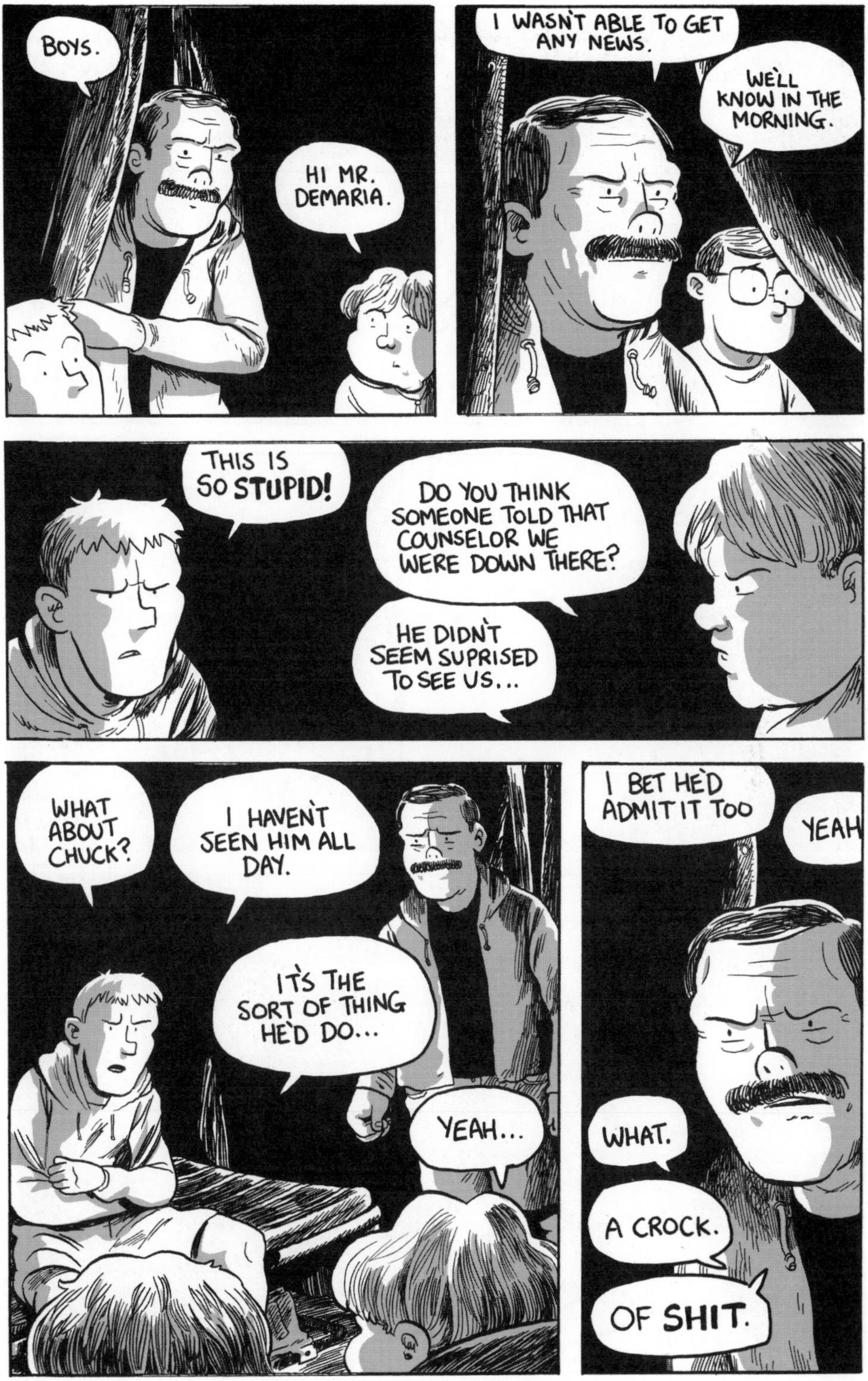
BOYS.
HI MR. DEMARIA.
I WASN'T ABLE TO GET ANY NEWS.
WE'LL KNOW IN THE MORNING.
THIS IS SO **STUPID!**
DO YOU THINK SOMEONE TOLD THAT COUNSELOR WE WERE DOWN THERE?
HE DIDN'T SEEM SUPRISED TO SEE US...
WHAT ABOUT CHUCK?
I HAVEN'T SEEN HIM ALL DAY.
IT'S THE SORT OF THING HE'D DO...
YEAH...
I BET HE'D ADMIT IT TOO
YEAH
WHAT.
A CROCK.
OF **SHIT**.

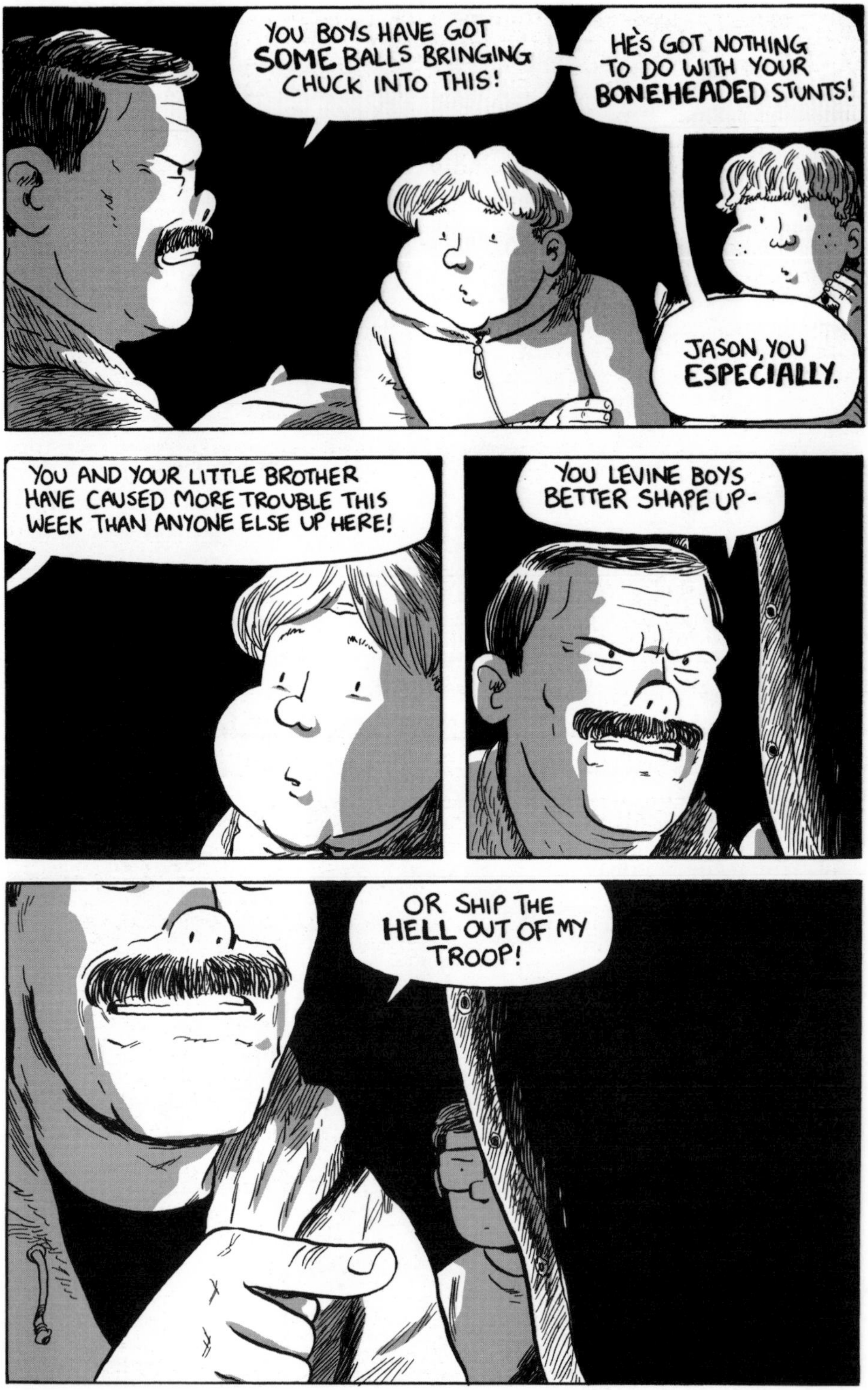
YOU BOYS HAVE GOT SOME BALLS BRINGING CHUCK INTO THIS!
HE'S GOT NOTHING TO DO WITH YOUR BONEHEADED STUNTS!
JASON, YOU ESPECIALLY.
YOU AND YOUR LITTLE BROTHER HAVE CAUSED MORE TROUBLE THIS WEEK THAN ANYONE ELSE UP HERE!
YOU LEVINE BOYS BETTER SHAPE UP-
OR SHIP THE HELL OUT OF MY TROOP!

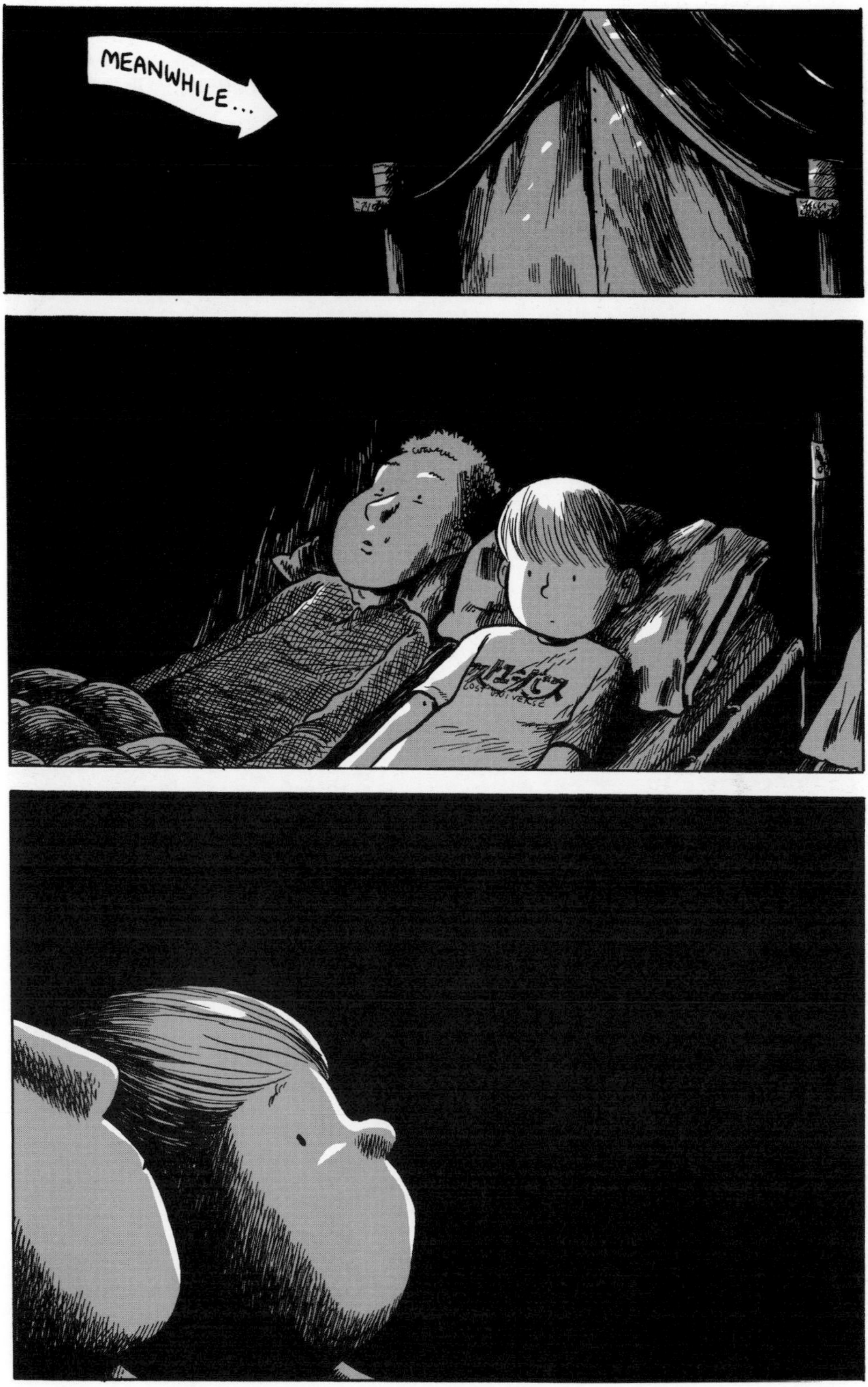
MEANWHILE...

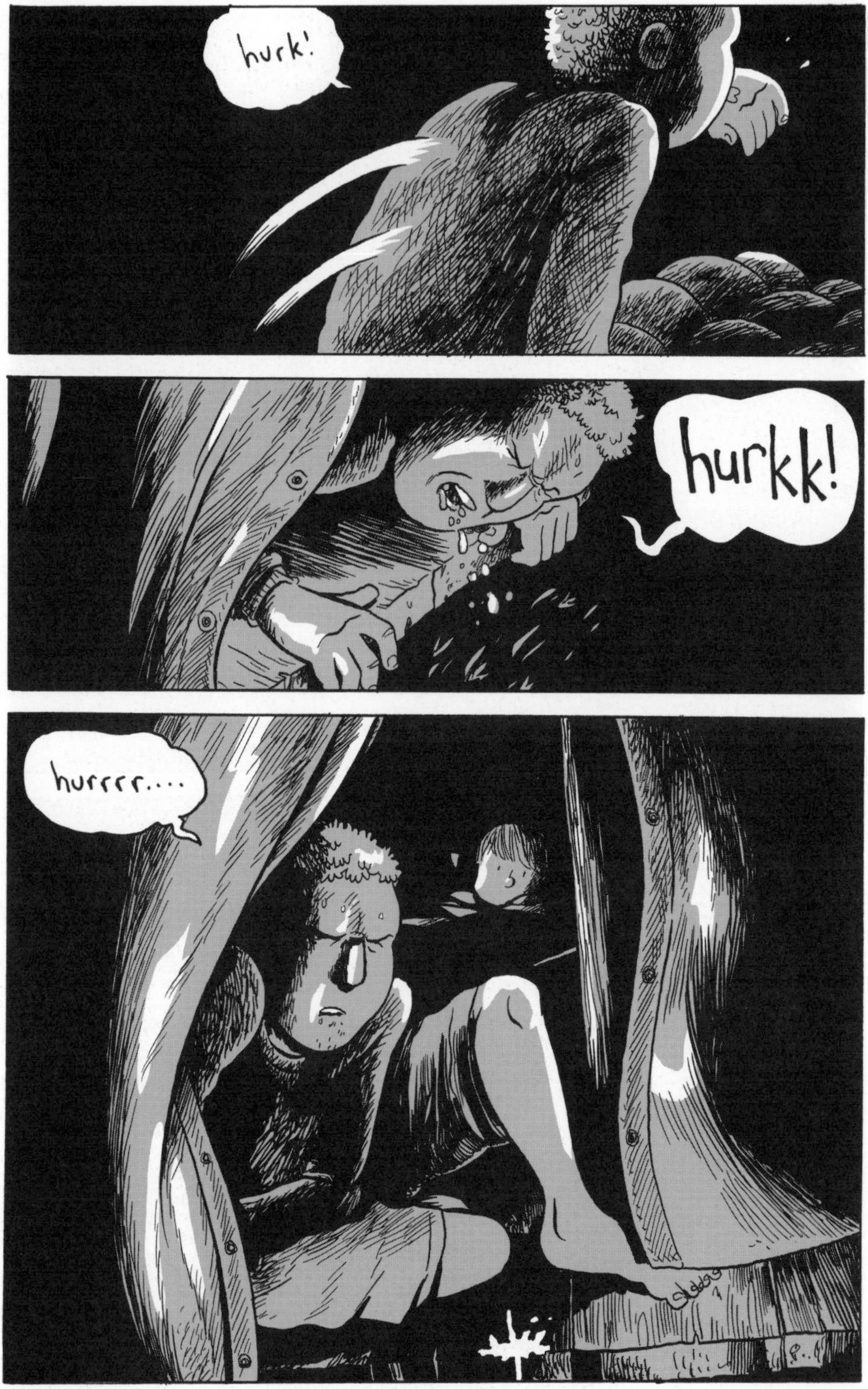
hurk!
hurkk!
hurrrr....

THURSDAY

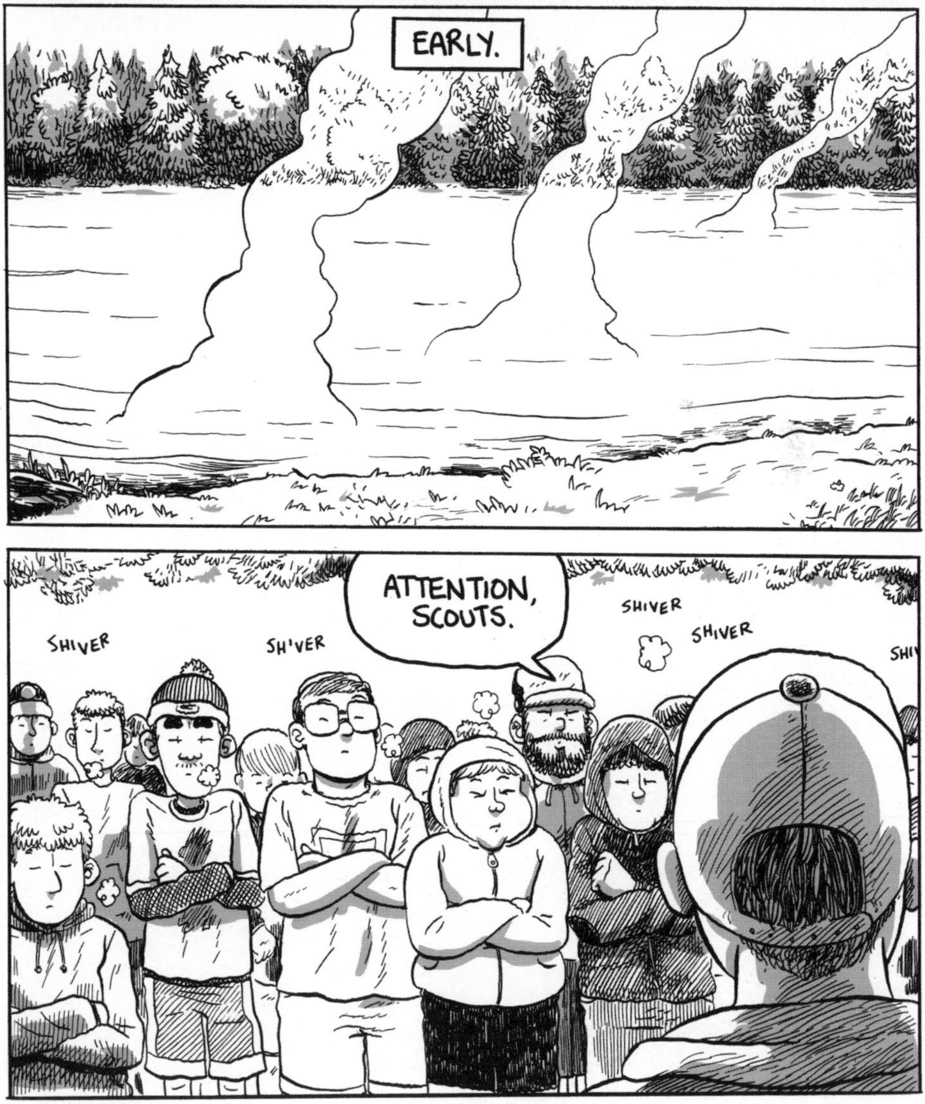
EARLY.
SHIVER
SH'VER
ATTENTION, SCOUTS.
SHIVER
SHIVER

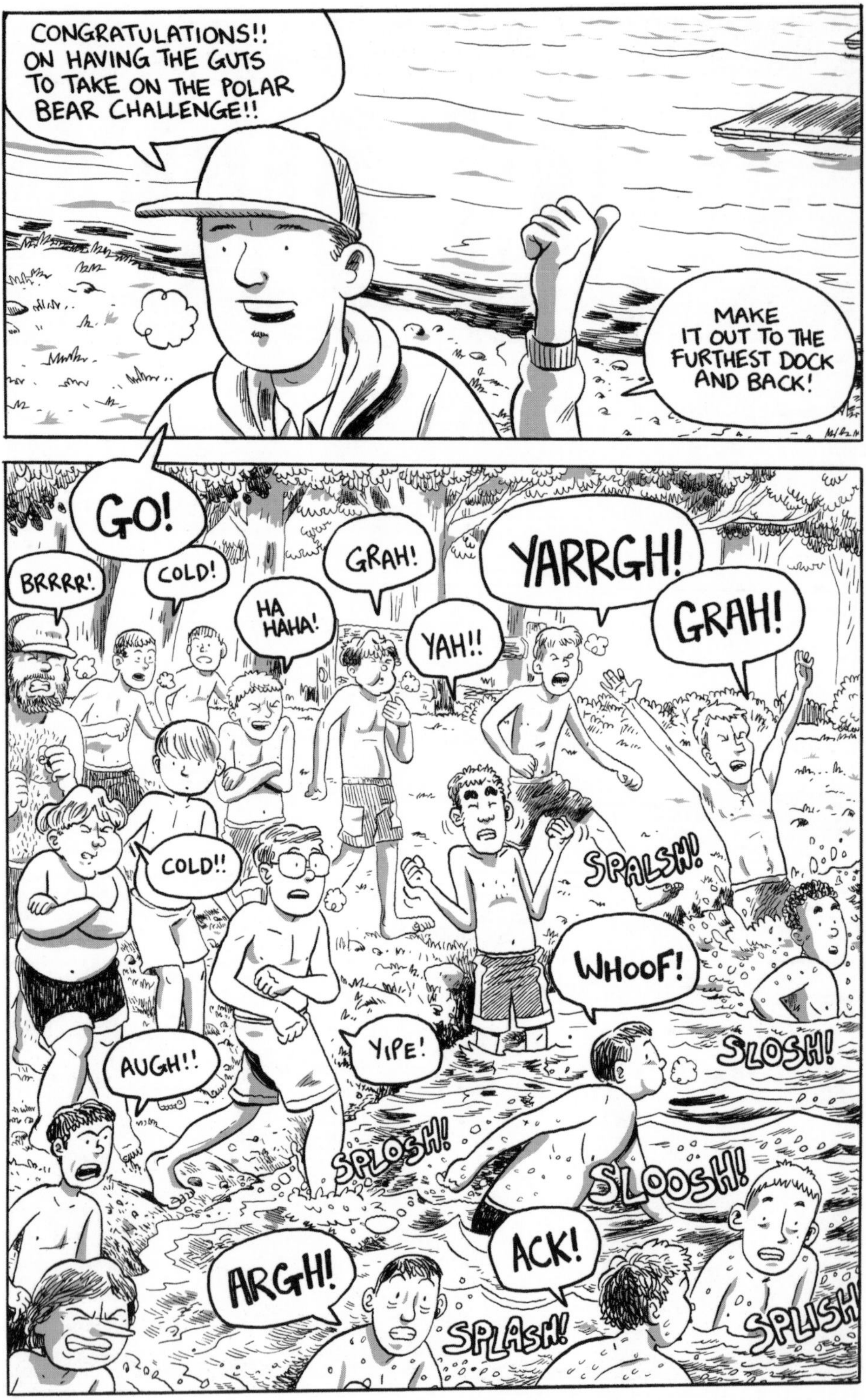

CONGRATULATIONS!! ON HAVING THE GUTS TO TAKE ON THE POLAR BEAR CHALLENGE!!
MAKE IT OUT TO THE FURTHEST DOCK AND BACK!
GO!
BRRRR!
COLD!
GRAH!
HA HAHA!
YAH!!
YARRGH!
GRAH!
COLD!!
SPALSH!
WHOOF!
YIPE!
AUGH!!
SLOSH!
SPLOSH!
SLOOSH!
ACK!
ARGH!
SPLASH!
SPLISH

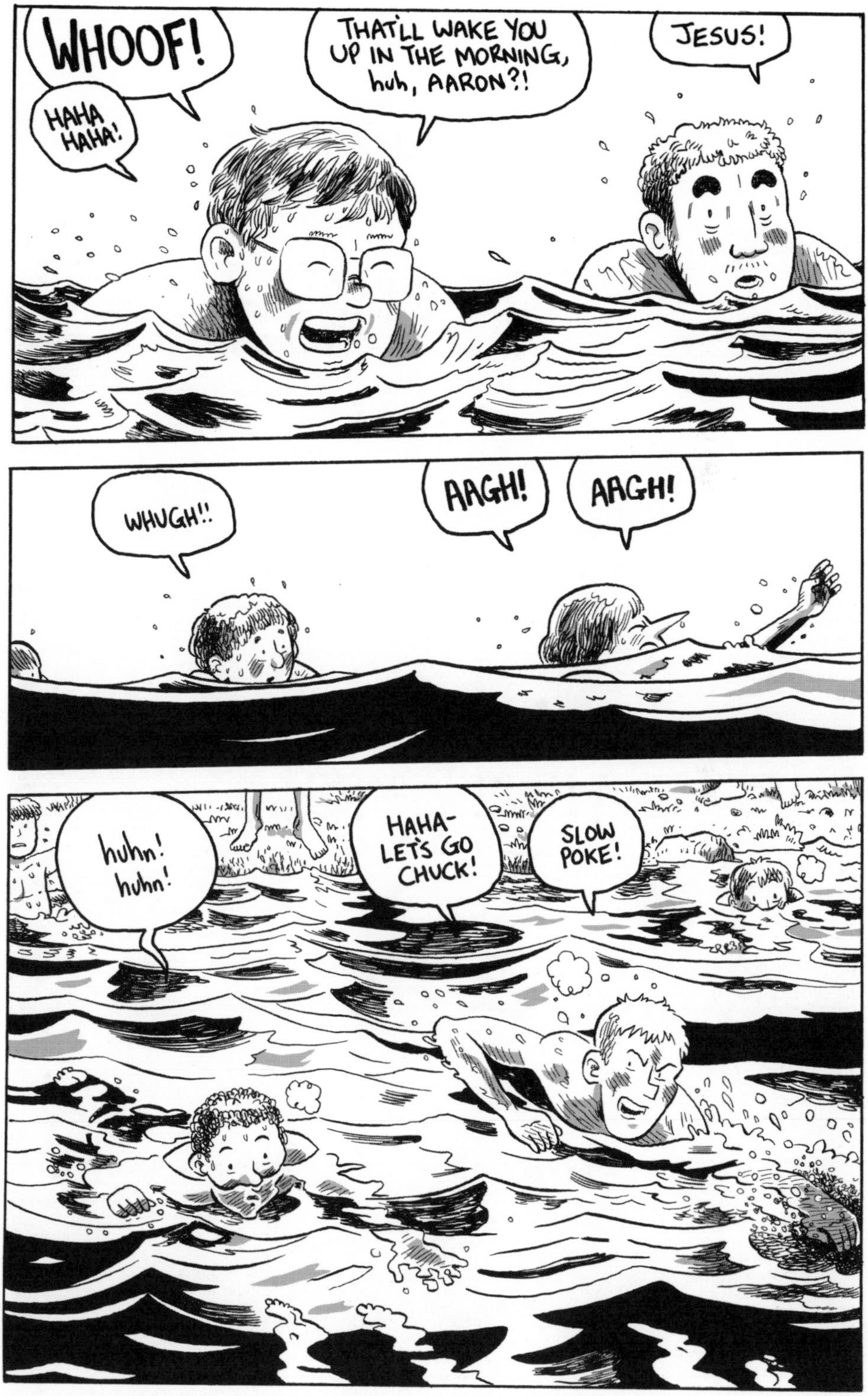
WHOOF!
HAHA HAHA!
THAT'LL WAKE YOU UP IN THE MORNING, huh, AARON?!
JESUS!
WHUGH!!
AAGH!
AAGH!
huhn! huhn!
HAHA- LET'S GO CHUCK!
SLOW POKE!

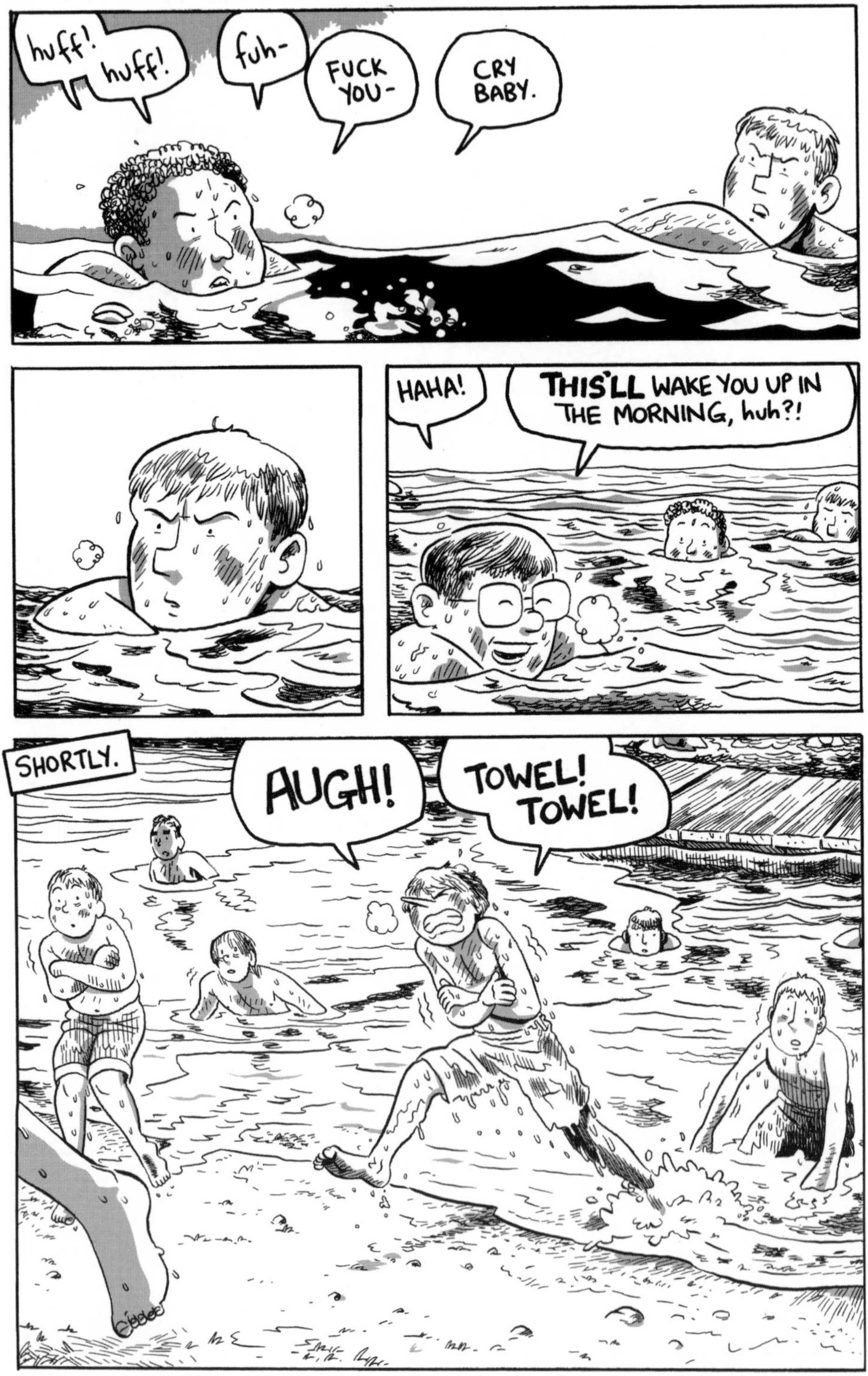
huff!
huff!
fuh-
FUCK YOU-
CRY BABY.
HAHA!
THIS'LL WAKE YOU UP IN THE MORNING, huh?!
SHORTLY.
AUGH!
TOWEL! TOWEL!

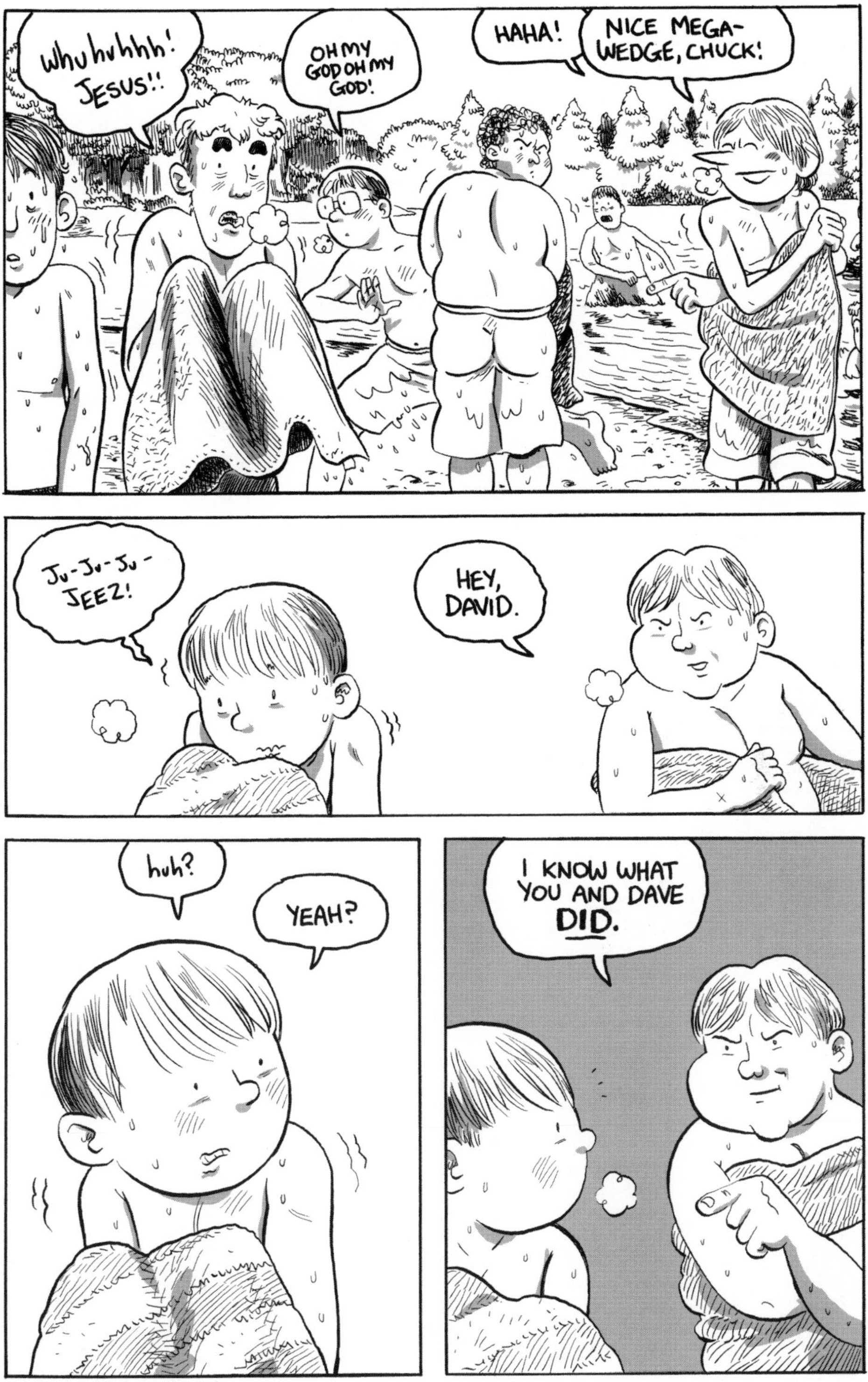

whuhuhhh! JESUS!!
OH MY GOD OH MY GOD!
HAHA!
NICE MEGA-WEDGE, CHUCK!
Ju-Ju-Ju-JEEZ!
HEY, DAVID.
huh?
YEAH?
I KNOW WHAT YOU AND DAVE DID.

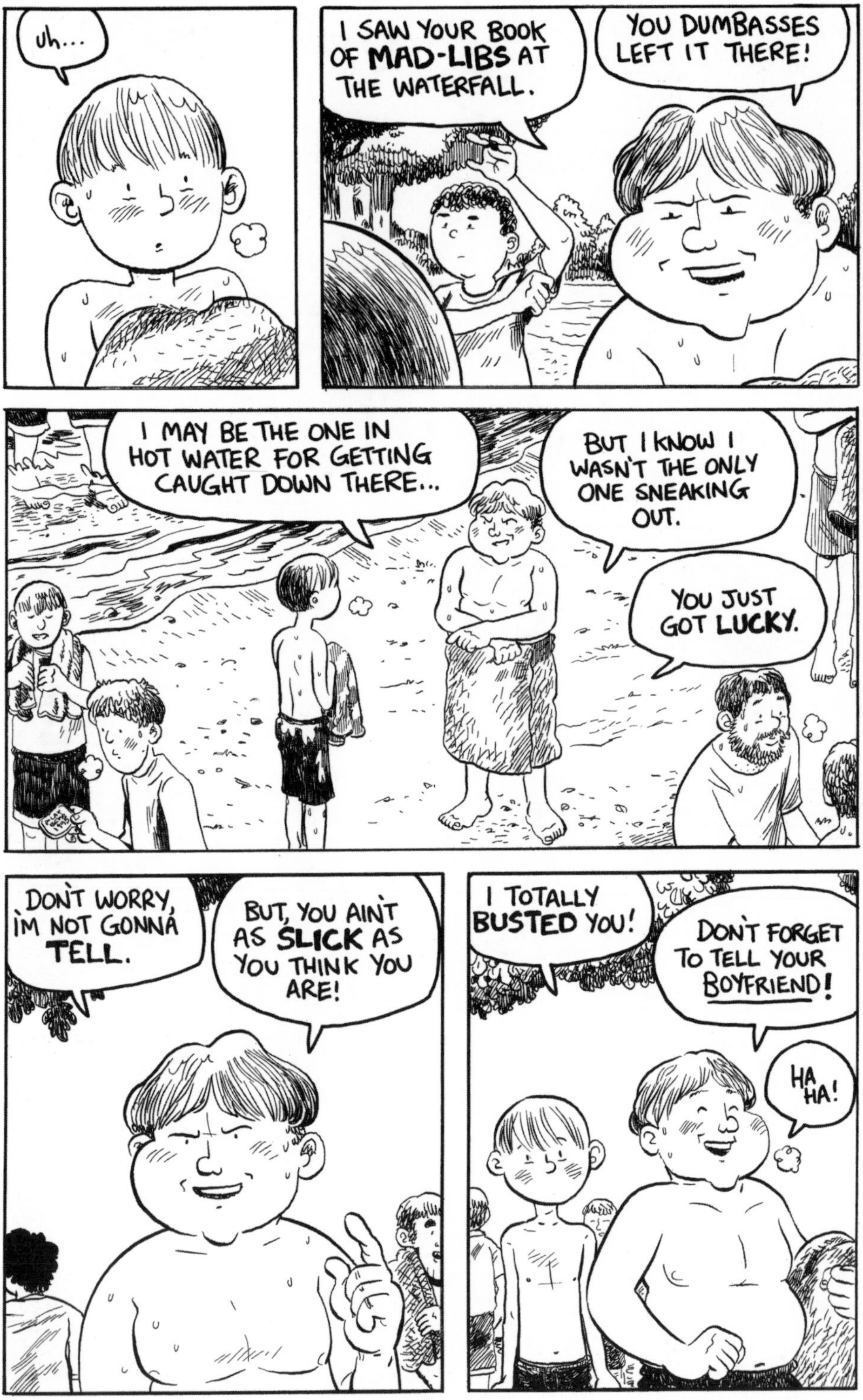

uh...
I SAW YOUR BOOK OF MAD-LIBS AT THE WATERFALL.
YOU DUMBASSES LEFT IT THERE!
I MAY BE THE ONE IN HOT WATER FOR GETTING CAUGHT DOWN THERE...
BUT I KNOW I WASN'T THE ONLY ONE SNEAKING OUT.
YOU JUST GOT LUCKY.
DON'T WORRY, I'M NOT GONNA TELL.
BUT, YOU AIN'T AS SLICK AS YOU THINK YOU ARE!
I TOTALLY BUSTED YOU!
DON'T FORGET TO TELL YOUR BOYFRIEND!
HA HA!

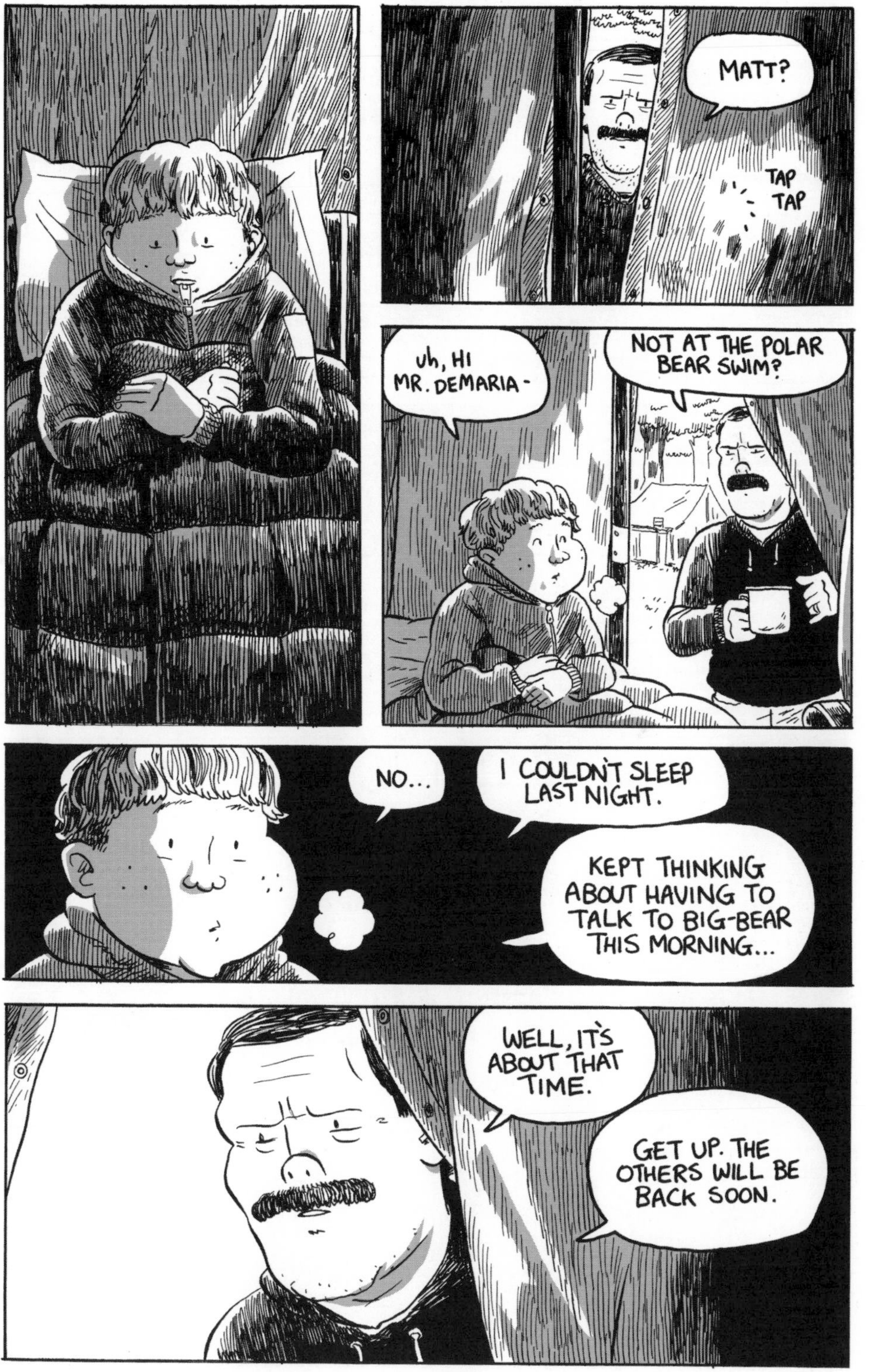
MATT?
TAP TAP
uh, HI MR. DEMARIA -
NOT AT THE POLAR BEAR SWIM?
NO...
I COULDN'T SLEEP LAST NIGHT.
KEPT THINKING ABOUT HAVING TO TALK TO BIG-BEAR THIS MORNING...
WELL, IT'S ABOUT THAT TIME.
GET UP. THE OTHERS WILL BE BACK SOON.

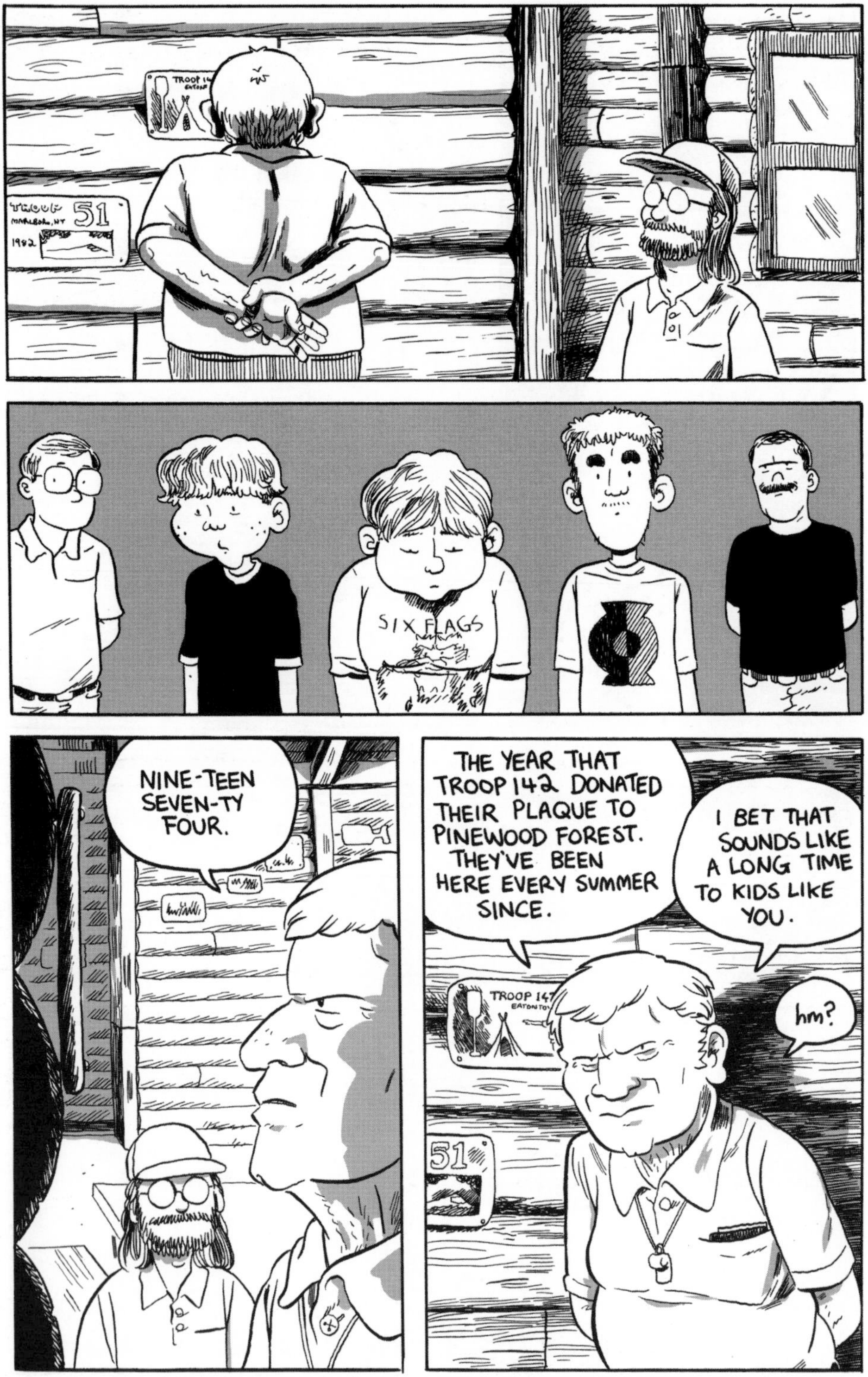
TROOP 51
1982
SIX FLAGS
NINE-TEEN SEVEN-TY FOUR.
THE YEAR THAT TROOP 142 DONATED THEIR PLAQUE TO PINEWOOD FOREST. THEY'VE BEEN HERE EVERY SUMMER SINCE.
I BET THAT SOUNDS LIKE A LONG TIME TO KIDS LIKE YOU.
hm?

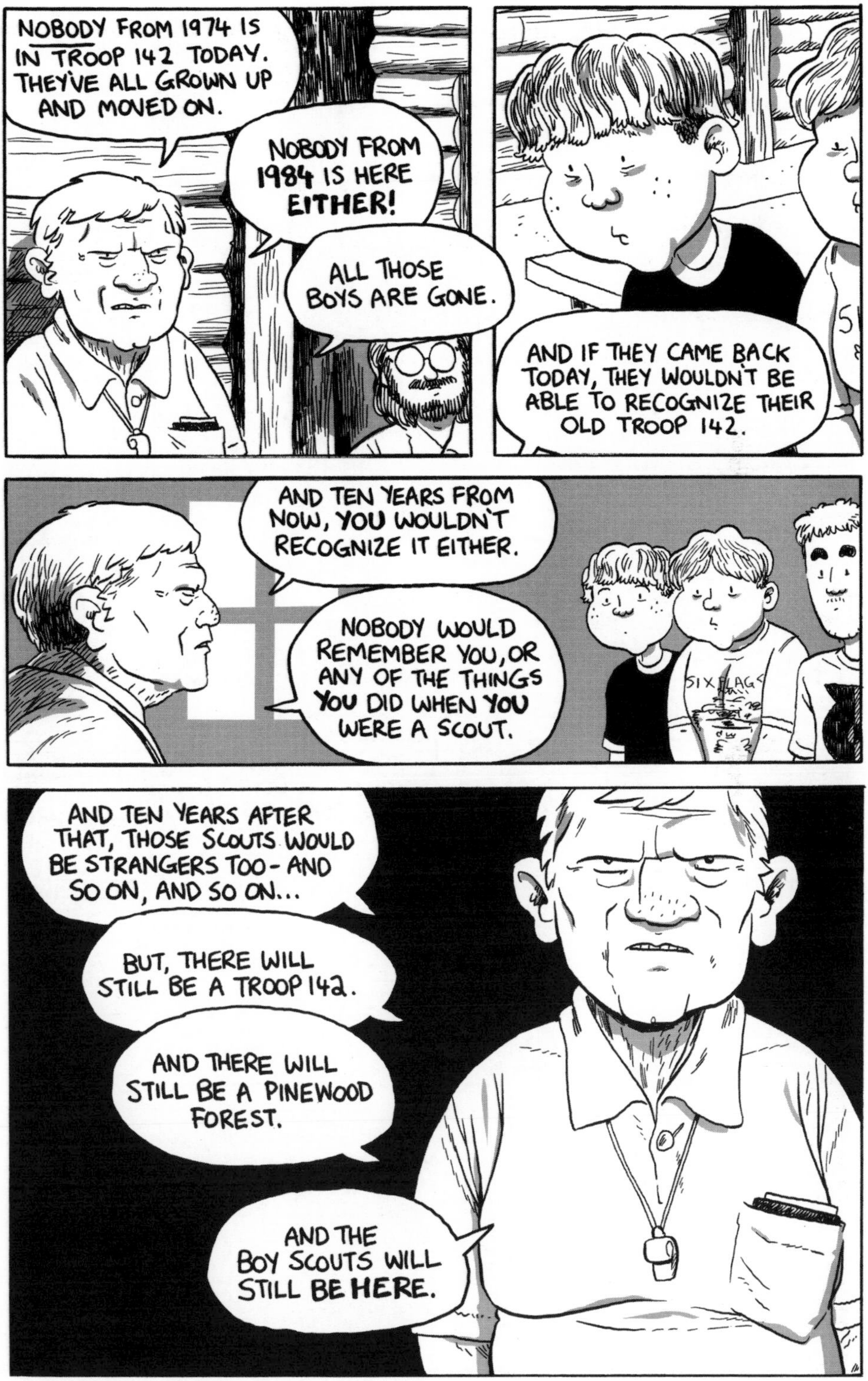
NOBODY FROM 1974 IS IN TROOP 142 TODAY. THEY'VE ALL GROWN UP AND MOVED ON.
NOBODY FROM 1984 IS HERE EITHER!
ALL THOSE BOYS ARE GONE.
AND IF THEY CAME BACK TODAY, THEY WOULDN'T BE ABLE TO RECOGNIZE THEIR OLD TROOP 142.
AND TEN YEARS FROM NOW, YOU WOULDN'T RECOGNIZE IT EITHER.
NOBODY WOULD REMEMBER YOU, OR ANY OF THE THINGS YOU DID WHEN YOU WERE A SCOUT.
AND TEN YEARS AFTER THAT, THOSE SCOUTS WOULD BE STRANGERS TOO - AND SO ON, AND SO ON...
BUT, THERE WILL STILL BE A TROOP 142.
AND THERE WILL STILL BE A PINEWOOD FOREST.
AND THE BOY SCOUTS WILL STILL BE HERE.

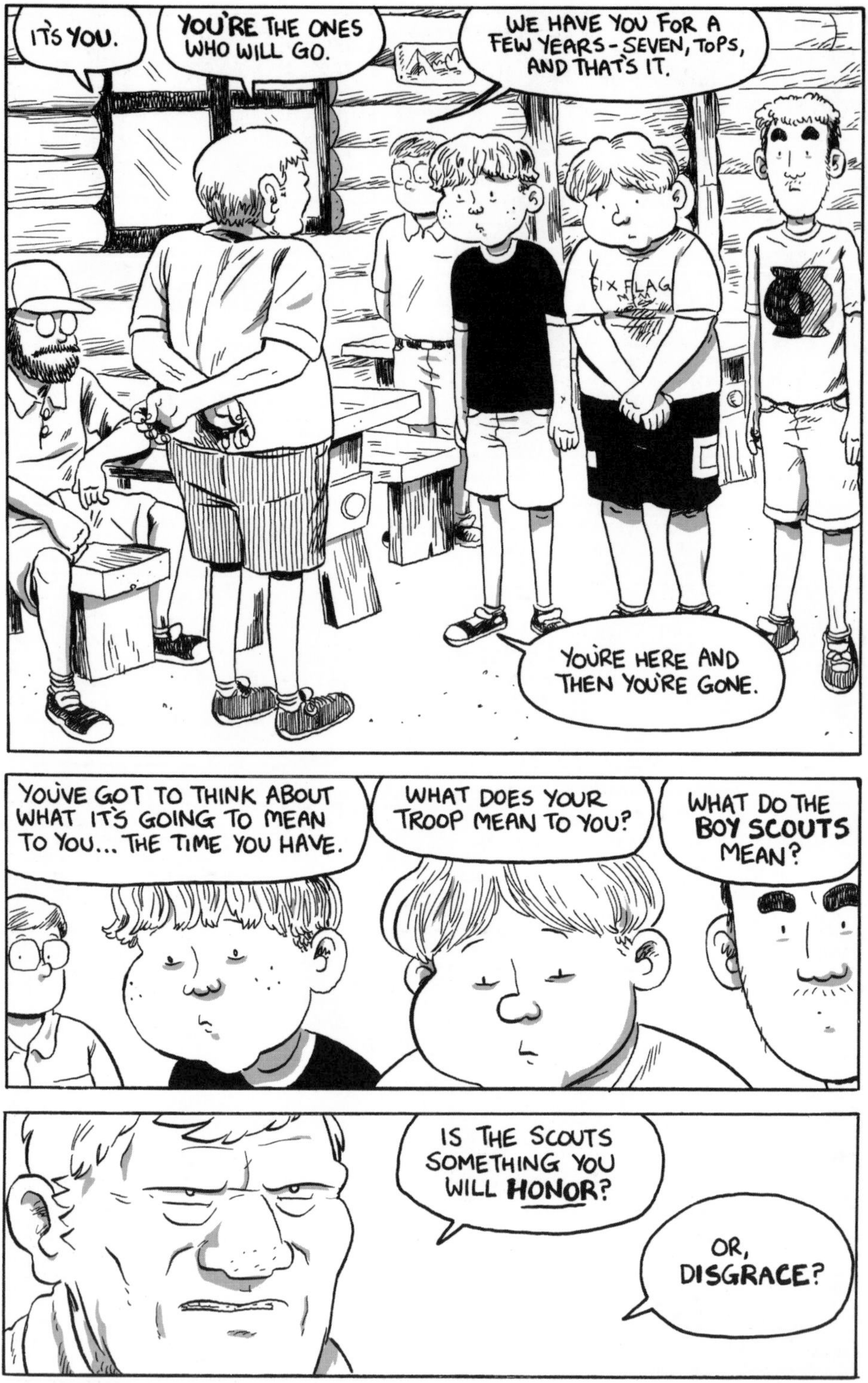

IT'S YOU.
YOU'RE THE ONES WHO WILL GO.
WE HAVE YOU FOR A FEW YEARS - SEVEN, TOPS, AND THAT'S IT.
SIX FLAG
YOU'RE HERE AND THEN YOU'RE GONE.
YOU'VE GOT TO THINK ABOUT WHAT IT'S GOING TO MEAN TO YOU... THE TIME YOU HAVE.
WHAT DOES YOUR TROOP MEAN TO YOU?
WHAT DO THE BOY SCOUTS MEAN?
IS THE SCOUTS SOMETHING YOU WILL HONOR?
OR, DISGRACE?

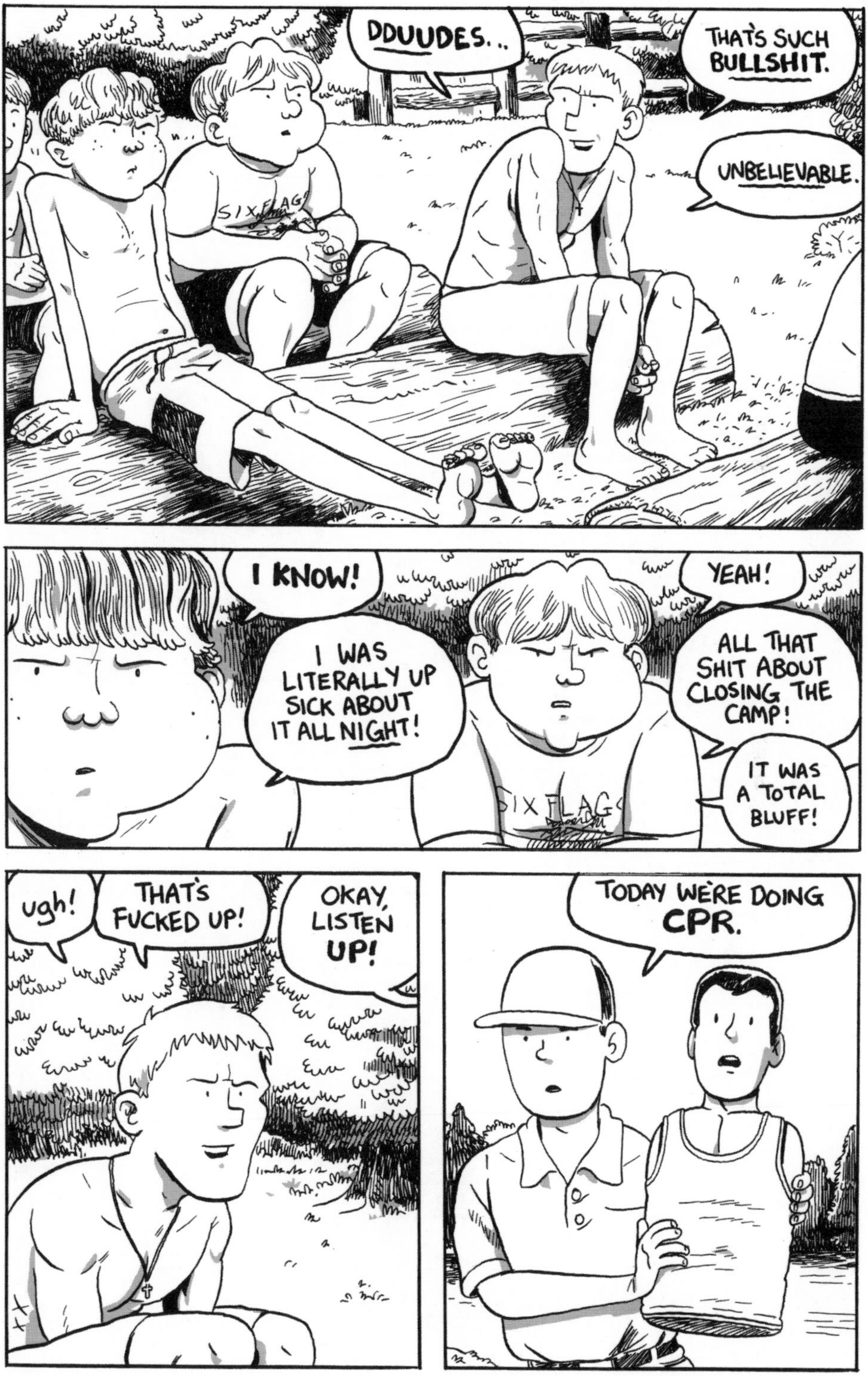
DDUUDES...
THAT'S SUCH BULLSHIT.
UNBELIEVABLE.
SIX FLAGS
I KNOW!
YEAH!
I WAS LITERALLY UP SICK ABOUT IT ALL NIGHT!
ALL THAT SHIT ABOUT CLOSING THE CAMP!
IT WAS A TOTAL BLUFF!
SIX FLAGS
ugh!
THAT'S FUCKED UP!
OKAY, LISTEN UP!
TODAY WE'RE DOING CPR.

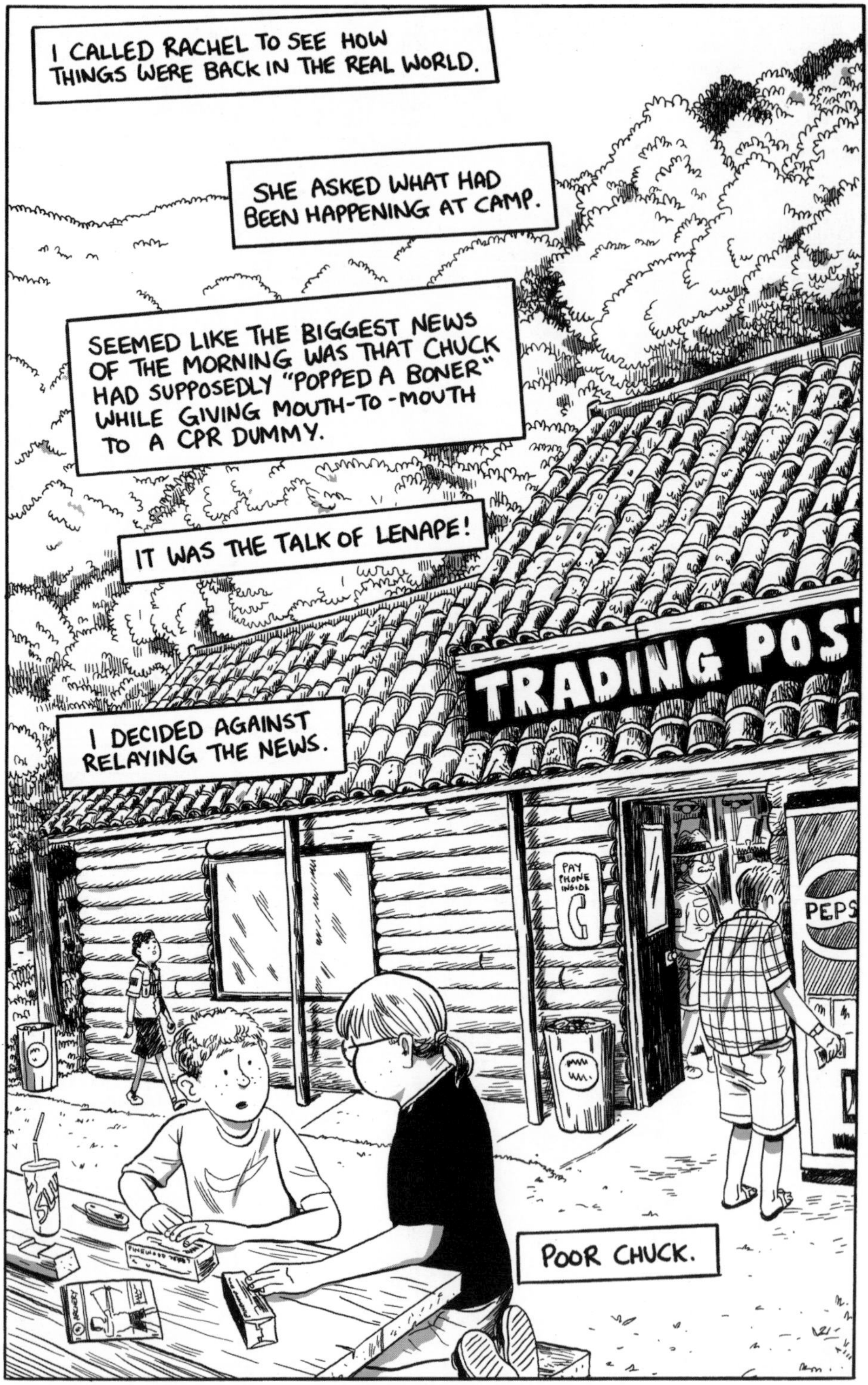
I CALLED RACHEL TO SEE HOW THINGS WERE BACK IN THE REAL WORLD.
SHE ASKED WHAT HAD BEEN HAPPENING AT CAMP.
SEEMED LIKE THE BIGGEST NEWS OF THE MORNING WAS THAT CHUCK HAD SUPPOSEDLY "POPPED A BONER" WHILE GIVING MOUTH-TO-MOUTH TO A CPR DUMMY.
IT WAS THE TALK OF LENAPE!
I DECIDED AGAINST RELAYING THE NEWS.
TRADING POS
PAY PHONE INSIDE
PEPS
POOR CHUCK.

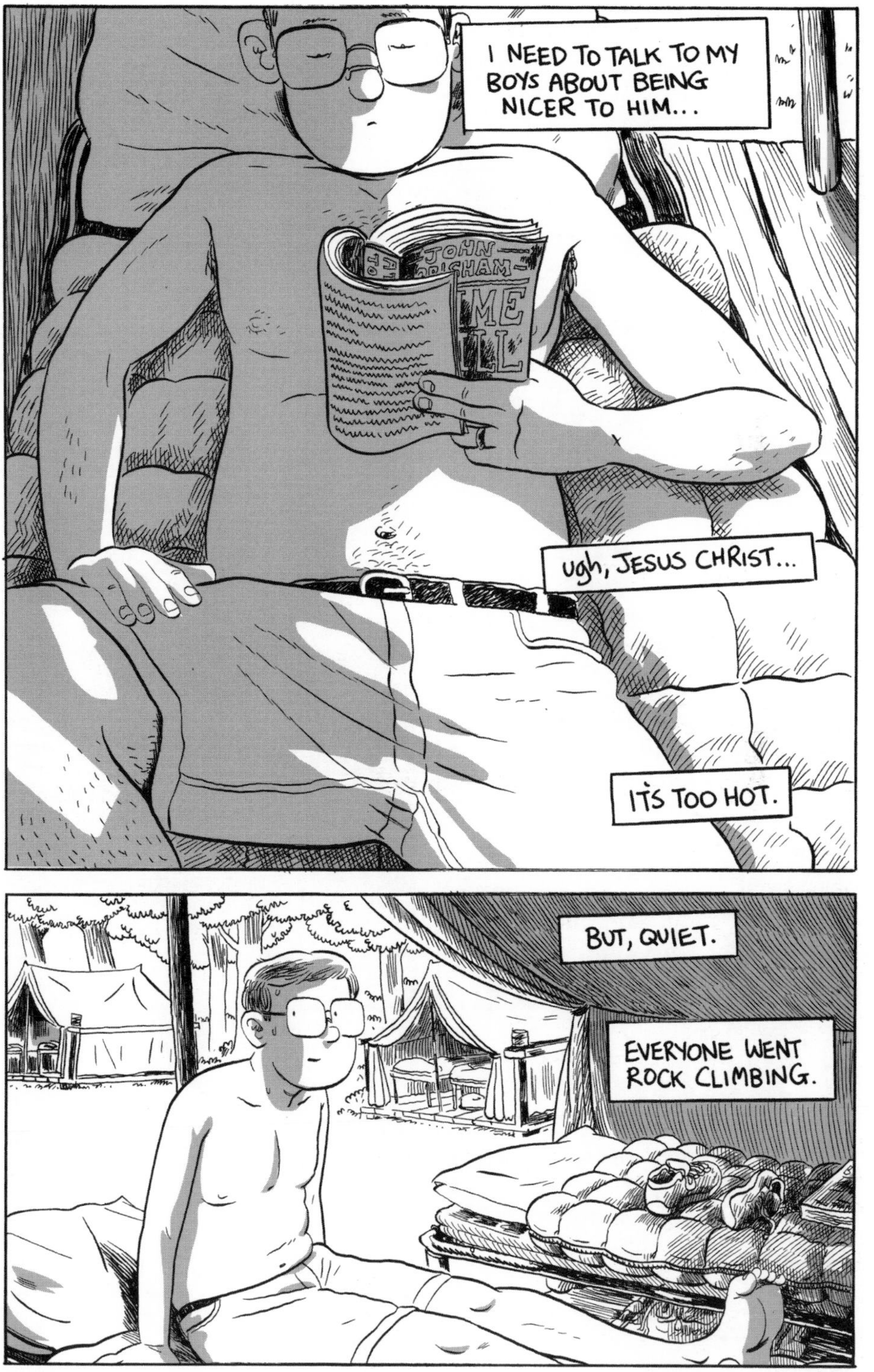
I NEED TO TALK TO MY BOYS ABOUT BEING NICER TO HIM...
ugh, JESUS CHRIST...
IT'S TOO HOT.
BUT, QUIET.
EVERYONE WENT ROCK CLIMBING.

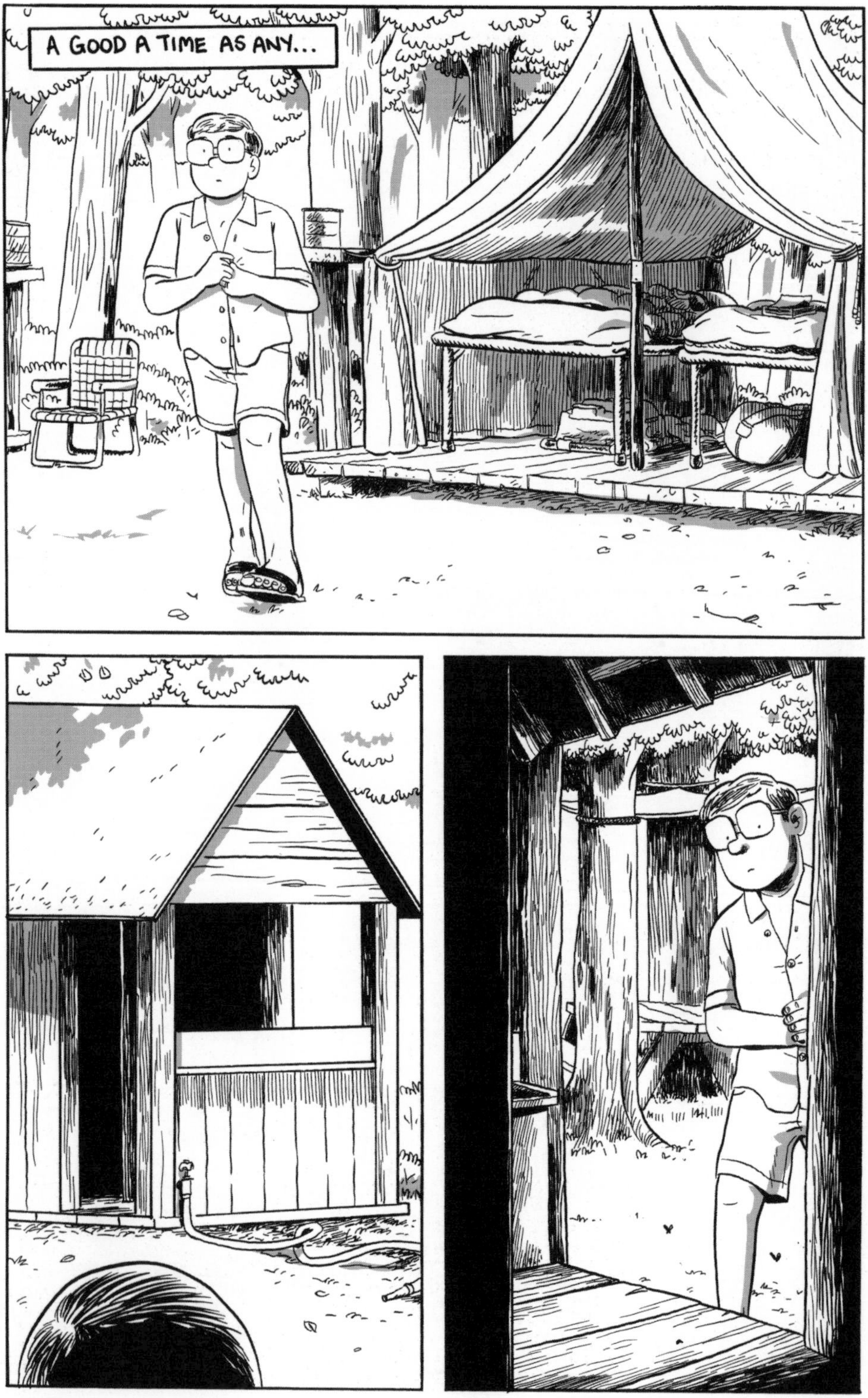
A GOOD A TIME AS ANY...

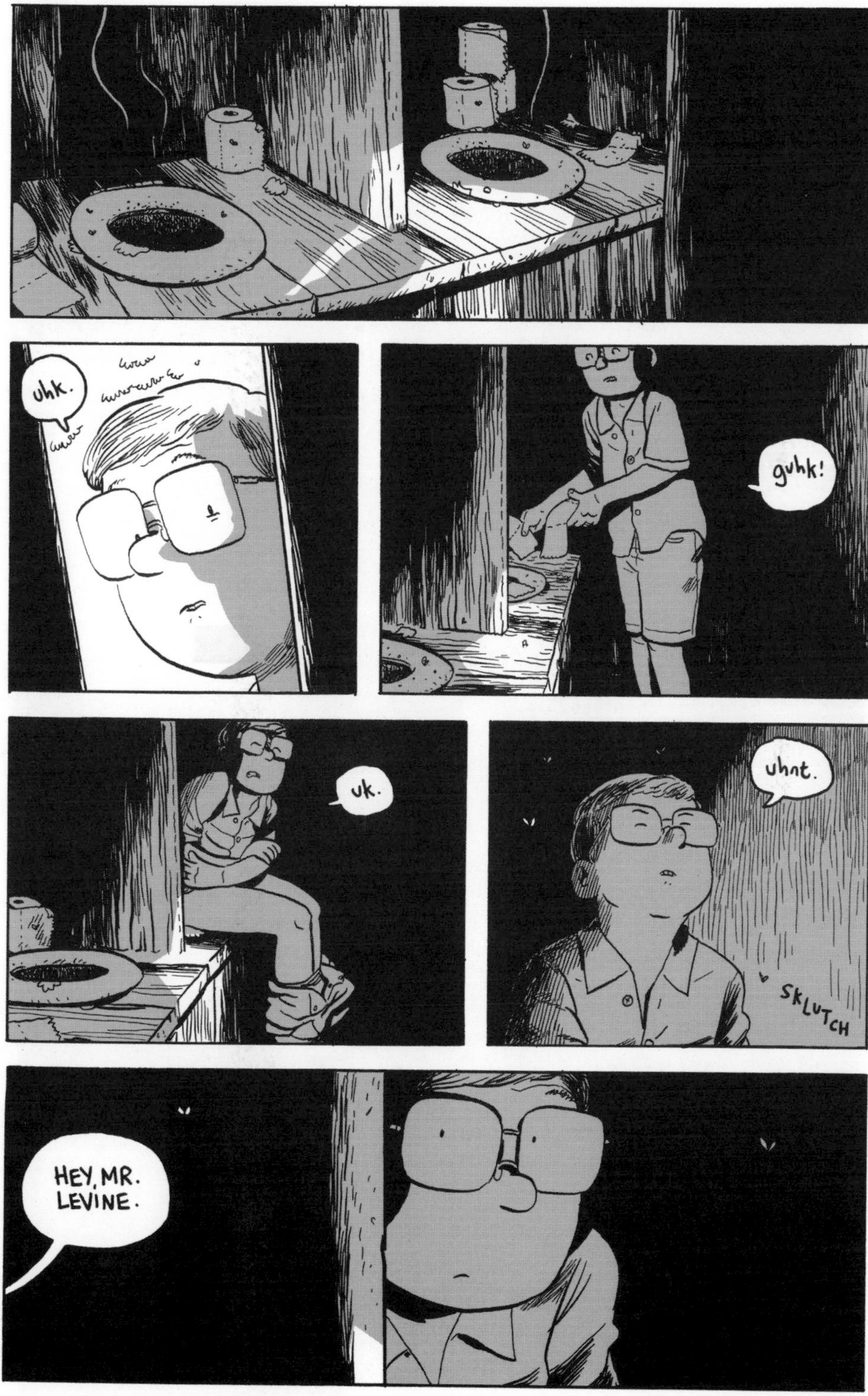
uhk.
guhk!
uk.
uhnt.
SKLUTCH
HEY, MR. LEVINE.

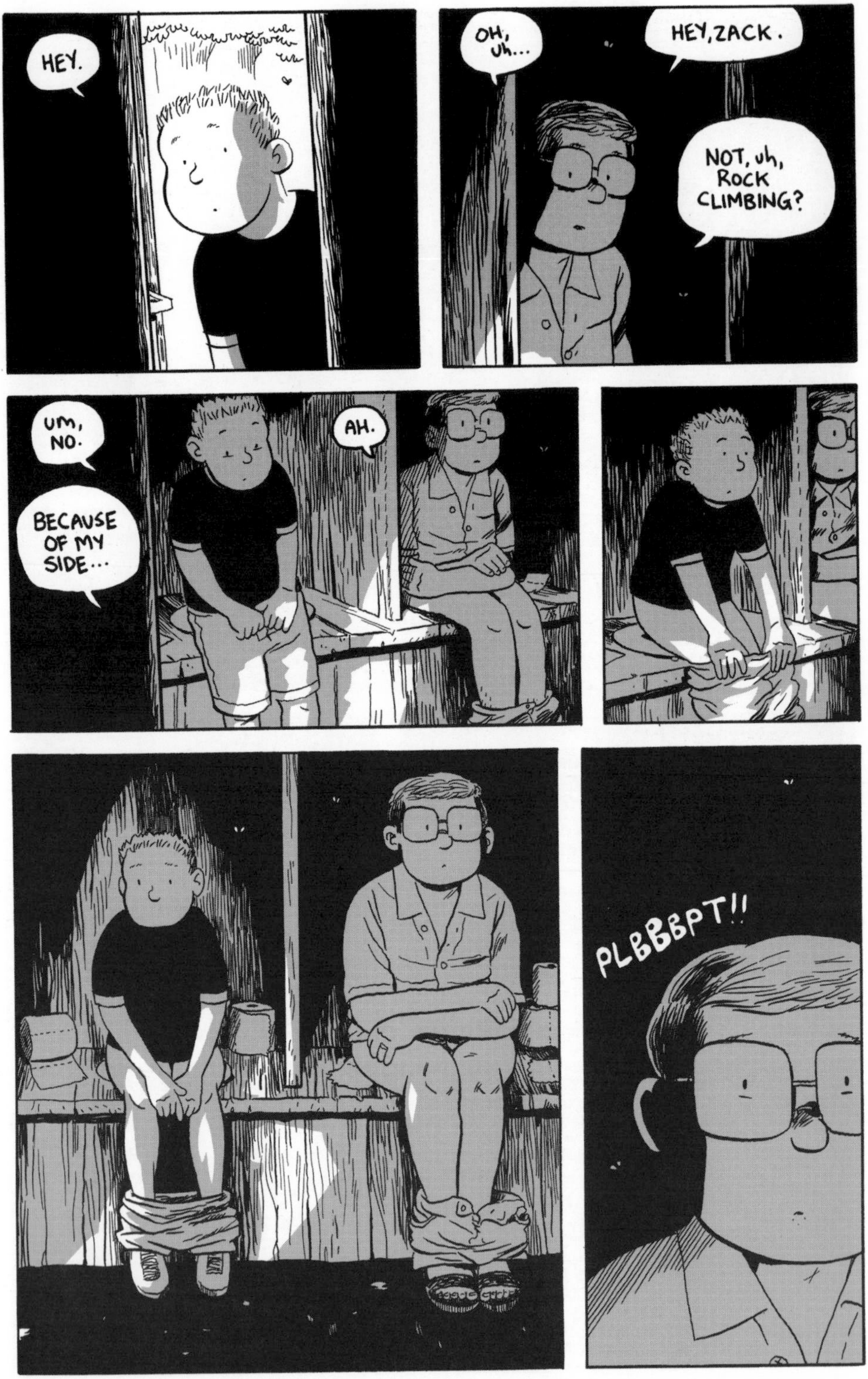
HEY.
OH, uh...
HEY, ZACK.
NOT, uh, ROCK CLIMBING?
um, NO.
BECAUSE OF MY SIDE...
AH.
PLBBBPT!!

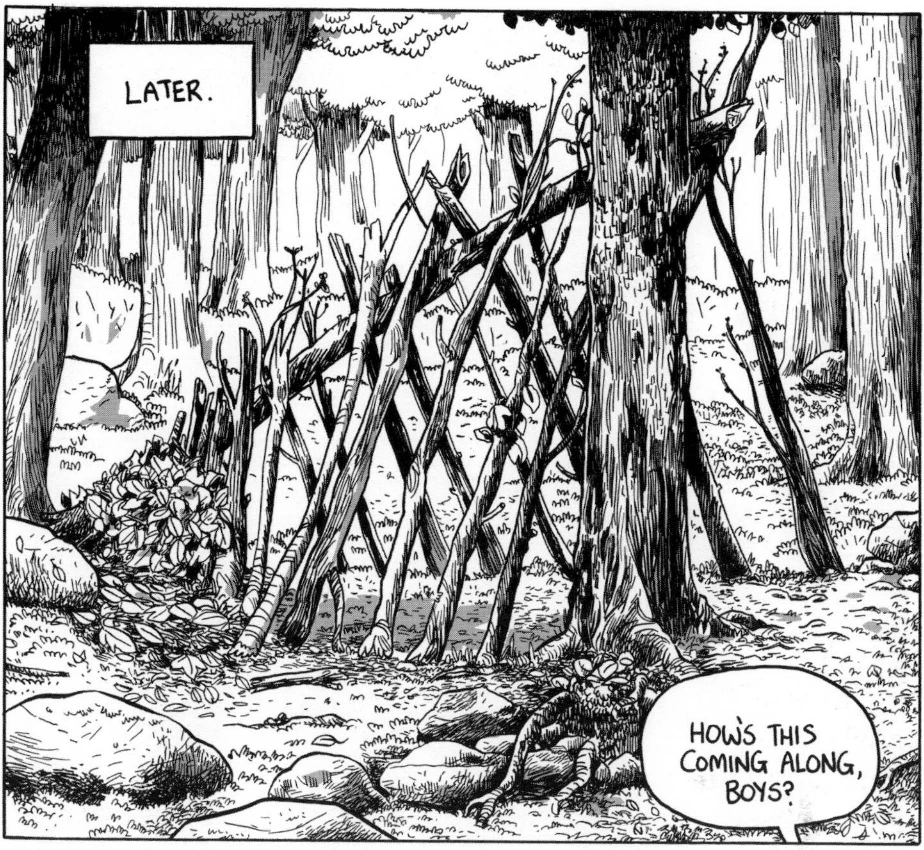
LATER.
HOW'S THIS COMING ALONG, BOYS?

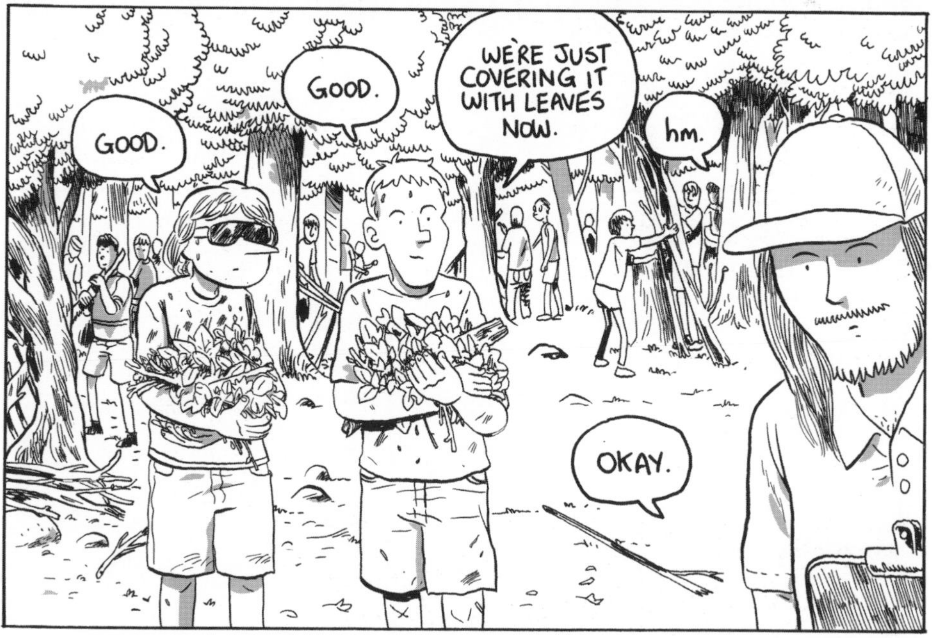
GOOD.
GOOD.
WE'RE JUST COVERING IT WITH LEAVES NOW.
hm.
OKAY.

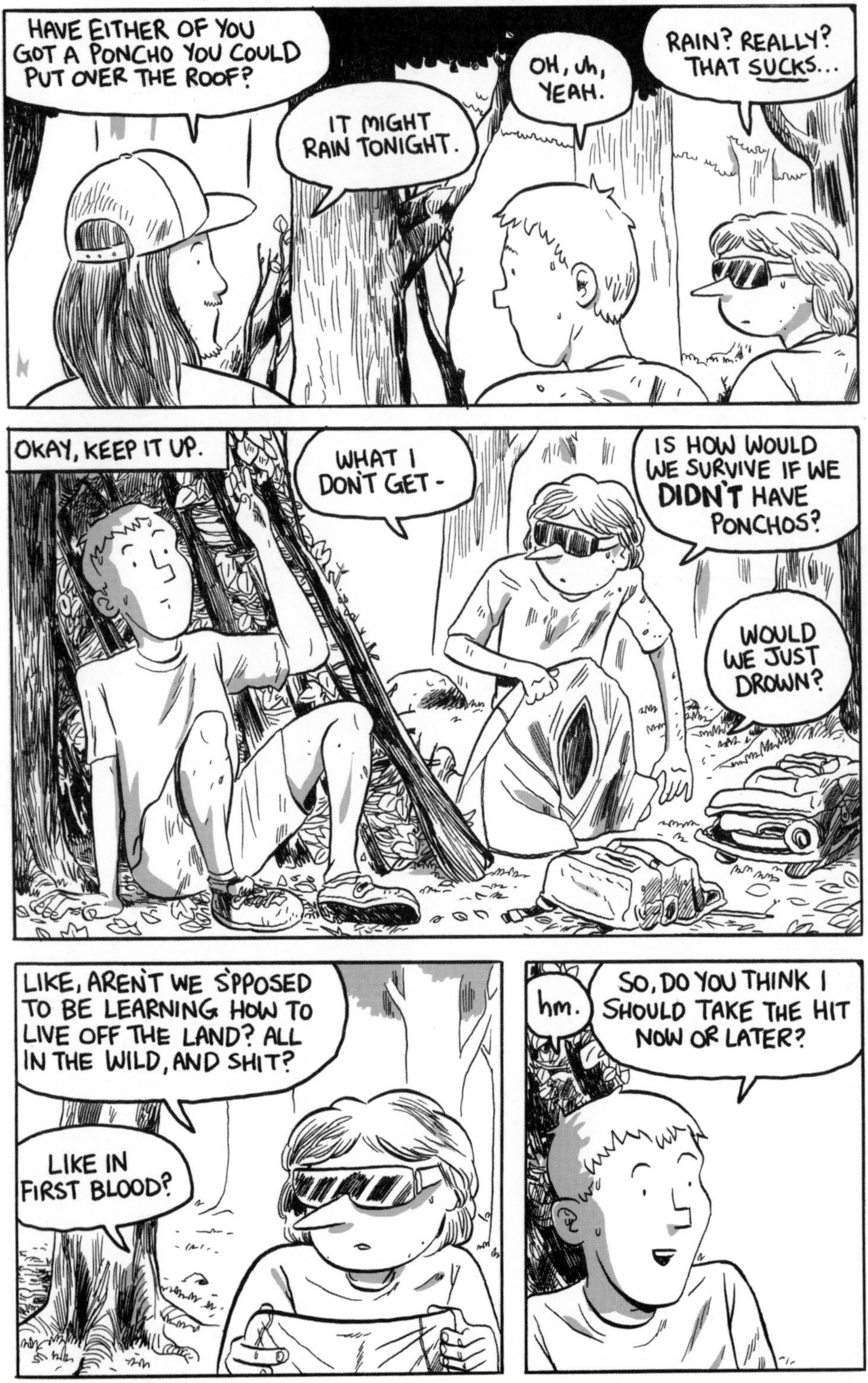
HAVE EITHER OF YOU GOT A PONCHO YOU COULD PUT OVER THE ROOF?
IT MIGHT RAIN TONIGHT.
OH, uh, YEAH.
RAIN? REALLY? THAT SUCKS...
OKAY, KEEP IT UP.
WHAT I DON'T GET -
IS HOW WOULD WE SURVIVE IF WE DIDN'T HAVE PONCHOS?
WOULD WE JUST DROWN?
LIKE, AREN'T WE S'PPOSED TO BE LEARNING HOW TO LIVE OFF THE LAND? ALL IN THE WILD, AND SHIT?
LIKE IN FIRST BLOOD?
hm.
SO, DO YOU THINK I SHOULD TAKE THE HIT NOW OR LATER?

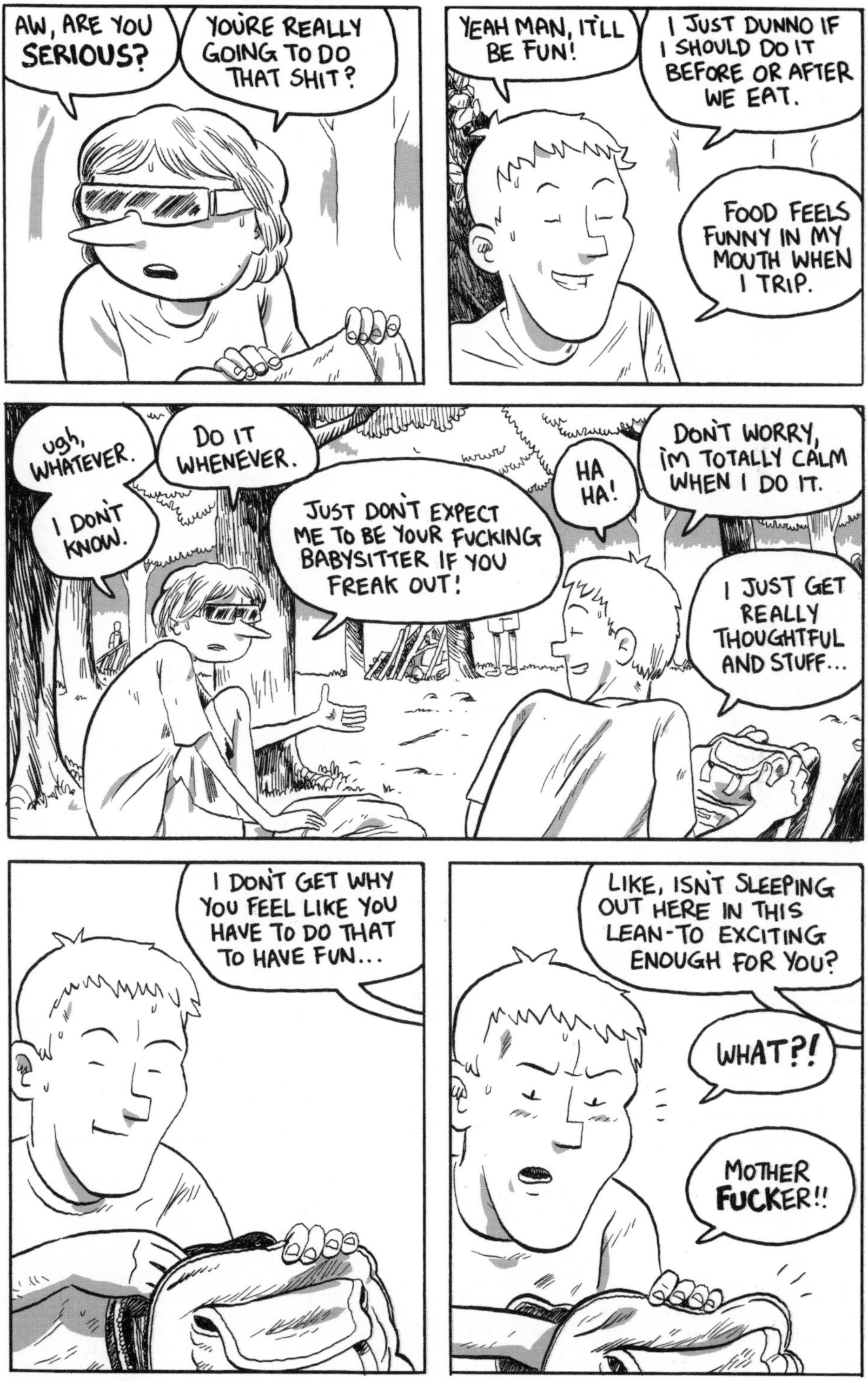
AW, ARE YOU SERIOUS?
YOU'RE REALLY GOING TO DO THAT SHIT?
YEAH MAN, IT'LL BE FUN!
I JUST DUNNO IF I SHOULD DO IT BEFORE OR AFTER WE EAT.
FOOD FEELS FUNNY IN MY MOUTH WHEN I TRIP.
ugh, WHATEVER.
I DON'T KNOW.
DO IT WHENEVER.
JUST DON'T EXPECT ME TO BE YOUR FUCKING BABYSITTER IF YOU FREAK OUT!
HA HA!
DON'T WORRY, I'M TOTALLY CALM WHEN I DO IT.
I JUST GET REALLY THOUGHTFUL AND STUFF...
I DON'T GET WHY YOU FEEL LIKE YOU HAVE TO DO THAT TO HAVE FUN...
LIKE, ISN'T SLEEPING OUT HERE IN THIS LEAN-TO EXCITING ENOUGH FOR YOU?
WHAT?!
MOTHER FUCKER!!

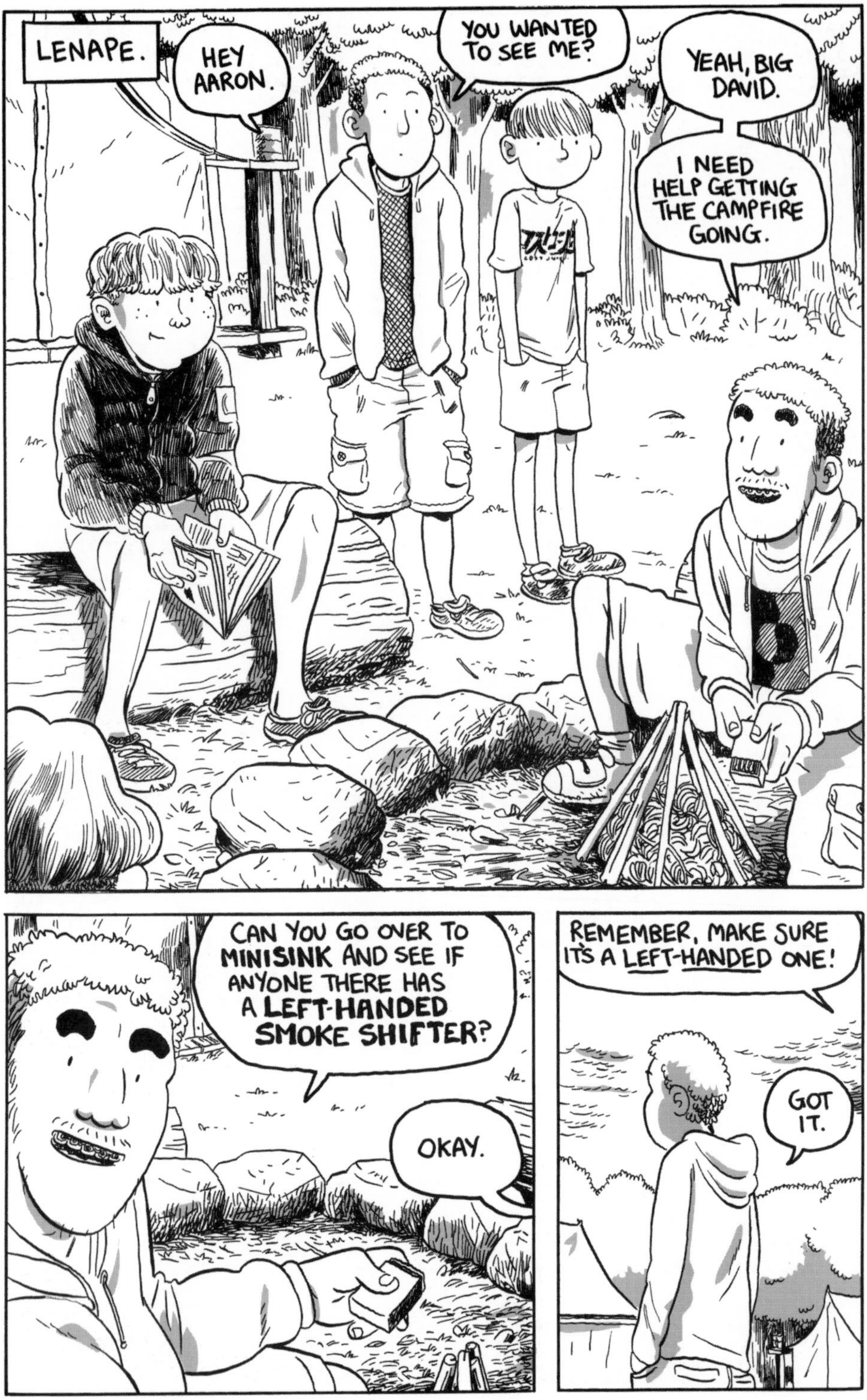
LENAPE.
HEY AARON.
YOU WANTED TO SEE ME?
YEAH, BIG DAVID.
I NEED HELP GETTING THE CAMPFIRE GOING.
CAN YOU GO OVER TO MINISINK AND SEE IF ANYONE THERE HAS A LEFT-HANDED SMOKE SHIFTER?
OKAY.
REMEMBER, MAKE SURE IT'S A LEFT-HANDED ONE!
GOT IT.

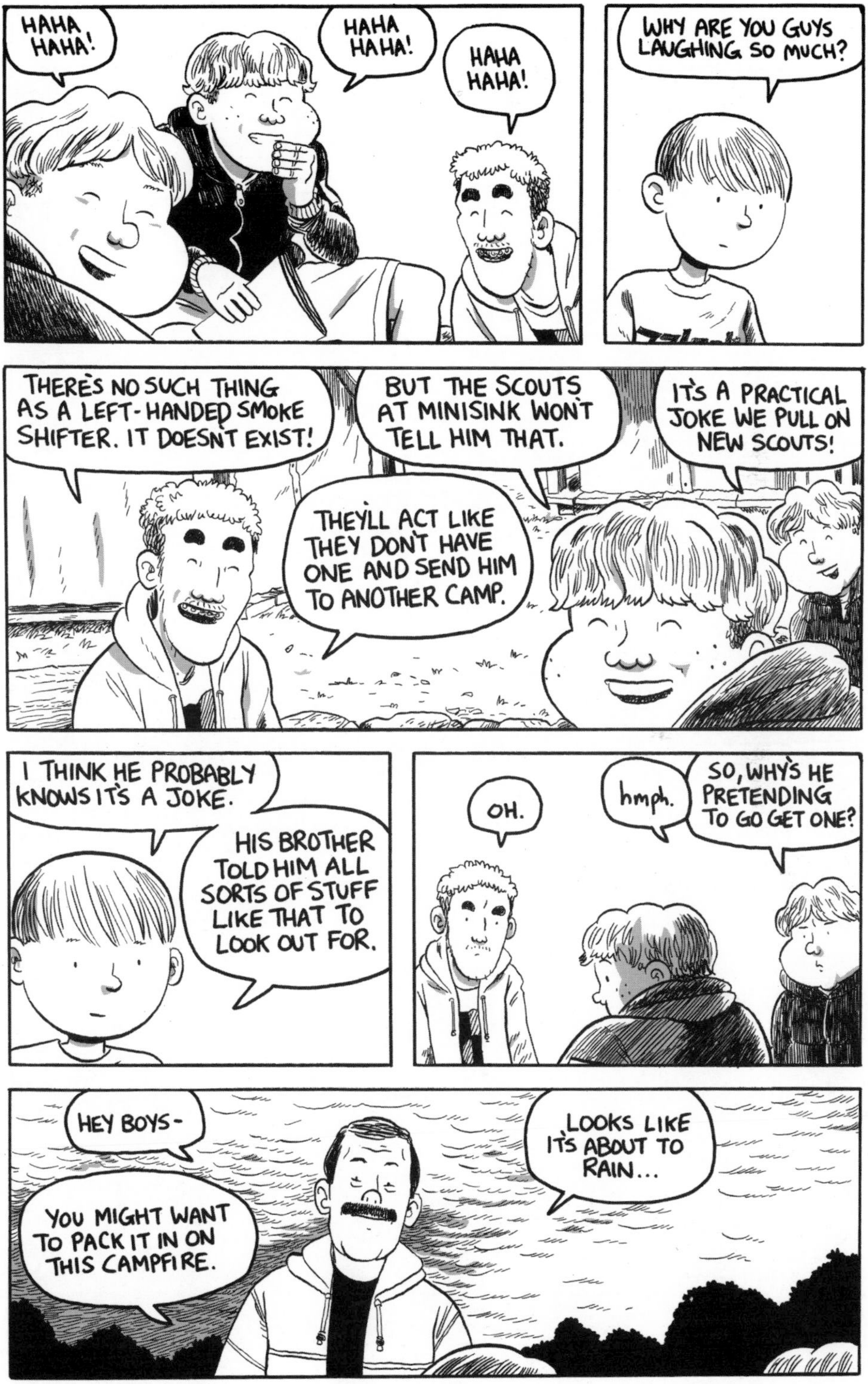
HAHA HAHA!
HAHA HAHA!
HAHA HAHA!
WHY ARE YOU GUYS LAUGHING SO MUCH?
THERE'S NO SUCH THING AS A LEFT-HANDED SMOKE SHIFTER. IT DOESN'T EXIST!
BUT THE SCOUTS AT MINISINK WON'T TELL HIM THAT.
IT'S A PRACTICAL JOKE WE PULL ON NEW SCOUTS!
THEY'LL ACT LIKE THEY DON'T HAVE ONE AND SEND HIM TO ANOTHER CAMP.
I THINK HE PROBABLY KNOWS IT'S A JOKE.
HIS BROTHER TOLD HIM ALL SORTS OF STUFF LIKE THAT TO LOOK OUT FOR.
OH.
hmph.
SO, WHY'S HE PRETENDING TO GO GET ONE?
HEY BOYS-
LOOKS LIKE IT'S ABOUT TO RAIN...
YOU MIGHT WANT TO PACK IT IN ON THIS CAMPFIRE.

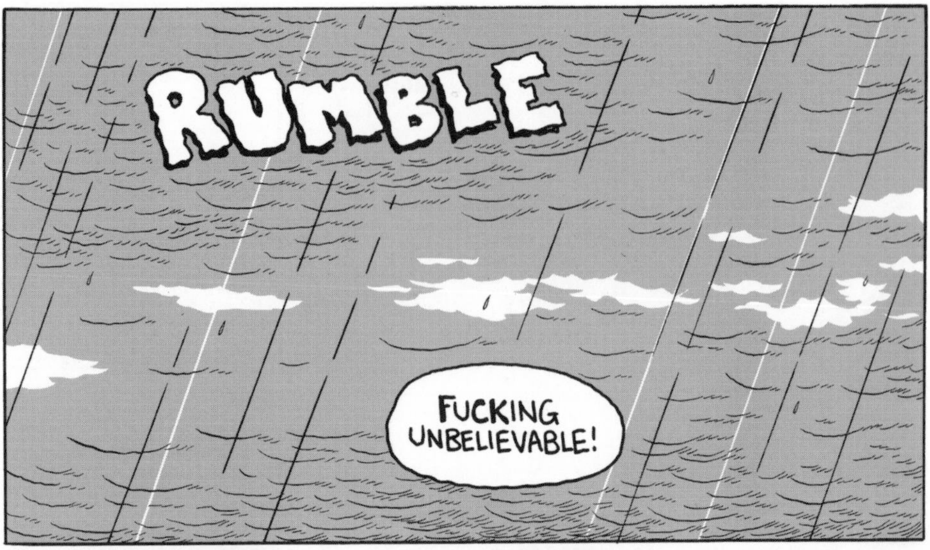
RUMBLE
FUCKING UNBELIEVABLE!
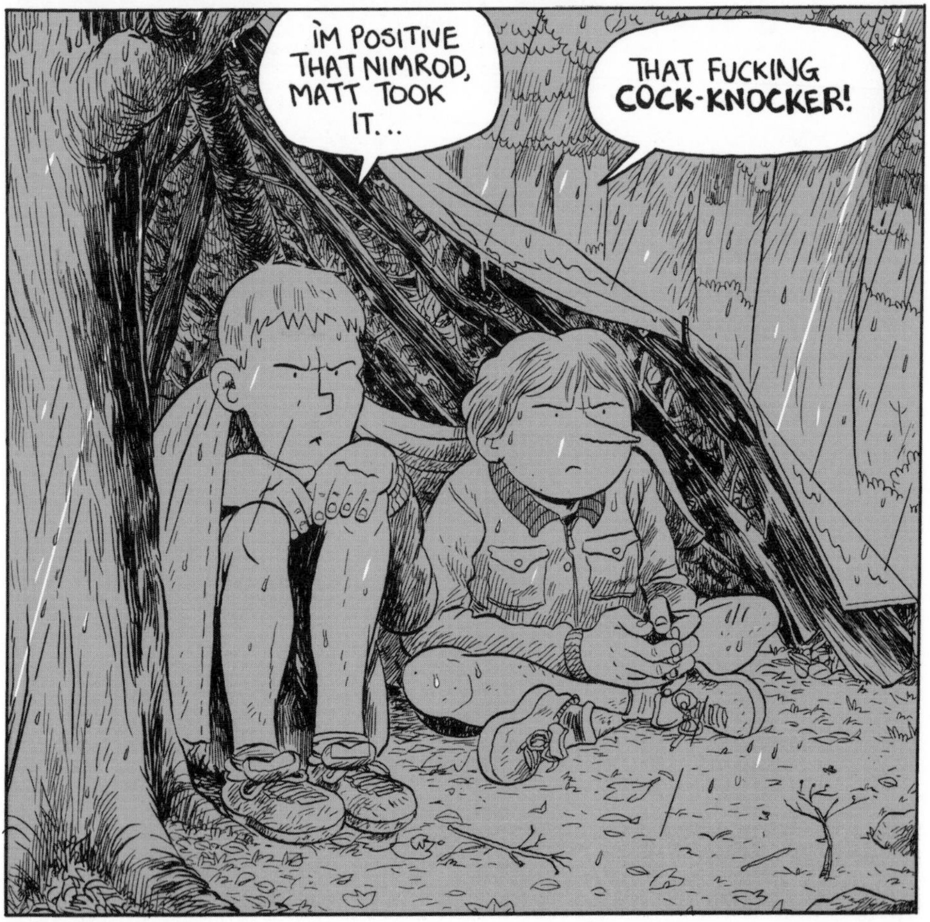
IM POSITIVE THAT NIMROD, MATT TOOK IT...
THAT FUCKING COCK-KNOCKER!

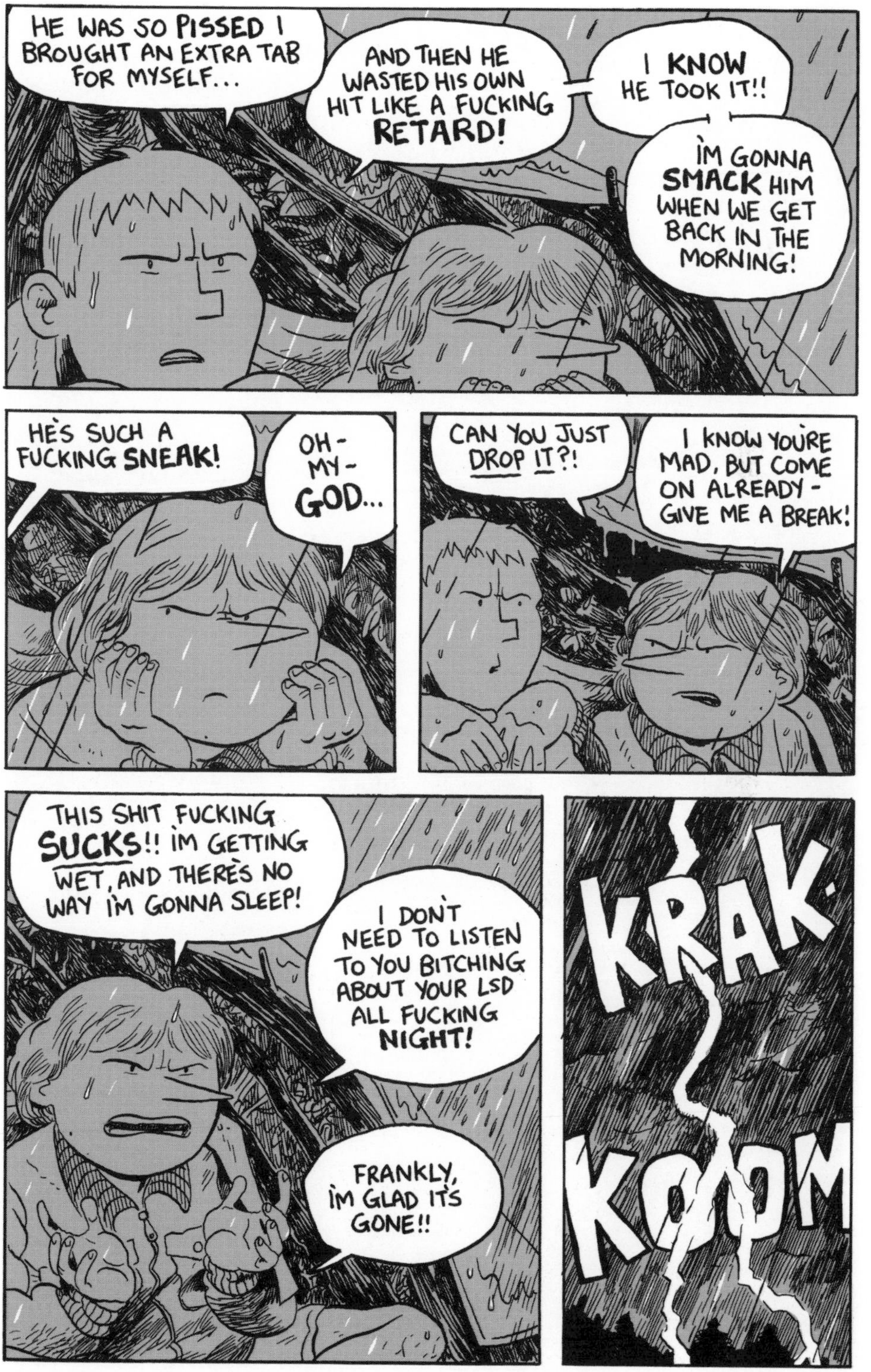
HE WAS SO PISSED I BROUGHT AN EXTRA TAB FOR MYSELF...
AND THEN HE WASTED HIS OWN HIT LIKE A FUCKING RETARD!
I KNOW HE TOOK IT!!
I'M GONNA SMACK HIM WHEN WE GET BACK IN THE MORNING!
HE'S SUCH A FUCKING SNEAK!
OH- MY- GOD...
CAN YOU JUST DROP IT?!
I KNOW YOU'RE MAD, BUT COME ON ALREADY - GIVE ME A BREAK!
THIS SHIT FUCKING SUCKS!! I'M GETTING WET, AND THERE'S NO WAY I'M GONNA SLEEP!
I DON'T NEED TO LISTEN TO YOU BITCHING ABOUT YOUR LSD ALL FUCKING NIGHT!
FRANKLY, I'M GLAD IT'S GONE!!
KRAK-KOOM

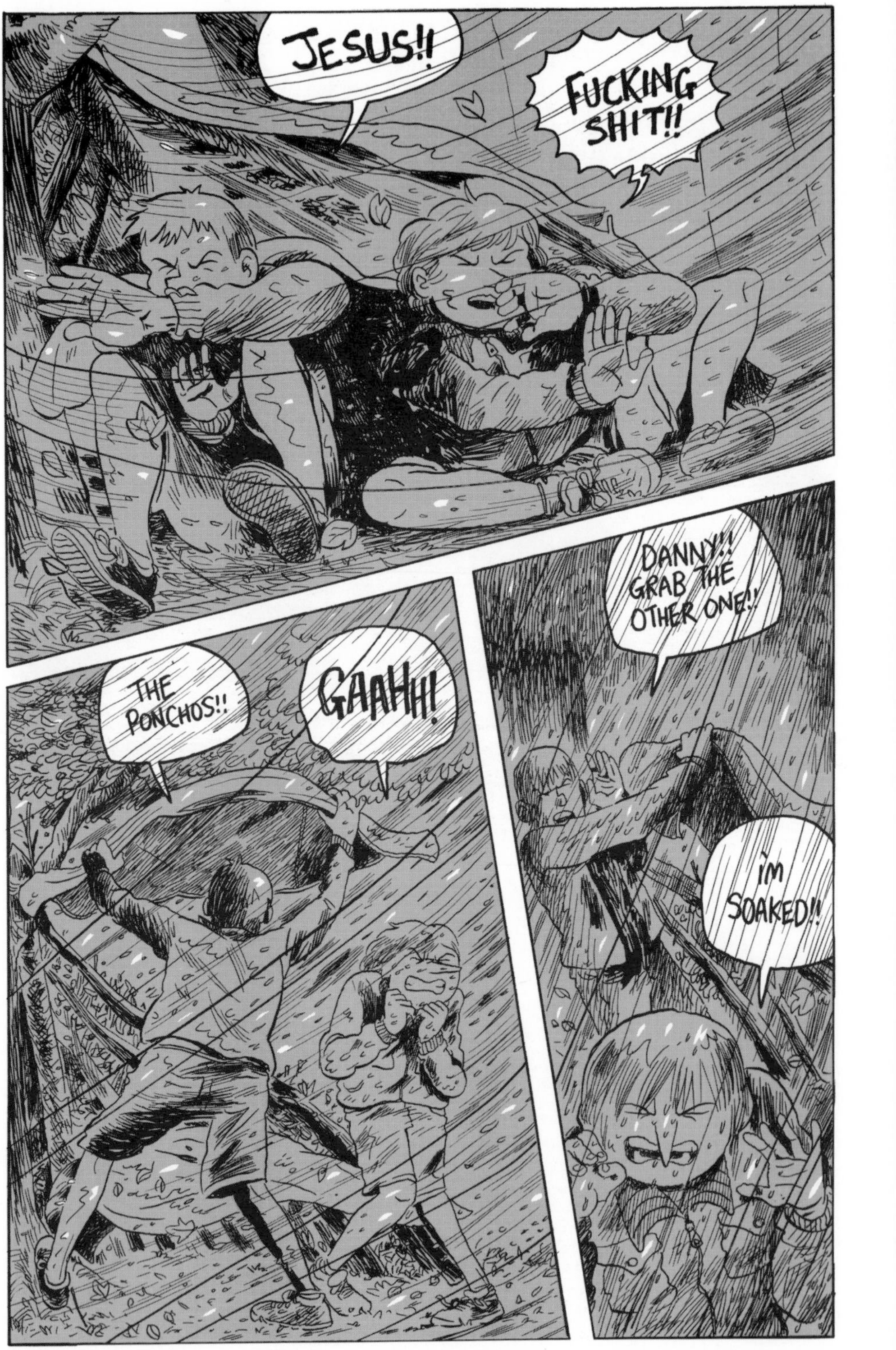
JESUS!!
FUCKING SHIT!!
THE PONCHOS!!
GAAHH!
DANNY!! GRAB THE OTHER ONE!!
I'M SOAKED!!

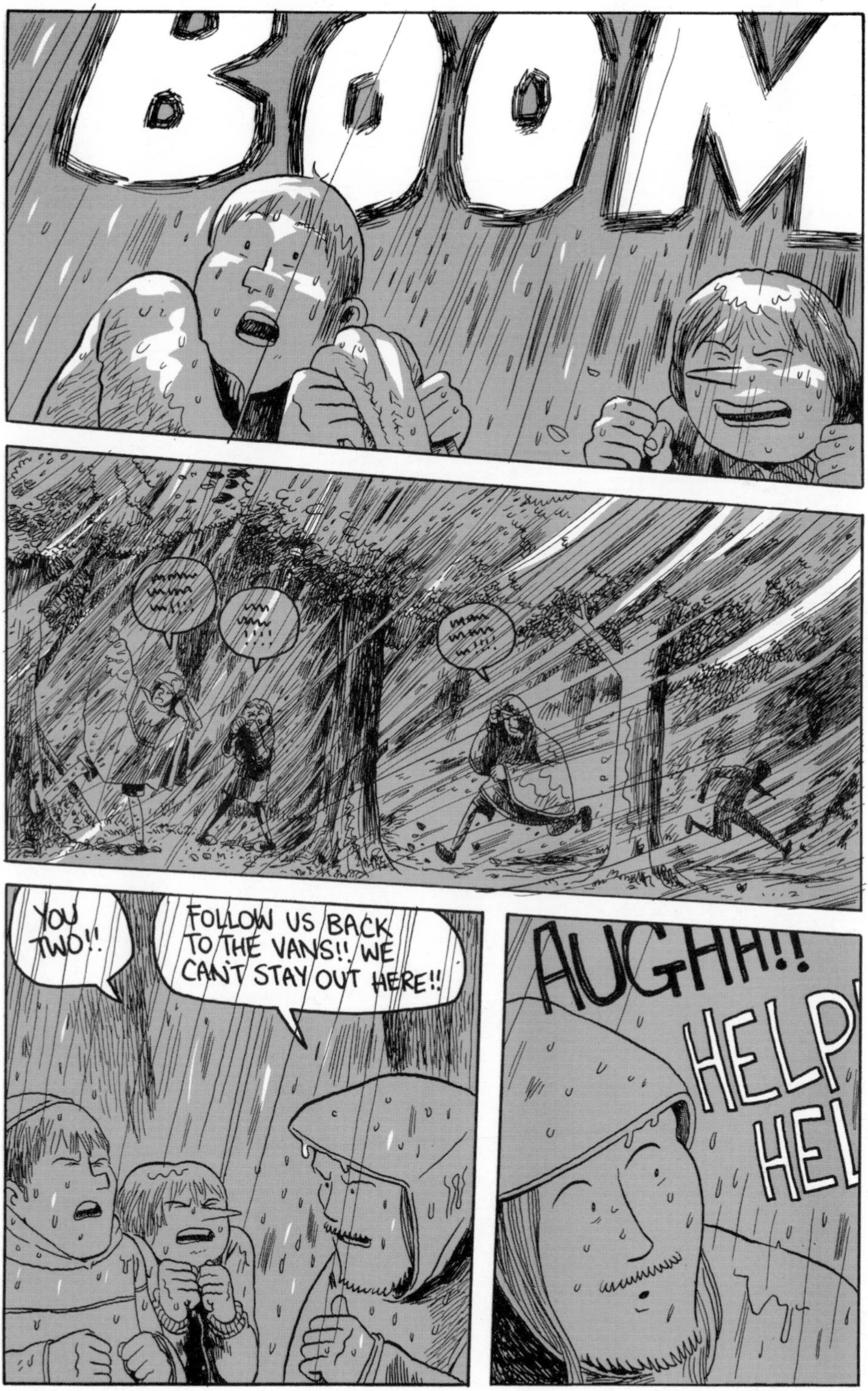
BOOM
YOU TWO!!
FOLLOW US BACK TO THE VANS!! WE CAN'T STAY OUT HERE!!
AUGHH!!
HELP
HEL

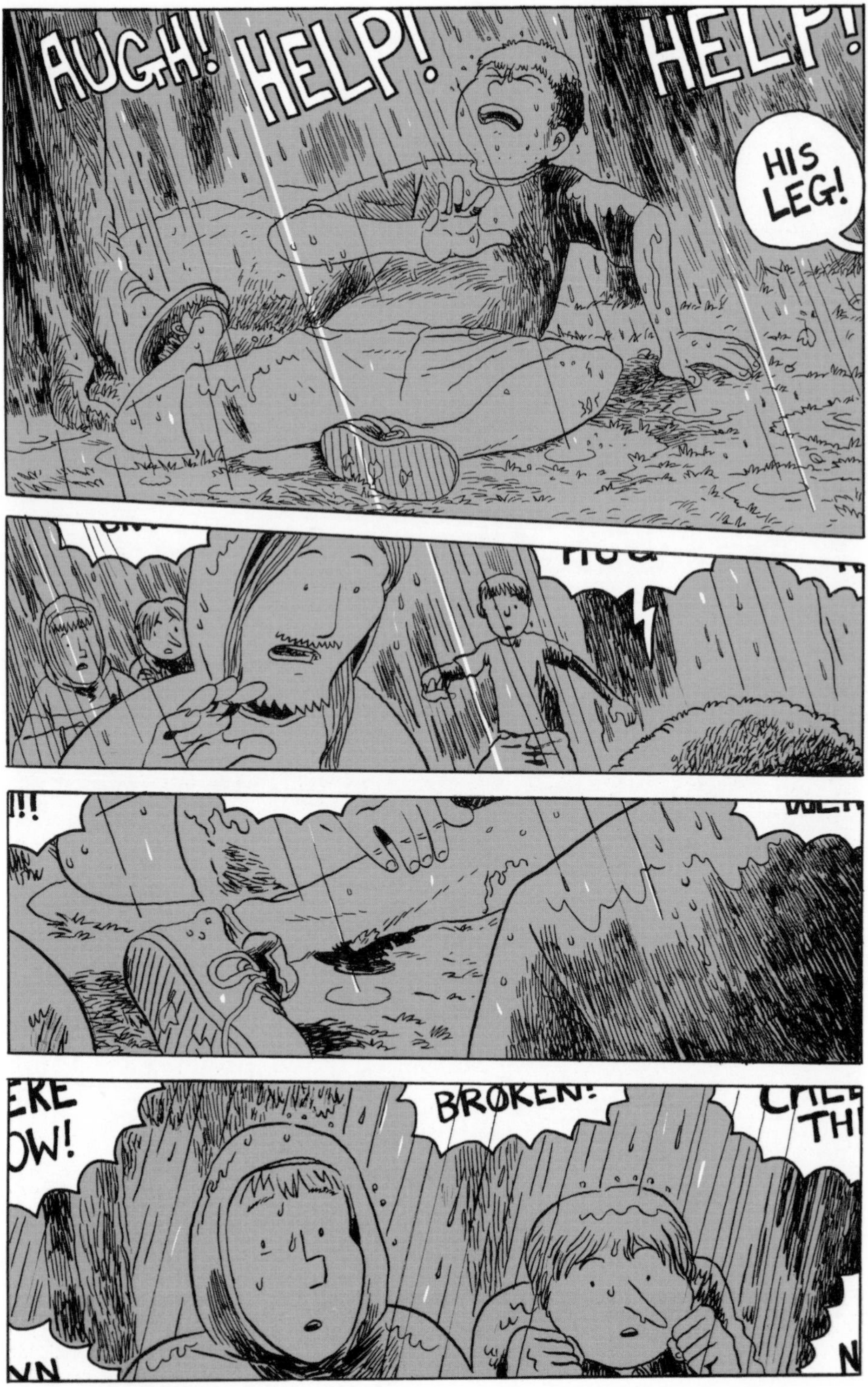
AUGH! HELP!
HELP!
HIS LEG!
BROKEN!

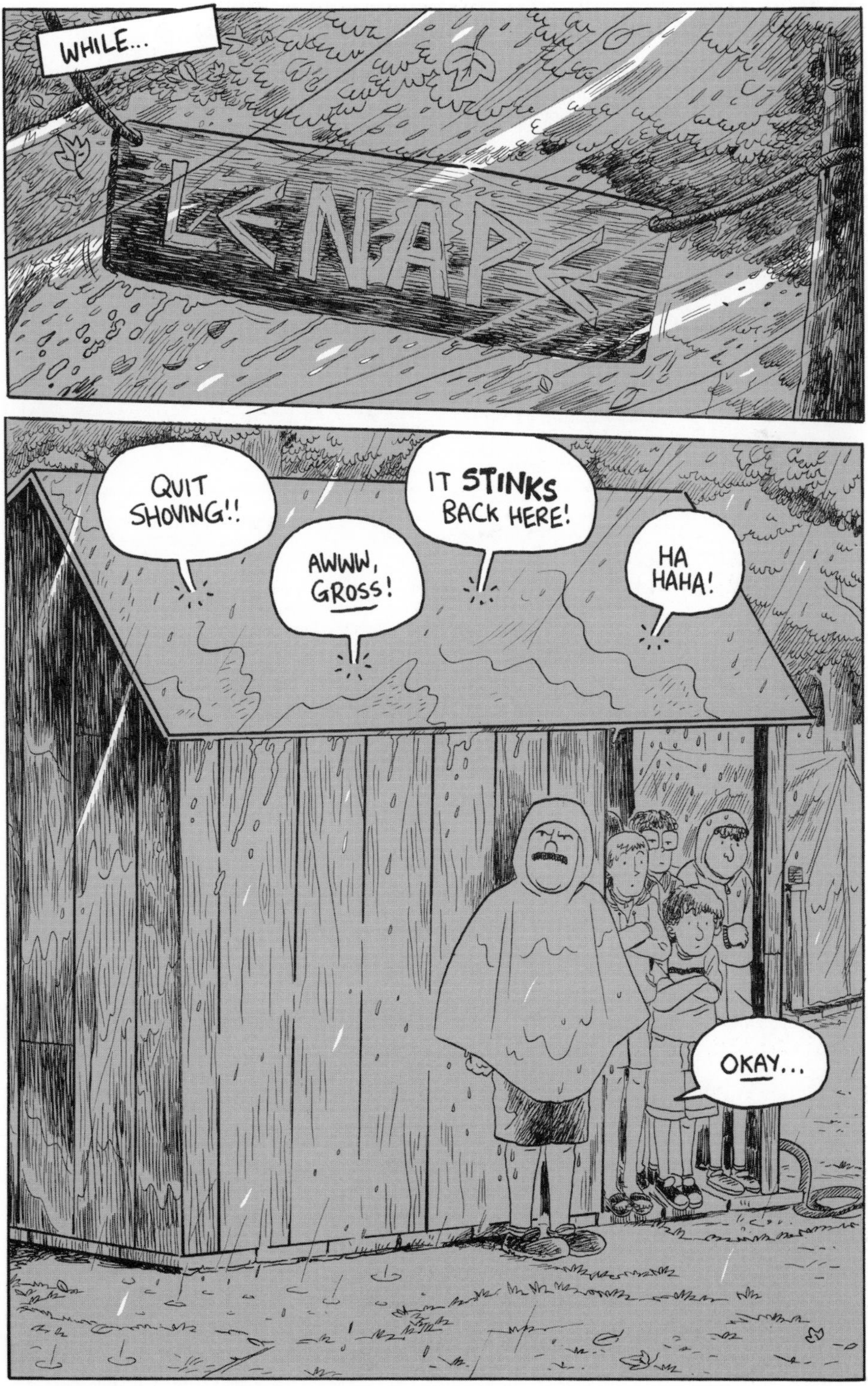
WHILE...
LENAPE
QUIT SHOVING!!
AWWW, GROSS!
IT STINKS BACK HERE!
HA HAHA!
OKAY...

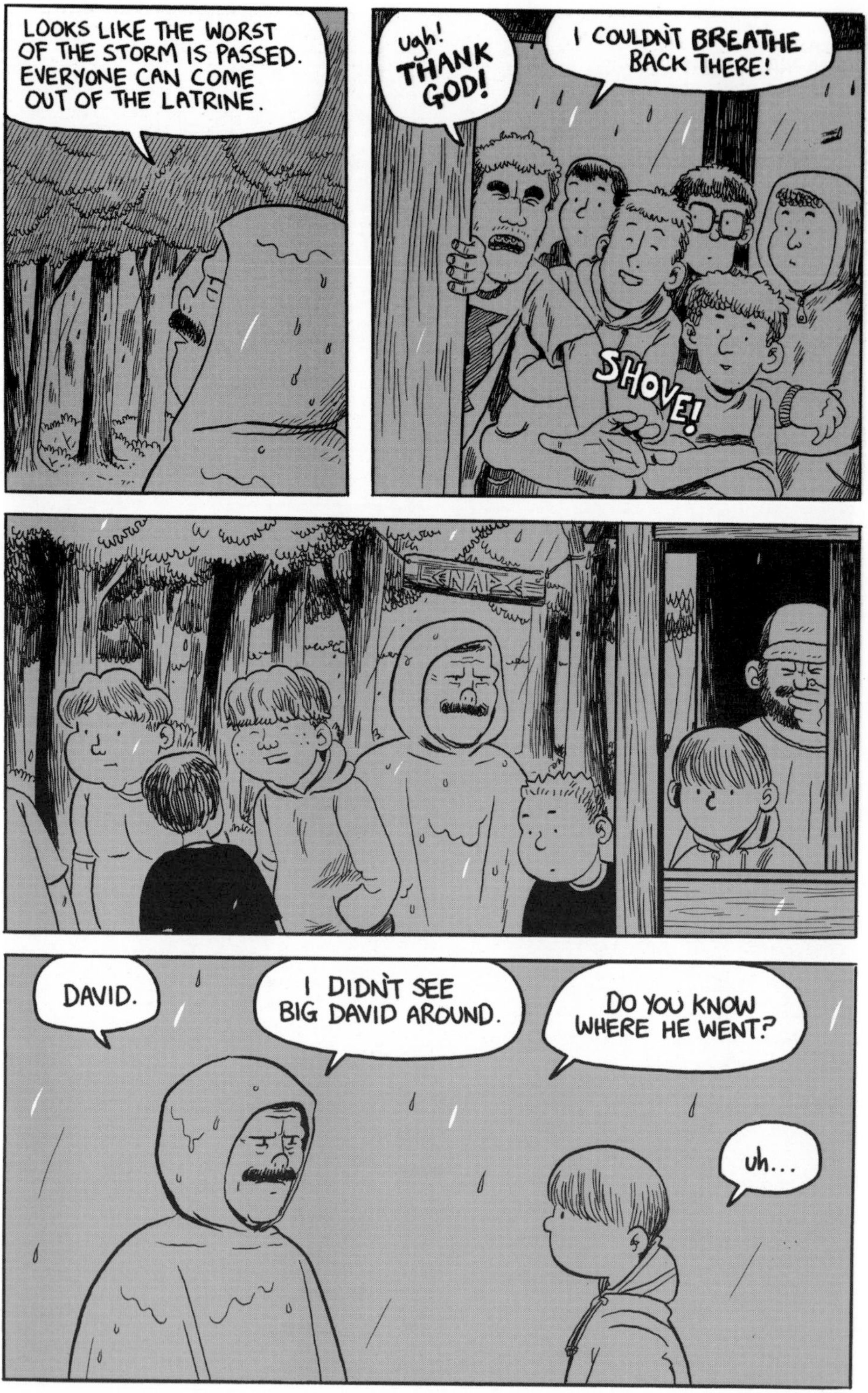
LOOKS LIKE THE WORST OF THE STORM IS PASSED. EVERYONE CAN COME OUT OF THE LATRINE.
ugh! THANK GOD!
I COULDN'T BREATHE BACK THERE!
SHOVE!
DAVID.
I DIDN'T SEE BIG DAVID AROUND.
DO YOU KNOW WHERE HE WENT?
uh...

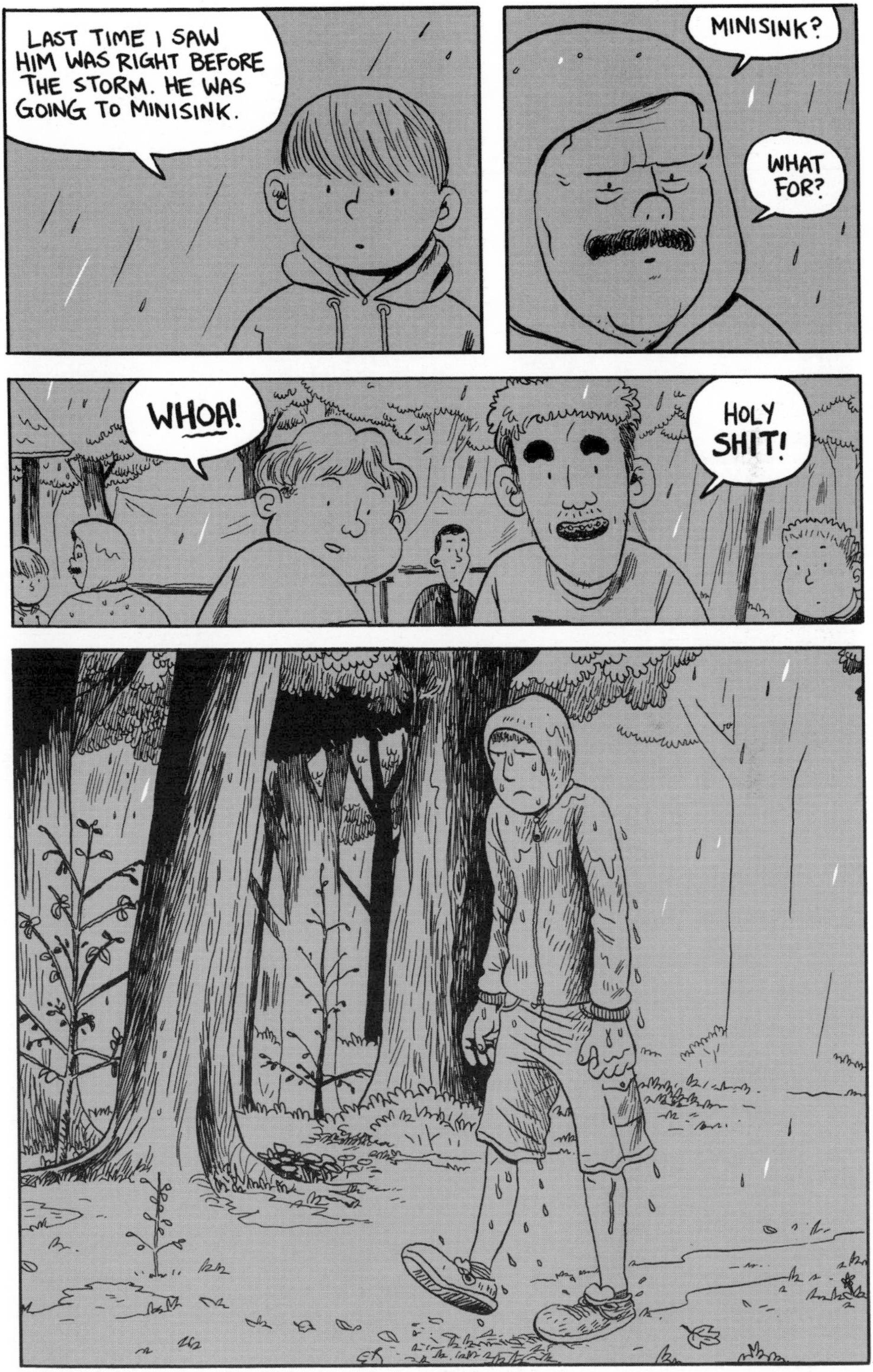
LAST TIME I SAW HIM WAS RIGHT BEFORE THE STORM. HE WAS GOING TO MINISINK.
MINISINK?
WHAT FOR?
WHOA!
HOLY SHIT!

HAHA HAHA!
YOU LOOK LIKE A DROWNED ANIMAL!
SHUT UP!
YOU GUYS ARE **DICKS**!
THERE'S NO SUCH THING AS A LEFT-HANDED SMOKE-SHIFTER!
I GOT CAUGHT OUT ON THE TRAIL!
HAHA HAHA!
HAHA
SORRY, DUDE, IT'S A RITE OF PASSAGE.
YEAH, AND WE DIDN'T KNOW IT WAS GONNA RAIN!
WHATEVER.
I GOTTA GET OUT OF THESE CLOTHES.
FRANKLY, I DON'T KNOW WHY IT TOOK YOU SO LONG TO GET BACK.
MINISINK'S NOT **THAT** FAR AWAY...
HAHA! YEAH.
HEY!
LOOK WHO ELSE IS BACK-

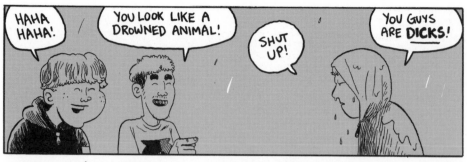

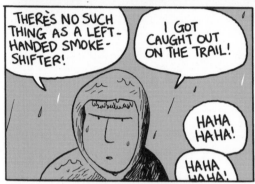

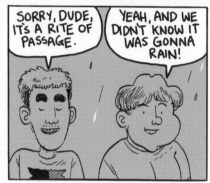

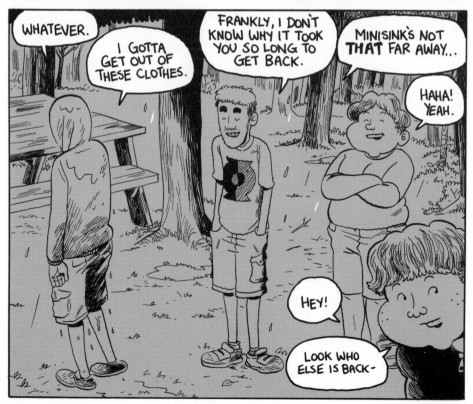

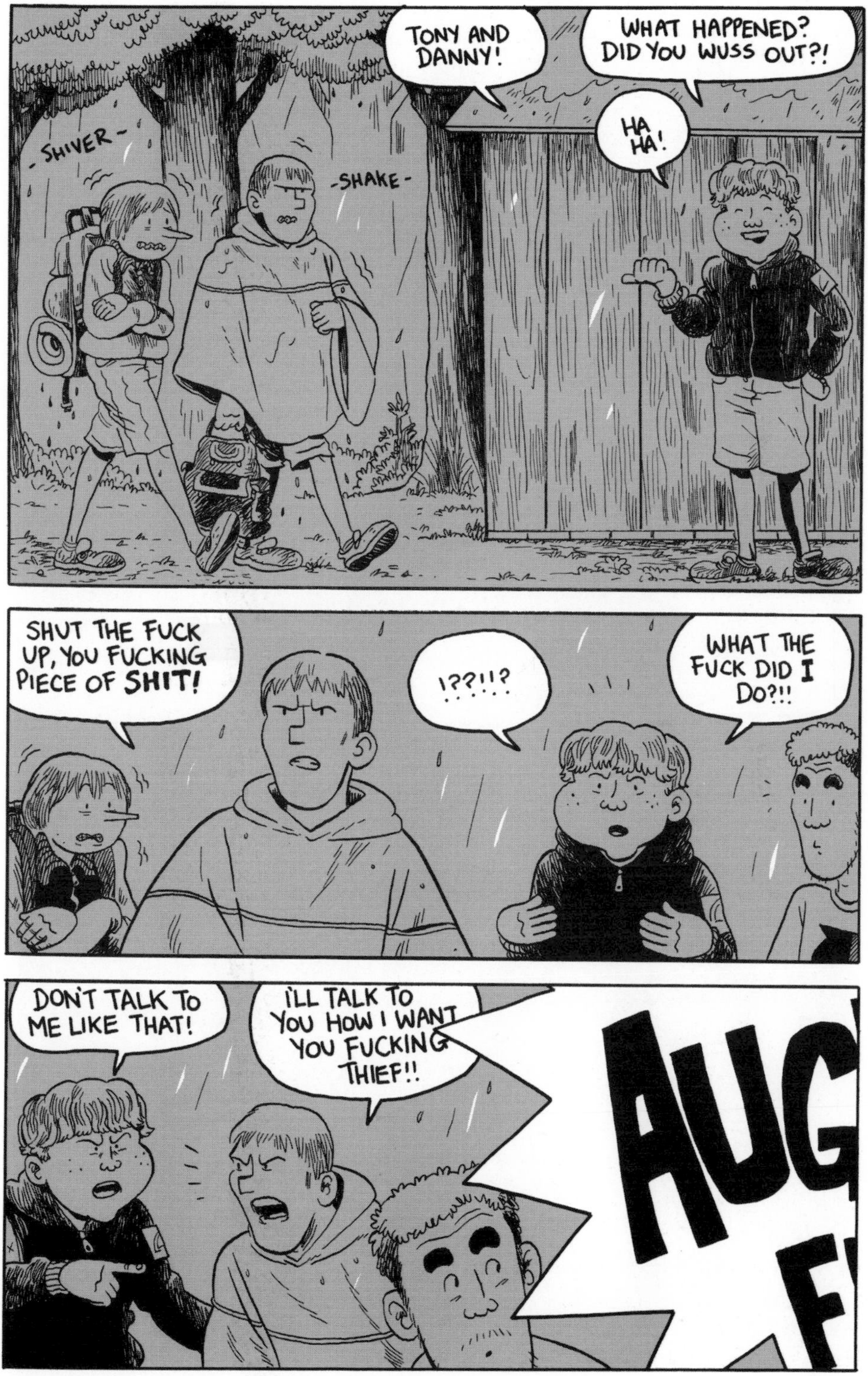

TONY AND DANNY!
WHAT HAPPENED? DID YOU WUSS OUT?!
HA HA!
-SHIVER-
-SHAKE-
SHUT THE FUCK UP, YOU FUCKING PIECE OF SHIT!
!??!!?
WHAT THE FUCK DID I DO?!!
DON'T TALK TO ME LIKE THAT!
I'LL TALK TO YOU HOW I WANT YOU FUCKING THIEF!!

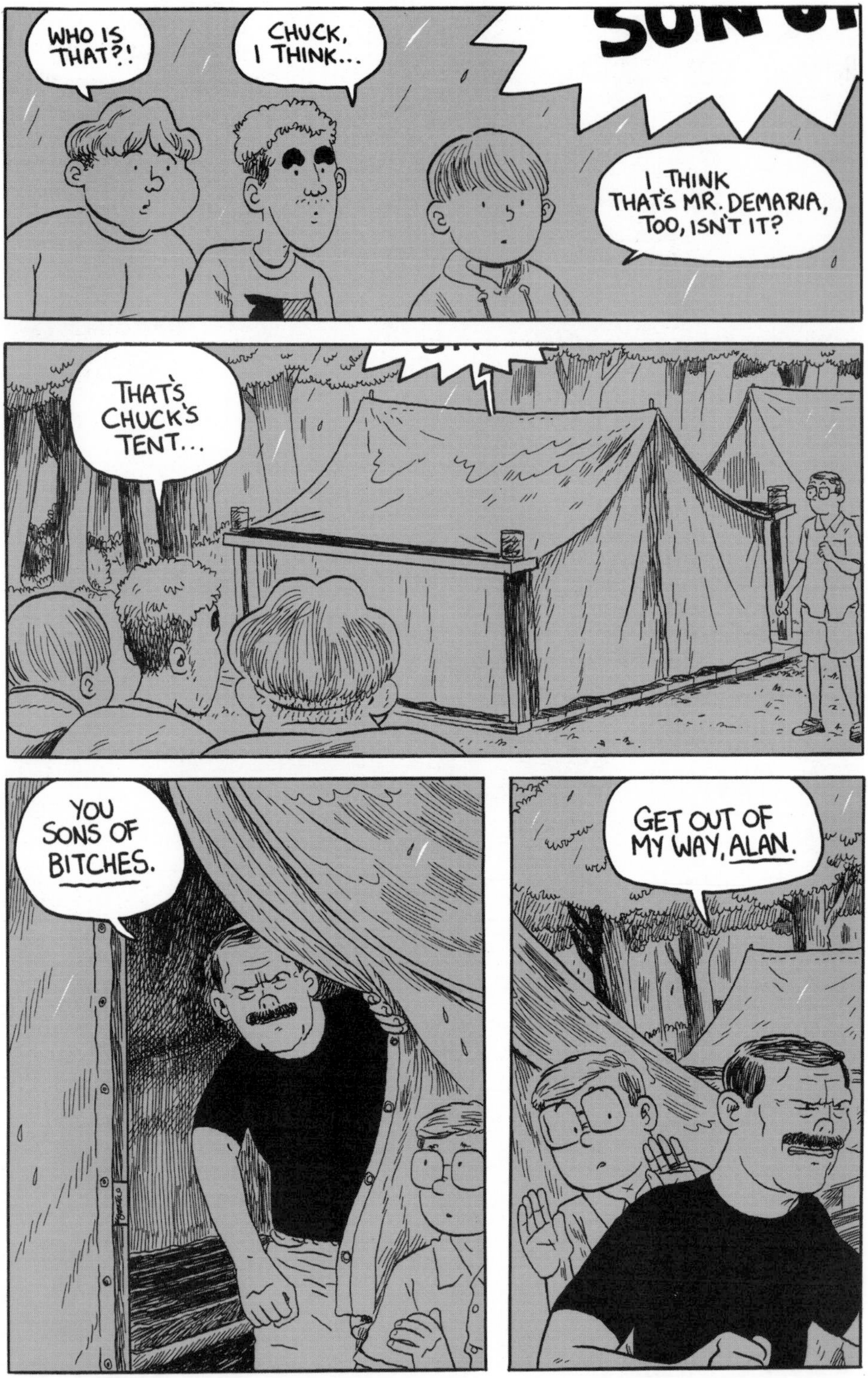
WHO IS THAT?!
CHUCK, I THINK...
I THINK THAT'S MR. DEMARIA, TOO, ISN'T IT?
THAT'S CHUCK'S TENT...
YOU SONS OF BITCHES.
GET OUT OF MY WAY, ALAN.

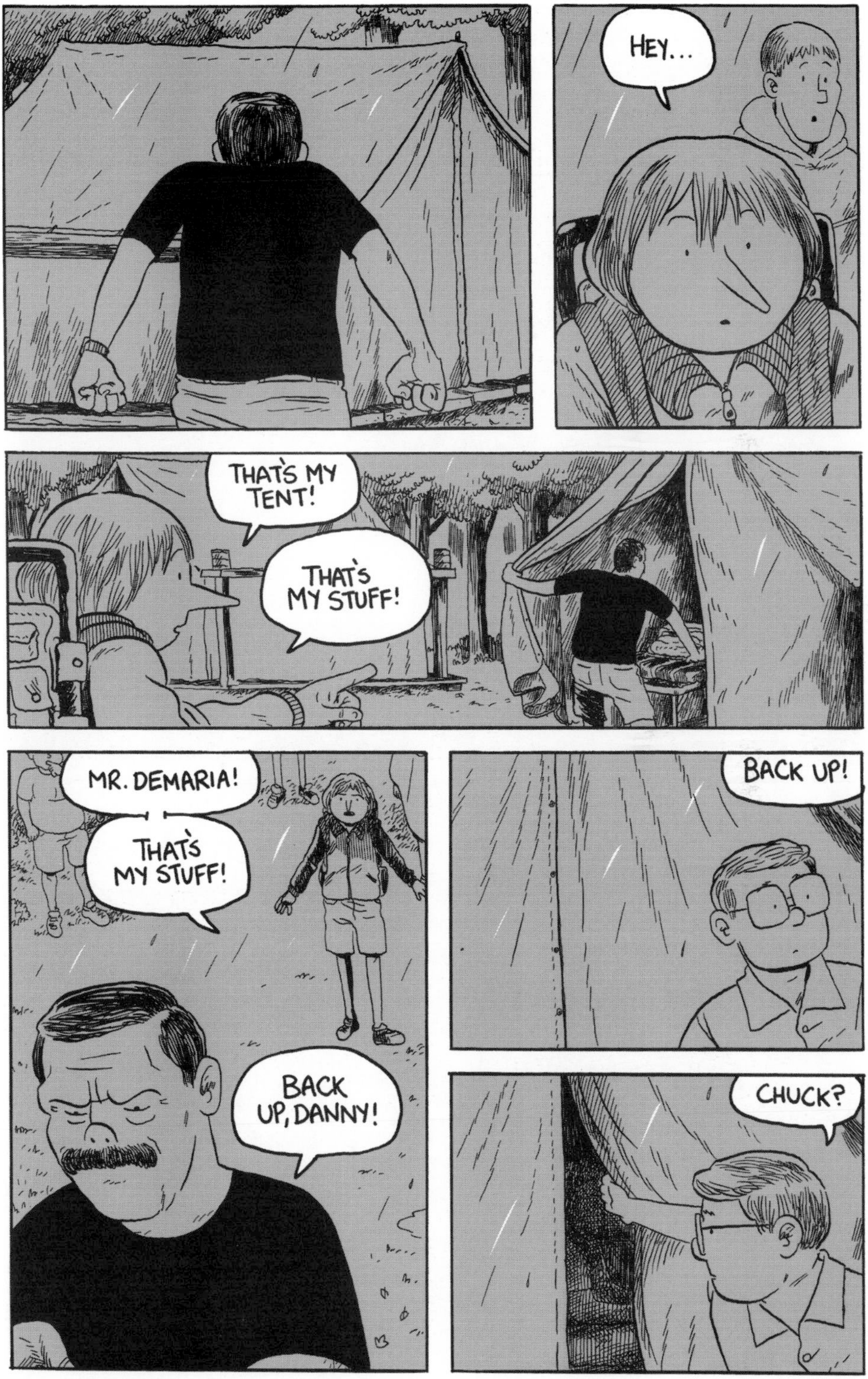
HEY...
THAT'S MY TENT!
THAT'S MY STUFF!
MR. DEMARIA!
THAT'S MY STUFF!
BACK UP, DANNY!
BACK UP!
CHUCK?

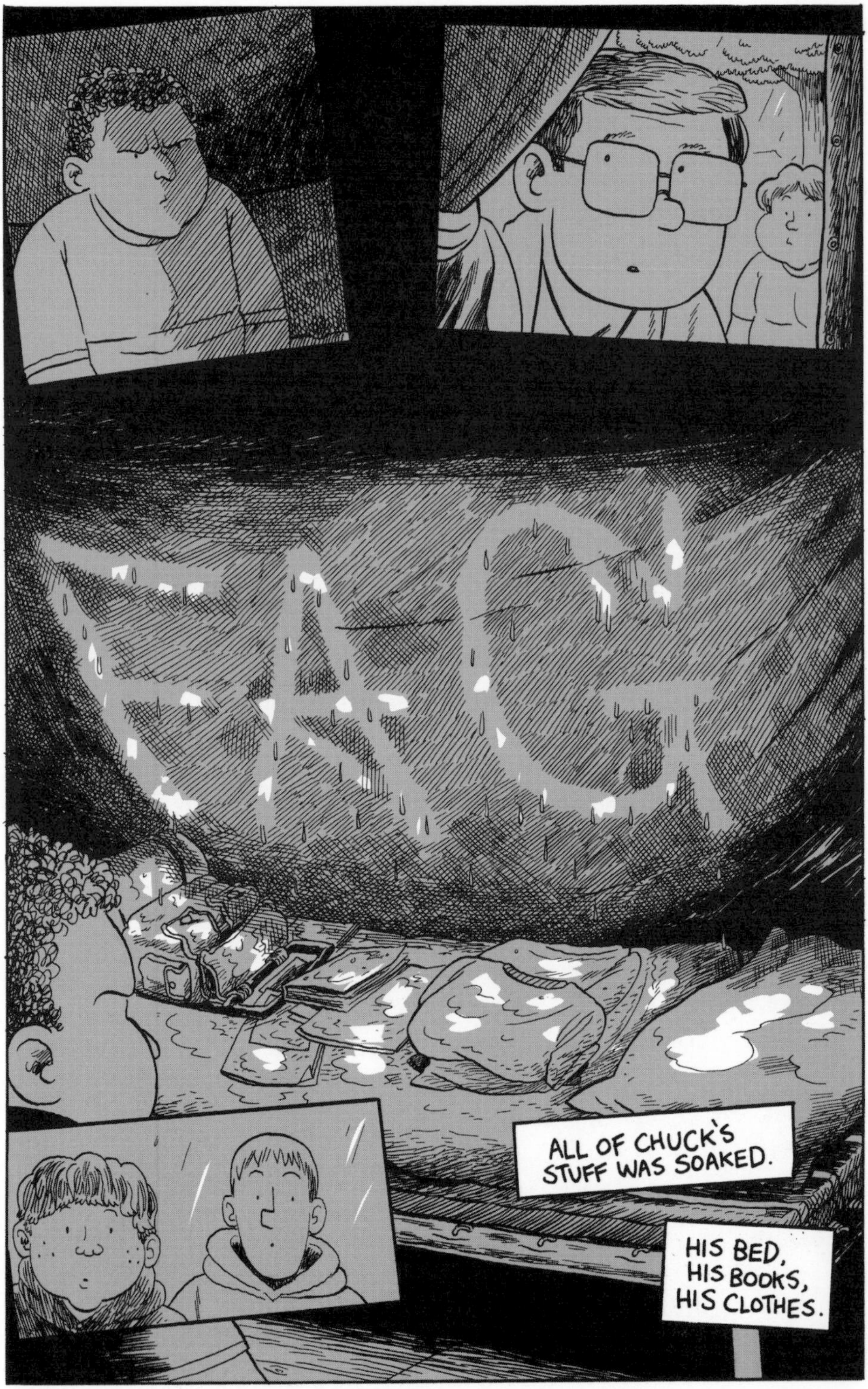
ALL OF CHUCK'S STUFF WAS SOAKED.
HIS BED, HIS BOOKS, HIS CLOTHES.

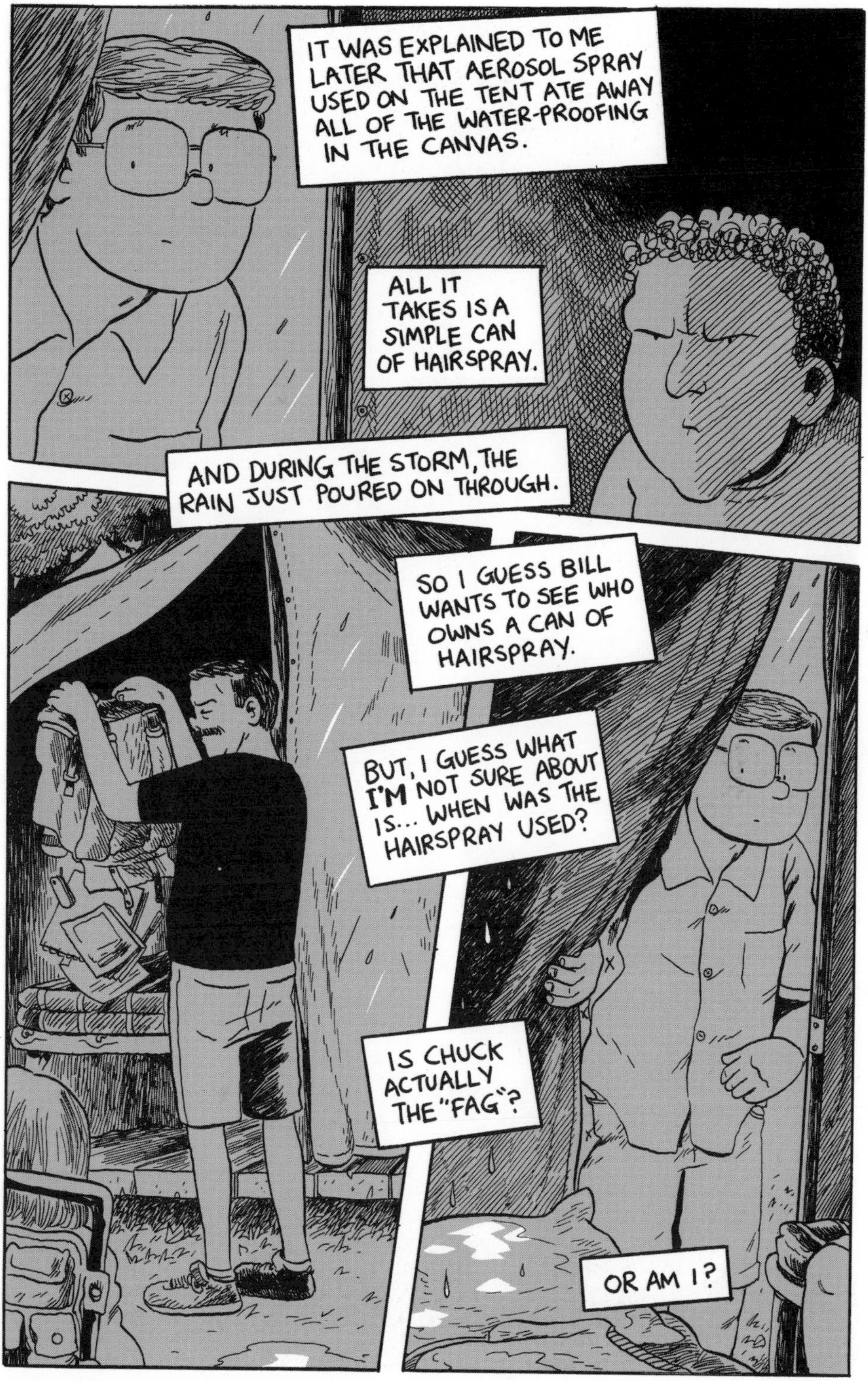
IT WAS EXPLAINED TO ME LATER THAT AEROSOL SPRAY USED ON THE TENT ATE AWAY ALL OF THE WATER-PROOFING IN THE CANVAS.
ALL IT TAKES IS A SIMPLE CAN OF HAIRSPRAY.
AND DURING THE STORM, THE RAIN JUST POURED ON THROUGH.
SO I GUESS BILL WANTS TO SEE WHO OWNS A CAN OF HAIRSPRAY.
BUT, I GUESS WHAT I'M NOT SURE ABOUT IS... WHEN WAS THE HAIRSPRAY USED?
IS CHUCK ACTUALLY THE "FAG"?
OR AM I?

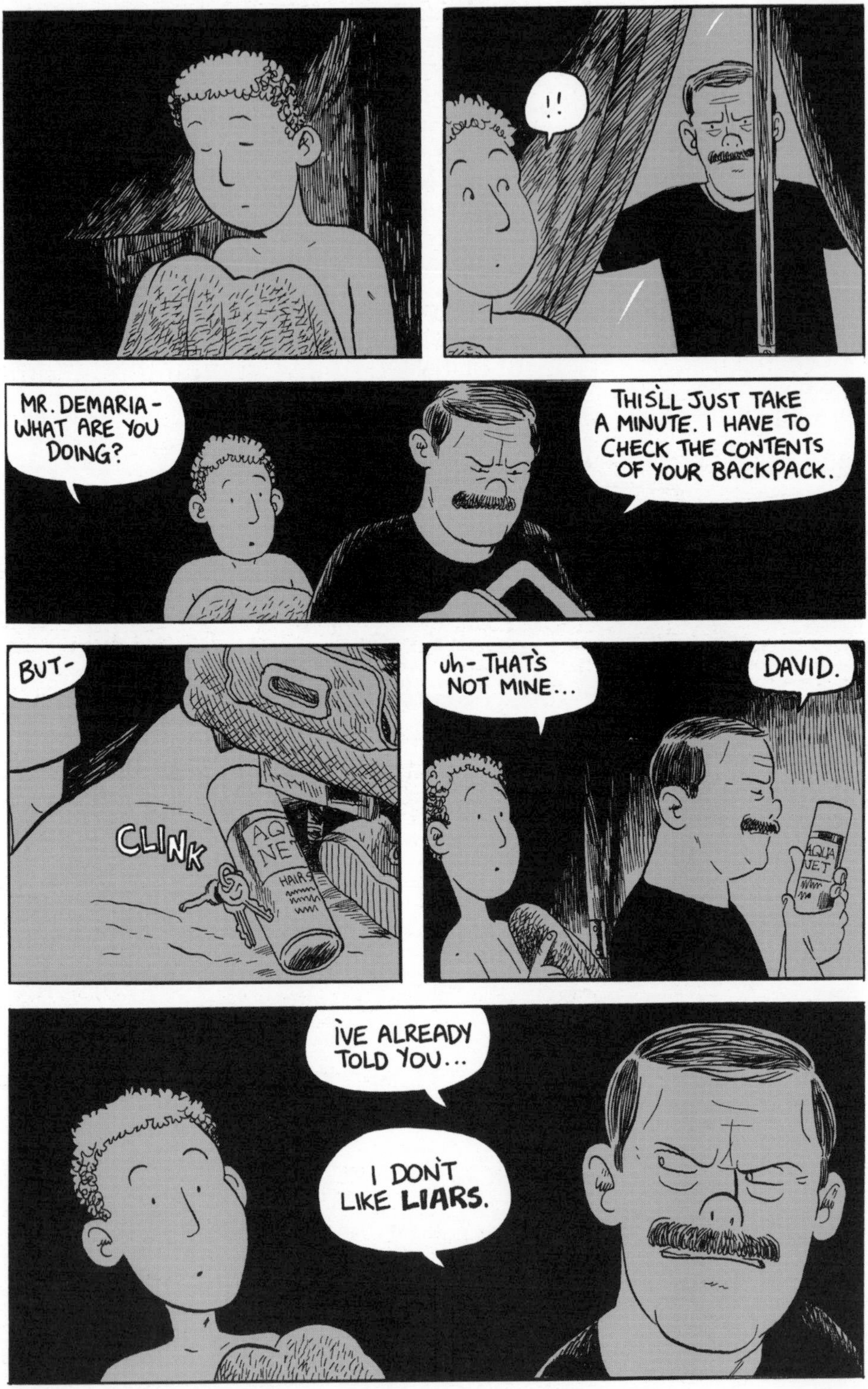
!!
MR. DEMARIA- WHAT ARE YOU DOING?
THIS'LL JUST TAKE A MINUTE. I HAVE TO CHECK THE CONTENTS OF YOUR BACKPACK.
BUT-
CLINK
AQUA NET
uh- THAT'S NOT MINE...
DAVID.
I'VE ALREADY TOLD YOU...
I DON'T LIKE **LIARS**.

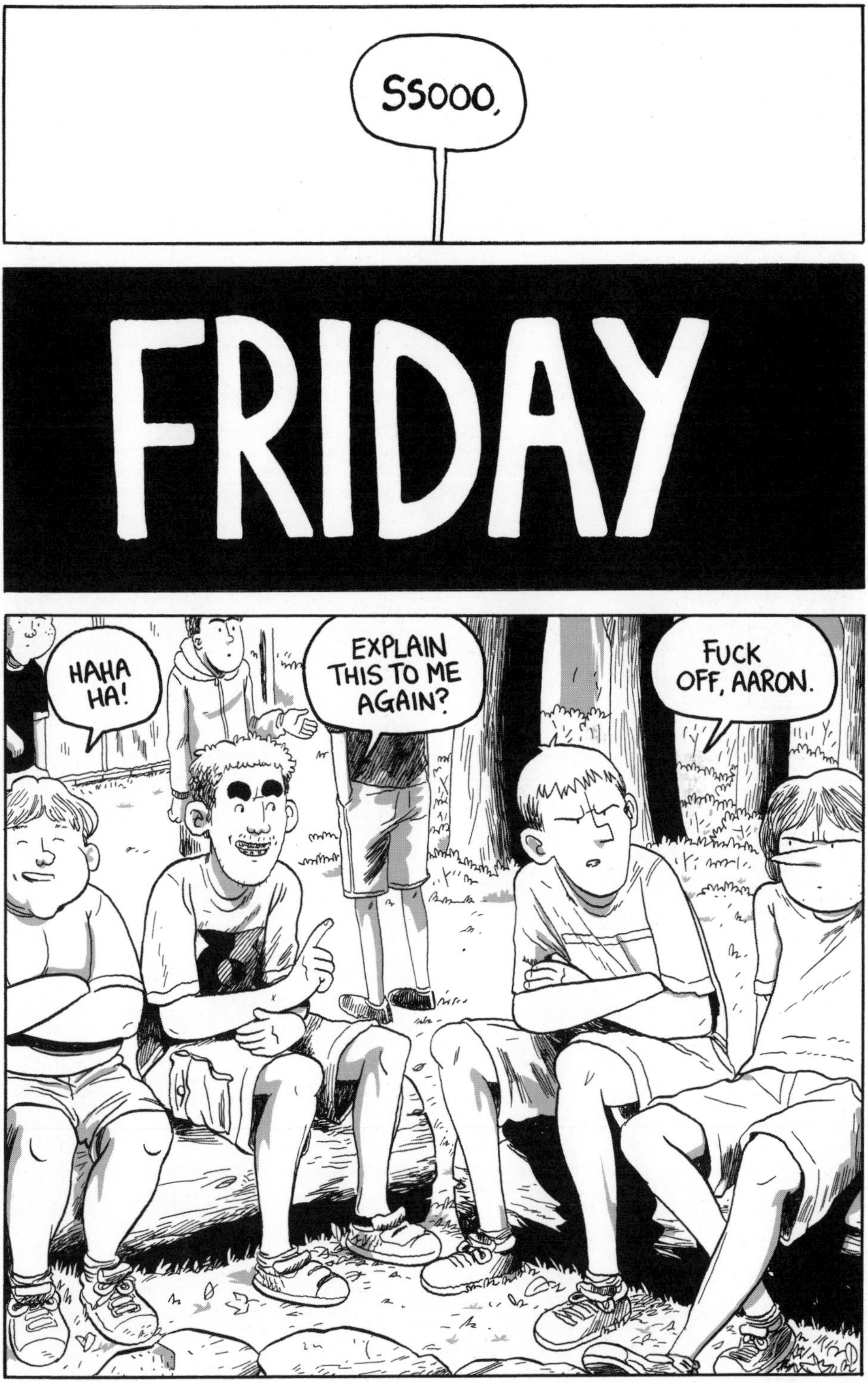
SSOOO,
FRIDAY
HAHA HA!
EXPLAIN THIS TO ME AGAIN?
FUCK OFF, AARON.

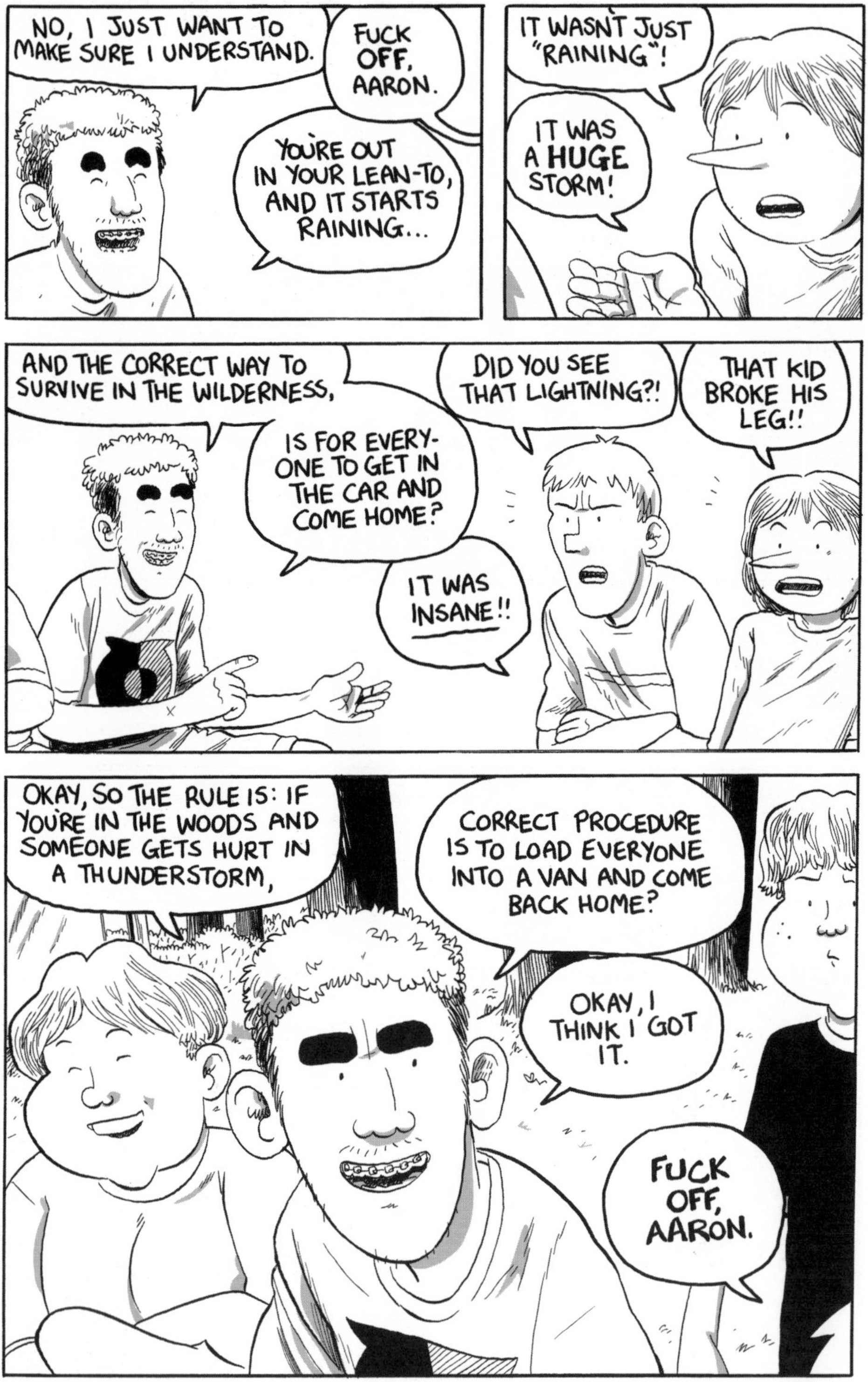
NO, I JUST WANT TO MAKE SURE I UNDERSTAND.
FUCK OFF, AARON.
YOU'RE OUT IN YOUR LEAN-TO, AND IT STARTS RAINING...
IT WASN'T JUST "RAINING"!
IT WAS A HUGE STORM!
AND THE CORRECT WAY TO SURVIVE IN THE WILDERNESS,
IS FOR EVERY-ONE TO GET IN THE CAR AND COME HOME?
DID YOU SEE THAT LIGHTNING?!
IT WAS INSANE!!
THAT KID BROKE HIS LEG!!
OKAY, SO THE RULE IS: IF YOU'RE IN THE WOODS AND SOMEONE GETS HURT IN A THUNDERSTORM,
CORRECT PROCEDURE IS TO LOAD EVERYONE INTO A VAN AND COME BACK HOME?
OKAY, I THINK I GOT IT.
FUCK OFF, AARON.

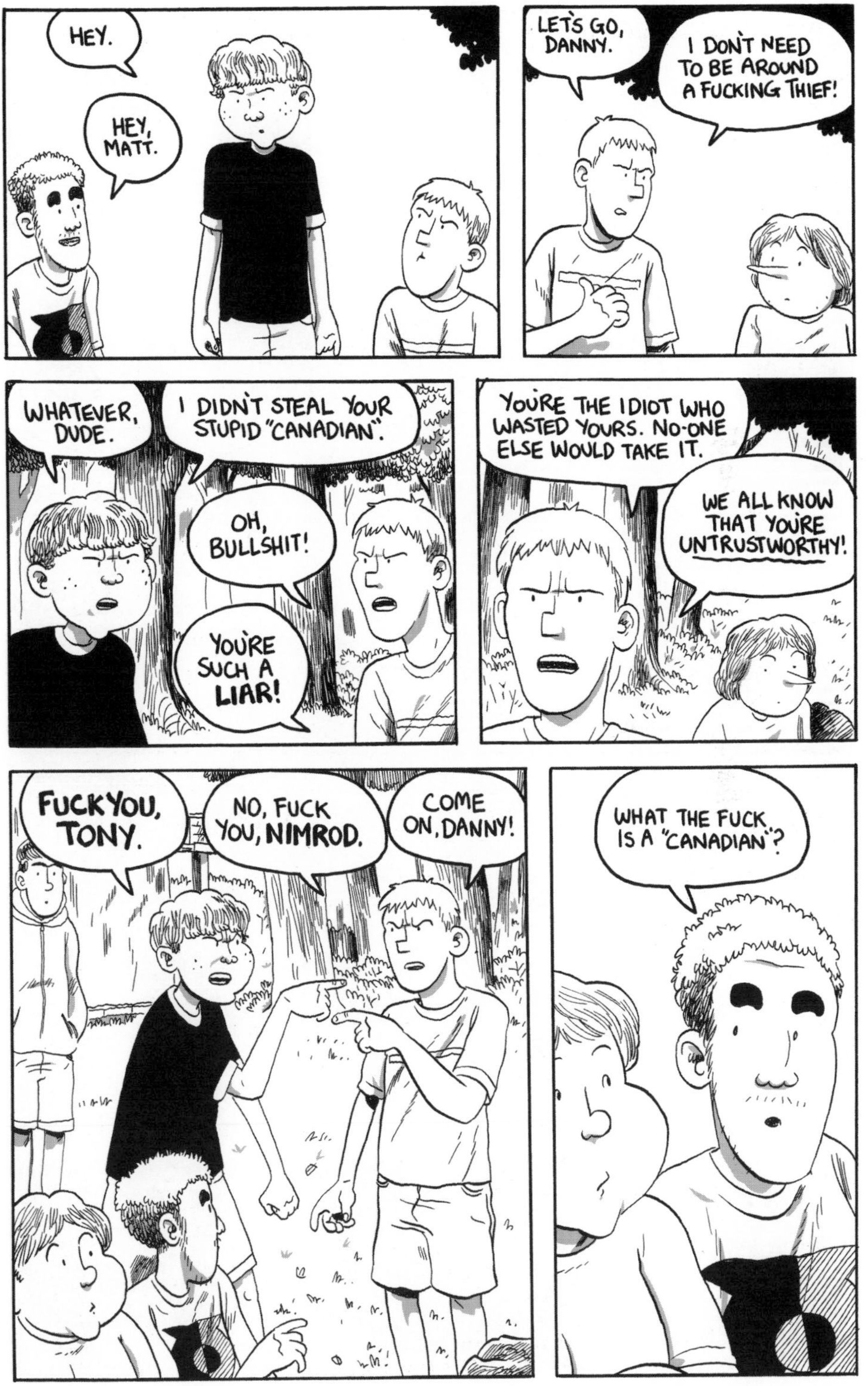
HEY.
HEY, MATT.
LET'S GO, DANNY.
I DON'T NEED TO BE AROUND A FUCKING THIEF!
WHATEVER, DUDE.
I DIDN'T STEAL YOUR STUPID "CANADIAN".
OH, BULLSHIT!
YOU'RE SUCH A LIAR!
YOU'RE THE IDIOT WHO WASTED YOURS. NO-ONE ELSE WOULD TAKE IT.
WE ALL KNOW THAT YOU'RE UNTRUSTWORTHY!
FUCK YOU, TONY.
NO, FUCK YOU, NIMROD.
COME ON, DANNY!
WHAT THE FUCK IS A "CANADIAN"?

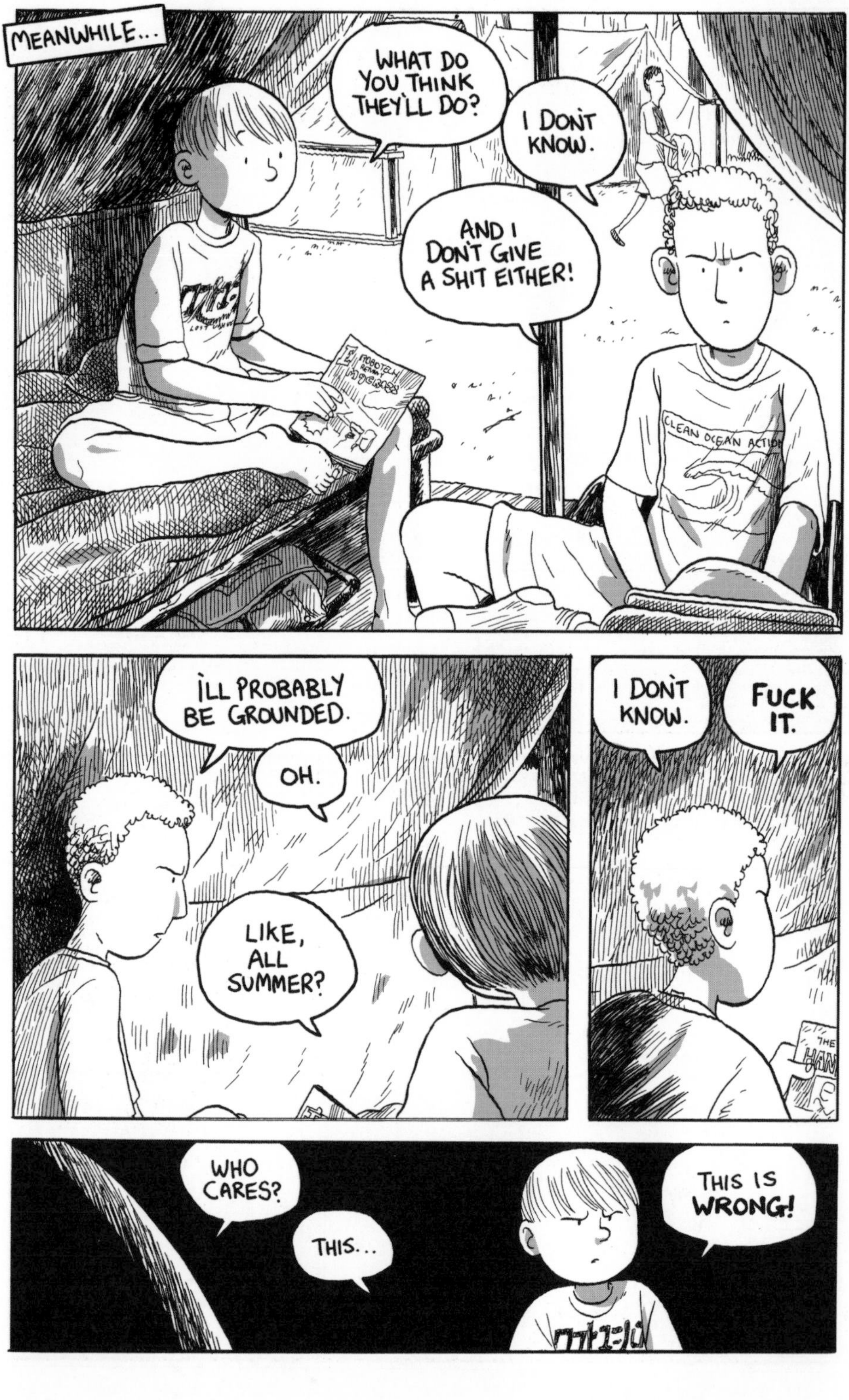
MEANWHILE...
WHAT DO YOU THINK THEY'LL DO?
I DON'T KNOW.
AND I DON'T GIVE A SHIT EITHER!
CLEAN OCEAN ACTION
I'LL PROBABLY BE GROUNDED.
OH.
LIKE, ALL SUMMER?
I DON'T KNOW.
FUCK IT.
WHO CARES?
THIS...
THIS IS WRONG!

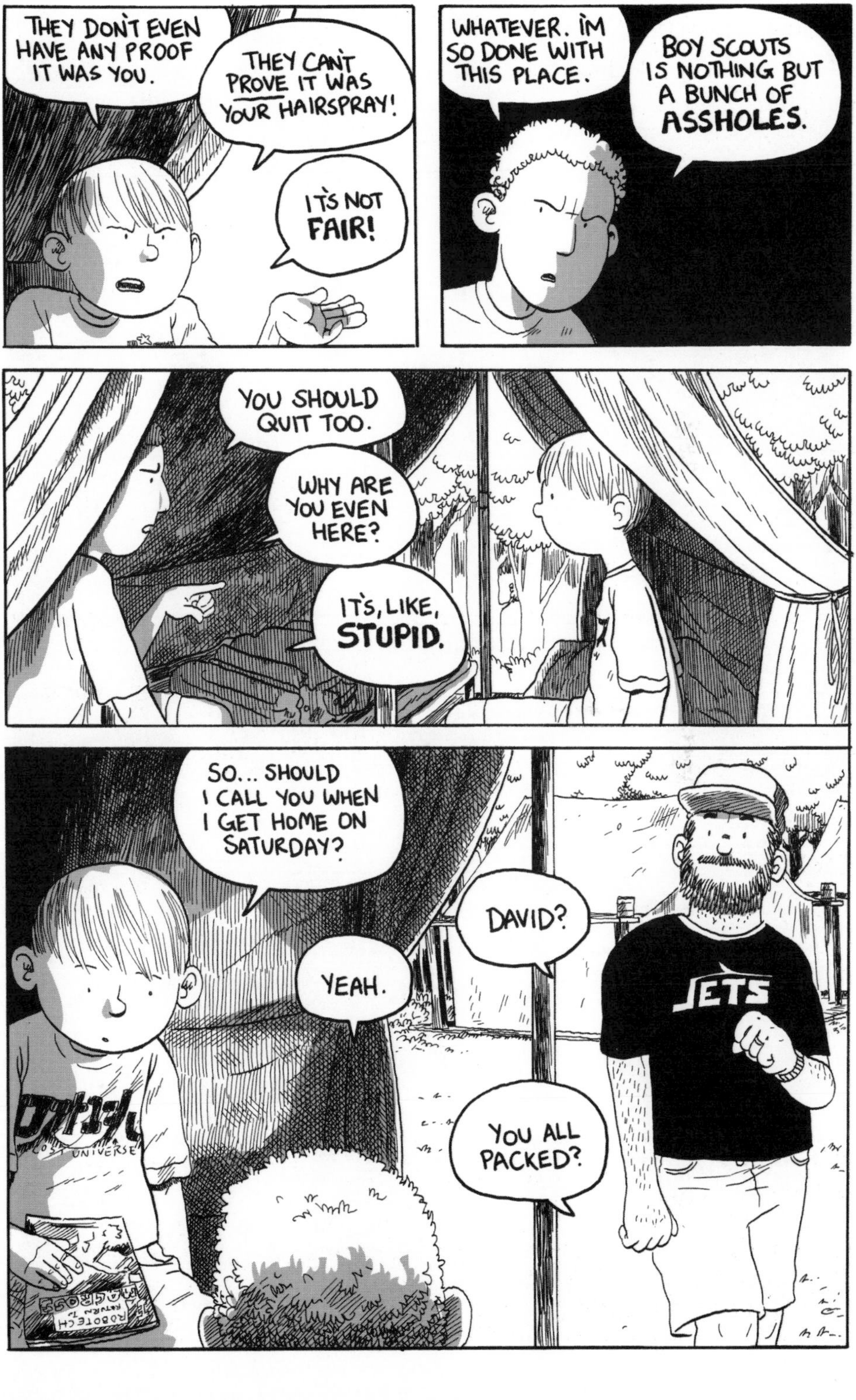
THEY DON'T EVEN HAVE ANY PROOF IT WAS YOU.
THEY CAN'T PROVE IT WAS YOUR HAIRSPRAY!
IT'S NOT FAIR!
WHATEVER. I'M SO DONE WITH THIS PLACE.
BOY SCOUTS IS NOTHING BUT A BUNCH OF ASSHOLES.
YOU SHOULD QUIT TOO.
WHY ARE YOU EVEN HERE?
IT'S, LIKE, STUPID.
SO... SHOULD I CALL YOU WHEN I GET HOME ON SATURDAY?
DAVID?
YEAH.
JETS
YOU ALL PACKED?

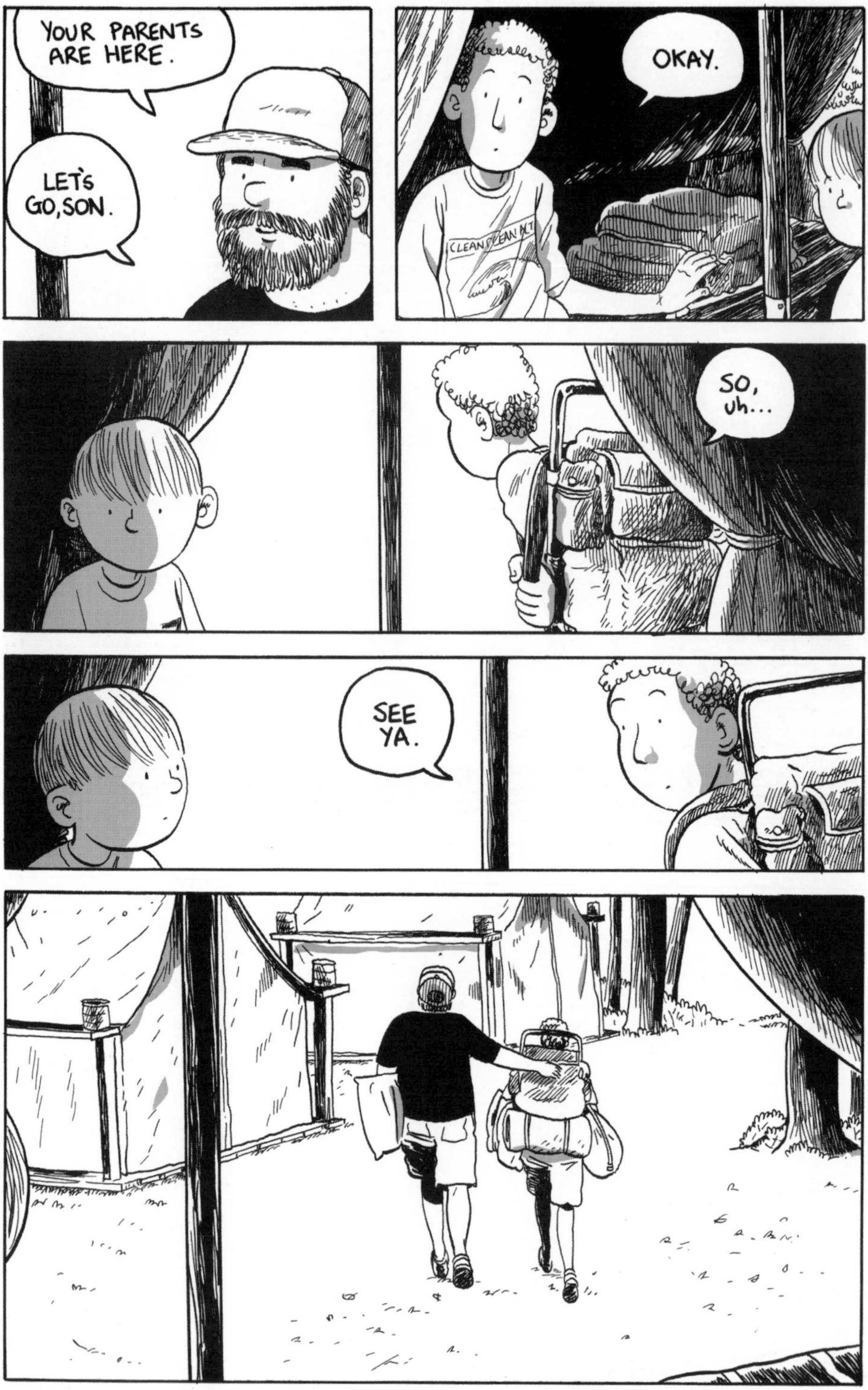
YOUR PARENTS ARE HERE.
LET'S GO, SON.
OKAY.
CLEAN
SO, uh...
SEE YA.

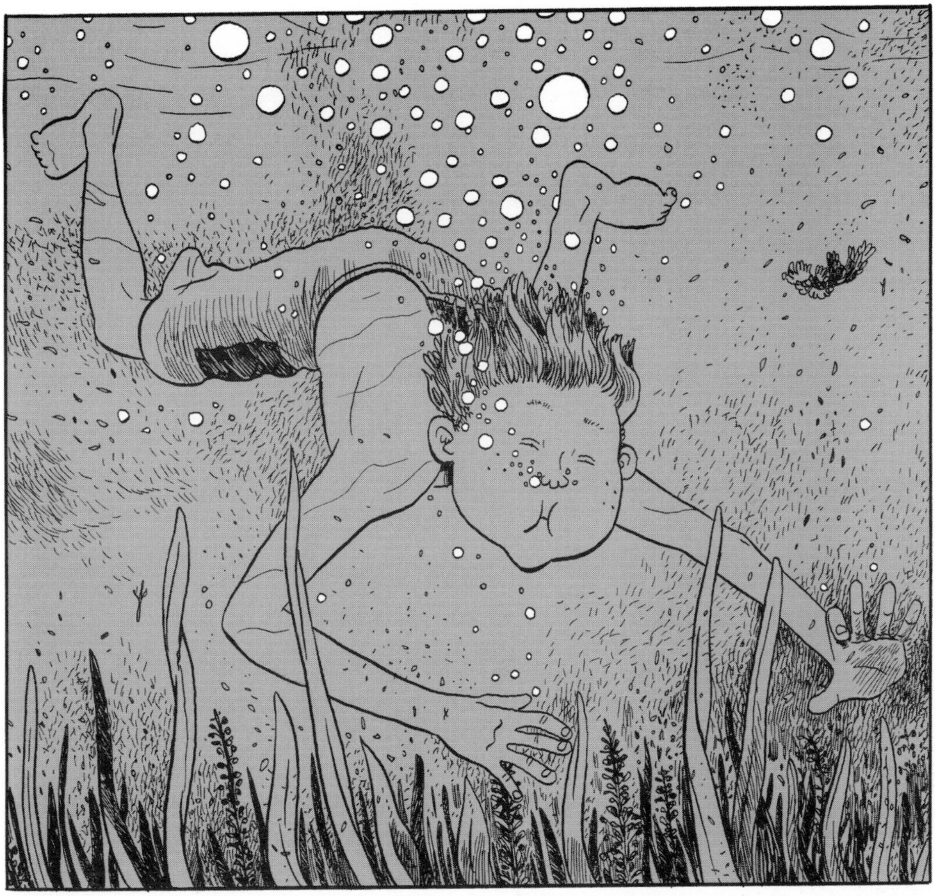

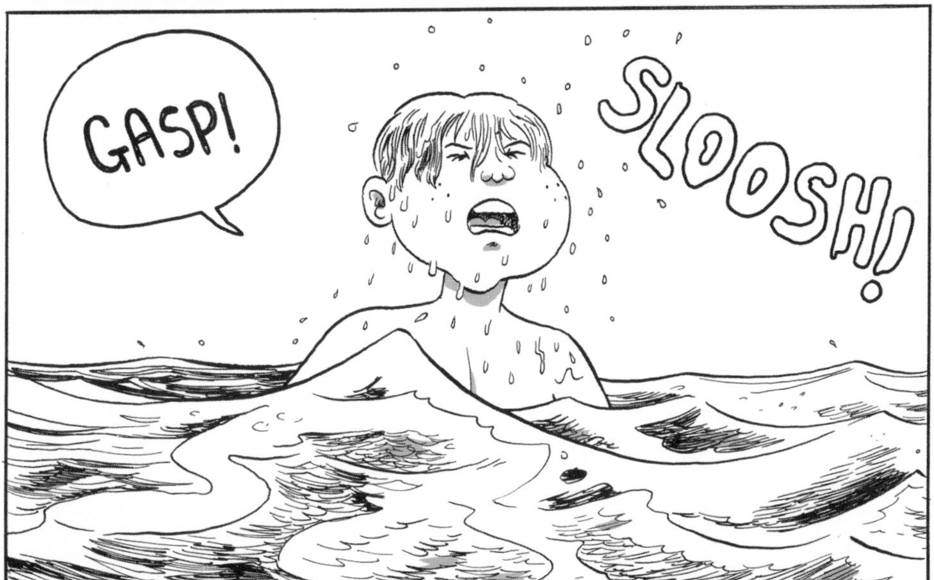
GASP!
SLOOSH!

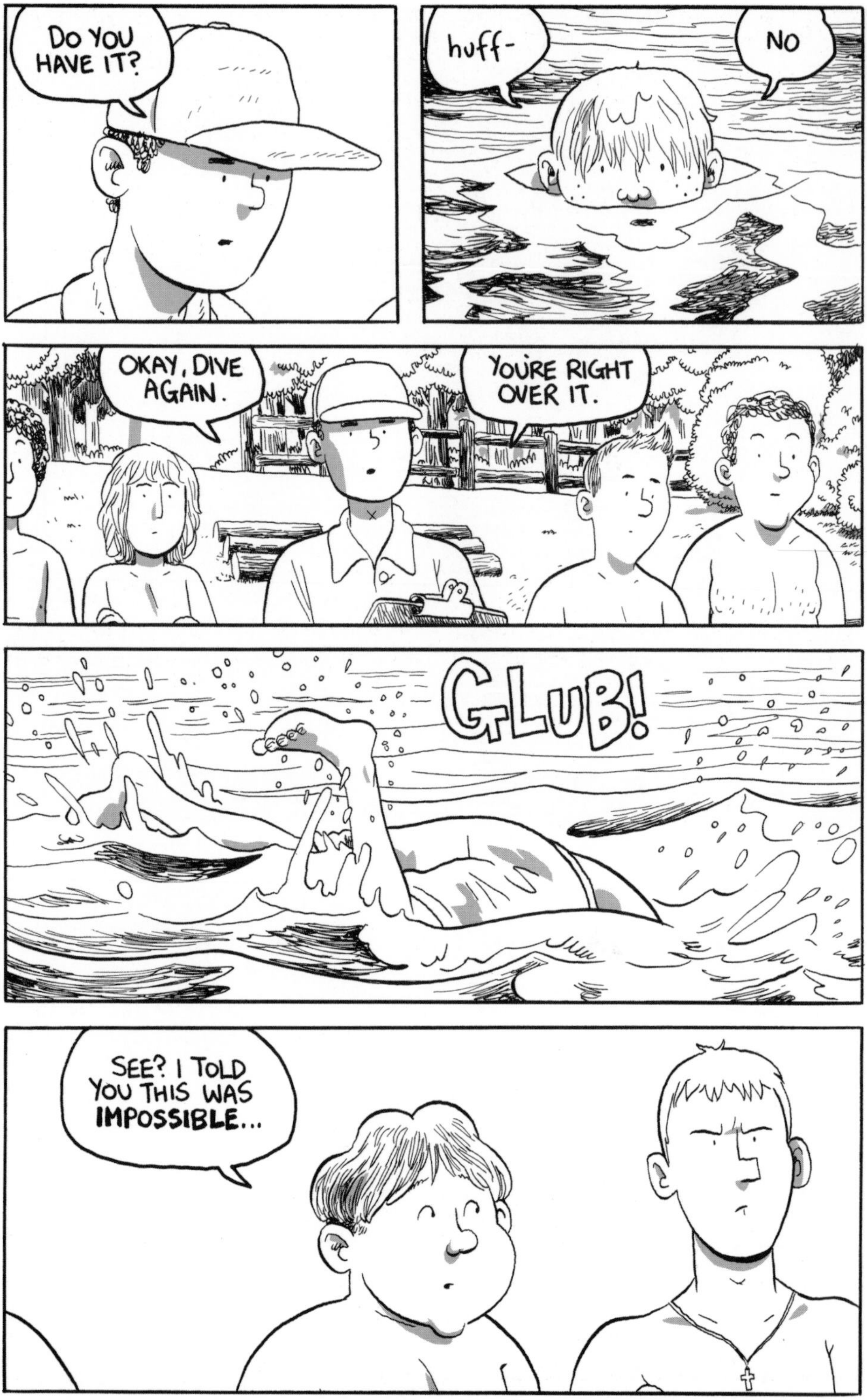
DO YOU HAVE IT?
huff-
NO
OKAY, DIVE AGAIN.
YOU'RE RIGHT OVER IT.
GLUB!
SEE? I TOLD YOU THIS WAS **IMPOSSIBLE**...

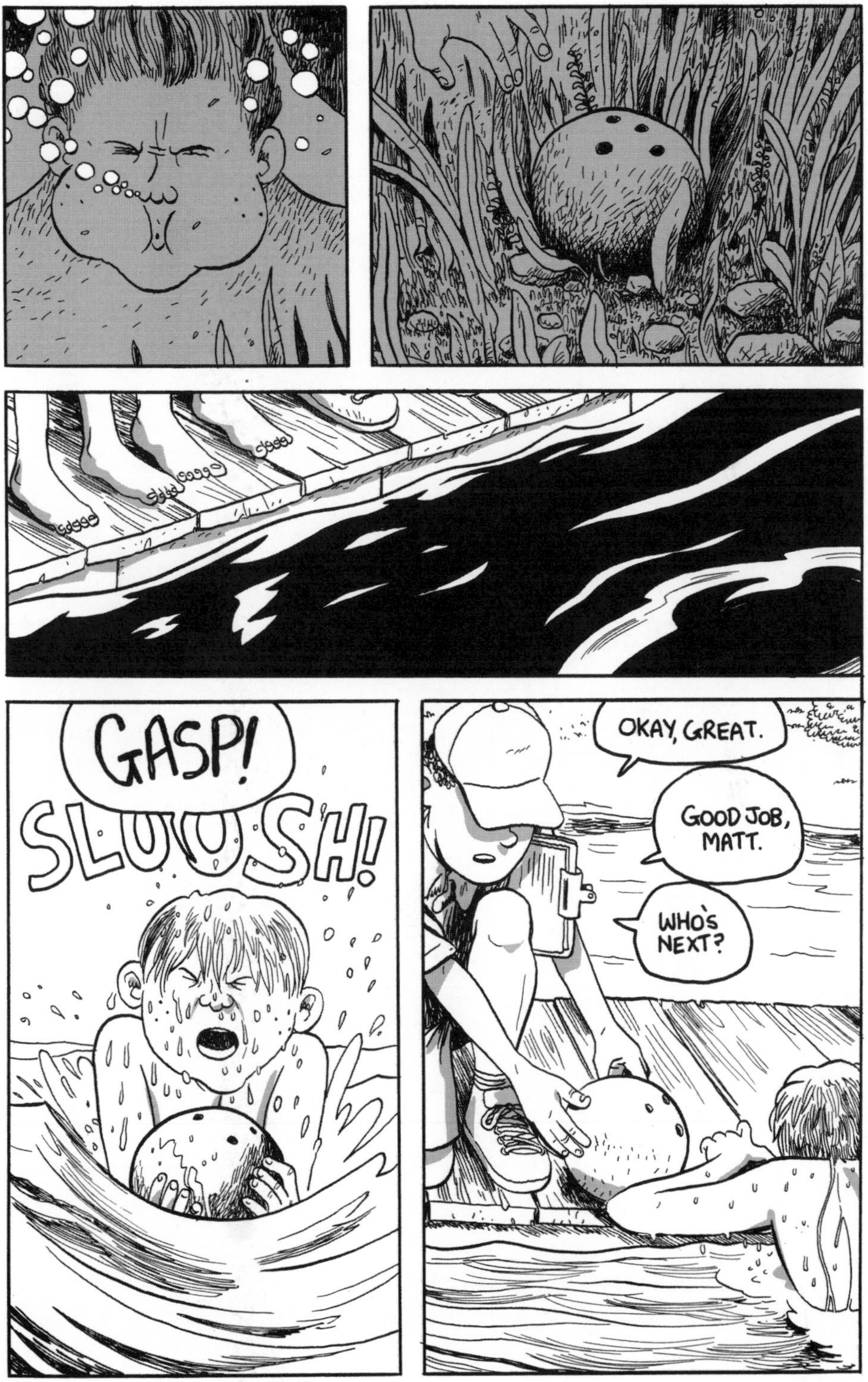
GASP!
SLUOOSH!
OKAY, GREAT.
GOOD JOB, MATT.
WHO'S NEXT?

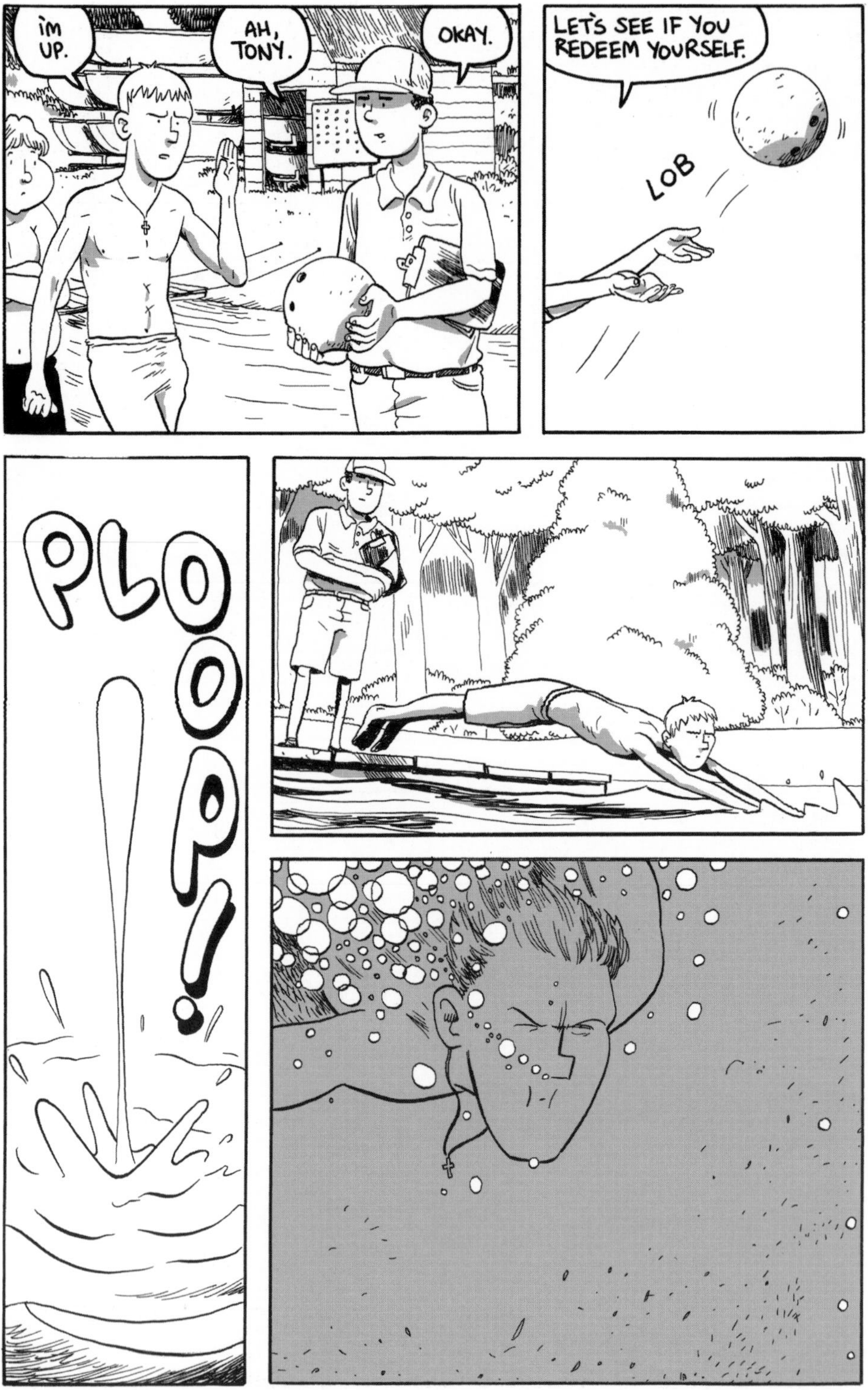
I'M UP.
AH, TONY.
OKAY.
LET'S SEE IF YOU REDEEM YOURSELF.
LOB
PLOOP!

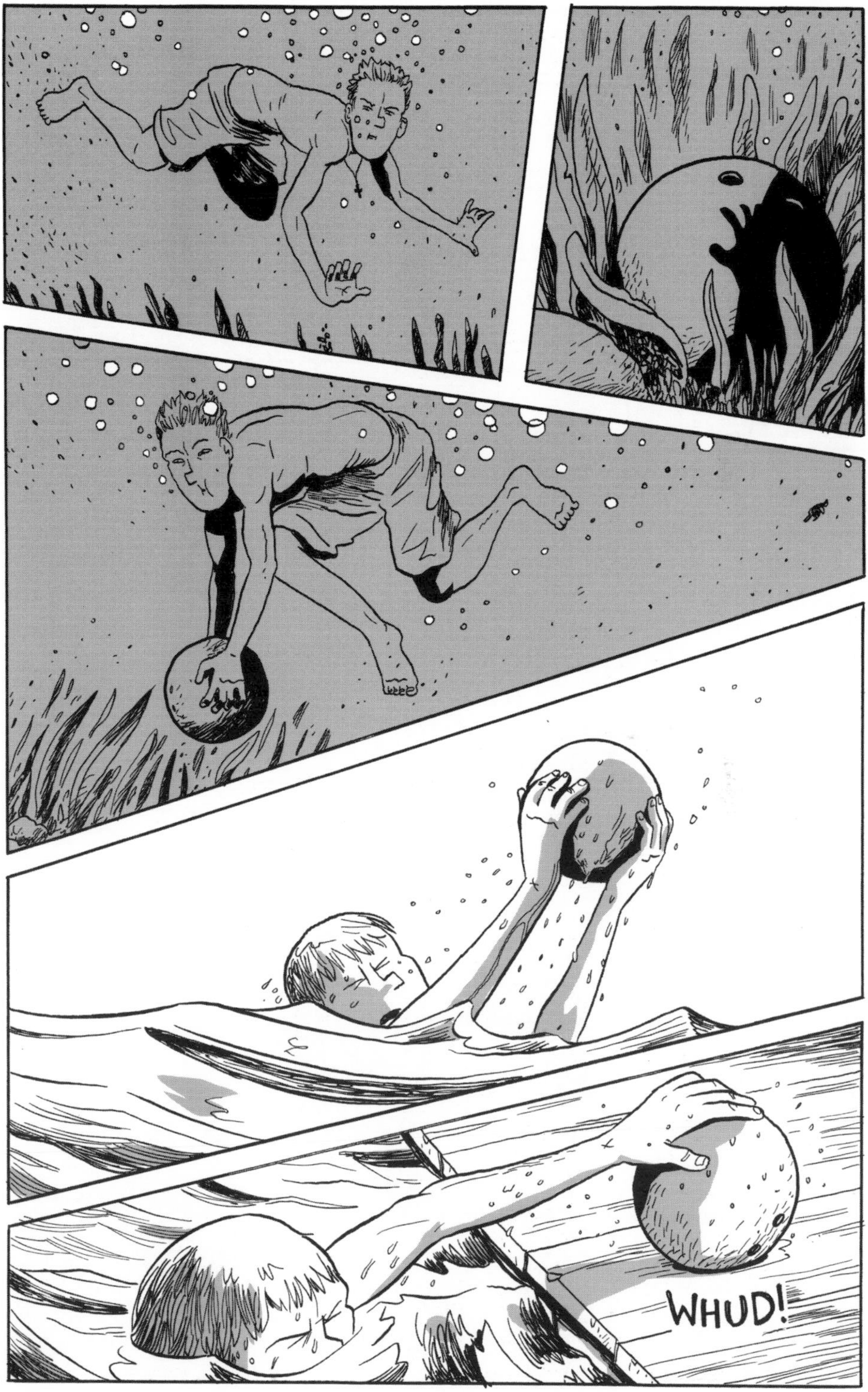
WHUD!

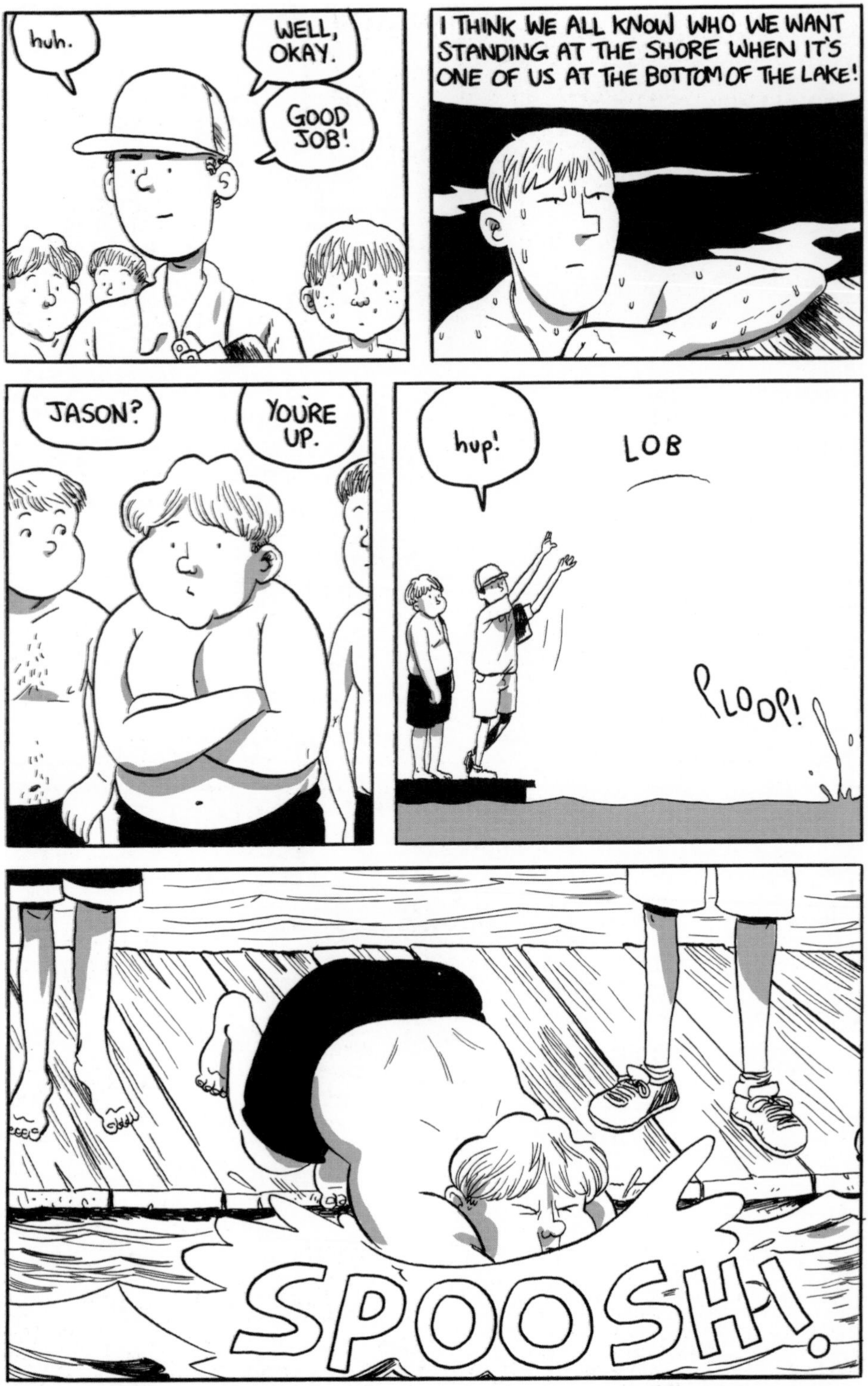
huh.
WELL, OKAY.
GOOD JOB!
I THINK WE ALL KNOW WHO WE WANT STANDING AT THE SHORE WHEN IT'S ONE OF US AT THE BOTTOM OF THE LAKE!
JASON?
YOU'RE UP.
hup!
LOB
PLOOP!
SPOOSH!

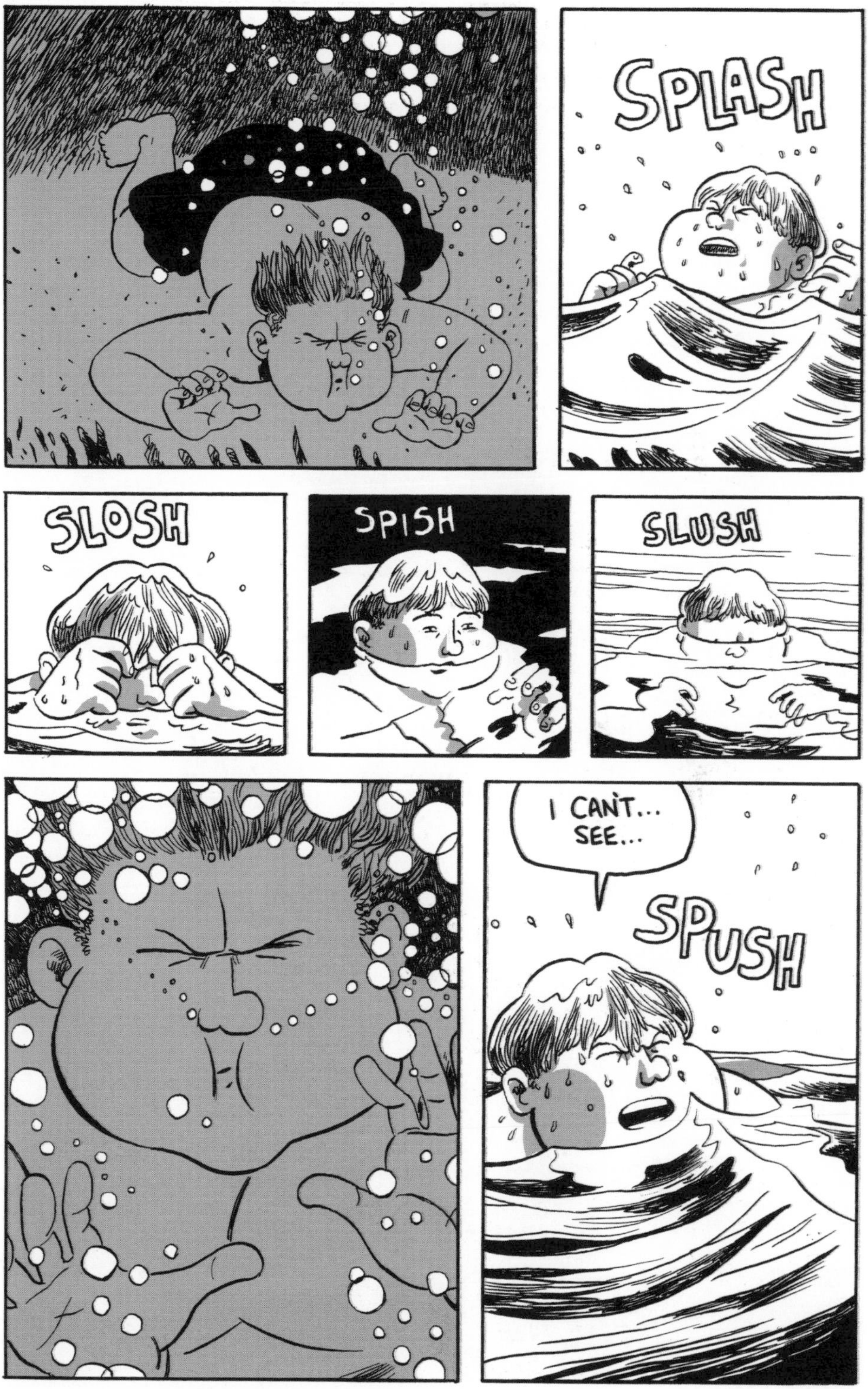
SPLASH
SLOSH
SPISH
SLUSH
I CAN'T... SEE...
SPUSH

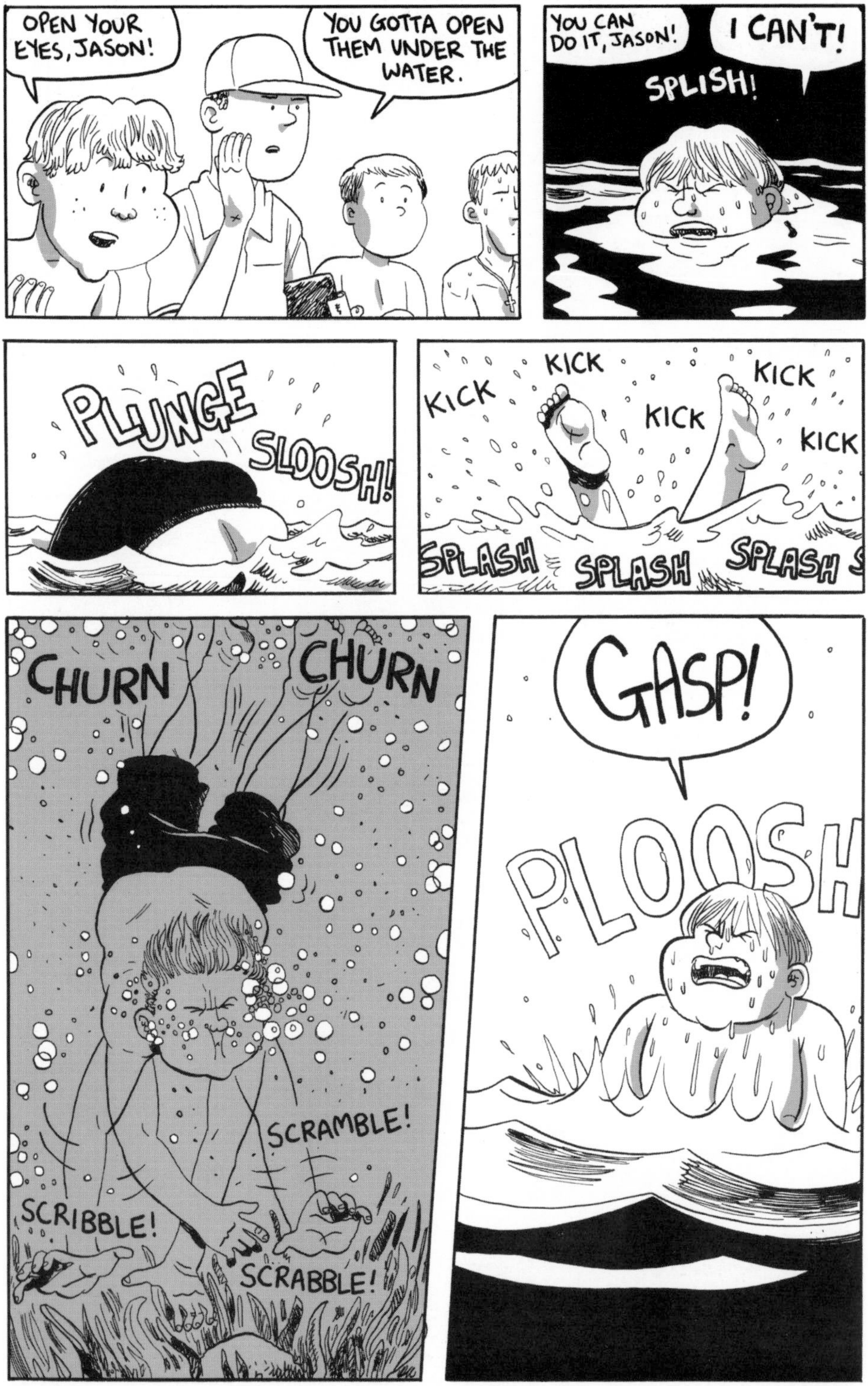
OPEN YOUR EYES, JASON!
YOU GOTTA OPEN THEM UNDER THE WATER.
YOU CAN DO IT, JASON!
I CAN'T!
SPLISH!
PLUNGE
SLOOSH!
KICK
KICK
KICK
KICK
KICK
SPLASH
SPLASH
SPLASH
CHURN
CHURN
SCRAMBLE!
SCRIBBLE!
SCRABBLE!
GASP!
PLOOSH

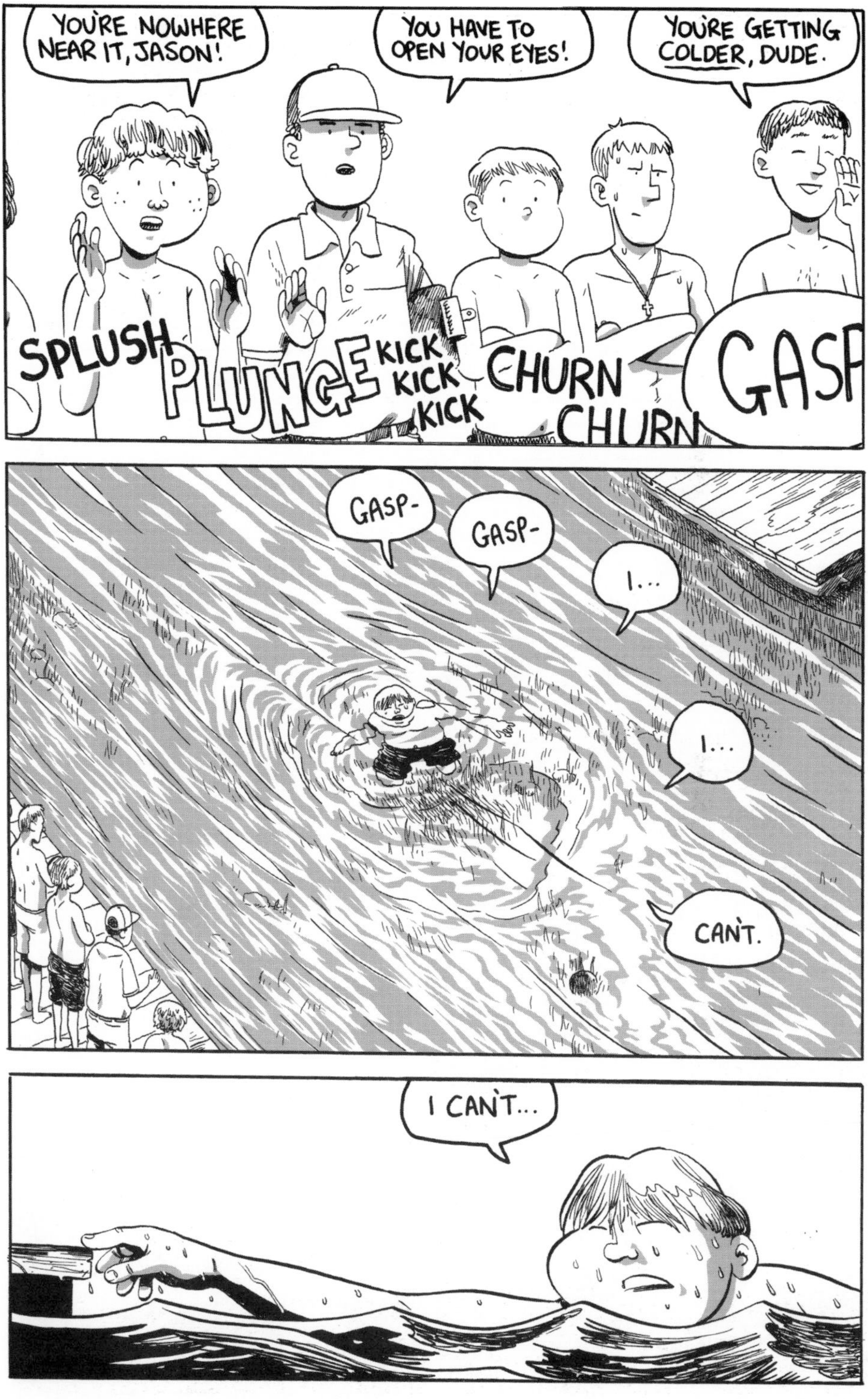
YOU'RE NOWHERE NEAR IT, JASON!
YOU HAVE TO OPEN YOUR EYES!
YOU'RE GETTING COLDER, DUDE.
SPLUSH
PLUNGE
KICK KICK KICK
CHURN
CHURN
GASP
GASP-
GASP-
I...
I...
CAN'T.
I CAN'T...

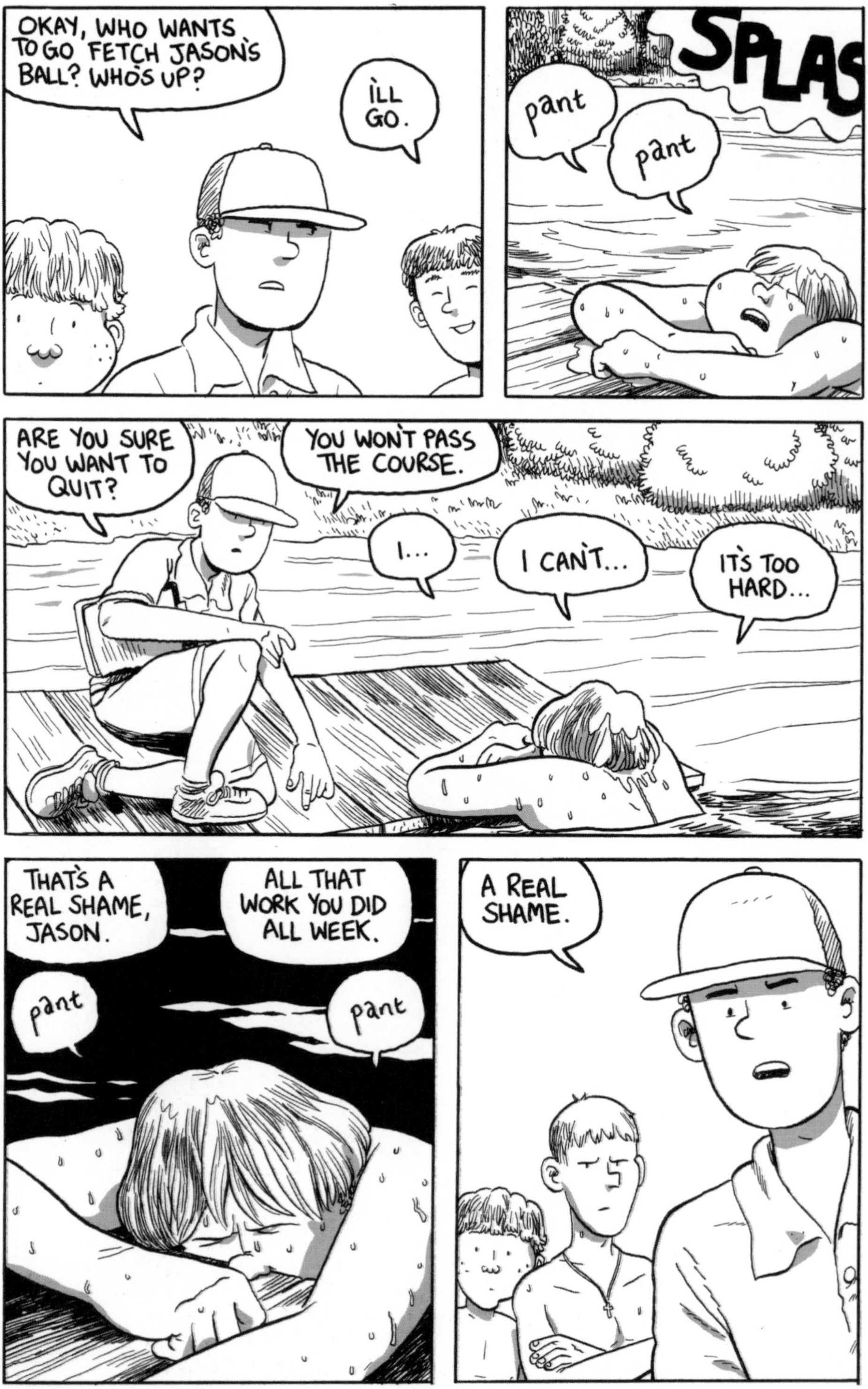
OKAY, WHO WANTS TO GO FETCH JASON'S BALL? WHO'S UP?
I'LL GO.
SPLAS
pant
pant
ARE YOU SURE YOU WANT TO QUIT?
YOU WON'T PASS THE COURSE.
I...
I CAN'T...
IT'S TOO HARD...
THAT'S A REAL SHAME, JASON.
ALL THAT WORK YOU DID ALL WEEK.
pant
pant
A REAL SHAME.

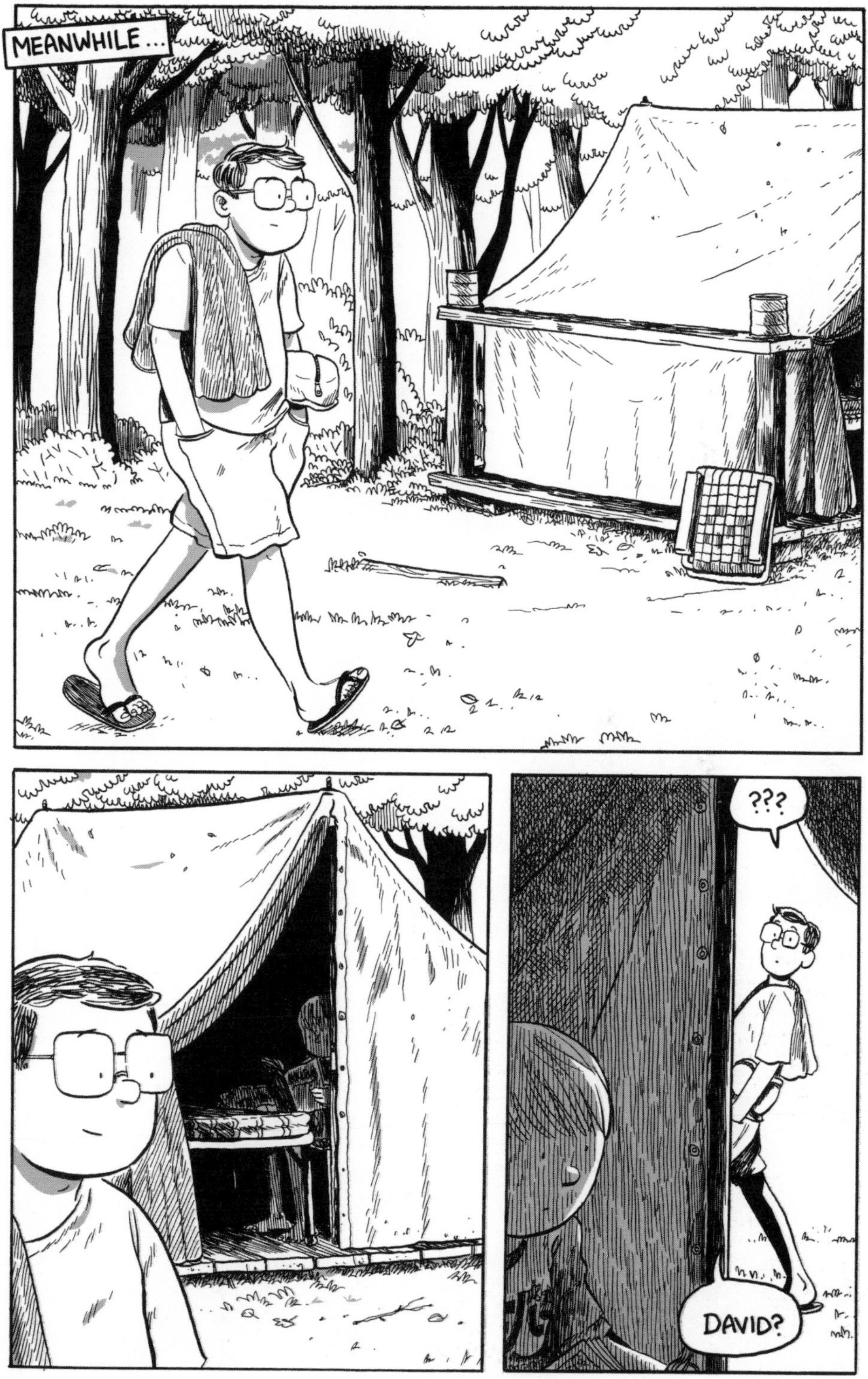
MEANWHILE...
???
DAVID?

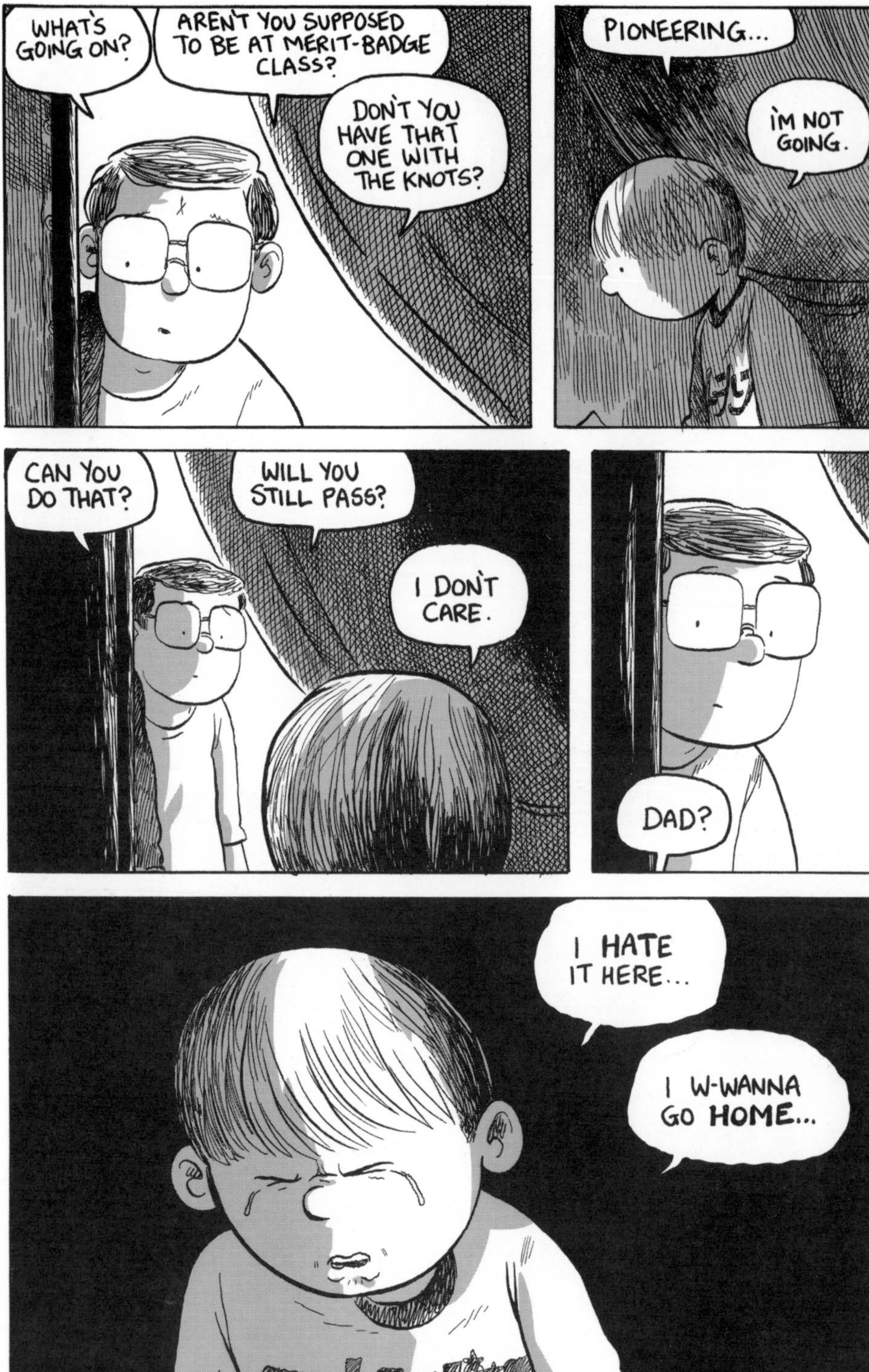
WHAT'S GOING ON?
AREN'T YOU SUPPOSED TO BE AT MERIT-BADGE CLASS?
DON'T YOU HAVE THAT ONE WITH THE KNOTS?
PIONEERING...
I'M NOT GOING.
CAN YOU DO THAT?
WILL YOU STILL PASS?
I DON'T CARE.
DAD?
I HATE IT HERE...
I W-WANNA GO **HOME**...

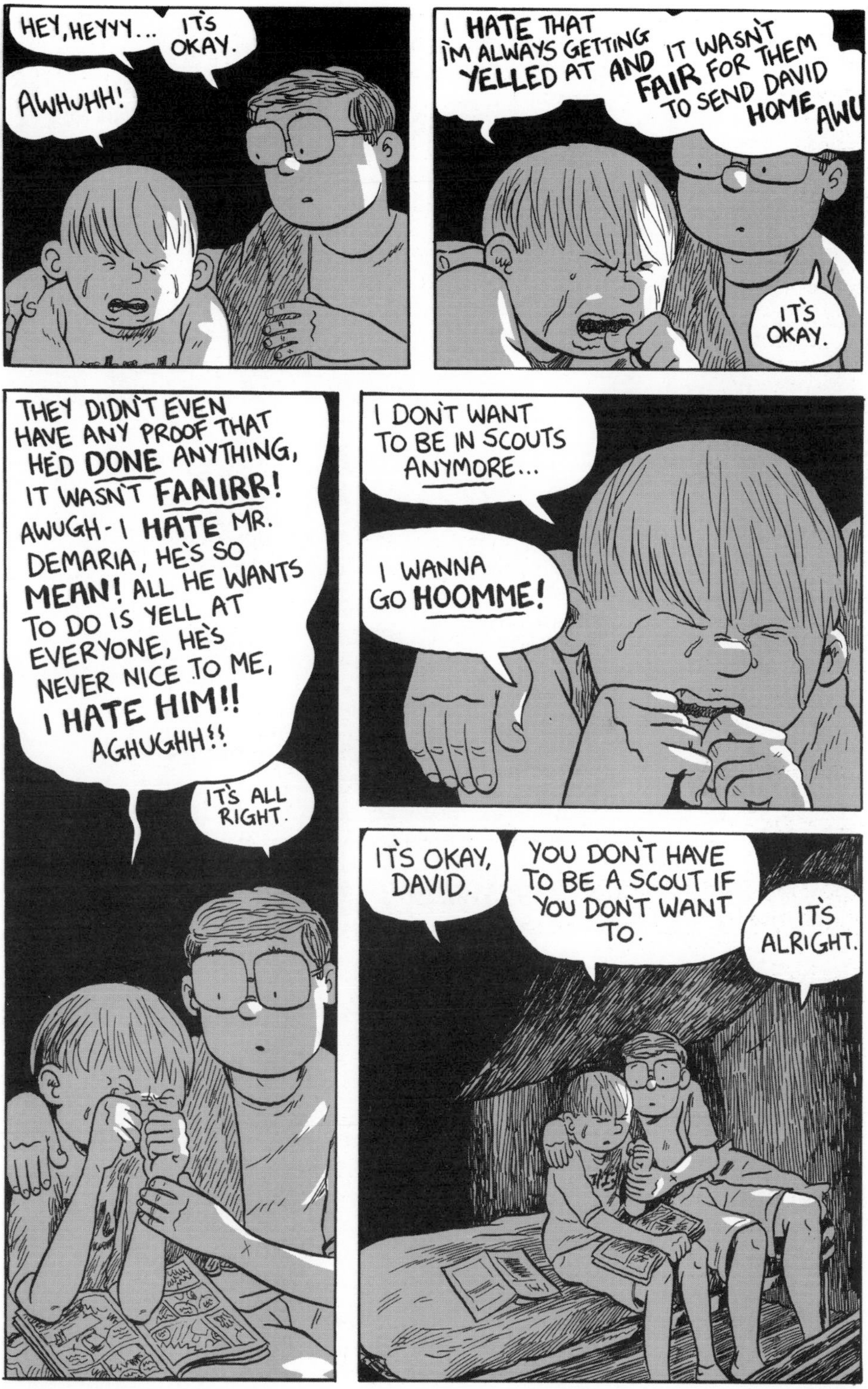
HEY, HEYYY...
IT'S OKAY.
AWHUHH!
I HATE THAT I'M ALWAYS GETTING YELLED AT AND IT WASN'T FAIR FOR THEM TO SEND DAVID HOME AWU
IT'S OKAY.
THEY DIDN'T EVEN HAVE ANY PROOF THAT HE'D DONE ANYTHING, IT WASN'T FAAIIRR! AWUGH- I HATE MR. DEMARIA, HE'S SO MEAN! ALL HE WANTS TO DO IS YELL AT EVERYONE, HE'S NEVER NICE TO ME, I HATE HIM!! AGHUGHH!!
IT'S ALL RIGHT.
I DON'T WANT TO BE IN SCOUTS ANYMORE...
I WANNA GO HOOMME!
IT'S OKAY, DAVID.
YOU DON'T HAVE TO BE A SCOUT IF YOU DON'T WANT TO.
IT'S ALRIGHT.

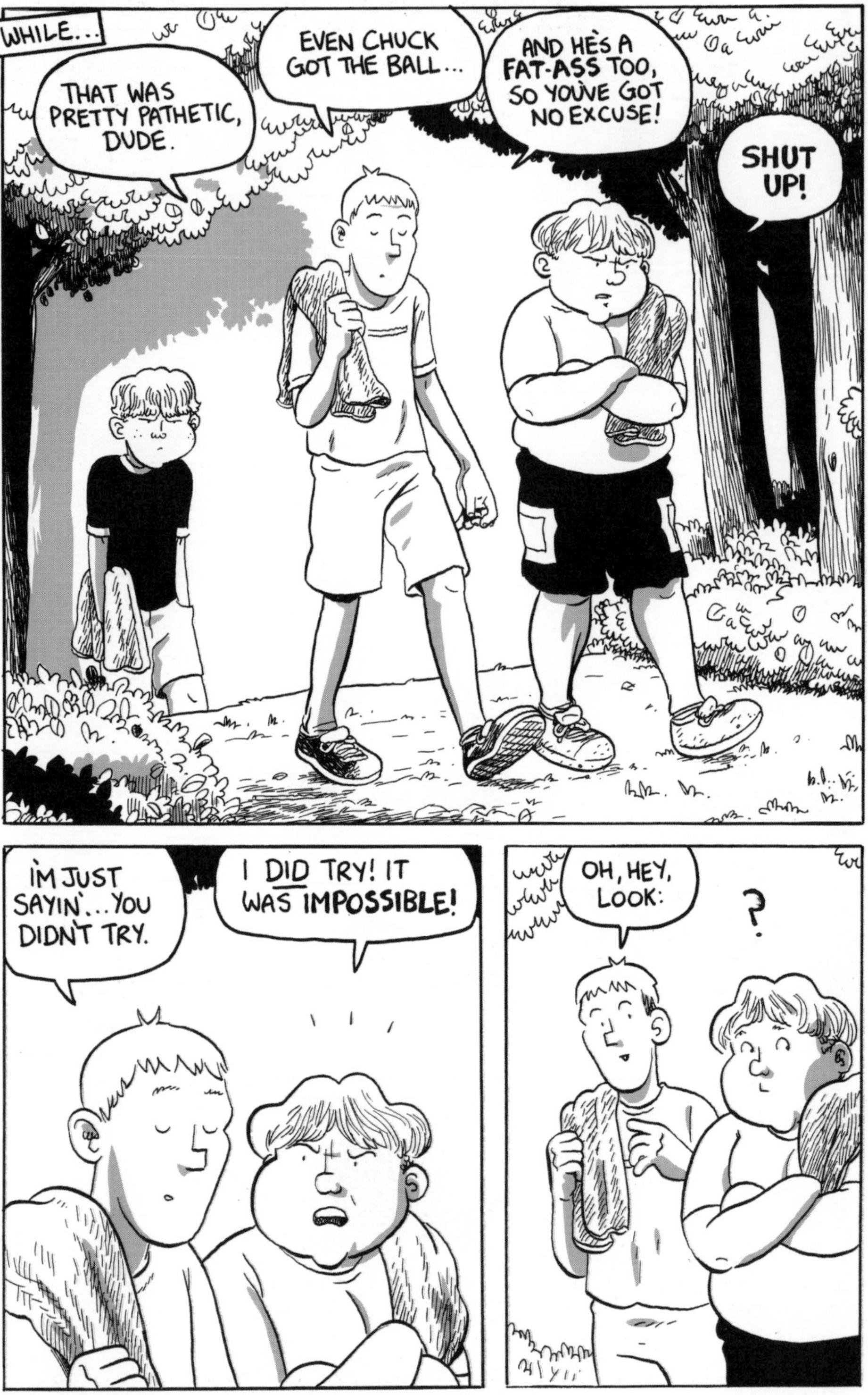
WHILE...
THAT WAS PRETTY PATHETIC, DUDE.
EVEN CHUCK GOT THE BALL...
AND HE'S A FAT-ASS TOO, SO YOU'VE GOT NO EXCUSE!
SHUT UP!
I'M JUST SAYIN'... YOU DIDN'T TRY.
I DID TRY! IT WAS IMPOSSIBLE!
OH, HEY, LOOK:
?

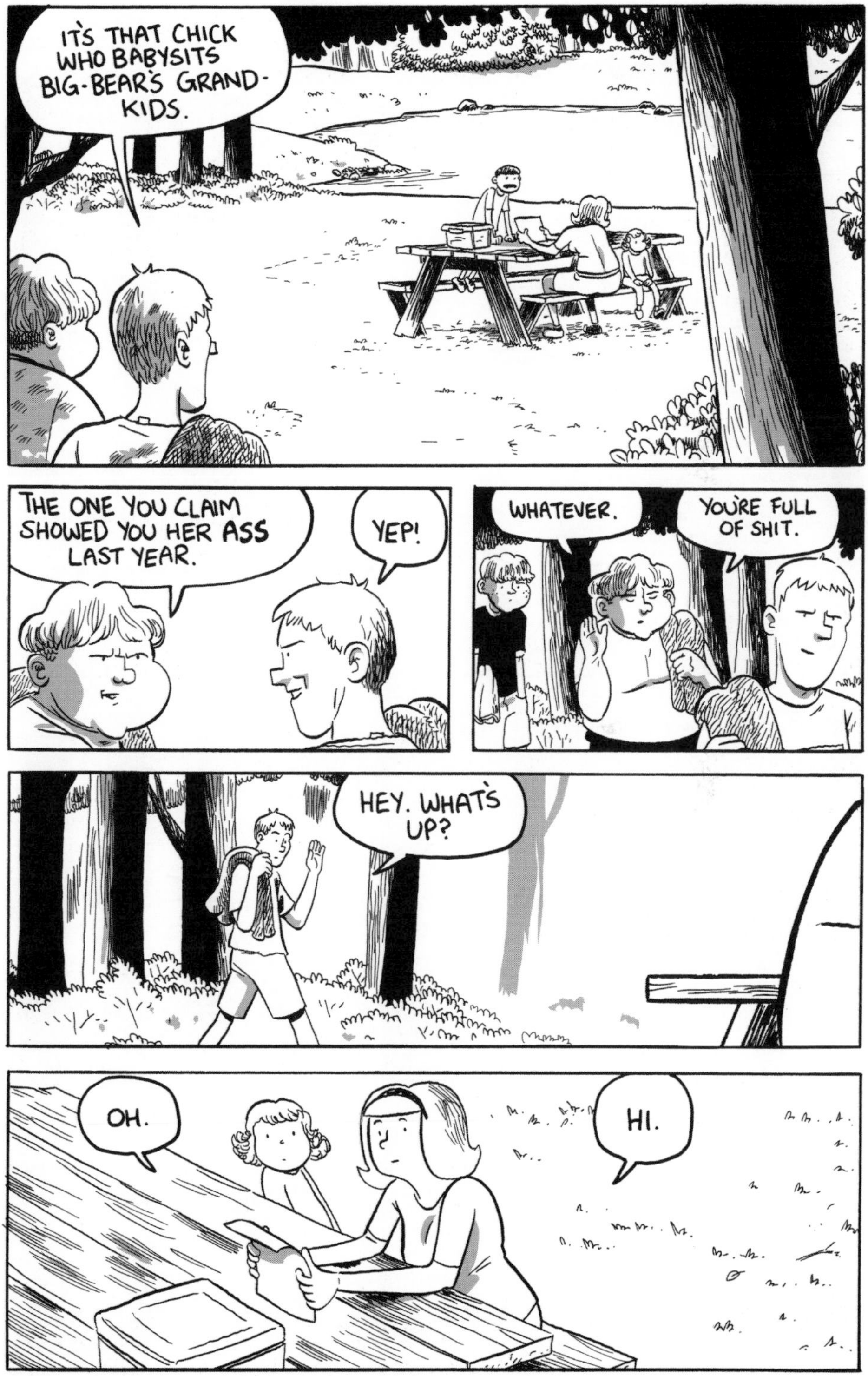
IT'S THAT CHICK WHO BABYSITS BIG-BEAR'S GRAND-KIDS.
THE ONE YOU CLAIM SHOWED YOU HER ASS LAST YEAR.
YEP!
WHATEVER.
YOU'RE FULL OF SHIT.
HEY. WHAT'S UP?
OH.
HI.

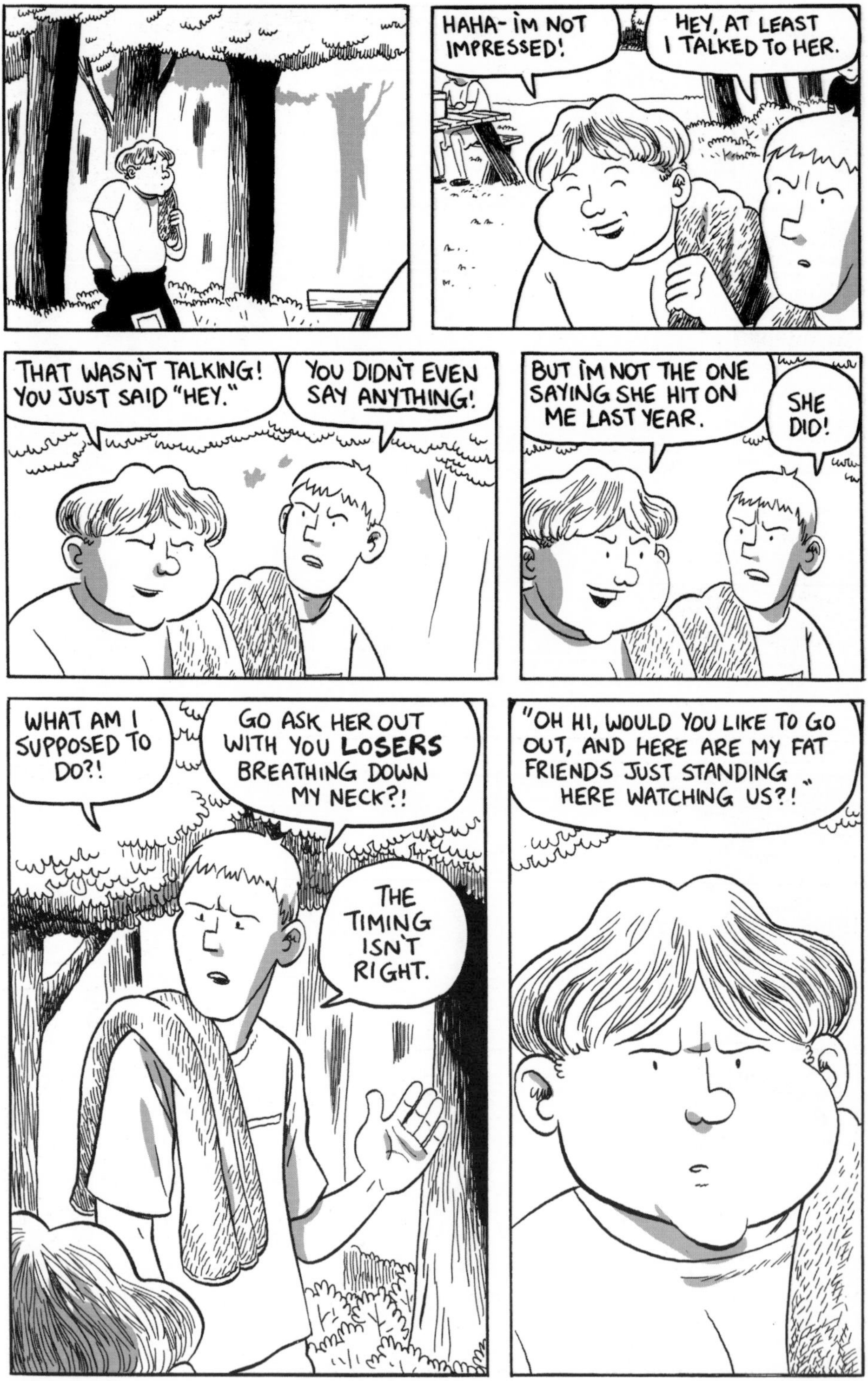
HAHA- I'M NOT IMPRESSED!
HEY, AT LEAST I TALKED TO HER.
THAT WASN'T TALKING! YOU JUST SAID "HEY."
YOU DIDN'T EVEN SAY ANYTHING!
BUT I'M NOT THE ONE SAYING SHE HIT ON ME LAST YEAR.
SHE DID!
WHAT AM I SUPPOSED TO DO?!
GO ASK HER OUT WITH YOU **LOSERS** BREATHING DOWN MY NECK?!
THE TIMING ISN'T RIGHT.
"OH HI, WOULD YOU LIKE TO GO OUT, AND HERE ARE MY FAT FRIENDS JUST STANDING HERE WATCHING US?!"

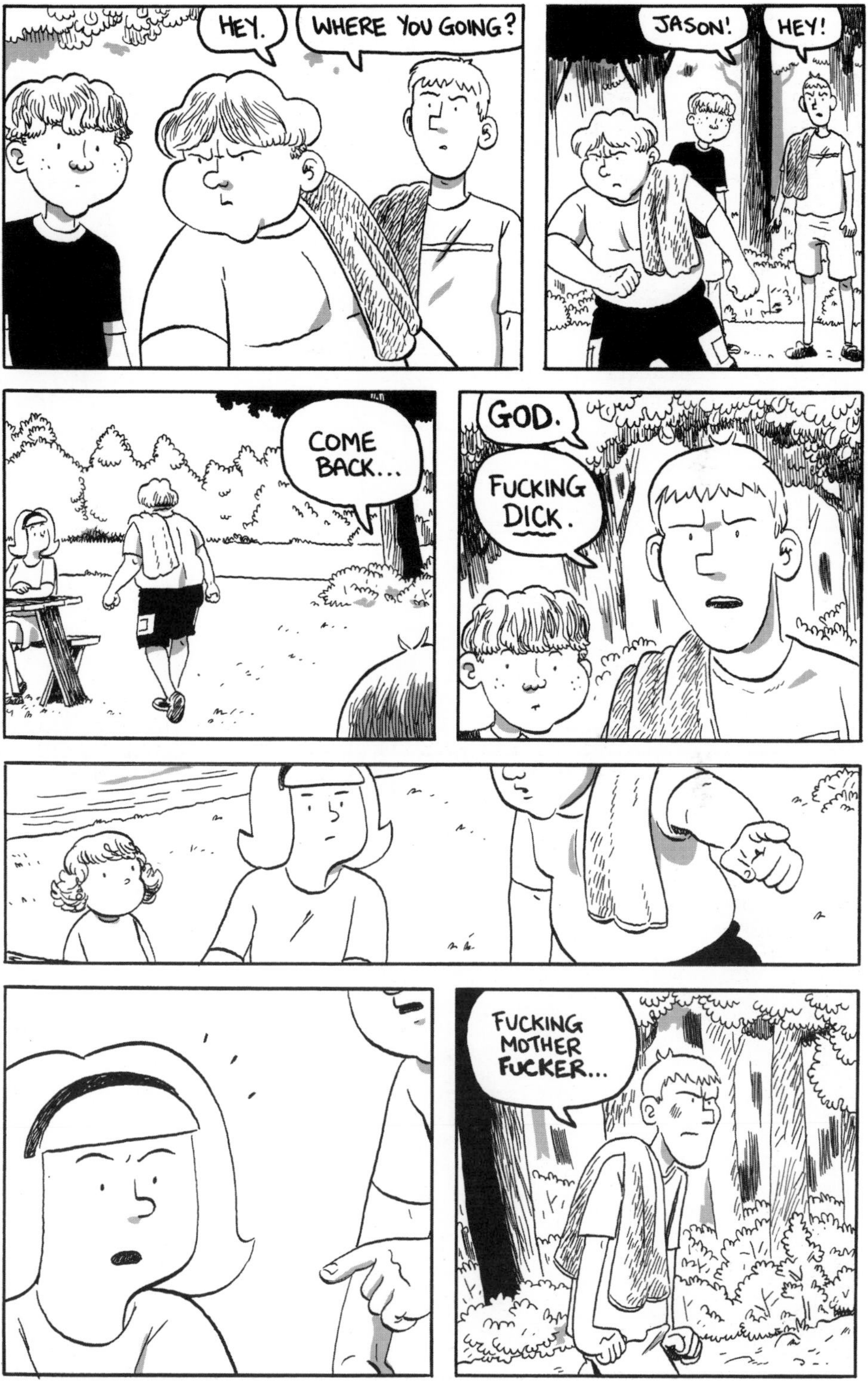
HEY.
WHERE YOU GOING?
JASON!
HEY!
COME BACK...
GOD.
FUCKING DICK.
FUCKING MOTHER FUCKER...

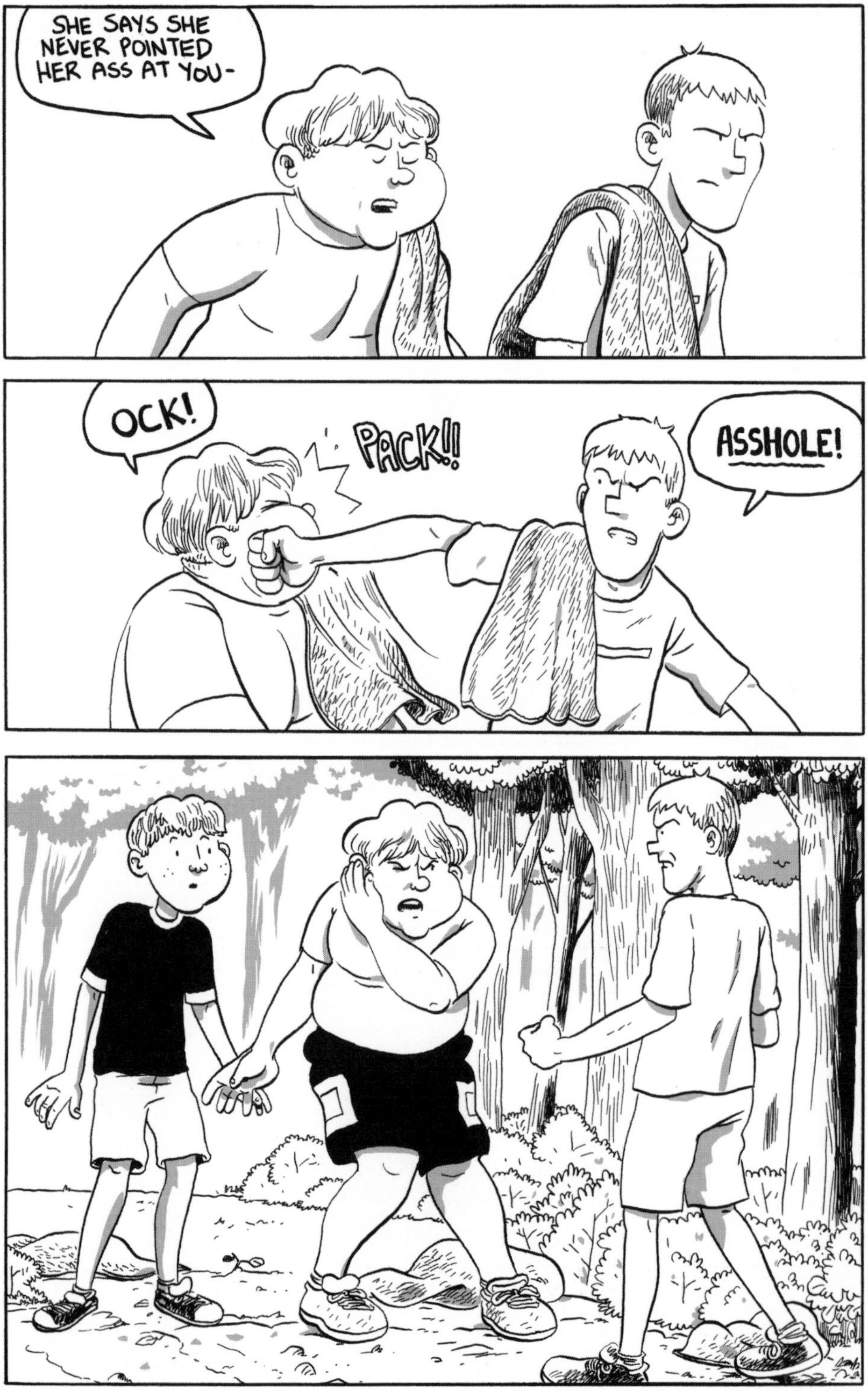
SHE SAYS SHE NEVER POINTED HER ASS AT YOU-
OCK!
PACK!!
ASSHOLE!

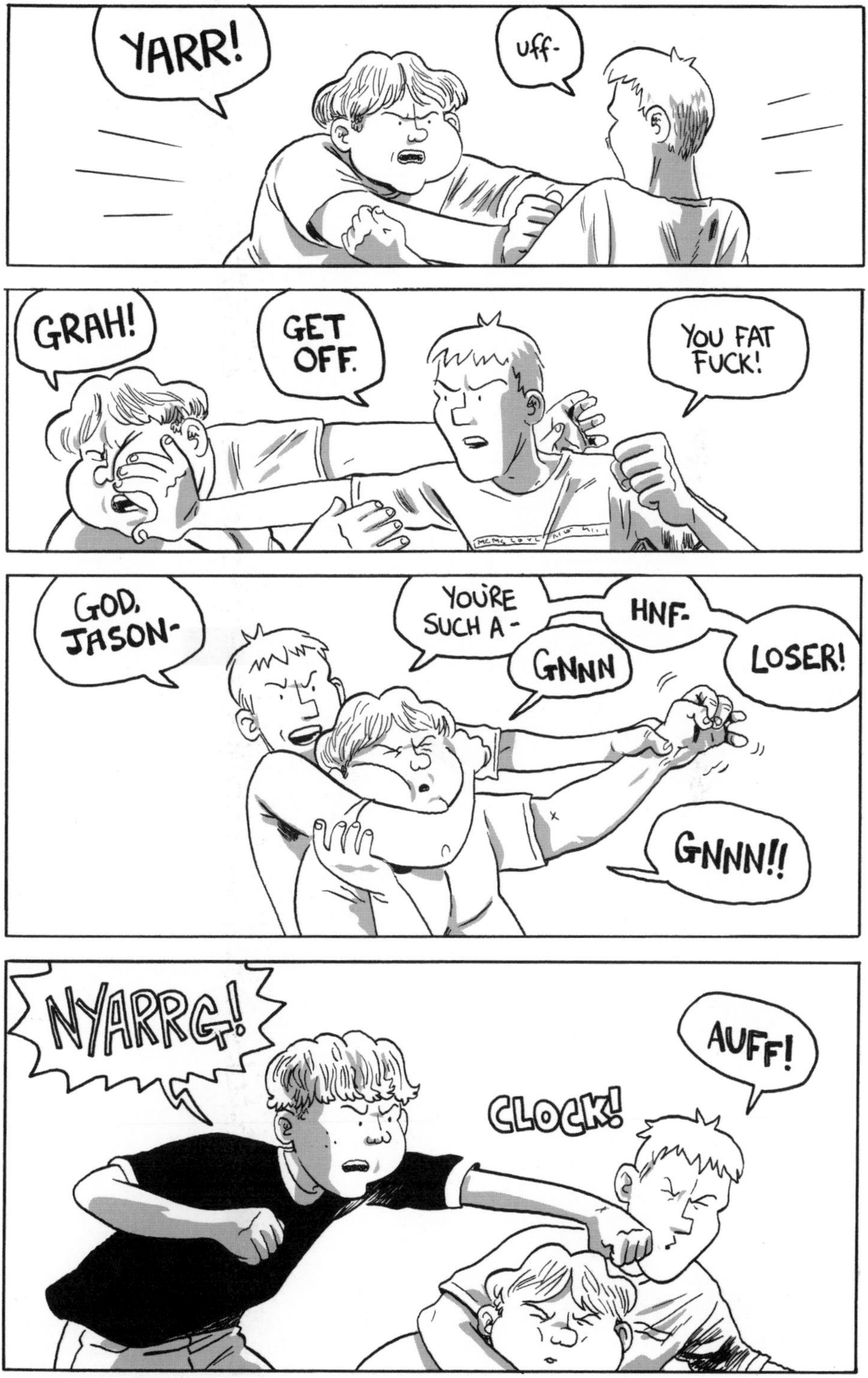
YARR!
uff-
GRAH!
GET OFF.
YOU FAT FUCK!
GOD, JASON-
YOU'RE SUCH A-
HNF-
GNNN
LOSER!
GNNN!!
NYARRG!
AUFF!
CLOCK!

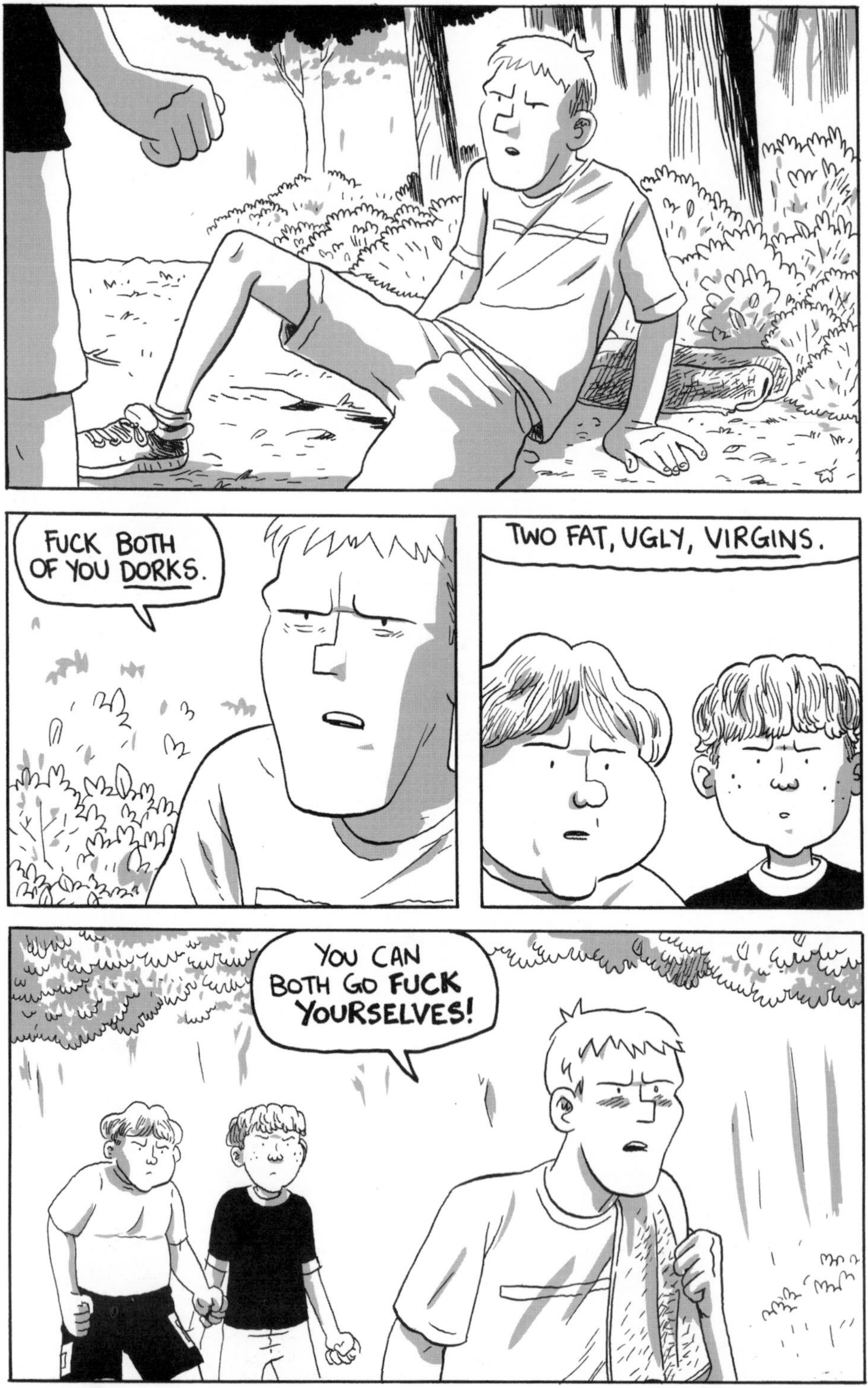
FUCK BOTH OF YOU DORKS.
TWO FAT, UGLY, VIRGINS.
YOU CAN BOTH GO FUCK YOURSELVES!

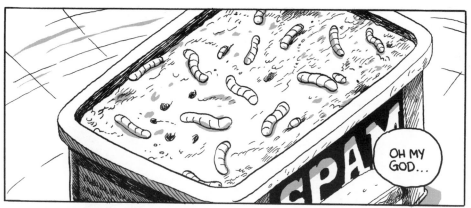

OH MY GOD...

GROSS...

OH, MAN, THAT'S NASTY!

HEY CHUCK, I TAKE BACK WHAT I SAID BEFORE...

BONG

IF YOU WANT TO EAT THE SPAM, GO AHEAD!

IN FACT, I'D PAY YOU FIVE DOLLARS!

YEAH!

HAH

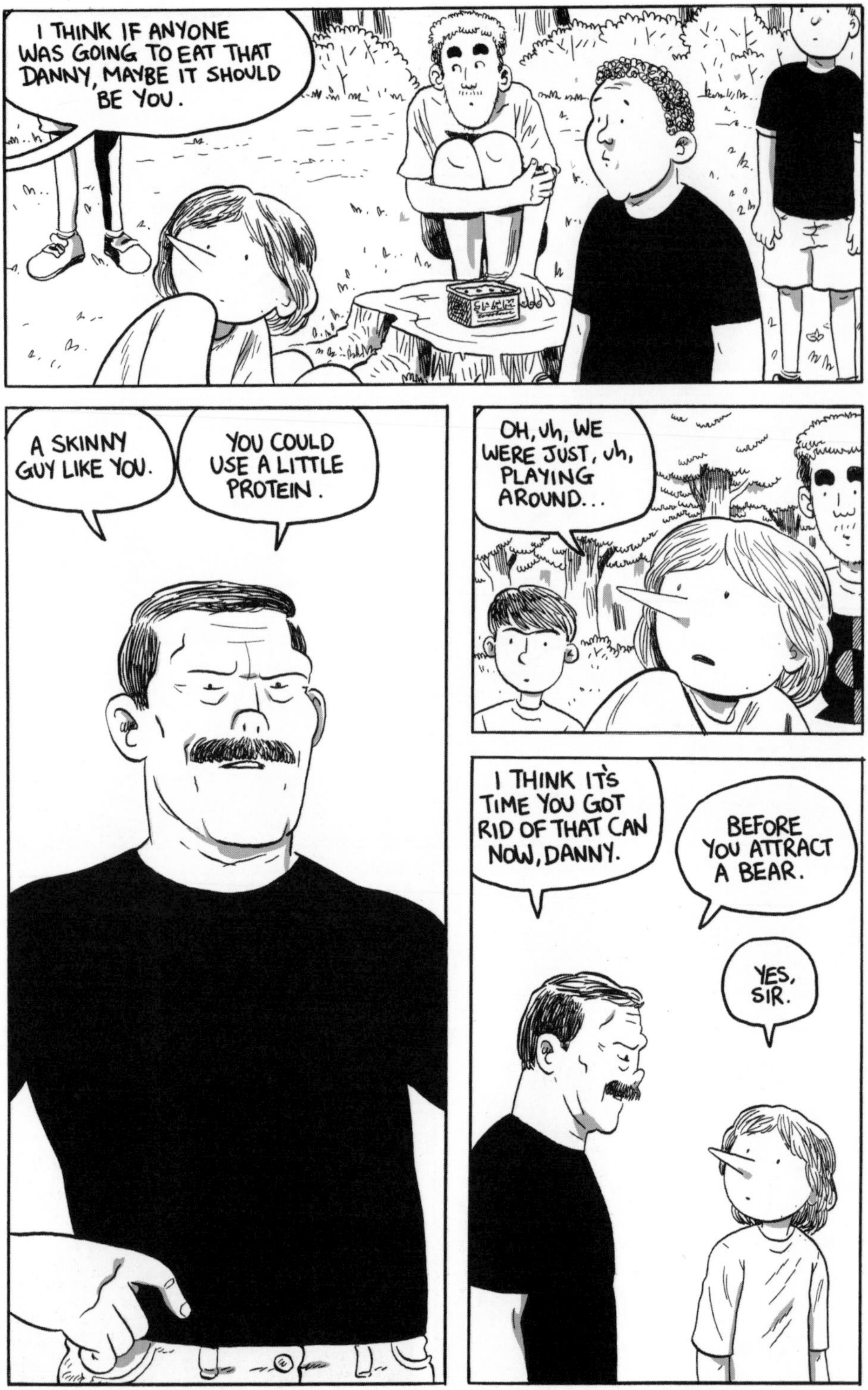
I THINK IF ANYONE WAS GOING TO EAT THAT DANNY, MAYBE IT SHOULD BE YOU.
A SKINNY GUY LIKE YOU.
YOU COULD USE A LITTLE PROTEIN.
OH, uh, WE WERE JUST, uh, PLAYING AROUND...
I THINK IT'S TIME YOU GOT RID OF THAT CAN NOW, DANNY.
BEFORE YOU ATTRACT A BEAR.
YES, SIR.

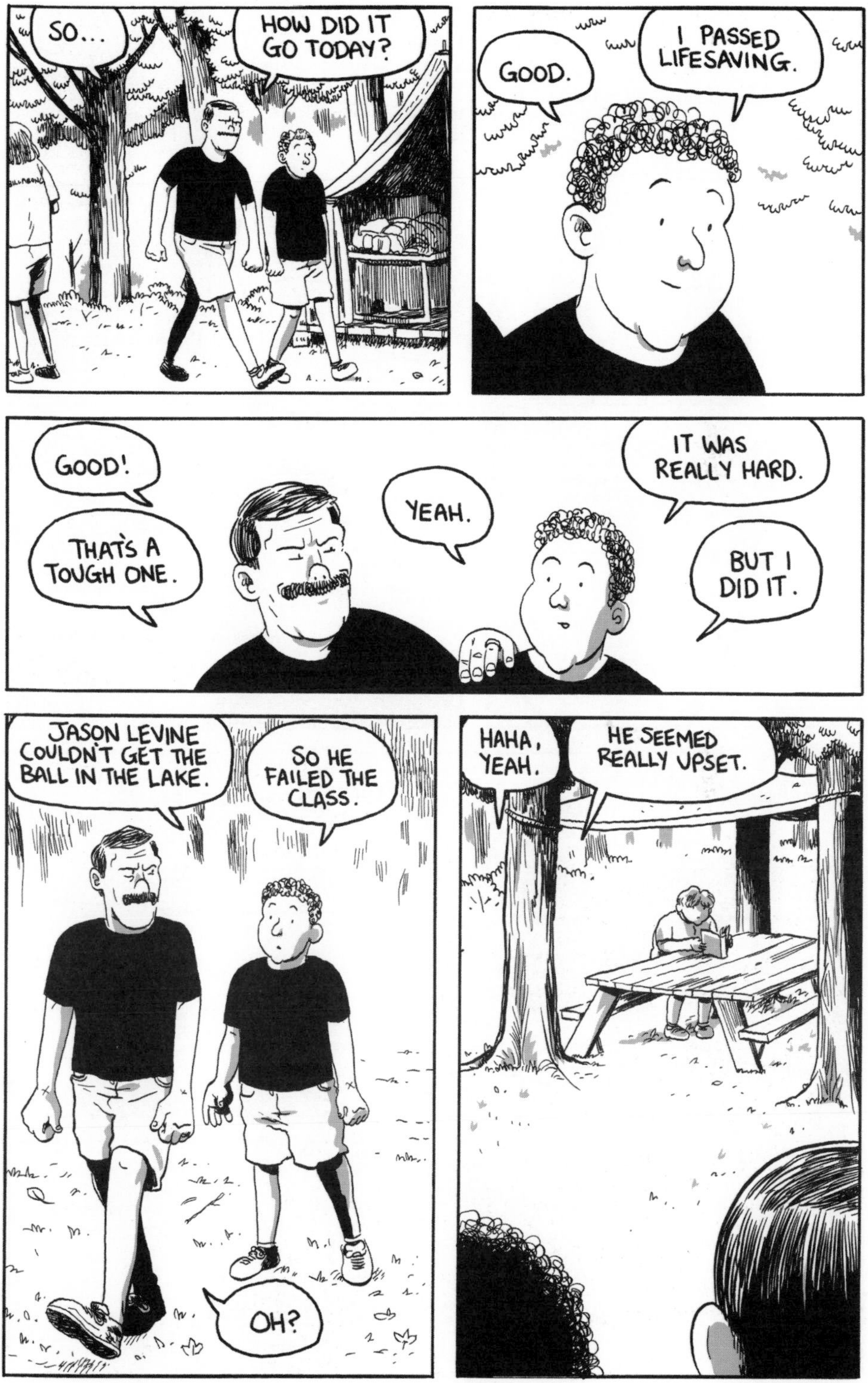
SO...
HOW DID IT GO TODAY?
GOOD.
I PASSED LIFESAVING.
GOOD!
THAT'S A TOUGH ONE.
YEAH.
IT WAS REALLY HARD.
BUT I DID IT.
JASON LEVINE COULDN'T GET THE BALL IN THE LAKE.
SO HE FAILED THE CLASS.
OH?
HAHA, YEAH.
HE SEEMED REALLY UPSET.

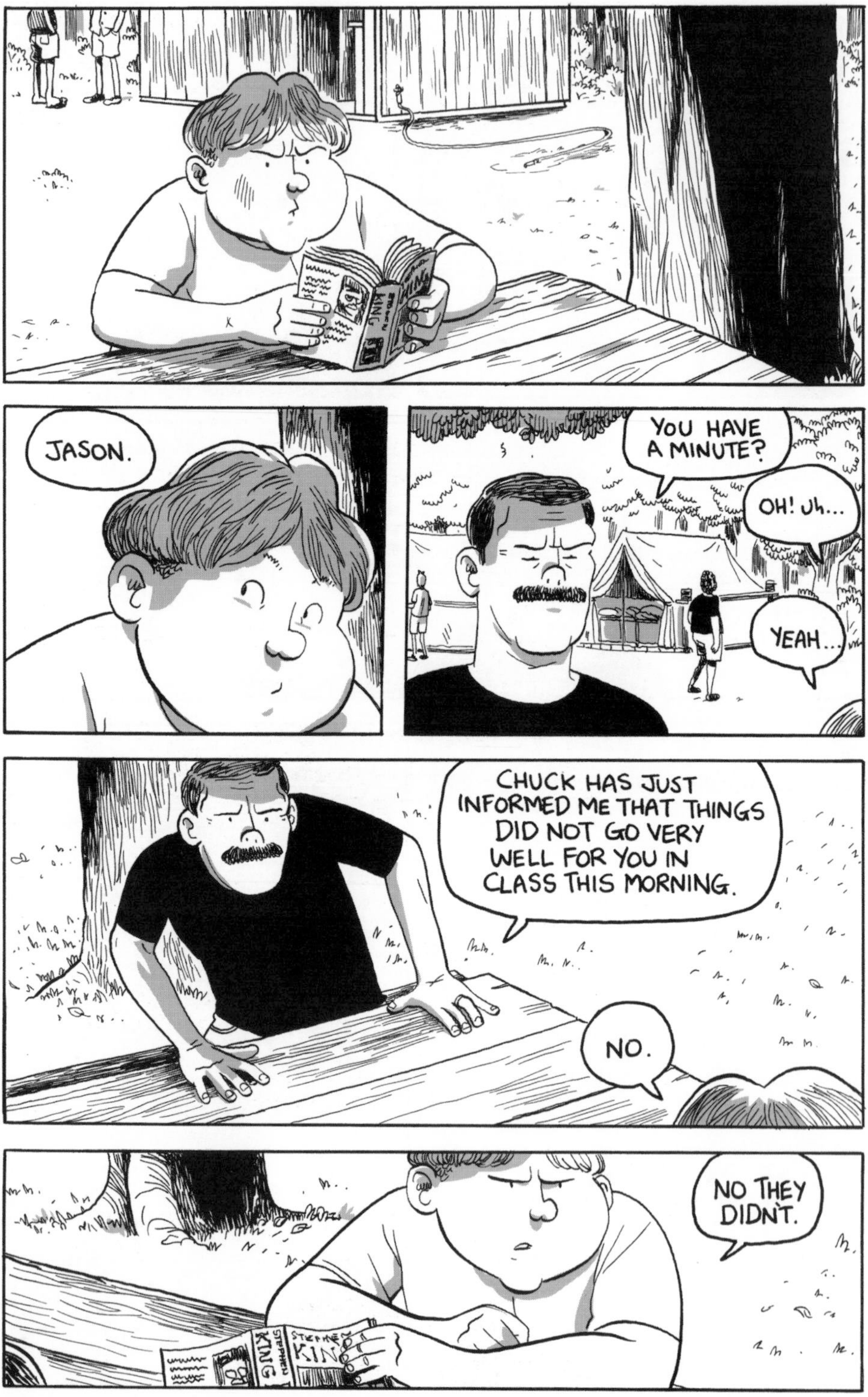

JASON.
YOU HAVE A MINUTE?
OH! uh...
YEAH...
CHUCK HAS JUST INFORMED ME THAT THINGS DID NOT GO VERY WELL FOR YOU IN CLASS THIS MORNING.
NO.
NO THEY DIDN'T.

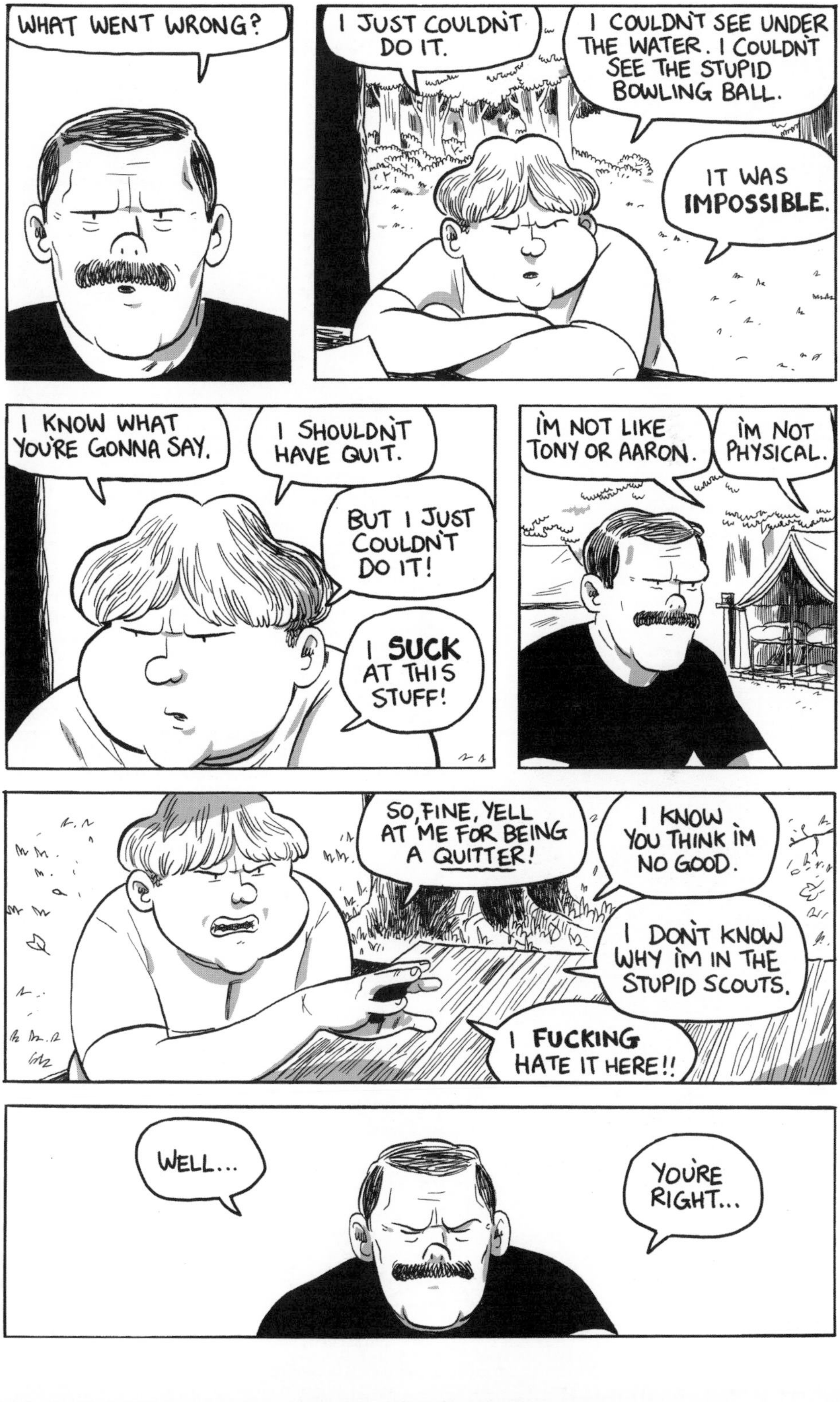
WHAT WENT WRONG?
I JUST COULDN'T DO IT.
I COULDN'T SEE UNDER THE WATER. I COULDN'T SEE THE STUPID BOWLING BALL.
IT WAS **IMPOSSIBLE.**
I KNOW WHAT YOU'RE GONNA SAY.
I SHOULDN'T HAVE QUIT.
BUT I JUST COULDN'T DO IT!
I **SUCK** AT THIS STUFF!
I'M NOT LIKE TONY OR AARON.
I'M NOT PHYSICAL.
SO, FINE, YELL AT ME FOR BEING A QUITTER!
I KNOW YOU THINK I'M NO GOOD.
I DON'T KNOW WHY I'M IN THE STUPID SCOUTS.
I **FUCKING** HATE IT HERE!!
WELL...
YOU'RE RIGHT...

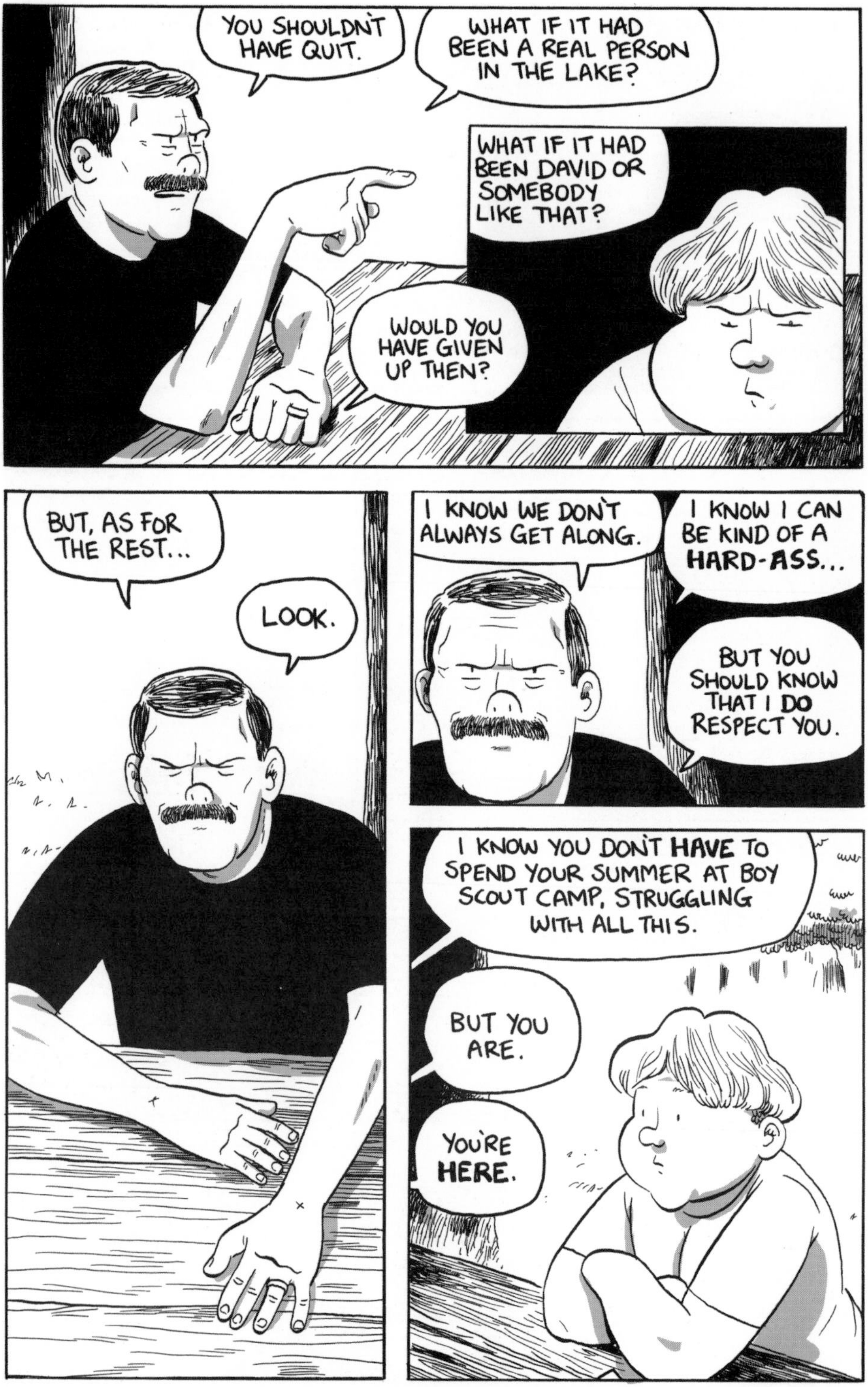
YOU SHOULDN'T HAVE QUIT.
WHAT IF IT HAD BEEN A REAL PERSON IN THE LAKE?
WHAT IF IT HAD BEEN DAVID OR SOMEBODY LIKE THAT?
WOULD YOU HAVE GIVEN UP THEN?
BUT, AS FOR THE REST...
LOOK.
I KNOW WE DON'T ALWAYS GET ALONG.
I KNOW I CAN BE KIND OF A **HARD-ASS**...
BUT YOU SHOULD KNOW THAT I **DO** RESPECT YOU.
I KNOW YOU DON'T **HAVE** TO SPEND YOUR SUMMER AT BOY SCOUT CAMP, STRUGGLING WITH ALL THIS.
BUT YOU ARE.
YOU'RE **HERE**.

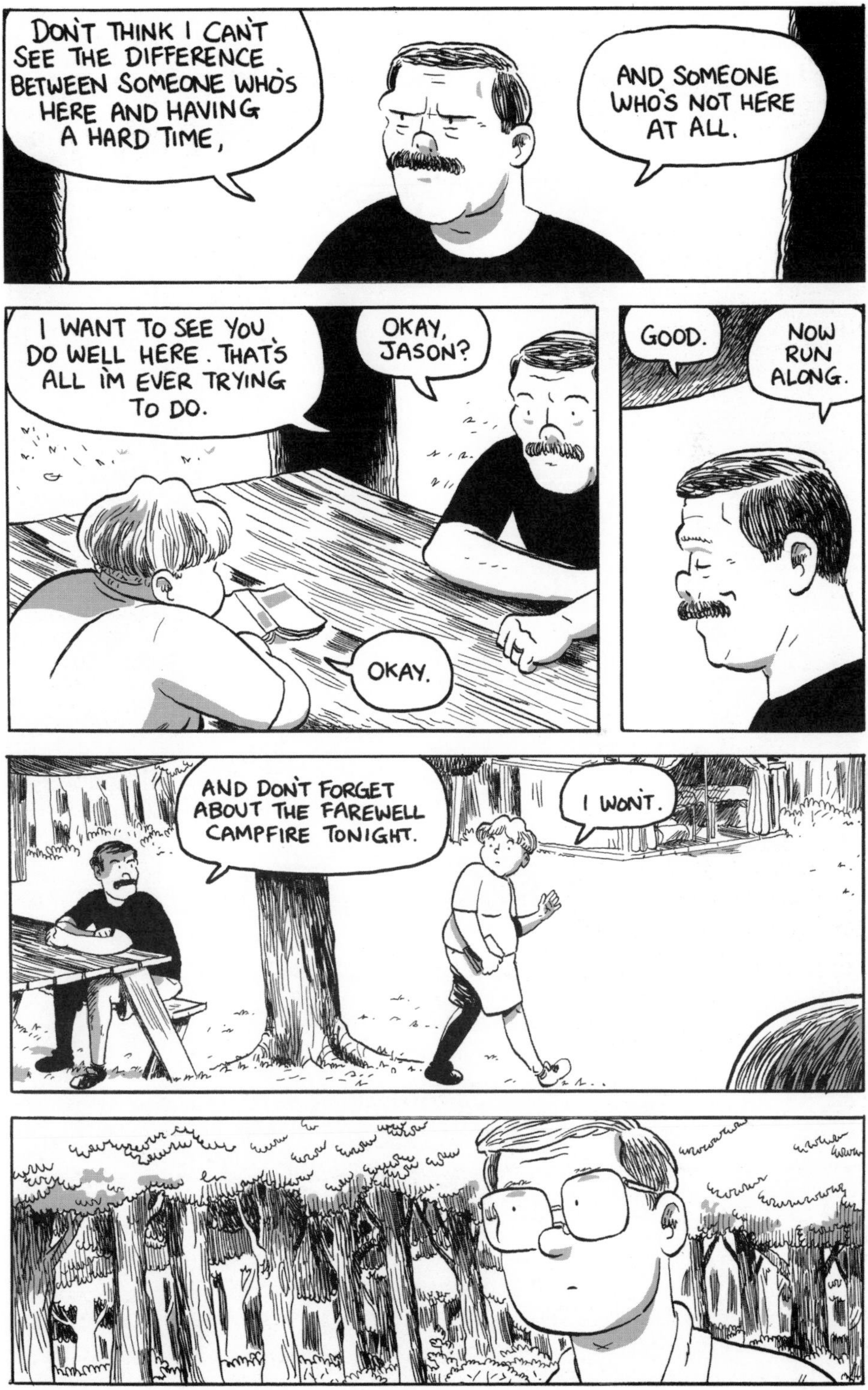

DON'T THINK I CAN'T SEE THE DIFFERENCE BETWEEN SOMEONE WHO'S HERE AND HAVING A HARD TIME,
AND SOMEONE WHO'S NOT HERE AT ALL.
I WANT TO SEE YOU DO WELL HERE. THAT'S ALL I'M EVER TRYING TO DO.
OKAY, JASON?
OKAY.
GOOD.
NOW RUN ALONG.
AND DON'T FORGET ABOUT THE FAREWELL CAMPFIRE TONIGHT.
I WON'T.

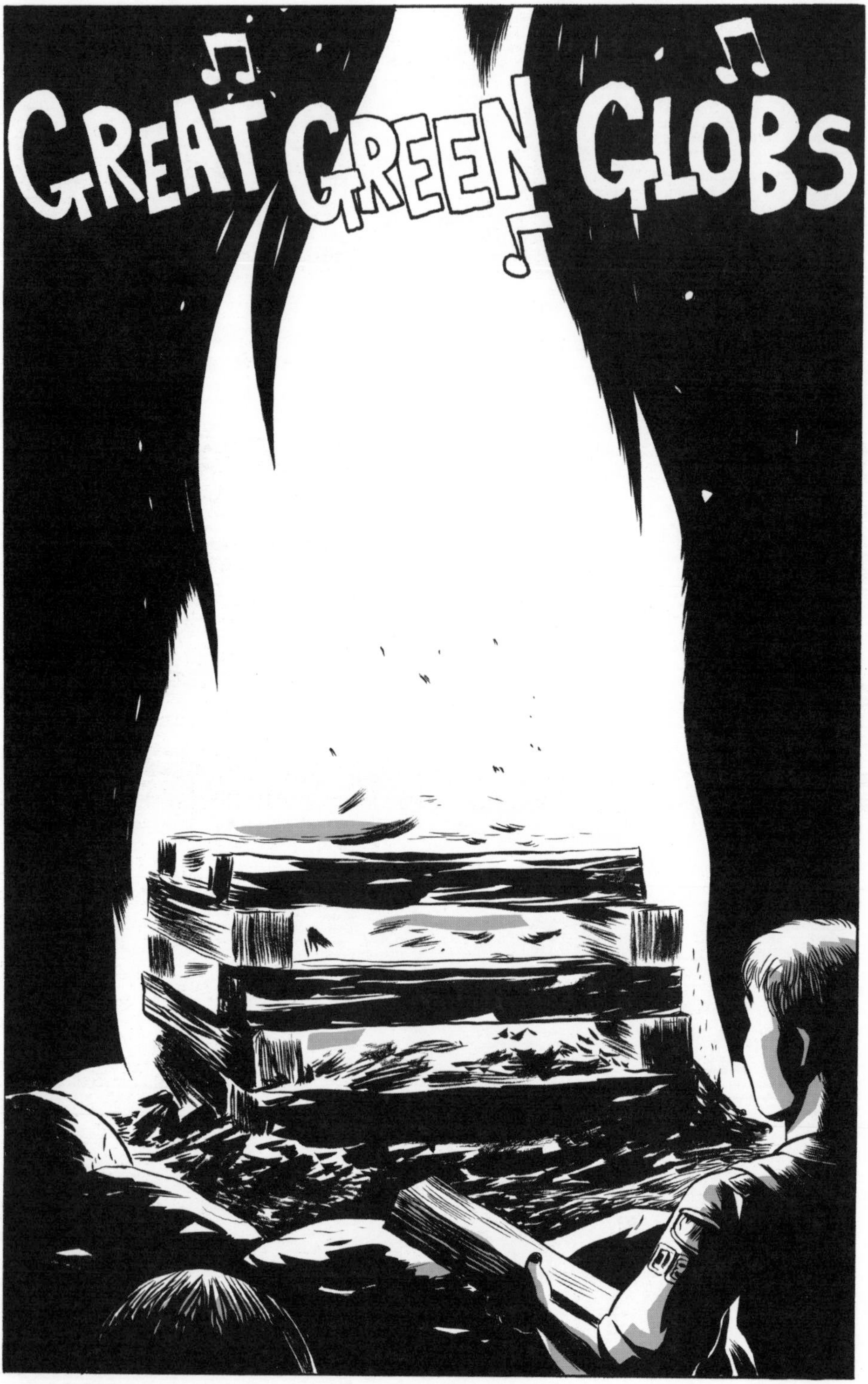
GREAT GREEN GLOBS

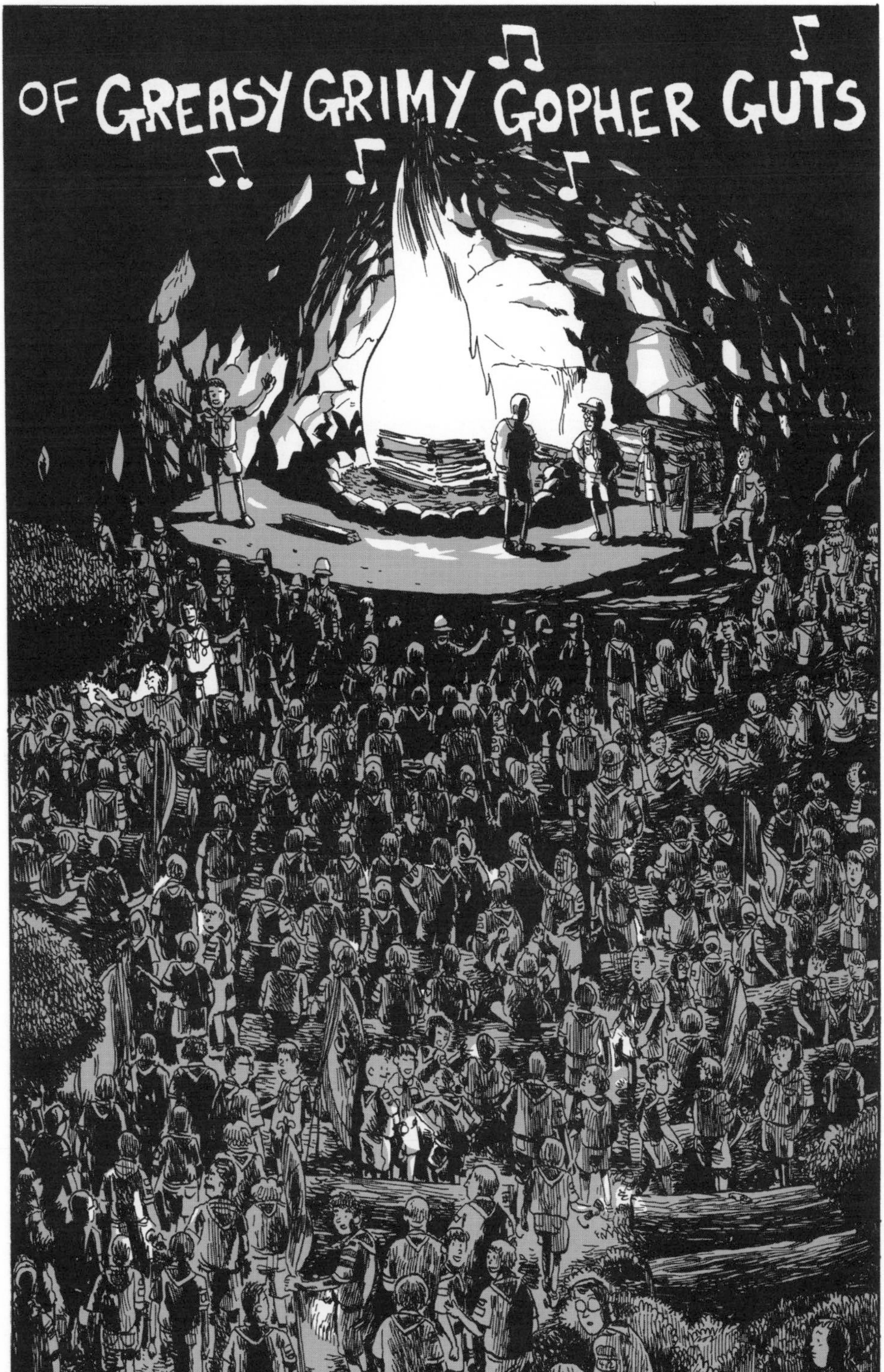
OF GREASY GRIMY GOPHER GUTS

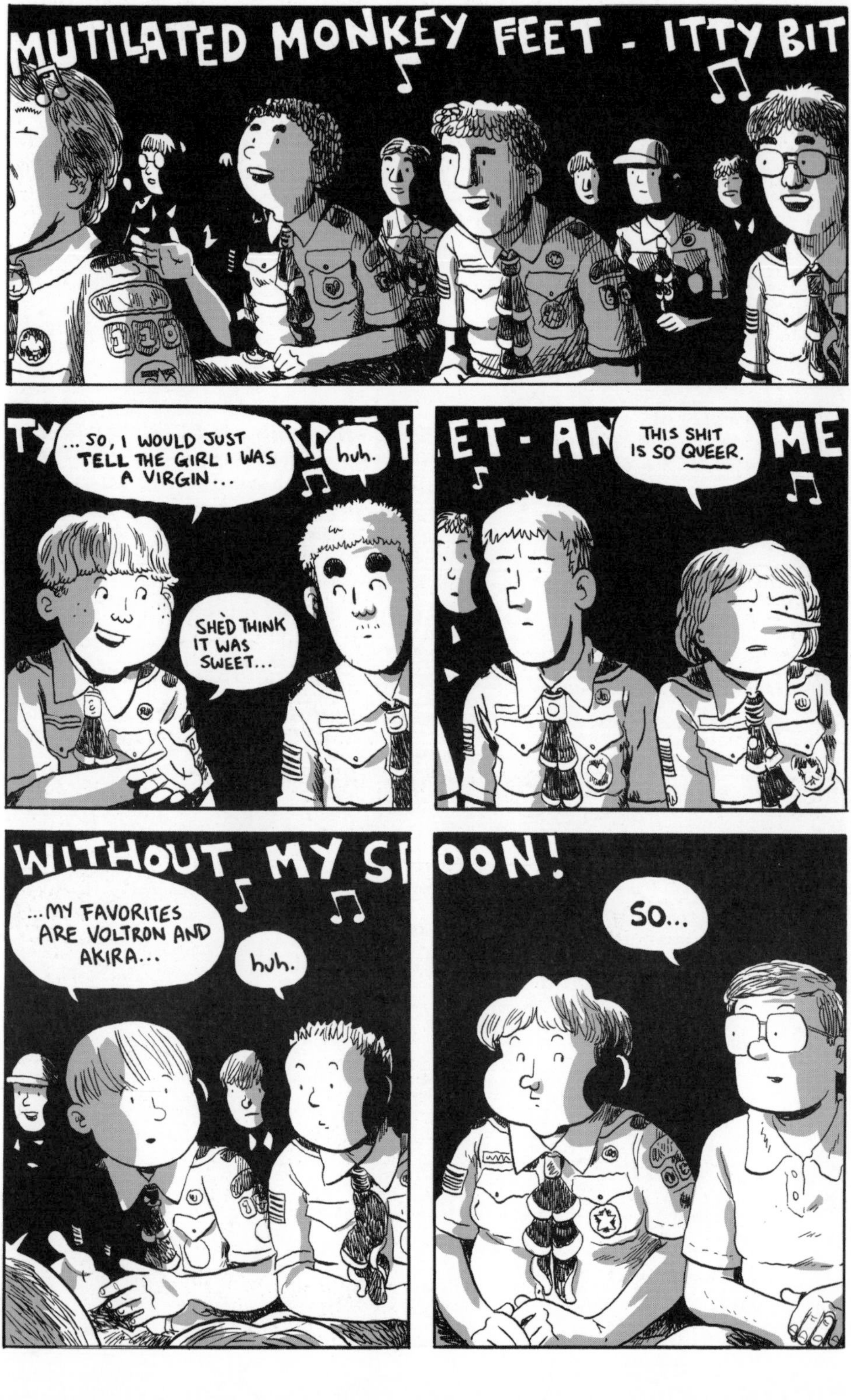

MUTILATED MONKEY FEET - ITTY BIT
...SO, I WOULD JUST TELL THE GIRL I WAS A VIRGIN...
huh.
SHE'D THINK IT WAS SWEET...
THIS SHIT IS SO QUEER.
WITHOUT MY S
OON!
...MY FAVORITES ARE VOLTRON AND AKIRA...
huh.
SO...

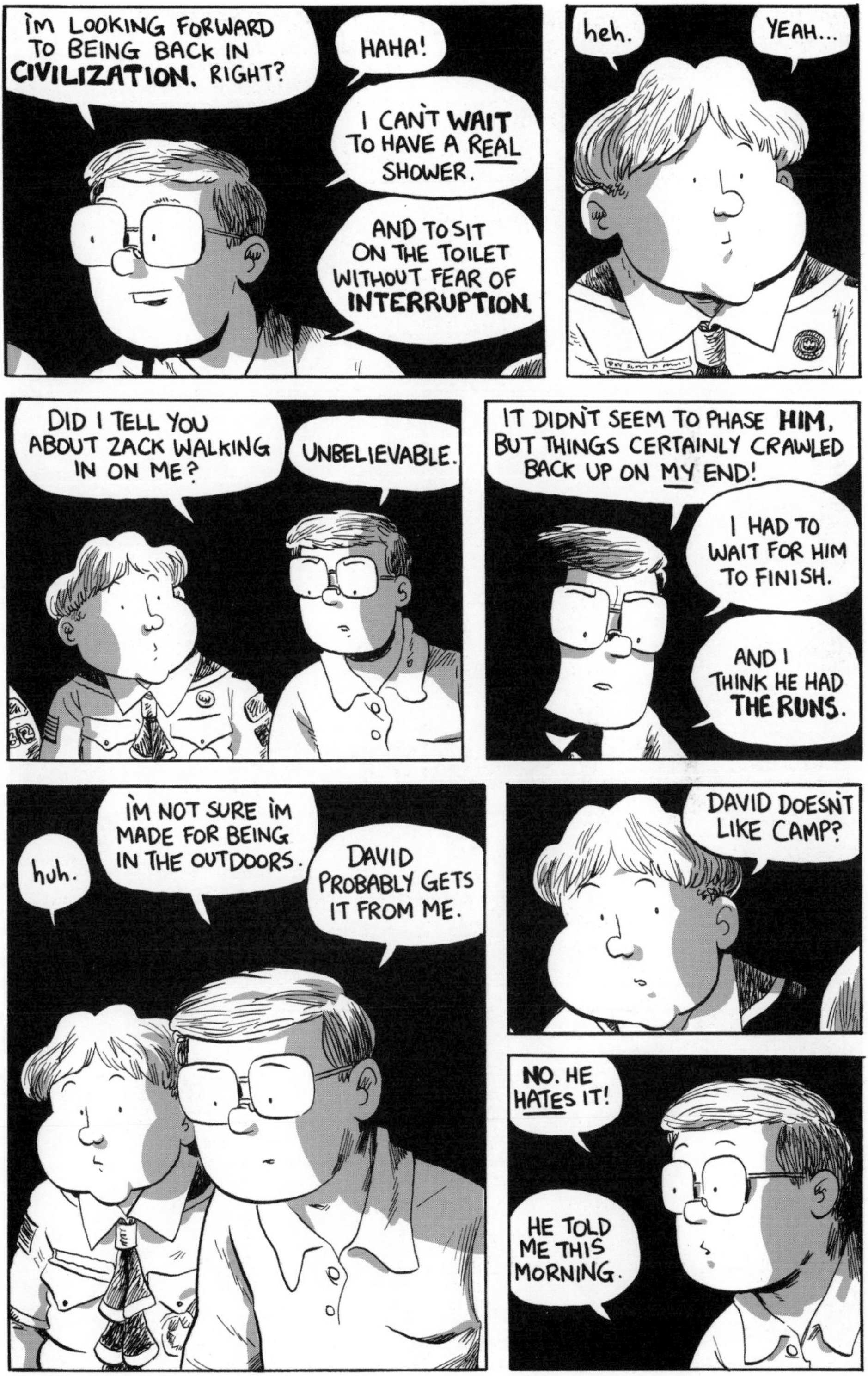

I'M LOOKING FORWARD TO BEING BACK IN CIVILIZATION, RIGHT?
HAHA!
I CAN'T WAIT TO HAVE A REAL SHOWER.
AND TO SIT ON THE TOILET WITHOUT FEAR OF INTERRUPTION.
heh.
YEAH...
DID I TELL YOU ABOUT ZACK WALKING IN ON ME?
UNBELIEVABLE.
IT DIDN'T SEEM TO PHASE HIM, BUT THINGS CERTAINLY CRAWLED BACK UP ON MY END!
I HAD TO WAIT FOR HIM TO FINISH.
AND I THINK HE HAD THE RUNS.
huh.
I'M NOT SURE I'M MADE FOR BEING IN THE OUTDOORS.
DAVID PROBABLY GETS IT FROM ME.
DAVID DOESN'T LIKE CAMP?
NO. HE HATES IT!
HE TOLD ME THIS MORNING.

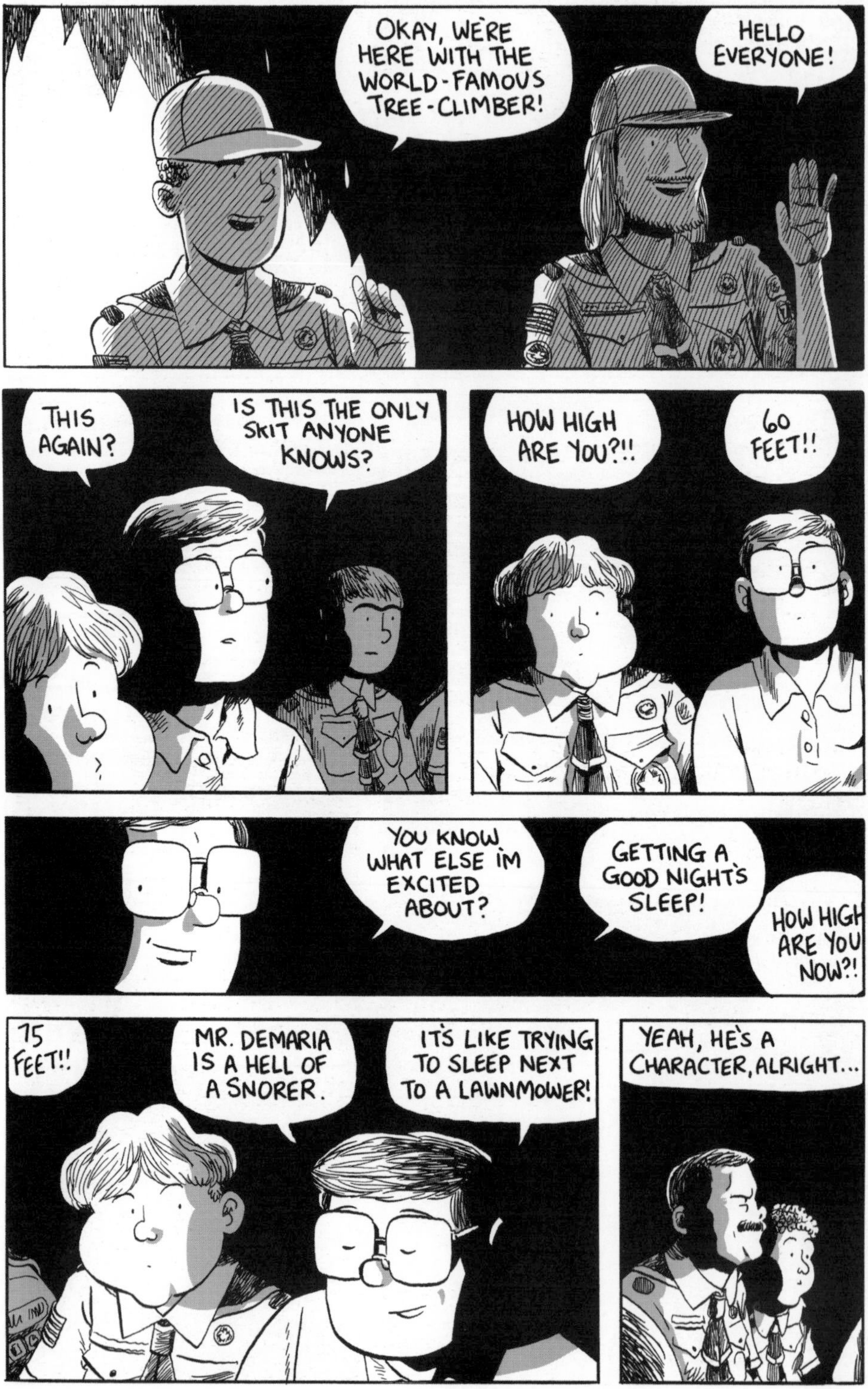
OKAY, WE'RE HERE WITH THE WORLD-FAMOUS TREE-CLIMBER!
HELLO EVERYONE!
THIS AGAIN?
IS THIS THE ONLY SKIT ANYONE KNOWS?
HOW HIGH ARE YOU?!!
60 FEET!!
YOU KNOW WHAT ELSE I'M EXCITED ABOUT?
GETTING A GOOD NIGHT'S SLEEP!
HOW HIGH ARE YOU NOW?!
75 FEET!!
MR. DEMARIA IS A HELL OF A SNORER.
IT'S LIKE TRYING TO SLEEP NEXT TO A LAWNMOWER!
YEAH, HE'S A CHARACTER, ALRIGHT...

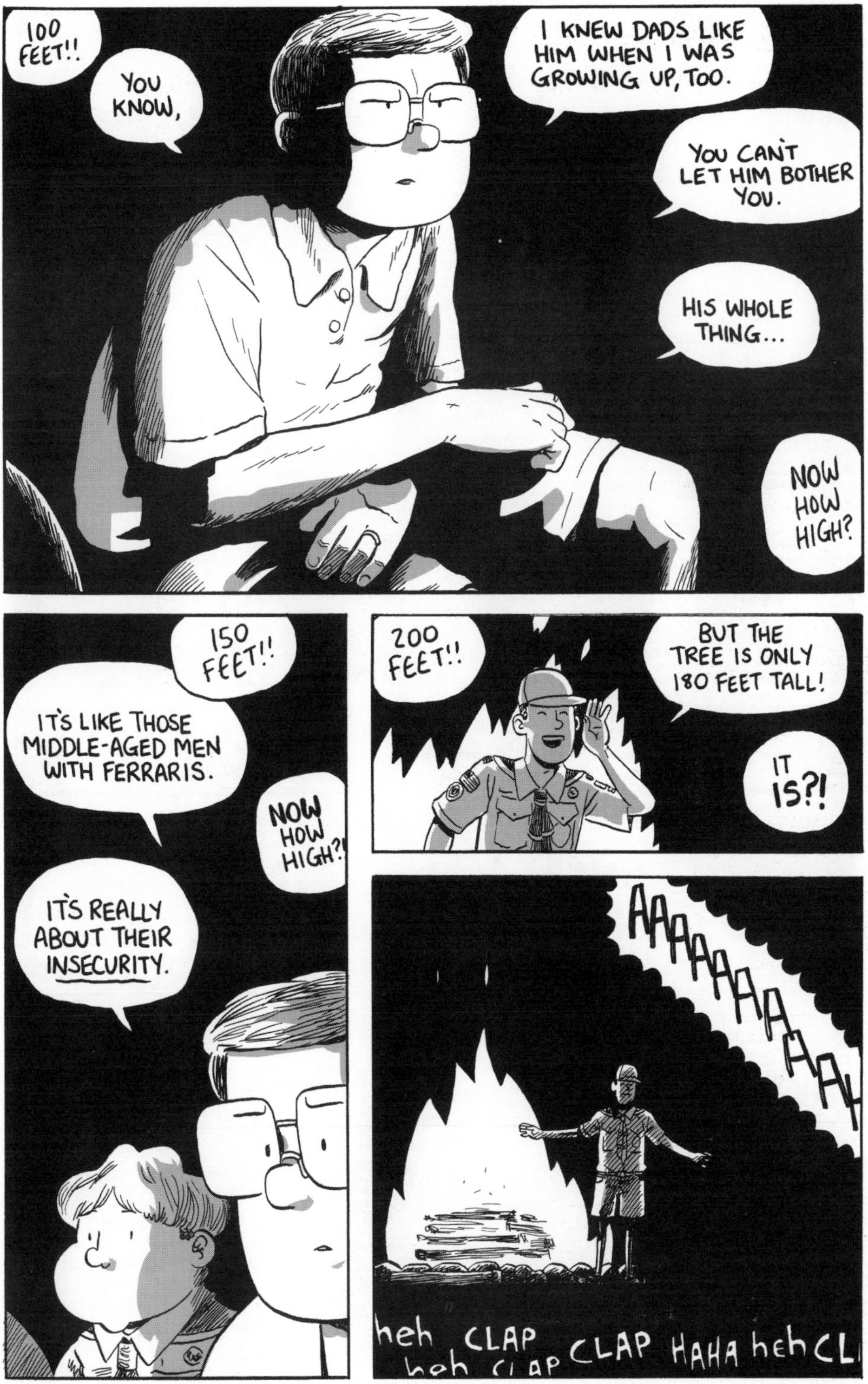
100 FEET!!
YOU KNOW,
I KNEW DADS LIKE HIM WHEN I WAS GROWING UP, TOO.
YOU CAN'T LET HIM BOTHER YOU.
HIS WHOLE THING...
NOW HOW HIGH?
150 FEET!!
IT'S LIKE THOSE MIDDLE-AGED MEN WITH FERRARIS.
NOW HOW HIGH?!
IT'S REALLY ABOUT THEIR INSECURITY.
200 FEET!!
BUT THE TREE IS ONLY 180 FEET TALL!
IT IS?!
AAAAAAAAAAH
heh CLAP heh CLAP CLAP HAHA heh

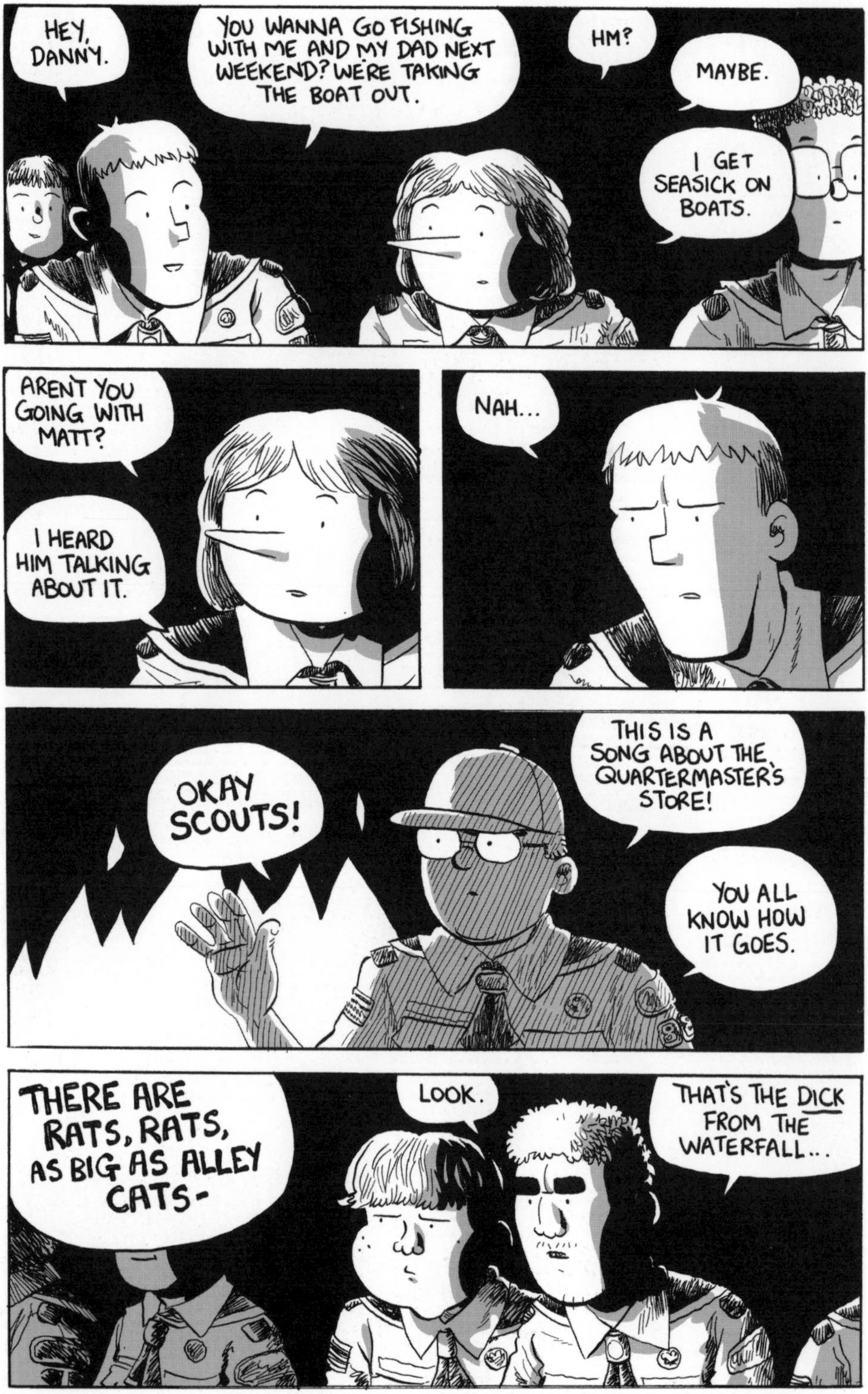
HEY, DANNY.
YOU WANNA GO FISHING WITH ME AND MY DAD NEXT WEEKEND? WE'RE TAKING THE BOAT OUT.
HM?
MAYBE.
I GET SEASICK ON BOATS.
AREN'T YOU GOING WITH MATT?
I HEARD HIM TALKING ABOUT IT.
NAH...
OKAY SCOUTS!
THIS IS A SONG ABOUT THE QUARTERMASTER'S STORE!
YOU ALL KNOW HOW IT GOES.
THERE ARE RATS, RATS, AS BIG AS ALLEY CATS-
LOOK.
THAT'S THE DICK FROM THE WATERFALL...

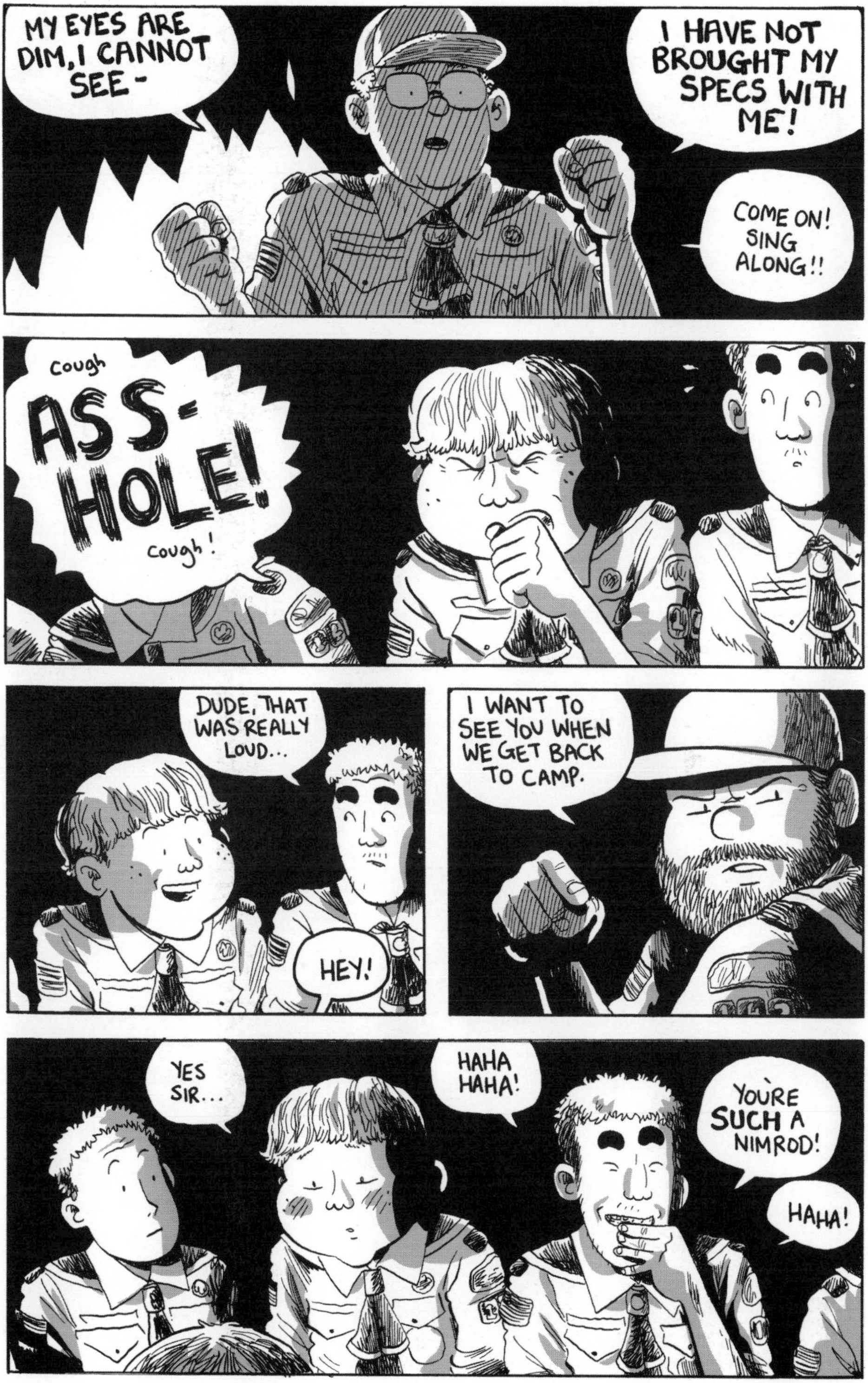
MY EYES ARE DIM, I CANNOT SEE -
I HAVE NOT BROUGHT MY SPECS WITH ME!
COME ON! SING ALONG!!
cough
ASS-HOLE!
cough!
DUDE, THAT WAS REALLY LOUD...
HEY!
I WANT TO SEE YOU WHEN WE GET BACK TO CAMP.
YES SIR...
HAHA HAHA!
YOU'RE SUCH A NIMROD!
HAHA!

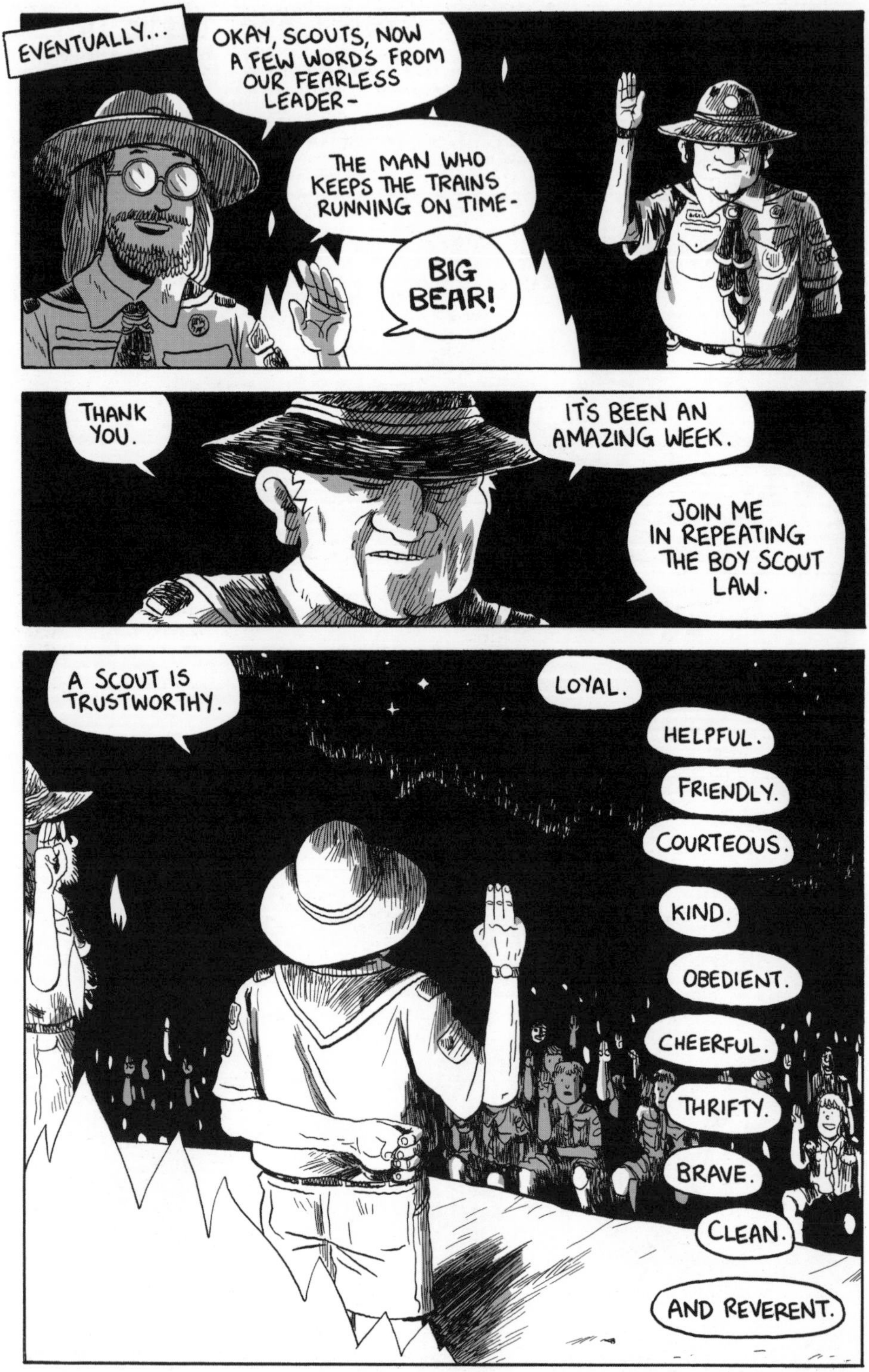
EVENTUALLY...
OKAY, SCOUTS, NOW A FEW WORDS FROM OUR FEARLESS LEADER-
THE MAN WHO KEEPS THE TRAINS RUNNING ON TIME-
BIG BEAR!
THANK YOU.
IT'S BEEN AN AMAZING WEEK.
JOIN ME IN REPEATING THE BOY SCOUT LAW.
A SCOUT IS TRUSTWORTHY.
LOYAL.
HELPFUL.
FRIENDLY.
COURTEOUS.
KIND.
OBEDIENT.
CHEERFUL.
THRIFTY.
BRAVE.
CLEAN.
AND REVERENT.

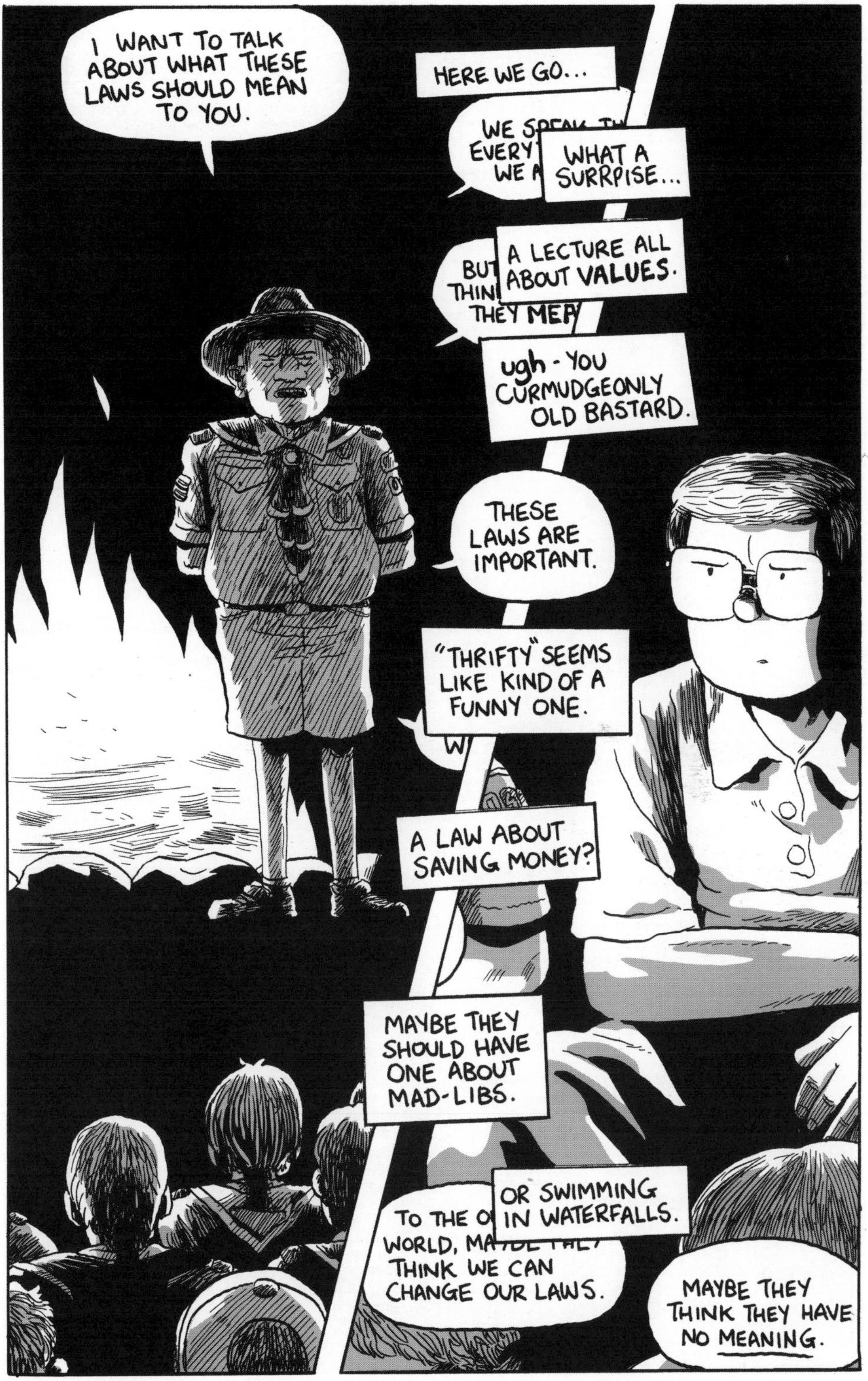
I WANT TO TALK ABOUT WHAT THESE LAWS SHOULD MEAN TO YOU.
HERE WE GO...
WHAT A SURRPISE...
A LECTURE ALL ABOUT VALUES.
ugh - YOU CURMUDGEONLY OLD BASTARD.
THESE LAWS ARE IMPORTANT.
"THRIFTY" SEEMS LIKE KIND OF A FUNNY ONE.
A LAW ABOUT SAVING MONEY?
MAYBE THEY SHOULD HAVE ONE ABOUT MAD-LIBS.
OR SWIMMING IN WATERFALLS.
THINK WE CAN CHANGE OUR LAWS.
MAYBE THEY THINK THEY HAVE NO MEANING.

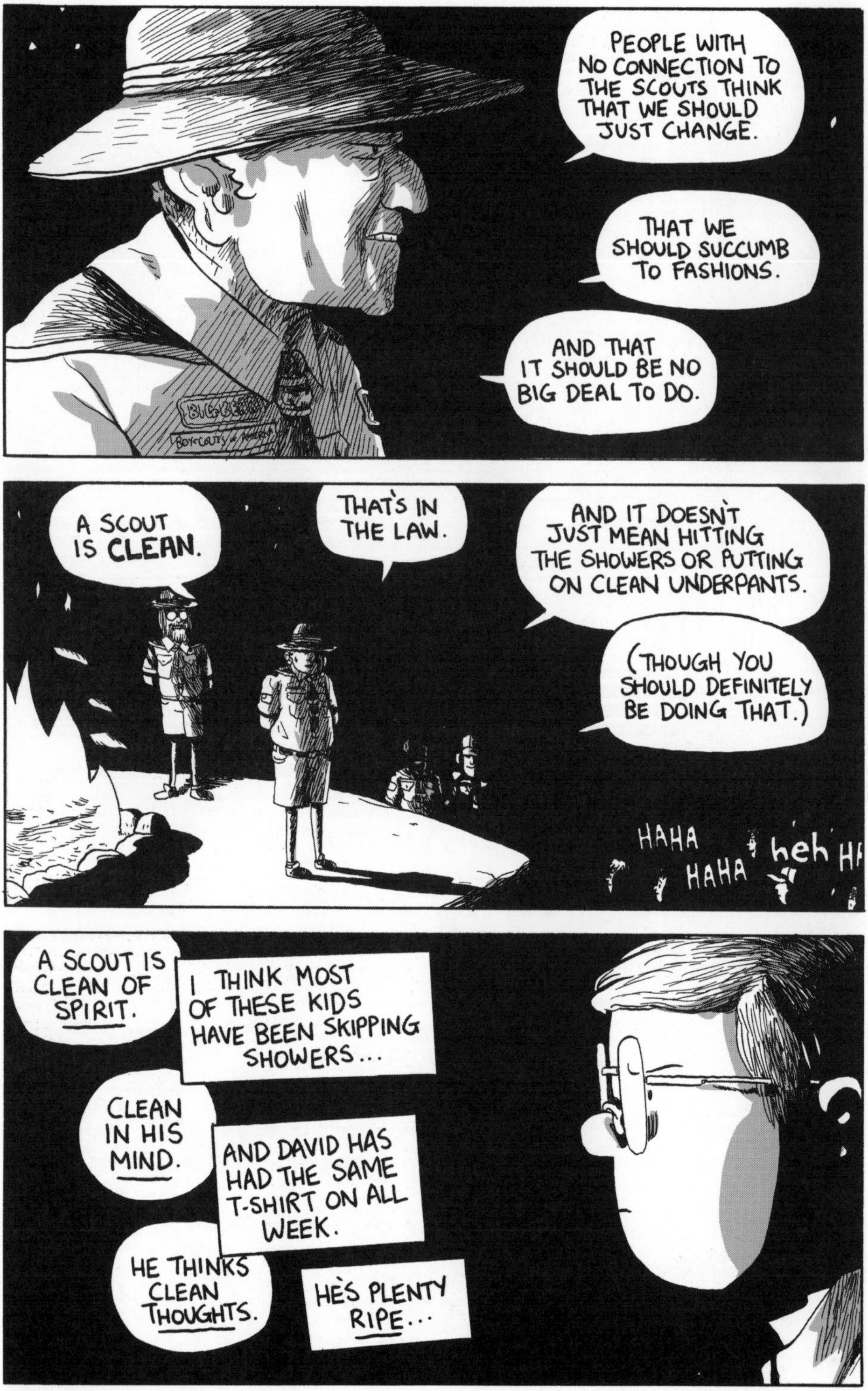
PEOPLE WITH NO CONNECTION TO THE SCOUTS THINK THAT WE SHOULD JUST CHANGE.
THAT WE SHOULD SUCCUMB TO FASHIONS.
AND THAT IT SHOULD BE NO BIG DEAL TO DO.
A SCOUT IS CLEAN.
THAT'S IN THE LAW.
AND IT DOESN'T JUST MEAN HITTING THE SHOWERS OR PUTTING ON CLEAN UNDERPANTS.
(THOUGH YOU SHOULD DEFINITELY BE DOING THAT.)
HAHA
HAHA
heh
A SCOUT IS CLEAN OF SPIRIT.
I THINK MOST OF THESE KIDS HAVE BEEN SKIPPING SHOWERS...
CLEAN IN HIS MIND.
AND DAVID HAS HAD THE SAME T-SHIRT ON ALL WEEK.
HE THINKS CLEAN THOUGHTS.
HE'S PLENTY RIPE...

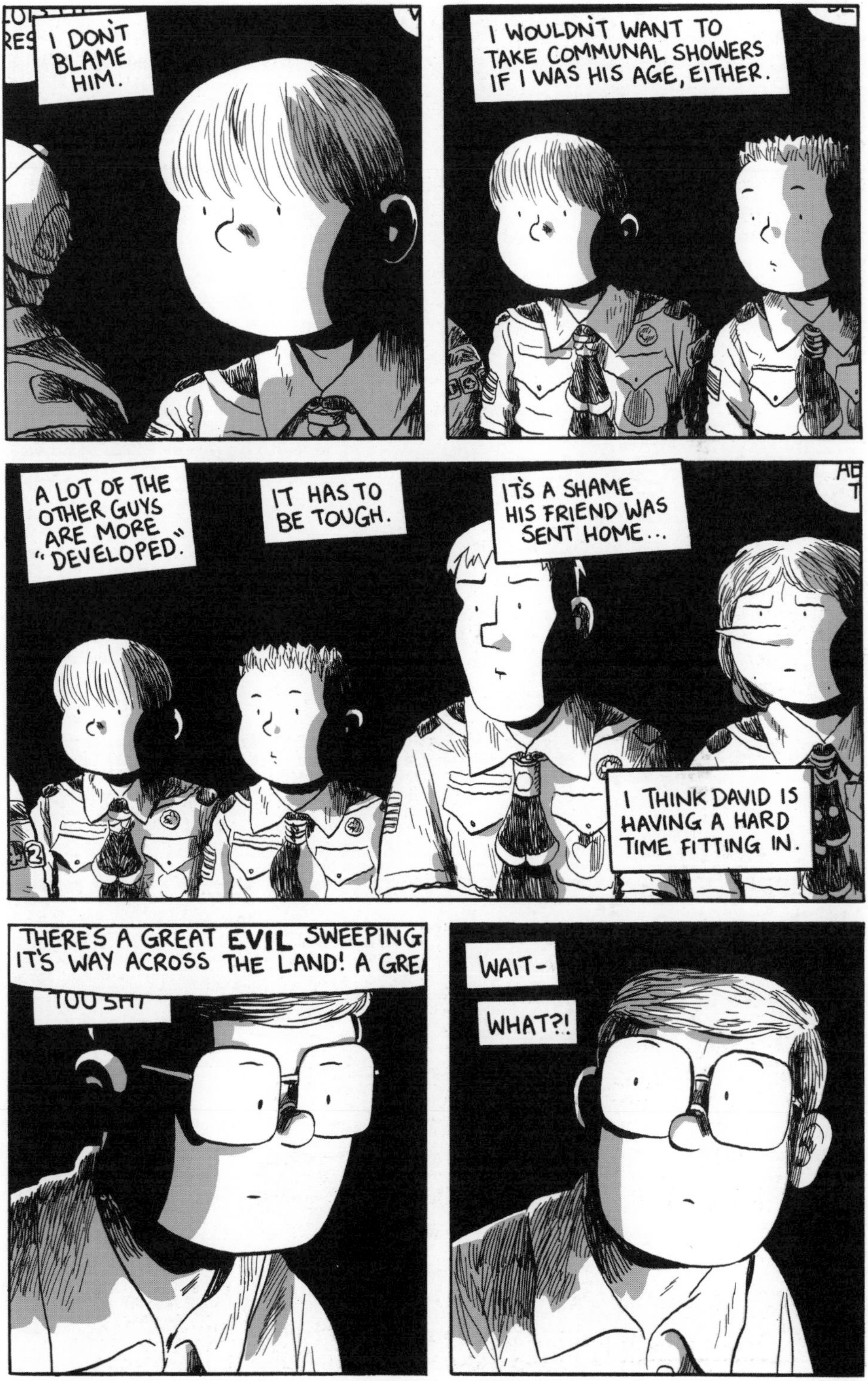
I DON'T BLAME HIM.
I WOULDN'T WANT TO TAKE COMMUNAL SHOWERS IF I WAS HIS AGE, EITHER.
A LOT OF THE OTHER GUYS ARE MORE "DEVELOPED."
IT HAS TO BE TOUGH.
IT'S A SHAME HIS FRIEND WAS SENT HOME...
I THINK DAVID IS HAVING A HARD TIME FITTING IN.
THERE'S A GREAT **EVIL** SWEEPING IT'S WAY ACROSS THE LAND! A GRE
WAIT-
WHAT?!

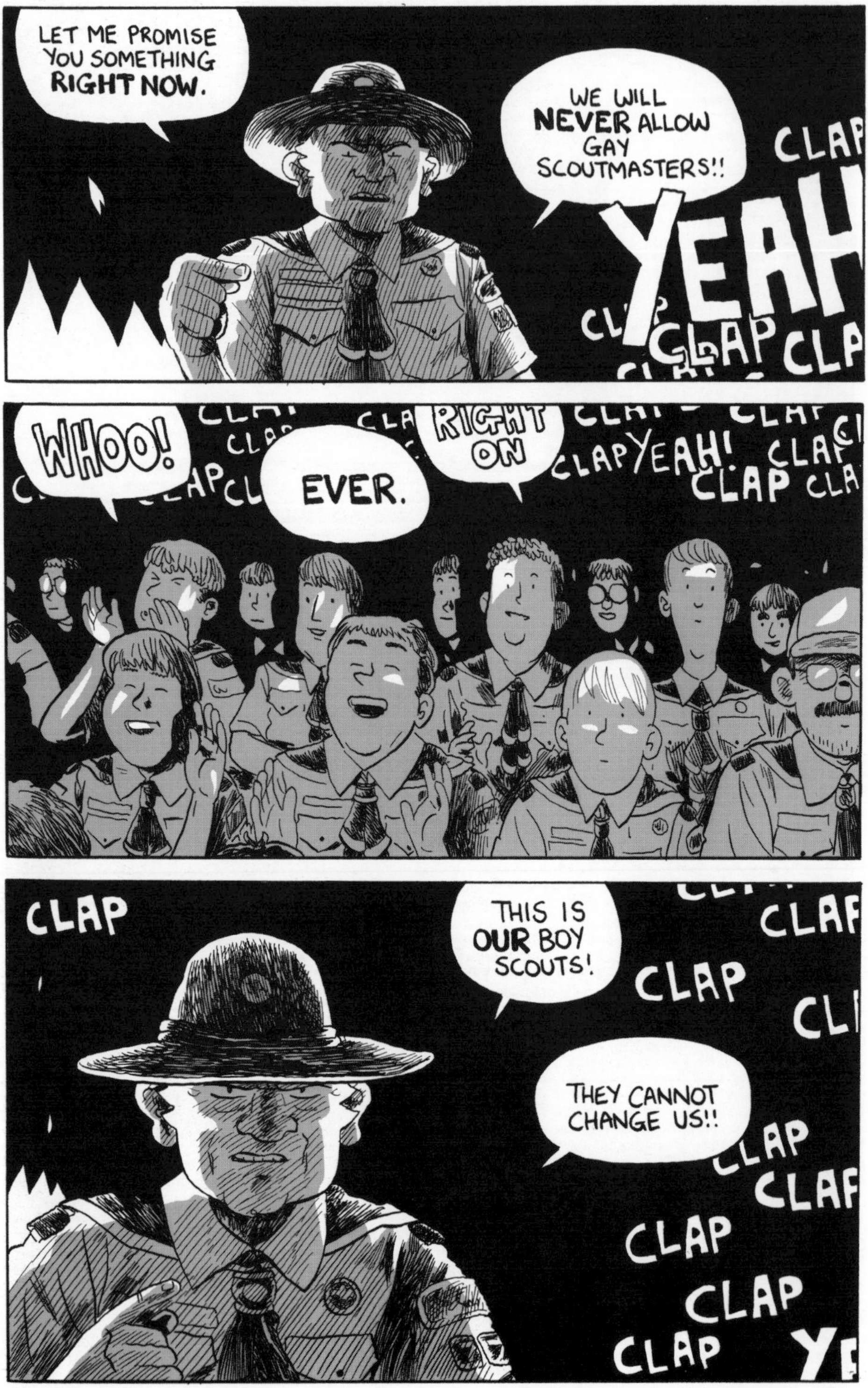
LET ME PROMISE YOU SOMETHING RIGHT NOW.
WE WILL NEVER ALLOW GAY SCOUTMASTERS!!
CLAP
YEAH
CLAP
CLAP
WHOO!
RIGHT ON
EVER.
CLAP YEAH!
CLAP
THIS IS OUR BOY SCOUTS!
CLAP
CLAP
THEY CANNOT CHANGE US!!
CLAP
CLAP
CLAP
CLAP

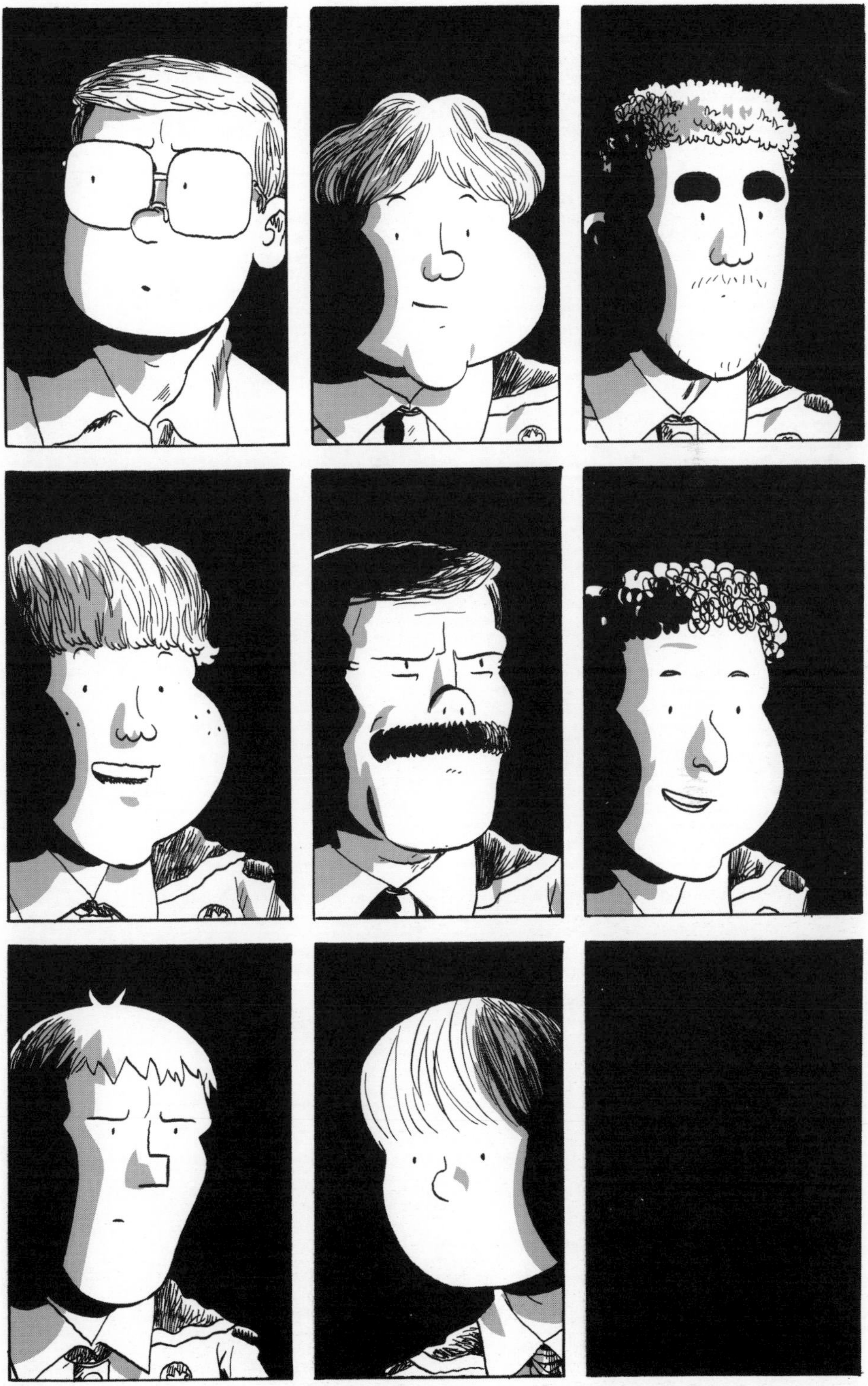

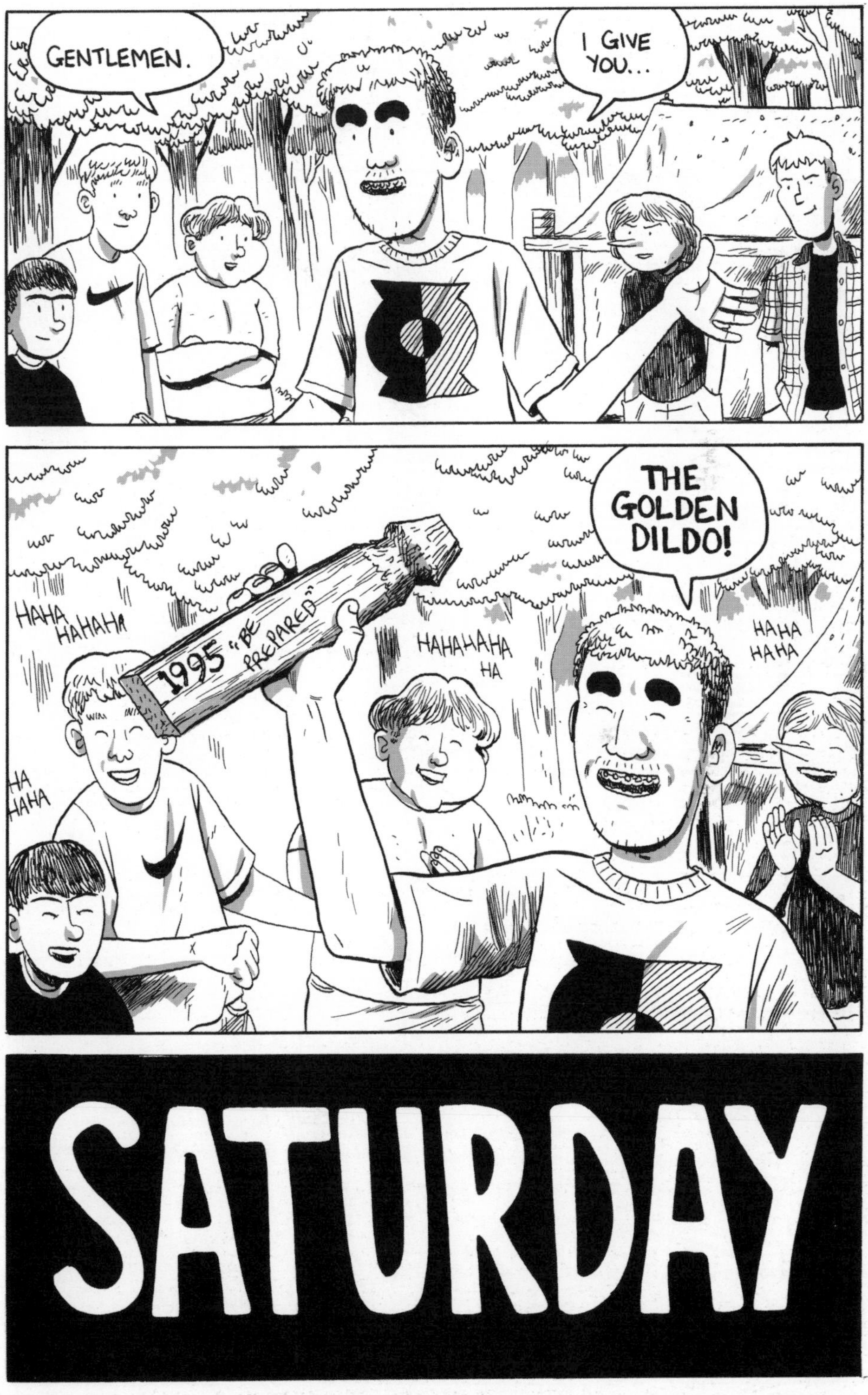
GENTLEMEN.
I GIVE YOU...
THE GOLDEN DILDO!
HAHA HAHAHA
1995 "BE PREPARED"
HAHAHAHA HA
HAHA HAHA
HA HAHA

SATURDAY

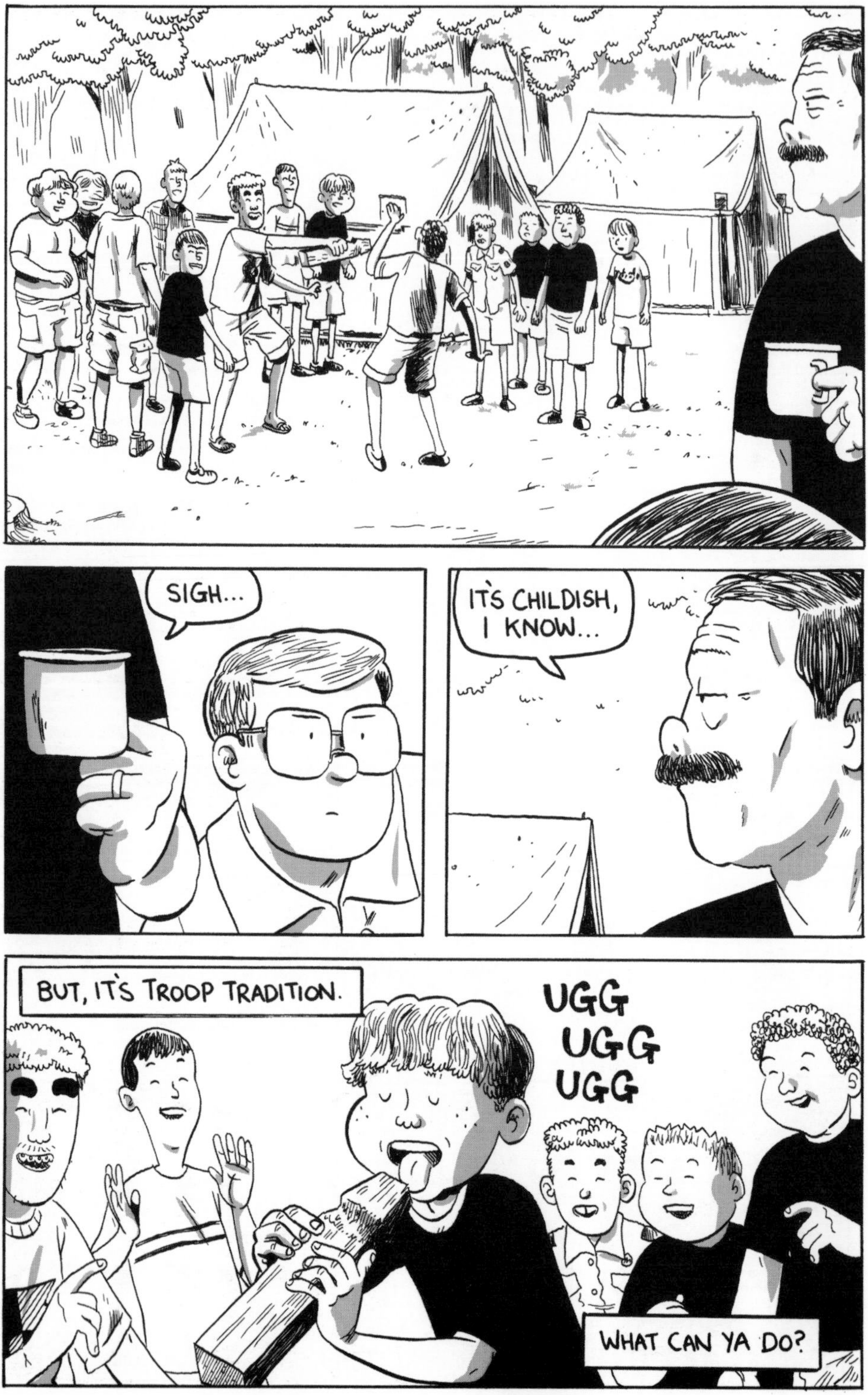
SIGH...
IT'S CHILDISH, I KNOW...
BUT, IT'S TROOP TRADITION.
UGG UGG UGG
WHAT CAN YA DO?

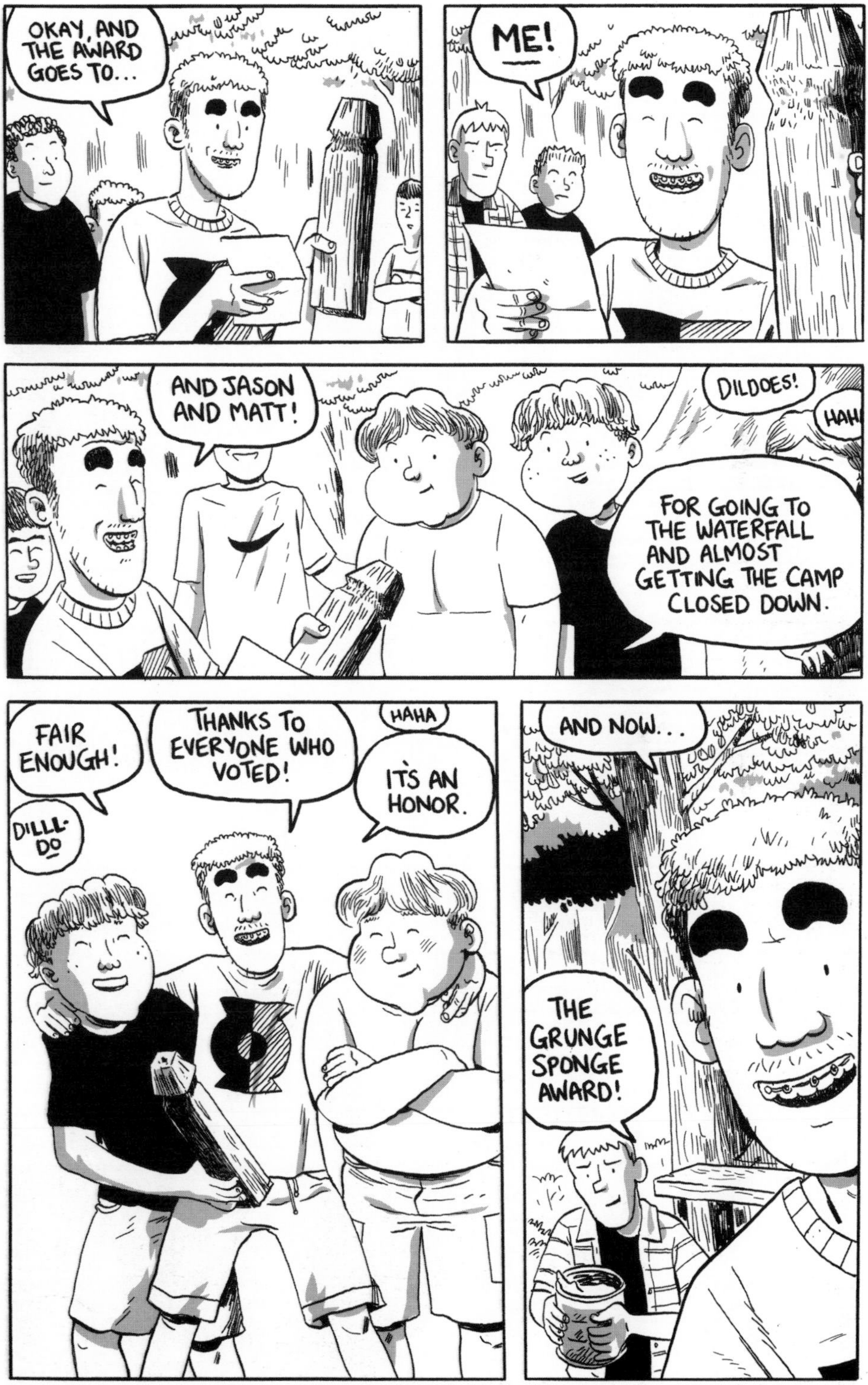
OKAY, AND THE AWARD GOES TO...
ME!
AND JASON AND MATT!
DILDOES!
HAH
FOR GOING TO THE WATERFALL AND ALMOST GETTING THE CAMP CLOSED DOWN.
FAIR ENOUGH!
DILLL-DO
THANKS TO EVERYONE WHO VOTED!
HAHA
IT'S AN HONOR.
AND NOW...
THE GRUNGE SPONGE AWARD!

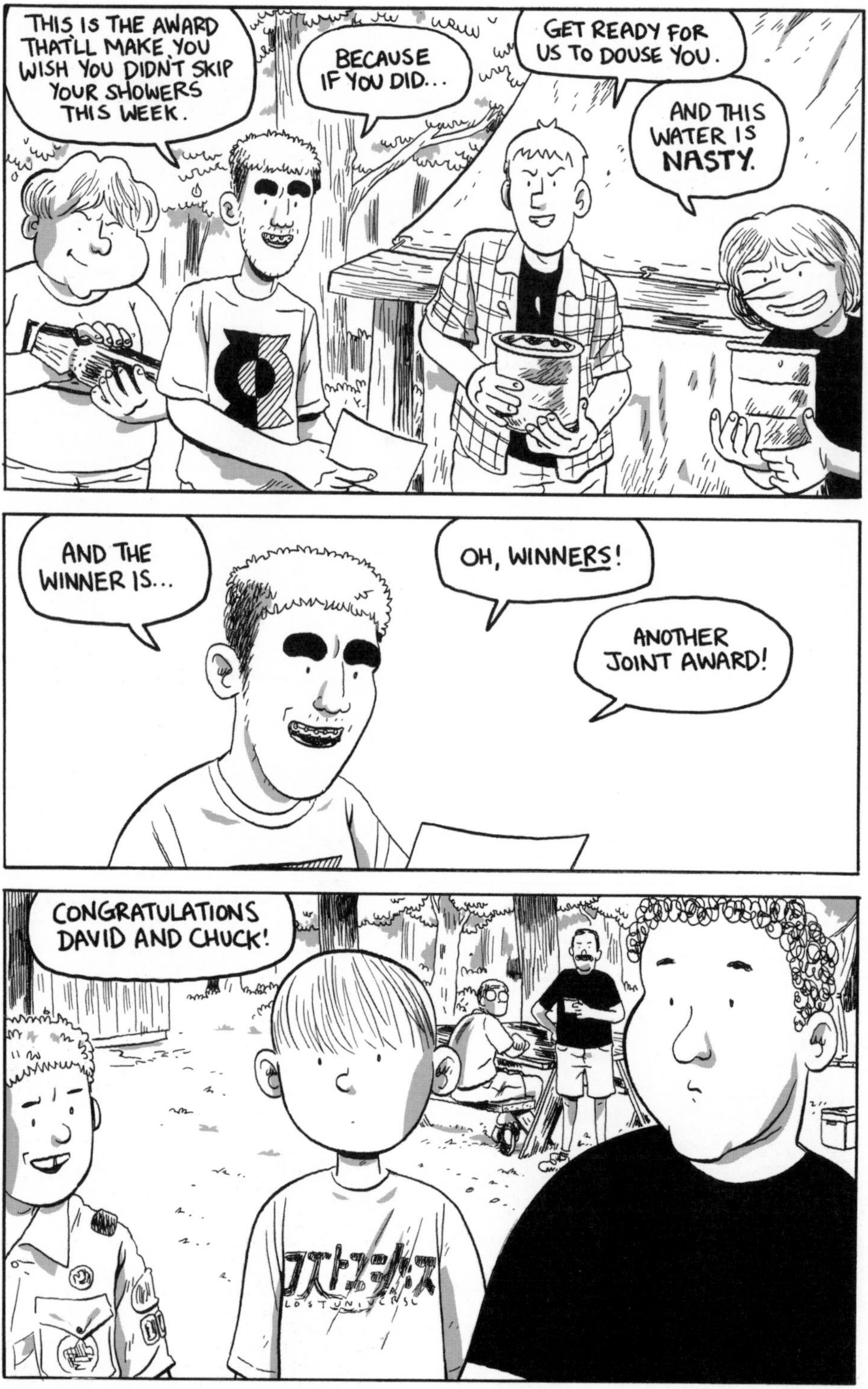
THIS IS THE AWARD THAT'LL MAKE YOU WISH YOU DIDN'T SKIP YOUR SHOWERS THIS WEEK.
BECAUSE IF YOU DID...
GET READY FOR US TO DOUSE YOU.
AND THIS WATER IS NASTY.
AND THE WINNER IS...
OH, WINNERS!
ANOTHER JOINT AWARD!
CONGRATULATIONS DAVID AND CHUCK!

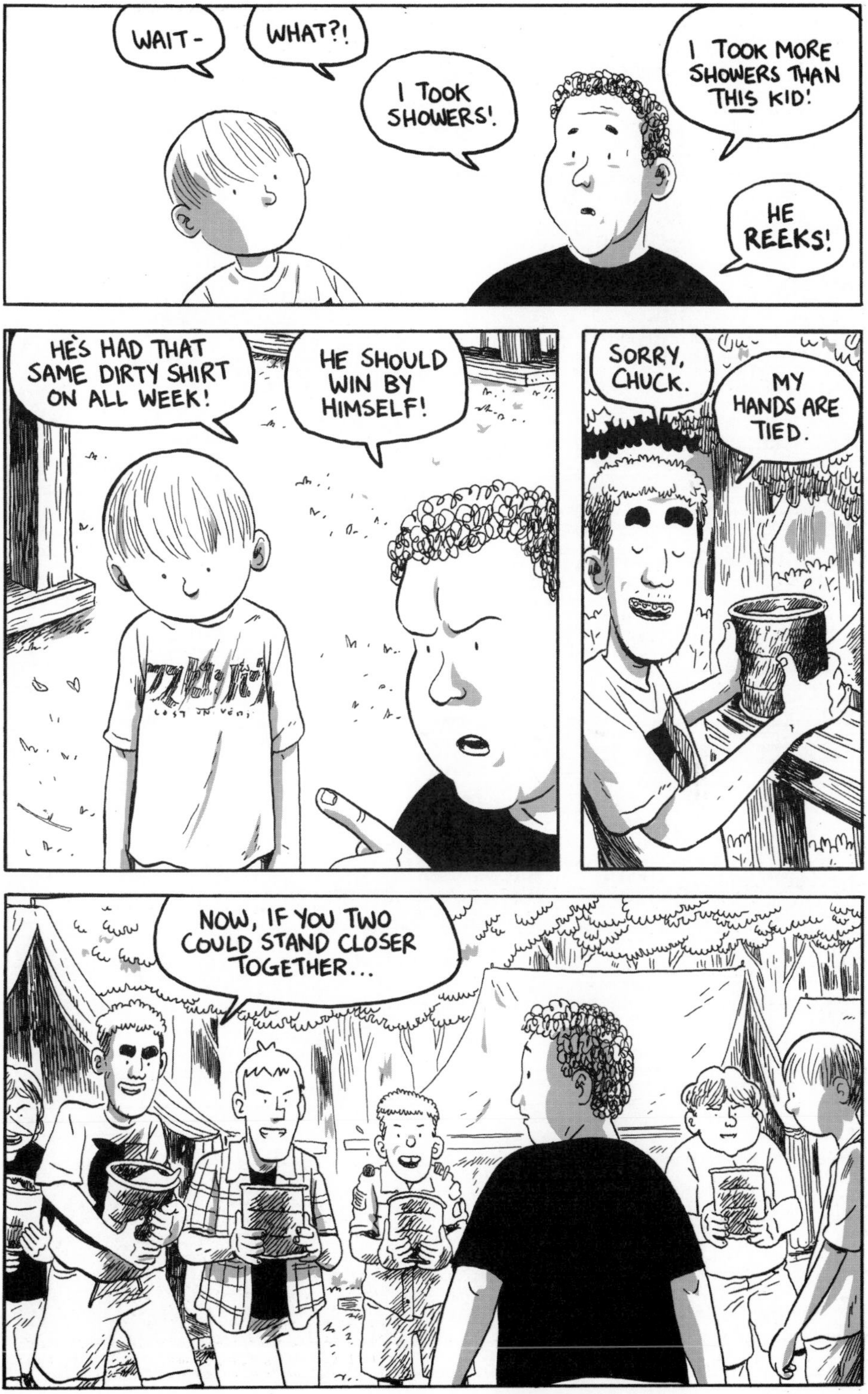
WAIT-
WHAT?!
I TOOK SHOWERS!
I TOOK MORE SHOWERS THAN THIS KID!
HE REEKS!
HE'S HAD THAT SAME DIRTY SHIRT ON ALL WEEK!
HE SHOULD WIN BY HIMSELF!
SORRY, CHUCK.
MY HANDS ARE TIED.
NOW, IF YOU TWO COULD STAND CLOSER TOGETHER...

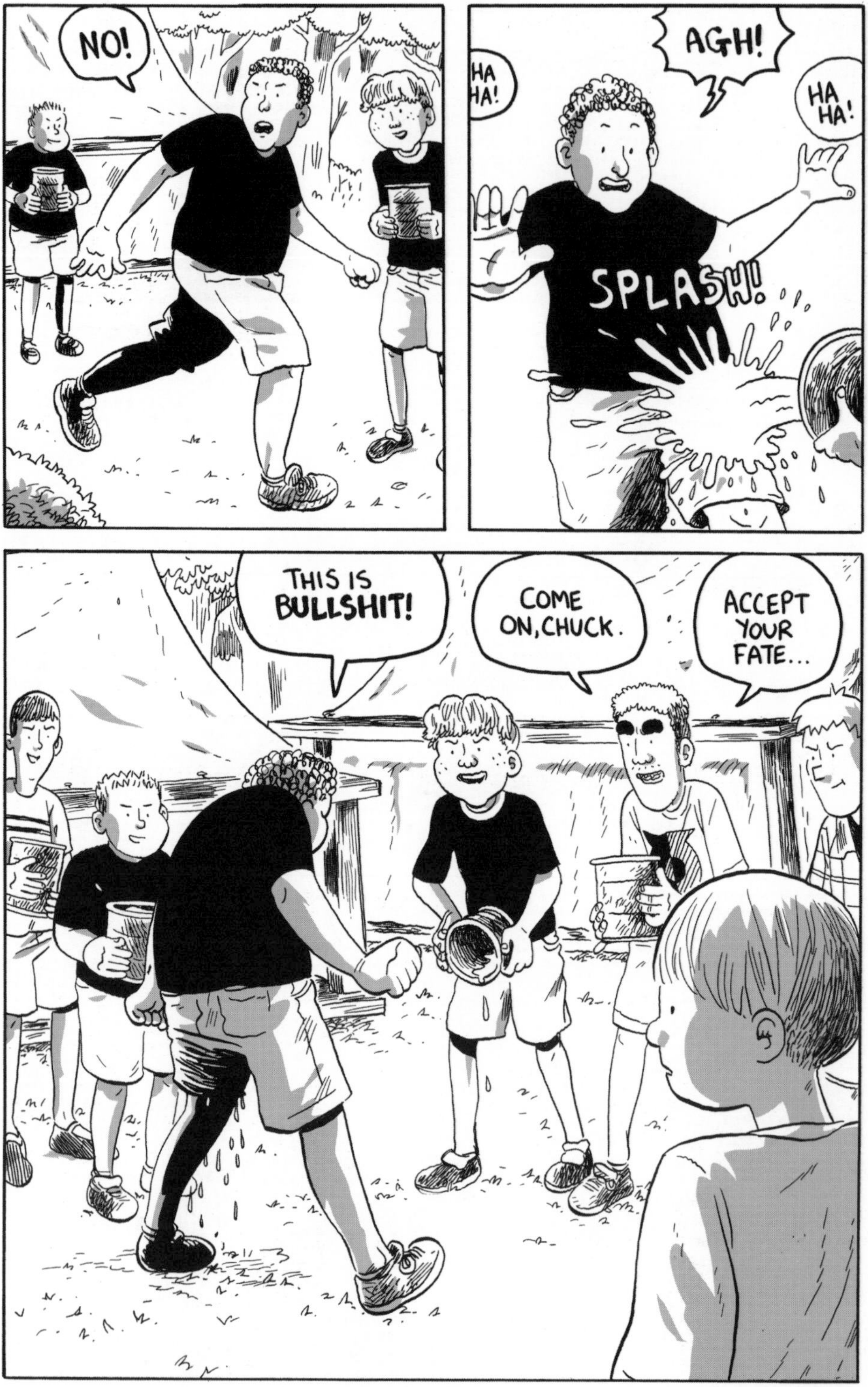
NO!
HA HA!
AGH!
HA HA!
SPLASH!
THIS IS BULLSHIT!
COME ON, CHUCK.
ACCEPT YOUR FATE...

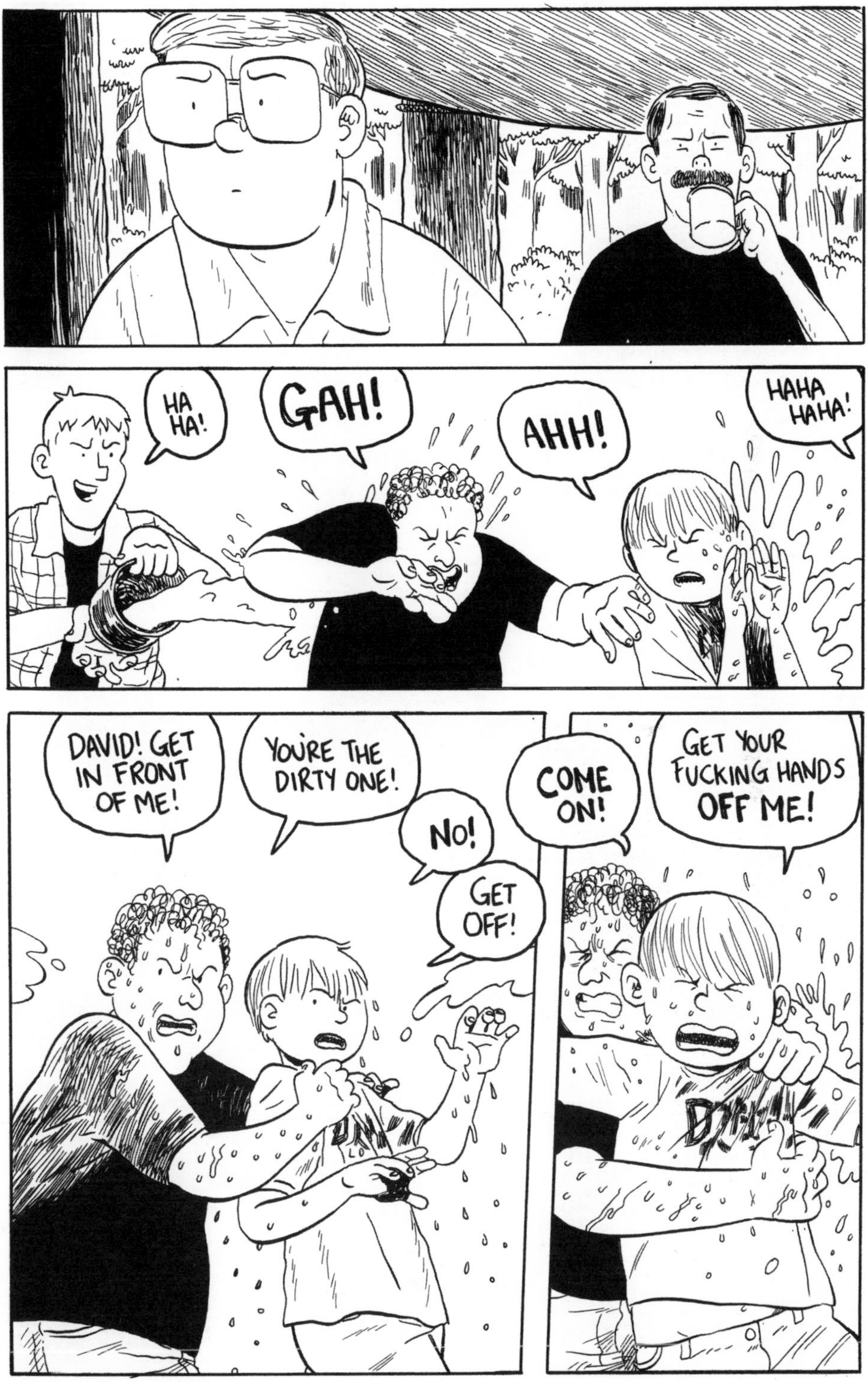
HA HA!
GAH!
AHH!
HAHA HAHA!
DAVID! GET IN FRONT OF ME!
YOU'RE THE DIRTY ONE!
NO!
GET OFF!
COME ON!
GET YOUR FUCKING HANDS OFF ME!

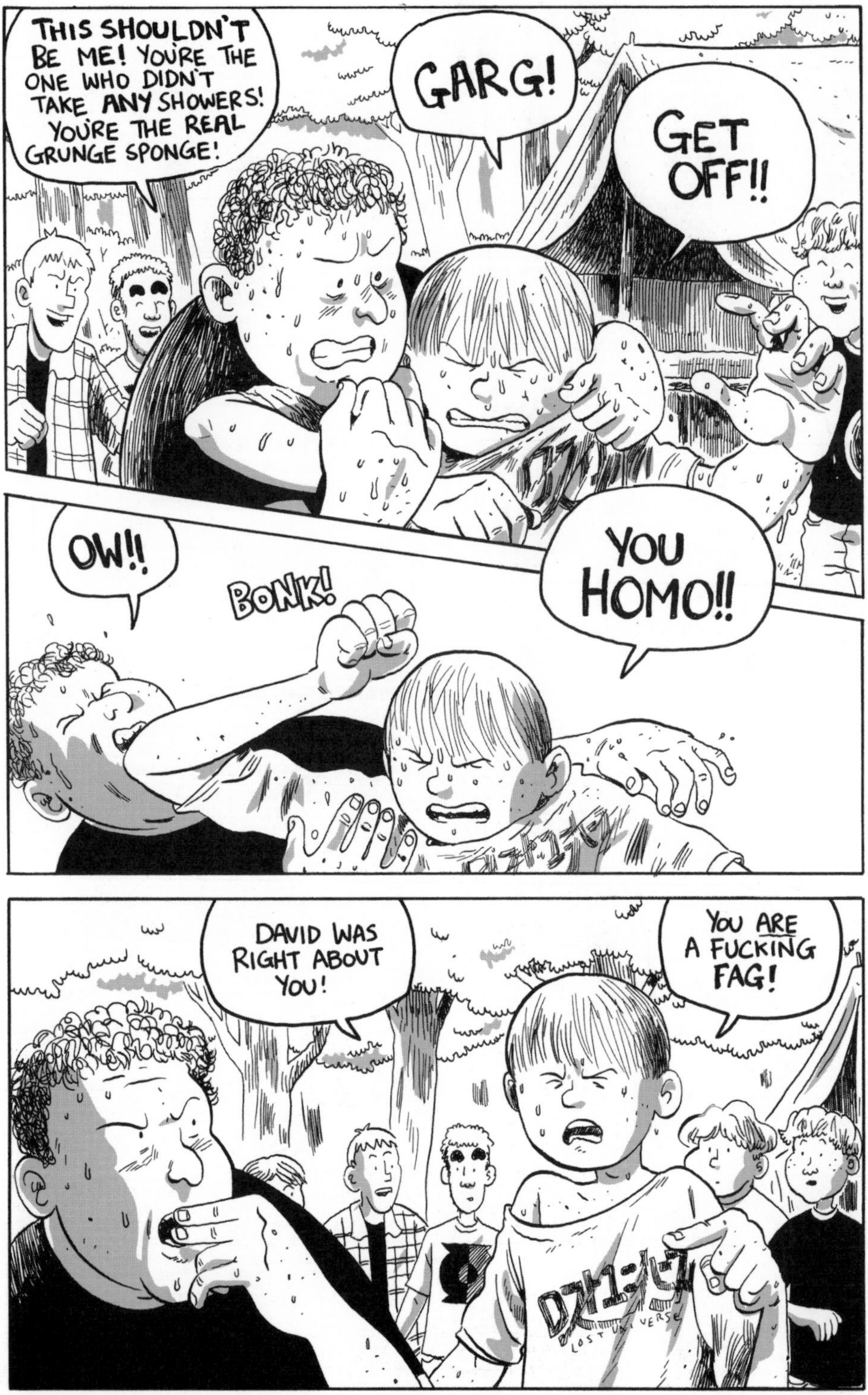
THIS SHOULDN'T BE ME! YOU'RE THE ONE WHO DIDN'T TAKE ANY SHOWERS! YOU'RE THE REAL GRUNGE SPONGE!
GARG!
GET OFF!!
OW!!
BONK!
YOU HOMO!!
DAVID WAS RIGHT ABOUT YOU!
YOU ARE A FUCKING FAG!

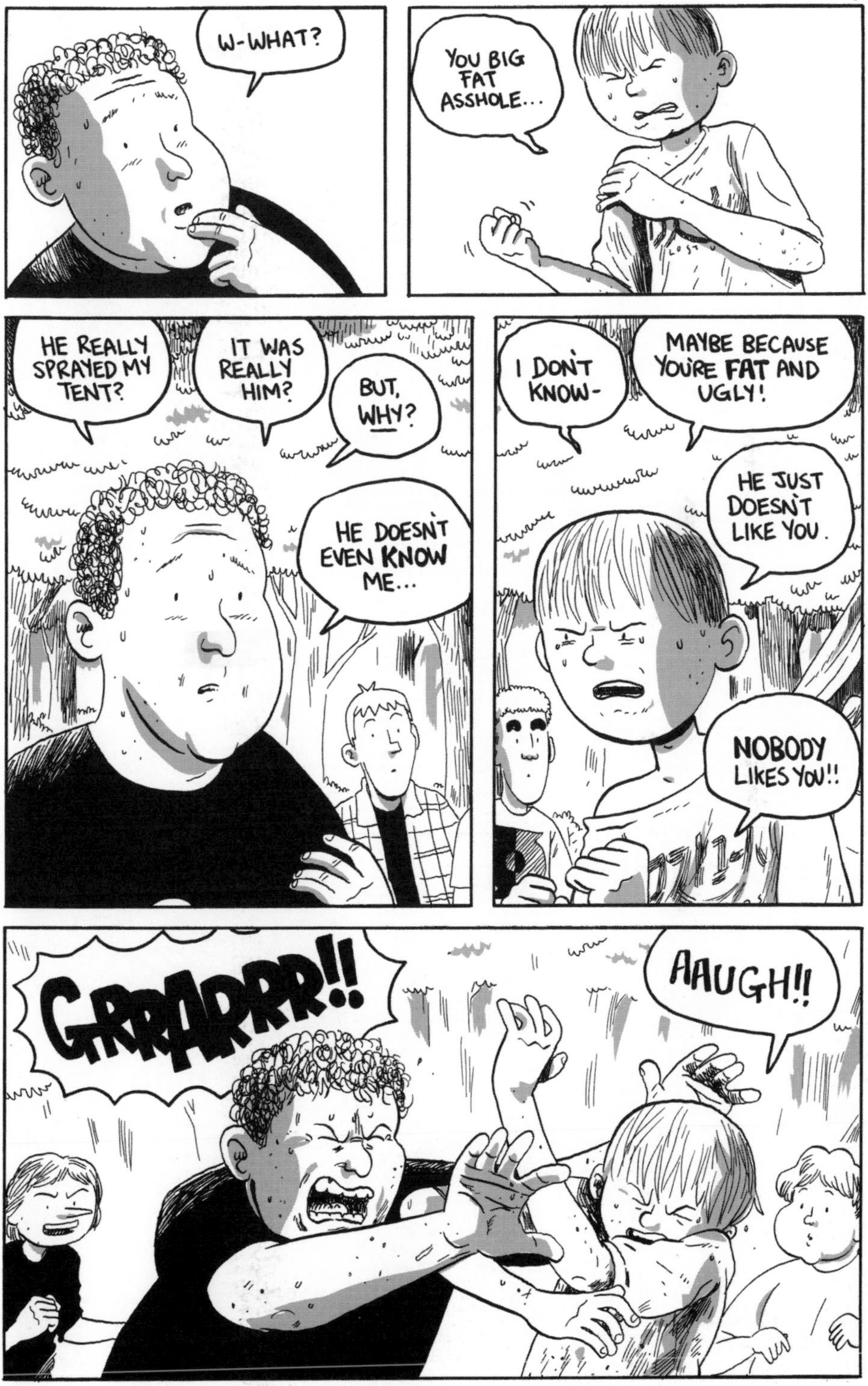
W-WHAT?
YOU BIG FAT ASSHOLE...
HE REALLY SPRAYED MY TENT?
IT WAS REALLY HIM?
BUT, WHY?
HE DOESN'T EVEN KNOW ME...
I DON'T KNOW-
MAYBE BECAUSE YOU'RE FAT AND UGLY!
HE JUST DOESN'T LIKE YOU.
NOBODY LIKES YOU!!
GRRARRR!!
AAUGH!!

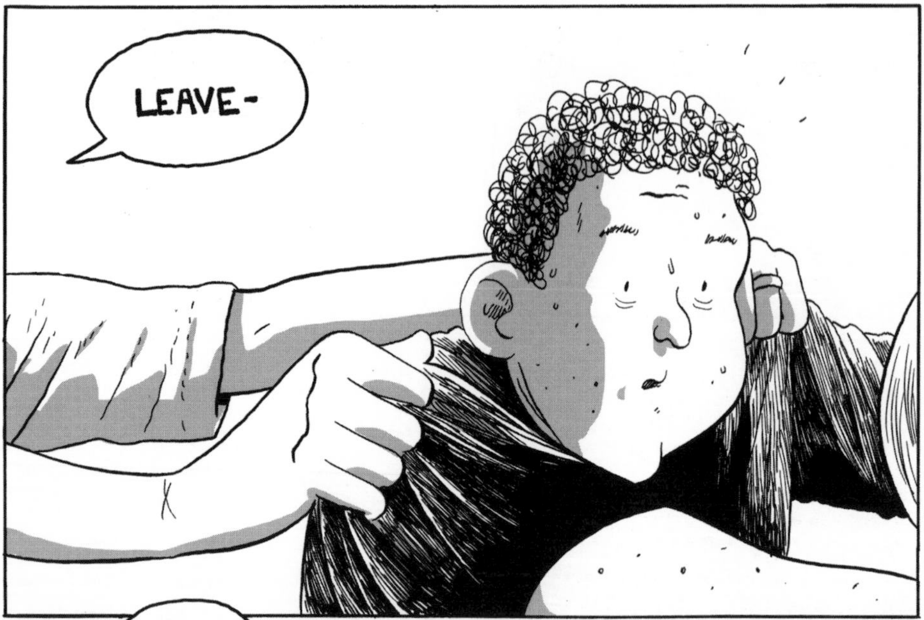
LEAVE-

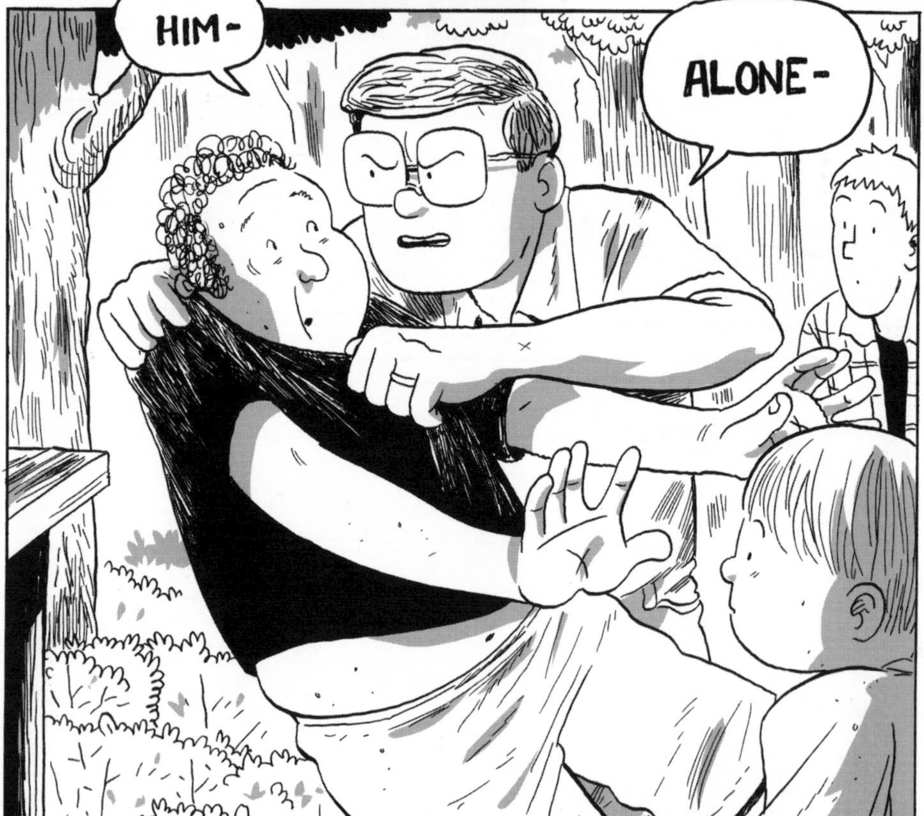
HIM-
ALONE-

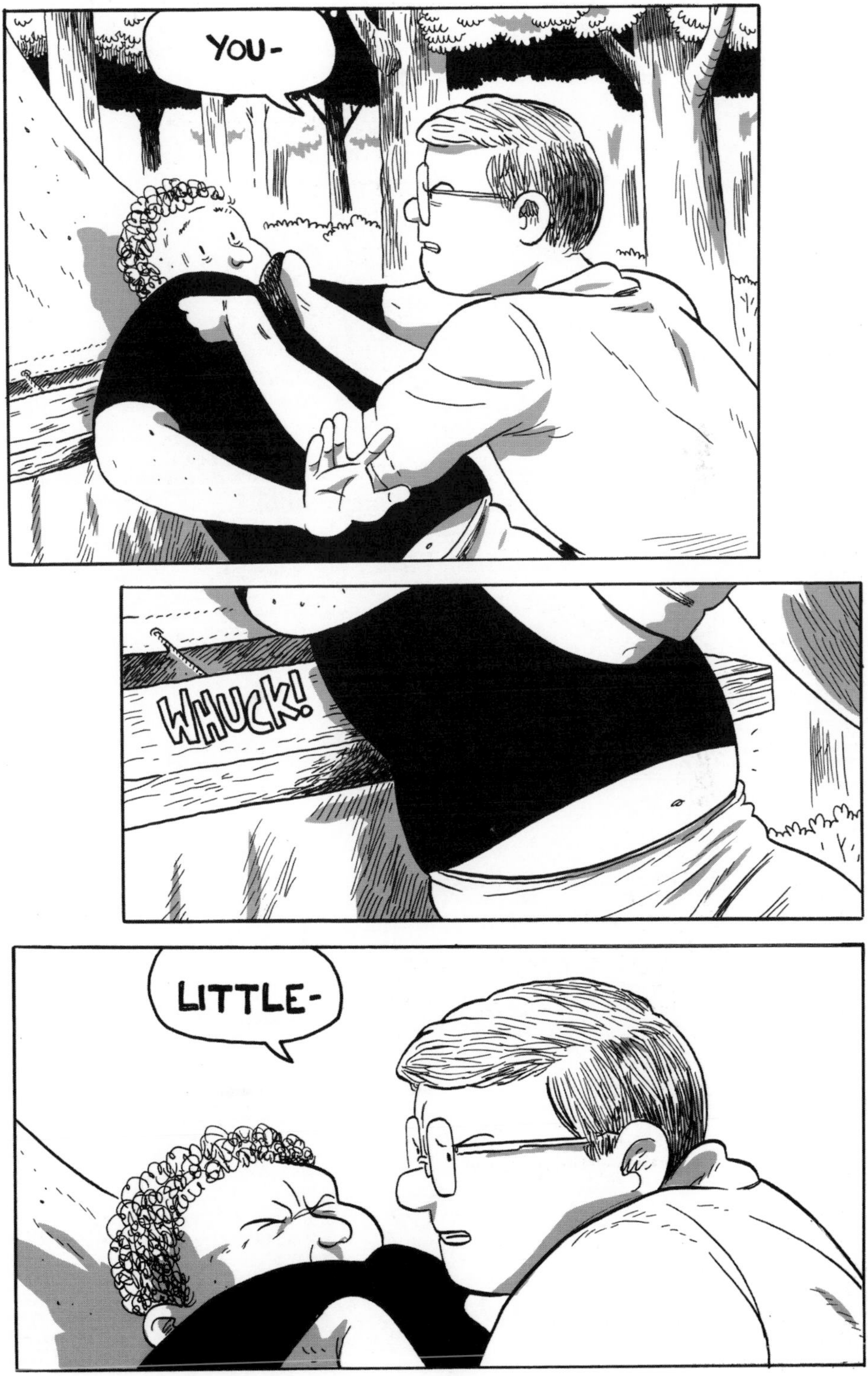
YOU-
WHUCK!
LITTLE-

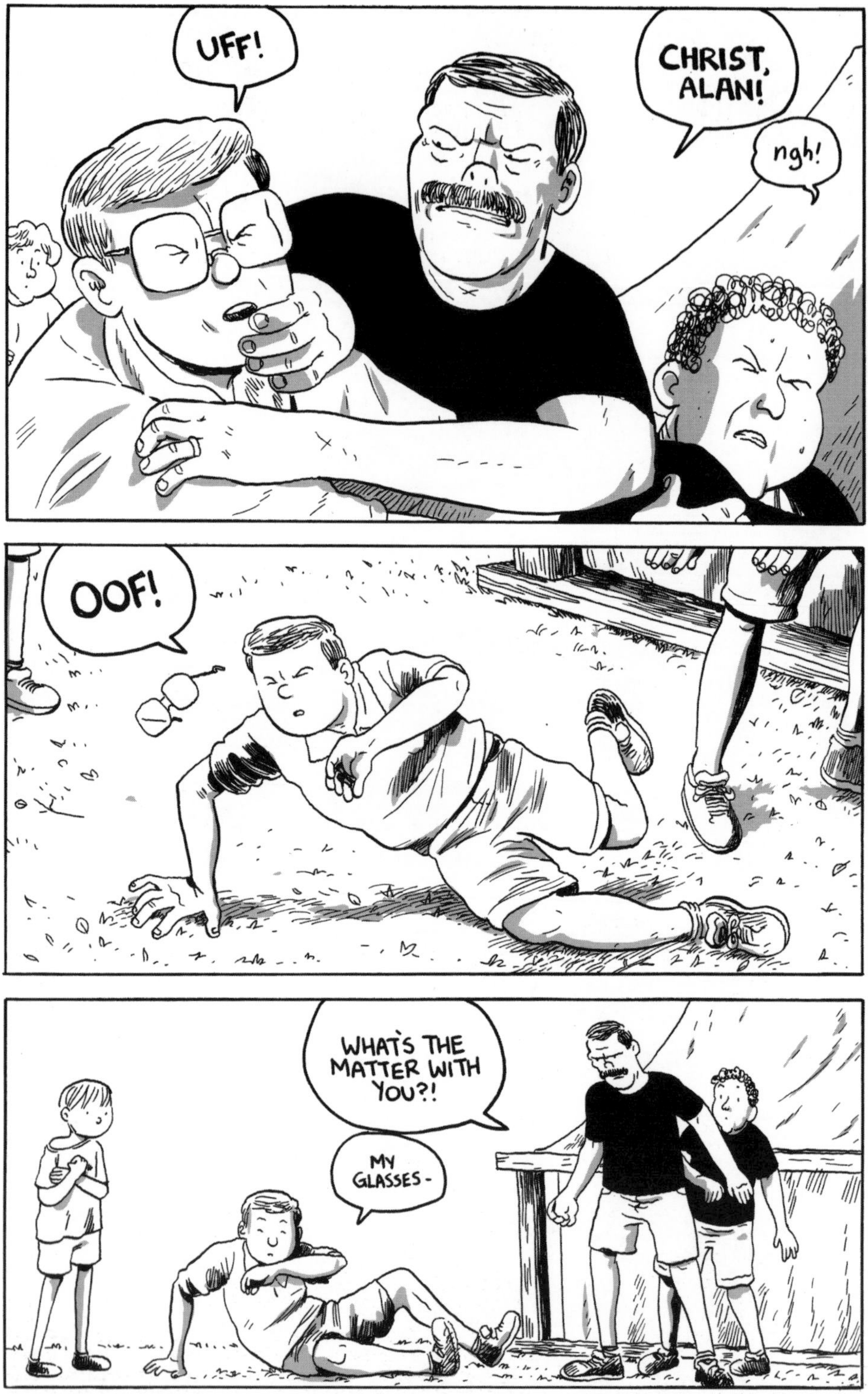
UFF!
CHRIST, ALAN!
ngh!
OOF!
WHAT'S THE MATTER WITH YOU?!
MY GLASSES -

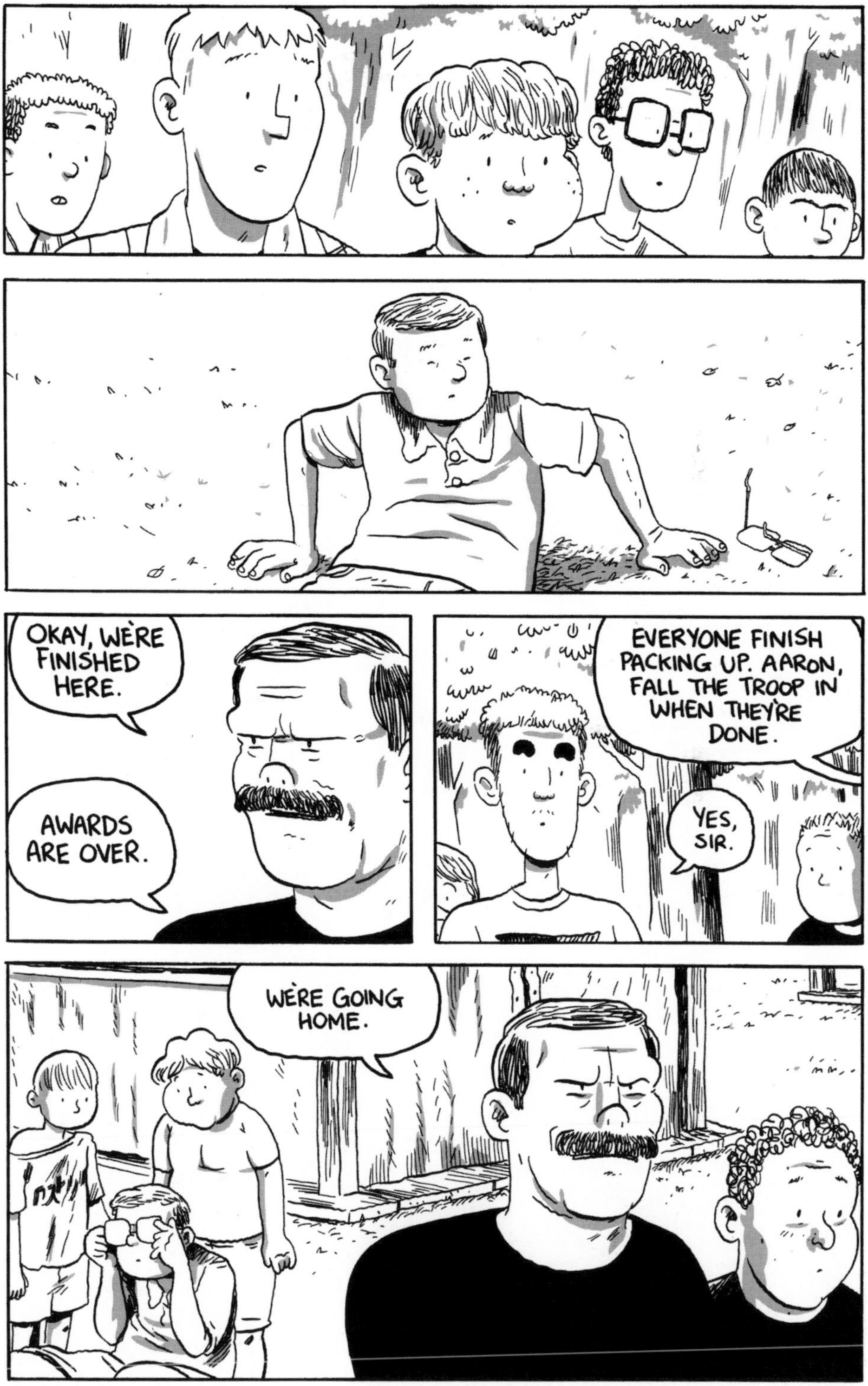
OKAY, WE'RE FINISHED HERE.
AWARDS ARE OVER.
EVERYONE FINISH PACKING UP. AARON, FALL THE TROOP IN WHEN THEY'RE DONE.
YES, SIR.
WE'RE GOING HOME.

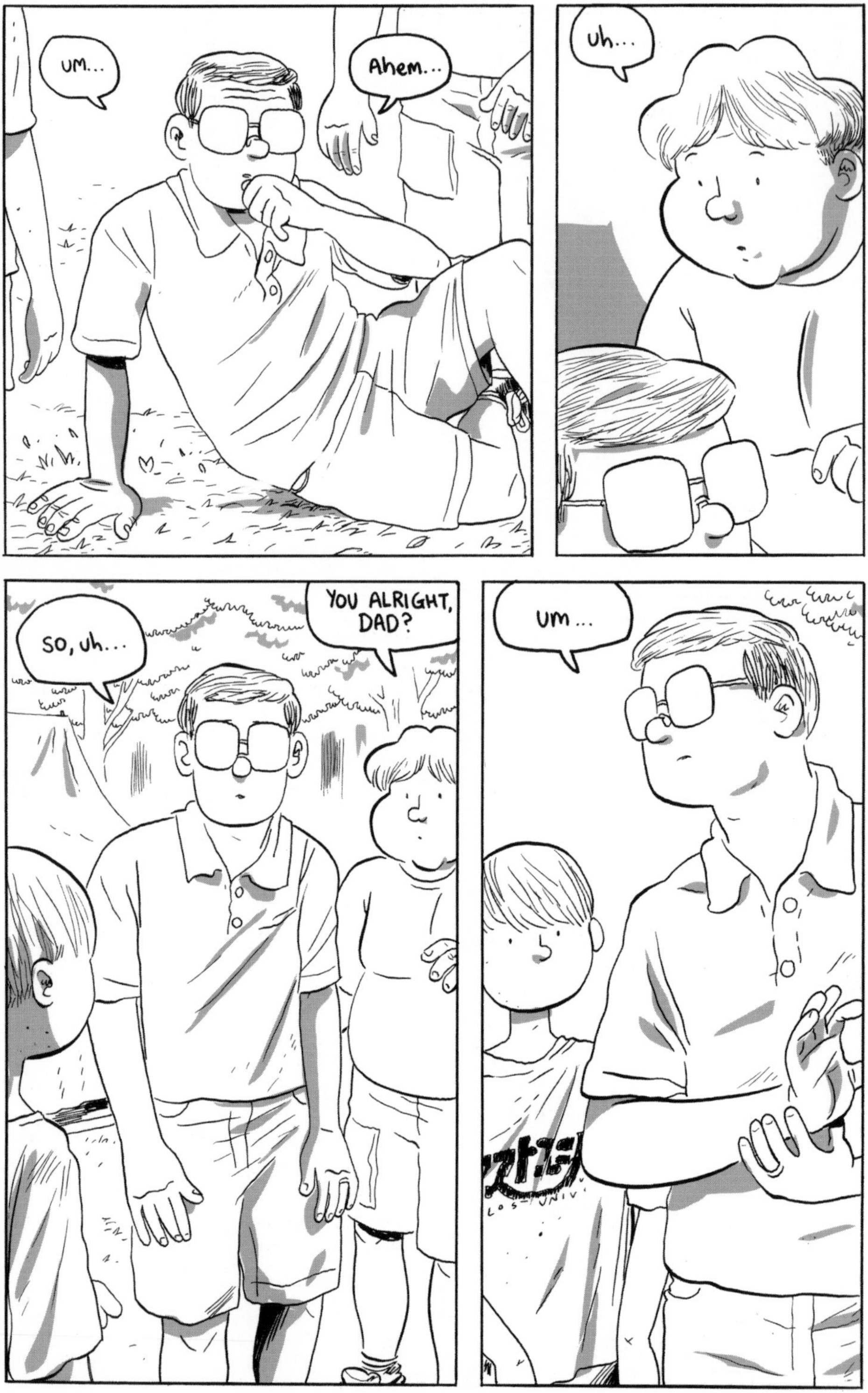
UM...
Ahem...
Uh...
SO, uh...
YOU ALRIGHT, DAD?
Um...

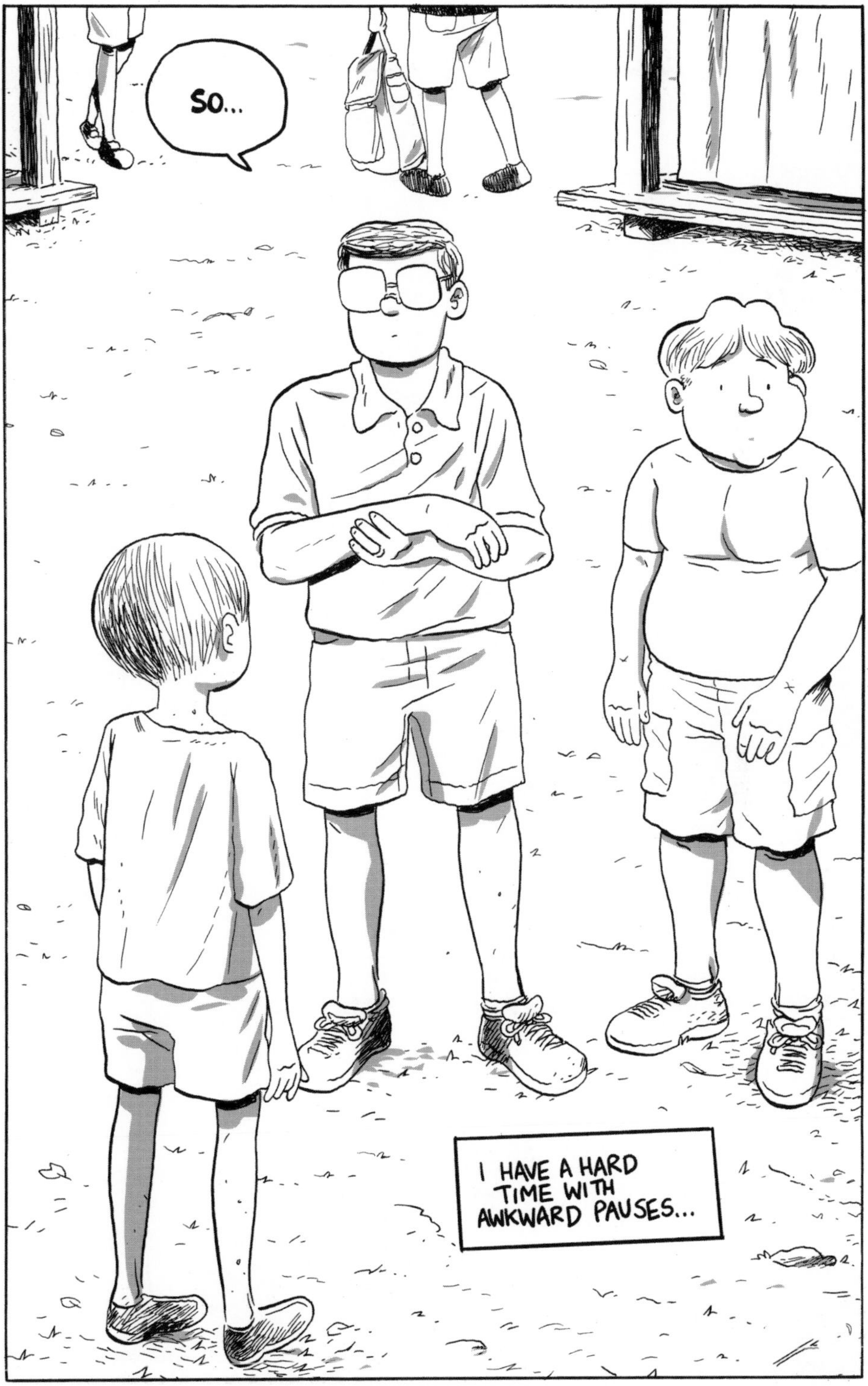
SO...
I HAVE A HARD TIME WITH AWKWARD PAUSES...

I BECOME AWARE THAT I'M STARTING TOO MANY SENTENCES WITH "SO..."

I REALIZE I MUST BE HAVING A BAD CONVERSATION.

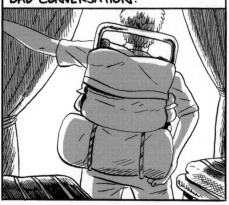

WE'RE NOT TALKING. IT FEELS LIKE I'M CONDUCTING AN INTERVIEW.

I BECOME OVERWHELMED WITH THE SENSE WE'RE NOT CONNECTING.

WHY IS THIS HAPPENING? CAN'T WE REACH EACH OTHER ON A DEEPER

HUMAN LEVEL?

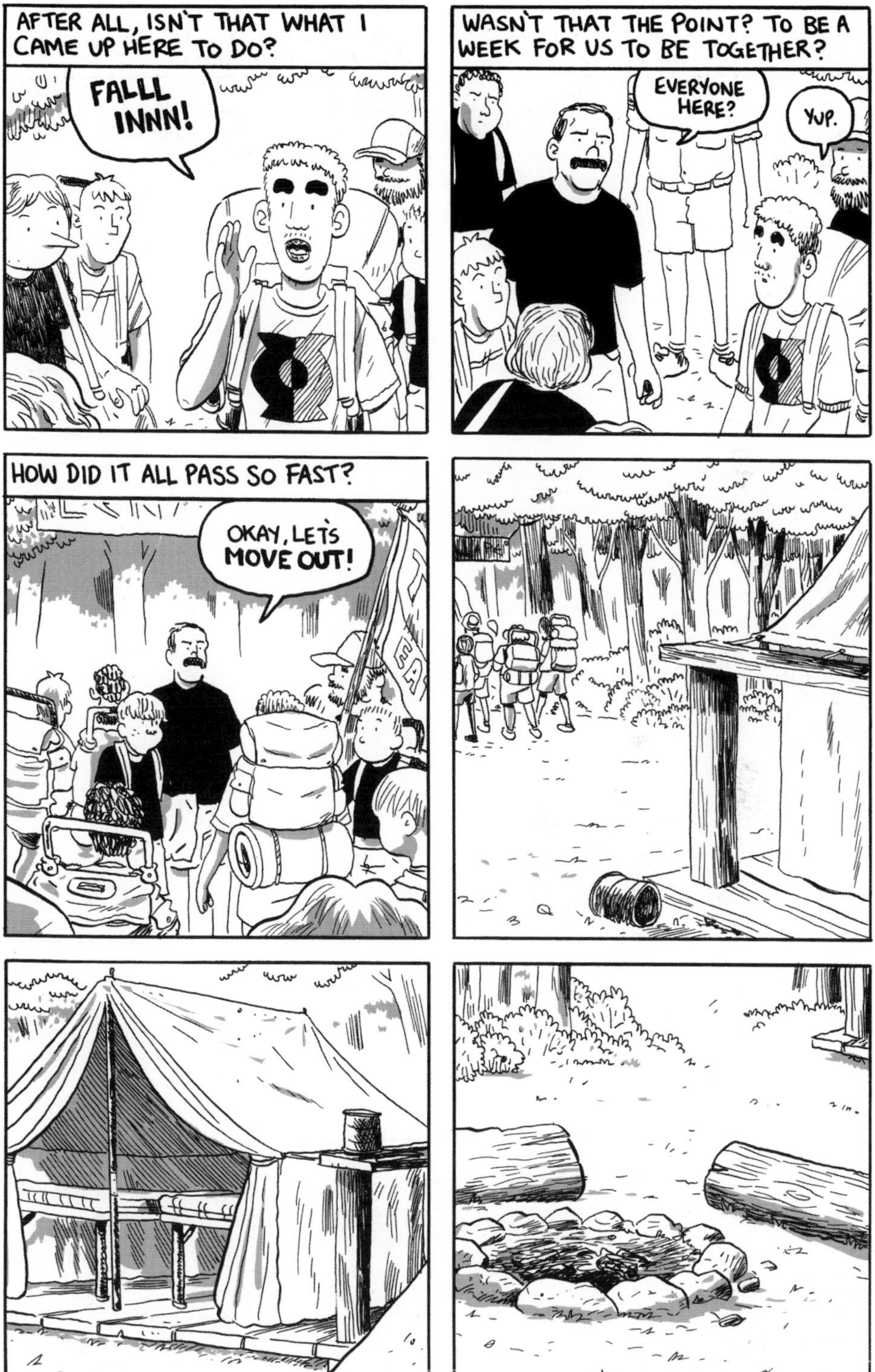
AFTER ALL, ISN'T THAT WHAT I CAME UP HERE TO DO?
FALLL INNN!
WASN'T THAT THE POINT? TO BE A WEEK FOR US TO BE TOGETHER?
EVERYONE HERE?
YUP.
HOW DID IT ALL PASS SO FAST?
OKAY, LET'S MOVE OUT!

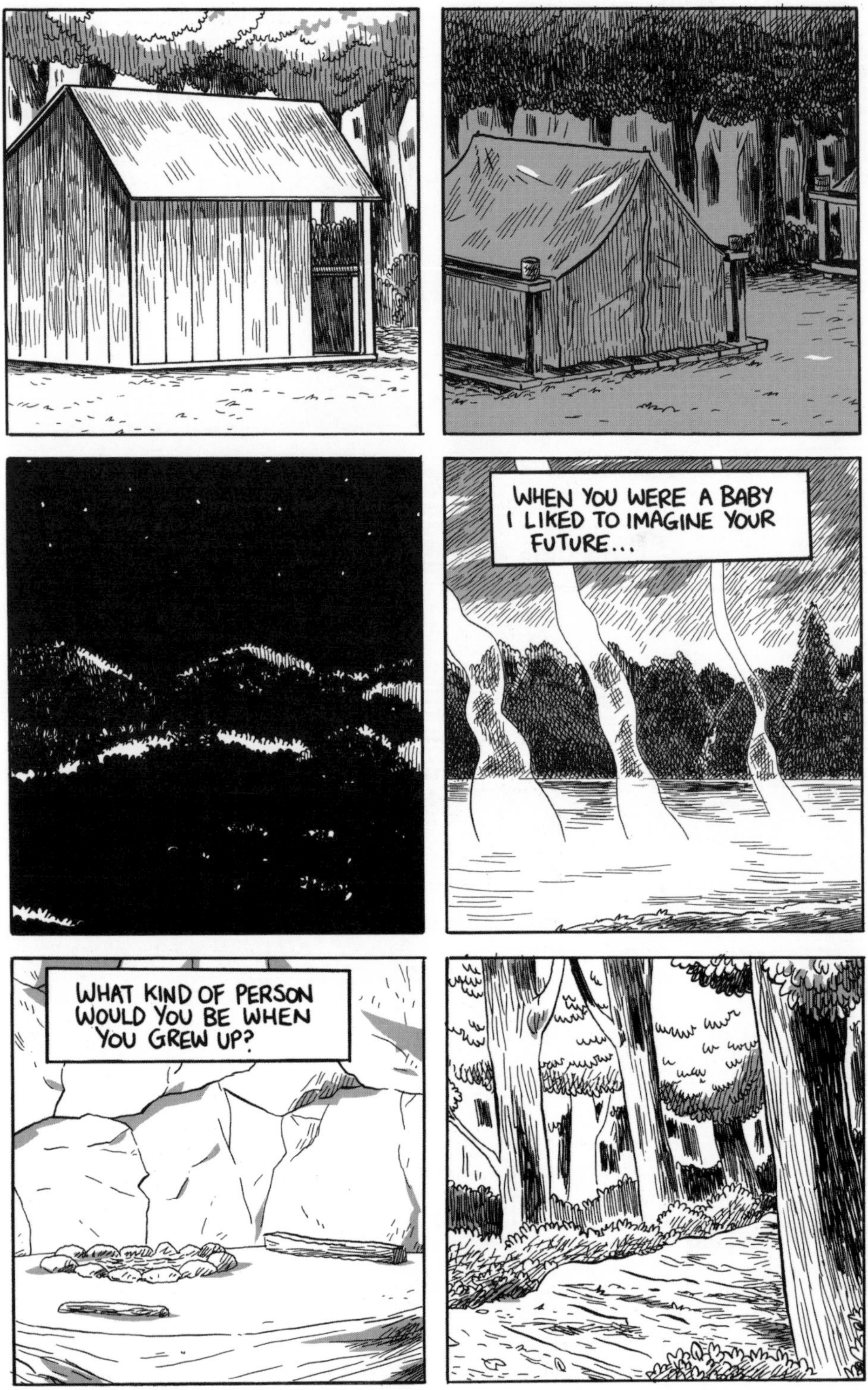
WHEN YOU WERE A BABY I LIKED TO IMAGINE YOUR FUTURE...
WHAT KIND OF PERSON WOULD YOU BE WHEN YOU GREW UP?

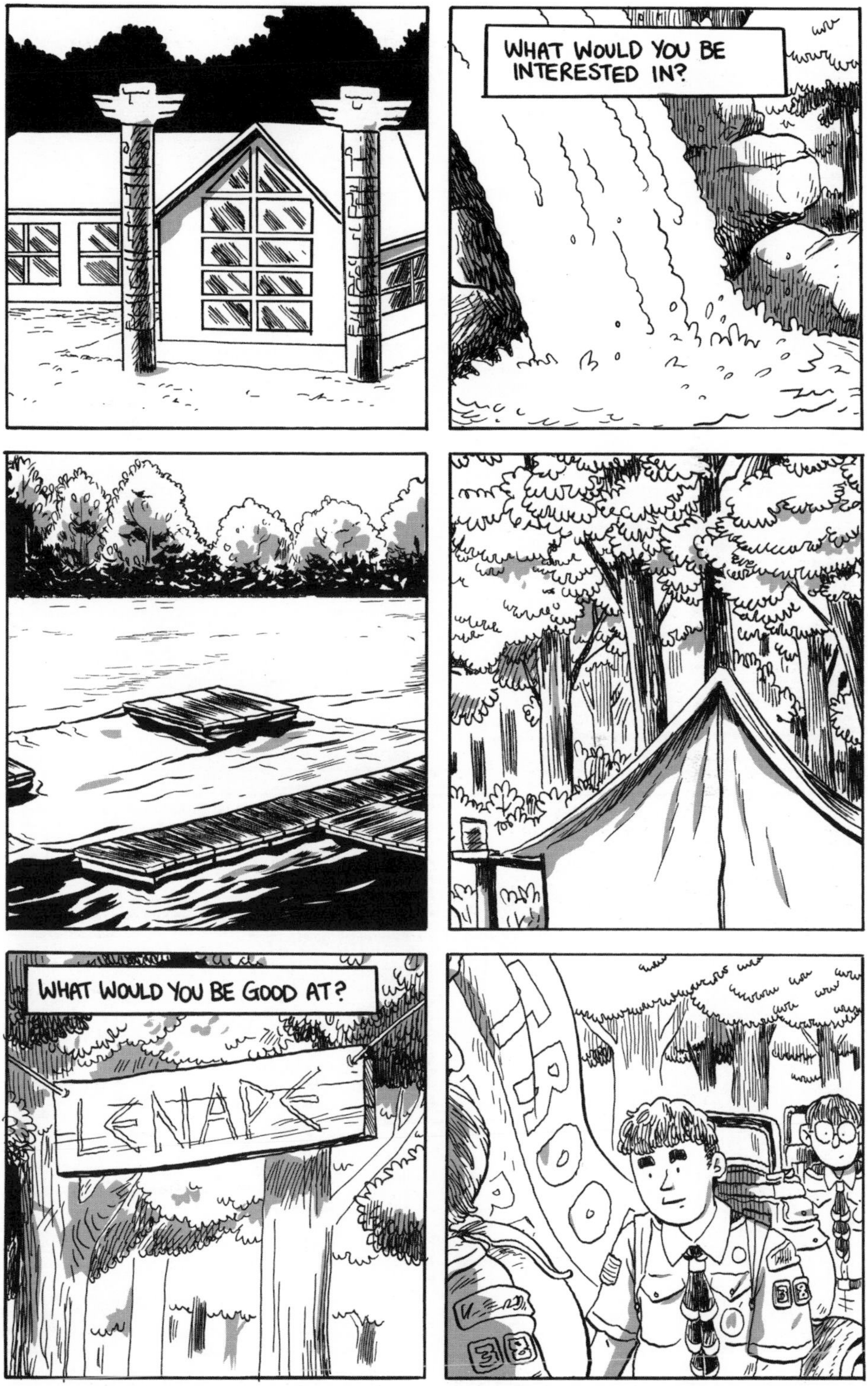
WHAT WOULD YOU BE INTERESTED IN?
WHAT WOULD YOU BE GOOD AT?
LENAPE

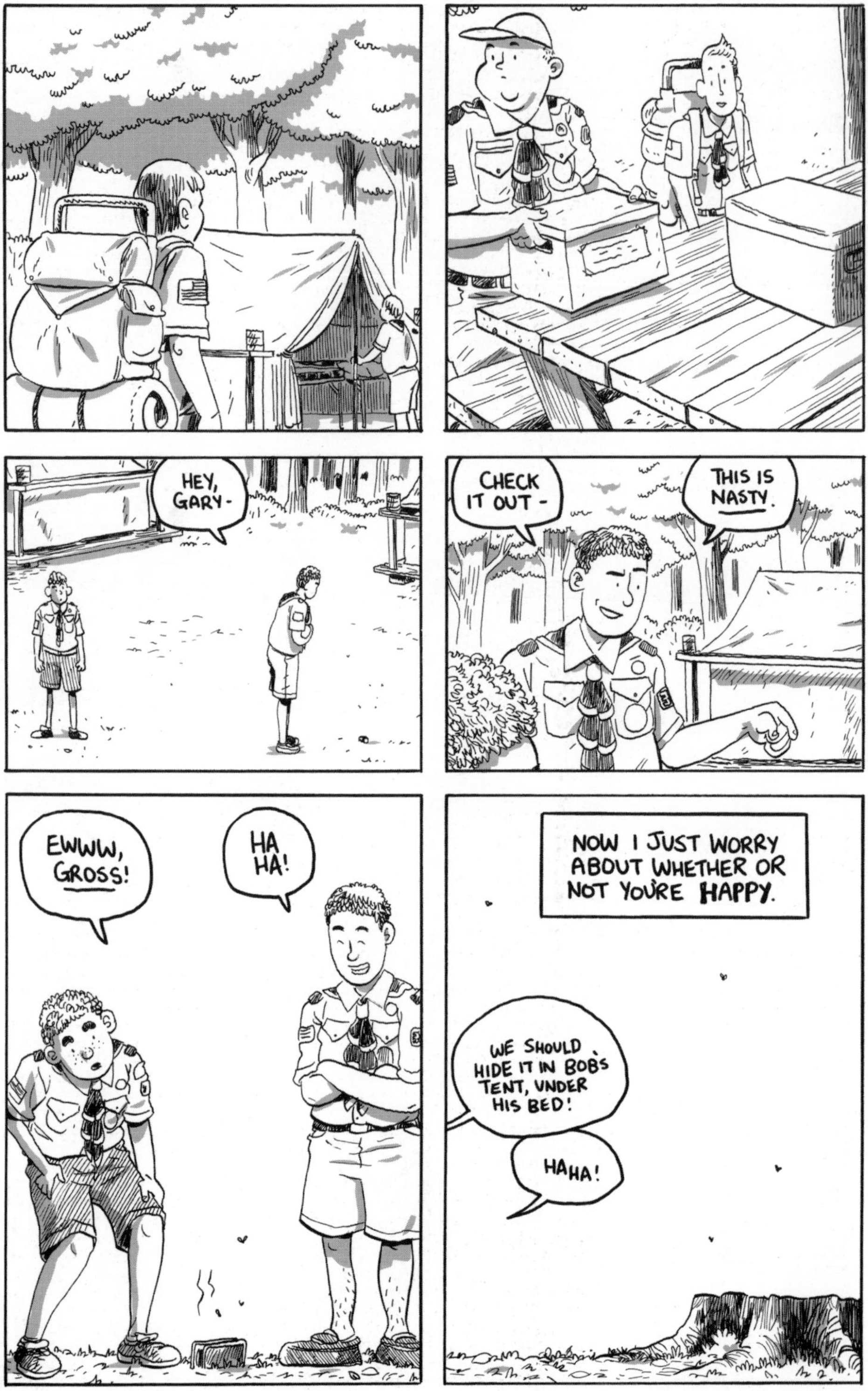
HEY, GARY-
CHECK IT OUT -
THIS IS NASTY.
EWWW, GROSS!
HA HA!
NOW I JUST WORRY ABOUT WHETHER OR NOT YOU'RE HAPPY.
WE SHOULD HIDE IT IN BOB'S TENT, UNDER HIS BED!
HAHA!

ONE WEEK LATER...

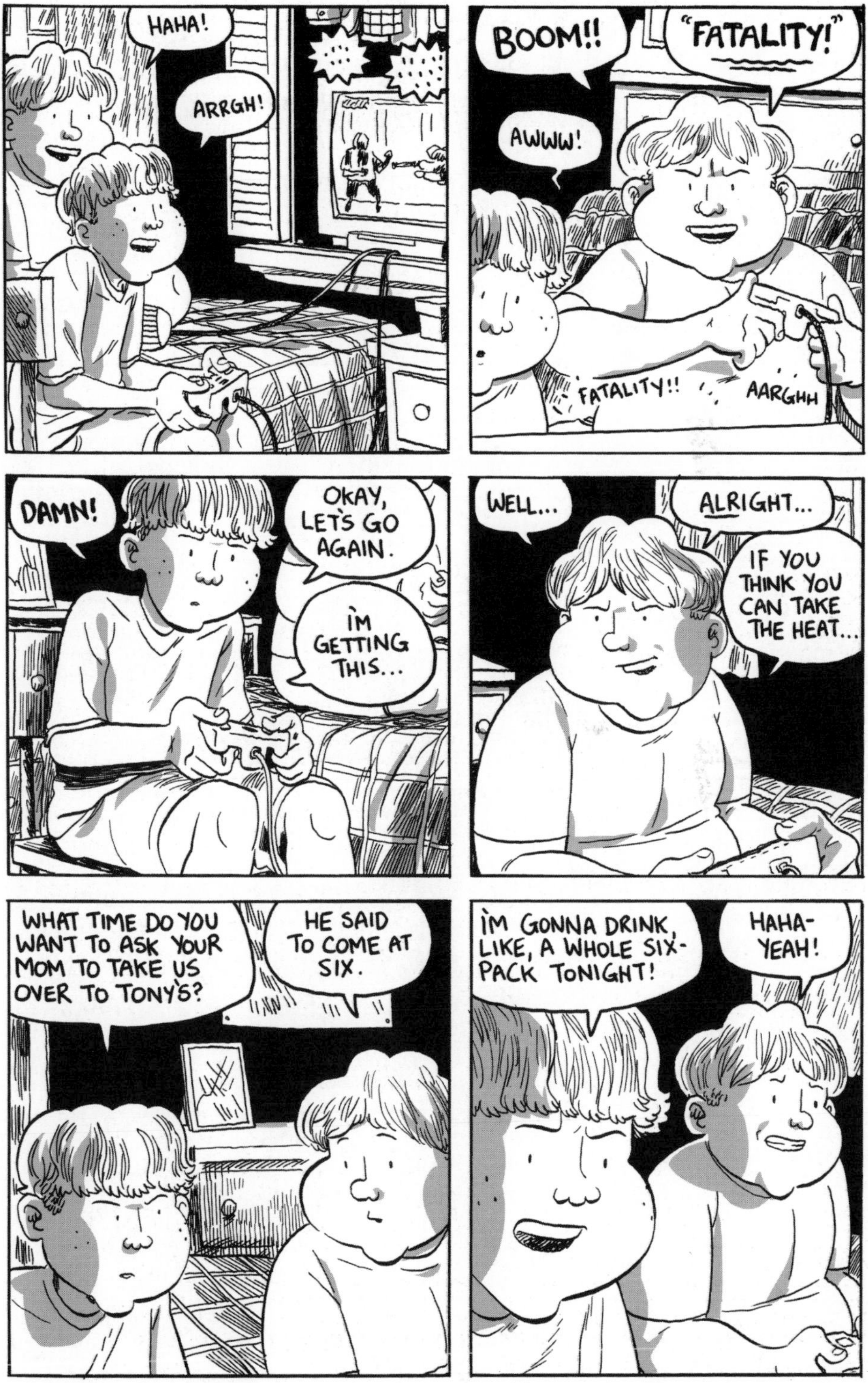
HAHA!
ARRGH!
BOOM!!
"FATALITY!"
AWWW!
FATALITY!!
AARGHH
DAMN!
OKAY, LET'S GO AGAIN.
I'M GETTING THIS...
WELL...
ALRIGHT...
IF YOU THINK YOU CAN TAKE THE HEAT...
WHAT TIME DO YOU WANT TO ASK YOUR MOM TO TAKE US OVER TO TONY'S?
HE SAID TO COME AT SIX.
I'M GONNA DRINK, LIKE, A WHOLE SIX-PACK TONIGHT!
HAHA-YEAH!

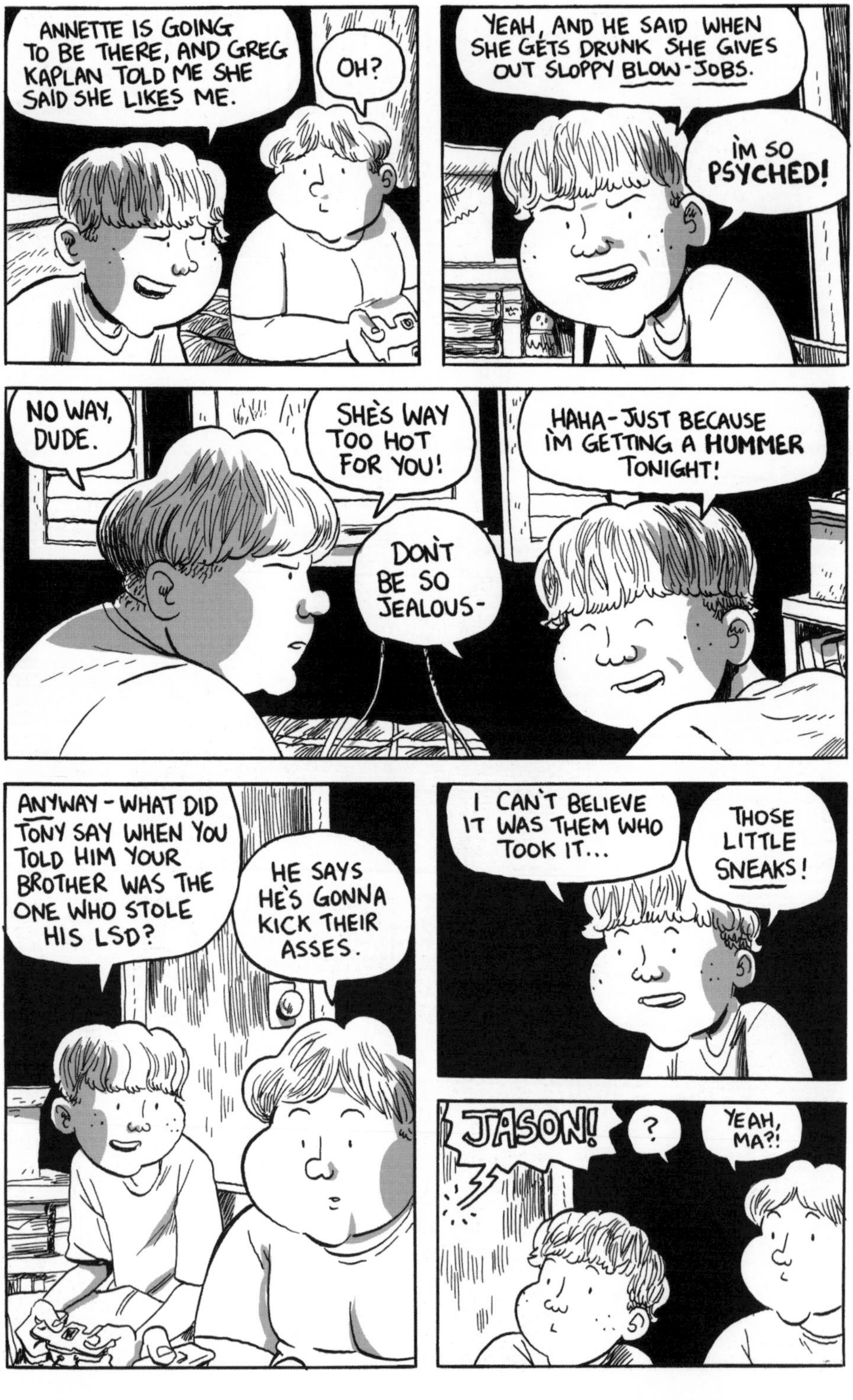
ANNETTE IS GOING TO BE THERE, AND GREG KAPLAN TOLD ME SHE SAID SHE LIKES ME.
OH?
YEAH, AND HE SAID WHEN SHE GETS DRUNK SHE GIVES OUT SLOPPY BLOW-JOBS.
I'M SO PSYCHED!
NO WAY, DUDE.
SHE'S WAY TOO HOT FOR YOU!
HAHA-JUST BECAUSE I'M GETTING A HUMMER TONIGHT!
DON'T BE SO JEALOUS-
ANYWAY-WHAT DID TONY SAY WHEN YOU TOLD HIM YOUR BROTHER WAS THE ONE WHO STOLE HIS LSD?
HE SAYS HE'S GONNA KICK THEIR ASSES.
I CAN'T BELIEVE IT WAS THEM WHO TOOK IT...
THOSE LITTLE SNEAKS!
JASON!
?
YEAH, MA?!

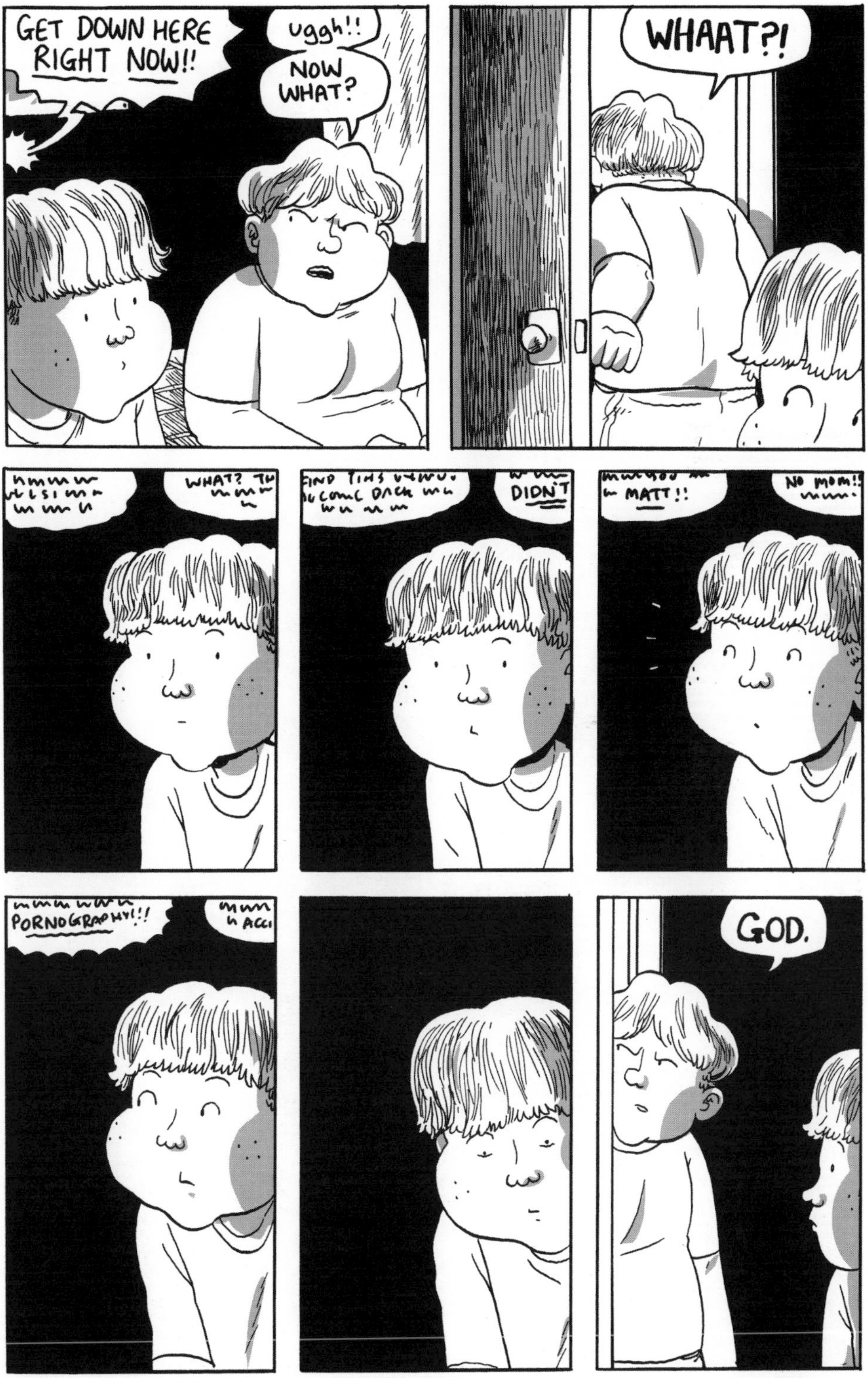
GET DOWN HERE RIGHT NOW!!
uggh!!
NOW WHAT?
WHAAT?!
WHAT?
DIDN'T
MATT!!
NO MOM!!
PORNOGRAPHY!!
GOD.

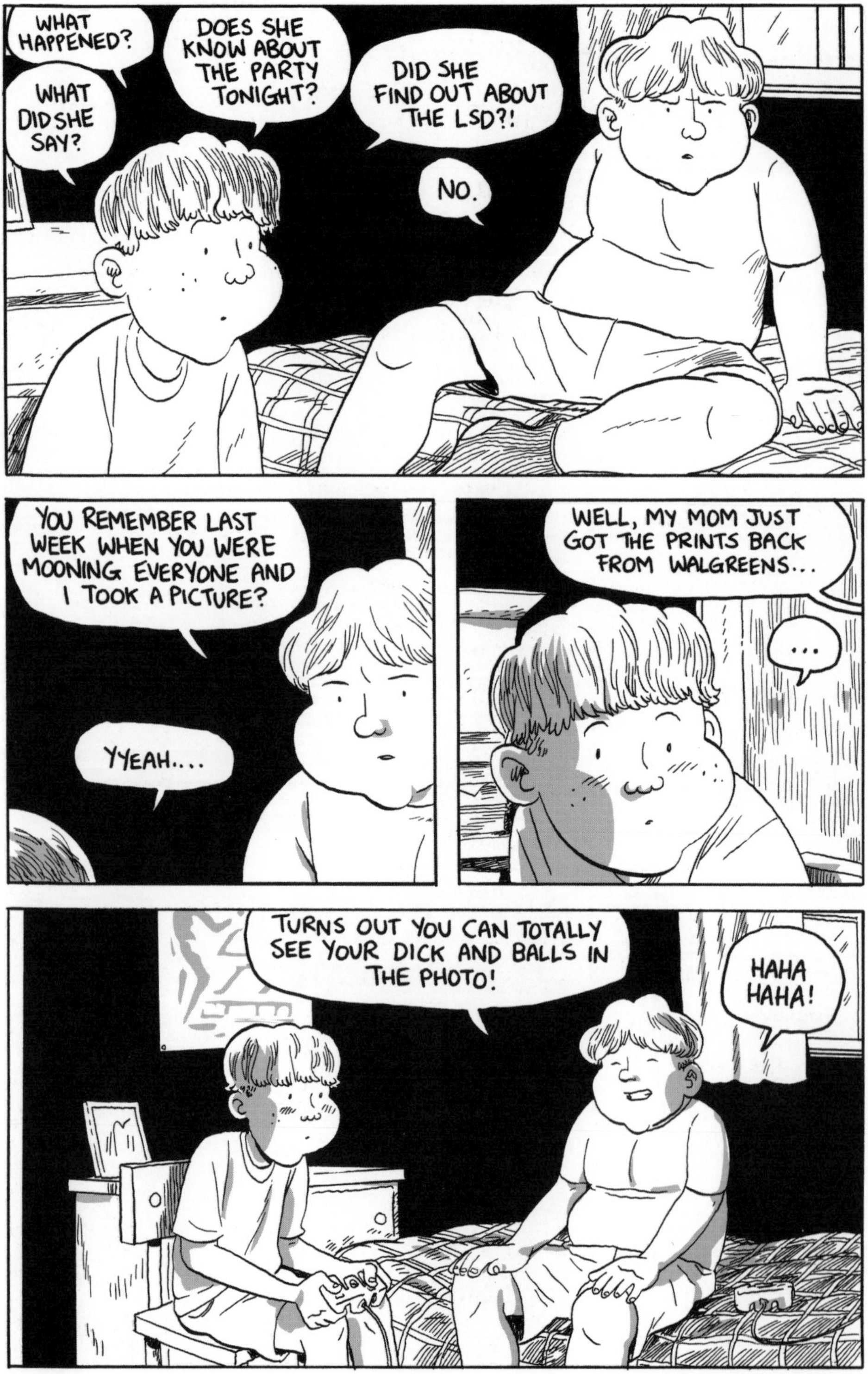
WHAT HAPPENED?
WHAT DID SHE SAY?
DOES SHE KNOW ABOUT THE PARTY TONIGHT?
DID SHE FIND OUT ABOUT THE LSD?!
NO.
YOU REMEMBER LAST WEEK WHEN YOU WERE MOONING EVERYONE AND I TOOK A PICTURE?
YYEAH....
WELL, MY MOM JUST GOT THE PRINTS BACK FROM WALGREENS...
...
TURNS OUT YOU CAN TOTALLY SEE YOUR DICK AND BALLS IN THE PHOTO!
HAHA HAHA!

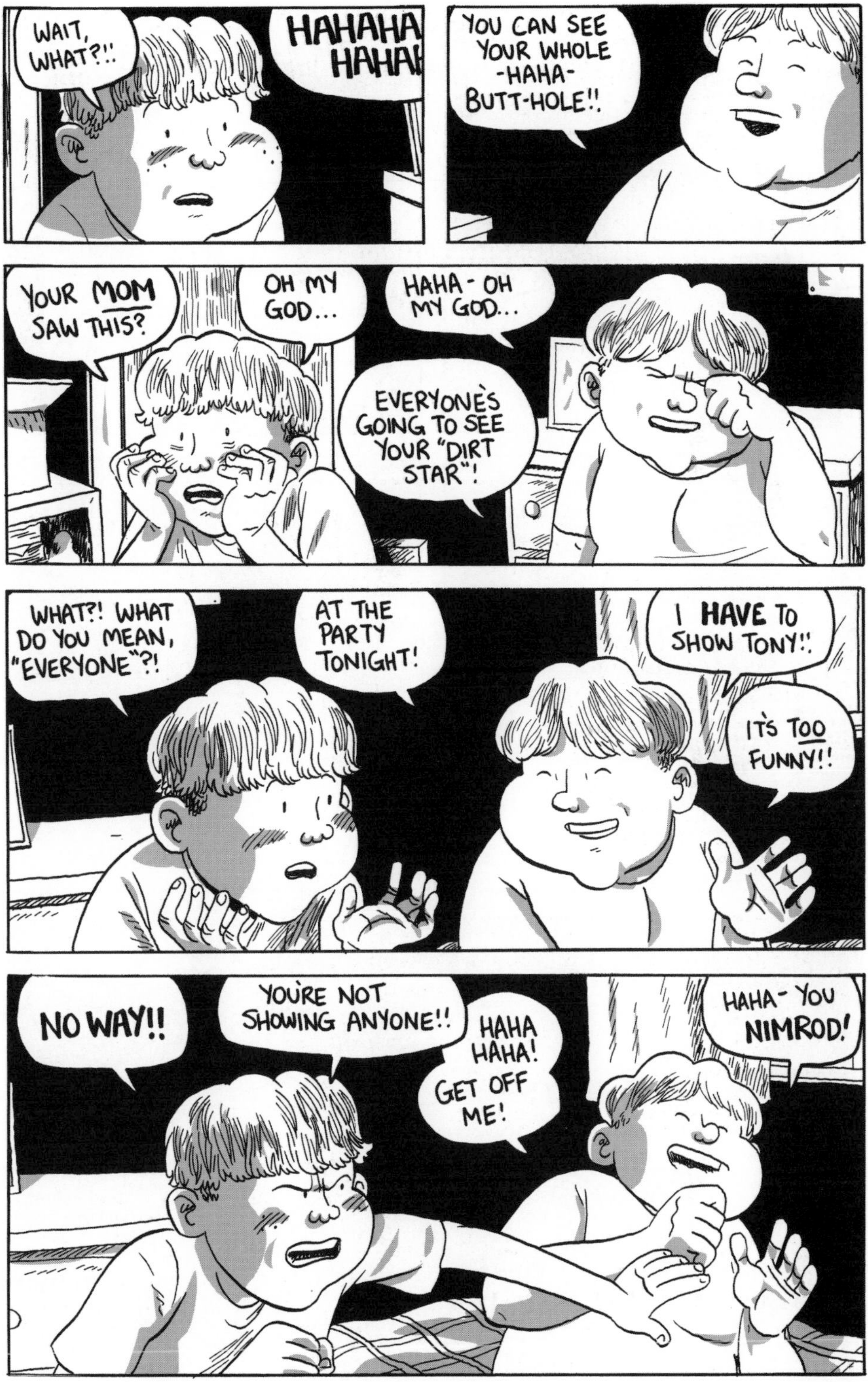

WAIT, WHAT?!!
HAHAHA HAHAH
YOU CAN SEE YOUR WHOLE -HAHA- BUTT-HOLE!!
YOUR MOM SAW THIS?
OH MY GOD...
HAHA - OH MY GOD...
EVERYONE'S GOING TO SEE YOUR "DIRT STAR"!
WHAT?! WHAT DO YOU MEAN, "EVERYONE"?!
AT THE PARTY TONIGHT!
I HAVE TO SHOW TONY!!
IT'S TOO FUNNY!!
NO WAY!!
YOU'RE NOT SHOWING ANYONE!!
HAHA HAHA! GET OFF ME!
HAHA- YOU NIMROD!

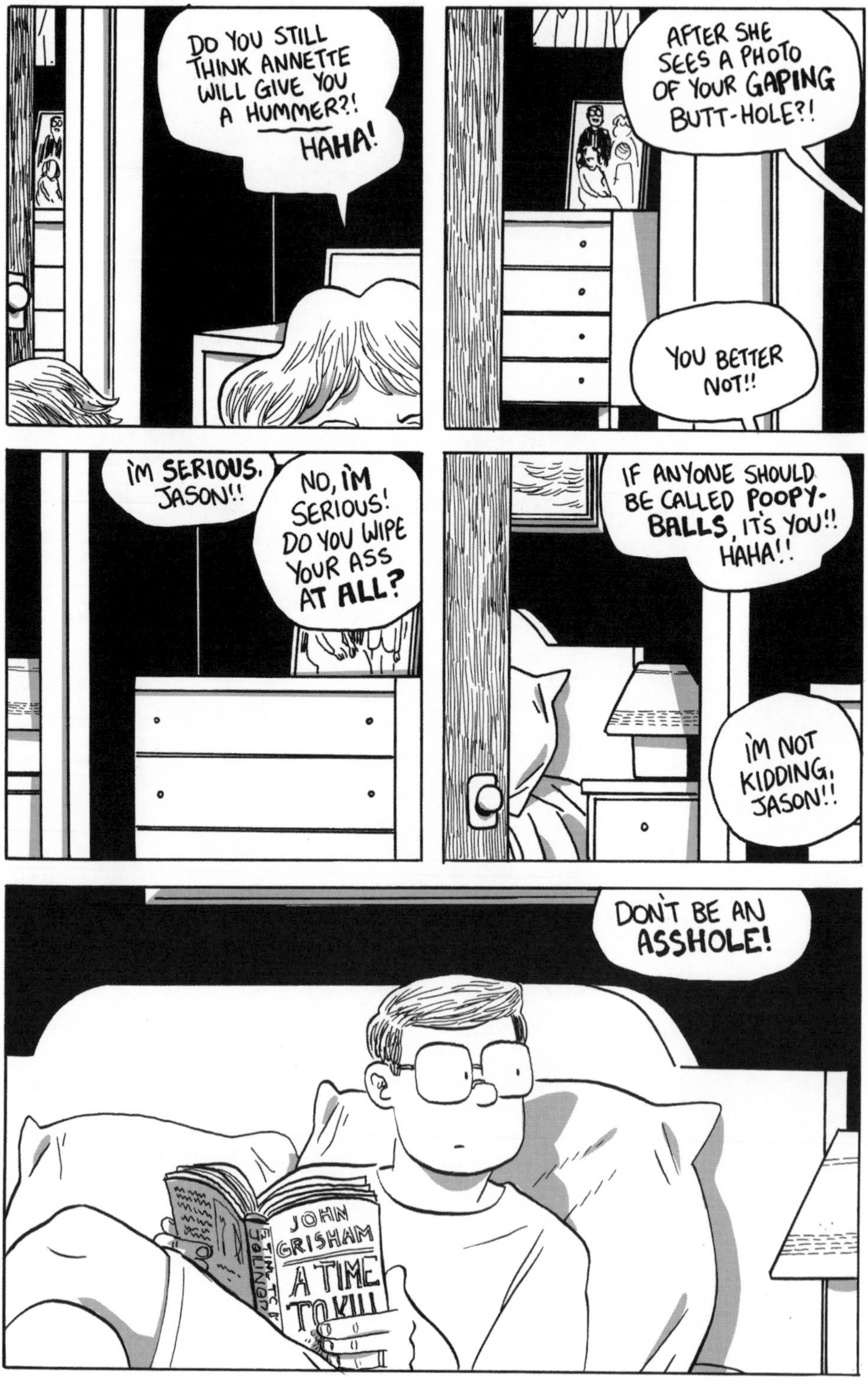

DO YOU STILL THINK ANNETTE WILL GIVE YOU A HUMMER?!
HAHA!
AFTER SHE SEES A PHOTO OF YOUR GAPING BUTT-HOLE?!
YOU BETTER NOT!!
I'M SERIOUS, JASON!!
NO, I'M SERIOUS! DO YOU WIPE YOUR ASS AT ALL?
IF ANYONE SHOULD BE CALLED POOPY-BALLS, IT'S YOU!! HAHA!!
I'M NOT KIDDING, JASON!!
DON'T BE AN ASSHOLE!
JOHN GRISHAM
A TIME TO KILL

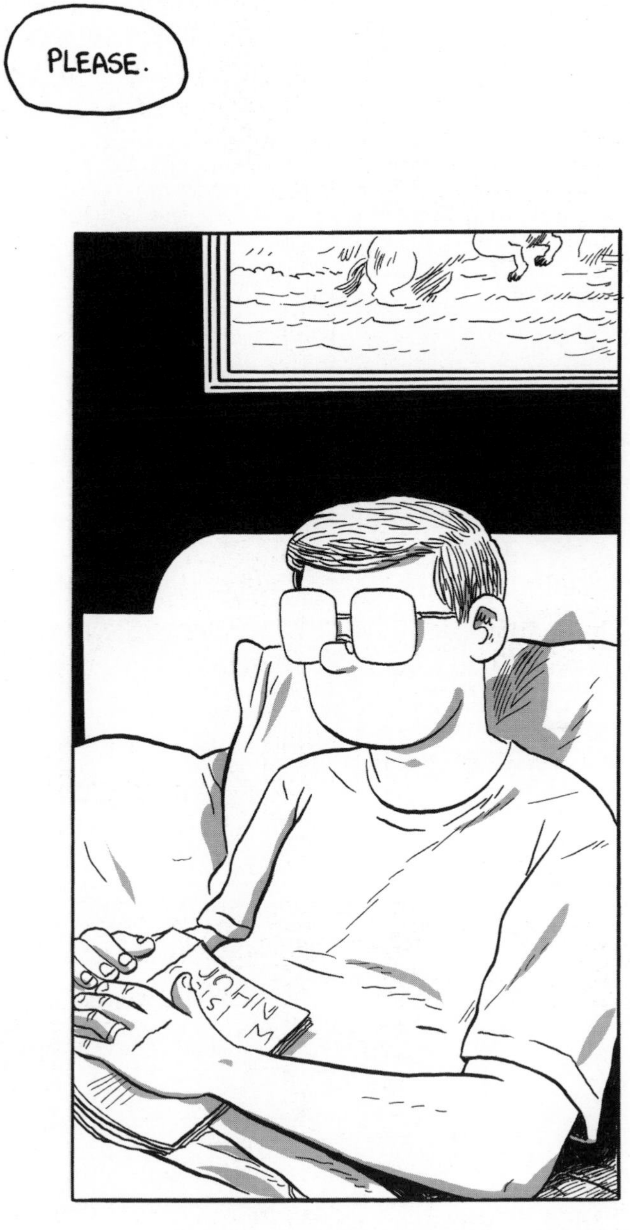

PLEASE.
DON'T.